Jessica Blair Omnibus

THE LONG WAY HOME
DANGEROUS SHORES

JESSICA BLAIR

piatkus

PIATKUS

This omnibus edition first published in Great Britain in 2010 by Piatkus

Previously published separately:
The Long Way Home first published in Great Britain in 2001 by Piatkus Books
Paperback edition published in 2002 by Piatkus Books
Reprinted 2009
Dangerous Shores first published in Great Britain in 2007 by Piatkus Books
Paperback edition published in 2008 by Piatkus Books

A CIP catalogue record for this book
is available from the British Library.

ISBN 978-0-7499-5381-2

Typeset in Times by Phoenix Photosetting, Chatham, Kent
Printed in Great Britain by Clays Ltd, St Ives plc

Papers used by Piatkus are natural, renewable and recyclable
products sourced from well-managed forests and certified
in accordance with the rules of the Forest Stewardship Council.

Mixed Sources
Product group from well-managed
forests and other controlled sources
www.fsc.org Cert no. SGS-COC-004081
© 1996 Forest Stewardship Council
FSC

Piatkus
An imprint of
Little, Brown Book Group
100 Victoria Embankment
London EC4Y 0DY

An Hachette UK Company
www.hachette.co.uk

www.piatkus.co.uk

The Long Way Home

FOR
JILL
WHOSE MAGIC INSPIRED
ME TO KEEP GOING

Chapter One

Lydia put down the fourth monthly part of *David Copperfield* with regret that she had finished it. The publishers had planned that this novel by the popular author, Charles Dickens, would continue through the remaining four months of 1849 and into 1850, so she looked forward eagerly to the next instalment, trying to anticipate its developments.

As she rose from her chair and walked to the window her mind was full of sympathy for Copperfield and the tragedies life had dealt him. But when she reached the window the story was cast to the back of her mind for from her room among the new houses high on Whitby's West Cliff she had a view which always moved her, or had these last three years at least since she was seventeen, the age when an appreciation of her surroundings had begun to play a part in her young life.

The sun this late-August afternoon flamed the red-tiled roofs of Whitby's east side where the houses, crowded one on top of the other, climbed the cliff. She could see the gaunt outline of the ruined Norman abbey on the cliff top where tomorrow afternoon she would ride with David Drayton. It had become a regular Friday activity for them since Easter, as it had done last year.

Their respective families approved of the friendship, seeing a future marriage between them as forging a closer

1

alliance between two mercantile businesses in Whitby's thriving port. Lydia knew this but kept her own counsel. She liked David a great deal and enjoyed his company, but did she love him? He had become a handsome twenty-one year old, standing just over six foot tall. His angular jaw gave him the appearance of a man who loved a challenge, and in Lydia he'd found a tempting one, for she always rebuffed his more amorous advances, desiring for now at least to keep their relationship to one of close friendship only.

David respected her wishes but went on telling himself that one day he would marry this pretty girl with hazel eyes and silky hair which shimmered like the peat-brown waters of a bubbling moorland stream. He knew that behind the pleasant, vivacious exterior there was a stubborn streak to Lydia, and this conflict in her nature he found unusual and appealing.

So he went on being attentive, escorting her to parties with friends, to the plays occasionally held in the Freemasons' Tavern, to lectures held by the Literary and Philosophical Society, and to other functions in the town, making no secret of his admiration and affection for her.

As she stared thoughtfully from the window Lydia acknowledged to herself that life with David Drayton would be comfortable, she'd want for nothing, since one day he would inherit his father's company. And the time would come when she, in her own right, would inherit a share in her own father's business together with her brother, Luke.

She pursed her lips. Should she agree to what both families saw as an ideal match, hold back no longer? Maybe tomorrow when they rode along the cliff top she would speak to David and embark upon a new stage in her life ...

Lydia's reverie was interrupted by a loud rapping on the front door which resounded through the house. The sound alarmed her with its urgency and persistence. She ran out on to the landing and heard a maid's footsteps scurry across the hall below. Stepping close to the banister rail she looked down and saw the alarmed girl open the front door wide.

'Mr Middleton, is he at home?' The words were spoken with such compelling force that the maid could only splutter something unintelligible. 'Quick, girl, is he?' The man stepped past her as if he would find out for himself, but she outmanoeuvred him and scampered towards the drawing-room door. He followed, paused while she knocked and opened it, then was into the room before the maid could make any announcement.

Lydia started for the stairs. She had recognised the man as Julian Briggs whom her father employed as clerk in the small office near the harbour from which he conducted his business. Briggs was usually calm and steady in even the most exacting circumstances. This unusual agitation must presage a major catastrophe.

She started down the stairs then stopped. In her haste to retreat, the maid had failed to close the door properly and Lydia overheard Briggs's shattering announcement.

'Sir, the *Mary Anne* has been lost!'

'What?' Tristram Middleton gasped in disbelief.

'Merchantman, the *Aurora*, bound for Newcastle, put in with the news. *Mary Anne* went down in a storm off the French coast. The *Aurora* tried to help but couldn't get near.' Briggs's voice broke as he added, 'I'm sorry, sir.'

There was total silence, the house filled with the stillness of tragedy. Earlier today her father had spoken of his high hopes for a successful trading voyage. Now disaster had blighted those hopes.

'Total number of lives lost?' Tristram asked weakly as he anticipated the worst.

'All hands, sir.'

There was a heavy silence again then Lydia heard her father's muttered words of dejection. Though the loss of the *Mary Anne* and its cargo of Spanish wine and lace would hit him hard financially, she knew that the fact there were no survivors counted far more with him. Each member of the

3

crew was personally known to him, he'd seen to that, believing that friendly and sympathetic relations with his crew members made for loyalty and good work. She realised that he would suffer anew with each meeting with the men's families, the wives, mothers, fathers, brothers, sisters and sweethearts of each sailor who had perished and now lay in a watery grave.

The men's voices became more distinct and Lydia could follow their conversation.

'Is there anything I can do, sir?'

'Thank you.' Her father's voice was firmer now. She pictured him squaring his shoulders, subduing his own sense of shock so as not to appear weak in the eyes of his employee. 'I'd like a list of the crew and the addresses of their nearest relatives. I'll have to visit them.'

'Yes, sir. I'll get that ready for you.'

'Thank you. I'll be at the office shortly.'

'Very good, sir.'

Lydia watched her father accompany Briggs to the front door.

'I'm sorry you had to be the bearer of such bad news.'

'So am I, sir.' The clerk tightened his mouth to a grim line. He gave his employer a deferential nod and left the house.

Tristram closed the door. When he turned, Lydia saw his shoulders slump. His face was grave and his footsteps dragged as he started across the hall.

It hurt her to see her father like this. She wished she was able to reassure him that things were not as bad as they seemed, but she couldn't. All she could do was offer comfort and sympathy and give him her unstinting support in the difficult days ahead.

Her footsteps, tripping quickly down the stairs, drew Tristram's attention. Seeing his daughter, he tried to disguise the despair which had settled on him, but realised it was too late. He could not fool Lydia, he knew from her expression that she had heard everything.

4

His heart filled with sorrow to think that even she, the daughter he loved so much, would feel the harsh effects of what happened so far from Whitby. He held out his arms as if to shield her from the harsh realities of the world, rather than to seek comfort from her.

'I'm so sorry, Father,' she said, her voice full of sympathy.

She was in his arms. They hugged each other, finding reassurance in their closeness. He held her for a few moments, controlling his feelings while he struggled to find a way of breaking even more catastrophic news to her.

Slowly he released her, placed his arm round her shoulders and led her gently to the drawing room.

'Father, I know it will be hard for you to visit the families of the missing men, but if it will help I'll come with you,' Lydia offered.

He smiled wanly. 'That is kind of you. You will be a great support and comfort to me, I'm sure.'

'I know Luke would do the same if he were here.'

'I'm sure he would.'

'He will be devastated when he hears the news.'

Tristram nodded. 'No doubt word will reach the iron workings before he leaves.' He changed his mind about revealing the extent of the tragedy now. It would be better to break the news when both his children were home. 'I think we should go and get this unpleasant task over.'

As they made their way to the older parts of the town, they sensed that Whitby had already taken on the mantle of mourning. The usual bustle of a busy working port was absent. Orders were toned down; people going about their daily lives spoke in hushed tones when they could not stay silent. Even the children, usually raucous in their play, were muted, their enthusiasm curbed by watchful mothers or stifled by an inbred understanding of the tragedy that can strike any port that sends its men to face danger on the sea.

Well known in the town as the owner of the *Mary Anne*,

Tristram Middleton received sympathetic glances from those who knew him by sight, brief words from those who were more familiar with him.

The Middletons had become a respected family in Whitby after moving there from Pickering, a market town sixteen miles inland across the wild North Yorkshire Moors. Tristram's father, John, had built up a successful merchant's business in the market town but had seen better opportunities in the growing port and moved his wife and two sons there when Tristram was five and his brother Nathan seven. Through perspicacity, good judgement and a little luck linked with a likeable personality, John had prospered. When his wife died the firm and his two sons became the be all and end all of his life. He found it trying at times to be both father and mother to two growing boys and many times wished he had his wife's help still to tame the harsh, sometimes vicious streak in Nathan which frequently brought him into conflict with his gentle younger brother. Nathan had an adventurous streak, was daring to the point of irresponsibility, and would cruelly mock the more cautious Tristram.

John found in his eldest son a sharp brain and an eager desire to shoulder responsibility within the family firm when he came of age. He had a flair for trading and, because of the adventurous side of his nature, sometimes secured business which even his father would have thought twice about soliciting.

Tristram, on the other hand, liked to play safe, which cast him always in the shadow of his brother.

It therefore came as a shock to both of them, though for different reasons, when their father's will was read to them by Whitby's leading attorney, Abraham Marsh, after John's funeral had taken place at the old parish church high on the East Cliff close to the ruined abbey.

Mourners eager to resume their normal routine and escape the chill wind which brought with it the threat of rain briefly commiserated with Nathan and Tristram and their families, and hastened from the cliff top. Closer friends came to the house on the west side where John had lived his brief married life and afterwards in his widower's state. His many virtues were mentioned in hushed tones by those who had known him well. Nathan and Tristram graciously accepted their comments, comforted by the knowledge that their father had clearly possessed considerable standing in the eyes of many in Whitby.

Once the mourners had left, the two brothers and their wives settled themselves with the attorney in what had been John's study. He had conducted most of his business from this room, leaving his clerk to handle the finer details from the harbourside office.

Nathan smiled in satisfaction as he settled himself in a comfortable armchair. He could see himself continuing to run the firm from this very room. Though he had little time for his brother, whom he personally considered weak, he would no doubt have to continue to employ Tristram. Well, he would tolerate his continued presence so long as his brother did not interfere in the new schemes Nathan was already hatching.

As Abraham Marsh intoned praises for the way John had clearly formulated his assets, making it easy to draw up a will respecting all his wishes, Nathan had a hard job curbing a desire to tell the attorney to get on with it. Tristram comforted himself with the knowledge that their father had obviously been well liked; he barely speculated about what might be coming his way. He was sure his father would have left him provided for while leaving the future control of the business in Nathan's hands. The prospect did not dismay Tristram.

'And so I come to the will itself,' the attorney continued. 'It is fairly simple and straightforward.' He cleared his throat, casting a quick glance over the four people before him, dressed in deepest black, who waited to hear the bequests which would shape their futures. '"I leave to my grandchildren, Nathan's daughter Isobel and his son

7

Christopher, the sum of two hundred pounds apiece. I leave the same amount to Tristram's children, Lydia and Luke. I thank them dearly for the joy they have brought me."' There were murmurs of satisfaction that John had seen fit to acknowledge his love for his grandchildren. '"I also thank my two daughters-in-law for being kind to me, especially in my loneliness after Martha died. To each of them I leave the sum of three hundred pounds.

'"I deliberated for some time as to how I should disperse the rest of my assets and after considerable thought have decided what would be most beneficial to Nathan and Tristram, both of whom, in their different ways, have been good and dutiful sons to me.

'"I leave all my properties, a list of which is appended, to my son Nathan, provided he and his family shall agree to reside in number sixteen Bagdale."'

This announcement brought a sharp gasp from Nathan for he had expected to take over this house, his father's residence. He exchanged a sharp glance with his wife who raised her eyebrows in surprise.

'"My son Tristram shall be allowed to live rent-free in my own residence, number twenty-one St Hilda's Terrace, for the duration of his life. Upon his death the property shall revert to his brother Nathan or his heirs. I also bequeath to Nathan the sum of three thousand pounds.

'"To Tristram I leave two thousand pounds plus all the assets of the business known as John Middleton, Merchant."'

This information brought an even louder gasp from Nathan. All his expectations of assuming his father's mantle in the business were destroyed with those few words. 'It can't be true,' he protested. A quick glance at his brother showed that Tristram too was surprised and he knew without a doubt there had been no conniving with his father which he could use to invalidate the will.

The attorney gave Nathan a disapproving look. 'I assure you it is quite true, Mr Middleton. I did not come here to read false statements.' Nathan smarted under the rebuke, mouth set grimly. 'May I go on?' Abraham Marsh turned to the will again.

'"I do this against the probable expectations of both my sons and feel it is only right I should furnish an explanation as to why I divide my assets in this way. Tristram does not possess the business acumen of his brother, but I believe, given the chance, and based upon the solid foundation I have laid, he can continue the success of John Middleton, Merchant."' The attorney ignored a contemptuous grunt from Nathan. '"I am sure that with the money I have left him my eldest son will be able to establish his own concern. I hope the two businesses will be run in a spirit of friendly competition rather than rivalry. Signed, John Middleton, and witnessed by Abe Dickinson and Tom Heathcote this day 12th August 1843."'

In an atmosphere that was heavy with surprise and disbelief the attorney saw Nathan's face darken with anger. He knew the eldest son had expected to take control after his father's death, and not without reason given his own hard work and the custom of favouring the eldest son. But such practices were not always followed in wills. Abraham had seen many similar situations and often they had led to family rifts. He could see John's thinking. Tristram was the more likeable person, but easygoing, someone who needed responsibility thrust upon him to develop a latent talent. That would never have happened with Nathan in control; he would not have allowed it but kept his brother strictly in his own shadow.

'Well, gentlemen, that is all.' Abraham broke the stunned silence, and provoked an angry outburst.

'The bloody sod!'

Abraham started, frowned and glared at Nathan. 'Do not speak ill of your father.' The words were heavy with reproof but Nathan was impervious to that.

'He must have been out of his mind to expect this nitwit to keep the business thriving!' His mouth tightened in

9

disgust. 'After all I've put into it, *this* is how I'm repaid.' He turned a contemptuous gaze on his brother. 'You played your cards right!'

'This is as much of a surprise to me as it obviously is to you,' returned Tristram quietly.

'So you say,' sneered Nathan. He rose from his chair and looked hard at Abraham. 'Get the funds sorted out quickly and lodge my share with my bank.' He looked back at Tristram, his eyes narrowed. 'Don't expect any future favours from me, and don't come crawling to me for help when you start to make a mess of things, as you certainly will.' Then, without so much as a 'good day', he headed for the door, flinging over his shoulder as he did so, 'And remember, this house reverts to me and mine so your family needn't get too comfortable in it.' He slammed the door behind him.

Tristram watched him go with no sense of triumph. In fact, he felt pity. He knew how badly disappointed his brother was, and inwardly wondered at the wisdom of his father's decision.

Little passed between the brothers during the next six years. Tristram had seen Nathan prosper quickly, using his inheritance to good effect to create a business which would have elicited their father's admiration.

Now, as Tristram walked through Whitby with a heavy heart, he wondered what his father would have thought of his handling of the family firm.

The next two hours were agony for him. He was lost for words to comfort the families who had lost someone on the *Mary Anne* and faced a future without a husband, son or father, the breadwinner snatched from them by the angry sea. He was thankful for Lydia's support. She was able to express their heartfelt sorrow even without speaking, for her eyes could speak volumes. The mourners appreciated a look or a gesture of sympathy from the owner's daughter whom they all knew, some having seen her grow from a gangling schoolgirl into the pretty, vivacious young woman

10

she was today. The younger ones, while 'knowing their place', saw her as a friendly lass with a ready sense of fun when she accompanied her father on sailing days or watched his ship return to the safety of her home port.

As they trudged homeward with steps as heavy as their hearts, duty done, Tristram realised that a little money would ease the immediate burden of those who had lost someone. How he wished he could help but the future looked equally grim for him.

When they reached home an anxious Luke was waiting for them. 'Father, I'm so sorry.' His eyes and voice betrayed how shocked he felt. 'I came straight home when I heard.'

'Thanks, son. We've been to see the families who ...' Tristram's voice faltered.

'I wish I had been here to go with you.'

'I know, but you had your work.'

'I'll get Maggie to make us some tea,' said Lydia. She headed for the kitchen while Tristram and Luke went into the drawing room. A few minutes later she helped Maggie bring in the heavy silver service and fine bone china.

As Lydia poured she was aware that something was seriously amiss with her father. He wasn't just sad over the loss of the men, he was in despair. Something was weighing heavily on his mind. She made no comment for she sensed that he would tell them what it was in his own good time.

Tristram stirred his tea and then, still staring into his cup, replaced the spoon carefully in the saucer. He looked up slowly. 'I have something to tell you both, and then we must decide what best to do for the future.' His voice was quiet, each word spoken as if it had been the subject of careful deliberation beforehand. 'Four investments I made shortly after the *Mary Anne* sailed turned out to be bad ones. I lost heavily – in fact every penny I had invested. I did not tell you because a successful voyage by the *Mary Anne* would have meant I would just about break even.' He paused to let the full significance of their situation sink in.

11

'The insurance will help,' suggested Luke.

Tristram shook his head and looked frankly at his son. 'The *Mary Anne* wasn't insured.'

'What?' Luke was astounded. That his father, usually the most careful of men, should have overlooked this was unbelievable. A sharp glance at his sister showed him that she too had grasped the enormity of the statement. 'You forgot?'

'No. I did it so that I could put the insurance money into those investments. I was assured they were sound and would bring a good quick return.'

'Oh, Father!' cried Lydia.

'Please don't condemn me,' he pleaded with tears in his eyes. The last thing he wanted was to lose the trust of his children. He needed their unwavering support and loyalty in this terrible crisis. 'I did what I thought was best.'

'We don't blame you, Father.' Lydia was quick to reassure him and offer comfort.

'How can we?' said Luke. 'How many times has the *Mary Anne* sailed without anything bad happening to her? You couldn't foresee this tragedy.'

'You weren't to know what was to happen.' Lydia was quick to lend weight to her brother's view. 'We'll work something out.'

'We won't be able to.' Both Lydia and Luke sensed doom in his tone, and tensed to receive more bad news as they waited for him to continue. 'You see, I borrowed heavily to add more money to those investments. I'm afraid I will be bankrupt.'

They stared at him in horror. This could not be true, yet there was no other reason for him to make this shattering statement.

Tristram read their shocked expressions. 'I'm afraid it's true,' he sighed. 'My creditors will take all the assets I have: the office, the warehouse, all the furnishings and contents of this house.'

'They can't!' cried Lydia. 'Not my beloved piano! It's a family heirloom.'

12

Tristram looked sadly at his daughter. 'I'm so sorry, but I'm afraid they will. They'll take everything to regain as much money as possible, and even that will be nowhere near what I owe.'

'But they can't take the house, it belongs to Uncle Nathan so we'll still have somewhere to live,' said Lydia, seeking some small crumb of comfort.

That was crushed by her father's next statement. 'I could go to prison.'

'Oh, no!' she gasped. 'Surely no one would seek retribution that way?'

'They wouldn't.' Though Luke made the remark as a statement it carried a note of query which he tried to dismiss as he went on, 'Your creditors will know you as an honourable man who will repay them in the future. If they put you in jail you would not be able to set about recouping their money.'

Tristram gave a little grunt of doubt. 'You never know which way people will turn.'

'There must be something we can do to help ourselves,' said Lydia, deeply disturbed by the thought of her father in prison for debt.

'What? Who will help?' he said with a sad shake of his head. 'If I tried to borrow more, and I doubt if there is anyone who would lend me money to pay off my debts, it will only worsen the situation. I'd face an exorbitant interest rate with no assets or possible source of income.'

Lydia saw there were other thoughts disturbing him. His lips tightened as he went on. 'What I regret most is what I have done to you, my children. I'd hoped, nay, dreamed of leaving you a thriving business which you both could run. Luke was already gaining a wide experience. And you, Lydia,' he glanced at his daughter, 'I know how interested you were in it, and you showed a willingness to learn. Together you'd have made a successful team of whom I and your grandfather would have been proud. But, now ...' His voice faltered. 'I've brought you nothing but poverty.'

13

He sank on to a chair, covering his face with his hands. His whole body seemed to fold in on itself, oppressed by the collapse of his world.

Lydia was quickly on her knees beside him, taking his hands in hers and drawing them down so she could look into his eyes with an expression of love to combat the guilt he was feeling.

'Father, you've given us your love and that is more important than anything.' She glanced at Luke who had also come to kneel beside him. 'We love you and nothing that has happened can destroy that.'

'We'll be here for you,' added her brother. 'Whatever we can do to help, we will. I earn only a little but it can go towards necessities.'

Tristram nodded. 'Thank you, Luke, but I must find a way to pay ...' His voice faltered as the enormity of his situation bore down upon him with unrelenting force.

It troubled Lydia to see her father like this. She knew that behind the easygoing exterior there was a proud man who would take this reversal hard. But worse even than the loss he had suffered, he would have an overwhelming feeling of having let people down: the victims of the tragedy, their families, his employees, herself and Luke. He believed he had failed his own father and betrayed John's trust. She had to show him he was wrong.

Her eyes brightened as an idea occurred to her. 'Uncle Nathan!' she cried. 'He'll help!' Why she had thought of their rarely seen uncle, why he had sprung to mind when they had never directly communicated since her grandfather died, she did not know, but his name was on her lips almost before she had thought it.

Tristram gaped at his daughter in astonishment. 'What on earth gave you that idea? You know we haven't spoken in six years, ever since Father left the business to me.'

'That may be,' said Lydia, 'but he's still family. He wouldn't see his own brother go to prison for debt.' She stopped then added a little cautiously, 'Surely?'

14

Tristram gave a wry smile. 'You don't know your Uncle Nathan. He never had any love for me even when were boys. He'll probably delight in my predicament.'

'But you've never been in a situation like this before,' said Luke, seeing a possible way out of their dilemma in Lydia's suggestion. 'Why not go to see him? He may say no, but he may agree.'

Tristram raised his eyebrows as if to say it was a preposterous idea.

Irritated by this attitude, Lydia spoke sharply. 'If you won't go, then I will.'

He recognised the stubborn streak in her, rising to the surface. He must stop her before she took matters completely out of his hands. He would not have her or Luke suffer the humiliation of asking Nathan for help.

'No,' he protested. 'You will do no such thing!' He glanced at his son. 'Nor you, Luke. I forbid it!'

'But why, Father?' asked Lydia.

'Because I know my brother.'

'He may have changed in six years,' Luke suggested.

'Not he.' Tristram straightened. 'Now, no more of this. Forget your Uncle Nathan and let us concentrate on more practical measures which will help us to a solution. First, we will list our assets.'

They got down to practicalities but their conclusions were not encouraging and when Tristram went to bed he was a very worried man.

For a long time sleep eluded him. His mind was too preoccupied with his problems. The future was a blank. When some sort of sleep eventually came it was broken by visions of his father, openly disappointed in a son who had brought a once thriving business to the point of bankruptcy. The disgust on John's face and the accusing finger he pointed sent Tristram cowering into a dark corner in an attempt to escape. There he found his brother laughing loudly, delighted at his downfall. The noise grew louder and louder until he woke up, shouting, arms lashing out to

15

ward off the condemnation of his father and the mockery of his brother.

It was a weary man who dressed the following morning, but by the time he walked downstairs his mind was made up. In spite of the hostile ghosts that had haunted his night, he realised in the chill of the morning that maybe they were adding their strength to Lydia's suggestion and that, for the sake of the firm and his father's memory, he should approach Nathan who surely would not want to see the family business ruined.

Lydia and Luke were already in the dining room and tried to make their morning greetings as bright and near-normal as possible. Tristram did not respond with his usual enthusiasm, meeting each day as a new adventure. Today there was a sober note in his voice. He poured himself some tea and sat down.

'Can I get you some bacon, Father?' asked Lydia.

'No, thank you,' he replied quietly, staring at his cup.

'Mrs Harrington has fried it just how you like it,' she tried to tempt him.

He shook his head. 'I'm not hungry.' He looked up and decided that the only thing to do was to inform them of his decision. 'It goes very much against the grain but I'm going to see if Nathan will help.'

'Good,' said Luke brightly. 'I believe it's the right decision. Uncle Nathan won't want to see the business Grandfather founded pass out of existence.'

'That is good news.' Lydia agreed her father was doing the right thing. 'I'm sure he'll help.'

'We'll see,' Tristram replied in a tone which showed he still had doubts. He rose from his chair, his tea untouched.

'Would you like me to come with you?' asked Luke.

'You have your work.'

'Mr Martin will understand.'

Tristram shook his head. 'Maybe, but it's important you make sure you don't jeopardise your job. No, you go to work.'

16

Lydia was about to suggest that she accompany her father but held back when she realised that he did not want either of his children to see him in the embarrassing role of begging his brother for help. She watched him walk from the room, his step lacking the usual briskness, his shoulders slumped under the weight of the situation. There was no final word for them as he left.

Chapter Two

'And what would it be you're dreaming of, Sean Casey?'
Eileen Nolan twisted over on to her stomach so that she
could lean on her elbows to catch his reaction. The sheet
slipped from her shoulders and her brown hair, shot with a
touch of gleaming copper, fell forward over her naked
breasts. Her blue eyes searched the day-dreamer's face for
an answer.

Sean continued to stare past her at the ceiling where he
saw beckoning horizons instead of flaking distemper
marked with Dublin soot and grime.

She poked him in the ribs to remind him that she had
asked a question.

Slowly brown eyes, soft as suede, met hers. 'Ah, sure,
your beautiful self, Eileen.' The Irish brogue rolled off his
tongue softly and caressingly, trying to lull any doubts she
might have about his answer. But he did not succeed.

'Away with you, Casey,' she replied, eyes sparkling with
delight that she had seen through his ploy and he knew it. 'I
wasn't in those thoughts. You wouldn't have held that
faraway look if I had been, they'd have lingered on closer
pleasures. Tell me and tell me now, what's that idle brain
of yours thinking?'

'Nothing that can't be set aside for more tempting
matters.' His fingers pushed aside her falling strands of hair
and ran provocatively over the smooth skin of her firm

breasts. His eyes danced with teasing laughter as he looked deep into hers, tempting her to forget her question.

'That's what you think, Sean Casey, but don't you believe it. You can't tempt me with anything until I know what's hatching in that brain of yours.' She saw protests spring to his lips but cut them short, eyes narrowing with suspicion. 'I hope it's not another of those wild ideas you had in the past?'

'Like emigrating to America?'

'Like emigrating to America,' she agreed.

Sean had met Eileen four years ago when they were both twenty-one. Their eyes had met across a crowded dance floor in Saint Patrick's Church Hall and from that moment their lives had come together. They could not live without each other. Being apart held no joy and within three weeks they had both left home in what was a respectable but poor part of the city, north of the Liffey. They had not gone far, having found rooms to rent in an area of similar reputation, though it was on the borders of a far worse district with rundown buildings and brawling tenants. They would have liked better but realised that in their circumstances they could not be choosey.

Their two rooms comprised one floor of what had once been an elegant eighteenth-century town house, one of a terrace built, among many others, for the elite of Dublin society by Luke Gardiner, a banker who had married well and seized his opportunity to buy land cheaply on the north side. Now the properties were of little interest to their owners, who saw them only as a source of income and did not care if they moved down the social scale to house the poorest poor like those in the near neighbourhood. There the dregs of Dublin lived, many of them driven to the towns and cities for reasons of sheer survival during the famine and now remaining there with nothing to entice them back to the land.

Sean's and Eileen's move was disapproved of by both

families, the local priest and the tongue-wagging neighbour-hood. But they considered only their passionate love for each other and were the envy of others their own age who had not the courage to go against convention.

They were ostracised by many, longer by some than others, but with their friendly, easygoing natures they soon laid the ghost of their mode of living, though the priest and some of his close supporters in the parish continued to look down their noses at them for 'living in sin'.

Sean had been in and out of jobs since he was fourteen. Born restless, he was always looking for the pot of gold at the end of the rainbow. When love hit him he regretted that he could not take Eileen to: 'The type of house you deserve, away from the impoverished side of Dublin, in one of the fashionable seaside places like Donnybrook, Blackrock or Kingstown.'

She laughed off his concern, saying, 'Houses don't matter, Sean, as long as I'm with you.' But she looked no further than Ireland. She rode the condemning looks, the snide remarks and the derogatory names she was called until they mostly ceased though there were still those, even among her one-time friends, who would have nothing to do with her.

She had quickly recognised that Sean cherished his freedom and had no desire to be tied down by marriage, at least not yet. She knew that if she wanted him she would have to 'live in sin' for the time being. He had charm, charisma, the gift of a flattering tongue that would tempt any girl. But she knew he would charm others but go no further, for without marriage ties she could walk away from any unfaithfulness and he would not want that. He loved her deeply, as much as she did him.

She did what she could to make their rundown home more comfortable though that was not easy with little money to spend except on necessities and sometimes it was hard even to get those. Jobs were not easy to come by and Sean took work here and there whenever it was available.

There were too many unskilled men like him chasing too few vacanices. But they managed and lived on love, determined that their circumstances would never detract from their powerful feelings for each other.

Now his fingers ran enticingly down her spine. Eileen shivered. Sean's lips twitched in amusement, he winked, and with one arm threw the bedclothes to one side.

'No, Sean!' She eased the prohibition by adding, 'Not yet. Not until I know what's in that brain of yours.'

He was a dreamer, always coming up with ideas to make their fortune. 'Some day, my love,' he would say, 'I'll dress you in the finest clothes and parade you before the gentry of Europe. They'll envy me your beauty and flock to meet you.'

At first she'd treated his words with a frivolous response, laughter on her lips, until she'd realised there was something deadly serious behind them. She loved a man who, though a dreamer, believed that one day he would do exactly what he promised. When he changed 'the gentry of Europe' for 'American society' she started to treat his ideas seriously. The prospect of travelling three thousand miles over water and then goodness knows how many on land was daunting. She was not going to go that far from home and she had told him so.

'Ah, Eileen, don't be so hasty. We'd escape this poverty and all the wagging tongues. There'd be no more disapproving glares and headshakes from Father O'Connell. We'd be far away where no one would know us.'

'Too far,' she had responded.

He had ignored this. 'And there'd be a fortune to be made. Think of it, me bonny – money. Rings on your fingers ...'

'Bells on your toes to trip us up,' she had cynically interrupted.

'Now, Eileen, me love ...'

She had tossed her head and snorted contemptuously. 'Don't be "loving" me, Casey.' She'd set her chin defiantly

21

at him and fixed him with an uncompromising stare. 'No! Not America!'

He recognised the signs, and, though he dwelt on the idea for many a day, had allowed it to fade gradually from his mind.

She knew she had won – but now? What scheme was hatching in the mind of the man who lay naked beside her? His mind was filled with but two things at the moment. One she would withhold until she knew the other. She inclined her head provocatively, promising much if he answered the quizzical light in her eyes.

'Well?'

His eyes sparkled in anticipation of what would follow after he had answered her question. 'England, me love, England.'

Her look of disdain was meant to dampen his eagerness. 'You've been listening to the likes of Seamus O'Leary and Kevin Harper.'

'No, no,' Sean put in almost too hastily.

'You have and I know it,' she insisted. 'They've filled your head with . . .'

'. . . real prospects,' he finished her sentence before she could complete it. 'They say there's a fortune to be made if you're not afraid of work. And I'm not frightened of that.'

'Bend your back with a shovel in your hand?' Her voice held disbelief. 'Is that for the likes of Sean Casey?'

'If needs be.'

Eileen looked doubtful, ignoring the soft touch of his fingers as they ran persuasively up and down her spine. 'And for how long? You've never been keen to pick up a shovel here in Ireland.'

'That's as maybe. But there's more money to be made over there than there is here. And the shovel is only a means to an end.'

'I might have known.' She raised her eyebrows heavenwards as if entreating the Lord to wipe the ideas, whatever they were, from Casey's mind. 'Dreams, dreams!'

22

'Now don't be hasty, me love. The shovel will get me to England and I'll be able to see what other prospects there are for me there. Sean Casey won't be slow in spotting them, believe me.' He gripped her shoulders and looked hard into her eyes. 'Don't you see? This is our chance to find a new life away from here, to better ourselves. Industry's expanding on the other side of the Irish Sea, it needs workers. Seamus and Kevin have money in their pockets now, money to spare. That's more than we have. I realise America is too far from home for you. I know you didn't like the idea of leaving Ireland forever. But this is on our doorstep.'

'It isn't Ireland,' said Eileen wistfully.

'I know, but what has Ireland to offer us? Me in and out of jobs, with no chance of anything permanent, no chance to move out of this trap. Think what there might be in England.' He saw he was making no headway. There was no spark in her eyes, no current of excited anticipation in her body. 'Let's compromise,' he suggested. 'Let me go first, see what the prospects are. If there's nothing for us, I'll come home. But if I think there is a chance for us, I'll come back to fetch you, let you see for yourself and then you can decide.' He put emphasis on the role she'd have to play, using his most persuasive lilt. 'Let me give it a chance?' he urged.

Eileen hesitated. Though she was reluctant to leave Ireland she knew there was some truth in what he'd said. There were opportunities in England. She had seen evidence of it in friends who had returned on brief visits home. Had she the right to put obstacles in Sean's way, to deny him his chance? Sean was a dreamer, which was part of his attraction, and dreamers sometimes fulfilled their dreams. Might not he do the same? Who was she to stand in his way? If she did, might she not wonder, for the rest of her life, what could have been?

'Please?'

Her mind spun under the soft caresss of his voice. But

23

she was not ready to commit herself for another doubt had sprung to her mind.

'I might lose you,' she said quietly, looking down at him with troubled eyes.

His arms came round her bare shoulders. 'Never!' he cried as he pulled her to him and his lips met hers with a passion which said his love for her was unbreakable.

She returned his kiss with equal ardour, vowing her love for him would prove stronger than any temptation that came his way.

Afterwards they lay entwined in silence for a few minutes, each wrapped in the wondrous love they had shared.

'Eileen Nolan, your loving tempts me to stay,' he said quietly as he stared at the ceiling.

She did not move but replied in a hushed tone, 'It'll be even better when you return for me.'

Sean twisted over to look down at her with eyes which danced with delight at her permission to embark on a quest to change their lives for the better.

'You'll let me go?'

She nodded.

He kissed her hard. Her arms came around his neck and held him there with a kiss he would long remember.

'When will you go?' she asked quietly.

'The day after tomorrow, with Seamus and Kevin. They know the ropes when we dock in Liverpool.'

Startled, she pushed herself away from him so that she could examine his reaction the better. 'Sean Casey, you've had this planned all along,' she said sharply.

'Ah, now, mavourneen,' he said lightly as if to brush aside her objection, 'maybe I did and maybe I didn't.'

'Maybe you did is more likely.' Her eyes flashed with annoyance. 'Did you figure on leaving without telling me?'

'Maybe I did and maybe I didn't,' he repeated teasingly, his eyes twinkling with amusement at her reaction. He saw anger clouding her face then. 'Ah, come here, my sweet.'

He grabbed her arm as he saw her move to slip out of bed and pulled her back towards him. 'Sure, would I be doing such a despicable thing as to leave without telling you? Would I jeopardise my chances with you forever by doing that? Of course not. But Casey likes it when you flare up, there's passion there.'

He brought her the final few inches until his lips met hers. For a moment she did not respond, but as his hands slid down her spine and round her waist she succumbed, and in their mutual giving they left each other with much to remember during their parting.

'There they are!' Sean's voice rose with excitement as, holding Eileen's hand so that they did not become separated in the crowd milling on the quay, he weaved his way towards Seamus O'Leary and Kevin Harper.

'Ah, sure, the little lady's coming with us. Couldn't bear to leave her behind?' queried Seamus with a teasing grin and an added insinuating wink.

'Away wi' ye, Seamus O'Leary, I wouldn't walk the same road as you, let alone get on board the same ship,' Eileen retorted.

'Oh, she's a mite touchy,' said Seamus, cocking his head on one side. 'Annoyed that what you have to offer won't keep Sean here?'

'Why? Are you jealous you've not had it offered to you?' she snapped.

'Ah, what would I want with that when there's a host of willing lasses the other side of the water?' Seamus's eyes twinkled as he added, 'Want us to keep an eye on Sean for ye?'

'A right bollox you'd make of that.'

'She'll be telling us next she trusts ye, Casey,' put in Kevin.

'And she can,' rasped Sean.

The two men laughed in disbelief. 'Wait 'til you see what we've seen.'

'You two's all mouth,' Eileen shot at them. 'I'll bet you wouldn't know what to do if it was offered you on a plate.'

They let out a great guffaw. 'If you won't test us we'll let Sean be the judge when he gets to the other side,' teased Seamus.

Sean put his arm round Eileen's waist. 'Take no notice of these two, me darlin'. I'll have no time for their antics when I'm setting about making a fortune for us.'

'Promising ye gold, is he?' asked Kevin. 'More likely all he'll get is blisters and a thick head.'

'I thought you told him there was money to be made in England?' said Eileen.

'Oh, they did,' put in Sean quickly, 'but I'll not spend it on drink and colleens, and there won't be any blisters.'

'There will from the shovels and picks, and you'll be so homesick ye'll find comfort in drink and ... you know what soon enough,' predicted Seamus.

Sean flexed his shoulders. 'Not Sean Casey. Better things await him.'

Kevin and Seamus looked at each other and raised their eyebrows. 'The great Sean Casey, still out to make his fortune,' they both said in unison.

'And he will one day,' said Eileen, wanting to spike their doubt.

Seamus and Kevin had no opportunity to respond with their glib teasing tongues. Sean cut in to change the subject as he saw Eileen beginning to seethe beneath her cool exterior. Looking around at the milling crowd, pressing towards the two steam packets lying alongside the quay awaiting passengers bound for Liverpool, he asked, 'Are all these people seeking work in England, and taking the whole family with them?'

'Good grief, no. Most of the families here will be bound for America,' explained Seamus.

'Why go via Liverpool? Why not direct to America?'

'The Coffin Ships, Sean, the Coffin Ships, remember?' said Kevin. 'There were once cheap passages direct from

26

these shores to America but the ships they used often weren't seaworthy and were manned by inexperienced hands. Many ships never reached America. Passages from Liverpool have a better reputation. They cost more but there are many willing to pay for a better chance of reaching America.'

'Most of the men on their own will be seeking work in England,' added Seamus. 'Some with the idea of making enough to take them across the Atlantic to a better life – they hope.'

'Haven't you two thought of doing that?' asked Eileen.

Seamus gave a laugh. 'Like to be rid of us, would you?' He gave a little shake of his head. 'Sorry to disappoint you, sweetheart, we're happy as we are.'

'Got your ticket?' asked Kevin, raising a querying eyebrow at Sean.

'Ticket?' He looked puzzled.

'Aye, to get aboard ship.'

'No one told me.' Sean looked around in panic.

Planks were being run out from the ships and the crowd surged forward. Passengers eager to make sure they got on board bustled each other. Angry voices rose in protest at being jostled or knocked unceremoniously by luggage. Mothers firming their grip on their children's hands screamed at them to hold tight as the crush bore down on them. Wives yelled at their husbands to do something to ease their burdens or take the strain of the bodies pressing around them.

'Where do I get one?' Sean's voice was full of anxiety as he envisaged being refused passage and having to watch the ship sail without him. That would be a tragedy after winning Eileen's approval.

'At the office,' said Kevin.

'Where's that?' yelled Sean, annoyed at Kevin's nonchalant attitude.

'Other end of the quay.' Kevin inclined his head in the direction of some buildings way beyond the crowd.

27

'Hell, will I ever make it?' Sean thrust the bundle, which he had been holding over his shoulder, to Eileen. 'Here, hold this.' As he turned Seamus stepped into his path. Sean made to go past him but Seamus once more blocked him. 'Out of the way, man,' snapped Sean. 'What the bloody hell are you playing at? Do you want me to miss the ship?'

Seamus spread his hands as if he had done nothing. 'Not I, man.'

Sean felt a tap on his shoulder and heard Kevin say, 'Nor I.' He swung round to see his friend grinning at him and holding up a boarding ticket. 'Yours,' he said, and then cast a mischievous glance at Eileen. 'We told you we'd look after him.'

'You pair o' eejits,' Sean snapped, and grabbed the ticket. He relieved Eileen of the bundle and glanced in the direction of the ships. 'Which one?' he asked.

'Take your pick,' replied Seamus, still grinning at Sean's irritation over the trick they had played.

Sean eyed him suspiciously but Seamus just shrugged his shoulders to indicate, 'I couldn't care which one.'

'The ticket isn't for a particular ship?'

'No. Now get on with it.'

'Right. The *Nimrod*.' Apart from the fact that cattle were bellowing on the *Sea Horse* and not the *Nimrod*, it looked that little bit sleeker than the other vessel and he could only put that down to the different-shaped bow. In all other respects the two were almost identical.

'Good choice,' agreed Seamus. 'No cattle for us, only freight, but it'll mean a bigger crush.'

'Come on then, let's get aboard,' said Kevin. He started to jostle his way towards the gangplank. Seamus and Sean were close behind. Eileen just managed to keep hold of Sean's hand as a burly passenger cannoned into her. Sharp curses sprang to her lips but she could not vent her feelings as Sean was pressing on.

He was about to step on to the gangplank when she cried, 'Hi, what about me?'

A contrite expression flashed across his face as he swung round. He grabbed her and pulled her to him. His kiss was hard and passionate. 'Look after yourself, and keep yourself for me.'

There were yells all around them as people wanting to get on board were irritated to find their way blocked.

Before Eileen could reply or return his kiss Sean was striding up the plank. She staggered under the pressure of the bodies surging around her, fought against the swelling tide of emigrants trying to get on board before a halt was called. She escaped the crush and scanned the vessel for Sean. Catching a glimpse of the three Irishmen making for the stern, she took her place among the folk lining the quay.

'Follow me!' called Kevin as he stepped on deck. He started towards the stern and, though the rail alongside the quay was already filling up, managed to find a space there into which the three friends could push themselves and their possessions.

'Wouldn't we be better below deck when we sail?' asked Sean as he scanned the people on the quay looking for Eileen.

Seamus gave an amused laugh. 'Can't go down there, we're deckers and on deck we remain, no matter what the crush or the weather. So make the best of it and hang on to the space we've got.'

Sean made no comment on this advice; he realised Seamus and Kevin knew what they were about. His attention was on the line of well-wishers, relatives, sweethearts and friends come to see their relations off on the first step to a new life in an unknown land.

He saw Eileen at the very moment she saw him. Their eyes locked and across the distance exchanged vows of love that needed no words. Each sensed the regret in the other for what was happening. Eileen's heart ached at their parting. She longed for Sean to jump ship and crush her in his arms again, never let her go. He longed for the touch of

29

her body again, wanting her to be with him, sharing a new adventure, seeking a new life. Together they could conquer the world. He wished the ship was just bringing him back from England with the news that their fortune was assured and he would be able to give her the best of everything and make the rest of Britain – no, of Europe – jealous of Sean Casey who could walk into all the best places with the most beautiful woman of them all beside him.

A sudden unexpected shrilling from the ship's steam whistle, which burst with piercing abruptness across the dock, shattered his dreams and brought him back to reality. Cries rose from those still trying to get on board as officials barred their way, yelling that the full complement of passengers had been taken aboard the *Nimrod*. Those refusing to believe it scuffled with the authorities. Others tried to step on the gangplank to prevent it being hauled from the quay.

'Try the *Sea Horse*!' the cry went up among those still without a passage. Most of the crowd took the advice and surged towards the other ship. A few hoped that, relieved of the crush, the officials would take kindly to them and order the plank to be run out again. But it was not to be and curses were heaped on their heads as orders came to cast off from the captain on his bridge who would not be delayed any longer.

He wanted to be clear of the harbour before the *Sea Horse*, for he knew her captain would show him no consideration, and would use all the power he could muster to reach Liverpool first.

Smoke which had been rising from the *Nimrod*'s solitary funnel now thickened as the boilers below were stoked in readiness for departure. Noise ground from the depths of the vessel. Slowly, the large encased paddles began to turn. Orders were shouted, sailors hurried about their urgent tasks, ropes were cast off, and the *Nimrod* began to ease gently away from the quay.

People shouted their final farewells, yelled good wishes, offered last-minute advice, urged their loved ones to write, waved, dabbed their eyes or wept openly. Tears streamed down Eileen's cheeks. She felt shattered, as if a part of her life was being torn from her. And yet, she reminded herself, this parting was nothing compared to that of some of the people around her. She would see Sean again before long, whereas for others this parting could be forever. She waved, trying to make her gesture one of approval of what he was doing, but she hated, with all her heart, the gulf widening between them as the steamer moved further and further from the quay.

Sean waved back silently, oblivious to the noise around him, his thoughts all on the girl he loved, the one who had brought meaning to his life when it had seemed to be going nowhere. She had instilled a purpose to his dreams, and now this ship was taking him on his first step towards achieving them. As he watched her growing smaller, he vowed he would never let her down.

When she was no longer in sight, Kevin broke the silence between them. 'Well, me boy, a new life for you.'

Sean, still looking downcast, nodded.

Seamus slapped him on the back. 'We'll soon have you a pretty girl to take yer mind off Eileen.'

'Don't want my mind taking off her, thanks. You go your way and I'll go mine.' His voice carried a warning that he wanted no meddling from them. He knew their ways, trusted them only so far. They could get up to all sorts of tricks and he knew that in Ireland they had had several brushes with the law but always managed to talk themselves out of trouble with their glib tongues. That wasn't Sean's idea of achieving his ambitions. Nevertheless, knowing that Seamus and Kevin had experience of life in England, he realised they would offer him useful advice.

Kevin held up his hands in acknowledgement. 'All right, Sean, we understand. But allow us to give you a few tips when we reach Liverpool. We don't want you being done over by the runners or the dock dollies.'

'The latter hold no interest for me.'

'Maybe, but they'll try to lure you on, manoeuvre you for pickpockets and thugs to do their thieving and robbing.'

'And what about the runners?'

'Well, they work chiefly on emigrants to America who are most vulnerable to their game. There's a gang of men known as the "Forty Thieves". They hang about the docks when the ships come in. They are well organised, pretend to be porters to help the emigrants.'

'Help?' put in Seamus with a laugh of derision. 'They have a vicious system worked out to deprive the emigrants of all the cash they have. They'll spin them a yarn of looking after their interests, telling them they know just the man to book them a passage to the New World. If they already have a passage, then they'll suggest they can arrange accommodation until the ship sails. The travellers'll want food, too, so these rogues will tell them they know just the man to direct them to the cheapest good-quality shops.'

'So they pass the gullible emigrant on to the runners who take them on their rounds, each time working with a passenger-broker, a shopkeeper and a proprietor of a boarding house. Needless to say the emigrants are over-charged, cheated and left in a parlous state.'

'Can't anything be done about it?' asked Sean, amazed at the unsavoury sound of Liverpool.

Kevin shrugged his shoulders. 'There's a token display of concern by the authorities but who cares about an Irishman and his family? Liverpool folk are against us, don't like us flooding into their city even though it's on a temporary basis, so the emigrants get the poorest dwellings in the city to house them until they move on. Nobody seems to care.'

'But surely not everyone in Liverpool can be against them?'

'True. There are the do-gooders who try to help and continually press the authorities to do more, especially about the overcrowded conditions which bring health hazards.'

32

Sean shook his head. 'I don't look forward to seeing Liverpool.'

'Oh, it's not all bad. And we are lucky we can pass through quickly, knowing where we're going.'

'There'll be men on the quay when we arrive, recruiting. They'll have placards offering work. You'll have to sign up but we won't as we have our old jobs to go to, digging out docks at Grimsby on the east coast. Stick by us, we'll have a word with Joe Sanders who'll be doing the recruiting for Grimsby. He signed us on when we first came and will probably hurry you through if you're with us. Bottle of Irish whiskey usually does the trick.'

'Thanks,' replied Sean. Before leaving Ireland he had made up his mind that once they reached England he would go his own way, but now he was weakening. If his companions were to be believed they could ease his way considerably once they were ashore. 'Seems I chose the wrong steamer,' he added, indicating the *Sea Horse* which was steadily gaining on the *Nimrod*. Thick black smoke belched from her funnel; her paddles churned the water with a regular thunderous pounding as if to show the *Nimrod* how it should be done.

'Well, if you want to get there first, yes, you have, but it doesn't matter in our case,' said Kevin, leaning casually against the rail. 'Relax, Sean, enjoy the sea air.'

Sean did just that, his mind dwelling on the girl he had left behind. It roused his determination anew that this 'adventure' to England should bear the fruit he wanted and that Eileen should enjoy it to the fullest.

The sea was calm, causing only the slightest rolling of the deck which did nothing to upset Sean and allowed him to enjoy his first voyage.

'Land ahoy!' The cry from the lookout sent a wave of excitement through the ship. Passengers strained to get their first glimpse of new horizons.

Sean saw the distant change of colour, a smudge 'twixt

33

sea and sky, but his attention was drawn to the *Sea Horse* which had not outdistanced the *Nimrod* as much as he had expected though nevertheless she would be first into Liverpool. He cast his eyes towards land, eager to see it grow clearer, his first sight of shores beyond his native Ireland. Excitement coursed through his veins. It couldn't be dampened by the sight of his two companions in casual conversation with an attitude of 'we've seen it all before'.

As the shore gew more distinct he looked to the progress of the *Sea Horse*. 'She's heading straight for that island,' he cried, drawing Kevin's and Seamus's attention to the ship whose wake had cut across the *Nimrod*'s course.

Both men give a short laugh. 'Not her,' replied Kevin. 'Looks like it but the captain will soon alter course to sail wide round what's known as the Rock.'

They watched, waiting for the manoeuvre to take place, but the *Sea Horse* ploughed on. The *Nimrod* shuddered as her captain altered course to give the Rock a wide berth.

'Captain of the *Sea Horse* is leaving it late,' observed Seamus.

'Aye, he is that,' agreed Kevin, his voice filled with concern.

Tension sparked as they concentrated on the progress of the other ship.

'My God, he's going to cut it fine,' cried Seamus. 'He'll be running very close to the Rock.'

Water churned more vigorously from the steamer's paddles, sending white foam streaming behind them.

'He's putting her under more speed,' cried Kevin, astonished at this latest change of pace with the vessel nearing the Rock. 'What the hell's he up to?'

'All to gain a few minutes,' observed Seamus in disgust.

The Rock was off the *Sea Horse*'s port side now.

'Good grief!' There was alarm and disbelief in Seamus's cry.

Another steamer had appeared, sailing in the opposite direction around the Rock. The two ships were closing fast.

Alarm ran through the *Nimrod* as passengers and crew saw that a collision was unavoidable. The names *Sea Horse* and *Eagle* would be emblazoned on their minds forever.

'There's no room for the *Eagle* to swing to starboard. If the captain tries it, he'll be on the Rock!'

The captain of the *Sea Horse* had ordered the helm to be thrown hard over but it was too late. There was a grinding crash, a rending of timber as the *Eagle* cut sharply into the port bow of the *Sea Horse*. She tore open under the force.

It seemed as if the collision would never stop. Her top-gallant forecastle was carried away, the deck split halfway across. There was pandemonium on her crowded deck. Passengers were tossed about by the force of the impact. Screams rent the air. Families were scattered. Panic-stricken mothers looked around frantically for children who only a few moments before were standing beside them, not knowing whether they had been tossed into the sea. Men and women clung desperately to whatever they could seize hold of as the vessel lurched, shuddered and juddered, throwing the *Eagle* aside before it finally stopped, to be left wallowing in a sea churned into tumult by the impact.

The captain of the *Eagle* did the only thing he could to save his vessel and those on board. Grasping the situation quickly, he assessed that the watertight compartment had held and headed for the nearest shore to beach his craft.

As soon as the captain of the *Nimrod* saw that a collision was unavoidable, he brought his steamer round to head for the stricken vessel which was taking in water quickly. Orders flew, clear and precise, boomed with an authority that demanded instant obedience. His crew were already moving with that instinctive calm born of an emergency at sea. His calls rose above the clamour of the passengers who had never witnessed a tragedy of this proportion. They felt the helplessness of people driven into shock, wanting to help, wanting to eliminate further horrors, but could only stand and stare or move in hopeless confusion.

The *Nimrod* came round on to a course which would take her close to the doomed ship. The captain, his eyes alert, took in the ever-changing scene. More people were thrown into the water or jumped, with the hope of surviving, taking their destiny into their own hands rather than allowing the *Sea Horse* to yield them to the mercy of the sea.

Passengers at the *Nimrod*'s side, numbed by the sight of men, women and children trying to cling to life in the heaving cauldron, were jerked out of their bemusement by the crew yelling at them to clear the rail and supplementing their orders with physical persuasion. Realising that the sailors were desperate to facilitate a rescue, several male passengers, including Sean, Seamus and Kevin, helped them in their task.

A mother cried out that she had lost her child. Sean, aware of what had happened in the crush and confusion, whisked a little girl off her feet and shoved her into her mother's arms. He gave the woman a broad smile and a wink in acknowledgement of the relief in her face and tears which streamed down her cheeks. Kevin persuaded an old man that he was too helpless to give aid in a physical way and suggested to the man's son that he would be better employed looking after his father.

The Captain concentrated on bringing the *Nimrod* as close as he dare to the people in the water without endangering their lives further. The ship's paddles could exact a vicious toll if he did not hold back. The crew were fastening ropes to the rail and dropping them overboard to dangle in the sea and provide support to any victim who managed to reach the *Nimrod*.

Sean grabbed a rope from one of the crew.

'Know how to tie that?' asked a sailor doubtfully. He did not want anyone's chance of rescue snatched away through incompetence.

'Sure, I can fix it as good as you.' With the dexterity of long practice Sean fastened the rope securely. He looked up, saw approval in the sailor's eyes, and grinned.

The man thrust three more ropes at him. 'Fix these. I'll get more.'

The *Nimrod* slowed, her engines quietening. The paddles turned just enough to keep the vessel under control. Boats were lowered, and as soon as they hit the water were cast off. Backs were bent at the oars to power the rescue vessels towards the sinking ship.

The air throbbed with the screech of the *Eagle*'s engines as she pounded her way to the beach. Heart-rending pleas for help came from those in the water and cut through the awful sound of the sea gulping at the *Sea Horse* as it sucked the vessel towards its doom.

There was tumult everywhere. Water foamed and boats swayed as sailors heaved victims over the gunwales into the sodden safety of the life-saving craft. People struggled for life. Heads bobbed, arms flailed as if trying to pluck support from the air, while others grabbed at any floating debris.

'Come on! Come on! Swim for it! Swim!' There was pleading in Sean's urgent cajoling when his eyes fixed on a man struggling to support a young woman who was floundering in the heaving sea. He realised that the man was only a weak swimmer and would never make it to the *Nimrod* unless he released his grip on the woman.

Seamus and Kevin hauled another man over the rail when he reached the top of one of the ropes, then followed Sean's gaze and joined him in his encouragement.

He straightened up from the rail, urgency in his movements as he threw off his jacket and tore off his boots. Before Seamus and Kevin were aware of what he intended he was on the rail and diving into the sea.

He went down and down, slowed, then kicked for the surface. He burst into daylight, water streaming from his hair. He trod water, brushed it from his eyes and took his bearings quickly. He found the man and relief swept over him when he saw that the woman was still supported. Sean struck out towards them, his strokes strong. As he neared,

37

he saw the man was weakening but his determination to keep the woman afloat superseded everything else.

Sean reached them. He trod water again and shouted, 'I'll take her!'

The man, breathing hard, was thankful to be relieved of the responsibility.

Sean took the weight of the woman on his left arm, holding her close to reassure her. 'Relax! Don't struggle, I've got you.' His words did nothing to banish the fear from her eyes, but she recognised that he might be her saviour and allowed him to take control.

'You all right?' Sean eyed the man.

He nodded, and when Sean started towards the *Nimrod*, followed.

Sean saw that their best chance of survival was to make for the narrow metal platform fixed to the paddle housing, just above the waterline. His stroke with his free arm was strong but, having to support the woman, his progress was slow. He appeared to be making no headway.

Sean's stroke faltered. The movement transmitted itself to the woman and he felt her tighten her grip on his arm and stiffen her body in alarm.

'It's all right,' he called encouragingly. 'Relax.' He felt her grip slacken in response. He knew how much she depended on him and hardened his resolve that the sea should not have them.

Slowly, ever so slowly, he drew nearer the *Nimrod*. He heard shouts from above and realised they came from Seamus and Kevin.

They had watched his actions, willing him to succeed. When they realised his intention, they hurried along the deck and clambered over the rail to drop on to the narrow platform. Gripping the paddle-casing, they shouted encouragement to their friend. Holding on one-handed they knelt down and reached out with their free hands when Sean began to tread water.

Realising that safety was within her grasp the young

woman made her own effort to aid the rescue. She slipped her right hand free from Sean and stretched it towards her would-be rescuers, but help was tantalisingly just out of reach. Her face contorted with the strain. One more push. Fingers touched and then she felt a strong grip. She freed her other hand from Sean and grabbed the fingers reaching out to her. Seamus and Kevin took her weight, paused, and then together pulled her out of the water as Sean gave a helping push.

Oblivious to the hard edge of the iron platform, she lay sprawled beside the two Irishmen, gulping air into her aching lungs, ignoring the sodden weight of her clothes and the lank hair clinging to her head. She was safe. Then she realised she was alone. 'Father!' Her scream reverberated with her worst fear. She sat up, twisting round to search the waves. 'Where is he?' Her eyes pleaded with the Irishmen to give her the reassurance she sought.

She felt a comforting arm around her shoulder, heard a rich Irish brogue close to her ear, and saw a finger point across the water. 'He's there. He'll be all right. Sean will rescue him.'

She saw her father battling to keep swimming, saw Sean strike out from the *Nimrod*, and was gripped by the scene unfolding before her which could end in tragedy or joy.

The older man was weakening, his face creased with strain. His body sapped of energy, still he tried to drive onwards until, overwhelmed by the effort, he threw up his arms as if making one last grab at some invisible support. An agonised cry for help was lost as he disappeared beneath the waves.

His daughter screamed and would have jumped into the sea had not Kevin and Seamus restrained her.

Sean dived, took three strong strokes. He saw the man underneath him, grasped his clothes and kicked for the light. Water streamed from their heads as they broke the

39

surface. Their lungs gulped greedily at the air. Sean got a better grip under the man's arms.

'Relax,' he shouted. 'Soon have you out.'

A few minutes later the strong hands of Kevin and Seamus hauled the man out of the water. Sean held on to the *Nimrod*'s side, thankful that his effort had not been in vain. His chest was still heaving as Seamus and Kevin pulled him from the sea to lie beside the man.

'Father! Father!' The young woman crawled the few feet to him.

'Sarah ...' Her father's voice was weak but it strengthened as he added, 'Thank God you're safe.' He felt the reassuring pressure of her hand on his shoulder and fear for her safety drained from him.

She looked round at Sean who was struggling to his feet. 'Thank you for saving us. We'll be ever in your debt.'

Sean gave her a heartening smile. 'Ah, now don't go on so, miss. It was nothing.' In spite of her dishevelled and sodden appearance, with face drawn by the ordeal and eyes lacking sparkle, he realised he was looking at an attractive young woman. Before his thoughts ran away with him he added, 'Come, I think we had better get you both back on deck and find you something warm to wear.' He held out his hand and, as Sarah took it, she felt uplifted. His touch was gentle but firm, imparting the feeling that she would be safe with this young man. She felt an empathy with him as their eyes locked for a moment before she turned them, and her concern, to her father.

Seamus and Kevin were helping him to his feet and giving him the support he needed after his battle with the sea. He caught his daughter's eye and nodded to confirm that, apart from his loss of strength, he was no worse for their ordeal.

The deck was packed with people and noisy with the cries of passengers struggling to be reunited with loved ones. Small boats crowded with survivors dragged from the edge of a watery grave scraped the side of the *Nimrod* as they rode the swell. Eager hands dragged women and children on board before turning to the men. Hysterics, anger, thankfulness and shock were apparent on every side.

Nimrod's crew and passengers did what they could to ease the suffering. Blankets were brought from cabins and from the crew's quarters. Male passengers took off their overcoats and jackets and women wrapped their shawls around the shoulders of the rescued to bring warmth and comfort.

Sean, who had retrieved his jacket and shoes, held the jacket out to Sarah.

She shook her head. 'No, you need it as much as I.' Her voice was soft yet firm with refusal.

Sean started to protest but at that moment a sailor hurried to them cradling some blankets in his arms. Sean whisked one from the pile and swung it around Sarah's shoulders. Kevin grabbed one for her father.

'Thanks,' he said, a grateful light in his eyes, and turned to Sean. 'And you, young man, Sarah and I will never forget what you did today, risking your life the way you did.' He held out his hand. 'James Langton, and this is my daughter, Sarah.'

Sean smiled and returned the handshake. 'Sean Casey,' he replied. 'And my friends, Seamus O'Leary and Kevin Harper.'

Any further exchanges were muted for the time being as a shout went up around the ship. 'There she goes!'

The *Sea Horse*, stern in the air, slid beneath the waves leaving a trail of heaving water in which debris and bodies were tossed around like corks.

Sarah was numbed by the sight. Only a short time ago the *Sea Horse* had been a proud ship, filled with passengers and crew facing a future full of hope. Now it had disappeared forever, leaving shattered lives in its wake.

41

No one spoke. A mantle of silent tribute hung over the *Nimrod* until it was broken by the captain who realised that there might still be survivors in the water. His orders rang clear across the waves for the *Nimrod*'s boats to continue the search.

When all the boats had done what they could and had reported back to their parent ship and been brought on board, the Captain ordered the *Nimrod* to get under way so that she could reach her dock with all possible speed.

News of the tragedy had already reached Liverpool and by the time the *Nimrod* docked every assistance for those struck by the catastrophe was already on the quay. Doctors and their assistants were ready with medical support as soon as the first victim was ashore, despatching the more seriously injured to hospital in ambulances. The less serious cases were shepherded into two warehouses where they received the necessary attention for shock and injuries such as broken limbs, minor cuts and bruises. They were helped into dry clothing which had been hastily assembled. Volunteers had also organised warm drinks which were welcomed by victims eager to drive the cold from their bodies.

In the warehouse set aside for male passengers Sean put on his own change of clothing which he had brought from Ireland. James, pleased to be out of his wet clothing, was thankful for anything, ill-fitting though it might be. When they were satisfied that he needed no further attention the three Irishmen accompanied him outside to await Sarah.

Five minutes later she emerged from the warehouse used by the female passengers. As she walked towards them, in spite of their efforts to stifle their laughter the four men could not do so.

Sarah's anger started to rise. She knew she must cut an amusing figure in the ill-fitting clothes she had been given. Her plain brown dress was about four inches

42

shorter than it should be and the waist sat oddly high. Her auburn hair, which could cascade like a mountain stream, was drawn severely straight back and tied in a tight bun at the nape of her neck.

Indignant at their laughter, she drew herself up only to stumble because of the ill-fitting shoes she had been given. Annoyed that her attempt at dignity in the face of adversity had been thwarted, her lips set in a hard line. She cursed beneath her breath, kicked off her shoes in a flare of temper and, setting her hands on her hips in a gesture of defiance, faced the four men.

'Laugh, would you? Well, it does you no credit. Laugh indeed! You should be showing compassion for a poor girl dressed in such clothes – all they could give me. It was take them or leave them, I had no choice. And what are you going to do about it?' The sharp tone was accompanied by flashing eyes which boded ill for anyone who continued to be amused by her plight.

'Oh, come now, daughter,' put in James quickly. He knew the signs and a major outburst of temper was imminent. It very rarely happened but, when it did, the tantrum could be fiery. He only hoped the three Irishmen read the warning in what he was about to say. 'We were not making fun of you.' He had stifled his laughter and replaced it with a more serious demeanour. 'We were just amused at the sight. My dear, we are concerned for you and you can be sure that I will lose no time in finding you more suitable clothing. We will delay our onward journey until tomorrow and stay overnight at the Imperial. That will give you time to choose yourself a complete new outfit and have the evening to recuperate.'

Sarah felt her anger subsiding with each additional suggestion he made. 'Thank you,' she said stiffly.

'Sorry, miss. We meant no disrespect with our laughter.' Sean had read James's intentions and made his own apology gracefully.

'Ah, sure now, miss, we meant no harm.' Seamus took his lead from Sean.

'They're right, miss, we did not intend to insult you. Besides, how could we? You'd look elegant in whatever you wore.' Though there was still a twitch of amusement at the corners of Kevin's lips and a twinkle in his eyes, Sarah could not ignore his expression which not only begged forgiveness but contained real admiration.

She tossed her head. 'You've all got glib tongues. I suppose I'd better forgive you, though thousands wouldn't.' Her temper was under control now. Her eyes lit up with mischief as she added, 'But, Father, it will cost you two dresses.'

'Two?' James spluttered. 'Now, see here, young lady . . .'

'Two!' There was a sharp, no-nonsense tone in her voice again. She knew she had the upper hand and would brook no refusal. 'And, it goes without saying, the best suite in the hotel.'

James raised his eyes heavenwards, as if pleading for someone to rescue him from this extravagance. He knew Sarah to be a determined young woman who would extract full payment for their mocking laughter. He glanced at the Irishmen. 'What can I do?' he pleaded.

'Nothing, I suppose,' said Sean, 'except agree.'

James grunted his assent. 'Young men, if ever you marry, don't have daughters. But if you do, make sure they can't twist you round their little fingers.'

'Now, Father, what kind of advice is that to give? You know you don't mean it. You enjoy our friendly disputes.' Laughing, Sarah came and linked arms with him in a loving gesture. 'Which always work in my favour.'

He pouted thoughtfully for a moment. 'I suppose I do,' he admitted, giving her a look of devotion. 'Now, we had better be on our way, but first we must acknowledge our debt to these three gentlemen, especially Sean

44

who risked his life.' He started to protest at the praise but James halted him with one upraised hand. 'It's true,' he said. 'I want to repay you in some way. I suppose all of you are coming to England seeking work?'

'Yes, sir,' replied Seamus. 'Well, that is, Sean is. Kevin and I have been coming over for two years already. We've been working at Grimsby, helping dig out the new docks.'

'And you are contracted for this year?'

'No, sir, not contracted, but we have an understanding that if we do return, after visiting our relatives in Ireland, there's a job for us if we want it.'

James showed a little surprise. 'Unusual terms. You must be good workers if they take you on that footing.'

'Ah, well, though I say it meself there's no slacking by Seamus O'Leary and Kevin Harper, and we don't care what we do,' put in Kevin brightly.

'And you, Sean, had you planned to go with your friends?' asked James.

'Well, sir, it's my first visit to England so as these two know the ropes, and I realised they could put in a good word for me, I was prepared to go with thcm.'

'Well, Sean, I can assure you of a job elsewhere.'

'You can?' Surprised, he added almost without thinking, 'Doing what? Where?'

'I'm managing the Bolckow and Vaughan bar iron manufactory at Middlesbrough, a new town on the south bank of the River Tees.'

'And as such you can guarantee me a job?'

'Oh, yes. I can hire and fire if necessary. I normally leave hiring the men to my overseer but if I make a recommendation he'll follow it.' He turned to Kevin and Seamus. 'If you're interested, the offer's open to you as well.'

'Thank you, sir,' said Kevin. 'A change will do us good.' He knew Seamus would agree whatever he decided.

'So you've three new employees,' said Sean. He had noted Sarah's rapt attention during this exchange. Had he really seen relief and approval cross her face or was he letting his imagination run wild?

'Good.' James nodded. 'Come to Middlesbrough. Anyone will direct you to the Bolckow and Vaughan rolling mill. Ask for me.'

'Thank you, sir,' echoed Sean and Kevin.

James turned to his daughter. 'Come, Sarah, let's get you out of those clothes.' His eyes twinkled as he spoke.

'Father!' Her sharp tone reminded him that he should not overstep the mark.

He held up his hands in mock surrender.

Sarah accepted it with an inclination of her head then turned to the three Irishmen. 'Thank you for what you did. Maybe we'll meet again in Middlesbrough.'

'Sure and that would be my pleasure, miss,' Sean replied with a warm smile.

Kevin pressed agreement with his eyes.

As she accompanied her father from the dock, Sean stood watching until Seamus gave him a dig in the ribs.

'Getting ideas?' he said with mocking amusement. 'Sure, you can't have designs on a manager's daughter – she's far above the likes of us.'

'Oh, I don't know about that,' replied Sean.

'Ah, now, don't you go forgetting Eileen,' admonished Kevin.

Chapter Three

Tristram had lost his customary briskness and usual happy demeanour with its accompanying smile which brought pleasure to friends, acquaintances and even strangers. Instead there were leaden feet, a worried frown and a sombre expression which gave no acknowledgement of the respectful greetings given to him by those who knew the tragedy that had befallen him.

The course on which he was now embarked caused his stomach to knot and brought a chill to his heart. To have to beg from his brother was bad enough, but to hear the mockery, which he knew would come, and be accused of letting their father down by destroying the firm he had so painstakingly built up, would inflict deep wounds on Tristram's mind and heart.

He made his way to the east bank of the river, hardly aware of the people around him or of the ships which usually drew his attention. The *Mary Anne* should have been one of them but now she lay with all hands at the bottom of the English Channel, victim of the storm that had brought him ruin and now humiliation.

He had chosen to visit his brother's office rather than his house, for he wanted privacy. His sister-in-law would not be around to nose out the reason for his visit after all these years. There would be no servants within earshot to snap up a juicy piece of news and boast to others that they were privy to certain facts. He hoped the clerks his brother employed would be far enough away from their master's room to hear nothing. His humiliation must not be evident to anyone but his brother and himself. To beg from a man who despised him, who had baited him in childhood and beyond, and who held him in contempt, would pierce like the thrust of a harpoon.

Reaching the building which proclaimed itself as housing the offices of Nathan Middleton, Merchant, he entered through an imposing door to find himself in a corridor which ran to the back of the building. A door on his right was open and he saw a man sitting on a high stool facing a sloping desk. He was diligently making entries in ledgers but paused when he became aware of Tristram's presence.

'I'm here to see Mr Nathan Middleton.' He tried to sound authoritative and confident but dread of the reception he would receive made it come out as a tentative statement.

'Yes, sir,' said the clerk seated near the door. He had no need to enquire the visitor's name. He knew Tristram Middleton by sight though he had never met him face to face for his employer's brother had never crossed the threshold of these offices. He slipped from his stool. 'If you'll follow me, sir.'

He led the way to the far end of the corridor where he gave a sharp knock on a door. A piercing call of 'Enter' reached them both. The clerk, who was wondering why Tristram was here, gave him a wan smile. He recalled rumours of a rift between the brothers, so serious that the elder had cut off all communication with the younger, even to the point of ignoring him should they ever meet in the street or in the company of friends. The clerk wished the two offices were nearer, but he'd take a chance and linger in the corridor. Raised voices could bring him knowledge that might prove useful in the future.

Tristram, on the other hand, was relieved that there was the length of the corridor between the offices. He felt sure there was little chance of the encounter with his brother being overheard.

The clerk opened the door. 'Mr Tristram Middleton to see you, sir.'

There was a moment's silence filled with disbelief, then an explosion as the unexpected announcement made its impact. 'What?'

'Mr Tristram . . .' the clerk started again.

'I heard you.' Nathan's voice was filled with irritation, making the clerk flinch. 'What the hell does he want?'

'I don't know, sir,' spluttered the clerk.

'Clown! Of course you don't know. He wouldn't tell the likes of you. Get out of the way, man, and let him come in.' Nathan waved one huge hand in contemptuous dismissal.

The clerk scurried out of the door and hesitated after Tristram had entered the room.

'Shut it, man,' barked Nathan. 'And back to your work.'

The clerk closed the door and hurried to his office. He had been at the receiving end of Mr Nathan's sharp temper more than once but had never seen such a wild expression on his employer's face as he had witnessed when he had announced Mr Tristram by name. Whatever had divided the brothers it must have been serious.

'Well?' snapped Nathan, leaning back in his chair. His dark eyes bored into Tristram with menace and contempt. They were cold, without any shred of comfort or brotherly love. 'If you've come looking for sympathy here because you've lost a ship, you'll get none.' His eyes narrowed, matching a voice that was filled with suspicion. 'But I wonder if it's more than that?'

These last words upset Tristram's plan of approach for they made him wonder if his brother already knew of the deep dilemma he was in. As he hesitated he glanced at the unoccupied chair on the opposite side of the desk from his brother.

'Oh, sit down if you must,' snapped Nathan. 'It can't be for long. I've work to do, if you haven't.'

Tristram sat down, trying to assume a firmness he did not feel. 'The ... er ... loss of the *Mary Anne* has hit me hard. I ...'

'It will have done. All hands, I hear. That's bad enough but think of the cargo, the profits that now lie at the bottom of the sea. You'll miss them, I'm sure, but the insurance money will go a long way to easing your burden.'

Tristram was shocked by his brother's callous attitude towards the loss of the crew. All he had focused on was the money. But this was no less than Tristram had secretly expected. However, it seemed his brother knew only of the loss of the ship.

'Well, you see, there is more to it than that,' said Tristram, shuffling on his chair.

'Must be for you to come here. Though how it can concern me, I have no idea.' Nathan riveted his eyes on Tristram. His curiosity had been aroused and he was enjoying his brother's unease. A slightly mocking tone came into his voice. 'Embarrassing, is it?' He pursed his lips, enjoying the taunt.

'I need your help.'

The bald statement made Nathan throw back his head in a laugh. 'You need *my* help?' He swung forward on his chair and slammed his fist down hard on the desk. 'You have the gall to come to me for help after you got what was rightfully mine?'

Tristram flinched, but the thought of Lydia and Luke strengthened his resolve. 'It was no fault of mine that I inherited Father's business,' he pointed out. 'He made the will, not me.'

'No doubt you played up to him.'

Tristram's eyes sharpened at the suggestion. 'I did no such thing.'

'So you say.'

'I didn't,' he said firmly. The accusation had had the effect of hardening his attitude.

Nathan gave a grunt of disbelief. 'You still haven't told

me why you need help,' he pointed out in a uninterested voice. But beneath the bland exterior he was curious. Tristram wouldn't have come here if the situation didn't go beyond even the loss of a ship with all hands. 'So tell me and then get out.' The last two words were spat with such venom that Tristram felt himself weakening. All his resolve to be strong was disappearing. He dreaded the attitude his brother would take when he learned the full truth. He was beginning to wish he had not come but he must put his case, for Lydia's and Luke's sake.

He drew himself up and squared his shoulders. His voice was hardly above a whisper when he said, 'I need money to survive.' The tremor in it made the words hard to distinguish, but Nathan caught them.

'You what? Your ship and cargo would be insured, surely?'

Tristram shook his head slowly.

For a moment Nathan stared at Tristram in disbelief. Then realisation of what his brother had done, or rather had not done, dawned on him. 'You weren't insured?' His face contorted with renewed scorn as he leaned forward over his desk, his expression full of incredulity. 'Why the hell not?'

Tristram started his sorry tale. Nathan did not interrupt but was not averse to shaking his head in disbelief or grunting with disgust at each further revelation. 'What a mess,' he commented when Tristram had finished. He paused for a moment then, with mouth set hard, poured scorn on his brother. 'You're a damned fool! How could you allow the business Father built up so meticulously to be destroyed in this way? He must be turning in his grave at such carelessness. Didn't you damn' well think of what might happen?'

'Can you foresee an act of God?' said Tristram weakly.

'No,' snapped Nathan, 'but I can be cautious enough to safeguard myself should one arise.' He stared hard at his brother. 'And I suppose you've come snivelling here to me expecting me to save you? Well, you'll not get a penny from me. You'll have to sink in the mess of your own making.'

Tristram shuddered under this scathing onslaught. 'Please, for Father's sake? To save his business?'

'Don't try to get round me by using him. It's no longer his firm. He left it to you. It's *your* business, and I couldn't care a damn what happens to it.'

'I'll have to sell everything and even that won't be enough. I'll be brought to court as a debtor and go to gaol. Surely you wouldn't see that happen to your own brother?'

'I could and I would,' snapped Nathan, revelling in the sight of Tristram squirming as each word of condemnation and denial hit home. 'You're an incompetent fool and should pay for it.'

'But the family name?' Tristram made what he felt must be his last appeal. Was there no way he could soften his brother's heart, change his outlook? 'Surely you don't want to see the name of Middleton dragged through court, see stigma attached to it?'

Nathan's pitiless eyes bored into him. 'It's the name of Tristram Middleton that will be bantered around the court, no other. It's you who'll be paraded for all to see, no one else. The dirt will be stuck to *you*. Folk know I don't own you, that I don't even regard you as family.'

He saw that his brother realised it was useless to pursue the matter further. He saw Tristram's eyes dull, his expression become forlorn, his shoulders droop. A defeated man sat before him and Nathan liked what he saw. He delighted in deepening the wound.

'You're a weakling. Couldn't even maintain what was handed to you as a successful business. There's not a drop of common sense in you. If there was you wouldn't be in this dilemma.' He gave a little laugh of derision and triumph. 'All that's left for you is the debtors' prison.'

Nathan savoured the pronouncement, delivered with slow deliberation, for he saw each word pierce his brother's mind, filling it with dread of the consequences of his folly.

52

Tristram flinched. He was utterly deflated, all energy drained from him. He hadn't the will to protest, nor to fight back. His brother had sapped the last of his resolve. The future was as bleak as it could be. He faced the horrors of prison, of being branded a debtor and failure. He would never be able to hold his head up again. Friends would shun him, others would point the finger at him, but worse than anything he had failed his daughter and son. How could he face them again? The thought of them made him turn to his brother with one last appeal. 'Please ...' But that was as far as he got.

Nathan cut in sharply. 'No! Get out of here, you whining good-for-nothing. I want nothing more to do with you or your family. Tell those two brats of yours not to come pleading with me either, as well they might. If they do they'll get short shrift from me.' Nathan's lips curled, his eyes blazed with fiery contempt. 'Now get out of here, destroyer of what should have been mine. I don't want to see you again – ever!'

Tristram reached the door a broken man.

Nathan leaned back in his chair and watched with satisfaction. Revenge for what he saw as the injustice perpetrated six years ago had come, but in an unexpected way. Nevertheless the spectacle was sweet. He chuckled to himself as he listened to Tristram's footsteps shuffling away along the corridor.

He was unaware of reaching the outside door and stepping out into Church Street. Nathan's scathing words still swam in his head, the condemnation burned deep. His brain was awash with self-accusation too. He walked unsteadily, unaware where he was, ignorant of normal life going on around him until the sounds began to penetrate his thoughts. Something of reality came back to him then but with it a greater horror. Lydia and Luke would be tainted by what was to happen to him. He didn't want that. He didn't want folk nodding in their direction saying they were a debtor's offspring. And there would be poverty, for there would be nothing left after all his possessions had been sold. Oh, why had he listened to those promises of a good investment?

Poverty – everything gone. His children destitute. Oh, Luke had a job but with that as their only source of income the outlook looked bleak. The comfortable lifestyle they had been used to would disappear. Oh, why had he been so stupid as not to take care of the insurance of his ship and its cargo before he had been tempted to make a quick profit? Insurance . . . Something stirred in his thoughts.

Oblivious to the people passing around him, his thoughts became more and more fixed on the future of his children. His mind was blank to everything else. It was as if he had become spellbound by a possible solution. It filled his mind to the exclusion of everything else and blotted out any consideration of the terrible deed it would entail. Those thoughts had a compelling effect on him, seeming to direct his very steps. His children must not know poverty, must not share the disgrace which faced him.

He was insensible to the wind strengthening as he moved along the west pier, away from the protection of the cliffs. He stopped at the end and stood for a few moments gazing out to sea, across the grey waves. They seemed to call to him, offering comfort in their undulating depths.

The solution was there. He turned as if to walk back. A fishing boat slid from the sea to the calm of the river. Along the pier two men watched it. He saw them move in his direction. His step faltered, he tottered. His hand came up to his chest. He doubled up and staggered sideways. His hands came up as if he was trying to save himself. Then he was falling. Falling. Down. Down. He hit the water and allowed it to take him.

'I would have expected Father to be back by now.' Worry was clearly visible on Lydia's face.

'Well, you don't know Uncle Nathan's views. He may have wanted a lot more detail about the business and

Father's assets before he committed himself, and that would take time.' Luke tried to offer comfort but secretly he too was worried.

'But two hours?'

'I know. It does seem a long time but . . .' He shrugged.

'I wish we'd gone with him.'

'Father didn't want that and we had to respect his wishes.'

'Yes.' Lydia bit her lip. 'Do you think Uncle Nathan will be more amiable?'

'Who knows? Maybe the years have mellowed him, though what I hear of his usual attitudes doesn't augur well.'

'And he's never attempted to get in touch.'

'Well, nor has Father.'

Lydia fidgeted. She couldn't settle to anything. She had sat down, paced the room, stared from the window, always with her thoughts on what might be happening between her father and uncle. Her uneasiness had permeated her brother and he became more and more anxious to know the result of the interview as each minute passed.

A loud rapping resounded throughout the house. Its suddenness and urgency startled them. For a brief moment they shared a glance of fear and doubt. There was something about that urgent knocking which spelt trouble. They started for the door together. Luke flung it open to see the maid hurrying across the hall.

She opened the front door and was met by a request. 'Are Mr Middleton's son and daughter here?'

Before she could reply Luke stepped across the hall. 'Yes.' He saw a solemn-faced member of the Watch standing there. 'What can I do for you?'

'May I come in, sir? I need to have a word with you.'

'Yes, yes.' Luke was a little flustered by this unexpected visit.

'Constable Isaac Smurthwaite, sir,' said the big, bulky man as he stepped into the hall.

'Come this way,' said Luke. As he started towards the drawing room, the maid closed the door and at a signal from him, hurried away to the servants' quarters at the back of the house.

Lydia was standing in the doorway. Though she realised her brother knew no more than she did she looked askance at him.

He pursed his lips and gave a slight shake of his head. After ushering the constable into the room, he closed the door and said, 'I'm Luke Middleton, and this is my sister, Lydia.'

The constable nodded. 'I know you both by sight but have had no cause to speak to you. I'm sorry that this first time must be the occasion of bad news.'

Alarm gripped Lydia. Her stomach felt hollow as if all sensation had been drained from her. Solemnity marked the constable's expression and the corresponding sadness in his eyes caused her face to drain of colour.

Luke shivered as a chill ran through his body. His mind was racing, trying to fathom the reason for this visit. He almost missed the man's words.

'Sir, miss, I'm sorry to bring bad news about your father. I'm afraid he's dead.'

Disbelief filled them. Luke stared at the man. Lydia wanted to cry out in denial. Her father had walked out of the house a little over two hours ago. He had been alive and well, weighed down by the problems he faced but healthy. He couldn't be dead. But the weakness of shock creeping over her told her this was true. Why should this man be here if it weren't?

'Oh, no!' She sank on to a chair.

Luke refused to accept the announcement. 'He can't be. There must be some mistake.' He was willing the constable to contradict himself, urging him to admit that what he had said was untrue. But it was no good. Breaking news such as this was part of the man's job, though not something he enjoyed doing.

56

'There is no mistake, sir. I'm afraid your father is dead.'

'How? What happened?'

'He fell from the west pier.'

'Fell from the pier?' Luke was incredulous. 'What was he doing there?'

'Well, sir, I was hoping you might be able to answer that. Had he gone for a walk?'

Before Luke could answer, Lydia broke in quickly, shooting her brother a look which she hoped he would interpret correctly. 'Yes, he went out just after breakfast.' She was relieved when Luke confirmed her statement. He had realised that if the visit to Uncle Nathan was mentioned the whole sad story of their father's losses might come out.

'Did he seem in good health?'

'Yes.'

'I know that he had lost a ship with all hands recently, might that have been preying on his mind?'

'It worried him as it would any man who had lost a ship, and he felt for the families of the crew. However, he had matters in hand.'

The constable pursed his lips thoughtfully as he nodded. He glanced at Luke. 'Would you agree with your sister?'

'Most certainly.'

'And would you say that Mr Middleton's health was good?'

'As far as we know.'

'But this loss had been a real shock to him?'

'He felt it deeply because of the crew.' Luke cocked his head suspiciously. 'What are you implying, constable?'

'Well, sir, your father fell from the pier and with what had happened to his ship . . .'

'Are you implying he committed suicide?' Lydia's voice was full of indignation.

The constable raised his hands in a gesture of apology. 'I'm sorry, miss. No, I'm not saying that, I'm only wanting to verify certain facts to tie in with our observations.'

'And what might those be?' she asked.

'Well, miss, he was seen at the end of the pier by members of a fishing boat returning to harbour, and also by two men walking there. He turned as if to walk back, staggered, seemed to grasp his chest and fell. It would seem from what these men say, and knowing of his recent loss, that your father had a heart attack. The boat manoeuvred quickly but it took some time to find him for he had been swept back out to sea.'

Luke and Lydia were silent, assessing the implications behind these words while still in shock at the news.

'I'm sorry to be the bearer of such sad tidings.' The constable broke into their thoughts. 'This is a tragic time for you both. I hope that you approve of what I have done and that it will relieve you of some of the pain of dealing with the situation.' He glanced at them both and then continued, 'I contacted Reuben Mason, the undertaker, and he has taken care of the body. He will call on you to make the funeral arrangements. I hope I did right?'

Luke nodded. 'Yes, thank you, constable.' The words were almost dismissive. After what the man had said he wanted time to consider the nature of his father's death and saw from the thoughtful look on her face that Lydia shared his feelings. 'Is there anything else we should know?'

'I don't think so, sir. I must thank you both for your frank statements. I am most grateful. They clear up any doubt about your father's death. I'm sorry I had to ask them but it is my duty. May I say before taking my leave that I often had a few words with your father whenever I met him in the street, on his way to work or whatever. He always seemed a pleasant, straightforward sort of man, one who valued his family and would do nothing to upset them.'

Lydia rose from her chair. She clasped her hands tightly together, keeping a grip on herself to hold her emotions in check until he had gone. 'Thank you for those kind words, constable. We are most grateful for them and for your thoughtfulness in trying to spare us the worst of this tragedy.'

Luke made his thanks too and escorted the man to the front door.

Lydia sat down slowly, hardly aware of the voices in the hall as the official made his departure. Part of her was still in a state of shock, but another part conjured up vivid mental pictures of Tristram's death. The numbness which gripped her body did not subdue them. It was as if she had witnessed them in the clear knowledge of what was happening. She sat perfectly still, fingers entwined on her lap, her fixed gaze unseeing.

Luke's footsteps approached the room. She did not move. The door opened and closed. Still she stared straight ahead.

As he turned from the door, he was saying, 'I can't believe this nightmare is true. Father gone? He was ...' His voice faded. Alarmed by the trance-like figure, he looked with concern at his sister. 'Lydia, are you all right?'

Her gaze remained fixed but she spoke. Her voice was low though it embraced the strong conviction that what she said was the truth. 'Father committed suicide.' The statement filled the room with tension.

'Lydia!' he gasped, astonished by his sister's bald statement.

'It's true.' Her voice never faltered. Her gaze remained fixed, as if she was witnessing her father's actions here and now.

Shocked, Luke stepped forward and sank on to his knees in front of her. He took her hands in his and looked into her face with sympathy and a desire to relieve her of such terrible thoughts. 'You can't say that, love. You don't know.'

Her eyes slowly met his. 'I do. I'm right.'

'No, Lydia. The constable said that witnesses saw Father grasp his chest and stagger before falling off the pier.'

She shook her head. 'That's not right. Oh, they related what they saw, and I don't question the truth of it, but Father was healthy, you know that.'

Luke had to concede the fact but added, 'But who can tell what the shock of the loss of the *Mary Anne* did to him?'

'I don't believe it gave him a heart attack.'

'Well then, what happened?'

'I've already said. He committed suicide.'

'Lydia, you must be careful what you say. You'll sully Father's name. The constable believes the witnesses. The verdict will be that Father had a heart attack, so let's leave it at that.'

A fierce light had come into her eyes. 'I won't leave it at that!' She raised a hand quickly to stem Luke's protest. 'I'll not make my views public but I will accuse one man to his face.'

While he was relieved by the first part of Lydia's statement, he was puzzled by the second. 'What are you getting at?'

'I believe that Father's interview with Uncle Nathan was a waste of time. He spurned Father's request for help. Imagine Father in that situation, desperate for money, facing ruin, disgrace and probable imprisonment.'

'You're saying that's what caused him to commit suicide?'

'No. Father wasn't the type. He loved life too much. What I'm saying is that in that situation he saw a way in which his debts would be cleared.' She paused a moment to let the meaning of her words sink in.

Puzzled, Luke prompted, 'Go on.'

'We know that Father had comprehensive life insurance – remember, he told us when he took it out three years ago?' She paused for verification. Luke nodded and she continued, 'Realising this, he saw that death was the only way he could clear his debt.'

Luke's words came out thoughtfully. 'So you're saying he faked an accident so we'd receive the insurance?'

'Yes, and by so doing saved us the stigma of having a bankrupt father, and ensured we would not be left completely impoverished as we would have been if he had stayed alive. Don't you see, Luke, he did it for us!'

He was battling to accept this. Harder still to take in that his father was dead. It was such a terrible thing. And to do it deliberately . . . 'But suicide?' He shuddered.

Lydia reached out and touched his cheek lightly. 'I know it's hard to take, but don't look at it as such. Look at it as an act born of love for us.'

Luke gave a little nod and pressed his cheek more firmly against her fingers, drawing strength to cope with their loss.

Lydia said nothing for a few moments, knowing that her brother needed time to accept her theory. She recognised that that was all it was but, nevertheless, she felt strongly that she was right. She would test out her ideas. She knew she could never receive definite proof that she was right but she needed to know for her own peace of mind if she was near the truth. And that meant finding out what had happened between her father and Uncle Nathan.

She stirred. Luke glanced up at her. 'I'm going to see Uncle Nathan.'

'He's the one man you said you would accuse to his face?'

'Yes. If Uncle Nathan refused to help then he is the cause of Father's suicide!'

Luke scrambled to his feet in alarm. 'Be careful, Lydia. Even if what you say is true, what can you do about it?'

'That remains to be seen,' she replied quietly. She stood up, smoothed her dress and started for the door.

'You're going now?'

'Yes.'

'Then I'll come with you. You're not facing Uncle Nathan alone.'

'Thank you.'

'Besides, I want to hear what he has to say.'

Within half an hour they were being shown into Nathan Middleton's office, having accepted the commiserations of the clerk when they'd announced who they were. Lydia

61

was pleased to receive them for it meant that news of her father's death must have reached Nathan.

When they entered his office, he stood up and hastened from behind his desk to greet them cordially. 'My dear young people, this is truly a tragedy. I am deeply sorry. My commiserations to you both.' He took Lydia's hands in his and kissed her quickly on the cheek then shook hands with Luke. He fussed as he showed each of them to a chair and then returned to his where he leaned back and clasped his hands across his chest.

Lydia plunged in, wanting to get straight to the point and avoid the crocodile tears. 'I believe my father came to see you earlier this morning?'

'He did indeed.'

'About the loss of the *Mary Anne*?'

'Yes.' Nathan was becoming concerned. He really did not care for his niece's tone of voice.

'He sought your help financially?'

'I think you know that's why he was here.'

'What was the outcome of his appeal to you?'

Nathan leaned forward. His eyes were cold. 'I don't think that is any concern of yours, young woman.'

Lydia straightened. Her eyes met her uncle's un-flinchingly. 'I think it is. Luke and I will now have to deal with our father's affairs and if you and he had any sort of arrangement, then we should know of it.'

'My sister is perfectly right,' put in Luke to lend support to her statement. 'We need to know just where he stood, and especially if you had agreed to make him a loan.'

Nathan was beginning to seethe at this line of questioning. 'I had done no such thing!' The words came out before he could check himself.

'You refused to help your brother?' Lydia feigned shock. It was as she had expected all along.

'Brother? He was no brother of mine.'

'Of course he was,' said Luke. 'You can't escape that fact.'

'In fact, yes,' conceded Nathan irritably. 'But in every other way he was not.'

'You still bore him a grudge over Grandfather's will?' queried Lydia.

'He took what was rightly mine,' snapped her uncle.

'And you refused him help because of that?'

'He made a mess of the business, he got what he rightly deserved. Nincompoop! Had no idea about trading. Destroyed the firm carefully built up by your grandfather ... Gone, just like that.' Nathan's face had grown red and flustered-looking. 'I told him straight what I thought of him. A failure, a weakling, a ...'

'Uncle Nathan,' cut in Luke sharply. 'We don't wish to hear any more of this. Father was none of those things. In fact, in compassion and love he far outshone you. The loss of the *Mary Anne* was unfortunate – not Father's fault.'

'But it was his fault he hadn't insured her,' exclaimed Nathan triumphantly.

'Don't tell me you've never taken risks,' insisted Lydia, quietly implying that she knew of some deals of his which had sailed close to the wind. Before he could react to this she went on, 'I believe his death was a direct result of your refusal to help him.'

Nathan threw up his arms in horror. 'How on earth can you jump to that conclusion?'

'The shock of being rejected.'

'A heart attack could have come at any time.'

'Father was extremely healthy.'

Suspicion had started to mount in Nathan's mind. 'What are you getting at, young lady?'

'We hold you responsible.' Her voice was cold.

He gave a harsh laugh of derision. 'Me? How could I be responsible?'

'Your refusal to help Father must have put a great strain on him.'

'It's not my fault he couldn't take my refusal like a man.'

He gave a scornful grunt. 'Tristram was a weakling all his life.'

'By not helping, you condemned him. You drove him to his death.'

'What are you implying, young lady? Are you suggesting that your father committed suicide?'

'Interpret it how you will, and live with your own conscience.'

Nathan got to his feet. His eyes were wary. 'If this should come out . . .'

'Your reputation would be severely harmed,' Luke finished for him. 'How would people view you, a man who refused to help his brother and drove him to take his own life?' Nathan looked startled, so Luke pressed home his point. 'Besides, the stigma of a suicide in the family wouldn't go down too well in this town.'

'But I heard there were witnesses to what happened?'

'True, but I think you realise now there could be a different interpretation of why Father fell from the pier. I don't think you will voice it, though, because of the possible repercussions. For it to be passed off as a heart attack will suit us all. Father's name will not be stained.'

A look of relief that his niece and nephew were adopting this attitude was wiped from Nathan's face as Lydia went on. 'But nevertheless, Uncle, we three will always have good reason to believe it was no accident. Though you are beyond any retribution from the law you will not escape ours. An offer of help could have saved Father but you refused him. It will have serious consequences for you.'

'Don't you threaten me, young lady.' He could not conceal the fury mounting within him.

'Feeling threatened, Uncle? Suffering from a guilty conscience?' Lydia gave a little smile of satisfaction.

Nathan stiffened and slammed his fist down hard on the desk. 'Damn you, coming here with your veiled accusations that I drove Tristram to his death!'

'Didn't you?' put in Luke quietly.

'Don't think we'll let you get away with it,' added Lydia in an equally meaningful tone.

Nathan looked from one to the other, wondering just what they had in mind. His eyes narrowed. 'You can do nothing to harm me. You won't voice your suspicions because you'd only sully your father's name. As his death is being passed off as a heart attack it will suit you to remain quiet. I emerge from this unscathed.'

Luke gave a knowing grin. 'Oh, there'll be ways of paying you back, you'll see.'

'Your business,' suggested Lydia.

Nathan read the meaning behind the words and gave a harsh laugh of amusement. Then his lips tightened. 'I've heard enough. Now get out!'

Lydia and Luke rose slowly from their chairs.

'We've said all we have to say. We've seen all we need to see,' said Lydia. As she stood there looking down at him the light from the window highlighted one side of her face, driving the other into a shadow. It added a touch of menace to her last words.

Nathan felt compelled to resist their attempt at intimidation. 'Under the terms of my father's will I now have legal title to your house. I will soon be moving in where I should rightfully have been since he died. I give you two weeks to settle your affairs and move out.'

'You can't mean it?' gapsed Luke.

Nathan leaned back in his chair, a grin on his face. 'I can and I do. Two weeks. If you're not out then I'll have you evicted.'

Luke started to speak again but was silenced by Lydia's hand on his arm.

'Leave it, Luke. This is typical of our uncle. This is how he treated Father. We'll leave you,' she continued, her gaze fixed on Nathan, then she moved it slightly to one side as if she was seeing beyond him into the future. 'Retribution will come and it will be sweet.' She pronounced the words slowly, letting them assume an ominous tone. She turned with head held high and walked from the room followed by a silent and dignified Luke. They had to show him that, his threat to dispossess them notwithstanding, he could not intimidate them.

Once outside, tension drained from them in spite of the cloud of uncertainty which hung over them. They started along Church Street in the direction of the bridge across the Esk.

'Well?' said Lydia after a few moments during which both of them turned over in their mind the confrontation with their uncle. 'Do you think as I do – he drove Father to commit suicide?'

'We could never prove it,' replied her brother cautiously.

'I know, but what do you think?'

'Weighing everything up, I believe it is the likeliest solution.'

Lydia's eyes gleamed with excitement. 'Good. I'm glad you share my opinion.' Her tone was virulent.

'Steady on, Lydia. We could be wrong. Besides it may not have been any deliberate intention on Uncle's part.'

'Maybe not, but it happened. He was responsible and in my view deserves to be punished.'

'You'd never get him into court.'

'I know, but there are more ways than one of avenging Father's death.'

Chapter Four

There was so much for Luke and Lydia to think about over the next three days that life crowded in on them, but Luke could not eliminate from his mind the vow of revenge his sister had made as they had left his uncle's office.

He knew her as a determined young woman who, in spite of being younger than he, always took the lead when they were together with decisions to make. Not that he sat back; he always made his opinion known but it was hers which generally prevailed. Now he determined to see that she made no rash moves which might bring devastating consequences. He sympathised with her attitude, for he felt the same animosity to their uncle. He too wanted revenge and agreed that there were more ways than one to achieve it. They must be subtle in their approach.

During the three days after their father's death they had to face enquiries from the authorities. But their tone was sympathetic and, having no doubt that Tristram had suffered a heart attack, they probed no further. There was also a stream of visitors to the house in St Hilda's Terrace offering sympathy and condolences.

With her world turned upside down, Lydia was pleased to see them. She was shattered by the loss of a man whom she'd loved dearly and to whom she had drawn close after the death of her mother. She found she needed support. She received this from Luke but knew that he too was suffering.

One of the first to visit was an anxious David Drayton, eager to be of assistance to the girl he admired and whom his family expected him to marry. Though he knew that his mother and father held a businesslike approach to the match, seeing it as of benefit to their own trading pursuits, he chose to ignore this motive, for Lydia had touched his heart.

She was grateful for his sympathy and for the steady and practical way he helped Luke to deal with the funeral arrangements.

That took place in the old parish church high on the East Cliff. The minister extolled Tristram's virtues to a church packed with people, there to pay their last respects to a man who was well liked in Whitby.

As Lydia followed the coffin to the burial site she marvelled that the weather had been kind to them, in keeping with her father's character. Even the wind, which could lash viciously across this exposed cliff top, was today but a gentle breeze. As it caressed her cheeks she could almost feel her father's soothing touch comforting her in her woes. There was comfort too in Luke's firm grip on her hand as they watched the coffin lowered into the ground. Though her mind was torn, her body aching with grief, she fought the tears. Two escaped and trickled down her cheek. The rest welled inside her and were shed there.

As they turned away from the grave people offered their sympathies in low, respectful tones or in silent looks. Once that ordeal was over Lydia and Luke set off down the one hundred and ninety-nine steps to Church Street.

Lydia broke the silence when they were halfway down. 'Uncle Nathan didn't even come to the funeral.' There was bitterness in her voice.

Luke expressed his disgust and added, 'I thought Cousins Isobel and Christopher would have come. They were always friendly whenever I came across them. They never forgot the childhood days we shared before Grandfather died and caused the rift between our parents.'

'No doubt Uncle Nathan forbade them to come and they daren't go against his authority.'

'I expect so,' agreed Luke. He grimaced at the thought of the disunity in a family which could have enjoyed a close and loving relationship, for he too liked their cousins. 'Thank goodness Father wasn't cast in the same mould as Uncle Nathan. We will always have happy memories of him in spite of what has happened.' He paused then added, 'We have a problem, Lydia, and we have to face it quickly.'

She sighed. 'I know, but it will have to wait until we've received our visitors. There are sure to be some mourners who will come to the house. I wish it was all over.'

'So do I, but we must go through with it, for Father's sake. I'm sure his last thoughts were of us. Our suspicions about how he died must stay our secret.'

The preparations for the funeral tea had been made earlier in the day so that Mrs Harrington, their housekeeper-cook, and three maids could fulfil their wishes to attend the service. They had not gone to the graveside, deeming it better to return to the house and make the final arrangements there before anyone arrived.

Lydia and Luke were most appreciative. They had nothing to do but to prepare themselves to receive callers.

David Drayton was the first to arrive. He gave his heartfelt condolences again without being over-effusive. He made them simple and left them at that. He was more concerned about Lydia and wanted to ease the ordeal for her as much as he could. She appreciated his consideration and felt reassured by his physical presence. He saw that she was never monopolised by any one person and insisted she should take some refreshments. Lydia was thankful that he steered his father Jonas away from making any direct enquiries about the future of the business. Its demise would become clear to the people of Whitby soon enough.

Guests were taking their leave when two more arrived.

When they entered the room Lydia's face broke into a smile of pleasure. She rose from her chair to greet her cousins.

'Isobel, Christopher, I'm so pleased to see you.' She hugged Isobel, remembering happier times they had been free to share until six years ago. Her arm still round Isobel, she held out her other hand. 'Christopher.' He took it and she felt in his touch the warmth of a friendship he still treasured deeply.

Isobel kept hold of Lydia's hand but stood back to look more closely at her cousin. She was pleased to see that Lydia, though a little pale, seemed in good health and appeared to be standing up to the ordeal well. 'We just had to come, had to let you know we do sympathise. We're only sorry we could not be at the church – Father forbade us.' Her regret at this ban and the one which had kept the cousins from close association was evident in Isobel's expression.

'Knowing approximately what time the funeral would be over, we made an excuse to leave the house and here we are,' explained Christopher.

'I'm grateful to you for coming,' said Lydia, a tremor in her voice. 'Luke will be pleased as well. Come, sit down. We must catch up on the news.'

They had been seated only a few moments when Luke and David came into the room. Surprised at seeing his cousins, Luke hurried forward and expressed his pleasure. David greeted them and then turned to Lydia. 'You will be more than occupied now so I'll take my leave.'

She held out her hand to him. 'Thank you for your kindness and support today.'

David made his farewells and the cousins settled down for a long chat. Over the past six years contact between them had been accidental and brief. In his bitterness Nathan had commanded his family to have no association with his brother's. Though hurt by the loss of a formerly deep friendship with their cousins, Isobel and Christopher dare not flaunt the iron rule of their father. But now, in adult-

70

hood, they judged that they could no longer abide by that rule on an occasion when Lydia and Luke were in mourning.

All four of them enjoyed the exchanges and reminiscences. Isobel and Christopher were pleased that they had brought smiles to their cousins' faces to counteract the sombre atmosphere which had reigned in the house before their arrival.

Inevitably the question of the future came up. 'Will you continue to run the business?' Christopher asked.

'Won't be able to,' replied Luke. 'The loss of the ship and its cargo is a great blow and, after paying some debts, there will be nothing left on which to rebuild. But we have a great deal still to sort out before we know the exact position.'

'But you'll continue to live here?' queried Isobel.

Lydia smiled wanly. 'We have to be out by the end of next week.'

'What?' Both Isobel and Christopher stared at her in amazement.

'Under the terms of Grandfather's will all his properties went to your father with the proviso that our father had a life interest in this house. Beyond that there was no provision made for his family.'

'I don't believe it!' gasped Christopher, though he knew his cousin had no reason to lie.

'It's true,' Luke confirmed.

'Then we must speak to Father,' said Isobel firmly, receiving a nod of agreement from her brother.

'No! Please don't.' Lydia was quick with her request.

'But we must.'

'We don't want you to,' she insisted. 'Please, don't let us fall out over this.'

'You've seen Father?'

'Yes, at his office.'

'And he said he wanted you out?'

'Most certainly.'

'I know there was trouble between him and your father, but surely he couldn't see you out on the street?'

'He can and he has. Please don't ask any more. One day you may know the full story.'

Isobel glanced at her brother and received a signal that she should comply with Lydia's wishes.

'Very well.' Isobel squeezed her cousin's hand in an assurance that she would do nothing to upset her. 'But where will you go?'

'Father's death and the funeral have occupied all our time. We really haven't given it a great deal of thought, but now we must.'

'If there is anything we can do to help, please contact us,' said Christopher.

'Oh, do,' Isobel added. 'And if you change your mind and want us to speak to Father, we will.'

'Don't think about it. You'll only bring his wrath down on your heads because he'll know then you've seen us. We wouldn't want to be the cause of any friction between you. After all, he is your father and we know from our early years how much he dotes on both of you.'

Isobel and Christopher recognised she was right and they agreed to keep their own counsel but made their cousins promise that if there was anything they needed in the future, they would not hesitate to ask.

'I'm so glad they came,' said Lydia as she and Luke returned to the drawing room after saying goodbye to their cousins. 'They made me recall the happy times we used to share. Father would have been pleased.' She paused halfway across the hall, drawn by the sounds coming from the dining room where refreshments had been laid out for any visitors. 'We must thank Mrs Harrington and the maids for taking care of everything today.'

When they entered the dining room they found the three young maids clearing the tables, supervised by Mrs Harrington. The girls hesitated on seeing their employer, uncertain whether to continue their work or not. They bobbed a curtsy and stood where they were.

Mrs Harrington came over to Lydia, smoothing her apron as she did so. Her round red face broke into an understanding smile. Lydia drew immediate comfort from the presence of this kindly, motherly person who had been with the family for ten years. At that time she had been recently widowed and had appreciated the kindness she was shown by the Middleton family. Mrs Middleton was seeking a cook and a housekeeper, as live-in employees, along with two maids. During the interview Mrs Harrington had shrewdly weighed up the position. Realising that Mrs Middleton was the type of person who would like to do a certain amount of supervision in her own household, she had suggested that she could combine both positions if Mrs Middleton employed a third maid. Mrs Middleton saw the wisdom in this suggestion and agreed to a trial period. Mrs Harrington's gentle but firm authority, her thoughtfulness for the welfare of the family and happy working relationship with Mrs Middleton, left her employer with no cause for anxiety and the trial period was quickly forgotten.

Two years after she had come to the Middletons' she was shaken by her mistress's sudden death. Without ever overstepping her position, she'd adopted the role of surrogate mother to Lydia and Luke. Her observance of the rapport between Mrs Middleton and her children enabled her to continue in the same manner, a fact much appreciated by Tristram.

She had seen the young Lydia blossom from a gangling, rather plain schoolgirl into a pretty, likeable young lady, and Luke into a handsome young man. She always had their interests close to her heart.

Now, knowing the ordeal they had been through, she came forward to offer succour. 'I hope it has not been too much for you, Miss Lydia?'

'No, it hasn't, thank you, Mrs Harrington.'

'You're sure you are all right?'

'Yes.'

'Good. Go to the drawing room then and have a nice quiet sit. I'll bring you both some tea. I'm sure you had very little when everyone was here. It's always the same.'

'Thank you, that would be welcome. But first I came to thank you all for the way you have managed everything today. We're sorry for all the extra work, but both Mr Luke and I appreciate what you have done.'

'All in the line of duty, Miss Lydia,' replied Mrs Harrington. 'Now, off with you, and I'll see to that tea.'

When she and Luke were settled in the drawing room, Lydia voiced her apprehension at one of the tasks they would now have to face. 'It's going to be dreadful having to tell Mrs Harrington and the maids that we can no longer employ them and that we must all leave.'

'It will be a blow to her and we're going to miss her terribly,' said Luke, a catch in his voice.

'I wish there was something we could do. She's been like a mother to us. I think I'll get it over with as soon as we've had tea. She and the maids must have time to adjust.'

Luke nodded. He tightened his lips and then said, 'I suppose so, but it's going to hurt.'

As they drank their tea and enjoyed Mrs Harrington's home-made cake, he brought Lydia up to date on developments with the business.

'When I was out yesterday I went to see the agent with whom Father took out his life insurance. Everything there will be straightforward. I also found out who advised Father about his unsound investment and went to see them – Mr Sleightholme and Mr Wear.'

Lydia raised her eyebrows in surprise. 'I would have thought their advice was genuine?'

'Oh, it was. There was no intention to deceive Father for their own ends. They thought the investment to be sound and they too have made losses though it hasn't affected them as deeply as Father. They kept within their means. They merely passed on the information to Father – it was

74

up to him to judge it and decide what he should do. He acted on the information and, like Mr Sleightholme and Mr Wear, made his investment through Chapman's Bank. I saw Mr Chapman and explained what money would be forthcoming to meet the debt. He agreed to waive any further interest on the loan.'

'That's good of him. I hope he will be discreet about the debt?'

'He will be, and I got Mr Sleightholme and Mr Wear to promise to say nothing about Father's difficulty. They readily agreed, don't want it known that they too made a bad investment.'

'That is some comfort,' said Lydia. 'Will the insurance money meet what Father owes?'

Luke shook his head. 'I'm afraid not. When I came home I made a quick assessment of our assets as far as I could. I did not want to trouble you with it the day before the funeral.'

'And?' she prompted anxiously.

'Father was right, we'll have to sell everything.'

'Not my beloved piano!'

'I'm afraid so, love,' replied Luke sadly.

'But it's a family heirloom.'

'I know.' He wished he could give her better news and wipe the anguish from her face. 'It's a wonderful instrument and should fetch a tidy sum. That and what we get for the rest of the furniture plus the insurance money should cover Father's debt.'

The thought of losing her piano had brought tears to her eyes but she felt some relief at Luke's final words. Then, almost immediately, despondency returned. 'We'll have nothing?'

'Not a thing, except a few pounds saved from my wages.'

The enormity of their dilemma hit her then. The loss of her father, dealing with sympathisers, the funeral arrangements and then the funeral itself had all taken precedence in her mind. Now, in the aftermath, their own predicament came to the fore.

'Luke, what are we going to do?' She was on the verge of tears.

He saw that he had better word his observations carefully or his sister, who had coped extremely well up to now, would succumb to feelings she had bravely kept suppressed.

'Lydia, love, we must take things one step at a time. If we do that thoughtfully and without panic I am sure we will cope.' He gave his advice steadily and assured her that he was in control of their affairs. 'Our first priority is to find somewhere to live. I'm sure Uncle Nathan will exact his legal right immediately our notice is up.'

Lydia gained strength from her brother. She dried her tears, straightened her back and smoothed her dress. Running her hands across the soft material gave her comfort. 'But first, we had better break the news to Mrs Harrington.'

Luke expressed his agreement by rising from his chair and pulling the long cord beside the fireplace.

A few moment later one of the maids appeared.

'Liza, please ask Mrs Harrington to come to see me,' Lydia instructed.

'Yes, miss.' Liza scurried away to do as she was told.

When the housekeeper arrived Lydia indicated a chair and said, 'Please sit down.'

Mrs Harrington said nothing, sensing the unease her young employers felt.

'We are in a dilemma, Mrs Harrington. We have something to tell you which we regret very much.'

Lydia paused as if searching for the necessary words. Mrs Harrington could see that her young mistress was both embarrassed and upset.

'We would ask you, first, that you keep strictly to yourself some of the things we have to tell you.' Lydia's words were accompanied by a steady gaze which required a pledge.

'Miss, you know my tongue will be silent as it always has been about the private affairs of this family, ever since the day your dear mother engaged me.'

'We know that, Mrs Harrington. And we do trust you, as we always have, but I had to mention it so that you would appreciate the gravity of our situation.' Mrs Harrington nodded but made no comment and Lydia continued, coming straight to the point. 'Because of the loss of the *Mary Anne*, we are penniless. Father had certain debts which must be met. There is no need for me to go into detail, but please believe me when I say our situation is serious.'

'I wouldn't want you to elaborate, miss.'

'When the obligations are met, we will have nothing. We will have to sell everything.'

'Even the house?'

Lydia gave a wan smile of regret. 'The house doesn't belong to us.' She saw the amazement in Mrs Harrington's eyes and explained. 'When my grandfather died he left all his properties to our uncle with the proviso that Father had a life interest in this house. Now that he is dead, Uncle Nathan has told us he wants the house.'

'Oh, miss, surely he couldn't turn you out?'

'He could and he has,' injected Luke bitterly.

'We have until the end of next week to sort things out,' added Lydia.

'But, miss, what does this mean for me and the maids? Will you no longer want us?' There was a catch in Mrs Harrington's voice as she contemplated the happiness she had experienced with the Middletons.

'I'm afraid we just can't afford to employ any of you any more.'

'Oh, miss.' Tears came to Mrs Harrington's eyes but she fought to keep them back. She did not want to impose her own woes on these two young people who had become so much a part of her life. She dreaded having to face a future in which this family did not feature.

'We are sorry about this,' put in Luke, 'but there is

77

nothing we can do about it. We would dearly like to keep you all in our employment but there just isn't the money. I'll have my wage but it is small at the moment. I was hoping to progress in the iron trade out of Whitby. Maybe I shall, but that won't solve our immediate problems.'

'I understand, Mr Luke. You both have enough to cope with without our predicament being thrust upon you. Do you want me to tell the maids?'

'No,' said Lydia. 'It would not be fair to put what is our responsibility upon you. Besides I'd rather the bad news came from me.'

'Very well, miss. When will you want us to leave?'

'We would be grateful if all of you would stay for the remainder of our time here.'

'You'll be paid, of course. We have made sure we can manage that,' said Luke.

'We'd willingly forego . . .' Mrs Harrington began.

'No,' Lydia interrupted, 'you must have your dues.'

The housekeeper knew better than to object any further. Miss Lydia was a strong-minded, independent young woman whom she knew would not want anything that smacked of charity.

'Very well, miss.' Mrs Harrington put her hand before her mouth as if plucking up the courage to voice a question which had just occurred to her. 'Miss, may I ask where you and Mr Luke are going to live?'

'You may ask, Mrs Harrington, but I can't give you an answer. We do not know ourselves.'

'With the last of the money we have, it will probably be a hovel on the east side,' put in Luke in a dispirited tone.

'Oh, Mr Luke, you can't go to one of those! They aren't fit for a beggar, let alone respectable people like yourselves. The squalor could be enough to finish you, but the degradation of living among the neighbours you'd find there would certainly destroy you.'

'Mrs Harrington, it can't be as bad as that.' Lydia gave a shaky laugh.

'Miss, you cannot go there.' The firmness of this statement reminded Lydia of the days when she and Luke were children and had been forced to obey Mrs Harrington.

'We might have to if nothing better turns up, and there isn't long to go.'

'But something *has* turned up,' said Mrs Harrington. She gave a knowing little smile as if she was pleased with the idea she was about to impart.

'What do you mean?' asked Luke. Lydia was as mystified as he.

'You know that when my husband died I kept our little house, anticipating there might come a day when I would retire? I haven't seen fit to do that yet. It's there still, just big enough for two, so I suggest you young people use it.'

'You mean, move in there?'

'Yes, it's furnished so it won't matter that you'll have to sell everything here.'

'But won't you want to go there?'

'It's only big enough for two. I needn't go there until you leave, and that must be whenever it suits you.'

'But what will you do?'

'I'll go to my sister. She's on her own and is ailing a bit so she'll be pleased of the company. I'll find work as a cook locally without having to live in, so you use my cottage for as long as you want.'

'What can we say, Mrs Harrington?' Lydia's eyes were damp with gratitude. 'This has taken one problem off our minds and will give us time to work out where our future lies.'

There were more tears when Lydia broke the news to the maids. They were sorry to have to leave a kindly, understanding employer and feared they would not find such a post again. They were only too willing to stay for the remainder of the allotted time.

The following Monday morning when David Drayton turned into St Hilda's Terrace he received a shock to see

79

activity around the Middletons' house and furniture being taken out of it and loaded on to carts. His step quickened and, finding the front door open, he hurried straight in. Lydia, with tears running down her cheeks, was standing at the bottom of the stairs watching the removal of her piano.

'Lydia, what's happening?' he gasped.

'We are having to sell everything,' she said wearily. 'Most is going today, the rest on Saturday.'

'But you love that piano.'

'I know, but it's got to go.' She started to sob.

He put a comforting arm around her shoulders and led her to the drawing room.

'Now tell my why?' he said as he closed the door.

She swallowed hard and dabbed her eyes with her hand-kerchief. 'We have to move out and can't take all this with us,' she answered cautiously. She wanted to keep her father's debts a secret if she could.

'But why do you have to move out? This house is yours now. Well, yours and Luke's.'

'I'm afraid it isn't.'

'Your father would naturally leave it to you. There's no one else.'

'But it was never his.'

David frowned in disbelief. Lydia explained the situation.

'And now your uncle wants it!'

She nodded.

'Surely he hasn't turned you out?'

'Yes. He wants to move in at the end of the week.'

'I knew he and your father had differences but I didn't know they ran so deep that he would evict his own niece and nephew.'

Lydia gave a little sigh. 'Then you don't know Uncle Nathan.'

'What are you going to do? Where are you going?'

'Mrs Harrington has kindly offered us her house in Wellington Square. We'll go there when we leave here.'

80

'Wellington Square?' David looked shocked. 'But that's not what you're used to.'

'Maybe not, but we'll have to get used to it for the time being.'

'It's a crowded area and just off Baxtergate. Goodness knows who you'll get snooping around.'

'I know it's not St Hilda's Terrace nor Cliff Street where you live, but being Mrs Harrington's it will be respectable and clean, and it's good of her to offer it to us until we can decide our future,' Lydia answered a little testily. 'Goodness knows where we'd have ended up if it hadn't been for her.'

'I'm not disparaging Mrs Harrington. I know how much she has meant to your family, and it's extremely kind of her to help in this way.' David changed the subject. 'Lydia, I haven't seen you since the day of the funeral. I've kept away thinking you might prefer some time to yourself but I could keep away no longer. I want to know how you are?'

Pleased with his concern, she smiled her appreciation. 'You are very kind. Physically I'm quite well. There's much to occupy my mind at the moment, but it's still hard to believe I will not see Father again.' A catch came into her voice.

He reached out and took her hand. She felt comforted by his touch and he thrilled to the contact. Desire surged in him. The girl he loved was in trouble and there flashed through his mind a way to solve her problems.

'Lydia, I know so soon after your father's death may not be the best time to say this, but I'm going to.' She heard the intensity in his voice. His eyes had come alive. 'Marry me and it will solve all your problems.'

For a moment she was taken aback by the suddenness of this proposal. She stared at him, speechless. Her mind whirled as difficulties and solutions occured to her, threatening to stifle her reason. There was an almost overwhelming desire to say yes, for this would indeed solve everything. There would be comfort, riches even, she would never want again. Luke had his job. But even as she made this quick appraisal, caution raised its head. Was this what she wanted? She loved David but would it appear as if she was taking an easy way out to solve her immediate problems? She did not want that. Then the facts of her father's death thrust their way to the fore and her mind churned with the desire to avenge him. If she married David, she dare not pursue that course. He would not want the cordial relationship which existed between his father's firm and her uncle's to be affected by her theories and accusations.

'Marry me,' he said again.

She hesitated. She could see that he was hanging on her answer, wanting her to say yes. She reached out and touched his cheek. 'That is sweet of you but I can't give you an answer now. With so much happening I must have time to think.'

He did not look disappointed but said in a tone of meek acceptance, 'If that is what you want then so be it. I'll await your answer eagerly.'

When Lydia broke this news to Luke he was surprised. He knew Lydia and David had felt a great admiration for each other since childhood but he had not realised that this had blossomed into true love. He knew David's parents had seen a link between the families as advantageous to the businesses, but what would their views be when they learned that Tristram Middleton's firm no longer existed?

'And what will your answer be?' he asked.

Lydia gave a shrug of her shoulders. 'I don't know. It would solve one of our problems. I would have a husband to look after me. You have your job and could pursue your ambition without the worry of providing for me.'

'Lydia,' Luke took on an extremely serious tone, 'I must not come into your calculations. It is your happiness that must count. I want that, and I know Father and Mother would have wanted it too. So it must be uppermost in your

82

mind. The real question is not how to solve your problems or ease our situation, but whether you love him or not.'

Lydia shook her head. 'Oh, I don't know. I like him. We've always got on well together. He's kind and considerate. He's asked me before but I was always evasive. He swore that one day he would get me to say yes. I've always thought I probably would, but is now the time? He doesn't know that we have lost everything, but has he maybe taken advantage of our homelessness, thinking it will make me grasp at any opportunity to escape it?'

'You must not marry for convenience. If you do you will never be happy.' Luke paused, but seeing that she had listened to his words carefully didn't press his opinions further. She would decide in her own good time.

David could not concentrate on his work. In mid-afternoon he left his office on the east side overlooking the harbour and crossed the swivel bridge, an improvement on the drawbridge it had replaced fifteen years ago. He walked along St Anne's Staith, through Haggersgate and on to Pier Lane. The afternoon had turned grey and the wind had freshened but David was well cloaked against its chill. He rather liked this sort of weather; it brought briskness to his walk along the west pier, drove sharp air into his lungs and stung his cheeks with a refreshing tang. It gave him a feeling of well-being which would be all the more enjoyable if Lydia would only say yes.

He breathed deeply of the salt air and strode towards the fluted Doric column of the stone lighthouse, an important addition to the harbour facilities in 1831. He approved of the continued employment of Francis Pickernell as resident Harbour Engineer, for it meant continual supervision and development which in turn meant improved amenities for the ships in whch his father had invested. There were now better methods of handling goods and facilities for storage. Lydia would benefit from all this if she married him.

The sea was running high, driven by the wind. From

the pier he could see it pounding the cliffs below the ruined abbey and beyond. In the other direction waves rolled their white caps towards the long stretch of sand running to Sandsend. They broke in a whirl of foam, sending their whiteness streaming up the beach. The water then ran back to meet the next white cap which was flung its way. Spray rose on the wind and lay across the scene as if cloaking a mystery. David revelled in the atmosphere and anticipated sharing the experience and his enthusiasm for it with Lydia.

The more she occupied his mind, the more sure he was she would say yes. Tonight over dinner he would break the news of his proposal to his mother and father. He reckoned they would be pleased for they had never disguised their hope that this would happen.

He knew that they saw such a marriage as bringing an alliance between the Drayton and Middleton firms, and thus strengthening their position within the trading fraternity of Whitby. They had never doubted that Tristram would approve of this equally. Lydia was the apple of his eye and would bring her share of his business with her when she married. But that situation had changed. With Tristram's death Lydia would surely get her share of the business sooner?

Thoughts of his son occupied Jonas Drayton's mind when he left the office. He was surprised to find that David had already gone and offered no explanation to the staff as to why he too was leaving early. He was a law unto himself and did not let them forget it. He ruled his firm with strict discipline and an iron resolve, being only marginally more tolerant to his son during working hours than he was to the rest of his employees. Jonas deemed this rigidity was good for him, breeding character which would manifest itself when David assumed full control.

With Jonas's departure the atmosphere in the office eased and the staff relaxed in the knowledge that there was no need now to keep their noses inside their ledgers, manifest papers and invoices.

Today Jonas's stride was measured but slow. He was satisfied with life. He ran a successful merchant's business with investments in ships which brought a good income. But it had not come about without the hard work of his early trading years and an astute mind for seeing and seizing an opportunity. He saw such an opportunity in his son's marriage to Lydia Middleton. Tristram Middleton's business was sound but it had lacked a man with flair to expand and develop it, something Jonas was certain he could do. His chance had come sooner than he had expected. Yes, life was good. Maybe a little celebration was called for. A call at the Angel Inn was merited.

Coaches had been running from the Angel in Baxtergate since 1795 and, as the route grew busier, the inn became a hive of activity, a meeting place, the site of social functions both public and private. With its good food and congenial atmosphere, businessmen of the town met here, either by appointment or casually to exchange notes and gossip. Jonas called in maybe once or twice a week, finding it advisable to keep up with local news and what was happening in the town.

He passed the time of day with the landlord when he entered the inn, called for his usual glass of brandy and made his way down some stairs to a snug. It was cosy and quiet, a place which seemed to call for hushed voices, a room with an atmosphere which encouraged the exchange of gossip and rumours.

Four tradesmen, well known to Jonas and he to them, were already enjoying their tankards of ale or glasses of spirits. They greeted him amiably as he lowered his tall, lean body into a chair at their table, and took him into their flow of conversation about proposed developments to the quays on the east side of the river.

'It's a pity Tristram can't give us his views, he was keen on certain aspects,' said a rotund man who leaned back in his chair as he made the observation.

'His loss is a tragedy,' commented another. 'And if what I hear is true his son and daughter are left almost penniless.'

Jonas started. His dark eyes, which had grown somnolent in this convivial atmosphere, now became sharp and searching as he glanced around the men seated at the table. 'Penniless?' His word was clipped. 'They can't be.'

The man who had offered this information spread his hands in a gesture of deference. 'Only rumours. I cannot vouch for their truth.'

'What have you heard?' asked the rotund man, anticipating a story to take home to his wife.

'Maybe Jonas knows more than I,' came the answer. He glanced at the new arrival. 'Your son and Miss Lydia Middleton see something of each other, I believe.'

'They do,' Jonas admitted. 'But I have heard nothing of what you imply.'

'As I say, they're only rumours.' The man added with a wise-owl look, 'But often truth will out after rumours are heard.' He continued when pressed by his companions, 'Well, I've heard tell that Tristram left debts which Mr Luke and Miss Lydia are having difficulty in meeting.'

'Debts?' Jonas put the query cautiously.

'Yes.' The man nodded. 'True or not, I've heard that he made some unwise investments and now there's nothing left. His children are having to sell everything.'

'If the rumour is true this is terrible news,' commented Jonas, hiding the real reason for his concern. 'Where did you hear it?'

'Sam Charters. Where he'd got it, I don't know, but a hint had been dropped somewhere, picked up and passed on to him because he had had dealings with Tristram in the past. He wondered if I had heard anything. I hadn't, so couldn't confirm or deny.'

'So it's just a rumour,' said one of the others dismissively as he placed his tankard on the table.

With that the conversation drifted to other matters, like

the vessels being built in the thriving shipyards, the shipment of iron ore out of Whitby, the state of the jet trade, the economies of the Peak alum industry, and the possibilities of further links with the Whitby-Pickering railway which would ameliorate the port's isolated position on the Yorkshire coast. All these nuggets of information were useful to the minds of men who saw in the development of the town a boost to their own fortunes.

But today Jonas had only half his mind on what was being said. The other was still trying to decide whether the earlier information was just unsubstantiated rumour or not. Maybe David knew something. Well, if he did, his father would have it out of him and chastise him for not imparting his knowledge sooner.

David was not at home when Jonas arrived and he took the opportunity to inform his wife, Eugenia, of what he had heard.

'Surely this can't be true?' she queried.

Jonas shrugged his shoulders. 'Who knows? But one thing is certain: if it is, David had better look elsewhere for a bride. I'm not having him marrying Miss Lydia without her bringing something to the marriage.'

'I should think not,' agreed Eugenia. 'You need her interest in the Middleton business to help us expand.' Eugenia had never gone against her husband. Meek and humble, some folks said with a sneer behind her back, but she was also shrewd. Agreeing with her husband bolstered his ego and that produced renewed confidence in his own ability to make deals which were profitable. And she liked profits. They gave her an extremely comfortable and leisurely lifestyle with all the assets that money could buy. And she liked the idea of these increasing further. Her hopes of a favourable development soon had now received a setback. But then her mind latched on to an idea.

'Jonas, there is another Middleton other than Miss Lydia,' she announced with a note of satisfaction.

87

'What do you mean?' asked Jonas.

'There's Miss Isobel.'

'Nathan's daughter?'

'Of course.'

Jonas greeted his wife's ability to see an alternative so quickly with pursed lips, bright eyes and a chuckle.

Eugenia smiled, content in the knowledge that her hint had struck home.

He nodded. 'That could well be better. Isobel is a good catch. It would make Nathan less of a rival, more of a friendly enemy, for he would have to drop his animosity to us and be more willing to exchange ideas. We would not gain the same overall influence we would have with Tristram, but Nathan is a shrewd judge of opportunities and he would want his daughter to benefit through us. I have no doubt he would see that we learned of anything worthwhile. Yes, if this rumour is true then David will have to set his sights on Isobel.'

'Don't rush in as soon as he comes home. Do it quietly towards the end of our meal. Let's have some special wine. Work him into a good receptive mood.'

'You're a crafty witch.' He laughed quietly, drawing her into his euphoria. Maybe there would be other ways to celebrate.

'And a tempting one?' There was suggestion in her eyes as she came towards him.

He laughed and spanned her waist with long thin fingers to draw her into his kiss.

She knew she had him under her spell and that he would handle their son in the way she had suggested.

By the time he reached home David had decided that he would choose the right moment to inform his parents of his proposal to Lydia. It would need subtlety to make them see that he did not want to marry to advance his father's business but wanted to do so for love. If the business was helped by that then it was all to the good, but if it wasn't then so be it.

Dinner was a congenial affair. The cook's special vegetable soup was followed by a succulent roast duck with an exquisite orange sauce, potatoes and green vegetables. There followed an apple pie and syllabub. Wine flowed freely, putting them all in a good mood.

David wondered why his parents were so exuberant but did not question it when he saw it working to his advantage. Relaxed in this way they would be more receptive to his news. At the start of the meal, preoccupied with what he wanted to tell them, he had felt a little strained but the good food and wine had banished his apprehension.

'Let's take coffee in the drawing room,' said Eugenia, rising from her chair. She indicated to the maid to bring it and received a nod of understanding from the girl.

Once they had settled, Jonas leaned back contentedly in his favourite chair. 'David, there is . . .'

At the same moment he started, 'Father, Mother, there is something I want . . .'

Father and son pulled up short with nervous laughs.

'What is it?' asked Jonas.

'No, sir, you shall have the first say,' replied David quickly, seizing on the chance to take a few more minutes to collect his thoughts about the approach he should make. Start gently in a roundabout manner or plunge straight in? But the answer to that question was speedily apparent.

'On my way home today I called in at the Angel and there I heard some very distressing news. I've already told your mother and she's just as shocked as I was.' Jonas paused. He saw he had David's concentrated attention. 'It was more a rumour that Tristram Middleton's firm is no longer operating because of debts he had incurred. Everything, even his personal possessions, furniture, the lot, is having to be sold to meet them apparently. You are close to Miss Lydia, I wondered if you can confirm or deny this rumour?'

David had not expected this and his hesitation in replying gave him away.

'You do know something?' pressed his father.

David nodded. 'Earlier today I visited Lydia, a courtesy call to see how she was. I was surprised when I reached the house to see all the furniture was being taken away to be sold.'

'And did you hear any reason for this?' his mother asked.

'Yes. Apparently the house was left to Mr Nathan when his father died but his brother had a life interest in it. Now Mr Nathan wants it for himself.'

'He's turning Lydia and Luke out?'

'Yes.'

'Have they bought somewhere else?'

'No. Mrs Harrington has given them the use of her house until they decide what they are going to do.'

'Did Lydia mention what will happen to the firm?'

David shook his head. 'No.'

Jonas looked thoughtful. 'If Miss Lydia and Luke are selling everything, then what I heard could be true.'

'But Lydia said it was because there was no room for their things at Mrs Harrington's,' David pointed out.

'That may be the reason she gave you, but tie it up with what I was told. If they were going to carry on the business they would have stored the furniture until such time as they were able to get another house. They would not be selling it. I reckon it's right it is being sold to meet part of the debts Tristram is said to have left. And no doubt the business is either being sold quietly for the same reason, or there'll be no money left to operate it and it will cease to exist.'

'If that is true Lydia will be penniless, so all the more reason for her to say yes to my proposal.' David spoke almost to himself but his words were audible enough for his mother to pick up.

'Proposal? What do you mean?' she asked sharply.

'I asked Lydia to marry me. I love her. I would have asked her sometime in any case.'

90

'What? You proposed marriage to a girl who will bring nothing?' Jonas spat.

'Yes, now seemed as good a time as any. Marriage would solve the predicament she is in, though she did not indicate it was as serious as you've heard.'

'And I expect she said yes! She'd grasp the chance to get your money behind her.' Jonas's tone was scathing.

'She's not like that,' David protested. 'You should know, you like her. You've always approved of our relationship.'

Eugenia gave a dismissive wave of her hand. 'People can change, especially when they face possible poverty. Lydia has never given you the same encouragement you have given her.'

'Mother, you don't know how close we are, and I'm sure she'll say yes.'

'Then she hasn't yet done so?'

'No.'

Jonas and Eugenia showed relief in their exchange of glances, but that was dashed as David continued.

'Not there and then. She said she wanted time to think as there was so much happening.'

Jonas seized on his words. 'So much happening. What was she implying by that? She told you they were selling the furniture because they couldn't take it with them, yet she talks about *so much* happening. What else? Seems like there's something to these rumours after all.'

'And when do you expect her answer?' asked Eugenia.

'When she is ready to give it. But I'll press her for it. The sooner she realises she needn't face poverty, the better.'

'You'll tell her no such thing,' said Jonas coldly. 'In fact, you'll forget any idea of marrying Lydia Middleton as from now.'

David was so taken aback by his father's blunt words that he was speechless.

'You heard your father,' said Eugenia, enforcing his command.

David nodded. 'I heard. But you can't forbid this. I love Lydia.'

'Love has nothing to do with it,' snorted Jonas.

'It has everything to do with it. I love her and I believe she loves me. There's no better reason than that to get married.'

'And what about advancement?' asked Eugenia quietly.

'Advancement?' he queried.

'You can't be blind to the fact that in our social circle marriages are made so that families may prosper by them. If love is there as well, then so be it,' Jonas pontificated.

'It's true, David. Don't look so surprised,' said his mother with a faint smile at his bewilderment.

He was shocked at their cynical view. 'Then it will be different in my case. If Lydia brings nothing to the marriage in the way of wordly wealth and goods, it doesn't matter. I love her for what she is, not what she has.'

'She would once have had a share of Tristram Middleton's business, and her share coupled with what you will inherit would have given you more power among the Whitby merchants.'

'I'm not bothered about power. I don't want ...' He paused. Behind the mask of disapproval on his father's face he saw a deeper meaning. 'Ah, I see it all now. You aren't concerned about my feelings in all of this. It once suited you very well that I had feelings for her, but only because it accorded with your plans for the business. Well, I'm sorry to disappoint you but you can forget them. I'm sticking to Lydia.'

Jonas's lips tightened. 'There are other girls who would enhance your prospects.'

'You mean yours,' snapped David.

'Ultimately benefitting you.'

'I'll marry Lydia and you'll have to like it.'

'I won't like it and you won't marry her!' Jonas's face reddened with anger.

'I will!'

'Very well, but from the moment you do your allowance will be cut off.' His father's voice was rapier-like, making each thrust at his son painful. 'You will no longer be employed by me and the firm will go to your cousin in Scarborough on my death.'

There was no mistaking that his father meant it. The signs were there in the deadly seriousness of his eyes which never wavered as he stared at his son. There was no re-action from his mother, no gasp of horror at the pronouncement, no plea on her lips, so David knew she was in full agreement with his father.

He was beaten but he was still defiant. He sprang to his feet and glared at Jonas, wanting to wipe the look of antici-pated triumph off his face. 'Then you'd better get used to not having a son.' There was no reaction from his parents and he started for the door.

When he reached it he hesitated as a voice spoke in cold, considered tones.

'Think again, son. Look elsewhere. Lydia's cousin Isobel would make a good catch and would be a joy to bed.'

Chapter Five

Still seething with anger, his body taut with defiance, David stormed up the stairs. The light from the candelabra in the hall sent his shadow swinging round the curved wall as it matched him step for step. It flirted with him momentarily when he reached the landing and then was gone as he moved towards his room.

He flung open the door and slammed it shut behind him. The oil lamp, which had been lit by one of the servants half an hour earlier, juddered as the table shook with the crash of the door. He sank his back against it, trying to control the rage heaving within him. His face was twisted with anger and exasperation. He cried out to the heavens to guide him from the corner into which he had been driven. Choose! The word clamoured in his brain. Choose! Gradually his breathing, heavy after his exertions, eased back to normal. He pushed himself from the door and sat in a chair.

He gave a sigh, rested his elbows on the table and held his head in his hands. He tried to assess his situation with a clear mind. As he did so, Lydia became more and more prominent in his thoughts. There was no doubt that he loved her but he was confused as to what form that love should take. Should he defy his father for the girl he loved and condemn the two of them to a life of poverty? He would go to her penniless whereas he had expected to be able to keep her in the style to which she had been accustomed. No doubt she was thinking he would be able to do that. But, in view of his father's stipulation, what would life hold for them if he did defy Jonas? Could David face seeing her scratching and scraping, day after day, to save a penny here, to save one there? Could he face the anguish that would bring him? He had never wanted for anything so could he cope with poverty and the continual struggle of trying to overcome it?

But if he bowed to his father's wishes he would have to face Lydia with a decision which could tear her heart in two. If only he hadn't mentioned marriage at this stage. Maybe if he explained the situation carefully she would consent to wait until he could persuade his parents that he loved her and would not give her up. They must be made to see that there could be an amicable solution which would negate the drastic step his father had proposed.

Tomorrow would be a day of decisions when the destiny of many lives would be forged.

That same night when Lydia went to bed she was still undecided about David's proposal. The easiest path would be to say yes and accept whatever the future brought. But she did not want a marriage born on the horns of a dilemma. When she made her vows in front of a priest it had to be alongside a man who loved her for herself, one who wanted to be there because his professed love came from the heart and not out of sympathy and a desire to help her in her troubles.

She fell into a fitful sleep, hoping that by the time David came for her answer she would have made the right decision.

That moment came sooner than she'd expected.

The following morning David waited in his room until he knew his father had left for the office. He did not want another confrontation on top of the deliberations he had subjected himself to during the night. He also avoided his mother by forgoing breakfast and leaving the house immediately he came downstairs.

The morning was sharp with a fresh breeze but pleasant enough as there were few clouds to hide the sun. The port had come alive with all the activities the day's trading brought. Ships were being loaded with foodstuffs for London, alum for Newcastle and London, and iron ore for the works on Tyneside and the more recent developments on the banks of the River Tees. Even though there were now more men working on merchantmen than at fishing there were still a number of cobles with lines ready to leave the safety of their moorings for the hazardous North Sea. The clash of hammers rose from the shipbuilding yards renowned throughout the shipping world for the reliability and soundness of their work.

But David was oblivious to all this as he hurried to St Hilda's Terrace, nodding only curtly to any friends and acquaintances he passed.

He jerked the bell-pull at number twenty-one and impatiently rattled the brass doorknocker shaped like a fish. When the door was opened anxiety about Lydia's reaction brought unwonted sharpness to his query. 'Is Miss Middleton at home?'

'Yes, sir,' replied the maid nervously. Although she had opened the door to him on many occasions, she had never seen him in such an agitated mood. She stepped to one side and closed the door after he had entered the hall.

'Well, where is she?' David snapped.

'In the dining room, sir.'

He strode across the hall, hoping Luke was not with his sister. What he had to say was for her ears alone. The maid scurried across the tiles trying to circumvent him but before she could announce him he was into the room.

Lydia, taken aback by the intrusion, looked up from her cup of tea. 'David, what a surprise so early. After yesterday I thought it might be a few days before you came for my answer.'

'You have one so soon? But I . . .'

'Let me give it to you,' she interrupted quickly, and he could do nothing but allow her to go on. 'I'm sorry, David, I cannot marry you now.' She hurried on with her explanation before he could react. 'Due to our change of circumstances there are certain things I need to do. If I married you and still did them it would not be fair on you.'

David felt an unmistakable pang of relief but at the same time sharp disappointment.

'What have you to do?' he asked automatically. 'Can I help?'

'No, you can't.'

'Tell me and let me decide?'

'No.'

He knew he should not pursue the matter. 'Very well, but if ever . . .' He shrugged his shoulders. 'Maybe this has turned out for the best. Your decision eases mine, and you said "now" so there is hope for the future?'

She nodded but said, 'That sounds as though you've had second thoughts about the proposal? Is there something you're not happy about? If so then we'll just forget you ever made it.'

'No, I don't want that. But waiting until I am in a position to give you the life you have been used to and deserve might be no bad thing.'

'Can't you give me that now?'

He shook his head dejectedly. 'No.'

Lydia was astonished at his answer. 'What are you implying?'

He went on to tell her of his confrontation with his parents and the ultimatum made by his father, but did not mention Isobel.

Lydia listened without comment until he had finished and then said quietly but tellingly, 'So you wouldn't give up your kind of life for one in poverty shared with me?'

'It isn't that, Lydia!' he cried. 'I want to be able to provide for you as I should. I can only do that if we wait until I persuade my parents that it is no good expecting me to marry where they decree.'

'They're so calculating,' said Lydia in disgust. 'I knew them to be snobs but was always pleased it hadn't rubbed off on you. They're thinking only of themselves and not of your happiness.'

'It's not like that,' David protested though inwardly sharing her opinion. 'We just need to be patient. We need to give them time to . . .'

'They'll never give in, but you will. You'll find someone more to their liking and that will be that.'

'No!' His voice rose. 'It's you I love. It's you I want to marry. We're both of the same mind so let's just wait.'

'But even then, won't it depend on your parents' attitude? I'll never be able to bring to the marriage what they want.'

'Waiting will give me time to change their minds.'

'You're sure you can do that?'

'Yes. I'll show them you would bring more to our marriage than mere money, more than the assets of a thriving company.'

Lydia extended her hand to shake his. 'Then we have an amicable arrangement to see how things turn out.' But secretly she wondered if David would still feel the same once Nathan had finally exacted his right of ownership and turned his nephew and niece out of their home.

When David had gone Lydia went to the kitchen and sat down wearily on a chair beside the table. She tightened her lips in exasperation. How her life had changed! From being comfortably off, living happily with her father in the expectation of a marriage which would see her want for nothing, she now faced life without parents and with little money, and having to wait for an eventual marriage to David Drayton if he could ever persuade his parents to allow it.

Her thoughts turned to David and his attitude. If he really loved her, wouldn't he have defied his father, forsaken the life he knew, married her and faced life's trials in partnership with her? He had said his decision was made because of her but was it rather because of himself? Could he really bear to give up his comfortable way of life?

If she had married him and continued to move in the same social circles, her desire to avenge her father's death could have had dire repercussions for a husband. If David had come to her on the other hand, ostracised by his father, shunned by society because of their poverty, her revenge could have been pursued relentlessly. But as he had chosen not to, best to set thoughts of him aside and concentrate on paying back her uncle, she decided.

When Lydia told her brother of David's visit his first concern was for her. 'Are you sure you have done the right thing?'

'Yes,' she replied firmly. 'But I am a little disgusted he did not defy his father and call Jonas's bluff.'

'Don't be too hard on him. You've always liked David and you know how demanding his father can be. Jonas wields an iron fist.'

'You really believe he'd cut David off completely?'

'Undoubtedly, if it came to it, but David has one thing in his favour. Jonas makes no secret of the fact that he hopes some day David's son will take over the business. At some point therefore David has to marry. If he can only hold out long enough Jonas will be forced to welcome you eventually. But if David walks away from his family now he'll lose everything.' Luke was careful to check that his sister fully understood her best course of action. 'Don't condemn David, I think he has done this because of his love for you. He wants the life for you that you deserve.'

Lydia looked thoughtful as she took his words to heart. 'Maybe you're right, but Jonas might bring pressure to bear on David to find someone else. We'll just have to wait and see.' Her eyes narrowed as her thoughts turned elsewhere. 'Unencumbered by marriage, at least I can concentrate on our plans for Uncle Nathan.'

'And just what do you propose?' asked her brother cautiously.

Lydia eyed him closely. 'Does that tone of voice indicate you are having second thoughts?'

'No, no.' He was quick to alleviate her suspicions. 'But it will be a hard task and could lead us into all sorts of trouble.'

Lydia recognised the side of her brother's character which at times made him over-cautious. It was then that he would let things slide. This could not be allowed to happen now. She must take the initiative and keep their objective constantly to the fore.

On Saturday morning the last items of furniture had gone from St Hilda's Terrace by ten o'clock. All that was left were Lydia's and Luke's remaining personal possessions.

They had just finished their breakfast and were having a final word with the maids in the kitchen when they heard the front door burst open. Footsteps stormed along the bare boards of the hall. Doors were flung open and then crashed shut. Surprised and curious at the intrusion, they hastily left the kitchen.

'Ah, there you are.' Nathan's voice boomed out, seeming to fill the denuded rooms and echo throughout the house. 'Time's up, so get out. This is *my* house now. I'm moving in today. The carpets will be here soon and the furniture later in the day. So out with you!' Smug with the satisfaction of having at last attained something he had always regarded as rightfully his, he gesticulated towards the front door.

'You've no right to come bursting in here,' protested Luke.

Nathan laughed. 'I have every right. This house is mine. It's you who have no right here.'

'You had a key?' Lydia was stunned by what this might imply.

'Yes.' He held it up triumphantly. 'Ever since I lived

100

here.' He saw the look of distrust on her face. 'Oh, no, my dear, don't give me that. I have never used it until today, I'd swear to that on the Bible. Now stop shilly-shallying. Leave!'

Lydia drew herself up. 'We will. I would not want to stay in this house another minute. You've tainted it by your presence. It no longer feels like home.' She turned and hurried back to the kitchen.

A few minutes later the maids had departed by the back door after a brief but tearful goodbye. With their few possessions in two bags, sister and brother, accompanied by Mrs Harrington, left without another word to their uncle.

When they reached her small house in Wellington Square, off the thoroughfare of Baxtergate, she started to apologise for its state.

'Mrs Harrington,' Lydia halted her excuses, 'this is simply delightful.'

'But it's so small and not at all what you have been used to.'

'It's cosy, comfortable, and I know we will like it here.' Lydia raised an eyebrow and gave a little smile. 'I suspect you have been coming here every day to get things to your liking.'

'And, I hope, to *your* liking?'

'Of course,' put in Luke, to add weight to Lydia's assurances.

Though they had only been in the house a few minutes they felt comfortable in its welcoming atmosphere. That feeling persisted as Mrs Harrington showed them round. From the front room, which gave immediately on to the street, they stepped into the back parlour which served as a kitchen with its black range of fire, oven and a boiler for water.

Noting the fire burning brightly, Luke said, 'How thoughtful of you to come here early this morning and light a fire, Mrs Harrington.'

'I thought it would look more welcoming,' she replied.

101

'It's so cheery, it seems to lighten our troubles,' said Lydia, her eyes damp.

'And such a nice table and chairs,' observed Luke, wanting to direct his sister's mind from the thoughts he knew still bothered her. These items of furniture occupied the centre of the room. A matching cupboard stood in a recess between the chimney breast and the outside wall.

'My husband made them.'

'A skilled man.'

'Woodwork was his spare-time occupation when he was not away fishing. He liked to keep busy between sailings.'

A window looked on to a yard, part of which was occupied by a scullery with access from the back room. Upstairs were two small bedrooms lively with brightly coloured crocheted bedspreads, the work of Mrs Harrington's never-idle hands.

'This is a lovely little home,' said Lydia appreciatively. 'We cannot thank you enough for being so generous in allowing us to occupy it until we settle our problems and can find somewhere we can afford.'

'Take as long as you like. My sister will be pleased to have me around.' She filled a kettle and hung it on the reckon over the fire. 'I think a cup of tea is the first thing you should have in your new home.'

The next half hour would be forever marked on Lydia's mind. They sat at the table together over a cup of tea, a fire dancing in the grate. A conversation which revolved round Mrs Harrington's childhood and marriage brought some sort of peace to Lydia.

But once Mrs Harrington had gone and they had chosen their bedrooms, Lydia taking the front and Luke the back, the changes she was forced to undergo almost overwhelmed Lydia.

She sank wearily on to a chair. 'Oh, Luke, what are we going to do?'

The girl who had generally taken the lead, making most of the decisions for them with a firm resolve, now seemed

102

to be bordering on despair. Luke knew he must be the rock she could lean on.

'We'll manage,' he said firmly, kneeling in front of her and taking her hands in his. 'At least I have work and we are lucky to have this house, thanks to Mrs Harrington.'

'I know, but it's all going to be so different.' Her voice choked with emotion.

'It will be, but we are strong enough to adapt to a new way of life.'

'Oh, Luke, are we?' Uncertainty rang in her words.

'Of course we are.'

'Without Father?' Her voice broke for a moment then strengthened with a resounding cry to heaven. 'Why, oh, why, did that ship have to go down?'

'Oh, love, I don't know. Who can see the reason in God's ways?'

'God? There can't be a God to let that happen.'

'Father wouldn't have liked you to talk like that,' Luke pointed out quietly. 'And he wouldn't . . .'

Lydia's eyes flared. She finished what he was going to say. 'Want me to take revenge?'

Luke nodded. 'He wouldn't.'

'What about you?' Her eyes were fixed on him unflinchingly.

'Like you, I believe that Uncle Nathan's refusal to help caused Father's death . . .'

'Then he will not go unpunished.' His sister's voice was cold and remorseless.

Lydia had never been used to household work but, capable as she was, having inherited her mother's qualities, she quickly adapted to it and established a smooth routine.

Once that work was done she had time on her hands. She had her own books and could borrow more from the subscription library which had been established on the quay as an important asset to the town. She now had to do her own household shopping, and made sure that she kept to the

103

daily walk she had been used to. When she attempted to make contact with old friends she soon found out who were the true ones. Some offered sympathy and encouraged a continued relationship in spite of her changed circumstances. But there were those who made no such offer, who got rid of her quickly and made it plain that she was no longer welcome – snobs who wanted nothing more to do with her now she no longer had the same standing in Whitby society.

She stored these experiences in her mind, noting who might innocently impart information about her uncle when she wanted it.

Much of the time her thoughts were fixed on the desire to see Nathan ruined. She had pangs of conscience about her cousins but forced herself to ignore the fact that other people too would suffer. She narrowed her mind along the tunnel of revenge.

But the more she explored her possible courses of action, the more frustrated she became. She realised she needed assets to put her into a position strong enough to challenge her uncle's business interests. She needed secretly to establish a firm to compete for trade with him. To outbid him in negotiations, financial strength was essential, while to outsmart him she needed to know his intentions and for that she must have inside information.

Time and again she and Luke discussed the matter for she made sure his desire for revenge was kept alive. But they always found themselves at a disadvantage through the lack of money. Luke's discreet enquiries to try to raise capital were met with polite refusal. As Tristram had run into debt no one would trust Luke not to do the same. He was regarded as unsound.

Lydia was tempted to seek David's help but after carefully considering what that might involve and what she would have to reveal, suppositions she was not prepared to voice to anyone but Luke, she decided against it. So David's visits to the house in Wellington Square remained social calls only and were carried out discreetly for fear his father should get to know.

Throughout the next two weeks Lydia felt constantly frustrated at having to curb her desire for revenge. She tried to draw some comfort from the fact that she was still in Whitby where she could keep a check on her uncle's trading activities, storing the knowledge for future reference when she would initiate her vengeance. Then, one day, when Luke arrived home from work, she received what seemed at first like a setback.

As Luke came into the kitchen where she was preparing a meal Lydia could sense his excitement. She looked up from the table which she was setting and saw the light of enthusiasm in his eyes. His face was alive.

'Lydia, I've been promoted!' he cried.

Her eyes lit up with joy for her brother. 'Oh, Luke, I'm so pleased for you.'

'It means more money and a better chance of advancement.'

She came to him and hugged him affectionately. 'You deserve it.'

'There's only one snag,' he added on a cautionary note, as if he expected her to disapprove of what he was about to say. 'I . . . well, we . . . must move to Middlesbrough.'

Lydia's joy turned to bewilderment and her expression was puzzled. 'Middlesbrough? But why?'

'Well, Mr Martin is so pleased with my supervision of the loading of iron ore and the way I handle the men that he wants me to take over at the wharves on the River Tees. The manager there appears to be losing his grip and the men are taking advantage of his weaknesses and not working to capacity. The result is a slower turnaround of Mr Martin's vessels which means loss of revenue and could even lead to his losing the contract.'

Lydia nodded. 'And you feel capable of putting things right?'

105

'Yes.'

'If these men have become used to an easier time under an overseer they can manipulate, you could make enemies,' she warned. 'Wouldn't you be better here among friends?'

'It's a challenge and one I want to face. Father sent me to Mr Martin to gain experience. He intended to move me on to other merchants in the town so that I gained knowledge of many sides of Whitby's trading before we took over from him. But now, with those prospects gone, Mr Martin's offer presents a fresh opportunity.'

'I can understand why you want to do this, but to leave Whitby . . .'

Lydia saw what a vast change it would make to them. They had lived all their lives in this Yorkshire port. She loved it and knew that Luke did too. It was in their blood. To move away to a new town would be a wrench, and living away from Whitby would make it more difficult to pursue her dream of revenge. Would that desire fade with distance?

'It's a new life, a new challenge. We can make a fresh start, forget all our troubles,' pressed Luke.

'Forget? How can we forget what Uncle Nathan did?'

'I'm not suggesting we do that. But a move from Whitby may make us see things differently.'

'You mean forget our revenge? Never!'

Luke realised that recent events were still too painful for his sister to tone down her attitude. He had had work to occupy his mind. While he still ached to teach their uncle a lesson, the chance of ever doing so seemed to be remote and had become even more distant as he had thrown himself vigorously into his task of supervising the ore ships. But Lydia had had time to brood and keep alive the grudge she harboured. So Luke toned down his attitude in a way which he hoped would placate his sister and make her see that this move might be used to their advantage.

'At present no one will finance an enterprise for us here, but who knows what opportunities might arise if we move

106

away from Whitby? This offer could be just what we want.' He emphasised the words and saw they were having an effect on Lydia.

She began to look upon the idea more enthusiastically. 'You think we might find someone to back a venture with which we could challenge Uncle Nathan?'

'Who knows? Middlesbrough is a new town, not yet twenty years old. There could be a boom time coming with the growth of the iron industry.'

'Do you think that's possible?'

'Well, Mr Martin's shipment of ore is steadily rising. He wants no unrest among the men, either here or on Teesside, and that's why he has offered me this job. Who knows what it might lead to?'

Lydia's nimble mind began to see that a move from Whitby might give her the chance to work secretly towards her objective. 'When would we go?'

'A week today.'

'All right, Luke, I'll come with you.'

'Good!' He grabbed his sister, swung her off her feet and twirled her round, laughing with relief. 'We'll make good,' he cried. 'You can be sure of it.'

She laughed with him, pleased that he was happy with her decision. As he lowered her to the ground she looked at him with a deadly serious expression. 'But, Luke, we must never forget Whitby and what it means to us.'

Behind those words he read the implied threat to their uncle.

Chapter Six

'Sure now, if you two aren't coming to Middlesbrough, I'm off tomorrow. I didn't come over here to skylark in Liverpool.' Sean spat the words angrily at Seamus and Kevin.

'What's y' rush?' Seamus slurred his words as he flopped down on to his bed after an evening spent exploring some of Liverpool's ale houses. 'Sure, an' haven't we given y' a good time, haven't we shown y' the sights?'

'Sights? Aye, and what sights!' retorted Sean.

Seamus struggled to sit up. His eyes narrowed drunkenly and he shook his head slowly. 'Sure y' should have stuck with me every minute and then ye'd have seen better entertainment than y' ever did see.' He licked his lips lasciviously. 'Or were y' frightened Eileen might find out?'

'She had nothing to do with it,' snapped Sean. 'I didn't want to visit a brothel and nor did Kevin.'

Seamus snorted with disgust. 'Y' both sissies. Neither of y' knows what a good time is.' He pointed a finger at Sean. 'I'll tell y' what ... yes ... I'll tell y' this an' I'll tell y' no more – that little lady of yours won't be giving a damned thought to y'. She'll be bedding all and sundry.'

Sean's temper flared. He struck out at Seamus but Kevin, knowing his friend's talent for goading people, was ready for this reaction. He grabbed Sean's arm as it swung forward.

'Don't,' he hissed. 'Seamus doesn't mean it.'

Sean swung round on him. 'Then tell that bugger to curb his tongue.'

'Sean's right, Seamus,' interposed Kevin. 'We should be getting to Middlesbrough now we know that Mr Langton and his daughter have left Liverpool.' He turned to Sean. 'You must admit it was a good job we decided to stay here until Mr Langton left, and that I sweet-talked the hotel receptionist into letting me know when he and his daughter had checked out. We'd have been high and dry if we'd reached Middlesbrough first. Now our contact will already be there.'

'So you're coming with me tomorrow, Kevin?' Receiving a nod of agreement Sean added, 'What that disgusting excuse for a man decides is up to him.'

'Y' right, Sean, right. What I decide, I decide, whether you like it or not.'

'I won't like it, whatever it is.'

'Well, then, y'll have to lump it.' He collapsed backwards on the bed, his arms wide, muttering, 'That little lady Sarah Langton'll see a lot of dear old Seamus. A lot!' He chuckled.

'She's a respectable young lady who'll have nothing to do with the likes of you,' warned Sean.

'Think so?' Seamus went on chuckling, amused by his own lewd thoughts.

'Watch your step,' warned Kevin. 'We don't want you messing up our chances after what Sean did for Mr Langton.'

Seamus made no reply. He was already snoring.

The following morning, still nursing an aching head which seemed frequently to go into a spin, Seamus was bad-tempered as the other two cajoled him into getting ready to leave.

'Shut your nattering. Yous two are like a couple of aud washerwomen,' he snapped as he tucked his shirt into his trousers.

109

'If we didn't natter you'd miss this train,' pointed out Kevin. 'You've missed breakfast as it is.'

'Ugh! Don't mention food.' Seamus gulped and clasped one hand to his forehead.

'Get a move on or I will,' threatened Kevin.

Ten minutes later, having paid for their lodgings, they headed for the station.

'Not so fast,' called Seamus who bumbled along behind Sean and Kevin.

They took no notice. There was a train to catch and catch it they would. A few minutes later, seeing Seamus dropping further behind, they glanced at each other and turned as one to head back to him. Without a word they stood close, one on either side of him, and took hold of him under the armpits, lifting him off his feet. They strode out. Seamus's feet moved in a running motion but without purchase on the paving. He protested at their rough handling but, when he saw that they were taking no notice, resigned himself to the ride.

At the station they dumped him, purchased the tickets, grabbed him by the arms again and bustled him on to the train. As they shoved him into a carriage he lost his footing and sprawled on the floor, bringing sharp protests and glances of disgust from the two females who occupied corner seats and had been looking forward to a carriage to themselves.

Sean and Kevin clambered in, yanked Seamus to his feet and shoved him into one of the vacant corners before stowing their bags. All the time they muttered apologies to the two ladies for the state of their friend.

The two men's rich Irish brogue and smiles which would have melted any female heart soon won the forgiveness of their two travelling companions who, they learnt, were going as far as Manchester. Seamus knew nothing of the conversation or the journey, however, for he fell fast asleep as soon as he was settled.

He slept most of the way for which Sean and Kevin were

thankful. Once they emerged from the station in Middlesbrough, Seamus was all for finding the nearest pub.

'Sure, and isn't that the bright idea?' said Kevin, seemingly with an air of approval. 'But not to drink.'

Seamus, who by now had his wits about him, eyed his friend in amazement. 'Sure now, an' what would you be doing going to a pub and not drinking?'

Kevin leaned towards him, bringing his face close. He raised a forefinger and tapped Seamus on the head. 'Seeking information, wise one, information.'

'On what?' Seamus's voice rose and his face twisted in disgust.

'We have to sleep tonight. For that we want a boarding house. The landlord of a pub is likely to know of one.'

Sean had been looking around him. 'We'll go this way,' he suggested.

He received no objection and the three of them set off to find a pub. They had not gone far when they entered the Iron Smelter. They found themselves in a room with a mahogany counter running along one wall and small tables set beside the other three, leaving a space in the middle for customers to crowd towards the bar. Though it was still daylight the room was dreary. Light barely filtered through the coloured glass at the window or from the clouded gas mantles.

The bar was busy but had not reached the point where the three barmen would be kept continuously filling glasses. That would come about shortly as workers anxious to slake the dust and heat of work from their throats packed in demanding beer after their shift.

Only cursory glances were cast at the three Irishmen as they crossed the sawdust-strewn floor to the counter. A burly red-faced barman with a long white apron tied at his waist came over to them as they dropped their bags on the floor and lined themselves up along the bar.

'Evening,' he said curtly, eyeing the newcomers with an assessing look. 'Beer?'

Seamus's face broke into a smile. 'Ah, sure now, here's a man after m' own heart. Three tankards of your best.' He glanced at his companions. 'You two aren't going to say no?'

'Just the one,' said Kevin firmly.

The barman looked up from the glass he had already started to fill. 'Just in from Ireland?'

'Aye, we are that,' returned Kevin.

'First time in Middlesbrough?' His gaze swept quickly over the three of them. He'd had trouble with some Irishmen but these three were reasonably dressed and had not swaggered into the pub as if they were kings of the world.

'Yes.'

'Looking for work?' The barman started on the second glass.

'We think we're fixed up,' replied Sean, 'but we are looking for lodgings. Can you help us?'

The barman did not reply immediately but watched the beer foam at the top of the glass, allowed it to run over and then carefully topped it up. He placed the glass in front of Sean. In those few seconds he had confirmed to himself his first assessment of the newcomers.

'Aye, lad, I might be able to do just that.'

'Good, we'd be obliged.'

The barman had picked up a third glass and now he started to fill it. Seamus had already drunk half of his in anticipation of ordering another but slowed when he received Kevin's warning look – no more. He knew his friend was recalling one time when they had arrived in Grimsby and he had escaped Kevin's clutches. Turning up at their respectable boarding house drunk had not been a good idea. Kevin did not want it happening again.

The barman waited until he had filled the glass. He had held back from imparting the required information and unobtrusively observed Seamus's consumption of his beer. He noted him slow up now and decided that the man had just been keen to quench his thirst.

112

He put the third glass in front of Kevin who pushed some pennies over. The barman took the money and then added, 'Try Mrs Hartley in West Street. She's my sister. Just lost three of your compatriots. Decided they'd had enough and moved up north.'

'Thanks,' all three of them said at once.

'Where's West Street?' asked Sean.

'Turn right out of here. The way you were heading when you came in – I'm supposing you'd just come from the station?' They nodded their confirmation. 'Keep right on into the Square – the Market Place. To the left is West Street. Number ten. Tell Nell Jim sent you.'

'Thanks,' they chorused as he moved away to serve some arrivals with whom he was familiar.

'Come on, drink up,' urged Sean as he picked up his glass. 'Let's find West Street. I reckon our luck's in.'

There were no protests from Seamus and in a few minutes they called their thanks again to Jim and left the Iron Smelter.

They took little notice of the busy shoppers as they headed up South Street. The Market Place was dominated by the tall-spired tower at the west end of St Hilda's church.

'Imposing,' commented Kevin. 'Better-looking than that.' He nodded towards the northwest corner of the Square.

'Can't be anything else but a chapel,' said Seamus in a tone which showed he agreed with Kevin's assessment of the building.

'West Street.' Sean brought their attention back to their purpose by pointing across the open space.

Within a few minutes they were knocking at the door of number ten. It was opened by a short, plump lady dressed in black with a white apron tied at her waist. Her brown hair was taken back and tied in a bun. Her cheeks were rosy, her eyes bright but filled with curiosity on finding three strangers on her doorstep.

113

'Good day, ma'am,' said Sean. 'Mrs Hartley?'

'Aye.'

'Jim sent us. Said y' might be able to give us lodgings.'

'I might. Seen our Jim, have you? Well, he doesn't let the grass grow under his feet, nor mine by the sound of it.' Nell Hartley knew her brother well. Older than her, he had looked after her interests when they were kids and was still doing so. 'Well, if he's vetted you, you'd better come away in and have a chat.' She turned back into the house, leaving the last of the Irishmen to close the door.

The passage led to a room at the back. They followed her and found themselves in a square room with a door leading off it to a scullery in which there was another door giving access to a yard with a high brick wall. The room they were in felt cosy. A bright fire burned in the grate of a kitchen range which was no doubt Nell's pride and joy for it was as bright as a new pin. A kettle puffed gently away on a reckon above the fire.

'Sit you down.' She indicated a sofa let into an alcove formed by the stairs rising from the passage. A pinewood table and four matching chairs were placed in the centre of the room. A mahogany press was set against one wall and a cupboard occupied a space beside the fireplace.

'A cup of tea?' suggested Nell, wanting to create a friendly atmosphere. She had summed these men up quickly and in her own mind confirmed her brother's judgement. 'Though if you've seen our Jim you'll already have had something a bit stronger.'

'A cup of tea would be welcome,' replied Kevin, sensing that acceptance of the offer would strike an agreeable chord.

Over that cup of tea Nell promised them lodgings, but first they had to agree to certain conditions and she warned that if they were broken their agreement would be terminated immediately.

'No drink will be brought into the house. That would threaten Jim's trade and I won't be party to that. I have no objection to your partaking of whatever liquid you like but – and this is a big but – you never enter this house the worse for it. No female will be entertained here either unless there is serious courting with whoever she be and I am first introduced to her.'

'You'll approve or disapprove our choice if it arises,' commented Seamus with an amused twitch of his lips.

'I will that,' replied Nell firmly. She eyed him seriously, having judged him to be the one who would cause trouble if trouble were to be caused, but she had already decided she liked the rogue in him. 'Now if you are agreeable to that and to my charge of ten shillings a week each for lodgings, board and washing, then I'll show you your rooms.'

'That seems highly satisfactory,' replied Kevin, 'and we thank you for your kindness and hospitality.'

Nell nodded. She liked the look of these three and felt there was something different about the one who had just spoken, but she kept her thoughts to herself. She opened the door into the passage and turned up the stairs. At the top she went into a room to the right. 'Two of you will have to sleep in here.'

A brass bedstead, a chest of drawers, a wash stand on which there stood a large basin and ewer with clean white towels laid beside them, were all the furnishings apart from two chairs, one on either side of the bed.

'You two in here,' said Sean quickly, wanting to be on his own and having no desire to come between two friends.

'Very well. You'll be just across the landing.' She showed Sean a room which was similarly furnished.

He had noted there were only two bedrooms. 'What about you and Mr Hartley?' he asked.

'Oh, there's no Mr Hartley,' she replied. 'He was killed in those newfangled ironworks. I hate 'em for that but I suppose they're progress. At least that's what we're told, and I must admit Middlesbrough wouldn't be here without them.' She cocked her head and looked wryly at him. 'I suppose you're wondering where I sleep?' She saw he was

115

embarrassed and went on quickly, 'I know you only mean well by that thought. When I have lodgers I sleep on the sofa in the kitchen. But don't worry, I'm used to it. I'm comfortable enough and it's warm there.'

When she had returned downstairs the three men emptied their bags then joined her in the kitchen. She was already making a meat pie.

'This will be ready for six o'clock. I suppose now you're going to try and find work?'

'We've been promised something,' replied Kevin. 'We need to find the Bolckow and Vaughan works.'

'Ah, then you'll be wanting those towards the river. You wouldn't be wanting their Witton Park works – they're way north of the river near Auckland.'

'We were told to come to Middlesbrough and contact a Mr Langton.'

Nell raised her eyebrows in surprise. 'My, you will be riding high. Important man is Mr Langton. Firm but fair. And kind to me when my husband was killed. Go back into the Market Place, go down North Street to Commercial Street then turn right. You can't miss the works.'

'Thanks, Mrs Hartley,' said Sean.

As they were leaving the kitchen she stopped them, saying, 'Being Irish, I expect you'll want a Catholic church on Sunday?'

The three men cast sharp glances at each other. True they had all been baptised Catholics and brought up in that faith as youngsters but all three would have to admit they had become less particular about their religion as they had escaped the influence of their families. But they were caught out now and wanted to keep on the right side of their landlady.

'We will that, ma'am,' replied Kevin quickly in case his companions made any adverse comment.

'Well, you needn't go looking. I'm a Catholic myself and you can come with me on Sunday.'

'That's very kind of you,' replied Sean.

116

'Sure, we've landed in good hands, Mrs Hartley,' commented Seamus in his smoothest Irish lilt. 'It's a comfort for three young men far from home to have someone to look after us bodily,' he nodded in the direction of the pie she was preparing so that there was no misunderstanding his meaning, 'and spiritually.'

'Off with you and take your smart talk with you. You don't fool Nell Hartley but I'm sure we'll get on well if we understand each other.'

The three men bustled out of the house without another word until they were outside with the door shut tight behind them.

'Sunday Mass!' Seamus raised his eyes heavenwards as if to plead exemption from a higher authority.

'I'll tell you this and I'll tell you no more,' said Sean, 'it won't do us any harm.'

'Ah, listen who's talking – the man living in sin with Eileen Nolan,' commented Kevin.

'Who casts the first stone?' Sean returned knowingly.

'Ah, well, maybe we're all tarred with the same brush,' said Seamus. 'None of us can preach.'

'So, don't let's any of us cross Mrs Hartley,' Kevin insisted. 'We've got good lodgings there. We've been lucky so far. Let's find these works and hope our luck holds good.'

They hardly needed Mrs Hartley's directions for once they had started along South Street the rising smoke from several chimneys was a guide in itself. The hum of industrial power and the bustle of its accompanying activity was a new world to the three men and by the time the works were in sight they felt caught up in the energy of this place, heralding a future as yet unknown.

They paused as they turned into the open space beyond the railway where pig iron was being unloaded and then taken to the long row of buildings above which rose the rolling mill's chimneys.

As a man came hurrying past, Sean grabbed him by the arm. 'Where will we find Mr Langton?'

117

'Yonder,' came his curt reply. He pointed in the direction of a door close to the east end of the buildings.

'Thanks.'

He was gone and the Irishmen, avoiding the bustle of men intent on their work, crossed the open space in the direction of the buildings.

As they reached the door a man came out. Unlike the other workers he wore a suit of brown serge. His jacket was unfastened to reveal a matching waistcoat spanned by a watchchain slung between two pockets. He was slapping a bowler hat on to his head as if it was a symbol of authority.

'Mr Langton?' queried Sean, who had taken on the role of enquirer.

'Second door on the right.' He cast an eye over them as he spoke but made no further comment and went on his way.

They entered the building to find themselves in a passage with several doors leading off it. They stopped outside the designated door and all automatically straightened their jackets and firmed their shoulders. Seamus and Kevin glanced at Sean and he took their silent inference that he should continue to take the lead. He rapped on the door and after the call of 'Come in', opened it.

James Langton looked up from the maps he was studying. His face broke into a broad smile and he pushed himself quickly from his chair.

'Sean Casey!' He came from behind his desk, his hand held out in greeting.

As Sean took it he felt a strong friendly grip.

'Good to see you, young man.'

'And you, sir,' returned Sean with a smile, responding to the kindly greeting he had been given.

James looked beyond him to see Seamus and Kevin stepping into the room. 'So you two decided to come after all?'

'We did that, sir,' replied Kevin.

'Couldn't let him go off into the big wide world alone,' chuckled Seamus.

'When did you get to Middlesbrough?' James asked.

'Just today,' replied Sean.

'You've wasted no time in looking me up then.'

'No, sir. We want jobs and you said you could probably help.'

'I did and I'm a man who keeps his promises. First, have you found lodgings?'

'Yes, sir.'

'Good. Then it's just the jobs that have to be arranged. You can have employment here at the rolling mill or at our blast furnace at Witton Park.'

'Where's Witton Park?' queried Kevin.

'About twenty miles west of here.'

'That would mean moving, and leaving the excellent lodgings we've found in West Street.'

'Not far away.'

'No. So we'll take any work you have here,' decided Sean.

'Right. It'll be mundane work, I'm afraid. You aren't frightened of physical labour, I hope?' James queried.

'Kevin and I have had it physical at Grimsby docks,' said Seamus, 'but I can't answer for this fella here.' He nodded at Sean with a teasing twinkle in his eye.

'Away wi' ye,' rapped Sean. 'I'll match ye any time.'

'I'm sure you will,' replied James with a smile. 'Come, I'll take you to my supervisor. He directs the workers as necessary. We're currently shipping iron ore in from Whitby. That's got to be unloaded from the ships for transportation by rail to the blast furnaces at Witton. There it's turned into pig iron and brought back here by rail to the rolling mills, so there's a lot of humping and grafting to be done. Maybe one day after you've seen how things are done here we'll find you a job in the rolling mill.'

He took them outside, pausing a moment to cast his glance around the activity taking place between the railway and the mill but did not see the man for whom he was looking.

'With that train just arrived, Eric Gilmore, the supervisor, won't be far away. He has five foremen under him, each of whom oversees a team of men in the loading and unloading of the trains.'

'How many in a team, sir?' asked Sean, determined to show interest.

'Varies depending on the work. We maintain a pool of men whom we can move around as required. Numbers are down at the moment and we've had to lay off a few.'

'How's that, sir? I thought the iron trade would be experiencing good times.'

'It has but we're suffering a bit of a setback at the moment.' James was impressed by this young man's curiosity which he judged to stem from a genuine interest in anything new. He was minded, therefore, to expand a little further. 'Two reasons. The deposits of iron ore close by the Witton blast furnaces haven't produced the quantity we expected, so we are having to ship in ore from Whitby which is adding to the cost. And there's trouble with the men unloading the ships. The Whitby firm insisted that their own workers be employed for this but at the moment those men are slow, only making a pretence at work. A weak overseer's the trouble. The men take advantage of him.'

'Can't you do anything about it, sir?'

'Not personally, but I have contacted the shipowner in Whitby and he has promised to replace the overseer. Because of the trouble Mr Bolckow and Mr Vaughan have been forced to cut back on production. If the new man from Whitby fares no better, they'll have to reconsider the situation.'

'Any danger of closure?' asked Sean.

James shook his head. 'I shouldn't think so. I'm sure Mr Bolckow and Mr Vaughan see a future in iron so long as they can overcome the present setback and keep supplies of ore coming.' He changed his tone. 'Ah, there's Mr Gilmore.' He indicated a man who had come out of the rolling mill, and raised his arm in a gesture which brought Gilmore in their direction.

They saw that this was the man in the bowler hat they had encountered previously.

'This is Mr Gilmore, our supervisor. Eric, I want you to employ these three men.'

He raised an eyebrow. 'I thought we weren't taking on any more hands for the time being?'

'In this case we'll make an exception.'

Sean noticed Gilmore's expression darken and was sure that where the employment of men was concerned he did not like to be told who should be given work and who shouldn't. His burliness brought a belligerent attitude with it and his stern, unsmiling features did nothing to foster a friendly feeling. Sean sensed that Gilmore revelled in wielding authority over his fellow human beings and in their capacity of labourers looked down on them. They wore flat caps, he wore a bowler.

'These are the men I told you about who saved my life and my daughter's. I promised to help them,' explained James. 'I'll leave them in your hands.' He turned to the three Irishmen. 'Mr Gilmore will look after you.' He gave them a friendly smile and headed for his office.

Gilmore ran his gaze over them. 'Who's who?' he asked curtly.

'I'm Sean Casey. This is Seamus O'Leary and Kevin Harper.'

Gilmore grunted and ignored Sean's proffered hand. He glanced across at the office and saw James disappearing inside. 'Don't come here thinking you'll get privileges for what you did for Mr Langton. You're just another three pairs of hands to me, and don't you forget it. Here you'll work as you've never worked before – if not you're out. And don't go whingeing to Mr Langton. He'll listen to me before you.'

Sean read jealousy of their personal tie with James Langton.

'You start work tomorrow morning at six o'clock.' The supervisor gave a little chuckle to accompany his knowing grin. 'Gus Arnold will be there with his team to move another load of pig iron from Witton.' Without waiting for acknowledgement he hurried away towards the train, leaving the three Irishmen staring after him.

'Nice fella,' commented Seamus, deep sarcasm in his voice.

'A new friend,' Kevin joined in with Seamus's assessment.

'We shan't have to step the wrong side of that bastard,' agreed Sean. He glanced at his two friends. 'Wishing you'd gone to Grimsby?'

'No.' But there was a note of doubt in their answer. 'We'll see a different life here, then we'll decide.'

Sean's eyes narrowed knowingly as if he was seeing the future. 'There's one thing for sure, Sean Casey isn't going to spend much time heaving iron ore. There have to be better ways of making a crust than that.'

Chapter Seven

'Now, my boys, nine o'clock Mass tomorrow,' Nell laid it down as if she would brook no objection, and they knew better than to make one. In the few days they had been with her they had come to respect and like her, and, knowing that they were fortunate to have found such good lodgings, were determined not to upset her.

Dressed in their best clothes, clean-shaven, boots highly polished, they duly awaited her in the front room, hardly daring to move on their seats for fear of upsetting the precise placing of the furniture: 'Just as Mr Hartley liked it.'

When she appeared they stood up as one.

Nell looked them over with a quick glance. 'My, we are looking smart,' she commented approvingly.

'Ah, sure, we are no better than y'self, ma'am.' Seamus made a bow. 'Indeed you're a picture.'

'Flatterer,' she replied with a dismissive wave of her hand, but inwardly she was pleased.

'It's true,' confirmed Sean and Kevin.

Nell drew herself up that little bit taller. It was a while since she had been paid endearing compliments by three young men.

In fact she had taken pains with her appearance as she always did for Sunday Mass. She wore black and it suited her. The woollen dress was plain, nipped in slightly at the waist and flaring to a bell shape. A grey ribbon drew the neckline close to her throat and fell away in a long streamer across her full bosom. A silk bonnet was shaped close to her head, its narrow brim trimmed with grey lace. She wore a waist-length shot silk shawl, patterned in grey, and black gloves.

'Shall we go?' she said.

'Yes, ma'am,' they chorused.

As Mrs Hartley locked the door, Seamus and Kevin donned their bowler hats but Sean bucked convention and went without any headgear. He noticed Mrs Hartley had observed this but the expected comment did not come.

Nell was amused. She knew Sean had seen her reaction and that he had expected a rebuke but she refrained. After all, hats would be taken off in church and did it really matter outside? Besides, she had taken to Sean more so than to the other two. Not that she didn't like them, she did. Maybe it was because he had that extra charm, that Irish twinkle in his eye and a way with words that would charm a woman of any age, and she was not above being charmed in a friendly way.

'No rushing away after Mass,' she ordered. 'I want you to meet Father O'Flaherty, the parish priest. He always says this Mass on a Sunday. His curates officiate at the others.'

Seamus raised his eyes heavenwards. He had been anticipating a dash to the nearest pub. He'd make his escape as soon as he could.

Crowds of people were converging on the dull exterior of the church, hemmed in by taller buildings on three sides. In spite of this, long lancet windows let in sufficient light to make the nave and chancel with their white-painted walls seem bright.

Knowing that the church would be full, Nell had left home early so that they would all be able to sit together.

They had been there about three minutes when she nudged Sean with her elbow. She leaned closer to him and whispered, 'I didn't tell you they were Catholics.'

He followed her gaze and saw Mr Langton and his daughter taking their seats nearer the chancel on the other side of the aisle.

As he waited for Mass to begin Sean's eyes kept straying to Sarah. He had a three-quarter view of her and was thankful that she wore the smallest of bonnets so that her face was not hidden.

He remembered that even amidst the chaos of the tragedy off Liverpool he had seen that she was an attractive young woman. Her soaked and bedraggled condition had not been able to disguise that. He smiled to himself as he recalled the laughter she had invoked when she came to join them on the quay, and the defiant stance she had taken then. Now, sitting beside her father, she looked so demure and calm. Her auburn hair was tied neatly at the nape of her neck below a bonnet made of the same material as her white muslin dress and patterned in small mauve motifs. The bodice was plain, coming into a point at the waist to offset the flounces of the skirt and the wide, bell-shaped sleeves.

Throughout the service Sean found his thoughts and eyes constantly straying to Sarah. With the service over he saw father and daughter leave their pew. Anxious to try to make contact with her, he itched to follow them but knew it would be bad manners to rush out before Mrs Hartley was ready, and her head was still bowed in prayer.

The few minutes that passed before she gave a little nod to her three lodgers to indicate that she was ready to leave seemed interminable to him.

Emerging from the church, Sean felt a surge of relief. Sarah and her father were talking to the priest who, in the midst of his conversation, acknowledged other parishioners as they were leaving. Nell hesitated, then held back.

But Sarah glanced up and saw the three Irishmen. Her face immediately broke into a broad smile as she saw them. With a quick, 'Excuse me,' she broke away from the priest and her father. 'Sean! Seamus! Kevin!' She was so friendly

125

and natural in her greeting they might have been the oldest of friends. 'Father told me you had come to Middlesbrough and I hoped I might see you all again. How are you? Getting settled?' She glanced at their landlady. 'Don't tell me they're staying with you, Mrs Hartley?'

'Yes, miss.' Nell was mystified as to how Miss Sarah knew her lodgers.

'Then you know what they did?' Sarah saw the woman's puzzled look and added, 'You don't? They've never told you?'

Nell shook her head.

'They saved my life and Father's.'

Nell looked even more astonished as if she did not comprehend the meaning of Sarah's words.

'That shipwreck off Liverpool – oh, maybe you didn't know about it? Well, we were thrown into the sea and would have perished but for Sean.'

The group had now been joined by Mr Langton and the priest.

'These three young men were on board another ship,' explained James. 'Sean dived overboard and saved us. And, thank goodness, there were another two pairs of hands to haul us out of the water.'

'Well, I never,' gasped Nell. 'To think I have heroes staying with me. What do you think of that, Father?'

The priest smiled. 'You're in good company, Nell, as are they.' He held out his hand to each of the Irishmen in turn, introducing himself as Father O'Flaherty.

As they all fell into conversation, Seamus gradually edged himself away until he could leave without anyone noticing.

Five minutes later the priest said his goodbyes and returned to his house near the church. It was then that Kevin missed Seamus. Knowing full well why his friend had disappeared, his mouth tightened in annoyance. Seamus's habit of a drink after Sunday Mass was not to be forgone even though he was in new territory. Recalling

126

some Sundays in the past when his friend might have ended up in the Liffey if Kevin hadn't been around, he hoped Seamus would not be upsetting Mrs Hartley later in the day.

As they left the church grounds, Sarah managed a quick quiet word with her father.

'A good idea,' he whispered. Then he stopped and addressed the men. 'Sarah and I would like to say a proper thank you for saving our lives, though what we propose is not really adequate. Please would you all come home with us and join us for Sunday dinner? We'll introduce you to Yorkshire pudding, made as it can only be made in Yorkshire.'

'Sir, there's no need. You owe us nothing for what we did. Besides you have already helped us by finding us work,' said Kevin.

'That's beside the point,' returned James with a dismissive shake of his head. 'We'd like to do it.' He turned his gaze on Nell. 'Of course, you're invited too, Mrs Hartley.'

'That is very kind of you, Mr Langton.' She was embarrassed by this invitation from a man she regarded as of a different station in life. Though social attitudes were changing, she felt they still had not gone far enough to permit such familiarity between the classes. From her experience when her husband was killed, she knew there was no snobbery in the Langtons but wondered if he would have made this offer if he had not felt beholden to the Irishmen. 'But I'm afraid I have an appointment with Mrs Stuart about the cleaning of the church and the arrangement of flowers for the coming week.'

'Oh, dear. I am sorry, Mrs Hartley,' said Sarah.

'That's all right, miss. I'll expect my boys when I see them. Thank you for the invitation.' Nell felt a little relieved as she walked away.

As they fell into step, Sean found himself walking with Mr Langton, and Kevin, to his delight, escorted Sarah.

'Not far to walk,' said James. 'We live on Queen's

127

Terrace, close to the Head Office of the Owners of the Middlesbrough Estate, an energetic body set up in 1830 to develop Middlesbrough. So, do you think you'll like it here?'

'Yes.' Sean's reply was firm. 'But I look beyond humping ore and pig iron.'

James gave a little smile. 'I thought so. Well, see how you get on. And if in the future I can be of any help, come to see me.'

'That's very kind of you, sir.'

'I found a kindly man in Mr Vaughan when I first met him. He was the manager of a small ironworks in Carlisle then, with a special gift for handling men. For some reason he took to me, gave me a helping hand, instilled the confidence in me to tackle a job which was new. And he persuaded me to come to Middlesbrough with him. I've never forgotten the lessons he taught me and I never shall. I see something of myself as I was in you, though of course I was older and had held responsible positions before I came here. Nevertheless there are lessons to be learned at all ages and I certainly learned from him.'

'He sounds to be a fine man.'

'Indeed he is. And so is Mr Bolckow, for that matter, but in an entirely different way. They are just right as business partners. Bolckow has the capital – a very rich man – and Vaughan has the more practical knowledge. We can learn from them both.'

'And I think from you, too, sir.'

'Well, I saw opportunities for promotion and took them. I don't regret being here. You know, I can see this town expanding fast. Maybe there's a setback for the company at the moment but I'm sure that will pass and then there'll be expansion on a scale never seen before. And, Sean, that means plenty of opportunities for young men with flair who are not afraid of work.'

'I'll be on the lookout for them, sir.'

'That's the right attitude.'

Kevin, who was enjoying Sarah's company, neverthe-

128

less, caught those words and stored them in his mind. If Sean could do it, so could he.

'You'll be well looked after by Mrs Hartley?' Sarah observed.

'Oh, indeed.' He concentrated again on the girl beside him.

'A kindly person. Such a tragedy that she lost her husband.'

'She mentioned an accident at the rolling mill. What happened?'

'A boiler exploded, ripped the roof off and brought some walls down. A number of workmen were hit and some trapped. Mr Hartley was killed by a falling beam.'

'Was he the only one?'

'No. Two others died. One suffered a horrible death – he was thrown under a burning furnace.' Sarah grimaced at the recollection.

Kevin noticed her distress. 'I'm sorry. I shouldn't have asked.'

She gave a wan smile in appreciation of his concern. 'That's all right. It's as well to know of the dangers. The whole town was upset by the tragedy. Mr Bolckow and Mr Vaughan were very troubled by it. They felt the loss almost as much as the families.' She switched the conversation to a pleasanter tack. 'Let's talk of brighter things. I can tell that young man in front is ambitious.'

Kevin smiled. 'Sean? Sure now, he has big ideas.'

'And you?'

'Not in the same way. But I can see my life here being different from digging docks in Grimsby. There was nothing to do there but watch them fill with water.'

Sarah laughed. 'Nothing beyond that?'

'Little.'

'And here there is?'

Kevin had a beautiful girl beside him and was not going to give her the impression he was a mere labourer with no higher ambitions. This girl seemed interested in him. Dare he hope ...? He had seen Sean eyeing her in church and somehow that had riled him. Sean had his Eileen, couldn't he keep his mind on her? He knew Sean had had a reputation for liking all the girls when he was younger and would flit from one to the other like a moth flirting with the flickering flames of a candelabra. Was that trait still there, dormant in him, even though he had established a steady relationship with Eileen Nolan? Was it surfacing again at the sight of a pretty girl now there was distance between him and his lover? Well, maybe Kevin Harper would have something to say about that.

'Oh, yes, Miss Langton. I can see this town growing and growth means new opportunities for those sharp and quick enough to exploit them.'

'You sound just like Father. He believes this will be a boom area, especially if more ironstone deposits can be found.'

'Then I'll find them for you, Miss Langton, and name the mines after you,' said Kevin with a lighthearted laugh.

'Miss Langton? Please don't be so formal. I'm Sarah. After what you saw on the quay at Liverpool, I should say formality was rather misplaced.'

They both chuckled at the memory.

'Then I'll have to call them the Sarah mines.'

She inclined her head gracefully and said, 'And Seamus? What of him? I'm sorry he disappeared after church.'

'A man with a big heart but his own worst enemy. He's so generous money runs through his hands like the beer he drinks. As long as he has the money for that he's a happy man.'

'And has a friend like you to look after him.'

Kevin shrugged his shoulders but made no comment.

Kevin studied the three-storey dwelling in Queen's Terrace as they approached it. Its red bricks exuded an air of solidity and seemed to lend the house a safe, welcoming atmosphere.

Ahead of him, Sean, still beside Mr Langton, was

promising himself that one day he would own such a house. It spoke of a world in which Sarah walked with ease. He wanted to do the same, to be part of it, but that would only come about if he threw off the mantle of labourer. He would have to show some special talents, but first he would have to discover them. Maybe with Sarah's encouragement ... He started. A voice within him reminded him of promises made to a girl in Ireland. They had not been idle ones. He had believed in his own ability and had won her belief too. Eileen, who had shared so much with him, who had defied convention because she loved him, deserved better than to be cast aside.

Had he really entertained such a thought? Ruthless ambition had temporarily blinded him. He'd made promises before he came here and Eileen Nolan was relying on him to keep those promises. He had sworn to take her out of the life they knew into the sort of life she deserved, with the world at her feet. Could his path to riches start here among the ironworks of Middlesbrough? Could Sarah Langton be a stepping stone on that path?

From now on he would be on the lookout for any opportunity to achieve his goal. He would listen and absorb, see and remember, talk and elicit useful information. He would prise open a world of possibilities and choose the best of them to turn that world into his oyster.

He was even more determined to achieve his objective when he stepped inside the house. Here was elegance and richness such as he had never seen before. Everything was of the best, yet he knew from Mr Langton's conversation on the way home from church that these things had not been gained easily. This life, with its trappings of luxury, had been achieved by Langton's hard work and determination to become a man of responsibility – a manager trusted implicitly by his employers. If this was the home of a manager, how must those above him live? They must inhabit a different world. Let there be a place in it for Sean Casey and Eileen Nolan!

131

Unused to this way of life, he was keenly observant of everything he saw here. In Dublin he had not been used to maids to take visitors' hats and coats, and to wait on table. Here the cutlery and tableware baffled him but he avoided any embarrassment by hesitating until Mr Langton had made his choice.

James, an astute judge of men, was aware that Sean had moved out of his class but saw in him something different from the usual Irish labourer who sought work in what was regarded as the booming economy of England. The difference was visible in Sean's bearing. James had been conscious of it on the quay at Liverpool and again when the Irishman had faced him in his office. If Sean had talent and ambition it would out and his present occupation would soon be a thing of the past.

Kevin was different. He was more at ease here, not obviously overawed as Sean was. Kevin could progress easily but he could equally well be held back by his friend Seamus. There was a loyalty in him which might force him to put his friend before his own interests, and Seamus would play on that as he probably had done ever since they had met. His contentment lay in a glass of beer. He could stare into the golden liquid, not caring for the world around him. That attitude led nowhere except possibly to trouble, but did he care as long as Kevin was there to help?

James knew his daughter was making her own assessments and thought it would be interesting to hear them later. He thrust his own speculations from his mind and became the attentive host.

The roast beef and Yorkshire pudding brought praises from the Irishmen. The apple pie, served in the Yorkshire tradition with Wensleydale cheese, increased their accolades for the cook.

It was mid-afternoon when Sean and Kevin left the house after offering profuse thanks for what had been a splendid meal and a pleasant occasion.

As he closed the front door, James took hold of his

daughter's hand and started towards the drawing room. 'Now, Sarah, come and tell me what you thought of them. No, don't tell me you weren't closely observing our two guests.' His voice carried a tone that said he would brook no denials.

Sarah smiled. 'There's no fooling you. But what does my opinion matter anyway when you have made your own?'

'Ah, come now, you know I value your thoughts.' He smiled at her. Father and daughter loved these moments of banter.

They reached the drawing room and sat down opposite each other beside the fire.

'Well?' he prompted.

'Setting aside the fact that they saved our lives, I like them both. Their Irish charm could win over anyone.'

'You're not suspicious of it?'

'No. I believe they're genuine. And Scan has a twinkle in his eye that could entice any female.'

'A man for the ladies? Could get him into trouble.'

'He's in control.'

'And, as a young woman, you would know?'

'He flirted with those eyes of his but he knew when to stop.'

James raised one eyebrow. His daughter was more worldly-wise than he had thought.

'From what he said I believe he has ambitions to better himself, but you probably know more about that than I. You had his company from church.'

'And you had Kevin's.'

'More dependable, more cautious, but there's something about him ... Whatever it is it makes me surprised that he's a labourer.'

'My sentiments exactly.'

'Maybe there's loyalty owed to Seamus for some reason.'

'From what we've seen of him, he's a typical Irish labourer. Which Kevin isn't.'

'Yes, did you notice his comments about the wine? I feel sure that knowledge was derived from a better background. I mean to solve the mystery.'

James made no comment but thought, I'm sure you will.

The week before they were due to leave Whitby for Middlesbrough was a hectic rush for Lydia and Luke. He had several interviews with his employer and was pleased with the authority he had been given.

'Keep your eye on what is happening in Middlesbrough,' Mr Martin instructed. 'If the iron industry is set to expand then we must try to find new sources of ore, and hope that they are near enough Whitby for us to take advantage of them.'

'I'll do that,' Luke reassured him. 'And I'll see that nothing holds up the unloading of the ironstone.'

'Good. I have every faith in you. I have a letter here introducing you to Mr James Langton who is manager of the Bolckow and Vaughan works. It was he who asked me to look into the reason for slow deliveries and hinted that the trouble might lie with our overseer, Jos Sigsworth. There is another letter authorising you to take over if necessary, and one recalling him to Whitby if you deem that a wise move.'

'Thank you, sir. They will make things easier for me.'

'But they won't ease the unrest among the men which Mr Langton has indicated. That will be up to you when you assess the situation and decide what remedies are needed.'

'I'll soon have things sorted out, sir, and get the movement of ironstone back to the capacity expected.'

'I'm counting on you, Luke.'

'And I'll not let you down, sir.'

'Now, I don't want to pry into your private affairs but you've had a trying time recently. If it's not too nosy of me, may I ask if your sister is going with you?'

'Yes. There is nothing and no one for her in Whitby so it makes sense for her to come with me and make a new life away from here.'

'That's sensible thinking,' agreed Mr Martin. 'You can always return, as I'm sure you will. After all, you're both Whitby born and bred and Whitby gets into the blood. A break will do you both good, though. I've naturally agreed to pay your fare to Middlesbrough, but as a gesture of goodwill I'll pay your sister's as well.'

'That's very generous of you, Mr Martin.' Luke was surprised at his employer's offer even though he had always got on well with him.

Mr Martin smiled. 'Just see you do a good job for me.'

Lydia was adjusting to the prospect of leaving Whitby when David called on her unexpectedly.

He was astounded when she broke the news and stared at her in amazement. 'Leave Whitby? You can't!'

Anger rose in her at the way he had worded this. It was as if her decision was seen purely as an affront to him. 'I can and I am,' she snapped. 'Why should I stay when there's no one here for me?'

'There's me.'

'But you won't marry me now.'

'You know why I can't. You know it's because I love you and care about our future together.' His voice was firm; there could be no compromise in what he thought was the right way for them to tackle their future.

'I've said I'll wait but I'm not prepared to sit around here while you try to persuade your father to be more reasonable. It may never happen.'

David stepped closer and reached for her hands. He took heart from the fact that she did not draw away. 'I love you, Lydia. It's going to be painful without you here. Do you have to go?' There was pleading in his voice.

'There's Luke to think of.'

'He can take care of himself.'

'There are things I have to do.'

'Can't you do them here and let me help you?'

She shook her head. 'No, I can't.'

'Are you sure you can do them in Middlesbrough?'

'No.'

David raised his eyes heavenwards as if he despaired of her.

'But I can try.'

'Try? What do you have to try to do?'

'I can't explain, and if I could I wouldn't expect you to understand all the whys and wherefores. But unless I try I will never be able to live with myself, believe me. Please don't ask me any more.'

His hesitation was only momentary. 'All right, I respect your wish. But don't forget me. And don't find anyone else.'

She touched his cheek and looked into his eyes, sorrowful at the thought of parting. 'Dear David, I promise you this. If what I want comes to be, I'll be back in Whitby that very instant.'

'That's a definite promise?'

'Yes.' She kissed him, confirming what she desired.

She would have broken away but he held her and his lips sought hers again. She yielded, and as she was swept up in his love regretted the circumstances which had forced their parting.

Later she offered him tea which he graciously accepted. Their talk was of friends but Lydia gradually eased the conversation on to the subject of Whitby's trading fraternity and the future prospects of those involved. She stored this information away and realised that in David's knowledge of mercantile activities in the port she could find vital assistance in any future campaign against her uncle.

'When will you leave?' he asked.

'A week today, by the morning coach.'

'Did you not think of the railway?'

'It would have been a long and tedious journey, having to go via Pickering and York. The sooner the talk of constructing a line between here and Middlesbrough becomes a reality the better.'

136

'I'll try to be there when you leave.'

'If your father will let you.' Irritated by the words 'I'll try', Lydia spoke before she realised what she was saying and in what tone. As soon as she did she wished she could unsay the words. She saw anger and hurt in David's face.

He held back the cruel words which came to his own lips and said instead, 'I'm here, aren't I? And Father does not know.' But there was annoyance at her attitude in his expression.

Lydia and Mrs Harrington were in tears when the time came for the coach to leave, but the parting had to be made and, as the four horses bent to the reins, Mrs Harrington extracted a promise from Lydia and Luke that they would visit her whenever possible.

Through the tears in her eyes, Lydia searched in vain for David, hoping that he would make an appearance even if it was at the last minute. The final words they had exchanged had haunted her and now thrust themselves more prominently into her mind. Had he taken them too much to heart? Had she hurt him so deeply that their relationship had been affected? None of this would have happened but for the loss of the *Mary Anne*. Silently she cursed the storm that had changed her life.

With a heavy heart she watched her beloved Whitby pass by as the coach climbed out of the town to the road to Guisborough and beyond to Middlesbrough.

'It may be a long road home,' she whispered to herself, 'but one day I'll be back.'

Their arrival in Middlesbrough did nothing to lighten the depression she had felt since leaving Whitby. The journey had been cold, even the rugs provided bringing no warmth to her. Her body was chilled and chilled it remained. The other passengers had been dour and the intermittent conversation at the start of the journey petered out into a silence broken only by the creak of timber and leather and the shouts of the coachman, urging his team to greater efforts. Luke had tried to instil some cheer into his sister but, when she made little response, had respected her desire to be left alone with her thoughts.

The weather deteriorated into a clinging dampness accompanied by low, unmoving, grey clouds which spread smoke from the works by the river across the town.

There was activity as soon as the coach pulled to a halt at the coaching inn. Knowing no one among the bustling people, Lydia wished she was back in the town she knew and loved. There at least she would have had a roof over her head; here she did not know where she would rest for even one night. She looked forlorn, standing beside their two bags which had been handed down to Luke from the top of the coach.

'I'll see if there are any rooms for the night here,' said her brother, starting towards the door to the inn.

At that moment a young man hurried out of the building. In his haste, his eyes on the team being released from their harness, he failed to notice the bags. He crashed into them, stumbled and automatically reached out for support. His hands grasped Lydia's arms. She staggered backwards under the impetus but managed to keep to her feet. He struggled upright, his face red with embarrassment as he relaxed his grip.

'I'm sorry, miss,' he gasped.

'No, no. It was my fault, I shouldn't have had the bags in the way,' returned Lydia as she shrugged her coat back into place.

'Sure, now, there's no reason for you not to have them there. I should have looked where I was going.' The rich Irish accent was so full of genuine apology that Lydia was drawn to make a gracious acceptance.

'You've just arrived on the coach, miss?' he asked in order to stay in the company of this pretty girl a few minutes longer.

'Yes. My brother has gone to see if we can get rooms for

138

the night, then we'll look for more permanent lodgings tomorrow.'

'You are intending to stay in Middlesbrough?'

'Yes. My brother's work has brought him here.'

'Maybe I can help, or at least my landlady might know of somewhere.'

'It would be wonderful if she did. A recommendation is better than speculation. Ah, here's my brother.' She paused then added as Luke joined them, 'You *are* looking gloomy.'

'There's only one room available so we'll have to start enquiring, and I don't relish walking these streets on a day like this.'

'We may not have to,' said Lydia. 'This young man might be able to solve our problems.' She turned to the Irishman. 'I didn't catch your name?'

'Sean Casey, miss.'

'Very well, Sean Casey, meet my brother, Luke Middleton.'

'Sure and I'm pleased to meet you, Luke.' Sean held out his hand in a friendly fashion. Luke wondered how much of that was born of a desire to get to know his sister better.

Sean turned a mischievous gaze on Lydia. 'And you, miss?'

'Lydia.'

'It's delighted I am to meet two such charming people.'

Lydia smiled to herself as all the blarney of the Irish made itself evident. But she did not mind. Already the dismal day had taken a turn for the better. She quickly explained about Sean's offer to Luke.

'Then we are grateful to you, Sean,' he said.

'You'd better hold your thanks until we see if my land-lady, Mrs Hartley, can help.' Luke and Lydia picked up their bags. 'Here, let me take yours,' Sean offered her, and would not take no for an answer.

Under his direction they made their way towards the Market Square.

'Lydia tells me your work has brought you here?' said

139

Sean without disguising his curiosity, for he had judged that this young man would not be humping iron.

'We're from Whitby where I supervised the shipment of iron ore. The operation is not running smoothly at this end and my employer has sent me here to sort things out.'

'I hope you can.'

'It affects you?'

Sean gave a small laugh. 'Well, indirectly, yes. I'm a humper of pig iron when it returns from the furnaces at Witton, twenty miles away.' He shot a glance at Lydia to see how she reacted to the information that he was merely a labourer, but saw that she did not hold that against him. He was pleased that there was no snobbery in her. 'When your men are bloody-minded – sorry for the expression, miss,' he read in her returned smile that there was no need for an apology, 'the amount of stone going to Witton slows and so the supply of pig iron is interrupted. It is at the moment, so some of us have been laid off temporarily.'

'That may be our good fortune,' put in Lydia, 'or we wouldn't have had your help.'

'It's an ill wind . . .'

'Sean,' put in Luke, his expression serious, 'I would prefer you to say nothing about the reason I am here. I want to make some first-hand observations for myself.'

'Sure now I understand. You can trust me. I won't breathe a word.'

Reaching West Street, Sean opened the door to the house and called out, 'It's just me, Mrs Hartley. I've brought someone with me.'

A door at the end of the passage opened and Lydia saw a plump, motherly figure appear wiping her hands on an apron.

'Mrs Hartley, I'd like you to meet Lydia and Luke Middleton. They've just arrived from Whitby and I think you might be able to help them.'

Nell had surveyed the newcomers quickly and thoroughly. She took to them at once, sensing that they were a cut above her usual lodgers and came from a good, respectable family.

'I'm pleased to meet you both. Come through here and tell me how I may help.'

Sean smiled at Lydia encouragingly, while she in turn was delighted with her first impressions of his landlady. This was enhanced when they went into the kitchen. Though he judged that Lydia had been used to servants, she immediately commented on the cosy homeliness of this room, and of the house.

'Sit down, my dears, and I'll make you a cup of tea,' offered Nell Hartley. 'You'll need it after a ride from Whitby on a day like this.' She bustled about getting cups and saucers and pouring water from the kettle, already boiling above the fire. At the same time she passed pleasantries, but once she had poured the tea and handed round some home-made biscuits, she sat down and asked, 'Now, how can I help?'

'Luke has been sent here by his employer in Whitby and he and his sister are looking for accommodation,' Sean explained. 'I bumped into them just after they arrived and thought you might be able to recommend somewhere.'

'Yes, I can.'

Even Sean was surprised by the immediate reply.

'I'm sorry I have no room here,' Nell went on. 'I'm full with Sean and his two friends, Seamus and Kevin, but I think Mrs Turnbull at number sixteen might be interested. She's been considering the idea of taking lodgers, and you two might be just the people she needs to help make up her mind. When you've finished your tea, leave your bags here and I'll take you along to meet her.'

Lydia felt a huge sense of relief. She had liked this woman from the moment she had entered her house. Even if Mrs Turnbull decided against taking lodgers, she knew Mrs Hartley would not abandon them until they had found somewhere suitable.

141

If Mrs Turnbull had not already reached a decision her mind was made up when she saw brother and sister. It was not her place to pry into the past but she judged they were used to better things than lodgings in a two-up, two-down terraced house. Their clothes were of good quality, well cared for, and their manner was polite and friendly. Very different from some of the tales she had heard about lodgers, though Mrs Hartley had never had any trouble.

Once Mrs Turnbull agreed to have them, Mrs Hartley left them to discuss terms, telling them to collect their bags whenever they were ready.

When they returned to number ten Luke managed a quiet word with Sean while Lydia and Nell were discussing how Lydia could occupy herself while in Middlesbrough.

'Are you working tomorrow morning, Sean?' he asked.

'No. Like I told you, I've been temporarily laid off.'

'Well then, might I ask a favour of you?'

'Ask away.'

'What time would the unloading of the ship from Whitby begin? I know it was due to arrive yesterday, late afternoon.'

'Should be started by eight.'

'Will you show me where?'

'Certainly. A jetty near the rolling mill is used exclusively at the moment for the Whitby iron ships.'

'I'd like to be close by when the men are due to start unloading.'

'Right. Be here at half-past seven.'

At precisely that time the next day Luke was knocking on the door of number ten. It was opened by Sean who was shrugging himself into a three-quarter-length thick serge coat.

'Top of the morning to you,' he said brightly as he looked Luke up and down. 'Glad to see you've put something warm on. It can blow cold off the river even on the warmest day.'

'I'm used to it at Whitby though here you are more exposed, lacking the cliffs which shelter the river at home.'

Sean grabbed a cap. 'Right, I'm ready. Let's away.'

They walked to the Market Square and crossed to North Street. Already people were about their daily business. Men heading for work greeted fellow workers and teamed up in twos and threes, some merging into larger groups. Joking banter passed between them, betting tips were exchanged in good faith, last night's activities were remembered and legs were pulled.

Luke and Sean were swept along by the flow and absorbed the atmosphere of jollity and friendliness. Luke's curiosity was raised when he noted that few greetings were made by Sean, whereupon he learned that the Irishman and his friends had been in Middlesbrough little more than two weeks.

After passing the Bolckow and Vaughan Ironworks fewer people were about. Luke caught snippets of conversation and judged that he was among Whitby men here. He noted that the atmosphere had changed. There was a lack of cheer; the pace here was slower as if they had no enthusiasm for the work to which they were going.

He remarked on this to Sean and added, 'Is there a place from which I can observe what is going on without drawing attention to myself?'

'I know a spot. When Mr Langton, our works manager, told me about the trouble at this jetty I was curious so I scouted around to see what was happening for myself.'

'You know Mr Langton?'

Sean grinned at the incredulity on Luke's face. 'Sure now, why wouldn't I?'

'Well, to be on such confidential terms . . .'

'With the Works Manager?' Sean finished for him. 'Well, I'll tell you this and tell you no more: when you've done a man a good turn you do tend to get a bit closer, no matter what your station in life. And I promise you, I'll not always be humping iron.'

143

'I'm sure you won't. But how ...'

'Ask no more, Luke, and you'll hear no lies.' Sean did not want to be bragging about his own heroics. 'This way.' He took a narrow path running beside the river and turned Luke back to the quest in hand. He halted at a point from which they could discreetly observe the ship, the jetty and the workers. 'This do?'

'Perfect.' Luke settled himself to watch.

It did not take him long to size up the situation. There was some work going on but in general the men were making a pretence of it. Ironstone was certainly being loaded into railway trucks but at a rate which meant the ship would not be cleared today. The captain was talking in an agitated fashion with a group of men. Voices were raised and Sean, catching the odd word, judged that the captain was pleading with the men to get on with the work quickly so he could clear the Tees on the evening tide. He appeared to be receiving no cooperation. The group drifted away from him and joined others who sat doing nothing or were playing toss the penny.

Having taken all this in Luke cast around for sight of Jos Sigsworth, the man whom Mr Martin had put in charge of the Whitby team unloading the ore.

'Seen what you want to see?' asked Sean.

'Aye, but not what I'd like to see. That bunch wants a stick of dynamite up them. And where's the man in charge? I want to see what happens when he comes. You go if you want to. Thanks for bringing me.'

Sean gave a grin and shook his head. 'I'll stay. I can see there's going to be fun when you try to get that lot back to work.'

'*Try*?' Luke raised an eyebrow. 'I won't be trying. I'll do it.'

They settled themselves more comfortably. Five minutes later Luke grabbed Sean's arm and indicated a man approaching the jetty at a leisurely pace, pausing now and then to gaze across the river.

144

'The overseer?' said Sean.

'Aye, Jos Sigsworth.'

They watched him near the jetty. He stopped to have a word with some of the men but there was nothing to indicate that he was attempting to get more of them to join those working slowly between ship and train. No orders were shouted, no persuasive powers used. The men just went on doing what they were doing. Meanwhile Sigsworth went to a hut which Luke presumed he used as some sort of office. He reappeared a few moments later carrying a chair, placing it in a position where he was in the sun and from which he could see the activity or lack of it shown by his so-called workforce.

'Right, let's go,' snapped Luke, his voice filled with irritation at what he had seen.

145

Chapter Eight

A tap on the door drew James Langton's attention. He looked up from the plans he had been studying and then jumped quickly to his feet.

'Mr Vaughan, a pleasure to see you, sir,' he said, coming from behind his desk to greet one of the owners of the ironworks.

'And you, James,' said Vaughan pleasantly. He was a man of medium build with no outstanding features and no immediate presence. But those who knew him, and James had come to know him well since their first meeting in Carlisle, were aware that he was a man of ingenuity and keen ambition which had brought him success in the iron trade and a partnership in the most important venture on the south bank of the River Tees. But he wasn't a man who had ridden roughshod over others to achieve his aim. He was a man with tact, one who could handle his workers and draw the best out of them. Because of these attributes he was liked by everyone.

'Sit down, James. There's something we must discuss.' Almost immediately Vaughan changed his mind. 'No, don't sit down, we can discuss the situation as we go.'

James knew better than to query what was on his employer's mind. He fell into step with him and they headed for the river.

'What's happening about our shipments of ore from Whitby?' asked Vaughan.

'I've had word from Mr Martin that he will send someone to look into the matter.'

'No one's come yet?'

'No, sir.'

'Then we'll have to see if we can do something about it ourselves. These supplies must come through quicker.'

'Yes, sir. But this is a Whitby operation, remember. We agreed that Mr Martin could employ his own workforce to unload the ships.'

'Yes, I was part of those negotiations. It's a pity we ever agreed. We'd have had more control if we'd been the direct employers as we are with the coal imports. However, what's done is done. Let's see what the trouble is, why the men aren't working to full capacity. We must try to sort it out ourselves without waiting for someone to come from Whitby.'

'Yes, sir.' Though James knew Mr Vaughan had a gift for handling men, he doubted whether it would extend to those under someone else's jurisdiction and who, in his opinion, were taking advantage of a weak overseer.

'We need the flow of ore to Witton to be continuous and if Martin can't supply us as was agreed, then we'll have to find someone who can. A pity because I like Martin, a good, honest, straightforward man. I believe he's being let down by his workers.'

As Luke and Sean walked purposefully towards Jos Sigsworth they drew only a cursory glance from some of the men. A few shot them a second glance but then doubt clouded their minds. A vaguely familiar face? Couldn't be. Luke Middleton would be in Whitby.

They reached the overseer to find him with his eyes shut, even this early in the day.

Sigsworth had become familiar with the men's go-slow attitude and accepted that he could do nothing about it. Not that he wanted to, he liked the way things were and was happy to let the situation go on to his advantage. And there was nothing the Bolckow and Vaughan officials could do about it. This was purely a Whitby operation, and Whitby and Mr Martin were far enough away.

So it came as a violent shock when a voice boomed in his ear, 'Sigsworth, on your feet!'

He almost fell off his chair as he jerked upright. His eyes widened and anger flared at this untimely disturbance. It faded quickly when he recognised the man before him. 'Luke Middleton!' Caught out in an embarrassing and compromising situation, he struggled to his feet, losing his hat and knocking over the chair as he did so.

'What the hell's going on here?' Luke's voice thundered across the open space, resounding off ship and train so that no man listening could miss that note of authority.

Sigsworth, trying to pull himself together, muttered something inaudible.

'Speak up man, I want an explanation.' Luke swung round, sweeping out one arm to encompass the sorry scene. 'All of you, over here. And that includes you men unloading ore with all the speed of dead lice.' The penetrating voice demanded obedience, and received it. The men moved closer. 'Some of you may recognise me. Those of you who don't will know me now. I'm Luke Middleton, sent by Mr Martin to get this operation moving properly again.'

In those few moments Sigsworth got over his shock. He sensed Luke's presence spelt trouble he did not want, so hit back quickly. 'You've no right to stick your nose in here,' he barked, eyes flaring with fury.

'Haven't I?' countered Luke. 'Read this.' He pulled a sealed envelope from his pocket and thrust it at Sigsworth.

He took it suspiciously, hesitated, then tore it open. Silence had descended over the whole scene. Tension hung over the men. They waited expectantly as Sigsworth read the letter.

The heat of the exchange reached Mr Vaughan and James

148

Langton who were within earshot of the jetty.

'What's going on?' wondered Mr Vaughan, at the sight of the workforce gathered in a group around three central figures, one of whom had his eyes fixed on a piece of paper.

After a few more steps, Vaughan stopped and put a restraining hand on James's arm. 'Wait, let's see what's happening.' He paused then added, 'Who's that young man holding centre stage?'

'Don't know him,' replied James. 'The man reading the paper is the overseer of this gang. The one to the young man's left is a new employee of yours from Ireland – Sean Casey. He, along with several others, is laid off until we get more ore moving through. What he's doing here I couldn't ...' He let the words trail away when Vaughan raised his hand for silence.

'Let's listen.'

Sigsworth, face draining quickly of colour, looked up slowly from the letter.

'I know the contents,' said Luke firmly before Sigsworth could mouth a protest. 'See that you are on this ship when it leaves for Whitby on the evening tide.'

The impact of what was happening hit the overseer hard but it brought rebellion to the surface.

'It won't be unloaded in time,' he sneered.

'It will.' There was a note of assurance in Luke's tone which would have wilted any man's resistance. But Sigsworth thought he would have his men's support. They had enjoyed an easy time under him.

An atmosphere of uncertainty had settled over them. Unsure what was happening, they looked askance at the man who had been their boss.

Sigsworth held up the piece of paper for all to see. 'This recalls me to Whitby, takes this job from me and leaves this upstart in charge. You've heard him. Thinks this ship will be ready to leave this evening. That means very hard graft. What do you have to say about that? Will you . . .'

Luke intervened. He wasn't going to permit Sigsworth to preach dissent and rally the men to his side. 'Before you make up your minds, consider this – anyone who doesn't want to work had better be on this ship too when it sails. And that will mean you have no job, no wages, nothing for your families in Whitby but hardship. If you stay here I can promise you hard work but you will earn money. The ore ships from Whitby must be turned round quickly. Iron ore is vital to the life of the Bolckow and Vaughan Ironworks. If you fail, or slow up delivery, then the workers here suffer. Consider your fellow workers. The quicker you deal with the ore ships, the better for all. And particularly your-selves, because I'm going to alter the wage structure. You'll now be paid piece rates for the quantity of ore you move.'

A buzz of interest went round the men.

'That will mean we're dependent on the shipments from Whitby and on the weather,' someone shouted. It brought a chorus of agreement from the crowd.

'It will,' agreed Luke, 'but that money will be on top of the wage you are already being paid which is not related to the amount of ironstone you move.'

This sounded an advantageous move and brought excited exchanges among the men.

'Does that include the rise we were promised three months ago?' someone shouted.

'You got that at the time promised,' returned Luke.

A ripple of denial ran through the crowd.

'I know it was paid. I checked the calculations with Mr Martin. The money was sent in its usual sealed container to Mr Sigsworth, and I know it arrived because the receipt for the unopened box came back to Whitby.'

'We got no rise.' The statement was repeated, and agree-ment ran through the men like a fire sweeping through dry tinder. Immediately the truth dawned on them.

'Sigsworth pocketed it!'

'Aye, must have done.'

'Bloody hook!'

There was ugliness in their attitude as these statements swept from mouth to mouth.

'Let's have him!' someone shouted. The hostility was echoed throughout the gathering.

Luke saw the makings of a lynch mob if things ran out of hand. 'Quiet! Quiet!' he yelled, holding his hands high in a gesture for calm.

'The bastard!' The crowd started to surge forward.

Luke held his ground in front of a quivering Sigsworth, who was suffering horrid visions of being torn limb from limb. Sean came to Luke's shoulder.

'Stop! Don't do this.' Luke's yell carried not only authority but the threat of what could happen if they ignored him.

There was a roar of disapproval but the men in the front had seen a determination to maintain law and order on the faces of Luke and Sean. They had also seen the two men's clenched fists and knew they would be the first to feel them. They stopped and the whole mob came to a halt behind them.

'That's sensible,' Luke approved. 'If any man steps out of line on this he'll be dismissed immediately. I don't like using threats but occasionally they are necessary. It appears Sigsworth has cheated you out of the pay rise that was sent to you, but there's nothing to be gained by using violence against him.'

'He told us it hadn't come!'

'Aye, so after a month we organised a go-slow policy. He said he had repeatedly asked for the rise but Mr Martin had taken no notice.'

'We heard nothing of this in Whitby. Thought everything was all right until just over a week ago when Mr Martin received a letter from the manager of the ironworks, asking us to investigate the slow delivery of ore. That's how I

151

come to be here. Now, let's get this matter settled and get that ore moving. What I have told you about payment stands. My report will go to Mr Martin and I'm sure he will pay you the back money you have missed. Does that satisfy you?'

There was only a moment's hesitation while this sank in and then a murmur of approval was like music to Luke's ears.

He breathed more easily. 'Right then, let's get that ore unloaded.' The enthusiasm in his voice brought the men to life. They scattered to set about their work eagerly, streaming away to shift the ore so the ship could sail on the evening tide and take the man who had cheated them to his just rewards.

'Well done, Luke,' said Sean. 'You handled a nasty situation well.'

He nodded. 'Thanks. It was touch and go. I was pleased to have you beside me. Your presence helped when that mob got ugly. Want a job?'

'Job?' Sean was puzzled. What could he do here? Another pair of hands humping ironstone? Not much different from what he was doing already.

Before he answered, Luke called to two of the workmen, 'Keep your eye on Sigsworth until I'm ready to deal with him.' He knew the overseer daren't try anything now or he would feel the wrath of the men he had cheated. Luke turned back to Sean. 'You've been laid off, you haven't a job, so I'm offering you one – permanently, or at least as far as I can see for a long time ahead.'

'But you know nothing about me, except that I'm humping pig iron when it gets back from Witton.'

'Someone who took pity on two strangers and found them lodgings can't be bad. And from what I saw then and this morning, you have a nimble brain and I don't think you would shirk responsibility.'

Sean smiled. 'Thank you for your trust. I'll decide when you tell me what . . .'

152

Luke saw Sean look beyond him and turned to see what had drawn his attention. Two men were walking quickly towards them. They were well-dressed, men of obvious substance and authority. Luke speculated quickly but came to no conclusion as to who they might be or what they were doing here. He was about to put a whispered question to Sean when the Irishman recognised James Langton. The other he did not know.

'Hello there, Sean. Didn't expect to see you here,' called James.

'I'm with Luke Middleton. Luke, this is James Langton.'

'Mr Langton? Manager of the ironworks?'

'Yes.'

'Then I have a letter for you from Mr Martin of Whitby.' Luke fished an envelope from his pocket and held it out.

'From what we have just seen I think this letter of introduction will be superfluous.' He shoved it into his pocket. 'I'll read it later. First I must introduce Mr Vaughan.'

'Holy Mother of God, the top brass himself,' muttered Sean under his breath, but there was sufficient strength in his words for them to be caught by the man himself.

Mr Vaughan grinned. 'I'm flattered that you invoke higher authority.' He held out his hand.

Sean felt privileged to shake the hand of the man who, with his partner, had brought industry and employment to the banks of the River Tees.

Vaughan shook hands with Luke. 'Pleased to meet you, young man. You handled that extremely well, and I appreciate the fact that you will have the ship cleared by this evening.'

'Thank you, sir, it's kind of you to say so. The situation was not quite what I expected when Mr Martin assigned me the job.'

'You have a way of handling men.'

'That's what Mr Martin tells me.'

'And I can confirm that, can't you, James?'

153

'I certainly can. You'll be an asset here.'

Mr Vaughan nodded his agreement. 'Will you accompany us to Mr Langton's office so that we can clarify the movement of ironstone from Whitby?'

At this request Sean said, 'I'll see you later, Luke, to discuss our little matter.'

Luke saw an expression of curiosity cross Mr Langton's face. 'Sir,' he said, 'I've offered Sean a job. If he'll take it, I would like him to be at this discussion.'

Mr Langton shot Mr Vaughan a look of enquiry. After all, it was he who had suggested this meeting.

'Very well,' Vaughan agreed.

James saw that Sean still seemed uncertain about Luke's proposal. 'You're not beholden to me, Sean. I'm sure Mr Middleton has offered you something better.'

'He doesn't know what I have in mind,' put in Luke.

'Then discuss it quickly and join us in my office.' He and Mr Vaughan left them.

First Luke spoke quietly to the two men guarding Sigsworth. 'Take him to his lodgings. Collect his belongings and return here. Don't let him out of your sight.'

As the men walked away with a very subdued Sigsworth between them, Luke turned to Sean. 'I can't always be at the jetty, so as well as a foreman on the site, whom I have yet to appoint, I need an assistant. I'm offering the post to you. Your first job will be to escort Sigsworth to Whitby, deliver him and a letter to Mr Martin. The letter will explain the situation here. You can confirm it, add any details requested and answer Mr Martin's questions. Will you take the job?'

'Sure, even the devil himself wouldn't stop me!'

The bargain was sealed with a firm handshake and the two new friends hurried after their superiors.

When they entered James Langton's office they were offered chairs.

'As you are here, I take it you have accepted Mr

154

Middleton's offer, Sean?' said James.

'Too good to miss, sir. It gives me some authority which I will relish.'

'Good, I'm sure you'll do well.' He turned to Mr Vaughan. 'The meeting is all yours, sir.'

'I have no jurisdiction over you so all I can do is apprise you of our situation and ask what you can do or suggest to help. Especially you, Luke. I don't expect Sean to be familiar with the ironstone yields that pass through Whitby.

'They are vital to us, Luke. As you know, our best ore comes from Grosmont. It is important that that supply continues to supplement our own source near our furnaces at Witton. But the seams there are not yielding what we expected so we'll need more from Grosmont. It's important we build up stocks in case bad weather halts the supply. I'd like to make sure Mr Martin is aware of all this?'

'I understand, sir, and will do my best. Sean is escorting Sigsworth to Whitby, leaving on the ore ship this evening. I will be writing to Mr Martin informing him of what has happened here and will now add what you have just told me. If necessary I will go to Whitby after that but I'm sure Sean will be able to confirm and emphasise what I put in my letter.'

'You can trust me to give Mr Martin a full report,' he said. 'I'll impress upon him the urgency of an answer relating to the delivery of the ironstone. Hopefully I'll have his reply when I return on the next ore ship leaving Whitby, which I believe should be the day after tomorrow.'

'No doubt that Irish tongue of yours can be very persuasive,' commented Mr Vaughan.

Sean smiled. 'Ah, sure now, isn't that what it should do?'

Luke and Sean left the meeting. They were in good spirits as they headed back for the jetty.

Luke felt he had got the situation in hand and hoped

155

that in a few minutes he would have it more firmly under his control. If his written word, supported by Sean's testimony, convinced Mr Martin then the future looked bright.

Sean was grateful for the opportunity he had been given. With Luke's help he had thrown off the role of labourer and was determined not to let his chance slip. He was on the first step towards the future he had dreamed about, the one which would enable him to free Eileen from the dead end they had faced in Dublin. He hoped that, when she heard what he was doing, she would believe that coming to England had been the right decision.

When they neared the jetty they saw that the men were dealing with the cargo efficiently. Minds relieved of all doubt about what was happening to their pay, they seemed cheerful.

'All right, everyone, ease up a minute,' Luke shouted. 'I have a few words to say to you.'

The men stopped work and focused their attention on him. They had taken to the way he had handled Jos Sigsworth and solved their problem over pay. They saw here a man they judged knew what he wanted and would get it without exploiting them unfairly.

'I've appointed Sean Casey, here, as my assistant. What I want now is a site foreman. Someone you trust, from whom you will take orders without resentment. Someone you can work with, to whom you can go with any problems and be sure you'll get a fair hearing without any bias towards either you or the firm for whom you work. Our man must have the interests of both sides at heart. I don't know you personally so I want you to name someone.'

There was a moment's silence at the unexpected decision they had to make and at the responsibility that had been thrust upon them. Discussion broke out among them which was silenced as someone shouted, 'What about Bob Chase?'

There was a roar of approval.

'Seems unanimous,' called Luke. 'Where are you, Bob?' He scanned the crowd.

'Here!' someone shouted, and a tall, broad-shouldered man stepped forward.

Knowing he was coming under scrutiny, he walked towards Luke and Sean with a purposeful step. His eyes, strangely dark, were fixed on Luke as if he was trying to weigh up his new boss, though what he had seen of the way the young man had handled Sigsworth in a tricky situation had already impressed him.

Bob Chase looked like a man who would stand no nonsense. Apart from his sheer size, he was muscular without an ounce of fat on him. His hands were big; clenched they would present a formidable fist. Even here, in the open, he had a commanding presence which he must have kept subdued when Luke first arrived. Now, with responsibility thrust on him, it came to the fore. Luke's initial reaction was that he was pleased with the men's choice.

'Right, Bob, you are in charge on site. You must work harmoniously with the men, and of course with me and Sean. Bring any complaints or situations you can't handle to either of us. But the most important thing is that you keep the ironstone moving and turn the ships around as quickly as possible. It is vital to the welfare of all of us. Fail, and Mr Vaughan and Mr Langton will look elsewhere for the ore.'

Bob nodded. 'We'll shift it.' He half turned to view the men. 'All right, stop gawping. Get on with it! Bend your backs! This ship has to sail this evening.'

Instantly the men were back at their task.

'Keep them at it, Bob. We'll be back later.'

'Right, sir.' He touched his forehead with the tip of his right index finger.

As he moved away Luke noticed Bob's eyes darting, taking in all the activity.

'I reckon we've got a good man there,' commented Sean quietly.

157

'My opinion too,' returned Luke. 'Right, back to West Street. You get ready to leave and I'll write the letters.'

Their immediate departure was halted by the return of the two men escorting Sigsworth.

'Get him on board and don't let him out of your sight until the ship's ready to sail,' ordered Luke. 'Then Sean will take responsibility. I've just appointed Bob Chase as foreman on site. Report to him and tell him what I've said.'

The two friends parted company in West Street. When Luke entered number sixteen alarm immediately crossed Lydia's face.

'Back so soon? I didn't expect to see you all day.'

He smiled. 'Wipe that worry away. Everything is all right.'

'No hostility?'

'Only from Jos Sigsworth.'

'So that's who was in charge?'

'Aye, but running things to suit himself.' He went on to acquaint her of the facts and how he had dealt with them.

'Well done, Luke.' She was proud of her brother, who had been so decisive.

'And what's more, I've engaged Sean Casey as my assistant. His first assignment is to escort Jos Sigsworth to Whitby and give my reports to Mr Martin. I must write them now.'

'Then he could deliver a letter from me to David?'

'I'm sure he would.'

Brother and sister set about composing very different letters which were safely in Sean's possession when he sailed on the evening tide.

As he watched the *Nina* head downriver Luke felt the satisfaction of a job well done. He was also pleased with his ability to step from the shadow of his sister and deal with a crisis in which she could play no part. He sensed the men too felt a touch of pride as well as relief. They gave a great cheer when the ship cast off and took the full flow of the river. He thanked them all, especially Bob who had organised his workforce so as to get the maximum effort from them in the shortest possible time.

'There'll be another ship in tomorrow,' Luke told them. 'Let's have her turned round quickly so that the jetty is clear for the return of the *Nina* the next day.'

'So she's gone! Now you might as well get her out of your head, concentrate on your work and look for a new prospect who will be an asset to this business.'

Jonas Drayton eyed his son with smug satisfaction that his wishes had been obeyed. The threat of what could happen to David's inheritance if he persisted in pursuing Lydia Middleton had paid off.

'And you made sure I didn't see her leave.' Disgust coloured David's voice.

'One of us had to attend that meeting. I couldn't because of a request from Nathan Middleton to see him on a matter of some importance.'

'Aye, and you no doubt engineered both meetings to take place at the same time so I wouldn't be free to say my goodbyes to Lydia.'

'Poppycock!' snapped Jonas. His eyes narrowed with warning as he looked down at David seated behind his desk. 'Entertaining such thoughts about your own father should be beneath you. What your mother and I have done for you has always been for the best.' He placed his hands on the desk and leaned forward to peer hard at David. 'You'll not be above bedding a pretty girl, so consider bedding Isobel. It would go a long way to cementing the relationship between my company and Nathan's. I believe we could work on some profitable schemes together.'

'And what exactly might those be?'

'Oh, nothing concrete but with trade expanding who knows what might arise? To have someone who might be interested in joining us in deals we could not handle alone would be beneficial. So you consider that lass. Now I'm for out.' He turned quickly and left the office, leaving David pondering his words.

Jonas started down the corridor towards the outside door. He heard voices coming from the clerk's office and slowed his pace so that he could overhear what was being said. A puzzled frown crossed his face when he heard an unfamiliar Irish accent.

'I'd like to see Mr David Drayton, please.' Sean put the request to the clerk with an authority he thought befitted his new employment.

'Yes, sir. Who shall I say?'

'Mr Sean Casey. He won't know me. Tell him I have a personal letter to deliver.'

'I can see that he gets it.' The deep full-throated voice came from behind Sean.

As he turned to see who had spoken he caught a glimpse of the expression on the clerk's face. It told him that the man in the doorway was the man's employer and that he dare not go one inch against him.

Sean immediately realised why the clerk was in awe for he found himself disliking the man's overbearing manner and piercing eyes which spoke of a determination to get his own way.

Sean stiffened. He ignored the hand held out for the letter. 'Sorry, sir, my instructions were clear and I shall carry them out. This letter will be given to no one but Mr David Drayton.'

'I am his father. I will see that he gets it.'

'That is not for you to decide, sir.' Sean's tone was defiant.

Jonas's eyes darkened. 'Whipper-snapper! These are my premises. I rule here. If I say so, I will deliver that letter.'

'Whatever you say, you will not.'

Anger reddened Jonas's face. His voice shook. 'Then get out of here!' he snapped. 'Or I'll have you horse-whipped.'

'Don't you threaten me, sir.' Sean's voice turned icy

cold. 'I have nothing but contempt for a man who so blatantly ignores a lady's wishes.'

'Ah, so it is from a lady.' There was triumph in Jonas's voice. Sean's reaction was to curse himself for letting the information slip. 'My surmise was right. How you come to be delivering a letter from Lydia Middleton I neither know nor care.' His tone had gradually become more conciliatory. 'But I ask you not to let my son have it. That lady intends nothing but mischief and my son would be harmed if the letter reached him.'

Sean, who did not know the true relationship between Lydia Middleton and David Drayton, hesitated for a moment in the face of the older man's plea. He tussled with his thoughts. The man sounded reasonable enough now but his previous tone was probably more characteristic.

Sean's mind then went back to Lydia when she had presented the letter to him. He had read behind the look in her eyes a desire to put something right with the addressee. A lovers' tiff? A rift that needed healing? The clarification of a relationship? Whatever it was it was no concern of his. He had made a promise to her and would see that he carried it out.

'Sorry, sir, the letter remains with me. If you won't allow me to deliver it to your son then I must return it to the sender. I have no more time to spare, I leave Whitby shortly.' Sean brushed past Drayton, hoping that his final statement had fooled him.

He lingered outside, using the movement of people going about their daily business to conceal his presence. He was sure that Mr Drayton had been dressed to leave the building when he had been halted by Sean's exchange with the clerk. He would nip back when the man left. But as the minutes ticked by Sean became more and more irritated. Jonas Drayton did not appear.

He cursed his own luck. The voyage had passed well so far. He had delivered Sigsworth to Mr Martin, given his report and received his new employer's gratitude. In the town he had found comfortable rooms at the Angel Inn as directed by Luke. All had gone smoothly until he had tried to deliver Lydia's letter. Now his determination strengthened. He would not be outdone. He'd fox old Drayton yet. But he could make no plan, only watch and seize his opportunity when it arose.

It did so half an hour later.

The clerk came out of the office and hurried away to his right, holding some papers he was obviously intent on delivering. Maybe, Sean surmised, he had been told that idling would not be tolerated and he should get back to the office as soon as possible. Sean could imagine Drayton checking his watch as if he knew exactly how long it should take his clerk to carry out the designated task.

Sean followed the man, keeping at a discreet distance from which he could observe without being seen. He matched his pace to the clerk's, shadowed him across the bridge to the west side and then up Golden Lion Bank to a building in Flowergate. Sean waited close by the door.

A few minutes later the clerk came out with a quick step to find his path blocked. He was startled.

'Hold on,' said Sean, putting a detaining hand on the man's shoulder.

The man's instant scowl at being stopped vanished as he recognised Sean. 'You!' he gasped. Fearing the worst, he added disagreeably, 'What do you want?'

'Just a word and a favour,' returned Sean.

'I can't get mixed up in anything to do with that letter.'

'Ah, sure now, you have a sharp mind. That should help you look out for yourself.'

'Look out for myself? What do you mean?'

'You could make yourself a little money.'

The clerk licked his lips at the thought but then shook his head. 'No, no, I stand to lose more if old Drayton finds out I've delivered that letter to his son. I suppose that's what you want me to do?'

Sean gave a little smile and shook his head. 'No. All I want is for you to give him a message.'

The clerk still looked doubtful so Sean pulled a shilling from his pocket. He flicked it into the air so that its brightness and movement caught the clerk's eye. As it fell, Sean grabbed it.

'Now wouldn't that be better in your pocket?'

The clerk's eyes gleamed with greed. As Scan started to return the coin to his own pocket the man said, 'Hold on a minute. You said a message?'

'Indeed I did.'

'You mean, not the letter?'

'Aye.'

'Nothing written down?'

'Not a single word.'

The clerk pursed his lips and rubbed his chin thoughtfully.

Sean sensed him weakening and pressed his point. 'All you have to do is to give a message from me to Mr David without his father knowing.'

'So there'd be no incriminating evidence?'

'None. Only me and Mr David would know and I don't think either of us is going to tell his father.' Sean flicked the coin temptingly in the air again.

The clerk watched it fall back into Sean's open palm and lie there gleaming as much as to say, I can be yours.

'All right,' he agreed.

'Now you're talking like a man.'

'Stop slopping around. I'm late already. What's the message?'

'Just tell Mr David that someone has an important letter for him from Middlesbrough. If he wants it, tell him to meet me at the Angel between seven and eight tonight.'

'Right.' The clerk grabbed the coin and made to start off.

Sean's strong fingers clutched the front of his coat and pulled him close. The man cringed from the frightening expression that Sean had adopted.

163

'There's one more thing. Breathe a word of this to anyone and you'll feel my fist. And, after I've finished with you, all the wailing banshees of auld Ireland will haunt you for the rest of your life.'

The man's eyes widened. 'Your secret will be safe with me!'

'See that it is and see that you deliver the message correctly.' Sean thrust the clerk away from him and the man scuttled off as quickly as his thin legs could carry him.

Chapter Nine

Sean seated himself so that he had a view of the door to the snug and waited patiently for David Drayton. The small room was cosy with its own bar. Illumination came from two oil lamps hanging from the ceiling and four set in wall brackets. A fire burned brightly in the iron grate and banished all thoughts of the cold damp evening outside. Fog had rolled in from the sea and hung over the river, thickening as the darkness intensified.

The buzz of conversation from the well-dressed drinkers at the other five tables rose and fell and was occasionally pierced by laughter or amicable disagreements.

Sean grew uneasy as the deep ticking of the grandfather clock beside the door reminded him that the time he had stipulated was fast running out. Had the clerk failed him? If not, was David Drayton ignoring the message? Or was he not prepared to come out on a cold foggy night when a comfortable chair in front of a roaring fire would be more appropriate? Had the word 'Middlesbrough' no pull on him? That must surely indicate that the message was from Lydia. Sean wondered what sort of a relationship they had.

His attention was held by the sentinel clock. Its tick and the movement of the hands, drawing ever nearer the hour of eight, were hypnotic. Staring at them, he picked up his tankard and raised it to his lips. He started. Its emptiness drew his attention away from the mesmerising clock. He cursed to himself and called to the barman to bring him another.

As the man placed a full tankard in front of him, Sean was aware that someone had come through the door and had stopped to survey the room. He was good-looking, or at least Sean reckoned women would see him that way. He had a self-assurance to him which Sean thought would be more in evidence in the company of men. A shy streak might come out when the ladies were present, but it would be slight and might well add to his attraction. If this was the man to whom he had to deliver Lydia's note, Sean could see why she might be attracted to him and want to keep in touch.

'Who's that?' he whispered in the barman's ear as he stooped to retrieve the empty glass.

The man glanced over his shoulder. 'Mr Drayton,' he replied.

'Mr David?'

'Aye.'

'Please ask him to join me.'

'Yes, sir.'

The barman crossed the room to David and inclined his head in Sean's direction as he delivered the message. David nodded, thanked the barman, and came to Sean.

He rose from his chair. 'Mr David Drayton?'

'Yes. You have the advantage of me.'

Sean gave a friendly smile. 'Sean Casey.' He offered his hand. They exchanged a handshake and sat down.

'You must have got my message from your clerk?' observed Sean.

'I wouldn't be here if I hadn't,' David replied a little haughtily, and then added in a mystified tone, 'What is this all about?'

'I'm sorry to have acted so mysteriously but after my heated exchange with your father, I had to take precautions.'

David frowned. 'My father? You've had altercations with my father?'

166

'Yes. I have a letter which I was asked to deliver to you personally. I came to your office. Your father said he would give you the letter but I refused to let him have it and he told me in no uncertain terms to leave. Hence the need to resort to subterfuge.'

'This becomes more puzzling by the minute.'

Their conversation ceased as the barman placed a bottle of brandy and two glasses on the table.

'I took the liberty of ordering when the barman pointed you out. I hope you'll take a glass?'

'I'd like nothing better,' returned Sean, though he couldn't remember when he had last tasted brandy.

David poured, allowing the heavy aroma to linger between them. 'Well?' he said. 'The rest of your story.'

'There is little more except to hand you the letter which I think will explain everything.' Sean drew the envelope from his pocket and handed it over. He realised instantly from David's brightening eyes that he had recognised the writing and knew who had sent it.

'Please excuse me,' he said, breaking the seal.

Sean nodded, took his glass and leaned back in his chair, his mind taken up with thoughts of Lydia and her possible relationship with this man.

Dear David,

I was sorry you were not at the coach to say goodbye and wish me well. I missed you then as I shall do in Middlesbrough.

What the future holds for Luke and me in this new town I do not know. One day we may return to Whitby, and hopefully under happier circumstances than those in which we left.

I am sorry that recently we have had our disagreements. Maybe one day the cause of those will be overcome and our relationship be what it once was before misfortune changed it. I will dwell on this no longer nor expand on what happened between us. I will

167

not hold it against someone who I feel has always been a very dear friend to me and, at times, perhaps more than that.

However, if during our time apart you find someone else, I will understand. I hope you will reciprocate the feeling.

Please keep writing to me with news of yourself and of what is happening in Whitby – still my hometown and dear to my heart.

My fondest regards,
Lydia

David sat staring at the letter, no longer reading words. He chastised himself for not being at the coach and cursed his father for putting obstacles in his way. Deliberately, he believed. Why hadn't he defied Jonas? But if he had, he and Lydia would have faced a life of hardship and possible poverty which could well have strained their love. If only she could see that his way offered a chance that his father would relent and their love could blossom in the sort of surroundings they had known all their lives. But she gave no indication of such understanding. The touch of hope in her letter had faded before the final words. She had never mentioned love, merely sent fond regards. She had even suggested he might find someone else.

David's mind was in a tumult. Someone else? He frowned. Maybe she had done that, even in this short time. Maybe this Irishman ...

He looked up slowly. 'Tell me, Mr Casey, how do you come to be the carrier of Miss Middleton's letter?'

Sean quickly related the circumstances in which he and Lydia had met. David listened carefully and realised that this man had charm, which was emphasised by his smooth Irish brogue. And he had been kind. He had put himself out to help a lady in distress; not everyone would have done that. Maybe there had been an immediate mutual attraction and Sean Casey had made the most of it.

168

As he was speaking Sean hoped for some hint of the relationship between this man and Lydia, but obtained nothing from David's response when he merely asked, 'When do you return to Middlesbrough?'

'Tomorrow on the *Nina*, with another cargo of ironstone. We sail at ten in the morning.'

'You are turning her round fast.'

'The ironstone is needed as quickly as possible.'

'You'll take a letter for me?'

'If that is what you want.'

'I'll come to the ship.' David stood up, paused and then sank slowly on to the chair again. He leaned forward and fixed his gaze firmly on Sean. 'Miss Middleton, is she well?'

'When I left she was.'

'Her journey had not been too uncomfortable?'

'She never mentioned it to me. When we met she was too concerned about where they were going to stay.'

'And you said that her lodgings are comfortable?'

'That's what I said.'

'Describe them to me.'

Sean gave him a description of Mrs Turnbull's terraced house.

David pursed his lips. 'Hmm, not what she has been used to. Luke is with her?'

'Of course.'

David hesitated a moment and then stood up. 'Thank you. I'll be on the quay tomorrow morning.'

Sean nodded and watched him go. He had gleaned a little and now surmised that the relationship between Lydia and David Drayton had been deeper than friendship but that something had happened to mar it.

He signalled to the barman who came to him. 'Tell me about Mr Drayton.'

The man quickly imparted what he knew which led Sean to ask about the Middleton family. The barman was only too ready to talk of the recent tragedy and when he had

169

finished left Sean contemplating Lydia's background and the life she must have been used to once, so different from the circumstances in which she now found herself.

As he walked home David too thought of Lydia and what had been said. He drew some comfort from his conclusion that there was nothing between her and Sean Casey, but then doubt began to sow its seeds. Wasn't there such a thing as love at first sight? Had they instantly experienced a rapport between them? How could he tell? Casey had not been forthcoming and his words had been delivered without any inflection that would betray his feelings towards Lydia.

As soon as he reached home David cast all such troubling thoughts aside to compose his letter.

Few words were exchanged on the quay from which the *Nina* would be leaving. Such as were spoken were curt, non-committal, and David sent no verbal message to Lydia. Sean put the letter safely in his pocket along with two for Luke from Mr Martin.

David thanked him and left. Sean went on board and from the rail watched all the activity prior to sailing, noting the efficient way in which the final loading was carried out. Mr Martin, who had been encouraging his men, went to have a word with the captain and then came to Sean.

'Tell Luke I would like him to stay in Middlesbrough certainly well into next year to see that everything runs smoothly. Maybe he might even like to be there permanently? Tell him so, but that I'll understand if Whitby has too great a pull on him.'

The *Nina* made a good voyage, using the breeze to her best advantage on a calm sea, grey as pewter.

Once the vessel was tied up at the jetty close to the rolling mill, Sean was quickly ashore. He threw a brief greeting to Bob Chase who was already marshalling his men to carry out the unloading.

Luke, who was standing at the end of the jetty, greeted Sean with a warm smile and a firm handshake.

'Everything work out?'

'Ah, sure now, and why shouldn't it? Mr Martin was pleased with the results you achieved so quickly. He would like you to stay on here, certainly well into next year and maybe even permanently.' Seeing no reaction from Luke, Sean went on, 'He'll deal with Sigsworth. He approved of my appointment, too, saying the onus was on you if I turned out badly.'

'See you don't,' laughed Luke, then added seriously, 'What about the supplies of ironstone?'

'Mr Martin will give it some thought and let you know.'

'Good,' he said, satisfied with all the messages and with the way in which Sean appeared to have handled the responsibility thrust upon him.

He handed over the two envelopes from Mr Martin and, realising that Luke must be curious about the third, said, 'For your sister.'

'Then you'd better be off and deliver it.'

Sean went straight to West Street where he found Lydia, anxious to learn all she could from Mrs Turnbull about the practical side of housekeeping, helping with some baking.

'Away with thee, lass, and read your letter. You've been on edge all morning.'

An excited Lydia took the letter and impulsively kissed Sean on the cheek. 'Thank you,' she cried, and scurried away out of the kitchen and upstairs to her bedroom.

Mrs Turnbull made no comment but smiled to herself when she saw Sean touch the place on his cheek where Lydia's lips had been.

Lydia's hands trembled a little as she slit the envelope open. What reaction would her words have elicited from David? She sat on the side of her bed to read the letter.

171

Dear Lydia

Thank you for your letter. I was pleased to receive it and to know that you had arrived safely in Middlesbrough. I am thankful you have found suitable lodgings there.

I regret that I was not at the coach at the start of your journey, business matters got in the way.

Your Father more like, she thought. And you hadn't spunk enough to sneak away. She gave a little wriggle of annoyance and continued to read.

I am sorry that you refer to me only as a very dear friend but draw some consolation from the fact that you say at times you felt I was more than that, though I had hoped that your feelings matched mine for you. You hold out hope for the future yet spike that with the thought that I may find someone else and that you would understand if I did. And you expressed a hope I would reciprocate such an attitude. Does that mean you think you will find someone else? Or maybe you have already done so, even in the short time since you left Whitby.

Lydia paused. She was hurt by his formal, cold attitude. She had hoped for something different, that he would take the lead to repair what had gone wrong between them. Instead he was suspicious she might have found a new love. He must be thinking of Sean, that a friendly gesture had blossomed into something else. Ah, well, let him think what he liked. She turned back to the letter.

So that our friendship is not lost and that something else may follow from it, I shall do as you request, so here is my first attempt to bridge the gap between Whitby and Middlesbrough.

I am well and the business keeps me occupied. Its future success can mean so much to me. There is a shortage of ships in Whitby. Your uncle is looking for new investments. My father thinks a closer relationship between the two firms might be advantageous to both. They have met two or three times but there have been no definite proposals yet.

I believe your uncle and his family are well. I ran into Isobel when I was in town yesterday and she is concerned for you. I said if ever I had any news of you, I would let her know.

So please continue to write. Communication can keep us close and maybe help you to see why I chose the path I did. I think the best way to pass letters between us is by the ironstone ships. I am sure the captains would oblige and they could keep the letters from you until I collect them.

Lydia gave a little smirk. So your father doesn't know, she thought.

I look forward to hearing from you again. I hope there is no one else.

I am your devoted,

David

Lydia sat, not knowing how to react. The letter had not been the declaration of passionate love which would surmount his father's objections that she'd longed for. 'Devoted' was the strongest word he had used.

'Oh, David,' she whispered, 'our whole lives could pass us by before your father relents. I understand your concern for me – or is it for yourself? That could destroy our relationship. In fact, I can feel it happening, even so soon.' She pulled herself up sharp.

Yes, it may be happening but she must not allow it to sever all communication between them. She needed infor-mation out of Whitby and David could provide it innocently. The desire for revenge against her uncle still lay deep within her, crying out to be fulfilled. And already she had some information on which she could build. Already she had an unwitting spy. She must continue communicating with him.

The following Sunday morning Sarah vacated her pew before the priest had reached the sacristy after saying Mass. Concerned because she was alone, Kevin followed her before any of the others were ready to leave. Outside, he saw she was already hurrying away. He hesitated a moment then, chiding himself for doing so, ran after her.

'Miss Langton,' he called.

She stopped and turned.

'Miss Langton,' he gasped when he reached her, 'your father is not with you. Nothing wrong, I hope?'

She smiled. 'Nothing. But thank you for your concern. He came to early Mass as he wanted to visit a sick friend this morning.'

'Oh, good.' Kevin spluttered as he went on, 'I mean, good about your father, not good about the sickness.'

Sarah's merry laughter caused his head to spin. 'I knew what you meant, Kevin, and I'm grateful for your enquiry. It was thoughtful of you.'

Kevin, a shade embarrassed by her words, managed to say, 'You are alone, may I escort you home?'

Sarah inclined her head in gracious acknowledgement. 'I will be glad of your company.'

'You were in a hurry. I don't want to slow you down.'

'You won't. It was just that I did not want to be delayed by conversation outside the church.'

'Maybe you would rather be on your own?' suggested Kevin shyly.

'Kevin!' There was a note of reproach in her voice. 'That's not true. Someone who helped save my life will always be welcome company to me.'

'Thank you, Miss Langton.'

'And I prefer Sarah to Miss Langton.'

174

'Very well,' he returned, pleased to be on more intimate terms.

They fell into step, Kevin matching her pace which she slowed to a Sunday morning stroll while enjoying the sun and fresh autumnal air.

'Are you settling here in Middlesbrough?'

'Yes.'

'And the work?'

He gave a shrug of his shoulders. 'We were laid off for a few days, but now the flow of ironstone is back to normal so is the pig iron and we are back to full-time work.'

'Father tells me that it is due to a man sent from Whitby, Luke Middleton, and that he has employed Sean as his assistant. Quick promotion for him.'

'It is that, but that's what Sean wants. He's a dreamer.'

'Will he realise his dream?'

'Who knows? But give him his due, he'll try.'

'Because of a girl?'

Kevin gave a half smile. 'He's always been one for the girls, but recently he has been going steady with a Dublin girl, Eileen Nolan. Maybe it's because of her he wants to fulfil his dream and escape from poverty.'

'And you? Where do your ambitions lie?'

He spread his hands in a gesture of uncertainty.

'Oh, come, Kevin, I'm sure you have some. The work you are doing is obviously different from what you have been used to.'

'To be sure it's different from digging docks. I don't know which I'd say I preferred except that humping iron has brought me into contact with a charming young lady.'

Sarah made no comment on this. Instead she said, shooting him a searching look, 'And neither iron nor clay is really what you're used to.' The words were issued as a challenge. She saw him start and then become embarrassed like a naughty schoolboy caught out in some misdemeanour.

'What do you mean?' he asked warily.

175

'You weren't brought up to manual work. Oh, I've no doubt you could stand alongside any man and do it,' she added hastily as she saw the protests rising on his lips. 'But you are not what you outwardly portray.'

Kevin did not answer. Should he deny Sarah's statement? If he did he might wreck a relationship he would prefer to cultivate. And would she believe any denial? He felt sure the answer would be no for she struck him as a young woman who knew when she was right.

'What makes you say that?' he asked tentatively.

'A feeling I had from our first encounter in Liverpool. Then, when you and Sean came to dinner, he was hesitant at table, watching Father and me before he made a move. But you weren't. You knew exactly how to behave. Sometimes you let your guard slip. Sean and Seamus don't because they don't have one. They are what they are all the time while you are not.' She had been watching him intently while she was speaking but he had avoided her gaze until now when she continued, 'I would say you have had a better upbringing. So why are you here, doing rough work, when you could be doing better things?'

Kevin gave a wan smile and a shrug of resignation. He felt unmasked and knew it was no use trying to cover up the truth. He nodded. 'You are a shrewd young lady. It's true that I'm not from the same background as Sean and Seamus. They're Dubliners through and through, while I only assumed that background after I met Seamus. He and I have been together for five years.'

'But why?'

He hesitated, wondering where to begin and how much to reveal. But he liked Sarah, who was a good listener, and found her easy to talk to. His story unfolded.

'You're right in what you say. My people have land, a large estate about ten miles outside Dublin. I have an elder brother who loves the estate and enjoys managing it as Father has trained him to. I was the second son and really had no role there, or not in the way I would have liked.

176

Father and my brother did everything and I was merely a lackey, carrying out their orders. I had no incentive, no objective towards which to direct my own talents.'

'And you have now?' There was criticism in Sarah's tone.

'Ah, well, no, I must admit I haven't, but I still nurse the ambition that one day, some time in the future . . .'

'Why wait until then?'

'Because ..' His voice trailed away.

'Because?' she prompted, sensing that he had ceased to speak not because he was reluctant to reveal what had happened, but because his thoughts had drifted back to the past.

'Well,' he continued, 'when I realised that a future on the estate would bring me little but comfortable inertia and that there was a whole wide world apart from the Irish countryside, I decided to leave home. I must say my father was understanding. While he did not want to see me go, he gave me his blessing and some money, and said goodbye.

'I lived in Dublin for a while, not knowing what I wanted to do or where I really wanted to be. Adventure beckoned – America, Australia – but unlike many who sought new lives in those places they were too far away for my liking. It was then that I realised my roots were in Ireland, that I did not want to go far from the country of my birth. Adventure came to me in a strange way. I'd explored Dublin thoroughly, seen the seamier side of the city, met snobs who thought themselves above everyone else, experienced the ruthlessness of many who had money and were not beyond exploiting the lower classes to gain more.

'I saw that spill over outside a factory. The workers were angry there had been a cut in their pay, and were calling for the owners and making threats. The owners appeared, accompanied by a bunch of thugs, supposedly bodyguards. In reality they were there to make the trouble erupt into violence so that the bosses could teach their employees a lesson.

177

'They picked on a small wiry man towards the front of the workers. He was obviously the worse for drink which led to his shouting obscenities he would never have uttered sober. His yells inflamed the mob so he was immediately singled out as a ring leader. Four of the so-called bodyguards made a sudden rush and barged their way unceremoniously through the crowd to get him. They dragged him to the front. People were incensed by their actions and began to retaliate. The remainder of the bully boys moved in and scuffles and fights broke out. Meanwhile the man who had been hauled to the front was being beaten about the head and body and, though he tried to fight his assailants off, he was no match for them. He fell to the ground and they started kicking him with their heavy, steel-capped boots.' Kevin's voice faltered at the recollection.

'It was then you intervened to save Seamus,' said Sarah.

Kevin nodded. 'You guessed?'

'I think anyone would who had met the pair of you. What happened next?'

'I got him away.' Kevin did not want to enlarge on the action he had taken. 'I escorted him back to my lodgings, got a doctor and nursed him for two weeks, by which time he was up and about again.'

'And you've been together ever since?'

'Yes. I got to know him well in those two weeks. He isn't the wild man he appeared that day, drink had got the better of his tongue, but he will stick up for what he thinks is right. I found him to be a big-hearted man who would do anything for anyone he took to. He was extremely grateful for what I did for him that day, and we stayed together. I could see that he needed my help. Drink was his demon but I managed to get him to take less. He likes his beer but I feel he is now in control which is why I don't hang around him all the time. This isn't to say the relationship has been all one-sided. He's done me many a good turn.'

'I dare say he has,' commented Sarah. 'Does he know your background?'

'Yes, and so does Sean, but I swore them to secrecy. It made for a better relationship amongst ourselves, but also did not damage our standing with the people we worked alongside.'

'And you were prepared to sacrifice your own prospects to see that Seamus was all right?'

Kevin shrugged his shoulders as if to say, I don't see it as a sacrifice. 'One day, maybe, I'll get around to shaping my life differently.'

'I think you should start thinking about that now,' said Sarah wisely.

'But I can't desert him,' Kevin protested.

'There would be no need. I take it that you believe he could move no further than labouring?'

Kevin gave a sad shake of his head. 'I don't think he could, and I believe he knows it. He sees labouring as his role in life and therefore looks upon it as important, which of course it is because where would we be without the likes of him? And he's happy in what he does, asks no more from life.'

'Then if he's happy, there's no need for you to confine yourself,' said Sarah. 'Are you any good with figures? Any good at letter writing?'

'Sure now, didn't my father see that I had the best education he could provide?'

'Good. Then I'll give away a little information which won't be officially revealed until next week when an advertisement will be placed in the local newspaper. Or maybe it need never appear.'

'You are being very mysterious,' said Kevin, his interest aroused.

'My father is finding the paperwork he must deal with too much for him. There are constant meetings with Mr Bolckow and Mr Vaughan, as well as negotiations with the ironstone suppliers and several other affairs he must attend to. He is spending less and less time around the rolling mill and having to leave more and more to Eric Gilmore, whom

179

I believe is not the ideal assistant. I know Father would like to reorganise things so as to spend less time in the office and this would be the first move. Interested, Kevin?'

She had seen the light of anticipation brighten his eyes so it came as no surprise when he said, 'Of course I would.' But before she could say more he added, 'But I can't desert Seamus.'

'You wouldn't need to. You are both still working in the same place. In fact, from your office you would be looking across to where the pig iron is unloaded. You'd both still be in the same lodgings, so you'd be able to keep a closer eye on him there. Besides, you've said you don't have to be with him all the time now that he has his drink problem under control. I think it would be a good move for both of you, and I'll bet Seamus would want you to do it.'

Kevin smiled. 'You're a persuasive young lady.'

She laughed, delighted that he had taken to her suggestion. 'Then I'll tell Father what I've told you and have no doubt that tomorrow he'll want to meet you. See you convince him. Don't let me down.'

'I could never do that to the sweetest person I've met outside Ireland.'

Sarah laughed and, mimicking his Irish accent, said, 'Away wi' you. I bet you tell that to all the young ladies you meet.'

Kevin laughed with her. Then he became serious. 'But there's only one to whom I mean it.' His eyes were locked on hers and she knew who that was.

'Harper!' Gilmore's voice barked across the open space.

Kevin straightened up from shifting pig iron. He exchanged a glance with Seamus.

'Over here, and quick about it!'

'What's that bastard want?' muttered Seamus.

'I'll soon know,' returned Kevin. He peeled off his leather gloves, tossed them to Seamus, and wiped his sweating hands down his rough trousers. He headed for

Gilmore who was standing outside the door to the offices.

He glared at Kevin. 'Mr Langton wants you. Get in there quick, and see you're straight back on the job when he's finished with you.'

Kevin said nothing but brushed past him and entered the building. He knocked on Mr Langton's door and went in.

James was sitting behind his desk, elbows resting on the arms of his chair and hands steepled in front of his chin in pensive fashion.

'Sit down, Kevin.' He slowly lowered his hands to the desk, all the time his eyes fixed firmly on his employee. 'My daughter has told me what she learned about you yesterday. I make no comment on that for I am sure any appraisal would only embarrass you and I do not want that.'

'Thank you, sir,' replied Kevin, relieved.

'You should not be in a dead-end job humping iron, you are worthy of a better position with better prospects. I have a job you might be interested in. It would mean taking responsibility for practically all the paperwork here. At the moment a lot of it is being done by Gilmore but he really should be spending more time outside, particularly in the rolling mill. Between you and me, he uses it as a chance to take things easy and doesn't keep on top of things. Are you interested?'

'Yes, sir,' replied Kevin.

'Good. You can start tomorrow, eight o'clock. I'll show you what's what and then you can devise your own system and organisation.'

'Very good, sir, and thank you for this opportunity.'

James nodded. 'Give Gilmore a call. I told him to wait outside until I'd seen you. And you come back with him.'

Gilmore didn't like being summoned by a mere labourer, someone he regarded as beneath him, but he had no time to make an issue of it. Mr Langton wanted him. He disliked it even further when Kevin accompanied him back into the office.

'Eric,' said James Langton, leaning back in his chair.

181

'I've decided all the paperwork is getting in the way of your duties outside and in the rolling mill, so in future you'll do none of it. Harper will be taking all that over. He'll be my assistant inside the office, you'll be my assistant outside.'

Gilmore seethed but dare not voice his feelings. This whippersnapper of an Irishman hadn't been here five minutes and he was in Langton's good books. He'd sneaked a job Gilmore had found convenient for taking things easy when he liked, especially when Mr Langton was engaged in meetings and negotiations. Now that easy time was gone and Gilmore didn't like it. He bit back the torrent of harsh words which would have jeopardised his job and merely said, 'Yes, sir.'

'So Harper is off your gang as from now.'

'Yes, sir.'

'That is all.'

Once outside the office block, he gave a snort of contempt. 'Still living off the past, Harper?'

'I didn't ask for the job,' replied Kevin coldly. 'Mr Langton offered it to me.'

Gilmore sneered. 'No doubt you did a bit of crawling.'

'It's no concern of yours, Gilmore. Think what you like, no doubt you'll get it wrong.'

'That other bastard Irishman escaped me, and now you. Ah, well, I've still got the little runt.' There was a note of menace in his laughter which seemed to hang in the air as he headed for the rolling mill.

When Kevin rejoined Seamus he refused to take back his gloves. 'You keep them, Seamus, I don't need them any more.'

'Why?' Seamus looked astonished. 'What's happened?' He was alarmed by Kevin's serious expression.

'I no longer have this job.'

'What? Kicked you out, have they? That bastard Gilmore been telling lies about you? I'll get him.' The words poured out so fast that Kevin could not interrupt. 'I'll see Mr Langton. He can't do this to you, to us. Maybe Sean will give us a job, or at least put in a good word for us with Middleton.'

Kevin raised his hands to quieten Seamus. 'Hold on, hold on. It's nothing like that.'

'Then what is it? Why don't you need these gloves?'

'Mr Langton's offered me a different job, handling all his paperwork. Assistant in his office.'

For a moment Seamus looked astounded then, comprehending, his face broadened into a grin of delight. 'Good for you.' He slapped Kevin on the arm. 'That's one in the eye for bloody Gilmore.'

'That's as maybe, but you'd better look out, there'll be only you on whom to vent his dislike now. Maybe I'd better turn this offer down?'

'Y'd better not. Sure, isn't it right you shouldn't be labouring alongside me anymore? Never should have been.'

'But, Seamus, you and I . . .'

'You've done enough for me. I'm all right now, and you know it. So don't feel bad about this. Besides, you'll be around. We'll still be in the same lodgings.' Doubt came into his eyes as he added, 'We will, won't we?'

'Of course. Where else would I go? Mrs Hartley's is good enough for me.'

'Well, there you are, so best o' luck in your new job.'

'Thanks, Seamus. You watch out for yourself. Don't let Gilmore rile you.'

Seamus made no comment on that but winked and turned back to his job.

Kevin walked away with a heavy feeling he'd deserted a friend. Since the day outside the factory in Dublin they had shared much together without a single harsh word passing between them. They had taken life in their stride even in the toughest of times. Seamus realised that Kevin had come from a better background but never queried it and took the attitude that if his friend wanted to tell him about it he would do so in his own good time.

He was grateful to Kevin for weaning him off his hard

183

drinking, subtly, without criticism. Seamus still loved his beer and stout but, under Kevin's eye, had come to know his limits and keep within them.

Now he was pleased for Kevin, but, as he bent his back to the pig iron, his heart was heavy at the feeling of suddenly being alone.

Chapter Ten

'Had a good day, Father?' Sarah asked, turning from the small table where she had just poured him his usual measure of whisky.

This was a routine only occasionally broken. Recognising his opening and closing of the front door she would break off whatever she was doing and prepare his drink.

She knew that these moments at the end of a day's work were precious to him. They had been started by her mother to help him relax and dismiss the cares of responsibility. They had talked about the trivialities of the day, exchanged local news and gossip, indulging in the pleasure of being together, or sharing a silence which only true lovers know how to do.

When her mother had died, Sarah had resolved to keep up the tradition. Though she knew she could never step into her mother's shoes and take over the togetherness her parents had shared, she brought a different bond of love, that between daughter and father.

'Yes,' James replied, kissing her with fatherly affection on the cheek. He stretched, easing the tension of the day from him, and thanked her as he took his glass and went to his favourite chair. He sat down, drew a deep breath and sank back into its soft luxury. 'Highly satisfactory.' He gave a little nod as if agreeing with himself.

'Kevin settled in?'

'Oh, yes,' he replied with enthusiasm. 'He did the very first day. Eased my burden greatly by giving me more time to see to things I was beginning to neglect.' He took another sip of his whisky. 'You know, it was a good day when we met up with those Irishmen even though the circumstances were fraught. Kevin you know about, and Sean is doing well with Luke Middleton. He tells me the young man from Whitby has a real way with the men, gets the best out of them without any antagonism. He's certainly organised the turnaround of the ironstone ships from Whitby to our benefit.' He pursed his lips thoughtfully. 'Maybe we should invite him to dinner, meet him socially. It could help things.'

'A good idea, Father. Give me a date and I'll alert Mrs Jepson.' Sarah knew that their cook would be only too delighted to provide something more than the usual meal for two.

'What about next Tuesday?'

'Very well.'

'By the way, Luke Middleton has a sister. We'll ask her too, then you won't be burdened with men's talk all evening.'

Sarah smiled at his consideration for since her mother's death he was always trying to ease what he considered her lonely life, though she never complained.

By the following Tuesday Sarah and Mrs Jepson had devised a simple but mouth-watering menu. Sarah had had difficulties in trying to keep the cook from over-elaboration. 'Maybe another time,' she had said to soothe Mrs Jepson's disappointment that her range of kitchen skills was not to be fully exploited. 'Maybe Christmas.'

The evening was crisp, a hint of the first frost in the air. It sharpened Lydia's and Luke's appetites and made them pleased to enter the warmth of the house in Queen's Terrace. Sarah and her father were pleasant hosts, sweep-

186

ing away any doubts they had had about this visit.

James greeted Luke with a hearty handshake. 'Pleased you could come. And you, my dear,' he added, turning his welcoming smile on Lydia.

'Thank you, it is most kind of you to invite us.' Her reply was soft but sincere. She turned her eyes to the young woman beside him. 'You must be Sarah? I have so looked forward to meeting you ever since Kevin Harper told me about you.'

The flush which came to Sarah's face told Lydia the admiration was not one-sided.

'Indeed,' said Sarah, as the maid took the coats from the guests. 'All good, I hope.'

'Nothing but, Miss Langton,' replied Lydia.

'Sarah, please. I hope there will be no formalities between us.' She had felt an instantaneous liking for Lydia. Although the girl was a stranger, Sarah felt she had known her all her life.

Lydia held herself with the confidence that comes from mixing with many people, obviously someone who had enjoyed an active social life. Sarah was curious. She knew from her father that the Middletons had come from Whitby and wondered what sort of life Lydia had led there.

'Thank you for your kind welcome. I had heard about you, Mr Langton, but did not know that you had such a charming daughter.'

James gave a proud smile but said teasingly, 'She's a bossy-two-shoes really.'

'I'm sure she isn't,' chided Lydia.

'If I am, I'll boss you all to go into the drawing room,' said Sarah. 'There's no need to stand here when we can be more comfortable.'

They entered the room and Lydia, who was chatting to Sarah, pulled up sharp and let her remaining words go unspoken. Sarah glanced quickly at her new-found friend, fearing there was something wrong.

'Oh, a piano!' gasped Lydia. There was no mistaking the

ecstasy in her expression as she gazed at the highly polished black grand piano that stood in one corner of the large room.

'You play?' asked Sarah.

'She certainly does,' replied Luke when his sister seemed to have lost her tongue.

Lydia started. 'May I look?' she asked hopefully.

'Of course,' replied James.

There was an air of excitement about her as she crossed the room. Her fingers tingled, anticipating the feel of the keys. She stopped in front of the instrument, admiring it for a few moments before allowing her hands to caress the smooth wood lovingly.

'Open it.' Sarah was beside her. The words, delivered softly, enticed Lydia.

She hesitated only a moment then slowly raised the lid to reveal the contrast between black and white. She ran her fingers lightly across the keys.

'You must play for us later, my dear. Come now and have a glass of Madeira.' James innocently broke the spell which had lured Lydia into another world.

Slowly she lowered the lid and glanced at Sarah. 'You play, of course?' she said.

'Not very well,' came the reply. 'The piano was my mother's. She played extremely well. Taught me.'

'Sarah could have been her equal,' put in James, 'but I'm afraid she did not get all the practice she should have done. You see, it was too easy for her to persuade her mother to play. She so loved to do that.'

'And I loved to listen,' added Sarah with a reminiscent smile.

'I've tried to encourage my daughter to spare more time for it now, but I think the lack of someone competent with whom to share the joy holds her back. Maybe you . . .' He left the implication hanging in the air.

The meal passed off pleasantly with a growing familiarity between hosts and guests.

James admired the serious intellect behind Luke's easy conversation. Inevitably talk turned to their work.

'Shipping the ironstone from Whitby to your jetty, then by rail to Witton and back again as pig iron for the rolling mill, must be a costly operation?' he observed.

'No doubt about it,' agreed James. 'What we really need is to find ironstone in a more convenient situation.'

'On your doorstep.'

'Exactly. Cut out the shipping costs.'

'That would be a big blow to Mr Martin.'

'Progress in one trade inevitably harms another,' James commented, then added, 'It may never happen, and we'll go on as we are for as long as it is viable.'

'Now that's enough work talk,' chided Sarah firmly. 'This is a relaxing social occasion. We must make that a priority for our guests.'

'You have made it so already,' said Lydia. From the way she'd conducted herself all evening, Sarah deducted that this young woman and her brother had left a similar world behind. She wondered why?

Throughout the remainder of the meal Sarah subtly drew from them the information she wanted. In imparting the story of their life in Whitby, Lydia was careful to avoid the facts surrounding her father's death or her subsequent desire for revenge.

With dinner over everyone felt a pleasing sense of contentment. James drained his glass, leaned back in his chair and said, 'Shall we relax in the drawing room with some coffee or tea? And then maybe Lydia will play for us.'

'Are you sure you want me to?' Although the desire to play was strong, she felt she had to put the question. She was not setting herself up as an equal to Mrs Langton and wanted to avoid causing Mr Langton painful memories.

'It would be better if the piano were played more often,' he replied.

189

Lydia knew this was directed at his daughter, but also guessed that Sarah had refrained from playing out of respect for her father's feelings. Maybe she could help them both.

Lydia, accompanied by Sarah, went straight to the piano while the two men sat down. Sarah raised the lid, Lydia made herself comfortable on the piano-stool, flexed her fingers, paused for a moment with her fingers held above the keys, then filled the room with notes of sweetness.

Lydia was entranced. To her it seemed there was only the piano and herself in the room and they were as one. The others were bewitched by the flow of the notes which drew them into a different world.

Two maids came in with trays of coffee and tea. Hearing the music, they opened the door quietly, glided across the floor without a sound, placed the trays on a table and left as silently.

The coffee and tea remained untouched.

Lydia went from one piece to another. No one spoke to break the flow or mar the spell. The music went on and on. No one wanted it to stop, but then Lydia started. She suddenly realised how the music had taken her over and that she was monopolising the evening. She swung round on the stool, blushing as she uttered her apologies. 'Oh, I'm sorry I've gone on so, but I was lost ... I shouldn't have allowed myself to get carried away.' Her words came out in a rush.

'Don't apologise, my dear. That was enchanting,' said James. 'You held us under the magic of your touch.' He glanced at Luke. 'You were right, she certainly can play.'

He smiled, proud of his sister.

'Splendid, splendid!' cried Sarah, jumping up and giving Lydia a hug. 'I loved it so, I could listen to you all night.'

'I would love to play all night,' laughed Lydia, giving Sarah's hand a squeeze of appreciation.

190

'You must miss your piano?'

'It was the one piece of furniture I regretted having to part with. It nearly broke my heart.'

'Then your heart shall be properly mended,' said James. 'Please come and play here whenever you want.'

'But I couldn't impose,' said Lydia as she and Sarah sat down beside each other on the sofa.

'Of course you could.'

'And I will be pleased to see you at any time,' added Sarah.

'Your kindness overwhelms me, but I'm afraid my time will be taken up. I will have to find a paying occupation.'

'From what you have told us of your life in Whitby, to do so will be foreign to you,' said James. 'I have a suggestion to make. A genteel occupation for you.'

As he paused, Lydia looked curiously at him. 'Mr Langton, you have the advantage of me.'

He smiled. 'I don't want you to take up this idea merely because I have suggested it, nor to regard it as charity for there is an ulterior motive behind it. Using that piano, you can give music lessons.'

For a moment everyone was speechless. The sense of this proposal hit Sarah first. 'Father, that's a splendid idea. You must accept, Lydia, you must!'

'But, Mr Langton, I cannot accept such a generous offer. It would be an imposition. And remember, you'd have strangers coming into this house.'

'They would only be strangers at first. You would get to know them, and no doubt Sarah too. And the power of vetting would be in your hands. With Sarah's assistance, if you like.'

'It will work, Lydia, I know it will. I just know it!' Sarah was passionate about the idea.

'Before you make up your mind, I must impose one condition.'

James's serious expression brought a sharp glance of

191

surprise from Sarah. What was he going to say that might wreck what she saw as a chance of close friendship with this talented girl?

'I would like you to encourage Sarah to practise more and improve her playing.'

'Nothing will give me greater pleasure.'

'Good, then it's settled. I will leave all the arrangements to you and Sarah.'

'Mr Langton, you are too kind to someone who is a stranger.'

'From what I have observed this evening and in my dealings with Luke, I can no longer regard you as such.'

The following morning as Lydia hurried to Queen's Terrace she recalled those words with delight and satisfaction. She had taken to Mr Langton and his daughter. With his kind and gentle manner she had seen in him something of her father, while in Sarah she had seen the friend she had craved ever since her direct ties with Whitby had been broken. She was looking forward to planning this piano venture with Sarah and getting to know her better.

The maid who admitted her directed Lydia to the drawing room as she had been instructed.

After expressing their delight at seeing each other again, and recalling the previous evening, they quickly fell to making plans to publicise the lessons which Lydia was prepared to undertake. Sarah thought she knew of several people who might be interested in having their daughter learn the piano and it was agreed that she should mention the project by word of mouth.

'And we must not forget you,' pointed out Lydia. 'I must fulfil your father's wishes. Come, let me hear you play.'

With Lydia's ability in mind, Sarah was shy about her own playing and a little hesitant in her fingering. Lydia watched her carefully and when Sarah had finished a piece by Chopin she announced, 'There is nothing to stop you becoming a good pianist. You need to brush up on some basic aspects, practise and play often. If I am the means of you doing so then I will be satisfied with what I have achieved.'

'You really think I can be good?'

'Certainly.'

Sarah was pleased. She had always dreamed of emulating her mother.

'I believe you have not played as much as you would have liked because you thought it might remind your father of the past,' Lydia went on.

Sarah nodded.

'Well, with his kind suggestion that I give piano lessons here, he has cleared the way for you. You must not miss this chance, I am sure it will please him.'

'You are right. I should no longer be afraid of hurting him by playing the piano.'

So the plans were made and within the week Sarah had mustered enough pupils for Lydia to take two a day, four days a week.

Through her visits to Queen's Terrace a strong bond grew up between the two young women and they began to share the thoughts that only people in such close acquaintance-ship can exchange.

Yet Sarah felt she was not getting to know the whole person. But do you ever? she wondered. There was some-thing about life in Whitby that Lydia was holding back. Why she got this feeling Sarah was unsure, for Lydia appeared to be perfectly open.

'Couldn't Luke have taken over the business after your father died?' asked Sarah when Lydia had finished telling her about her life as a merchant's daughter.

'That was Father's intention but alas the debts were too great for the business to survive. Everything had to go, even my beloved piano. If there had been half a chance of keeping the firm alive, I would have encouraged Luke to take it. I would have helped him and I'm sure

193

we could have made a success of it.'

'Help? You mean in a practical way?'

'Yes. My father intended it, so why not? I'd been around his office and knew his ship and the way he traded. I think it came about because I wanted to be different from other girls who were content to follow in their mother's footsteps. After mine died I was more or less in a man's world.'

'Would you like to go back to that world?'

'Tomorrow if I could. It was more exciting than sewing, tea parties and gossip. Who knows? Some day I might be able to do it.' A wistful look had come over Lydia's face, but Sarah could not know that behind it lay a burning desire for revenge.

Observing the regularity of Lydia's visits with letters to the masters of the ironstone ships, Sean made it his business to be around at those times. His rich Irish brogue thickened in an assiduous display of charm and Lydia found herself looking forward to the exchanges which passed between them.

One day when he suggested that the following Sunday they might take a walk in the country, Lydia, not wanting to appear too forward, held back her answer.

Fearing she was on the point of refusing, Sean hastily decided, for the sake of decorum, to add, 'We can ask Sarah and Kevin to come along too.'

She readily agreed.

That was the start of regular outings for the four friends. Enjoyable as they were, they raised a problem in Sarah's mind. According to Kevin, Sean had a girl in Dublin and she wondered if she should warn Lydia of this.

One day with the piano lessons finished Sarah and Lydia were enjoying a cup of tea when Sarah casually remarked, 'You seem to enjoy Sean's company?'

'I must admit I do,' replied Lydia, stirring her tea thoughtfully.

'Was there no one in Whitby?'

Lydia hesitated.

'Ah, I can tell that there was,' said Sarah. 'Do you still feel affection for him?'

'Yes and no,' replied Lydia evasively.

'And which is the stronger, the yes or the no?'

Lydia shrugged her shoulders. 'I don't know.'

'Has being with Sean confused you?'

Again she shrugged her shoulders. 'Maybe.'

'Did you love this person?'

'Yes.'

'Do you still?'

'That's where the confusion arises.' Lydia went on to tell Sarah about David. 'So you see, I felt let down. I thought he would marry me in spite of my changed circumstances.'

'Does he still love you?'

'He says so and that he took the course of action he did to ensure our eventual marriage.'

'And he may be right,' Sarah pointed out. 'What do you know of Sean?'

'He has all the charm and glib tongue of an Irishman and can certainly weave a silver thread around a girl's mind. Beyond that I know very little. He has told me virtually nothing about himself.'

Sarah wondered how much she should divulge. Should she reveal what Kevin had told her? But she did not know how deep the relationship in Dublin was. Sean had never even mentioned the girl. Sarah decided that the best course, at this stage, was to say nothing and leave things as they were unless a situation arose where she deemed it imperative to interfere.

She smiled. 'Well then, I shall enlighten you on one aspect.' She went on to tell her friend about the accident off Liverpool and how Sean had rescued her and her father.

'I don't think Luke knows about that. Sean helped us to find somewhere to stay when we arrived in Middlesbrough, then showed Luke the way to the jetty where the ships unloaded the ironstone. Luke took to him and offered him a job as his assistant.'

195

'And he's very capable from what I hear. The next time you come for the evening you must bring him along and I'll invite Kevin too.'

Sean's conscience pricked him. He had been neglectful of Eileen – only four letters since leaving Ireland. He glanced at the clock. He just had time to pen a brief note before his appointment with Lydia. He wrote:-

My dear Eileen,

Thank you for your letter. I am sorry I have not written more regularly. You are right to rebuke me. As I explained, things happened here so fast that I was reeling with the shock of my good fortune and, not wanting to waste it, everything else got set aside. I know you will understand that this can only be for our good and will help to fulfil the dream I have for our future together.

With more responsibility thrust upon me I can't see that I will be able to come to Dublin for some time so be patient, love.

You ask about Kevin and Seamus. They are well. Kevin is revelling in his role as assistant to the rolling mill manager, but poor Seamus takes some stick from his supervisor, Mr Gilmore, who did not like being ordered to take us on by the manager when we first came here. Now Kevin and I have escaped his clutches, he has only the one scapegoat. Seamus is being careful about retaliating and away from work Kevin keeps an eye on him, so that his hard drinking does not return.

I must close now, but first I must answer your words – 'Don't forget me.' How could I forget the feel of your warmth against me, the temptation I could not resist? No one could ever compare to my blue-eyed colleen.

Soon we will be together.

Love,
Sean

*

196

In the brisk air of a December Saturday morning he quickly walked the few yards to number sixteen West Street.

His knock was answered by Mrs Turnbull. 'Ah, good morning, Sean. Lass is ready and waiting.' She called over her shoulder, 'Lydia, he's here.'

Immediately Lydia appeared, dressed in a warm top coat, sealskin hat and matching gloves.

'Good morning, Sean,' she said, obviously pleased to see him.

'And to you,' he greeted her, eyes twinkling merrily. 'What's it to be this morning? Window shopping?'

They made their way along Sussex Street, pausing every now and then to look in shop windows while carrying on their light teasing banter. On the way Sean posted his letter.

Eric Gilmore knocked on the door of Mr Langton's office in response to a summons by the manager. James looked up from some papers he was studying as the burly man entered.

'Gilmore, some serious allegations have been made about your attitude and behaviour towards the men.'

'Sir?' answered Gilmore, putting on a puzzled expression.

'There's no use denying what I have to say though I will give you an opportunity to answer these charges. I have already investigated the allegations, privately and unknown to you. I have more than one witness as to your behaviour towards certain of your men, and one in particular. From what I have learned your treatment of Seamus O'Leary is unwarranted. You try to cover your vindictiveness by mistreating and bullying others, though not to the same degree as you bully O'Leary. What have you to say?'

'But that's rubbish, sir,' protested Gilmore gruffly.

'I told you it was no use denying these charges,' returned James coldly. 'Can you justify your actions?'

'He's a poor worker, needs bullying to get the best out of him.'

'Not from what I have observed. He does his share.'

'But he's crafty and needs watching, otherwise he'd slack.'

'Again, not what I've noticed. He's never late and looks for no more time off than anyone else.'

Gilmore's lips tightened. His temper was beginning to fray. 'Who are you going to believe? I think you've already made your mind up that I'm in the wrong and he's right.'

'O'Leary has made no charges against you.'

'Damned Irishmen,' muttered Gilmore to himself, but said loudly, 'I've always got good results out of my men, haven't I?'

'Yes.'

'Then let me do it my way.'

'Not unless you stop hounding O'Leary.'

'You're mollycoddling the little runt! I know how best to handle him.'

'No, you don't,' returned James, eyes boring into the man who stood before him. 'I'll not have intimidation and bullying on this site.'

Gilmore's face reddened as his anger boiled to the surface. 'You've favoured those damned Irishmen ever since they came here, gave Harper my job and now you're listening to that runt O'Leary. No doubt he's egged others on to talk against me.'

'That's not true and you know it,' James replied, his voice level.

'I bloody well don't!'

'If that's your attitude, you're fired. Get out and don't let me see you around here again.'

Gilmore set his lips tight. For a moment he glared down at the manager then he hissed, 'Someone will pay for this, and don't you forget it.' He banged his fist on the desk. 'Damn you, Langton! You and that bastard O'Leary have just spoilt my kids' Christmas!' He turned and stormed out of the room, slamming the door behind him.

If he'd thought the mention of his children and Christmas would make his superior reconsider his decision he was mistaken. James Langton had carried out a thorough investigation not only into the man's working practices but also his home background. He had found out that Eric Gilmore kept his wife short of money, and, in spite of her efforts to protect her children, ill-treated them. In reality Christmas would mean nothing to a man like him. James hoped that the money he was proposing to send secretly to Mrs Gilmore to help her over this period would be kept to herself and not end up being poured down Gilmore's throat.

Outside the manager's office Gilmore strode with angry strides towards the men unloading pig iron. They could sense trouble even before he reached them. They stopped work and watched him approach, his fury plainly visible.

He went straight to Seamus. 'You little runt,' he snarled. 'Lose me my job, would you?'

The fire in his eyes warned Seamus what was coming. As Gilmore's huge fist swung, the Irishman ducked. The blow flashed close to his head and Gilmore, even more enraged, threw himself forward. Seamus skipped lightly out of the way. Gilmore staggered under the momentum of his own weight. He saved himself from falling and turned quickly, hoping to gain an advantage over the smaller man. As he did so he caught a glimpse of Mr Langton coming out of his office. He knew he would be in even greater trouble if he persisted. The constable might be called. Rage burned in him as he hissed, 'I'll get you, O'Leary. As sure as you're a bloody Irishman, I'll get you,' and stormed away.

An uneasy silence settled over the men as they watched him go.

The Saturday evening before Christmas, still three days away, was sharp with frost, but as yet there was no snow. It didn't even threaten for the sky was clear and brightly lit with stars.

Lydia, Luke, Kevin and Sean were thankful for such a fine night for it made their walk to Queen's Terrace much more pleasant.

Lydia revelled in her escort of three young men as they weaved their way through the crowds flocking around the market stalls and filling the streets with their usual Saturday-night forays.

Noise from the pubs penetrated the shouts of the stall holders and the protests of irritated customers waiting to be served. But the four friends were not worried by the din. Laughter was on their lips and their hearts were light in anticipation of pleasant company, good food and an enjoyable evening with Sarah and her father.

After a welcoming drink in the drawing room there followed a sumptuous meal with which Mrs Jepson had excelled herself. Conversation flowed smoothly with descriptions of the life the Langtons had led before they moved to Middlesbrough, the lighter side of Whitby, and general praise for the beauty of the Irish countryside which could never be marred even by the desecration wrought by famine. Tall tales interspersed the serious, and laughter flowed as friendships deepened. The merriment continued into the drawing room where, after a few minutes' relaxation, Lydia and Sarah were called upon to play the piano.

Sweet notes filled the room as each of them played their own particular favourites and the occasional Irish air for the pleasure of the Irish guests. The magic of the season crept into the room as note blended with note, enticed from the keys by delicate fingers. The piano came alive. It became one of them, bringing happiness and tranquillity, and transported both mind and imagination to other climes.

Luke felt the pull of home as he had known it in Whitby. How many Christmases there Lydia had played happily like this and their future had seemed bright.

Sean was drawn to remember Christmases spent with

Eileen, when even his dreams of a new life for them both could hardly better the love she gave him as a Christmas present. But the music also made him query his feelings now. Shouldn't he have sent for her when he received promotion? Was he betraying her with his weak excuses? His eyes settled on Lydia at the piano. He knew of her genteel past as the daughter of a merchant. Maybe this woman of talent and refinement would be a more fitting mate if he could bear to break his promises to Eileen.

The lilting notes transported Kevin back to a country house in Ireland. He had not realised how much he had missed such civilised entertainment until now. The music and the convivial atmosphere brought an urgent desire to be home again. And how he longed for Sarah to see his home, and meet his mother and father. Maybe one day ...

Their thoughts were interrupted by a loud hammering on the front door. Lydia stopped playing and looked at Sarah. The rest of them exchanged uneasy glances.

They heard a maid hurry across the hall, the front door opened and there was an urgent exchange of conversation. All eyes were on the drawing room door in anticipation of the maid's appearance. James was already on his feet when, after a barely audible knock, she burst in.

She was flustered, hardly able to get her breath as she announced, 'I'm sorry, sir, but Mrs Hartley said it was urgent. She's in a terrible state.'

Before anything else could be said the men's landlady was pushing past her, breathing hard from her exertions, face contorted with distress. 'I'm sorry to barge in, Mr Langton, sir, but it's a matter of grave importance.'

'What is it?' James spoke quietly to calm her as he moved to take her arm and lead her to a chair. 'Sit down and tell us in your own good time, Nell.'

Sarah and Lydia came over to lend their support.

'Oh, sir!' She looked up with tear-filled eyes. 'It's Seamus ... he's dead.' This wasn't the way she had

201

planned to break the shocking news. It wasn't the way she had rehearsed it as she'd rushed through the streets to Queen's Terrace. But now the words were out, stark with their chilling news.

'What?' Everyone gazed at her in disbelief. Kevin and Sean exchanged glances of horror. This couldn't be true. Their friend couldn't be dead. He had been at Mrs Hartley's before they left and in very good humour, asking them to thank Mr Langton for the invitation he had refused four days ago. Although Kevin had tried to persuade his friend to accept Seamus would not, saying he had other things planned for that evening. But Kevin knew the real reason: he did not want to find himself in a situation in which he would feel out of place. Now Kevin wished he had been more persuasive. If he had, Seamus would still be alive.

'What happened?' asked Luke, posing the question they all wanted to ask but seemed incapable of voicing in their shock and distress.

'He was found in an alley beside the Iron Smelter, badly beaten. Jim came looking for Kevin and Sean, and told me. I knew where you were so I came straight away.'

'Did he tell you any more?' pressed Kevin.

'He said there'd been trouble earlier. Seamus was having a quiet drink when Eric Gilmore and his cronies came in.'

'I knew it!' Kevin exploded. He struck his fist into his palm. 'Why wasn't I there?'

Sarah moved quickly to his side. She laid a hand on his arm. 'You weren't to know what would happen.'

'Go on, Nell,' prompted James.

'My brother said that Gilmore acknowledged Seamus in a friendly sort of way and bought him a drink, asking him to let bygones be bygones. Seamus said he held no grudges and hoped Gilmore didn't either. For ten minutes all seemed well but then Gilmore offered Seamus another drink which he refused, saying he'd had enough. Gilmore then took offence. His cronies crowded Seamus and forced him to take two more pints.'

Kevin's lips tightened in distress. Seamus had conquered his hard drinking. Knew when he had had enough. But bullies like Gilmore wouldn't be ignored.

'Jim tried to calm the situation but Gilmore took no notice. He started accusing Seamus of costing him his job. Seamus denied it and Gilmore threw a punch at him. His cronies closed in but Jim had anticipated this and signalled to a couple of his friends who always stand by on a Saturday night in case of trouble. They moved in and, in no gentle fashion, removed Gilmore and his cronies from the pub. My brother advised Seamus to stay where he was, in fact all night if he wanted. Seamus was there for about half an hour and then Jim noticed he had gone. An hour later he was found in the alley.' Her terrible story told, Nell Hartley seemed close to fainting.

Lydia, kneeling beside her, put a comforting arm round her and offered words of solace. Sarah quickly organised a cup of tea.

'I must go,' said James, starting for the door.

'Wait, sir.' Kevin's voice was firm. 'There is nothing you can do. Sean and I will go, he was our friend.'

'I'll come too,' offered Luke.

'It would help us more if you and Lydia would see Nell home when she is ready.'

'Very well, but if you need any further assistance let me know.'

The two friends spoke little as they hurried through the town. People still went gladly about their Saturday night revelry. Though the news of the Irishman's death had swept quickly through the town, many chose to ignore it. As far as they were concerned it was just another street brawl.

'Morbid vultures,' hissed Kevin with contempt when they reached the Iron Smelter and saw folk still hanging

203

around the end of the alley, heads together, tongues wagging under pretext of having inside knowledge of what had happened. They pushed their way through and entered the pub.

When Jim saw them he motioned them to come through to the private quarters. With the door closed, shutting out the noise which rose from the bar as if nothing had happened, he said, 'I'm very sorry about this.'

'Your sister told us what had happened,' said Sean, seeing Kevin was too shaken to speak.

'I thought she would know where you were.'

'Gilmore? Did they get the bastard?' There was venom in Kevin's voice when he spoke.

Jim shook his head. 'Nobody saw the killing so we can't be certain it was him.'

'Can't be certain?' Kevin's voice was filled with derision. 'It was him all right.'

'After what happened in here, my finger would point at him,' said Jim firmly, 'but I couldn't prove it and nor can anyone else.'

'And so the authorities will do nothing,' snapped Kevin. 'Well, I can.'

'Steady on, don't land yourself in trouble. Seamus wouldn't want that,' insisted Sean.

'So I just let him lie there, cold, without doing anything?'

'Gilmore will never admit it,' Sean pointed out.

'He won't,' agreed Kevin, 'but maybe one of his cronies will talk. Who are they, Jim?'

'I'm not saying. I don't want you confronting them.'

Kevin's lips tightened. He glared at Jim. 'If you won't tell me, I'll find out from someone else. There are always those who'll talk if the price is right.'

'Kevin, forget it!' Sean insisted.

Kevin's eyes flared with annoyance. 'I thought you'd understand. I thought you'd want to do something. We can't let Seamus's murderers go unpunished.' He turned his burning gaze on Jim. 'The names?'

Jim hesitated, moistened his lips while he weighed up what he should do, then nodded. 'All right. I want to see those bastards dealt with as much as you do, but I don't want you taking the law into your own hands. That will only cause more trouble and grief.'

'Jim, I only want the truth. If they did it, or Gilmore, I want to know so the authorities can be told.'

Jim nodded. 'Very well. He has three main friends, all of them present tonight. Jack Jardine, Fred Sykes and Matt Forbes.'

'And where do I find them?'

Jim shrugged his shoulders. 'Who knows? Used to live around here, then in Stockton. Then I heard of them moving to Yarm. Anywhere where there was work, though they always looked for the easy jobs. Came down here from Newcastle I believe, so, if they were involved in what happened in the alley, they could easily have gone back north and that'll be like looking for a needle in a haystack. Forget them. Gilmore's the man you want. He was the ringleader.'

Kevin nodded grimly. 'Maybe you are right. The law can deal with them after I've found Gilmore.'

'Not tonight,' put in Sean. 'In your state of mind you'd only do something rash.'

'Maybe that's what's needed.' Kevin started to walk away.

Sean grabbed his arm. 'Leave it for now. Remember you said you'd go back and report to Mr Langton? Do that and nothing else. I'll come with you.'

'No! You'd better go home to Nell. She was so upset.'

'Lydia and Luke are with her.'

'I know, but they may want to get back to Mrs Turnbull who will no doubt have heard the news.'

Reluctantly Sean agreed, but only on condition that Kevin promised not to pursue Gilmore that night.

*

Kevin hurried to Queen's Terrace, his thoughts full of revenge. If he did not seek it he would never rest easy with himself.

Reaching the Langtons, he quickly acquainted them with the situation and his theories as to who might have perpetrated the crime.

Sarah became more and more alarmed as she listened for she recognised that a desire to avenge his friend's death burned deep within Kevin. If he fulfilled that, other lives too would be ruined and she did not want that. She did not want him committing another crime as heinous as that which had happened in a lonely alley beside the Iron Smelter. Kevin was carving out a decent career for himself at the rolling mill. Her father had told her that he foresaw a time when Kevin could take over his job, or else take advantage of the growth in trade along the river. Nothing must mar his future. She must do all she could to soothe his anger.

James was quick to advise a cautious approach. 'If there were no witnesses it's going to be difficult to prove who did it,' he warned.

'I know, sir, but there are ways and means.'

'And are you prepared to circumvent the law?'

Kevin shrugged his shoulders.

'If that is the only way.'

'No!' cried Sarah. 'You might end up like Seamus.'

He gave a wry smile. 'I can look after myself.'

'Seamus would have said that,' said Sarah, her face grave, on the brink of shedding tears.

'The odds will be stacked against you,' warned James. 'There's more than one man involved, remember.'

'I know, but Gilmore won't have gone far. He's married, remember.'

'I don't think that would stop him leaving and staying away until things cool down here.'

'Even so, I can pay his house a visit. If he isn't there Mrs Gilmore may know where he is.'

'Be careful, young man. Don't get yourself into a situation you may later regret. Go home and sleep on it.' James looked hard at him. 'I want a promise that you will, and I want to see you at work Monday morning at the usual time.' He saw Kevin hesitate. 'Do you promise?' he demanded.

Kevin nodded. 'Very well, sir.'

'Good.' James received this with a sense of relief, for he judged Kevin to be a man of his word. He did not see that the Irishman had crossed his fingers.

'Good night, sir.'

'Good night, my boy.' James diplomatically stayed in his chair while Sarah accompanied Kevin to the front door.

She grasped him by the arms and looked up into his eyes pleadingly. 'Please don't do anything rash. I saw your crossed fingers when you made that promise to Father.'

He gave a wry smile but that did not soften the fierce anger she saw burning in him. She pressed on, 'Don't take the law into your own hands. There'll be investigations, enquiries, and you'll end up on the wrong side of the law.'

These words had the opposite effect from what she'd intended. They fanned his need for revenge and it showed. 'Gilmore must be made to pay. We know he was behind this.'

'You can't be certain. Someone else may have done it. Even if it was Gilmore, you'll never prove it. Never!'

He wanted no more of this attitude. All his friends were adopting it. Well, so be it. He'd go it alone.

She tightened her grip on his arms. 'Don't, Kevin. Please! Don't seek revenge.' She stretched up and kissed him on the cheek.

He felt her hands relax their hold. He hesitated, wanting to declare his love even though he may go against her wishes. Impulsively his arms came around her and pulled her hard against him. His lips fastened hungrily on hers with a passion born of fury. His kiss was hard and long as he held her tight. Sarah's heart pounded. This was the

207

Kevin she wanted, the man she'd loved almost from the start. She responded and hoped her gentle kisses would show him that in their future together there was no place for revenge.

He suddenly released her, opened the door and stepped out into the frosty air. She shivered and watched him stride down the street. He did not look back but was lost to the night.

Chapter Eleven

On Monday morning, from records in his office, Kevin was able to learn Gilmore's address. He kept this information to himself, and throughout the day gave James no indication that he still harboured a thirst for revenge.

He played that side of things down when James tentatively broached the subject of Seamus's murder, for he judged he was being tested.

'I'm pleased,' the manger concluded. 'Sarah thinks a lot of you and I wouldn't want her to be hurt.'

'I think a lot of her. Admiration and respect go hand in hand and I would not want to do anything that would upset her.'

Nevertheless, early the following morning Kevin made his way to the Gilmores' house. It was one of a row west of the Market Place, the bricks already showing traces of grime spewed from the chimneys of the rolling mill. It was an area of the town that even in this early stage of its existence was beginning to look rundown. It had an atmosphere that spoke of poverty, of people who didn't care how they looked and had no pride in their homes.

It came, therefore, as no surprise to Kevin when, in answer to his knock, the door was opened by a woman whose hair hung lank and untidy, her face smudged as if she had wiped a sooty hand down her cheek. Her eyes were blank, her shoulders drooped. She held a young child whose face and hair were equally dirty. Her dress, marked where the bairn had dropped its food, hung like a sack, down-at-heel shoes splitting at the seams. Yet Kevin detected in the high cheekbones, the set of her mouth and delicate nose that, given encouragement and the will and money to better herself, she could have turned heads. Maybe she had one day but unfortunately the wrong man's.

'Mrs Gilmore?'

'Aye.' She looked at him suspiciously.

'I'm Kevin Harper. I would like a word with your husband.'

'He ain't here.'

'Do you know where he is?'

'I ain't seen him for two days. Went out saying he had some business to see to, but didn't tell me what or where. Now, if that's all, please be on your way.'

Kevin saw her glance quickly along the street in both directions. Automatically he did the same and saw that already there were several nosy neighbours scrutinising him.

'I'd like to talk to you a bit longer if you don't mind,' he said.

Her first instinct was to shut the door in his face, but she'd been raised to be more polite than that in her old life before she'd married Eric Gilmore.

'Then you'd better step inside, Mr Harper, out of sight of that gawking lot. Though what interpretation they'll put on this visit, I think you can guess.'

'Then I'll make it brief so they can't think the worst of you.' She stepped aside to let him in and then closed the door.

She led the way to the kitchen, which was a scene of chaos. Dirty pots were piled in the stone sink. The table was still littered with food and a poor fire struggled against the ashes in the grate.

'Do you know when your husband will be back?'

'Never do. I have to take him as he comes.'

'Does he often go off like this?'

'Not when he's in work, but now . . . Don't know why he got the sack. Never told me but I did hear him ranting on about "some little runt called Seamus", as he put it.' She was about to go on when she pulled up sharp and stared with widening eyes at Kevin. 'The murdered man I heard about was called Seamus too . . . You don't think . . .'

Kevin nodded.

'Oh, my God.' Mrs Gilmore slumped on a chair. 'And you . . .'

'I am the murdered man's close friend. I know your husband believed that Seamus got him the sack.'

'And now you think my husband did him in?'

'Well . . .' Kevin felt a little embarrassed. 'I have no proof.'

'Eric wouldn't,' she protested.

'We can't always predict how people will react in anger.'

'But Eric wouldn't! He's loud-mouthed and a bully and wears that bloody bowler hat 'cos he thinks it gives him authority and power. He ill treats me and the bairns . . . but murder?' Her voice rose. 'No, he wouldn't!' Tears started to stream down her face.

Kevin realised that she didn't want to believe it possible even though she feared it might be so. In spite of Gilmore's rough ways and lack of affection, she still loved him.

'I'm sorry, Mrs Gilmore, if I have distressed you. I'll be off.'

She gulped. 'Please, Mr Harper, leave this alone.'

'Maybe I can't.'

'Think what will happen to me and the bairns. Look around you. You can judge he gives me little enough as it is but I do my best.'

'Then he's a brute for not giving you more. Except, I suspect, his fists.'

211

She flinched. 'He'll find more work. He's not afraid of it. He'll still keep most of his money for himself, expecting me to work miracles on a pittance, but I do know he helps his ageing mother.' She saw the questions springing to Kevin's lips. 'Before you ask, I'll not tell you where she lives except it's not in Middlesbrough. Now, please go.'

He nodded and said, 'I'm sorry to have taken up your time.'

He went down the passage to the front door. As he did so he heard her call out, 'Please, leave it, Mr Harper. No good will come of this. You'll only bring misery on me, his bairns and his mother.'

Her words were still ringing in his ears as he walked down the street.

The following morning, the wind drove glowering clouds across the river and over the salt marshes. It swirled through the graveyard, emphasising the chill of the loss the mourners were feeling. Kevin was filled with grief as he watched Seamus's coffin lowered into the ground.

Sarah slid her hand into his and gripped tightly as she felt the tension in his body. The coffin reached the bottom, the ropes were retrieved and the priest said the necessary prayers. It was all a blur to Kevin. He was picturing the friend he had known. Seamus had had eyes which could dance with merriment, and a way with words, ever-appreciative of the effort his friend had made to rescue him from the oblivion of drink. Kevin cursed himself now. He had saved Seamus from one set of thugs only to allow him to fall victim to a different gang. The desire for revenge which had abated with Mrs Gilmore's final words welled up inside him again.

He splashed the coffin with holy water from a pewter bowl held by a server and turned to depart with Sarah by his side. There were few mourners, but who in Middlesbrough had really known his friend? He appreciated the kindness of those who had come to pay their last

212

respects and drew strength from Sarah and Sean's presence. Then his eyes settled on a lone figure, holding a child in her arms, standing a little distance away.

Their eyes met for a brief second and in that moment her words returned to him. Like Seamus, Mrs Gilmore was an innocent. If he acted against her husband he would shatter her life too.

Christmas came and went, not as cheerfully as it might have done but they all recognised that life must go on. As Kevin said, 'Seamus would not want us to mourn, but rather give thanks for his life and remember him in happier days.'

The bond between Kevin and Sarah had deepened and, when it was known that Gilmore was back in Middlesbrough, she was fearful of what might happen. She was not certain that her pleas to Kevin to forget all thoughts of revenge had been successful.

The news that Gilmore was back did indeed revive Kevin's thoughts of vengeance but it also brought back memories of his interview with Mrs Gilmore and for a few days a battle raged in his mind over which course of action he should take. He did not want to risk losing Sarah's good opinion.

Until one day, on his way to work, he saw Gilmore at the gates to the rolling mill yards. Kevin's step faltered. Hatred for the man left him feeling breathless. His body tensed. Why should this man, whom he felt sure was a murderer, be alive while Seamus was cold in his grave? Oh, why was there no evidence to prove it?

Gilmore glanced round and met Kevin's cold-eyed gaze. Kevin received a shock then. He'd expected to see the Gilmore of old, all bullying bombast and foul-mouthed aggression. But this man cringed before him, and he was bare-headed, the customary bowler hat gone. Whatever had happened since Gilmore had been sacked, and wherever he had been, it had had a sobering effect. Then doubt sprang

213

to Kevin's mind. Was this act put on for some reason or other?

'Gilmore.' Kevin's voice was curt, his eyes challenging the other man to tell the truth. 'What are you doing here?'

'I hoped to see you, sir.' The last word came out a touch reluctantly as if he did not relish thus addressing a man who had once been under his thumb.

'Me?'

'Yes. I hoped you might be able to help me.'

'And why should I do that even if I could?'

'I can't give you a reason. Wouldn't blame you if you told me to get the hell out of here. But I hoped you might help me get a job. Oh, not my old one – I couldn't expect that.'

'You certainly couldn't,' snapped Kevin.

'I'll do anything, anything at all.'

Kevin had been studying the man closely. All the old bravado was missing, the desire to throw his authority around gone. His eyes no longer roved about as if seeking out some fault for which he could inflict punishment. This man had been shaken to the core by something. Could it be the murder of Seamus?

'Do you deserve my help after the way you treated three Irishmen on their arrival? Do you deserve it after Seamus's murder?'

'You think I did that, don't you?' Gilmore's voice was calm. There was no immediate denial, no words of protest. 'My wife Kate told me you did.'

'I'll not deny it.' Kevin's eyes narrowed. He leaned slightly forward. 'And let me tell you this. If I'd found you that night, I'd have given you the same treatment as Seamus got.'

'And you would have punished the wrong man, brought endless misery on my wife and bairns, and likely ended up on the gallows yourself with the real perpetrators still alive.'

He answered in such a matter-of-fact way that Kevin

found himself reluctantly accepting this as the truth. He reeled under the impact of what might have happened if he'd carried out his threat of revenge. His mind was in turmoil. Then he realised that Gilmore was still speaking.

'I'll not deny I was close to it, believing that Seamus lost me my job. I'll not deny that I and three cronies roughed him up in the Iron Smelter, but he was all right when we left and we didn't linger outside. Someone else must have thought he was ripe for the picking after we'd put too much liquor in him.'

'Then you are almost as bad as the murderers,' snapped Kevin.

'Maybe that's the way you see it, but we weren't the killers.'

'Then why did you leave Middlesbrough?'

'Because I knew what some people would think, and I didn't want Kate and the bairns to be involved in the trouble that would follow. I hoped that while I was away the real culprits would be found. Maybe I was wrong to go, but I'll tell you what, Mr Harper, it's had a sobering effect on me. I'm a different man nowadays. So please, for the sake of my wife and kids, try and get me a job.'

Kevin hesitated. Though it hurt him to admit it, he was sure now that Gilmore was telling the truth. It would be easy to deny him his request for his old cruelty to Seamus, but would there be any satisfaction in that? Would he not always suffer himself from the knowledge that he had helped deprive Kate Gilmore and her children of a better chance in life?

'All right, I'll see what I can do,' he growled.

Gilmore's eyes lit up. 'Thank you, Mr Harper. I'll not let you down.'

'I don't know whether I'll be able to persuade Mr Langton, mind. However, I'll do my best. But, and this is a big but, I want a promise from you that most of your wage will go to Mrs Gilmore to help her keep a better home for

215

your children. I think she could do that, given the money and the chance.'

'My Kate's a good woman. I know I've not been right to her.'

'Then you promise that you'll treat her better?'

'Aye.'

'Right. Be here this time tomorrow and hopefully I'll have some good news for you.'

'Sir, there's a marked change in the man.' Kevin made his point forcefully as he faced a doubtful James Langton.

James's eyes were fixed unseeingly on an envelope on his desk. He did not reply immediately. He had listened carefully to Kevin's account of his meeting with Gilmore. At first mention of the name he had shaken his head in disbelief that Kevin had even considered talking to the man, but he let him have his say.

Now he looked up slowly until his gaze met Kevin's. 'You really think a leopard can change its spots?'

'In this case, yes. I believe what he told me, and I truly think that Seamus's murder has shaken him to the core.'

'I don't know. I don't want a disruptive presence among my workers.'

'He won't be. I think he's had a terrible shock, and I believe his wife has greatly influenced his reform. I haven't mentioned this to anyone but, in an effort to trace him, I went to see her.'

'You did what?' James was taken aback by this admission. 'That was a risky thing to do when you didn't know the woman.'

'Maybe but I'm glad I did.' He went on to relate his interview with Kate.

Once again James listened patiently. When Kevin had finished, he was satisfied.

'All right,' he said, 'we'll take Gilmore back. You said you had an assurance that he would treat his wife right? Make him understand that if we hear anything to the

216

contrary, or if he causes any upset here, he will be dismissed immediately.'

Later that morning Kevin was called into James's office.

'Ah, Kevin, about this evening, I have been instructed to attend a meeting with Mr Bolckow and Mr Vaughan.'

'Very well, sir. I'll change my plans.'

James chuckled. 'Don't look so disappointed, my boy. The invitation for you to dine with Sarah and me still stands, but I won't be there. In fact, I want you to tell her I won't be home until late.'

'Yes, sir.' Kevin visibly brightened. 'I'll do that, sir.'

'Well, it's no good cancelling the whole evening. After all, our cook will have started her preparations. Besides,' added James with a twinkle in his eye, 'I wouldn't want to disappoint Sarah.'

'Er . . . yes, sir. No, indeed,' spluttered Kevin.

'Ah, away wi' y' now,' laughed James, mimicking Kevin's accent. 'And wouldn't y' know I'd be wanting y' to give my daughter a pleasant evening?'

When the maid admitted Kevin to the house on Queen's Terrace he heard the gentle sounds of the piano. 'Don't bother,' he said as the maid started towards the drawing-room door to announce his arrival.

'Very good, sir,' she said with a half smile before hurrying away to the kitchen to inform the cook that Miss Sarah's young man had arrived. The servants had come to regard Kevin as such and tacitly approved, hoping that nothing would upset the relationship.

He opened the door quietly and saw Sarah engrossed in her playing. Even with his small knowledge of music he could tell how much she had improved since Lydia had been instructing her. He stood quietly inside the door until she had finished the piece. As the last note faded away he started to clap.

Startled, Sarah looked up quickly. 'Kevin! I didn't hear

you arrive.' She was swiftly on her feet and coming towards him, her face showing her pleasure at seeing him. 'You're here before Father.' She kissed him on the cheek.

'I know,' he returned, hands coming to her waist so that she could not move away. 'He told me to tell you he had received notice to attend a meeting at Mr Bolckow's and would probably be late.'

She looked up at him. A twinkle had come into her eyes. 'And?' she prompted when he paused.

Kevin's mouth twitched. 'Your father said he did not want to spoil your evening and that I was to give you a pleasant time.'

She reached up and kissed him on the lips. 'Just being with you does that,' she whispered.

Their eyes met with that intensity which only comes between two people deeply in love. She slid her arms around his neck, he pulled her to him, and they kissed passionately.

A few minutes later Sarah reluctantly broke away, saying, 'I must inform Cook that Father won't be dining with us this evening.' She let her outstretched fingers trail through his before they parted enough for her to pull the bell-cord.

She gave the message to the maid, and as the door closed again Kevin said, 'I saw Gilmore today.'

Alarm crossed Sarah's face. She had dreaded such an announcement, knowing it might reignite Kevin's desire for revenge.

'Where?' she asked.

'At the works.'

'What on earth was he doing there?'

'Looking for a job.' Kevin went on to explain his encounter and its outcome.

When he had finished Sarah was suffused with relief. 'Oh, I'm so glad that your wish to avenge Seamus has burnt itself out.'

'When I was convinced he was telling the truth I realised that taking revenge would only cause misery to many people, especially you.'

She came and put her arms around him. 'I am so relieved, Kevin.'

'If I had done anything, my heart, soul and mind would have been tainted forever.'

'Thank goodness you were true to your real self. The one I love so dearly.' She kissed him in joy and relief that there was no hatred left in his heart now, only love for her.

Lydia laid out the letters on the small table in her bedroom. She had carefully numbered them on the envelopes as she had received them. They had come regularly once a week until winter storms interrupted the delivery of ironstone from Whitby. Then they had been spasmodic until the new year brought the first signs of spring.

Her flow of letters to David in Whitby had followed the same course. She expressed her feelings for him in terms which, though vague, were calculated to engender hope in the recipient. And they'd had the effect she desired. Interpreting them in his own way he was pleased with their tone and pandered to her constant requests for the latest news of Whitby.

Now, as she fingered the envelopes, she dwelt on visions of a time when she would achieve her fondest desire and wreak revenge on her uncle. But what she needed first was a ship and for that she would need financial backing. Maybe that would come from the names she had noted in David's letters, people who had been friendly with her father about whom she had elicited information. She knew who was doing well, who might have cash to spare, who might be interested in investing in a new enterprise. And Lydia had noted that a fast-growing town beside the Tees, built on the back of the iron trade, offered other possibilities for trading which in turn could give her the chance to outwit and ruin her uncle. But she needed something more than speculation to attract investors to her, she needed to be able to offer them something concrete, something from which they could anticipate a return. But what?

When the answer came three days later it almost caught her unawares.

Luke arrived home early in a state of agitation.

'What's wrong?' she asked.

'I'm summoned to Mr Bolckow's this evening.'

'Mr Bolckow's?' Lydia gasped. 'Whatever for?'

Her brother shrugged his shoulders. 'I don't know. No reason was given, I was just told to be there at six.'

'But you don't work for him.'

'No, but indirectly I am of importance in seeing that the supplies from Whitby are dealt with efficiently. And that's what worries me. I know Mr Bolckow would like to see another ship engaged in the trade. That suggestion has been put to Mr Martin but I've received word, via the ship that arrived this morning, that Mr Martin is seriously ill and therefore nothing can be done about another vessel at the moment. I'm wondering if Mr Bolckow has heard this.' He paused, frowning, then as he realised the time said with a touch of irritation, 'Lydia, I can't stand here gossiping. I must get ready.'

He left her pondering on what he had said. Another ship? Could she do something about that? If so, it would be her opportunity to re-enter the old family trade. Her mind spun with endless possibilities. By the time Luke reappeared her thoughts had calmed with the recollection of David's letters. Could she capitalise on this knowledge? The glimmer of a plan began to form in her mind.

'Luke, you do look smart, you'll impress Mr Bolckow no end,' she said when he came into the room.

'I've got to. We don't want to lose the ironstone trade.'

'You won't,' she said with conviction.

'Don't be too sure,' he said with a half laugh.

'But I am.' Lydia's voice filled with excitement as she went on, 'If Mr Bolckow is worried about another ship then tell him we'll get one.'

'Us?' Luke was astonished at her unexpected suggestion.

'Yes, why not?'

'We haven't the capital.'

'We'll get it.'

'How? Nobody would back us when we were in Whitby.'

'Because we had nothing definite to offer them. People were suspicious. They thought their money might go the way Father's did. But now we have something to offer: definite shipments of ironstone from Whitby. A ready market. It's an investment that can't lose. Mr Bolckow needs all the stone he can get. We can add to that supplied by Mr Martin.'

Luke appeared doubtful but Lydia knew he was impressed by her suggestion.

'And, don't you see, if we are able to do this, we will have the means of expanding further, taking us into an area in which we can directly challenge Uncle Nathan!'

Luke stiffened. 'You still harbour the idea of revenge? I thought that living here in Middlesbrough, among new friends, you had forgotten.'

'No! Never!' Her eyes widened. 'Don't tell me you have?'

His lips tightened. 'Well, no, but I don't want to jeopardise my future here.'

'You'd be risking nothing. You'd keep this job. I'd see to the business side of our new venture.'

'You?'

'Why not? I knew as much about Father's business as you did. He encouraged us both to take an interest in it. Hoped we would run it together after he died. Well, that was not to be but here is an opportunity to get back into trading and recreate his dream. You'd be here to help me, Luke. We must try it, for his sake.'

'This needs some careful thinking about,' replied her

221

brother, trying to inject caution into her enthusiasm. He held up his hand to stifle the words of persuasion. 'I haven't said I'm against it, and I would like to see Uncle Nathan pay in some way, but we can't be certain that he caused Father's death.'

'As near as can be,' rapped Lydia.

'But revenge can ruin lives.'

'Or bring satisfaction.'

Luke shrugged his shoulders. 'I must be off, I don't want to be late for this meeting. We'll talk about it again.' He started for the door.

'Luke.' The sharpness in her voice stopped him. 'Don't miss a golden opportunity. If it's a question of a ship, tell Mr Bolckow I'll see that he gets one. You needn't say that you will be directly involved. It wouldn't do for him to think you are trying to steal Mr Martin's trade. I will merely be supplementing it.'

Her words were uppermost in his mind as he walked to the house on the corner of Cleveland Street and Lower Gosforth Street. Lydia was a determined young woman when she got the bit between her teeth. But there were possibilities in what she suggested. And with this scheme they would return to the trade they knew. Maybe if she got involved in this venture her desire for revenge would ease, something he devoutly wished would happen. They had a new life here in Middlesbrough, with new chances to succeed. And the meeting with Mr Bolckow could be one of them.

Luke had passed this house several times but had taken little notice of it. Now, summoned there, he observed it with different eyes and interest.

He knew it served as the home of both Mr Bolckow and Mr Vaughan as well as being used for their offices. For those reasons it was large. It stood three stories high, each of the upper floors having six sash windows. Stone columns supported the lintel above the centrally placed door which was painted a rich dark green, showing off the highly polished brass knocker.

As Luke waited to be admitted he wondered why he had been summoned here. He had got the ironstone deliveries running smoothly. There had been no more disruptions and the ships were turned round quickly. The only interruptions had been due to winter storms which had held up some of the sailings. He knew, through Mr Langton, that these delays had been of concern to Mr Bolckow for the constant flow of ore was essential to the continuous production of pig iron at the Witton works to keep the rolling mill at Middlesbrough busy enough to meet demand. But there was nothing he could do about the weather, that was in God's hands.

The small fox's head on the right-hand doorpost he judged to be the bell-pull. That he was right was proved a few moments later when the door was opened by a butler.

Luke was determined not to show any nervousness at being called here by a man people held in awe. 'Mr Middleton to see Mr Bolckow.'

The expression on the butler's face became a shade more respectful. 'Please step inside, sir. You are expected.'

Luke found himself in a lofty hall, the sheer scale of which he had never before experienced. He had lived in a fine house in Whitby, but nothing like this. There was money to spare here and it confirmed everything he had heard about Mr Bolckow being an astute businessman.

'Can I take your coat and hat, sir?' Luke was startled out of his reverie. Once the butler had disposed of the garments in a small cloakroom, he said, 'Please follow me, sir.' He led the way across the hall to a door at the far right-hand corner. He knocked, paused, then opened it. 'Mr Middleton, sir,' he announced, and stood to one side to allow Luke to enter the room.

'Ah, Luke.' Mr Bolckow rose from his chair and came forward with hand extended. He smiled but his eyes were

223

openly appraising his visitor. 'You don't mind me calling you Luke?'

'No, sir,' he replied, awed nevertheless at being in the presence of the man who controlled the iron trade on the Tees.

Since coming to Middlesbrough Luke had learned that Mr Bolckow had made his money from speculative dealings in the corn trade while living in Newcastle, having gone to live there at the invitation of a friend in 1827. He had met Mr Vaughan when the two men were courting sisters. Mr Bolckow was looking for a new investment, and Mr Vaughan, who was at the time a manager of an ironworks at Walker, persuaded him to invest in the iron industry. The two men subsequently became partners and in looking for a suitable site for their enterprise had become friendly with Joseph Pease, a partner in the Owners of the Middlesbrough Estate.

Though Middlesbrough was then a settlement of only a few houses, Mr Pease had seen the potential of its situation on the River Tees. He encouraged Bolckow and Vaughan to move there by offering them cheap land. The two men jumped at the chance to achieve their ambition and in 1841 their rolling mill commenced operations. The blast furnaces at Witton followed and continued success seemed assured. But a crisis in the supply of ironstone was now threatening to disrupt their venture. Luke knew this was the likely reason for his being invited here, along with Mr Vaughan and James Langton.

'You have already met Mr Vaughan, I believe,' Mr Bolckow continued. 'He has told me about the way you handled the tricky situation with the Whitby men. Very commendable, and we are highly appreciative of the way you have kept the ironstone flowing ever since. And, of course, you know Mr Langton.'

Both men gave Luke a pleasant 'Good evening' and he responded.

'Sit down, my boy.' Mr Bolckow indicated a vacant

chair, one of four which had been drawn up around a small table on which stood a decanter of wine and four glasses, only one of which was empty. 'A glass of Madeira?'

'Thank you, sir,' replied Luke, aware that the other two men had their eye on him, though in the friendliest of ways.

Mr Bolckow poured the wine and handed the glass to Luke. 'No doubt you are wondering what this is all about?' he said as he resumed his chair. 'Well, I'll come straight to the point. We are gravely concerned about our ability to keep sufficient iron coming through to the rolling mills. As you know, that depends on the supplies near our blast furnaces being supplemented from the mines of North Yorkshire. The shipments from Whitby have been adequate until recently. You solved part of our problem there but we do need to increase our capacity. I believe it was mentioned to you, and that you were going to communicate with Mr Martin?'

'Yes, sir, that is correct.'

'Well, we are in need of his answer. If he can't do anything, let him say so and we'll have to look to another supplier to supplement his deliveries.'

'Sir, there has been a shortage of available ships in Whitby. I know that was of grave concern to Mr Martin. He wanted to do all he could to help you. I know he has been trying throughout the winter but I am sorry to say, sir, he has been unsuccessful. And just today I have had further word from him which is a grave setback.'

He had the undivided attention of the other three.

'And what might that be?' Mr Bolckow's expression was serious.

'Mr Martin has been ill these last three weeks. The news is not good. His condition is serious. As a result he is unable to give his full attention to solving your problem.'

The three men exchanged glances of concern.

Mr Bolckow frowned. 'This is indeed bad news. I am sorry that Mr Martin is ill and hope his recovery will be

225

soon and permanent. Please communicate these sentiments to him.'

'I will, sir, and I know he will appreciate your kindness.'

'Is there no one else who can take over the role of negotiating for another ship?' asked Mr Langton.

'No, sir. No one else in the Martin family is engaged in the business and his manager would not have the necessary connections to negotiate outside Whitby, which I know is what Mr Martin intended to do.'

'Then we are going to have to find someone else who can guarantee another ship,' put in Mr Vaughan. 'The existing supplies through Mr Martin's firm will continue, I suppose?'

Luke nodded. 'Certainly, sir. Mr Martin's manager is quite capable of arranging that.'

'Luke, you know the merchants in Whitby, how do you see the situation?' asked Mr Langton.

'The word is that there is a shortage of ships in the port for this sort of work. I believe that has come about because of increased shipments to the Tyne. So the situation is difficult.'

'Could we bribe one away from that trade?'

'I doubt it, sir. I've had word from two of the captains that there are rumours persisting in Whitby that your venture into the iron industry is failing.'

Mr Bolckow's face darkened. 'Rubbish! Who starts these rumours?'

'Hold on, Henry. You must admit things are a bit precarious at Witton because the supply of ironstone in its vicinity did not come up to expectations. Such facts do get out,' pointed out Mr Vaughan.

'And if I may say so, sir,' said Mr Langton, 'they are blown up out of all proportion and so affect traders' outlook. If things sound uncertain they become wary.'

'So what's the answer?' asked Mr Bolckow.

'Find a ship elsewhere, sir.'

'How do we do that? Can *you* do it?'

226

'Maybe yes, maybe no,' replied Luke.

'What sort of an answer is that?' snapped Mr Bolckow.

'Well, sir, I could try but the real negotiator would be my sister.'

Mr Bolckow stiffened. His swift glance at Mr Vaughan was not lost on Luke. He knew which word had instantly sprung to Mr Bolckow's mind. Female? A female dabbling in a man's world?

'Surely not?' he said.

'Let's hear him out,' returned Mr Vaughan, intrigued by this unexpected development.

'Very well, young man. Explain.'

Luke went on to tell them of Lydia's background and the experience she had gained from her father's business. He also gave brief details of the collapse of his father's business and the reason they had come to Middlesbrough. 'So you see, sir, she has experience, she knows people in the trade, and with her feminine charm would be much more persuasive than I.'

'And it sounds as though she knows the predicament we are in?'

'Yes, sir. I told her the latest news about Mr Martin and she realised it could be a blow to your enterprise. She is anxious to be back into trading and suggested that she might help.'

'Well, I must say, it's unusual to receive an offer like this. But we should not spurn any attempt to relieve our desperate need for more ironstone.' Mr Bolckow paused momentarily. The others sensed that he was making a decision and awaited his words. 'Can you bring your sister here tomorrow evening?'

'Yes, sir.'

'Very well. We'll all meet here at six.' He glanced at Vaughan and Langton and received their nods of agreement. 'James, why not bring Sarah? Mrs Vaughan and Mrs Bolckow will enjoy entertaining her while we discuss business with Miss Middleton. Besides Sarah's company throughout dinner will make the occasion less formidable for Luke's sister.'

His invitation left everyone with the hope that the next evening would be profitable as well as enjoyable.

Chapter Twelve

When Luke reached the house in West Street he found that Mrs Turnbull had gone to bed but Lydia, anxious to know the outcome of his visit, was awaiting his arrival.

'I wouldn't have slept, wanting to know what happened,' she explained when he expressed his surprise that she had not retired.

'It was a pleasant evening,' he declared, shrugging himself slowly out of his coat.

'And?' she replied irritably.

'Give me time to sit down.' He kept up his teasing. 'It was an enjoyable walk . . .'

'Luke! Tell me!'

'Mr Vaughan sends his regards . . .'

She stamped her foot. 'Stop it.'

'So does Mr Langton . . .'

Her mouth tightened with exasperation and her eyes flared with annoyance. Luke knew it was time to stop teasing.

'You are invited to meet Mr Bolckow tomorrow evening.'

There was a split second when the announcement didn't seem to have registered. Then the full meaning of Luke's statement struck home. Her eyes widened. She flung her arms around his neck. 'You did it? You told them?'

'Yes.'

'And they want to see me?' She needed his original statement verifying to prove she wasn't dreaming.

'That's what I said.'

'Oh, Luke, you're wonderful!' She gave him an extra hug, then pushed him into a chair. 'Now tell me all about it?'

He explained what had gone on and gave her the views of the three men. 'And I told them that, apart from your business knowledge, your feminine charm would be an asset, but I think Mr Bolckow wants to judge that for himself.'

'What about Mr Vaughan and Mr Langton?'

'Well, Mr Langton knows and likes you, so that will be in your favour, but of course he doesn't know how much influence you can bring to bear in getting another ship. Mr Vaughan is just as much at a loss about you as Mr Bolckow and those two are very close so you will have to impress them both.'

'I will!'

When Lydia came down the following evening she was arrayed in her best dress, pale grey silk with a motif of roses, the skirt flared from the waist. The wide neckline plunged from the shoulders to reveal a jet necklace. The sleeves puffed from the shoulders and came tight to her wrists. Her hair was held by a broad red ribbon matching the rose print. She carried a pale grey woollen shawl ready to drape around her shoulders against the chill air.

'You'll certainly catch their attention,' said Luke with undisguised admiration.

Mrs Turnbull was equally fulsome with her praise and her mind swept back to her own young days before she came to Middlesbrough. Though Lydia and Luke had not disclosed the reason for their visit to Mr Bolckow's, Mrs Turnbull knew it must be something special, for people from this area of town never usually got to dine with the owners of the ironworks.

Even though she knew Sarah would be present, Lydia

had butterflies in her stomach as she and Luke waited at the door of Mr Bolckow's residence. From her brother's description of his visit the previous evening she was prepared for the size and elegance of the entrance hall. The furniture was of the very best, not too much, not too little, each piece able to stand on its own merits. It was the same when they entered the drawing room. Lydia assessed it at a glance. That was all the time she was able to spare for her entrance had brought Mr Bolckow and Mr Vaughan to their feet. Mr Bolckow, smiling broadly, came forward to welcome her.

'Miss Middleton, I am pleased to see you. Your brother told me a lot about you yesterday evening and I have so looked forward to meeting you.'

'It is my pleasure too,' replied Lydia softly, her eyes appraising the man who took her proffered hand and bowed as he did so.

'Come, meet the others.' Mr Bolckow led her further into the room. 'Mrs Bolckow, my wife, and her sister, Mrs Vaughan.'

Lydia counteracted the assessment these ladies were making of her with expressions of delight at meeting them, exuding a charm she knew would win their acceptance. Something that was essential if she was to win the men over to her ideas.

A moment or two later, when she was introduced to Mr Vaughan, she turned her charm to flattery with a touch of flirtation. She knew immediately that she had the two gentlemen under her spell.

She was under no illusion that this alone would win their support. Luke had described them as hard-headed business-men. He had said they were kind, charming, able to share a joke. But when it came to considering investment ventures, they would need to be convinced of any scheme's merits.

Wine was poured and handed round. The sisters engaged Luke with queries about Whitby while their husbands were extolling the charm of the neighbouring countryside, conversations which established contact and enabled initial assessments to be made.

Five minutes later Sarah and her father arrived and merged easily with the company. Lydia managed a brief word with her friend before Mrs Bolckow whisked Sarah away to meet Mrs Vaughan. In that brief exchange Lydia gleaned that Sarah knew the reason for this invitation and hoped that it would lead to a return to the life Lydia had once known.

The dinner passed off with the most pleasing rapport between everyone. The sisters got on well with Sarah and Lydia, and enjoyed the younger company. Mr Bolckow was pleased to have his wife's approval of Lydia. It would make things easier, for he too had fallen under the spell of the pretty young woman.

He was pleased that he had decided not to meet Lydia in a purely business atmosphere. Relaxing around a dinner table, sharing a meal, had given him a chance to study at his leisure the young lady who had claimed she could solve his problem of bringing more ore to the Tees.

As they left the dining room Mr Bolckow managed to have a quiet word with Mr Vaughan while Lydia was engaged in conversation with his wife and the others had their attention on Sarah. 'Well, John, what do you think?'

'If her business sense is as pronounced as her charm then she'll not fail us.'

'My sentiments too. Well, we'll soon find out.' He crossed the hall to Lydia. 'Miss Middleton, this has been a most pleasant and interesting evening so far, now we come to the more serious aspect of it. If you'll come to my study, we'll join the gentlemen.' He inclined his head in the direction of the other three who were parting from Sarah and turned briefly to his wife. 'We'll be with you as soon as we can.'

She gave him a smile, and Lydia saw that it carried not only love but admiration.

'Very well, dear.' She turned away to join her sister who

had taken charge of Sarah and was about to enter the drawing room.

When Lydia walked into the panelled study she found five chairs had been placed around a low circular table on which stood an assortment of glasses, decanters of whisky, brandy and wine, and small dishes of sweetmeats.

Mr Bolckow escorted her to a chair and, as the others settled down, poured them the drink of their choice.

Lydia began to feel a fluttering in her stomach. With the serious business of the evening looming, she found she had tensed and apprehension began to gnaw at her. She faced four men and, though she expected Luke to back her ideas, she still had to convince him, and even more so the others, that they would work, and that she was capable of carrying them out.

She took a grip on herself. She must show no doubt, no weakness, she must sound convincingly at home in a man's world.

'Well, Miss Middleton, I expect you know our position from your brother or you wouldn't be here. You apparently suggested that you might be able to help us.'

'Mr Bolckow, the word is not might but can. I CAN help you.'

The words were out almost before she knew it, but her voice was firm and she drew strength from that.

Mr Bolckow raised his eyebrows. Lydia was aware of him exchanging a quick glance with his partner, but it was so quick she was not able to interpret it.

'Well, young lady, I must say you are brimming over with confidence, but can you bring that confidence to fruition to the benefit of us all? Let us hear what you have to say.'

Lydia sat upright, her eyes fixed firmly on Mr Bolckow at first, but as she spoke she let them take in everyone with a glance that made each listener in turn feel he was the really important one.

'Well, gentlemen, let me first sum up the situation so

233

that there is no misunderstanding on either side. You want Mr Martin's shipments of ironstone supplemented so that your furnaces at Witton can supply the required amount of pig iron to meet the orders you already have and attract more.'

'Exactly,' admitted Mr Bolckow.

'Agreed,' said Mr Vaughan.

Mr Langton nodded.

She continued. 'Mr Martin has been unable to fulfil your request for two reasons. The poor man is ill, and there is a shortage of suitable ships in Whitby.' She gave a brief pause to emphasise what she was about to say next. 'And you do not know where to look for one.'

'That's not strictly true, young lady,' Mr Bolckow's voice was curt. He did not like his business acumen being questioned. 'We are not devoid of contacts who could tell us where to look. Last night your brother was invited to bring us up to date regarding Mr Martin's dealings. His information led us to agree to look elsewhere for another ship. It was then that he mentioned what you had said. We were surprised to say the least, but he sang your praises as a determined young woman who knows what she wants and can get it because she has contacts. So we agreed to listen to you before pursuing other avenues.'

Lydia groaned inwardly. She hoped Luke hadn't piled on his praise too thickly and that, whatever he had said, she could live up to it. She met his glance and received an encouraging nod.

'Please go on,' prompted Mr Bolckow.

'You do not mind where this ship comes from?' She put what sounded to be a silly question but she needed a moment to re-order her thoughts after Mr Bolckow's interruption.

'A ship is a ship, Miss Middleton. It carries goods and that's all that matters,' Mr Vaughan pointed out.

'As long as it can navigate the Tees and tie up at our jetty,' Mr Langton added practically.

'Of course.' Lydia inclined her head in acknowledgement of these facts. 'To buy a ship takes money.'

'Ah,' said Mr Vaughan, 'and you can't supply it?'

'I never said I could, sir. I merely stated that I could get you a ship.'

Mr Bolckow eyed her suspiciously. 'Are you expecting Mr Vaughan and me to finance the enterprise?'

'No,' Lydia was quick to reply, hoping her sharpness would eliminate any doubts the men might have. 'I did not suppose you would but I was hoping you might take some shares in the ship.'

'Young lady,' Mr Bolckow's countenance was stern, 'you should not surmise any such thing in business. Neither I nor Mr Vaughan is interested in shipping as an investment. We are industrialists, iron our principal interest. The trade has a great future and our enterprise on the Tees must succeed. It will if we can increase our supply of ironstone. That is the only reason we are interested in ships.'

Lydia cast a quick glance round the others to see if she had any support. Mr Vaughan showed agreement with his partner. Luke wore a worried frown. Mr Langton was impassive.

She moistened her lips and recovered her poise. 'Sir, it is precisely because you need the ironstone that you should invest in something that would guarantee your means of supply. I am not suggesting that you and Mr Vaughan finance the whole enterprise on your own – I intend to seek out other investors as well. If it was known that you and your partner had taken shares in a ship, I am certain I could persuade others to do so as well. With your names involved I am sure there would be no problem.'

Mr Bolckow was silent. He stared at his hands, face wreathed in thought, and shook his head slowly.

Lydia's heart sank. Further words of persuasion sprang to her lips but she did not express them. She saw concentration in Mr Bolckow's eyes and knew better than to break it.

He looked up slowly and met her gaze. He saw hope

there. He realised how much success meant to her. He sympathised, recalling similar moments in his own career, then pulled himself up sharp. He chastised himself, Silly old fool, falling for a pretty face. But am I? he questioned himself. Didn't she make sense?

He ran his hand across his forehead and said, 'Miss Middleton, if – and I must stress *if* – we agree and you succeed in interesting other people, where will you find a ship? Haven't we been already told there are none available in Whitby?'

'There are other ports, Mr Bolckow. My father had several connections with shipbuilders in Hull and Newcastle.'

Mr Bolckow made no comment but glanced at his partner, seeking his opinion.

Mr Vaughan did not give it immediately. Instead he asked, 'Miss Middleton, the question I am about to ask implies no disrespect to you. I admire your acumen and vision, but do you think people will be prepared to deal with a woman? Won't they have doubts about your being able to cope in a man's world?'

For a moment Lydia bristled but quickly realising that he meant no affront to her capabilities, replied in a steady voice, 'Mr Vaughan, I am capable of putting my proposals as clearly as any man.'

'I am sure you are, but will people listen to them?'

'If they don't then they are not worth dealing with, poor narrow-sighted fools. It will be their loss. I am sure that this venture, if you and Mr Bolckow back it, will not fail. And let me remind you that I will have the counsel of my very capable brother readily available at all times.'

'Would he be deeply involved in this?' asked Mr Langton. 'None of us has any direct authority over him but I know Mr Bolckow and Mr Vaughan will be very much in agreement when I say I would not like to see him leave the job he is handling so successfully. And his authority will be needed all the more if there are further deliveries to oversee.'

'Mr Langton, I would not wish to relinquish my present

236

job. I see it as vital to the smooth running of Mr Bolckow's and Mr Vaughan's ironworks. Another ship will mean I will need more men and overseeing them will be more demanding, but if my sister needs advice I will give it to the best of my ability.'

'Behind those words I detect a great faith in her capabilities,' commented Mr Vaughan.

'Indeed, sir, I have. And I know my father saw her as a prospective equal partner in his business whenever we took it over. Alas, that was not to be. But the tragedy of his death and the loss of his concern has not diminished Lydia's enthusiasm, nor the ability she will bring to the venture she is proposing.'

'Ably put, young man, but it is only natural that you should sing her praises,' said Mr Bolckow. There was a tone of dismissal in his voice that indicated he was not yet fully convinced.

'Sir, I have seen more of Miss Middleton than either you or Mr Vaughan since she became friendly with my daughter,' said Mr Langton. 'I have seen the enthusiasm and thoroughness she brings to everything she does, weighing up possibilities and situations very carefully before venturing to the next stage.'

Luke saw that the two men were puzzled. 'May I explain?' he put in. 'Mr Langton is referring chiefly to the piano lessons she is currently giving after he kindly gave her the opportunity.'

Mr Langton took up the explanation, readily expounding Lydia's virtues.

Mr Bolckow glanced at Mr Vaughan and received a look of agreement to his unspoken question.

'Young lady,' he said, 'you have sat quietly through these praises from Mr Langton and your brother, showing admirable modesty. Your replies to our questions have impressed us.' He paused momentarily as if finally weighing up his thoughts. 'Very well, we'll ask you to go ahead with your proposals.'

237

A broad smile of satisfaction appeared on Lydia's face. Her eyes carried a new brightness, behind it triumph and satisfaction at her success. 'Thank you, Mr Bolckow. You will not regret it.'

'I hope not. When do you propose to start?'

'Right here and now,' she replied, catching them all unawares with this unexpected statement. 'By persuading you to take shares in the ship.'

'One that doesn't yet exist?' Mr Bolckow threw up his arms in horror. He had never dealt with anything so risky before. There had always been something tangible in which to make an investment but here there was nothing, a ship which existed only in the mind of this slip of a lass.

'Ah, but it does, sir. Somewhere there is a ship just right for us. I can find it but cannot obtain it without financial backing.'

Mr Bolckow smiled to himself. He liked the confidence of this young woman. 'Very well, I'll take an eighth share in whatever ship you find.'

'Thank you. That is a good start.'

'Then you'd better put me down for the same,' put in Mr Vaughan.

'Thank you. That makes it a very good start.'

'I cannot match those two proposals,' said Mr Langton, 'but I'll certainly take a sixteenth.'

'Thank you, Mr Langton. That makes it an excellent start.' She reached for her glass and raised it. 'Gentlemen, my thanks to you. And may I propose a toast to the new company – Tees Shipping.'

As they raised their glasses, Mr Bolckow said, 'A name already? That shows confidence. To your success and our mutual benefit.'

As they walked back to West Street, Lydia felt the warm glow of satisfaction that comes with the attainment of a desire. Her smile was wide as she held up three pieces of paper, memoranda of the shares the three investors had taken in the ship.

'Those, Luke, are our passport back to what should rightfully be ours.'

She had found a way back into her father's world. With this initial ship, which she was confident of finding, she could resurrect the firm of Tristram Middleton, albeit under a different name and in a different location. She would challenge those people in Whitby who had shown no trust in either her or Luke after their father had died, and she would build herself a position from which to destroy her uncle. Then her father could rest easier in his grave.

'We've done it, Luke, we've done it!' She gripped his hand and he felt her sense of triumph. 'Now we have the chance to do what Father hoped we would do, and more. We'll have power!'

Her tone and choice of words disturbed him. He frowned.

'Don't look so worried, Luke. You should be pleased. This is a great day. One we never expected to see so soon after coming to Middlesbrough.'

'You certainly did well,' he agreed, but in the gaze he turned upon her there was concern. 'But how far do you want to go?'

'All the way. To the ultimate,' she replied, eyes sparkling with a vision of the future.

'And the ultimate is?'

'Uncle Nathan's downfall!'

'Lydia, don't get carried away with this idea. Don't use other people to attain it. It could destroy you and hurt others. I don't want to see my dear sister consumed by a burning passion for revenge.'

'I won't, Luke, really I won't. But I want your support.'

'You shall have it,' he promised. 'But remember, as much as I want to see Uncle Nathan pay if he was responsible for Father's death, we still need definite proof and that will be hard to find.'

239

'Proof? We don't need proof. We *know* it. We *feel* it. That's good enough for me.'

Lydia began to lay her plans and by the following morning had a scheme to raise the remaining capital. She seized on a chance offered innocently by her brother.

'I'll be sending Sean to Whitby after the weekend to appraise the situation regarding the Grosmont ore. He'll be able to deliver your letter to David personally. That is, if you still want to correspond with him?'

'Of course I do. I get all sorts of valuable information from him about trading conditions in Whitby.' The revelation was out before she realised it.

'You what?' Luke was astounded.

'Oh, just the usual gossip from around the port.'

But her brother had read the real implications. 'You've been gathering information to use once you had reached a position in which you could exploit it. You've had something like this in mind ever since we left Whitby, Lydia, you've *used* David.'

'No, I haven't,' she protested. 'I just wanted to keep up with our home town.' Exasperated by her own slip, she changed the subject. 'I'll go with Sean. I'd like to see David, and I can make enquiries about raising the rest of the capital in Whitby.'

'Who'll be likely to help us there after we were refused help when Father died?'

'We have notes of agreement from our three existing investors. They'll help swing things our way.'

'They could,' Luke agreed. 'But there's one other thing. Uncle Nathan will hear about your visit and he'll wonder what is going on after the accusations we made. He won't like you recreating Father's firm in Whitby, even if it is under a different name.'

'We won't operate from Whitby. We'll register the ship in Middlesbrough and our name won't appear on the documentation.'

'I can see it might be possible to do that but he'll hear about you trying to raise money in Whitby.'

'He won't even hear that.'

Luke was puzzled. 'What's going on in that pretty little head of yours?'

Lydia smiled. 'I think Sean could be very useful to us here.'

'Sean?'

'Yes. Why not? He has the Irish gift of persuasion.'

Luke was taken aback by this suggestion but his active mind was fast seeing possibilities in her proposal.

'Supposing he doesn't want to help?'

'Oh, he will. Just leave him to me.'

'Lydia, be sure you make him a genuine offer and give him a proper explanation. Remember, I don't agree with using people for your own ends.'

'I won't, dear brother.' She gave him a reassuring kiss on the cheek.

Lydia arrived early to give her piano lessons at the Langtons' that same afternoon.

Sarah sensed the excitement still gripping her friend when she was shown into the drawing room.

'I'm so pleased everything went well for you last night,' she said.

'Now I've the chance I've dreamed of much sooner than expected,' replied Lydia.

Sarah reached out and grasped her hands. 'I'm delighted that you've got what you want.' Worry clouded her face. 'But it's a man's world, isn't it?'

'Aren't we just as capable?'

Sarah looked doubtful and said without a great deal of conviction, 'I suppose so, if we are given the chance.'

'And this is *my* chance. I'm going to succeed.'

'You're a very determined young woman.'

'And why not?'

Sarah felt herself being caught up in Lydia's enthusiasm.

241

'Yes, why not? So have you a ship in mind, or do you know where you might find one?'

'Not yet. I need to be assured of the capital first.'

'Where are you going to raise that?'

'I made a start last night. Mr Bolckow, Mr Vaughan and your father have all taken shares.'

'Father told me. I'm surprised he did, I've never regarded him as a speculator. Who else will you approach?'

'Whoever might be interested.'

'Try Kevin.'

'Kevin?' Lydia was puzzled by this suggestion, and the tone of her voice betrayed the fact that she believed he would not have money to invest. She knew that Sarah and Kevin were seeing more of each other and for that, of course, must have Mr Langton's approval. But for her friend to suggest that someone who had come to England as a labourer might be a possible investor . . .

'Kevin isn't quite what you imagine,' replied Sarah. 'What I tell you must be kept strictly to yourself. I do not want him to think I betrayed his trust.' She went on to reveal his background. 'So, you see, he may well have money he might be interested in investing.'

Lydia had listened carefully. 'I didn't know any of this. There's nothing I'd like better than to have people like him included in this venture. I'll ask him.'

'No, please don't, I'll do it. Then it won't look as if I've told you anything about his life.'

'Very well,' Lydia agreed. 'And then if he's interested I'll give him more details.'

'I suppose this will mean the end of our piano lessons?' said Sarah. There was no mistaking the regret in her voice.

'Of course not. Obviously there will be other things which will need my attention but I want to keep up the lessons. They help me relax. Besides, I don't want to lose the pleasure of seeing you.'

'That need not happen if you gave them up.'

'I know, but they mean we'll enjoy each other's company frequently, and that I value.'

'So do I. I'll ask Kevin for you, and if there is anything else I can do, please say.'

When Luke left for work the next morning Lydia accompanied him as far as number ten. His knock was answered by Sean who'd expected him, for Luke's timing was impeccable every morning.

'Top o' the morning to you.' No matter what the weather, Sean's greeting, accompanied by a smile, was always the same. The words were out before he realised that Lydia was with her brother. He turned his smile on her and added with an exaggerated bow, 'And top o' the morning to you too, fair lady.'

Lydia, amused by his effusive greeting, responded with a merry laugh.

'Ah, miss, that laughter is music to my ears. It will accompany me for the rest of the day and keep me sane while this brother of yours nags and nags me.'

'Enough of your flattery, you dummy,' admonished Luke with a friendly grin.

Sean raised his eyebrows. 'Flattery, is it?' He assumed a hurt expression. 'And who do you think keeps the ore ships moving?' He turned to Lydia. 'Now, miss, you don't think I'm a dummy, do you?'

'Not at all. You certainly won't act the dummy when my brother tells you he wants you to go to Whitby next week, will you?'

'Sure I won't, miss.'

'Good. And you won't act the dummy when he asks you to escort a young lady on the voyage?'

'Ah, sure now, I will not. It will be my pleasure and will greatly relieve the monotony of the voyage.'

'And would you mind if that young lady were me?'

'Not at all. It would double the pleasure.'

'Then that is settled.'

'Whatever the time of sailing I'll be there, awaiting your fair presence, and you can rest assured that your safety will be my foremost concern.'

'Thank you, kind sir.'

Luke saw more effusive words springing to Sean's lips so intervened quickly. 'An end to this backchat or we'll get no work done today.'

Sean sprang to attention and saluted. 'Sorry, sir. We shall end this delightful conversation now.' He turned to Lydia. 'I look forward to the voyage when we may converse without being interrupted by this clod of a fellow.' He bowed to her. As he straightened up he caught her eye and winked.

In a flash he was after Luke who had started along West Street towards the Market Place. Sean sensed Lydia's eyes on him and his ears registered the light laughter which floated along behind him. He wondered what the voyage might bring.

The following morning when Lydia reached the Langtons' the maid ushered her in quickly out of the rain. She shrugged herself out of her cape and handed it to the maid along with her bonnet and umbrella. When Sarah hurried into the hall to greet her friend, Lydia sensed she had something to tell her.

'I've news,' she cried, taking Lydia's arm and hurrying her into the drawing room. When she had closed the door she could hold back no longer. 'Father and I persuaded Kevin to take a share in your ship.'

Lydia's face broke into a broad smile. She grasped her friend and hugged her. 'That's wonderful!' she cried excitedly. 'I just know this is going to succeed, I feel it in my bones.'

'But there's more.' Sarah's eyes sparkled.

'More?'

'Yes. Kevin said he would have to go to Ireland to see his family and arrange for the transfer of some of his funds.

244

And guess what? He's asked me to accompany him and meet his people.'

'Splendid,' cried Lydia, swept along by her friend's enthusiasm.

'Father approved.'

'When do you go?'

'This coming weekend.'

'Meeting his family ... Does this mean what I think it might mean?'

'Who knows?' laughed Sarah. 'I wouldn't say no.'

As she snuggled closer to Kevin in the coach as it rumbled towards Dublin, Sarah looked back on her visit to Ireland with satisfaction.

Though she had approached the meeting with nervousness and apprehension this was soon swept away by the family's warm and friendly greeting. Throughout their three-day stay she had been thoroughly spoilt. Kevin's mother, having taken to her immediately, was pleased and relieved that her son had found such a charming and modest girl, and one with a practical head on her shoulders. His father fussed around her, delighted that his son had brought a pretty girl to their home. She had felt at ease immediately with his brother and sister who involved her in their own pastimes and pleasures.

'Enjoy yourself?' asked Kevin.

'Never more.'

'And I know my family loved you, but who couldn't?'

'Flatterer.' She smiled.

'We have a hotel in Dublin for the night and sail in the morning. This evening, I want to try to find a girl.'

Sarah was taken aback by this statement but then she saw the twinkle in his eye and knew he had phrased it in such a way as to tease her.

'And why might that be?' she returned, countering his tease with a feigned haughtiness.

Kevin changed to a more serious tone. 'She's Eileen Nolan. Sean's girl.'

245

'I didn't know he had one. I thought he was making eyes at Lydia.'

'Well now, that might just be the case and that's why I want to see Eileen. Sean always had an eye for the girls but Eileen was permanent, if you get my meaning. Sean was always a dreamer and he said he was going to make his fortune and whisk her away to a land of riches. Well, he's made progress since coming to Middlesbrough, but he might just get carried away by Lydia's scheme and forget Eileen.'

'But is it right to interfere?'

'It might be wrong not to do so. People might get hurt if I don't. Eileen's a nice lass. Sean has promised her so much that I should hate to see her let down. He did promise to send for her as soon as he saw what prospects there were in England. Well, he's had time to do that but he's shown no sign of sending for her so far.'

'Maybe he has a reason.'

'Maybe, but if that reason's Lydia, I think he's wrong.'

'She's nice enough,' protested Sarah, quick in defence of her friend.

'I'm not saying she isn't,' returned Kevin quickly. 'I've nothing against her. I like her. It's Sean I'm bothered about. I don't think Lydia is right for him whereas Eileen is another matter.'

Sarah shrugged. 'You know her, I don't. But be careful. Don't play matchmaker.'

'I don't like to see people lose the happiness they once had. And Sean and Eileen are right for each other.'

'Can I come with you to find her?'

'If you wish, but we will not be in the best part of Dublin. It's respectable but on the edge of poverty, not far from the dereliction and destitution of an area called the Liberties.'

Sarah saw what he meant when they made their way through streets lined on either side by identical houses, some shabby with refuse stacked outside, others boarded up. Alongside those were others where an attempt had been made to wrest some decency from the poverty around them. Sarah felt eyes watching them every step of the way. Men lounged on street corners, children in rags raced past them, and from behind curtains at unwashed windows faces peered out. She was thankful when they turned a corner where the houses showed signs of being better cared for, though some of these were beginning to verge on the shabby. At least many of them showed attempts to keep windows and curtains clean.

Kevin glanced at the numbers until he came to the one he was looking for. He rapped hard on the door and then, as they waited, gave Sarah a faint smile.

When the door was opened Sarah saw immediately why Sean had been attracted to this girl. Not only was she pretty but there was a jaunty air about her. She was the sort who would never let life or the knocks it dealt her get her down. Though her dress showed signs of wear she wore it as if it was new and designed to make the best of her figure.

'Kevin!' Her face lit up and her blue eyes danced with pleasure.

'Eileen, it's good to see you.'

'Sean? Is he here in Dublin?' Her voice was filled with eager anticipation.

Kevin shook his head. 'No, I'm sorry, he's not.'

'He's all right?' Eileen's eagerness changed swiftly to concern.

'Yes. May we come in?'

She was flustered by her own seemingly inhospitable behaviour. 'Of course, I'm so sorry. Come in, come in.'

'This is Sarah.' Kevin made the introduction as they stepped inside.

The two young women exchanged polite greetings. Kevin noted that Eileen was appraising Sarah's clothes and by her automatic gesture of smoothing her skirt he knew she felt shabby alongside the visitor.

'Sean? Tell me about him,' she pressed, eager for

247

first-hand news as she indicated for them to sit down. 'His letters say that he is doing well and that he will come for me before long, but he never names a date so I can tie things up here. Not that that would take long. I'd walk out now if he said so.'

'He is doing well for himself, better than he expected when he left Ireland.' Kevin went on to give Eileen an explanation of what had happened to them since they had last seen her, his narrative only faltering when he told her of Seamus's death.

'Then why hasn't Sean come for me or even sent for me?' she asked when Kevin had finished. 'Has he found someone else?'

Kevin hesitated.

'He has!' Eileen's voice soared with fury at the thought that she might have lost Sean.

'There isn't and there is,' replied Kevin. 'He is very friendly with the sister of the man who gave him employment as his assistant and took him away from labouring. I think Sean believes that he should be friendly with her.'

'Maybe,' said Eileen, 'but friendship can sometimes develop into more. Is she keen on him?' She looked to Sarah for an answer, judging that a woman would recognise this more readily than a man.

'I know she likes him, is smitten by his charm, but she has a young man in Whitby where she came from.'

'He's not in Middlesbrough, Sean is.' Eileen's mind had been racing, trying to find ways of counteracting Sean's interest in this other girl. She immediately voiced the best of these ideas. 'I think I'd better come to Middlesbrough. Can I travel with you?'

Both Kevin and Sarah were surprised by the swiftness of this decision.

'Of course,' he replied, 'but haven't you things to see to here?'

'They don't matter. All I need are a few personal belongings. I could pack them now.'

248

'Then come with us to our hotel. We'll all be together to sail in the morning,' suggested Sarah.

'But I couldn't afford . . .'

'I'm sure you could fix it, Kevin.'

'You get your things and come with us,' he said kindly. 'I'll take care of the expense.'

'But I couldn't let you . . .'

Sarah, realising that Eileen knew nothing of his background, said, 'Kevin, you'd better explain.'

He nodded and went on to do so.

Eileen listened with interest and, when he had finished, said, 'I always thought there was something different about you, Kevin Harper, but I couldn't put my finger on it. You're a lovely man, so you are, particularly for what you did for Seamus. Take care of him, miss.'

'Sarah, please.'

Eileen saw friendship in Sarah's eyes and was pleased to have that comfort as she set sail for England and her reunion with Sean.

Chapter Thirteen

'You mind and look after my sister, Sean,' Luke ordered as they stood at the foot of the gangway of the *Nina*, bound for Whitby. In five minutes the ropes would be cast off and the ship would be free of the jetty. Backs would bend to oars as she was towed into midstream and taken downriver until her sails could catch the breeze in safety.

'Sure now, she'll come to no harm with me,' replied Sean. He glanced at Lydia. 'These ore ships offer no comfort for passengers but the captain has made his cabin, such as it is, available to you.'

'Thanks, Sean, but more than likely we'll spend the time on deck this fine day.'

'Be sure you keep well wrapped up,' advised Luke. 'See she does, Sean.'

'Brother, stop fretting,' said Lydia, an edge to her voice which showed she was irritated by the fuss. She was thankful that, almost at the same moment, a cry of 'All aboard!' put a stop to any more talk. She kissed Luke quickly and hurried up the gangway.

Sean exchanged a handshake with Luke. 'I'll confirm that the Goathland mines are still able to meet our needs.'

'Good, and clarify the situation with Mr Martin. Give him my best regards and my hope that his prolonged illness has turned the corner.'

'I will,' Sean took long strides up the gangway.

'Best of luck,' Luke called after them.

There was an element of backchat in their conversation and observations as the ship proceeded downriver.

With the sea in sight, Sean said tentatively, 'Are you a good sailor?'

'Yes. Occasionally, if my father was going to London on his ship, Luke and I would go too. We loved it.'

Sean looked surprised. 'Your father's ship?' he queried as if he had not heard her correctly.

'Yes, he was a merchant in Whitby. You did not know?'

'No.' Sean did not want to disclose the snippets of information he had picked up on his previous visit to Whitby. He hoped his denial would lead Lydia into revealing more.

'Luke has never said anything about our background?'

'No. I thought he had come here as an employee of Mr Martin.'

'So he did. Father had him gaining experience in all manner of trading so that his knowledge would be wide when he and I took over the business, but sadly with Father's death that was not to be. There were debts.'

'I'm sorry about that.' Sean expressed his commiserations then added with a touch of doubt, '*You* were going to be actively engaged in the business?'

'Yes. Why not? I was close to my father. I'd seen how he organised everything, met the people he dealt with. I knew what had to be done. So, as I say, why not?'

Sean shrugged his shoulders. He had no argument against what she had said except that it was a man's world, but he certainly wasn't going to voice that opinion after sensing the determination of this interesting and attractive young woman. He agreed, 'Why not? Though I've never thought of a charming female running or helping to run a business.'

'Well, you see one here who is going to prove it can be done.'

Sean saw the fire of ambition in her eyes. He also read desire and resolve.

251

'You want the old life back?'

'Oh, yes, and I'll get it.'

There was a ruthlessness in her tone that was foreign to Sean's easygoing nature. It made him think. She had dreams of the future, just as he had. But had he been wrong in his approach? Should he have had the same attitude as her?

'Do you want to help me?'

The question, torn away by the wind as the ship met the first waves, caught him by surprise. Even so it echoed the thoughts he had just been entertaining.

'What do you mean?'

'Let's go to the cabin for a few minutes, then I won't have to compete with the sound of the wind in the rigging.'

Sean nodded and escorted her below deck. The cabin was small, containing two chairs and a table on which there were some charts. The bunk was neatly made with bedclothes ready for the captain's use whenever longer voyages were incurred.

Sean looked at Lydia questioningly after he had closed the door.

'My visit to Whitby is not just for pleasure,' she announced.

'I thought you must be going to see the friend to whom you write and to whom I delivered a letter on my first visit.'

'David.'

'Yes.' Sean hesitated a brief moment and then put the question. 'You had an understanding with him before you left Whitby?'

Lydia tensed. What right had he to ask such a probing question? Sharp words sprang to her lips but she suppressed them. She had need of him and should not alienate him. Rebuke him and all cooperation could be lost.

'We'd known each other all our lives. People took it for granted that we would marry,' she answered quietly.

'And will you?'

Lydia paused before answering, 'I'm not sure.' She gave a wistful shake of the head as she remembered her last days in Whitby. 'Things were confused when we left. David did not come up to my expectations then.'

'You don't see him in the same light nowadays?'

'His attitude hurt me, but you can't wipe out a lifetime's feelings.'

'But other things happen. You meet other people.' He stepped towards her. His eyes held hers. A tension, sparked by attraction, rose between them. He reached out to rest his hands on her shoulders. She did not pull away. She felt pleasure in the contact. Since their first meeting she had grown used to his company, enjoyed his Irish sense of humour and revelled in the attention he gave her. There were times when she had wondered if her feelings ran deeper. But always thoughts of David, and the wish that he had defied his father, intervened. But now they did not. She was lost in a welter of emotions as Sean drew her close and his lips met hers gently. His hands moved slowly to her waist and held her tight. Her fingers slid round his neck, caressing it sensuously, and her lips moved in a passionate response.

These moments sealed Lydia's conviction that Sean would meet the request she was about to make.

As their lips parted, Sean felt a sudden pang of guilt. Eileen! She thrust herself into his thoughts, but he tried to ignore the memories as Lydia brushed his lips temptingly again. Then, as he was about to take her to him, she spun out of his arms with a teasing, coy look that brought longing to his eyes. He reached out for her.

'No, Sean, we have serious things to discuss.'

He recognised that this was no prohibition of a future embrace but whatever she had in mind had to come first. To step over the present boundary could sour everything between them.

'Serious?'

'Yes. I have business to attend to in Whitby but I need your help.'

'My help?'

'Yes. Will you give it?'

'Anything for you.'

Lydia smiled gratefully. 'Thanks, Sean. You'll not regret it. You'll be suitably rewarded, especially if I achieve what I want. No, not if but when.'

She sat down and he did likewise. His curiosity was roused by her reference to the future and what it might mean.

'What I have to tell you must be kept strictly confidential. I want you to promise me that it will?' She cocked an eyebrow at him, turning the statement into a question.

'It will go no further than this cabin,' he replied. 'By the Holy Mother of God, my lips will stay sealed.'

She nodded and continued. 'As you know, Mr Bolckow is concerned about the supplies of ore. You know the details so I won't go into them. I met him a few nights ago because I had indicated that I could find another ship to deliver additional supplies. That needs financing. Mr Bolckow, Mr Vaughan and Mr Langton have taken shares but I need more investors.'

'I'm afraid I have no money for that purpose,' put in Sean.

'That's not what I want of you. Because of the loss of my father's ship and the subsequent collapse of his business on his death, my standing and Luke's are not high in Whitby. We could find no one to back us to revive his business.'

'And you are here to try again?'

'Not me, you.' Lydia was very clear about this.

'Me?'

'Yes. I want you to be the person looking for investors in Tees Shipping, a new company which you propose to run from the Tees with the immediate prospect of shipping ironstone but expansion into other trading in mind. You must not mention me or Luke. If you do, the whole enterprise would be suspect.'

Sean was beginning to appreciate the role he would have

254

to adopt. 'I will need briefing about who to approach. I surmise you have that all worked out?'

'Yes. That was one of the purposes of my corresponding with David. I kept in touch with commercial life in Whitby.'

Sean made no comment but suspected that Lydia had had this move planned for some time and had probably worked towards it ever since she'd arrived in Middlesbrough. He was surprised to realise that he found that just a touch alarming, but he dismissed the thought immediately. There was really nothing in what Lydia had said to justify that feeling, and those thoughts were already being supplanted by speculation of his own. Maybe he could use this situation to further his dreams.

'I'm sure you can do this, Sean. Your Irish charm will work wonders.'

His ready smile in response held a promise that he would work his magic in whatever capacity it was needed.

She took three envelopes from her handbag. 'And these will help to persuade those you approach.'

'What are they?'

'They are proof that Mr Bolckow, Mr Vaughan and Mr Langton have taken shares in the ship as yet to be purchased. Their names, especially those of Bolckow and Vaughan with their reputation in the iron industry, should lend weight to your argument that the proposition is a sound one.'

He took the envelopes from her.

'They are precious. Be careful with them,' she warned.

'They will never leave my person. Now, you must tell me as much as you can about the people you want me to see and about the commercial life in Whitby.'

The next hour was spent on this briefing. At the end Lydia made the following stipulations. 'You must not approach David and his father, nor Nathan Middleton and his family.'

'A relation?'

255

'My uncle.'

'I would have thought he would have been the first person on your list.'

'There are personal reasons why I don't wish that. There's no need for you to know what they are. Heed my words, Sean, do not approach those I have mentioned. They will no doubt get wind of you and what you are seeking. If they approach you, you must make some excuse for not entertaining them. That is vital to my scheme.'

'Do your present investors know of this stipulation?'

'No. Only you, Luke and I know. That is how it must stay. If it doesn't there could be serious consequences.' She saw other questions coming to his mind and quickly interposed. 'Ask no more about that side of the business. It is a private matter and there is no reason for it to intrude on the straightforward matters I wish you to deal with.'

'Very good,' Sean readily agreed, for the icy tone which had come into her voice when her uncle was mentioned had not been lost on him. It had raised his curiosity. Maybe he should find out more. And why hadn't David to be approached? This whole affair was growing more intriguing by the minute. His astute brain was already wondering if the embrace of about an hour ago was genuine or had it been employed to trick him into agreeing to help her? Well, he had done so, so he was committed. No matter, he'd play along. And be ready to turn any opportunities to his own advantage.

'Good.' Lydia still had not relaxed. Concerned that every aspect of her plan must be dealt with, she went on. 'In Whitby we do not know each other except as acquaintances who happened to take the same ship from Middlesbrough. The only person likely to make an association is Mr Martin and he is ill so will not see me there.'

'What about David Drayton? Remember, I carried a letter to him from you. If he sees us, even separately, he may draw conclusions which would not be far from the truth. He's bound to hear I'm trying to raise interest in a ship sailing out of the Tees.'

'Leave that to me. If by any chance he does question you, deny that I know anything about it.'

Seamus nodded and asked, 'When do we return?'

'You, when you have done all you can. Luke knows about this and is expecting you to be away a few days. We must not leave together. I will spend four days here, leaving on the fifth. That should give you plenty of time to raise the necessary interest.'

'And you would like to know of my progress before you leave?'

'Most certainly. In fact, every day.' She paused thoughtfully. 'I will be staying at the Angel Inn. It will be best if you stay at the White Horse on Church Street.'

'Not together? Not even in the same inn?' He looked disappointed.

She gave a wry smile and shook her head slowly, her eyes intent on his.

Did he read in them a promise beyond this refusal? He decided to test her. 'Not even discreet contact at either?'

'Well, who knows?' She let the words convey a subtle suggestion, but what followed was said in deadly seriousness. 'But nothing must get in the way of the success of this venture, Sean. It means a lot to me that I get this ship. More than I can tell you – much more.'

The sharpness in her voice, the tension in her body, emphasised her words and Sean read there an obsession born in the past. It made him wonder if there was more to this young woman than he had seen.

'Very well,' he acquiesced. 'When do we meet for my first report? And where?'

'Let's say the day after tomorrow. I'll be on the west pier at three o'clock. If it is raining I will send an envelope to you at the White Horse by two. It will contain an address at which you can meet me, again at three o'clock.'

'Very well. You seem to have covered most things except two – do I mention a specific ship, and have you a list of the people you think might be interested?'

'You can indicate that you are close to making a deal for the ship, but it is a matter of getting enough interest in the rest of the shares. If necessary you can mention the name Slater, a small but reliable firm who build sound ships on the Tyne.' As she was speaking she opened her handbag and withdrew two slips of paper. She handed one to Sean. 'That is the list you want – I have put the names in the most likely order of interest.' She paused while he gave the paper a quick glance then went on, 'Remember five-sixteenths have already gone and three more are spoken for. One for me, one for Luke and one for you.'

Sean's expression was a picture. 'Me?'

'Yes.' She smiled encouragingly. 'To keep you interested? To make you work harder to get others to invest? As payment for your work? Describe it how you will, I think you deserve a sixteenth.'

'But I have no capital,' replied Sean, still bewildered.

'Neither have I. Neither has Luke. We lost everything on Father's death.'

'Then how . . .?'

'My dear Sean,' she began, as she held out the second sheet of paper, 'unknown to them the rest of the shareholders will have paid for the three-sixteenths we cannot finance. You'll see my calculations on that paper, the cost of the ship, the fitting out, crew's wages and so on, plus the fact that there will be three shares which cannot be paid for.'

It began to dawn on Sean what a dangerous game she was playing. This was a most unequal venture with some investors financing Luke, Lydia and him as well as themselves.

'See the figure you must quote? Commit it to memory,' Lydia instructed. 'I want those calculations back.'

I'll bet you do, thought Sean. It wouldn't do for this sheet of paper to get into the wrong hands. He memorised the figure and returned the paper to her.

258

'Don't let me down, Sean. This is dearer than life to me. If I control that ship, I can fulfil a dream.'

He noted that a coldness had crept into her voice which almost carried a threat. But to whom? Certainly not him. There was no cause. Besides, she had taken him a long way into her confidence. He wondered what lay behind all her schemes. Such thoughts were forgotten in a host of more pleasant speculations as she stepped closer to him.

'Business is over, Sean. There are other things in life.' She cupped his face in her hands and kissed him passionately.

Sean thanked the captain for a safe voyage. He raised his hat and called his goodbyes to Lydia who was coming along the deck. Neither showed any trace of the emotion they had felt on the voyage.

When he stepped ashore, Sean tossed a coin above the heads of a crowd of urchins who clamoured to take his bag.

The coin spun temptingly. Cries of excitement rent the air. Youngster jostled youngster as they all leaped up with arms outstretched, grabbing at the tantalising coin. One arm seemed to stretch above the others. One urchin seemed to hang in the air longer. His fingers closed round the money.

'It's mine! It's mine!'

The cry brought groans from the others who immediately turned their attention to Lydia who had started down the gangway.

'Where to, mister?' The sharp query came from a tall, skinny boy who looked as if a good feed would do him no harm.

'The White Horse on Church Street,' replied Sean.

'Follow me.' The boy started off.

His pace was brisk as he threaded his way through the frantic activity on the quayside. He kept up the same pace when they moved into the more residential area away from the river.

Sean called a halt.

259

The boy looked anxious.

'Your name?'

'Tim, sir,' he replied. His eyes showed a fear of reprimand, though he could not think what he had done.

'Very well, Tim. What's your hurry? Eager to get this job done and find another? Maybe carrying a housewife's shopping, a basket for the fishmonger, planks for a carpenter ... or maybe picking pockets?' Sean had seen all these activities taking place after they had left the quay.

'Not the last, sir. I never do that. It's dishonest.' Shock that he should be thought capable of picking pockets showed on Tim's face.

Sean nodded. 'Right, I believe you.'

'I do any other job, sir. Why not? I have to make an honest penny as quickly as possible or my income falls.' Confidence had returned to Tim's voice.

Sean smiled. 'An honest penny, eh? Sure now, that's commendable. I'm here on business and don't know Whitby. I don't want to waste time looking for various offices, so will you show me around?'

'Yes, sir,' replied Tim, his eyes bright at the prospect of an assured income for a few days.

'Right, on your way.'

With urchins crowding round her, Lydia could not move from the bottom of the gangway.

'Stop!' she shouted. Her command was piercing.

The urchins gradually stopped pushing when they realised it was going to get them nowhere and that this lady demanded respect. Their shouts subsided into quiet murmurs of 'Miss ... miss ...' until they too died away to leave only expectant expressions on dirty faces.

'That's better,' called Lydia, placing her two bags on the ground. She straightened and cast her eyes over the group. She almost fell into the trap of hiring them all thanks to the woebegone faces and pleading eyes. But, realising that this was all a part of the tricks of the trade, whenever passengers disembarked, she stopped herself. She cast her gaze over them then said, 'You, and you.'

The rest moaned and turned away, trying to ignore the triumphant shouts of the chosen two.

'To the Angel,' Lydia ordered.

The two boys picked up her bags and started off, mocking the unlucky ones.

Lydia was welcomed by the landlord of the Angel and found herself allocated a most comfortable room. The bed looked inviting after her voyage so she slipped out of her dress and lay down. In her mind she started to make plans for the next four days. There was no business to attend to apart from meeting Sean at the allotted times. To all outward appearances this was a visit to see her old friends. Lydia dozed and fell into a deep sleep.

Sean settled himself in his room and then went downstairs to partake of the landlord's recommended ale, a hunk of cheese and some home-made bread, layered with butter from a local farm. He had much on which to ponder.

The voyage had revealed sides to Lydia he had never suspected. Apart from the sweet, endearing female he knew as Luke's sister, there was also a person who was comfortable among people like the Langtons, an accomplished pianist, someone who had been used to a comfortable life in very different circumstances from those in which she was living in Middlesbrough.

Now he had learned that a deeply ambitious woman lay below the surface. A capable one who had learned about ships and trading by being acutely observant of her father and his business. And he had detected a devoted daughter who had been stunned by his death. And that death, he had come to think, was linked to her desire to make a success of this investment in which he had become involved. For her father's sake? To resurrect the firm he appeared to have lost? Sean felt somehow there was more than that behind her desire to succeed.

But what else could there be? Why was she so particular that her uncle should not be approached to take shares in the ship? Was there some sinister reason behind the stipulation that she had emphasised should be strictly observed? Was there anything in this that he could turn to his own advantage? If there was would it be straightforward or would he be dabbling in things best left alone?

He had progressed since coming to Middlesbrough, he should be careful not to destroy his achievements. They were such that he could build on them, especially the share Lydia had promised him. But were they a sop to entice him into a web of intrigue being spun around him? And was part of that web the endearing things she had said during their passionate loving in the captain's cabin, or did she really mean them? Even here he felt himself being drawn into a quagmire of his own making. Hadn't he used his charm to persuade her to allow him to be her escort in Middlesbrough? Had that resulted in the advances she had made on board ship? Were they made for her own ends or was she really attracted to him? And where did his own feelings lie? With Lydia or with the girl he had left behind in Dublin?

Lydia came awake slowly. The moment of wondering where she was was replaced by realisation which brought her wide awake. She swung from the bed, felt the pain of hunger and, after refreshing herself and dressing, went downstairs to the dining room. She chose a table which occupied one corner of the room and gave her a view of the door and the rest of the tables.

She ordered broth to be followed by game pie with potatoes, accompanied by wine.

When the soup was brought Lydia was deep in thought and, for a moment, not fully aware that she was being served.

In that moment the maid spoke. 'Why, it's Miss Lydia.'

Startled at hearing her name, Lydia looked up to see a

girl who used to be in her father's employ, 'Maggie,' she said.

'Hello, miss. It's nice to see you again.'

'And you, Maggie. I'm pleased you found another job.'

'It's all right, miss. Brings in the pennies but it's not as pleasant as when I worked for you.'

Lydia smiled. 'It's good of you to say so.'

'Miss?' Maggie hesitated. 'Do you mind if I ask you something?' Her face went red.

'Of course not. What is it?'

'Well, seeing you here, I wondered if you were coming back to live in Whitby?'

Lydia gave her a sympathetic smile. 'No, I'm afraid not. Well, not for some time. I've just come on a short visit to see some friends.'

'If ever you do, please think of me.'

'Of course I will, but you may be snapped up by some nice young man before then.'

Maggie blushed even deeper. 'Don't think that'll happen, miss.' Before Lydia could comment further Maggie scurried away.

While they had been talking Lydia's view of the door had been obscured but now she was aware of two people sitting down at a table further along the room. The man had his back to her and blocked her sight of his female companion, but Lydia could tell he was making a fuss of her. As he sat down he half turned and gave Lydia a view of his friend.

'David! Isobel!' she gasped. She stared as if to convince herself that the man who had said he loved her was wining and dining her cousin. Lydia felt her heart thump a little. Was she jealous? She stiffened and chided herself for thinking such a thing. No. Hadn't she set down in writing that she would not blame him if he found someone else? But . . . her cousin! Really! Lydia stamped her foot in irritation at herself. She picked up her spoon and started on her soup. She must occupy her mind with something else. But her eyes, in spite of her effort to keep them fixed on what she was doing, kept straying to a particular table where the serving girl was taking their order.

As the girl moved away Isobel looked beyond her companion to see who else was dining at the Angel. Her eyes rested on Lydia. For one moment she stared in disbelief then she jumped to her feet, saying something to David as she did so, and hurried across the dining room.

'Lydia! This is a surprise.' She leaned forward and kissed her cousin on the cheek. 'What are you doing here? When did you arrive?'

'Just a few hours ago. A short visit to see my beloved Whitby.'

David thought he had caught the word 'Lydia' when Isobel had left the table but wasn't sure. But as he turned in his chair to let his gaze follow Isobel it was confirmed. He jumped to his feet and joined the cousins.

'I don't believe it. What brings you back?' he asked.

'Just arrived on a short visit, nothing special.' Lydia smiled to herself for David was blushing like a naughty boy caught in some misdemeanour.

'She was pining for Whitby,' trilled Isobel, her eyes sparkling with laughter and pleasure at seeing her cousin. 'You are just starting your meal. Come and have it with us.'

'I don't want to intrude.'

'You won't be. Will she, David?'

'No, of course not. I'll arrange it.' He turned away and a moment later was in earnest conversation with one of the servers.

Once they were settled Lydia immediately asked about her uncle and aunt.

After what she had said when she and Luke were turned out of their home by Nathan, Isobel knew it was only a courtesy enquiry.

'They are very well, thank you.'

'And Cousin Christopher?'

'He is in good health too and will be thrilled to know I have seen you.'

264

'And your mother and father?' Lydia queried of David.

'The same,' he replied stiffly, knowing that Lydia had no liking for them either.

'I do not send my regards to them nor to my uncle so neither of you need tell them you have seen me.'

There was a moment of silence.

'Very well, Lydia,' said Isobel. 'Now we have those enquiries out of the way we can talk without rancour about ourselves. You know, I do miss you so.'

'And I you,' Lydia returned, letting her eyes stray to David and wondering how he'd interpret her look. Would he take it as a reproach for his attitude when she'd left Whitby?

'Tell us how you are getting on in Middlesbrough. What's it like? How is Luke? Does he like his job?'

Isobel rattled out these questions as the meal proceeded and Lydia answered without giving any information away about the recent scheme she had instigated.

Their talk moved to what had been happening in Whitby since she had gone to Middlesbrough. Though she knew some of the gossip from David's letters Lydia made no reference to receiving them.

Gradually she steered the conversation to the commercial life of the port. 'Anything new or exciting happening?'

Isobel chuckled, 'You always were one to take an interest in your father's business.'

Lydia shrugged her shoulders. 'That's the way I'm made.'

'Things are very much the same as when you left,' put in David. She felt that he said it with a little more haste than was necessary. Was he trying to hide something?

'I'm not sure about that, David,' said Isobel. 'Your father and mine have had several meetings but I don't know what they were about.'

Lydia was alert to this snippet. 'Really?' She registered her surprise. 'I thought Uncle was very much a loner.'

'He is but . . .'

265

'I don't think there's been any real progress,' put in David. 'Father hasn't said anything to me.'

Though she would have liked to probe further, to test if David was covering something up, Lydia thought better of it and asked for news of the Chambers family who had become noted for their marine paintings, one of whom had depicted one of her father's ships at sea.

The rest of the evening passed amiably and a relaxed atmosphere transcended recent tensions as friendly childhood days were recalled.

When Isobel and David were leaving, Lydia managed to whisper to her cousin, 'Come to tea, three o'clock tomorrow.'

Isobel squeezed her hand in acknowledgement.

With that little intrigue over, she smiled to herself when David seized his moment to say in an urgent, don't-deny-me tone, 'I must see you. Tomorrow, ten o'clock?' She read his relief as she pressed his elbow, conveying her acceptance.

The timepieces of Whitby were showing the hour of ten when David strode into the Angel the next morning to find Lydia waiting for him.

'Good morning, my love.' He deliberately used the endearment as he swept his hat from his head and bowed to her. He hoped that it would counteract the term he had used when addressing Isobel the previous evening.

'Good morning,' returned Lydia in a tone into which he could read nothing. But her heart had given a little flutter when she saw him and she realised she still held a deep affection for him.

'I see you are anticipating a walk?' he said, noting her three-quarter-length, waist-fitting coat over a full-skirted dress. Their colours of brown and beige complemented each other and were brightened by red velvet trimmings. Her bonnet was small, worn to the back of her head, revealing hair flowing neatly from a centre parting. A red ribbon, tied under the chin, secured the bonnet to her head. 'And might I say how charming you look.'

Lydia smiled. The same David, attentive, observant, oozing charm to match his handsome, neat appearance. 'That's a new coat since I saw you, David.' She admired his redingote-style overcoat with its astrakhan collar. His trousers were striped in muted colours and his hat grey to match his coat.

'You are observant and have a good memory. It gives me pleasure that you remember.' His eyes were searching for her reaction but Lydia gave nothing away.

'Shall we walk?' he said, and offered his arm.

She took it and they left the hubbub of the inn.

'You've escaped your father's eye,' she said, and immediately regretted the touch of sarcasm in her voice.

'Things have changed, Lydia,' he replied, a slightly hurt note in his tone.

'I'm sorry, David. I shouldn't have said what I did.' She felt contrite. 'How have they changed?'

'I have much more authority within the firm.'

'I am pleased to hear that.'

'I insisted that if Father expected me to take the interest he was demanding then it should be with more responsibility.'

'Good. And does that include courting Isobel?' Lydia could not resist the question.

David ignored it. Instead he suggested that they walk on the East Cliff. 'It's more private,' he added.

'And we need privacy, do we?'

'I would like it.'

'Very well, the East Cliff it is.' Lydia felt a little flutter inside. This had always been one of their favourite walks.

They left Baxtergate and crossed the bridge to the east side. The streets were thronged with folk going about their daily business but David was expert at guiding her among them. It brought back memories to Lydia.

They reached the one hundred and ninety-nine steps

267

leading up to the ancient parish church and climbed them steadily, pausing now and then to look back over the red roofs of the houses which climbed the cliffside as if they were reaching for the sky and freedom from the crowded conditions below. At the top they turned along the path among the graves, memorials to lives dictated by the sea. Beyond the cemetery the path took them to the cliff edge, dominated by the ruins of the ancient abbey, home to Benedictine monks in Norman times. Lydia, as she had always done when walking beside it, imagined them singing their office and finding peace in their communication with God.

But this path also brought back personal memories of the day when David had first told her he loved her. Then the future seemed to be mapped out for them, their marriage certain. But the death of her father and David's reaction had stunned her and changed all that. Was he now wanting to make amends for his treatment of her, or was there another reason for his wanting to see her this morning? Was he going to tell her that Isobel was now the girl in his life, the girl he would marry? He still had not answered the question she had put before they decided to come to the East Cliff.

She paused and looked out over a tranquil sea. The waves hardly broke at the foot of the cliffs. The breeze was slight but it held a sharp nip and she turned up the collar of her coat for extra warmth around her neck. She breathed deep, feeling a sense of well-being as the cool sea air filled her lungs.

'I miss this, David,' she said wistfully. 'So different from the grime and smoke pumped out by the ironworks.' She sighed. 'But that's where Luke's job is.'

'Maybe you'll return here one day.'

'Who knows what life holds?' She shook off the nostalgic feeling. There was something she had to know. 'You didn't answer my question about Isobel?'

He tightened his lips as if reluctant to answer. Eventually

he did. 'The answer is no, but I have been seeing her quite a lot lately.'

'Why, if you are not courting her? You seemed on intimate terms yesterday evening before you knew I was there.'

'We're very good friends.'

'Does Isobel see it as just that?'

'I don't know.'

'David! You don't know?' Lydia frowned at him.

'As far as I am concerned our two families have always been linked by the ties of friendship.'

Suspicion was instantly roused in Lydia's mind. 'What are you telling me, David? Friendship between two members of merchant families such as yours and Isobel's often means someone somewhere is wanting to take advantage of a marriage.'

David looked embarrassed. Lydia saw it and knew she had struck home.

'That's it! Your father again. I can see him behind this.' Her voice had risen, her eyes blazed angrily. 'I was all right for you until I had nothing, no firm and no trade to bring as my dowry. Now it's Isobel he wants for you because my uncle has a thriving business. I thought you said things had changed?'

'They have! They have!'

'Oh, yes, you may be right about having more authority but you're still dictated to by him for his own ends. David, be a man and leave him.'

'I can't. My whole future is with the business. Leave and I have nothing and never will. I'll be cut off forever. That's no future for us.'

'Then you see a future with Isobel?' she cried.

'No! I'm only complying with his wish to be friendly, no more. Father would like a closer relationship between the two firms. Isobel means no more to me than that.'

'And when this deal between your parents, whatever it is, is completed, your relationship with Isobel will end?'

269

'Yes.'

Lydia looked disgusted. 'You're using her to meet your father's demands.'

'No, that's not the way of it. You know that your cousins and I have always been friendly, even when you were here.'

'But now I'm not in Whitby, has something stronger developed between you and Isobel?'

'No, Lydia, no. You are the one I think about. You are the reason I am trying to win my father's favour so that he will be more easily persuaded that I should marry you, the girl I love.'

'Will he ever agree, I wonder?' There was a contemptuous note in her voice.

'Just give me a chance to work this out my way. Everything will be all right eventually and I will be able to give you the life you deserve.' As he was speaking he took hold of her shoulders and eased her closer.

She did not pull away. Realising that she had not resisted, she knew she still felt something for him, that she wanted to believe him and that their future lay together.

'Lydia, it's you I love. I always have, even since schooldays. You know that. The future will be right for us ...'

'So long as I bring something to satisfy your father,' she broke in.

'I want only you,' said David. His eyes never left hers as he pulled her close and let his arms slide to her waist. His lips came down to her willing upturned mouth. They met hers with a ferocity born of passion as if he was determined to convince her of his love for her.

Lydia strove to let his kiss banish the confusion from her mind, where images of her father, her uncle and David's father were obliterated by Sean's smile and the words he had said to her in the small world of a ship's cabin.

Their lips parted. 'I love you.' His words were whispered but each was clear and filled with devotion.

Then their lips met again and Lydia longed for her own

270

feelings to match what he had just expressed. Maybe Sean's success would bring her riches enough to surmount Jonas's opposition. It was on the tip of her tongue to tell him she was involved with Mr Bolckow but she held back, remembering that this venture must be kept a secret so that she could manipulate it as a tool for her revenge.

Thoughts of what had happened on the cliff were still occupying Lydia's mind when she awaited the arrival of her cousin that same afternoon.

She had asked that Isobel be shown to her room on arrival and that tea should be served ten minutes later.

Affectionate greetings were exchanged on Isobel's arrival, and after she had shed her outdoor clothes they fell into an animated conversation filled with local gossip.

The flow was halted when the maid, neat in her black dress and white apron, brought them tea with fresh scones and home-made cakes.

Lydia seized her chance to ask her cousin, 'Do you and David see much of each other?'

'We have lately,' replied Isobel.

'You like him?'

'Like is probably the right word.' Isobel's lips were touched with a small smile. 'Are you wondering where you stand with him?'

Lydia shrugged her shoulders, trying to convey the impression that she didn't care.

'Oh, come now, cousin,' said Isobel. 'You were sweet on him until you went to Middlesbrough. Now you're wondering if I'm stepping in.'

Lydia gave a grunt. 'Things changed when Father died. Because I was left with nothing, his father forbade talk of marriage and pressured David to forget me. David should have stood up to him. However, that's the way things are. I thought when I saw you two together yesterday evening . . .'

'David's very attentive, kind, considerate, fun to be with. I enjoy his company. We have some pleasant times

271

together but I don't feel any more for him than friendship.'
She gave a thoughtful little pause. 'You know, Lydia, there
are times when I think I am being used. No, not by David.
That both of us are being used.'

'How do you mean?'

'That our relationship is being encouraged.'

'By both sets of parents?'

'Yes, but more as if the fathers are behind it.'

'A business alliance through a family union?' suggested
Lydia.

'If that is so then David would have to know about it,'
Isobel pointed out.

'Maybe he does and is a willing partner.'

'But he has never mentioned marriage.'

'Maybe he will. Maybe the time is not yet right. It might
be if your fathers initiate a business partnership.'

Isobel looked thoughtful. 'I suppose you could be right.'

'Then pressure will be brought to bear on you and
David.'

Isobel showed anxiety.

Lydia, keen as she was to know what her cousin's
answer would be, suppressed that desire and instead fished
for information she thought more vital to her at this
moment, but quickly realised that Isobel knew nothing of
any use to her.

Although there were many questions teeming in Lydia's
mind to which she would dearly love answers, she deemed
it unwise to press further. Besides, she doubted her cousin
would have the details. She would have to find other ways
to elicit the information she desired.

Chapter Fourteen

Sean had had a contented night's sleep but when he awoke his mind was filled with the events of yesterday and the questions which had been raised in his mind. He decided that his enquiries might go further than strictly required by Lydia.

After enjoying a hearty breakfast he went outside to find Tim waiting for him.

'I've a number of people I want to see. I want you to take me to them.' Sean held out a piece of paper.

Tim ignored it. His head drooped. 'Can't read,' he muttered.

Sean cursed himself for overlooking that possibility and embarrassing the boy. 'Sorry about that,' he said.

Tim, worried that he might lose the chance of earning, looked up quickly. 'Read 'em out, sir. I've a good memory.'

Sean seized on this suggestion to get him out of what had become an awkward situation. 'Right, listen carefully.' He looked at the sheet of paper. 'Mr Wesley of Wesley and Harcourt.'

'Grape Lane,' put in Tim quickly to impress his employer.

'Correct,' replied Sean, and continued, 'Mr Brewster of Baxtergate. Mr Wright, Cliff Street.'

'Which Wright?' interposed Tim.

273

'Ah, yes. L.'

Tim nodded.

'Mr Medd, Church Street. Mr Parker of Parker and Parsons, Market Place. Mr Brook, Old Market Place. Mr J. Murray, Flowergate. And Mr B. Webster, also of Baxtergate.'

'Got them,' replied Tim brightly.

'Good. Now, I don't mind which order we visit the rest but I must call on Mr Wesley first,' Sean said, in order to follow Lydia's instruction that this gentleman must be his first contact.

'Right, sir, follow me.'

Tim started off from the White Horse along Church Street in the direction of Bridge Street. Whitby's population was already about its daily business. Shops were open and shopkeepers were shouting their wares to attract custom. Dock workers hurried to the ships they were to unload; others had already bent their backs and flexed their muscles to fill the holds with produce bound for London. Boats were trying up, bringing bustle to the quay, so that their night's catch could be brought quickly to young women eager to earn a penny or two gutting fish.

Before they reached the bridge Tim stopped at the corner of Grape Lane.

'Yonder,' he pointed at the second door on the left, 'Wesley and Harcourt.' Sean nodded. 'Ask for Mr Wesley. He's just gone in.'

Sean raised his eyebrows at this information. 'Know your merchants, do you?'

'Aye, I keep my eyes and ears open.' The boy gave a knowing little smile.

'Wait here for me.'

'I'll see you come out even if you don't see me.'

No doubt you will, thought Sean as he walked to the door to the offices owned by Messrs Wesley and Harcourt.

When he reached it, Sean hesitated. He felt a little flutter of nervousness. This was something new to him. He had

274

rehearsed in his mind how he would go about the approach he would make, but now his boldness seemed to have vanished. He was on the threshold of a new chance to advance himself, another step on the road to his dreams. Lydia had . . . He cut off that thought. No! This was a move towards fulfilling the promises he had made to Eileen. But if that became known to Lydia would it stall the chance she had given him? He drew in a deep breath and put his own problems firmly to the back of his mind.

He opened the door and entered a small room with a counter. A clerk looked up from the ledger in which he was writing, pinched the spectacles from his nose and came to attend to Sean. He was a thin man with slightly hunched shoulders. He blinked as he said, 'Good day, sir. What can I do for you?'

'I would like to see Mr Wesley,' said Sean, firmly but politely.

'May I ask your reason?'

'Please tell him that Mr Sean Casey wishes to discuss matters concerning Tees Shipping, a firm actively engaged in trading in the North East.'

'Yes, sir.'

The clerk disappeared through a door behind him to re-emerge a few moments later. 'Would you like to come this way, sir?' He raised one end of the counter to allow Sean to pass through. He then opened a door and announced, 'Mr Casey, sir.'

The office was a large square room with two mahogany desks set aslant across each corner of the room and facing the door, with a long window set in the middle of the wall opposite Sean. On one desk was a neat arrangement of papers, pens, pencils and notebooks. The other was completely empty.

'Good day, sir,' said Sean, as he crossed the room towards the man coming from behind his desk to greet him. 'It is kind of you to see me.'

'And good day to you.' The man's smile was cheery,

broadening what was already a round chubby face. There was a bright and friendly air in his pale blue eyes, but Sean felt their assessment of him and knew that their charm probably hid the workings of a shrewd mind.

'Tees Shipping? I've not heard of them,' said Mr Wesley as he indicated a chair to Sean.

'We are based at Middlesbrough and see great prospects in the development of trade on the river.'

Mr Wesley nodded thoughtfully as he returned to his seat behind the desk.

'How might that interest me?'

'Well, sir, the name of your firm came to us as one interested in maritime investments. If your partner is due in later today, maybe it would be best if I returned then.'

'Ah. Your informant has somewhat misguided you. I am the sole owner of the firm. There is no Mr Harcourt now. I need not go into detail, sufficient to say that he had to move to the south of England. So, Mr Casey, I am the one to make all decisions. And, yes, it is true I am interested in sound investments. But you'll have to convince me.'

An hour later the two men shook hands over a deal and Sean had in his possession a note that Mr Wesley would take three-sixteenths share in the new vessel.

'I suppose you are making this offer to other merchants in Whitby?' said Mr Wesley.

'Yes, sir, the sooner all the shares have been taken, the sooner we can start trading.'

'Oh, I think you'll find receptive minds in Whitby, Nathan Middleton would certainly be interested, but I warn you, he'll cast a very probing eye over the enterprise.'

'And his brother?'

'Ah, sadly, no. He died and his firm no longer exists.'

Sean put on a look of surprise. 'Oh, dear, my informant is certainly not up to date.' He made a little grimace. 'And no family to carry on?'

'Well, there was a son and a daughter. I've no doubt they would have done well but they could get no backing because their father had left the firm in deep debt and the bankers feared they might do the same.' Mr Wesley shook his head sorrowfully. 'Real tragedy. Tristram's ship was lost with all hands and that broke him. There were those who said he had committed suicide but, if that had been the case, his children would not have received the insurance money.'

'So they were able to pay off his debts?'

'Aye, but had to sell everything to make up the balance. They were left penniless. And to pile on the agony, Mr Nathan turned his nephew and niece out of the house in which they were living.'

'But could he do that?' queried Sean.

'Apparently the house belonged to him and he wanted it.' Mr Wesley shrugged his shoulders. 'And that was it. A great pity. Mr Tristram was a much kinder man than his brother, liked by everyone. So now you know the type of man you have to deal with if you go to Mr Nathan Middleton.'

'Well, thank you for that, sir. Maybe I won't have to approach Mr Middleton,' said Sean, rising from his chair. 'And thank you for your time. I am certain you won't regret investing with Tees Shipping.'

'I hope not, Mr Casey. I trust you will make sure I am satisfied with the investment I have made.'

The two men shook hands and Sean left the office. He was pleased with himself. His patter and charm had worked. He had persuaded Mr Wesley to take three-sixteenths, better than he had expected. If he could do it once he could do it again. His confidence was high. But he had also gained some new knowledge regarding Lydia's father and what had caused her to leave Whitby. In the light of what he had seen of her yesterday that knowledge was worth considering, even investigating.

When he stepped outside Tim was nowhere to be seen but within a matter of moments he was by Sean's side.

He saw two other possible investors that morning, one of

277

whom took a sixteenth share while the other showed no interest whatsoever.

He saw one possible client in the afternoon who was willing to take another sixteenth. Sean then decided that Tim should show him something of Whitby, during which he located the place appointed to meet Lydia the next day.

As they walked on the west pier, Sean put a question to his guide. 'Do you know Mr Middleton?'

'There's two,' returned Tim quickly, then corrected himself. 'Nay, one, t'other's dead.'

'Oh,' said Sean in feigned ignorance.

'Aye. Mr Tristram died. It's Mr Nathan . . .' Tim cocked an eyebrow at Sean. 'But he ain't on the list you read out.'

'I know. But I've had his name mentioned to me.'

Tim gave a grunt. 'Wouldn't recommend seeing him meself,' he growled. 'Nasty man. Gave me a clip round my lughole rather than pay me for an errand I ran for him. Said I'd been too slow – I hadn't, it was an excuse so he didn't have to pay.'

'Was his brother like that?'

'Nay, not him. Always free with his pennies. Pity it wasn't Mr Nathan that drowned.'

'What happened?'

'Fell off the end of this pier. Though there are those who said he jumped 'cos he'd lost his ship.'

'Do you know where he fell?'

'Aye. Near the lighthouse at the end of the pier.'

When they reached the spot Sean looked it over carefully. He realised that losing one's footing here could prove fatal, but the situation set his mind exploring other possibilities for Mr Tristram Middleton's death and he tried to link them with what he knew of Lydia.

Even as he lay in bed that night they kept drifting back into his mind. Supposition followed supposition with little to commend them, but Sean let them come and go, taking the view that sometimes the unlikely proves to be the truth.

*

278

The following morning Tim was waiting for him outside the White Horse. He remembered there were four names remaining on the list and led Sean to the first of them in Baxtergate.

By one o'clock Sean could look back on a satisfactory morning. He had found two more interested parties, each willing to take a sixteenth share in the ship. Only one more to dispose of but, with two refusals, he had exhausted the names he had been given. Maybe Lydia would make another suggestion when he saw her in two hours. He paid Tim, bringing an extra wide smile to the youngster's face when he doubled the money he'd promised. Then Sean returned to the White Horse, where he dined on bread and cheese and apple pie washed down with a pint of the land-lord's best ale.

With his hunger assuaged, and having the satisfaction of knowing he had almost achieved his task, he was in a state of well-being as he strolled across the bridge. Oblivious to the flow of people, he paused a moment to survey the activities along the river banks and wondered what part in all of this Lydia was preparing to play. He had come to the conclusion that there was more in her mind than merely shipping ironstone from Whitby to Middlesbrough. She had seen her father trade on a much broader horizon. Was she set on emulating him? Or was there something more to it than that? She would rival her uncle for whom he knew she had no love, having been turned out of her home. But was she intent on developing that rivalry for more sinister purposes? Was there a link here to her father's death?

Sean continued his stroll. He turned into Saint Ann's Snaith, unaware that he had caught the eye of David Drayton who was nearing the bottom of Golden Lion Bank.

David's footsteps faltered, suspicion flooding into his mind at the sight of the man from Middlesbrough who had brought him that first letter from Lydia. What was he doing here? Was there some connection with Lydia's presence or was it mere coincidence? His lips tightened as he recalled

279

the questions which had come to his mind when the letter had been delivered. He had wondered then if she had a liking for the man she had entrusted with the letter. Now they were both in Whitby at the same time. Yesterday Lydia's kisses had allayed any doubt he had of her love for him, but now ... David took a watch from his waistcoat pocket and glanced at it. He gave a nod of satisfaction. He had time.

He diverted from his intended path and turned into St Ann's Snaith. He could make out Sean a short distance ahead and matched his pace.

They went down Haggersgate with high buildings rising on both sides, imparting a claustrophobic feeling. This was relieved as they emerged on to the Promenade.

David hesitated. Was this just a pleasure stroll? Was the Irishman on an errand which would mean nothing? He was about to turn back when he noticed Sean quicken his pace. It was much more purposeful now, as if he had suddenly realised he was late for an appointment. David decided he would continue his shadowing.

When Sean walked beyond the projection known as Scotch Head it was obvious that he was making for the west pier. David modified his pace. In the more open space and with fewer people around it was easy to see Sean. A few moments later David drew up sharply. A lady was standing at the side of the pier looking over the waves rolling on to the beach. She turned. Lydia!

David stiffened and his lips tightened into a grim line when he saw her smile, take Sean's arm and fall into step beside him as they strolled towards the end of the pier. He watched them for a few moments. They were in earnest conversation. They stopped. She kissed him!

Fury almost overwhelmed him. He half started forward, but thought better of making a public display of his disappointment. He swung round and walked briskly back the way he had come, anger in every step.

*

280

'I hope I haven't kept you waiting,' said Sean when he reached Lydia. 'I got carried away by the sights of Whitby.'

She shrugged. 'I've been here only a few minutes. I was enjoying the sea air, and it also gave me time to think.' She took his arm and he matched his stride to hers as she turned along the pier. 'Well?' she asked eagerly. 'How have you got on?'

'All shares taken except one-sixteenth,' he replied, a note of satisfaction in his voice.

'What?' Lydia stopped and stared at him with a touch of disbelief.

'It's true,' he proclaimed. 'A spot of Irish charm worked wonders.'

'That's marvellous.' She pushed herself on to her toes and gave him a quick kiss, her joy temporarily overcoming the dictates against such a display in public.

Sean's hands came to her waist. He held her close, eyes dancing with pleasure. For a moment she hesitated then slipped free from him but, still holding his arm, continued their stroll.

'Tell me who?'

Sean related in detail what had happened, leaving out the details he had gleaned for his own purposes.

'So, if you have anyone else in mind who I can approach, I'm sure I'll be able to dispose of the final share. What about your uncle? Surely he . . .'

'I told you, not my uncle.' Her voice was sharp. He could even detect hatred there. Did that link up with what he had learned?

'Mr Drayton then?'

'Nor him.' Her voice still held that sharp edge.

Was there some connection between the two men that roused this feeling in her? Sean was anxious to know more but he could not question her, for he knew from her demeanour that he would receive no answers.

'There's no need for you to try to sell the remaining

281

sixteenth. It slipped my mind to tell you that it is likely that Kevin will invest with us.'

'Kevin?' Sean feigned surprise.

'Yes. When Sarah's father was interested she thought Kevin might be too.'

'Then it's as well I didn't sell the remaining share otherwise Kevin would have been disappointed. But are you sure he can raise the money? After all, he is just . . .'

'. . . not what you think,' broke in Lydia. 'His family in Ireland are quite well off.'

Sean raised his eyebrows. 'You know?'

'Yes, there's no need to keep his secret from me.'

'So what now? Do I return to Middlesbrough tomorrow, or do we return together?'

'Not together. You go tomorrow. I have other things to see to here.'

Other things? Sean's curiosity was roused. He would dearly love to know what they were but his chances of finding out would be curtailed by leaving unless . . .

'Do we celebrate this evening?' he asked hopefully.

'No.'

This was obviously the person in control speaking, the person who was running the enterprise. Sean felt he had been put in his place. He sensed she held a secret she did not want him to know about, and that it had its roots in Whitby.

Throughout the rest of the afternoon, David could not concentrate on what he was doing. His actions were automatic. He contributed nothing to the meeting of a committee set up to encourage expansion of trade through Whitby. His mind was too preoccupied with what he had witnessed on the west pier, and whether he should disclose this knowledge immediately on seeing Lydia that evening.

His attention was sharpened only after the meeting closed and members sat around chatting in general terms while finishing their drinks.

'Anyone been approached to invest in Tees Shipping?' someone asked.

Two members indicated that they had.

'Seemed a very sound investment with Mr Bolckow and Mr Vaughan backing it,' commented one of them.

'Likeable young Irishman,' added the other. 'He certainly had the gift of the gab, but he was sound enough with his facts and figures.'

David's mind was brought sharply to what was being said.

'Neither I nor my father was approached,' he put in casually.

'The Irishman ...' The speaker hesitated slightly as if trying to think of a name. 'Er ... Sean Casey was looking specifically for investors in a ship which he was proposing would move ironstone from Whitby to Middlesbrough. All the shares must have been taken before he got to you. Bad luck, David.'

He gave a nod, accepting the explanation. 'But Martin is doing that.'

'Seems Bolckow and Vaughan need more.'

'I've never heard of Tees Shipping,' said David. 'Has it been trading long?'

'Newly founded as far as I could gather but there must be potential for the two iron men to invest.'

The conversation drifted but the facts were turning over in David's mind. They were still doing so when he returned home to prepare to meet Lydia for dinner at the Angel. He did not like what he had heard and seen and was now determined to tackle her.

'You are looking exquisite, my dear.' David was his usual polite and charming self when he arrived at the Angel.

But Lydia saw a difference in his eyes. Usually tranquil on such occasions, this evening they were tinged with a sharp expression as if they were searching. For what?

'A new dress?' he noted.

'Purchased today, especially for your visit,' returned Lydia, her voice smooth.

'I'm flattered.' He ran his eyes over the light blue twilled silk with wide borders of dark blue velvet. The square neckline came to the top of her breasts and the puff sleeves were tight to her wrists. She wore a jet necklace and carried a white shawl. 'You've had a pleasant day?' he asked.

'I enjoyed seeing Whitby again and visited Mrs Harrington.'

'She would be pleased to see you,' he said as he escorted her into the dining room.

'Yes. I was glad to find her in good health.'

They were shown to a table already set for a meal. He remained standing until he saw she was seated comfortably.

'You saw Isobel again?' he asked as he sat down.

'Yes, we had tea together.'

'Here?'

'Where else? You know I would not step over my uncle's threshold, and especially now that he has moved into the house I still regard as mine.'

'He has the law on his side,' David reminded her.

Lydia frowned. She knew he was right. 'The idea of him in that house which Father thought so much of galls me.' The venom in her voice was not lost on David. He had hoped her time in Middlesbrough would have eased her hatred, but it appeared not to have done so. And her return to Whitby, even for just a visit, had apparently only heightened the way she felt.

'And you'd do anything to get it back?'

'Of course!' The words came out sharply and before she could stifle them. She chastised herself. She must be careful not to give too much away.

'Have you something in mind?'

Lydia eyed him cautiously. He was probing too much. She merely shrugged her shoulders, and was thankful that the serving-girl came for their order.

During the meal conversation drifted between Whitby

284

and Middlesbrough until David's enquiries about Luke and his work enabled him to mention Sean in a casual way.

'The Irishman who delivered your first letter to me after you had gone to Middlesbrough . . .' He halted as if searching for a name.

'Sean Casey,' Lydia automatically prompted.

'That's him. I hear he's in Whitby raising interest in a ship.'

'Is he?' She feigned surprise.

David fixed his eyes on her. He needed to observe her reaction to what he was going to say next. 'You know he's in Whitby.'

Lydia tensed. 'What do you mean?'

'Exactly what I said. I saw you with him on the west pier.'

'Oh.' There was casual regret in the way she uttered the word, and David read the same in her expression.

'Then you don't deny it?' The edge to his voice was sharpened by her relaxed attitude, as if she didn't care that he knew. 'How could you after what we said to each other yesterday?' His eyes bore hurt and anger.

'It's not what you think, David.'

Unable to detect whether her outward sincerity was real or assumed, he gave a contemptuous sneer. 'That's what I expected you to say.'

She placed her knife and fork on her plate and leaned forward, resting her arms on the table. She adopted a purposefully no-nonsense attitude. 'From what you saw, and I presume you are including the kiss I gave him, you could not begin to understand what it was all about.'

'I conclude from what I saw that you have feelings for this man,' he said coldly.

'Not in the way you mean. I like him. He has done a good job for me, and for that I am grateful and respect him.'

'Job?' He gave another little laugh of disbelief. 'What are you dreaming up now to exonerate yourself?'

285

Lydia stiffened at the disbelief in his voice. 'Hear me out. If you still don't believe me or don't like what you hear then I'll walk away, out of your life for good.'

David read determination in her delivery. He knew that in moments of crisis Lydia was her own woman. She would stand or fall by her decisions, or by the things she had caused to happen. There was nothing he could do but listen to her or their relationship, which he had thought strong again, would be destroyed forever. He nodded. 'Convince me that what I saw meant nothing.'

'It was a spur-of-the-moment reaction. I was pleased to hear what he had achieved for me.'

'Achieved for you? Was I not here in Whitby? Could I not have done whatever it was?' There was still anger in his voice.

'No, you couldn't. What Sean did will in the end benefit you and me, David.'

'Me?' He was puzzled. How could he be involved in whatever had gone on, or was still going on, between Sean Casey and the woman he loved?

'Yes. Now hear me out. I needed to get people interested in investing in a new ship.' She went on to tell him how this had come about. 'When Luke and I needed to raise capital after Father's death no one would back us. You can't have forgotten that? Now, if I had come to Whitby to try to raise capital for a new ship, I believe I would still have been regarded with suspicion. So I had to have someone else to do it – Sean Casey. When you saw us on the pier he was making his report to me, and highly satisfactory it was. He had disposed of all the shares in the first ship to be owned by Tees Shipping.'

David had concentrated on her every word. They all sounded so convincing. But there was one thing left unexplained. 'You said that what you were doing would be for my benefit also, but Casey didn't approach me.'

'I told him not to.' She did not proceed to enlighten him on this but said, 'Don't you see, David? If what I am doing is a success your father can have no objection to our marriage.'

His eyes brightened with the realisation of what lay behind her scheme. 'But why not come forward now?'

'Two reasons. The enterprise might fail, and I don't want that humiliation again. If it was known in Whitby that I was involved in Tees Shipping, my uncle would know and he would not be pleased that I was in opposition to him. He would take every precaution to offset any harm I might do him. Try to see that we did not succeed.' At the mention of her uncle her voice had grown cold. 'I do not want you to mention what I have told you to anyone. It must be kept a strict secret between us.' Her tone left him no doubt that she was serious.

'You have my oath,' he said, a solemn promise in his voice which was matched in his eyes. He picked up his glass and raised it to her. 'May you succeed for the sake of our future together.'

Chapter Fifteen

Sean stood at the rail as the *Nina* was manoeuvred down-river on the noon tide towards the sea. Sailors went about their allotted tasks under the watchful eye of the captain with an efficiency he admired.

As his gaze scanned Whitby's east side, he had a pleasurable sense of achievement at having completed Lydia's task to her satisfaction. Not only that, he was pleased he had gained some new knowledge about her, though it disturbed him.

He liked Lydia. In the light of what had happened in the captain's cabin on their voyage to Whitby he had thought they might even enjoy a deeper relationship. But from her attitude towards him in Whitby he had begun to wonder if that interlude had been only a means of persuading him to help her. What he had learned since only strengthened that view. It had shocked him. Was Lydia a manipulator, using people for her own ends? He had known there was tough-ness behind that ladylike exterior, but now he wondered if it was tinged with ruthlessness and a determination to get her own way at any cost.

His gaze settled on Burgess Pier and the smoke rising from the kipper houses situated at its head. A figure moved along the pier. His eyes narrowed as he stared into the distance. Lydia! Was she there on purpose to see him sail? As a lover saying goodbye? Or to make sure that he had left

Whitby? He let his gaze settle on her, travelling over the water as if it was not there. She must have felt his eyes upon her. She lifted her arm and gave a small wave of her hand. He raised his and then doffed his hat in return. He bowed his farewell and when he looked up again could sense the amused smile on her lips, though she was too far away for him to see it clearly.

With the wish that he could came the return of his former troubled thoughts. As the ship met the first undulations of the sea and sails were unfurled to take advantage of the freshening breeze, away from the shelter of the cliffs, he wished he had someone he could confide in, someone with whom he could talk through his thoughts.

Luke? But he would support his sister. Maybe he was even involved in what Sean judged to be Lydia's schemes. Kevin? He would be a sympathetic listener, maybe even offer advice, but that would be tempered by his feelings for Sarah who was very friendly with Lydia. Kevin would not want to upset his sweetheart. But he was still the most likely to listen and offer advice about what Sean surmised and what he had gleaned from Drayton's clerk.

After his meeting with Lydia on the west pier, Sean had made his way to Drayton's office where he had kept watch for the clerk he remembered from his last visit.

He emerged finally and Sean followed him at a discreet distance. When the man held brief conversations with three separate people, and there seemed to be no urgency about his movements, Sean judged he was not about Drayton's business.

As they neared the Black Bull at the corner of the market place, Sean quickened his step and caught him by the arm. Startled, he reacted with annoyance that was soon replaced by alarm.

'You! What the devil. . .?'

'In there.' Sean propelled him towards the inn. 'I want to talk.'

'No more messages. I won't do it.' There was alarm in his voice and in his eyes. He tried to shake off Sean's grip.

'No messages,' rapped Sean. 'I just want some information, if you have it. We'll do it over some ale in a quiet corner.'

By then they were at the Black Bull and Sean shoved him inside.

Sean took in the scene with a quick glance. Tobacco smoke hung against the blackened ceiling like thin cloud awaiting a breeze. Several men lounged against the bar which ran the length of one wall. After calling for two pints of the best ale, Sean indicated a vacant alcove.

'Well, good to see you again, Mr . . .' he said heartily.

'Potter,' the man said automatically. He turned to go but Sean caught hold of him. Potter could do nothing but slide into one of the seats. Sean, his eyes never leaving the clerk, settled on the opposite side of the small table.

'I know nothing, Mr Casey,' muttered Potter, trying to wriggle out of any questioning which might land him into trouble.

'You remember my name. You must have a retentive memory.'

'Well, sir, there was something that made our previous meeting memorable.'

'And this one could be just as memorable, maybe even more so.'

The conversation was halted for a moment as a barman brought two tankards of ale and placed them on the table between them.

Sean raised his. 'Here's hoping your memory continues to be good.'

Potter gave a sly grin. 'Who knows?'

'You move around Whitby carrying messages for your employer. You overhear things outside and in the office. I think you may remember the time I want to know about.'

Potter screwed up his face doubtfully. 'Well, I don't know about that . . .'

Sean slid his hand into his pocket and drew out a shilling. He placed it on the table where no one could see it except Potter.

'What time are you talking about, sir?'

'The time of Mr Tristram Middleton's death.'

'Mmm.' Potter feigned deep thought.

'He lost a ship, I believe,' put in Sean.

'Aye, he did, with all hands.'

'It broke him?'

'In more ways than one.'

'What's that mean?'

'The debt he faced. I have it on good authority from a man who worked for Mr Tristram that the ship was not insured.'

Sean raised one eyebrow.

'I heard Mr Drayton . . .' Potter let the words hang in the air and glanced greedily at the coin. Sean slid it across the table and claw-like fingers closed over it. '. . . say that Mr Tristram had made some bad investments with the money he should have used for insurance.'

'So was there no one who could help him? Not even his own brother?'

Potter gave a grunt. 'Never got on, those two. Mr Nathan's a shrewd businessman but not liked. Why, he even turned his niece and nephew out of their house 'cos he wanted it.'

So it was true. Sean noted the confirmation he had received.

'And they had to sell everything to add to the insurance Mr Tristram had on his life so they could pay off the debts he had incurred.'

'Then his death was fortuitous if you care to look at it like that?'

'Aye, I suppose so.'

'Slipped off the pier, I hear.'

'Well, now, there's some that say so but . . .' Once more Potter let his words remain unspoken.

291

Sean read his intent and slipped another shilling across the table where a hand quickly removed it from sight. '. . . there are those that believe he fell on purpose but made it look like an accident so that the insurance money would help his children.'

Sean nodded his understanding of this theory.

'Mind you,' Potter put in quickly, 'them's only rumours. Whoever paid the insurance must have been satisfied that it was an accident.'

'One more question.' Sean leaned over the table and put it quietly. 'Did Mr Tristram approach his brother for help?'

'Aye.'

'That's the truth?'

Potter gave a little grin. 'Oh, I know with certainty.'

'How?'

'We clerks exchange news. Keep our ears open for items we might turn to our own advantage.'

'Like now.'

'If you see it that way.'

Another coin slid across the table.

'Mr Nathan's clerk saw Mr Tristram visit his brother the day after the ship was lost. Told me they had a terrible row, loud enough at the finish for him to hear. Mr Nathan refused to help his brother, called him names he didn't deserve and told him to get out in a voice that held hatred. The clerk saw him leave, said he looked a broken man. Not long after, Mr Tristram was seen to fall from the pier.'

Sean pursed his lips thoughtfully. 'And Tristram's children?'

Potter rose to the prompt, comforted by the three coins in his pocket. 'They visited their uncle. There were more harsh words, especially from Miss Lydia who accused her uncle of causing her father's death by refusing to help him. He laughed at her, but she persisted in her accusation and swore that one day she would get her revenge.'

Sean was gripped by this information.

*

It returned to his mind now as the *Nina* left the river and took to the sea.

He went over it again and again, trying to connect it with events he had witnessed since meeting Lydia. She and Luke had come to Middlesbrough with nothing. He had a job so they were not poverty-stricken but there was little she could use towards achieving revenge until the formation of Tees Shipping had come about. Now she had something she might be able to use against her uncle. But to compete with him would take time and even then what could she do? Unless she was able to turn circumstances to her advantage . . .

Sean was troubled. He had met a charming, likeable young woman, but he had also seen a hard, calculating side appear, one which could easily take over if her obsession became too much to control. If it did it could spell disaster for her and Sean did not want to see Lydia destroy herself.

It was early evening, the sky filling with low clouds scudding before a freshening breeze, when the *Nina* docked at Middlesbrough. Though its cargo would be unloaded the next morning, Luke was there to see that there had been no snags in Whitby or on the voyage. When Sean came down the gangway the two friends greeted each other with a warm handshake.

'Thought you might be away for a few days,' commented Luke as they walked away from the jetty, their shoulders hunched against the wind.

'So you must have known about the proposition Lydia was going to put to me?' returned Sean.

'Yes.'

'Therefore you must have approved of keeping her name and yours from being mentioned?'

'Yes. And I suppose she gave you a good enough reason?'

'Indeed.'

'And told you who you should and shouldn't approach?'

'Yes,' replied Sean and, with pride in his voice, went on to give Luke the names of those who had taken shares in the new enterprise.

'You did well. And you got no reaction from anyone else?'

'No. But it will soon get around that Tees Shipping is venturing into the iron trade. Are you expecting rivals?'

Luke was cautious. 'I think Mr Bolckow and Mr Vaughan will be glad of anybody entering the trade so long as it means more ore for them.' He quickly changed the direction of the conversation. 'When will Lydia be back? I thought she might have come with you.'

'She'll leave tomorrow. She thought it best we weren't seen together.'

Luke nodded. 'Very wise.'

'I suppose you know she offered me a share in the new vessel? And that Kevin is interested too.'

'Yes.' Luke smiled. 'I know all about Kevin. He's in Ireland now arranging his money. Took Sarah with him to meet his family.'

Sean raised an eyebrow. 'Looks as though those two ...'

'Yes. Sarah was very kind to him after Seamus was killed, and it seemed to bring them closer.'

'What happens now that Lydia has sold all the shares in the ship? She mentioned a shipbuilding firm, Slater's, does it really exist?'

'Oh, yes, it certainly does. And Lydia made sure they had a ship available. They have one nearing completion. Confident that she would raise sufficient investment, she's already negotiated to buy it.'

Lydia watched the mud flats and salt marshes slide past as the *Amanda* made her way up the Tees towards the jetty close to the Bolckow and Vaughan works. She saw potential in this desolate landscape, an expansion of the industry which these two men had established. Ship more ore, produce more pig iron, process it for all manner of goods, and prosperity could line the banks of the river. There was money to be made here. She would make sure that more ore was shipped from Whitby.

Her eyes narrowed with a vision of others following her lead to take advantage of the demand for ore, and if she knew her uncle he would be one of them. Then she would be able to exploit him. How? That did not occupy her at the moment. She would take advantage of the situation as it developed.

Luke and Sean were at the jetty when the ship docked. She came down the gangway with a quick step and an air of achievement. Sean watched her with desire, Luke with brotherly admiration.

'Sean will have told you of his success?' she said, excitement in every word.

'Yes, he has. He did well to gain support so quickly.'

She offered no further praise, merely nodded and gave Sean a half smile as Luke turned away to have a word with the captain.

'Did you have a good voyage?' asked Sean.

'Yes.'

'Better than the one to Whitby?'

'Neither better nor worse,' she replied, without a sign that she knew what he was hinting at.

'Mine was the poorer for being on my own,' he replied.

Again she ignored the inference. Instead, seeing Luke return to them, she turned in his direction.

'We have a lot to talk about, I'm sure Sean is capable of seeing to things here.' She linked arms with her brother as if she was taking possession of him.

Luke raised his eyebrows and shrugged his shoulders at Sean as if to say, I can't refuse my sister.

Sean said nothing. He watched them walk away, wondering at Lydia's coldness. It was as if nothing had ever happened between them. In fact, it had looked that way from the moment they had arrived in Whitby. Had she merely used him? Got what she wanted from him and was now casting him aside? Maybe he was making too harsh a judgement. He did not want to be too hard; after all, there were many qualities he admired in her. Maybe the cold, ruthless streak he had witnessed was foreign to her real nature and had only been brought about by the death of her father and harsh treatment from her uncle.

'So the whole visit was successful?' said Luke.

'Yes, far better than expected,' Lydia went on to tell him all that had happened. 'David has promised to keep me in touch with developments in Whitby.'

'No doubt he couldn't refuse you,' said Luke with a grin.

'I made sure of it. And I made him promise that no one should know that you and I are behind Tees Shipping.' Excitement charged her voice as she went on, 'Luke, I feel it in my bones that this is going to be our opportunity to hit Uncle Nathan hard and let Father rest easy in his grave.' Before he could comment she went on, 'I must go to Newcastle and get that ship underway.'

'A crew?'

'That's one reason why I stayed an extra day in Whitby. I saw Captain Anderson, persuaded him to raise a crew to take over the . . . we must have a name for her, Luke.'

'How about the *Ironmaster*?'

Lydia looked thoughtful as she pondered the suggestion. 'A good strong-sounding name. Why not? She'll lend strength to our cause.'

'Captain Anderson will take over the *Ironmaster* when she arrives in Whitby, having been brought there by a crew from the shipyard.'

'You had it all worked out.'

'Anticipation gets you on,' returned Lydia.

'Also Captain Anderson knows that our names should never be mentioned in connection with this scheme. He understands that he is employed by Tees Shipping, and, as far as anyone else is concerned, was hired by the gentleman raising the finance – Sean Casey.'

*

296

Lydia left the next morning by train for Darlington, where she would change to another for Newcastle. She'd had time to savour this turnaround in her fortunes and was determined that they would never go into decline again.

'Eileen, you'll stay with me and my Father.' Sarah made this announcement as their train approached Middlesbrough station.

'But I couldn't impose on you any more than I already have.'

'Nonsense. It's the best solution.'

'But your father . . .'

She was cut short by Kevin whose knowing smile confirmed his words. 'Don't worry, Sarah can twist him round her little finger.'

'It's a useful asset,' agreed Sarah, a twinkle in her eye.

'In any case, you'll like James,' said Kevin. 'He's a kind man and I know he'll take to you. You'll get on well.'

'Then it's settled,' said Sarah.

'When will I get to see Sean?' asked Eileen.

'If he's back from Whitby, I'll bring him this evening,' promised Kevin.

'Whitby? What has he been doing there?'

'Luke sent him to check on the supply of ironstone. He left the day before we did, so he should be back by now.'

'I'll arrange a meal for this evening, Kevin. Don't tell him Eileen is here, let it be a surprise.'

'Good idea.'

'And tell Luke and Lydia to come as well.'

'I'll do that, if she's back.'

'Where has she been?' asked Eileen tartly. 'Whitby, no doubt.'

Kevin, annoyed with himself for letting those words slip out, could only answer, 'Yes, she went to see friends.'

'I suppose they travelled on the same ship?'

'Yes. But I don't think that means anything.' Sensing Eileen's jealousy, Sarah tried to sound reassuring.

297

'I hope not.'

'Sure it's good to see you, Sarah,' said Sean when she greeted him in the hall after the maid had answered his knock on the front door. 'Kevin tells me you had a grand time in Ireland, short though it was.'

'We did,' replied Sarah.

Kevin gave her a wink as he came over. 'Lydia and Luke will be along shortly.' He kissed her on the cheek and whispered in her ear, 'Thought it best to bring him on his own.'

The maid took their coats.

'Father's in the drawing room,' said Sarah and led the way to the door. She opened it and stepped inside followed by Kevin and Sean. Sean closed the door behind him. When he turned round to greet Mr Langton he froze and stared in open-mouthed amazement.

'Hello, Sean.' Eileen's voice was soft but the words were delivered with an unmistakable depth of feeling for the man she addressed.

'Eileen! What? How?' He looked round to find faces smiling at his bewilderment.

She came to him, slotted her arm through his and kissed him on the cheek. 'Arrived today. Kevin and Sarah visited me on their way back and persuaded me to come with them. Not that I took much persuading. So here I am, and thanks to Sarah and Mr Langton more than comfortable.'

'And you are here to stay?' queried Sean, still bemused.

'If you want me to?'

Her query was made lightly but he knew what she was really saying. For one moment thoughts of Lydia loomed in his mind but then were dismissed. Here was the girl who had shared his life in Dublin, who had brought a sparkle to it even in the harshest times and in the face of public criticism. How could he ever have thought of abandoning her for someone else? If he had, his position would have been precarious, not knowing what Lydia really wanted from life. No, here was a girl who knew him, his ways and his

298

dreams, who would give him a devoted and secure marriage. When this last word sprang to mind it jolted him. But in the situation they were now in, among such friends, there were only two options – to part or to marry.

'Of course I want you to. I said I would come for you when things were better. Well, they are decidedly better. Kevin and Sarah have just beaten me to it.' He swung her round and kissed her unashamedly with a fervour that spoke of the old Sean she had known in Dublin. She knew then she had nothing to fear from any rival.

Half an hour later when Lydia and Luke arrived, they found a stranger in the house. Lydia hid her surprise when Eileen was introduced as Sean's sweetheart from Dublin, for he had never mentioned having a close relationship with anyone.

His fears about Lydia's reaction were allayed by the look she gave him. He knew their liaison on the way to Whitby would never be disclosed by her. For that he was thankful, but he also realised it was proof that she'd had no interest in him other than to use him for her own purposes.

'So, we are celebrating Eileen and Sean's reunion,' Lydia commented when she had been told how this had come about. 'Well, we have something else we can cele-brate. I returned from Newcastle yesterday evening. The *Ironmaster*, our new ship, will have sailed for Whitby today. The day after tomorrow should see her bring the first of what I hope will be many cargoes of ironstone for the Bolckow and Vaughan works. And that should mean good profits for those with shares in the ship.'

A buzz of excitement passed through the small gathering.

In a quiet moment, as James Langton charged glasses for a toast, Sean explained to Eileen what lay behind Lydia's state-ment. 'I have a share in that ship,' he concluded, though he made no reference as to how that had come about.

'Then you are on the way to the future you always dreamed of,' whispered Eileen.

'For you,' he returned.

'You're a fine man, Sean Casey.' There was love in the pressure of her hand on his.

With the *Ironmaster* fully loaded, Captain Anderson prepared to sail from Whitby.

A new ship in the port, built elsewhere, always raised interest locally. Captains between voyages studied the craft; sailors out of a job wished they had been chosen by Captain Anderson to crew her; shipbuilders cast a critical eye over her construction, wondering why, if the ship was to sail from Whitby, they had not been given the work of building her; while merchants were more interested in her cargo and whether they could embark in the same trade. Among them was Nathan Middleton.

He drew on his cigar. 'Another ore ship?' There was scepticism in his tone as he spoke to Aidan Wesley. 'Not Edgar Martin's, surely? He has two already, would have thought that enough for the trade.'

'No. New firm. Tees Shipping. Good prospects.'

Nathan, noting the keen edge to Aidan's tone, eyed him with curiosity. 'You sound enthusiastic. I'm surprised to see you here. Didn't know you had any interest in ships.'

'Ships themselves – not much. But they're part of the life of this port and in that respect I'm interested in what they do and the money they bring to boost Whitby's economy. That's of prime interest to us all.'

'True,' agreed Nathan. 'So why are you sounding so keen on this particular vessel?'

'Haven't you shares in her?'

'No.' Nathan looked mystified.

'You weren't approached?'

'No.'

'Young Irishman. Smart young fellow. Mind, he had a persuasive tongue but there was a genuine knowledge of the situation behind it. Seems there's a growing demand for ore along the Tees, more than Martin can supply, so this

Irishman was looking for investors in a new enterprise with the names of Bolckow and Vaughan also involved. Know them, do you?'

Nathan gave a little nod. 'I've heard of them.'

'Well,' continued Aidan, 'with their interest I thought the investment must be sound. I'm surprised you weren't approached.'

Nathan made no comment and a few moments later he said goodbye to Aidan. With his thoughts still on what he had just heard, he headed for his office. He'd make some enquiries about the demand for ironstone. Maybe a switch in his trading pattern would be profitable. If he was to have a closer working relationship with Jonas Drayton, he should also tell him what he had heard about the possibilities opening up in the iron trade.

Chapter Sixteen

My Dearest Lydia

I write again so soon in order to keep you abreast of events in Whitby, especially in connection with your venture.

The port is buzzing with excitement after three voyages by the *Ironmaster* alongside those of Mr Martin's ships. Rumours abound as to the quantity of ore needed along the Tees.

Your uncle has shown great interest and is annoyed that he was not invited to take shares in the ship. Father told him that all the shares may have been snapped up before the Irishman had a chance to approach him. This only heightened his interest. Your uncle is talking about switching his ships to the ironstone trade, and is trying to persuade Father that it will be a better investment than anything else they were discussing.

But Father won't consider doing that. He's being rather crafty. He sees that if your uncle did so the Middleton wine trade with Spain would be there for the taking. Of course, he cannot put that in hand until your uncle moves into the iron ore trade.

These are exciting times in Whitby. I wish you were here to share them. With your venture meeting such success it may be that you will soon be able to declare that to my father and so seal our future together.

I look forward to that day and until then, and beyond, my love is always yours.

David

Lydia read that letter with glee. Though she was reassured by David's declaration of his love, she was more excited to learn that her uncle was on the brink of moving into the ironstone trade. Make that final move and his trading would be in close proximity with hers, enabling her to watch and hopefully, before too long, make a calculated move against him.

Buoyed up by these thoughts and with the need to discuss the situation with her brother she persuaded him that as the day was warm and fine they should spend the afternoon together in the Eston Hills six miles south of Middlesbrough.

'It'll do you both good to get out into the countryside and the fresh air. You'll be away from all this grime and smoke and be able to hear something other than the din from the rolling mill,' said Nell when Lydia announced what they were proposing to do. 'I'll pack you a picnic – a few sandwiches and a piece of that homemade fruit cake you like. Then you needn't be thinking you'll have to be back by a certain time to eat.'

'You are so kind.' Lydia gave her a hug. 'And you're right, it will be good to get away from all this noise and smoke. I wonder how you stick it.'

'It's where I've lived for ten years, I'd miss it if I left, but you're different. When you returned from Whitby I could tell that you wished you could have stayed. I think you'll go back some day.'

Lydia smiled. 'I believe I will. Maybe one day soon.'

Luke passed a packet to his sister and started to open a similar one himself.

They had found a small outcrop of stones on the hillside and settled themselves on the flattest. The sun shone on

303

their backs. The air was clear and they had enjoyed its purity after the smoke that hovered over Middlesbrough. From where they were sitting they could see the chimneys of the works spewing out smoke which hung in a dense cloud over the houses and buildings. People, dependent on it for their livelihoods, grumbled about it but knew they must tolerate it. No smoke, no money. No money, no opportunities.

'This is wonderful,' commented Luke, looking over the hillside and drawing fresh air into his lungs. 'I'm glad you persuaded me to come.'

'Well, you haven't been outside Middlesbrough for months. It's time you did. Wouldn't you like to escape all that?' She waved in the direction of the smoke and grime.

'Who wouldn't?' he replied. 'But it was necessary to come here. We needed a living.'

'I know, Luke, and I'm proud of what you have done. But now we have a new chance.'

'You mean Tees Shipping?'

'Yes.'

'But I thought you didn't want our names mentioned in connection with it?'

'That's right, but only until the right moment, when our trading is successful and we will be in a position to avenge Father. That could be sooner than you think. Here, read this.' She handed him the letter from David.

He read it quickly and, with the implications dawning on him, again more slowly. He looked up and handed it back to Lydia.

'Well?' she said.

'I can't believe that Uncle Nathan will concentrate wholly on the ironstone trade.'

'Why else do you think I told Captain Anderson to extol its prospects every time he was in Whitby?'

'You did what?' Luke sat up in astonishment.

'I merely suggested that he might spread the word there were great chances for profits in the ironstone trade as

304

more and more stone is wanted.'

'But you don't know the capacity of the furnaces at Witton, nor if there will be any demand for the quantity they can turn out. Besides, it's a costly operation. At any time Mr Bolckow may decide it is too expensive to ship ore in from Whitby.'

'Where else can he get it?'

'True, he doesn't appear to have another source.'

'Then it's got to be shipped in.'

'But if it proves too expensive he may decide to close down the whole operation.'

'You're being gloomy.'

'No, only practical.'

'Well,' snapped Lydia, irritated by Luke's pessimism, 'that's not likely, in my opinion. Besides, what's more important to us is the fact that Uncle is prepared to invest heavily in the trade.' Her voice was harsh now, eyes narrowed as she dwelt on the vision conjured up by her next statement. 'And that will give us the opportunity to sink him.'

'Lydia!'

'Don't look so shocked, Luke. You have always known that is what I desire. You can't desert Father now!'

'As much as I would like to see Uncle pay in some way, I can't help wondering what Father would have wanted.'

'Revenge!' she cried, passion in her voice.

'Would he? I'm not so sure. Wouldn't he just have got on with life as we have done?'

'He didn't get a chance because of Uncle Nathan.'

'He did have a choice, but he chose . . .'

'A way to help us,' cut in Lydia sharply. 'Don't ever forget that, Luke.'

'You don't know for certain that it was a deliberate act on his part.'

'I believe it,' she cried. 'Surely you do?'

Luke shook his head. 'Lydia, I don't like what this thirst for revenge is doing to you. It is changing you, making you

305

into two people. There is dear likeable Lydia, the side you show to your friends and the sister I've always known. Then I see someone I don't like, a cold calculating person who is prepared to use people to achieve what she wants.'

'Use people?' She tossed her head. 'I don't do that.'

'You mean, you don't want to believe that.'

'Tell me, how do I?'

'David. You were disgusted that he would not forsake his position in his father's firm yet you played up to him so that he would supply you with information. I wonder whether you reciprocate the love he expresses in that recent letter?'

He waited for her to tell him but instead she prompted, 'And?'

'Captain Anderson. You got him to spread the word that more ironstone is wanted, and that information has only a thin foundation in truth. Sean, by some means, you persuaded to interest people in investing in the *Ironmaster*. As for the investors, your main aim was not to make money for them but to finance a company you could use as a means of revenge.' He paused and looked hard at her. 'Lydia, don't destroy the sister I know.'

She smiled at him, the smile he had always known, the smile filled with warmth and love. 'Luke, don't worry, that sister will always be here. The other woman you think you see will step back the moment I achieve my aim.'

'Very well,' he said, with a resigned shrug of his shoulders. 'If you say so. But be careful, don't antagonise anyone who might be able to hurt you.' With that veiled implication he let the matter drop, and they turned their attention to enjoying the rest of the day.

They took up the packages they had left untouched when Lydia had produced the letter from David, and sat in the warm sunshine enjoying the picnic.

'Yon must be the blast furnaces at Witton.' Luke pointed towards smoke rising in the distance across the river to the northwest.

Lydia acknowledged this and added a question. 'Then

306

why did Mr Bolckow and Mr Vaughan build the rolling mill at Middlesbrough?'

'That was established first when they were importing pig iron from Scotland. When the price of that rose they needed to find another source. They decided to build their own blast furnaces and make their own pig iron.'

'Why at Witton?'

'The proximity of coal in the Durham coalfields and an expected source of ironstone nearby.'

'And that didn't materialise?'

'The coal did but the ironstone didn't. Well, not in the quantity they had hoped, so they had to import Grosmont ironstone through Whitby.'

'And that's the situation now, the costly enterprise you talk about?'

'Aye. And it worries Mr Bolckow and Vaughan.'

They lapsed into silence, each surveying the scene before them. The slope of the hills gave way to green fields and grazing cattle, and beyond the river with its huge bend taking it southwards, and just to the east of that the new town of Middlesbrough between the river and the railway.

Street upon street of identical houses crowded together to house the workers of the rolling mill, the pottery and the coal staithes, as near to their workplaces as possible. Lydia could make out the towering chimneys of the rolling mill belching their smoke, creating grime which settled over land and buildings alike and polluted the air. But where it was there was money. Wages to be gained, money to make existence palatable if handled right. But there were those who couldn't, who had little pride in their homes and surroundings, and already sections of the new town were getting a bad reputation for their squalor and unruliness.

Lydia had witnessed it all. She wanted to escape back to her beloved Whitby where she could breathe fresher air and feel the tang of the sea in her lungs. Yet she knew there were other people who would not exchange this busy, grimy town. They enjoyed being part of the rapid growth of an infant industrial centre and did not know that there was every possibility their livelihoods could disappear and the town stagnate if the cost of producing iron could not be reduced.

'Let's walk a way.' Luke's suggestion, breaking into her thoughts, startled her.

He jumped to his feet and held out his hand to Lydia. She took it and he pulled her from the ground. She stretched, then smoothed her dress.

'Which way?' she asked.

He glanced from left to right. 'This.' He started to the right.

Their gaze continually roved across the landscape, speculating on this landmark or that. They aired their knowledge of the plants and grasses they saw and negotiated the occasional outcrop of rock or jumble of stones.

Lydia's foot caught on some stones half hidden in the grass. She stumbled and fell. Luke was beside her in an instant and stooped to help her up. His left arm came round her shoulders, his right gave her support, but at that moment he froze, making no effort to take her weight.

She glanced up at him. He was staring at the ground beside her, where the stones and rocks she had dislodged had scattered. 'What is it, Luke?'

He said nothing but helped her to her feet and then crouched lower, picking up stones and examining them. He discarded some, placed others to one side.

Surprised by his actions, struck by the intense concentration on his face, and sensing the tension which gripped him, Lydia put her question again.

He did not answer directly but said almost to himself, 'I don't believe it! I don't ...'

'What?' Lydia's tone was sharp.

When he looked up at her, she saw fire in his eyes.

'Lydia, this is ironstone!'

For a split second this announcement did not register, then as he repeated 'ironstone' the implications struck her.

'What? It can't be.'

'It is, I'll swear it. Look.' He pulled her down to crouch beside him, picking up one of the pieces of stone he had set aside. 'Look, the stones in this pile are different from those in the other. These have a green cast. They're like the stones we're bringing from Grosmont. Ironstone, here, right on the doorstep of the works.' His voice rose with excitement. 'Think what this means, Lydia!'

She already had. 'But there might not be any more,' she added by way of a caution and hoped she was right.

'And there might be,' he countered, springing to his feet. 'We must look around.'

He started off, stopping every few yards to examine more stones. Lydia made a pretence of similarly looking but her mind was on what it would mean if there was a huge supply of ironstone here. No more needed from Grosmont, no more shipments from Whitby. Announce a find now and Whitby ship owners, ready to invest in the ironstone trade, would retreat from doing so. Among them her uncle. And her chance of revenge would be lost!

'Come on, let's go this way,' Luke called and waved for his sister to follow him. She could do no other. When she caught him up he said, 'There's a depression yonder, I'd like to look there.'

Still locked in her own thoughts, she said nothing.

Luke paused on the rim of a hollow and surveyed it. It had the look of a small quarry to which grass was beginning to return and, in some parts, cling precariously to patches of soil between layers of rock.

'Over here,' he said, and started down the slope. In a few moments he was examining the places from which rocks had been taken. Stones lay scattered around. Lydia saw his eyes brighten with excitement. The greenish cast was unmistakable. Luke started to scrape at an area of exposed rock on the side of the quarry.

'Yes!' he yelled. 'Yes!' He swung round to face his sister. 'What a find!'

309

'Don't get excited too soon,' she warned him. 'You can't be sure how much there is.'

'I know, but I reckon we've stumbled on to something big. Mr Vaughan will instigate a proper exploration as soon as I tell him. Come on, Lydia.' He grasped her hand. 'We must get back.'

She resisted. 'Wait, Luke! Wait! Think what this means.'

'Wait? Why?' He was astonished by his sister's reaction and the desperation which clouded her face.

'Think, Luke. This will alter everything.'

'I know it will,' he broke in. 'It will lower the cost of transporting the iron ore and make Mr Bolckow's and Mr Vaughan's production less costly.'

'No, I don't mean that,' returned Lydia irritably.

'What then?' he demanded.

'It will set back our chances of avenging Father's death.'

'What?' Luke was astonished at this connection.

'I showed you the letter from David. Uncle Nathan is seriously considering switching everything to the iron trade.'

'If what we've found reveals big deposits then Uncle had better think again.'

'Exactly. But if we say nothing about this until he is fully committed, this revelation will ruin him.'

Luke shook his head. 'He'd switch back to his contacts in the Spanish wine trade.'

'Not if we'd cornered his market there.'

Luke stared at her, taking in the implication behind her statement. 'You mean, we take his wine trade, knowing he's let it go in favour of the iron trade, then reveal what we have found today?'

'Exactly. Uncle will face ruin.'

'But we can't keep this to ourselves. It could affect many more people. Supposing, because of the expense, Mr Bolckow decides to close down the works? What happens to all the workers? This find could prevent all that, save them hardship, keep them from ... You're using people again for your own ends again.'

310

'It won't come to that,' protested Lydia.

'How can you be sure? No, Lydia, we can't do this. We can't play with so many lives.'

'We won't be. Uncle is on the point of investing. As soon as his ship has made one voyage we will tell Mr Vaughan of our find.' Luke looked doubtful. 'Just keep this knowledge between us for a little while.' She saw doubt in his eyes. 'You want Uncle to suffer for what he did, don't you?' He did not speak. 'Don't you?' she pressed.

He gave a little nod. 'Yes,' he said quietly. 'But not at the expense of other people.'

'Then just give me time,' she said. 'Everything will be all right.'

He bit his lip, still reluctant to agree.

'Please, Luke. For me?'

He met his sister's pleading gaze. They had been so close all their lives, especially since their mother had died. He had never refused her anything, never opposed anything she proposed, he had always been there to help and support her. He could not refuse her this wish.

'All right. But if people's jobs are threatened, livelihoods put at risk, then we must reveal what we have found today.'

'Very well.'

'And I ask you again: be careful, don't destroy yourself nor anyone dear to you.'

'I won't. All I want is for Uncle Nathan to know that Father has been avenged.'

'. . . and your uncle is finally committing himself to the iron trade. Father tried to make him see that he should not put everything into it, but he was adamant.'

Lydia reread the paragraph in the letter she had received from David the day after she and Luke had discovered the iron ore. Excitement gripped her. Things were beginning to fall into place. Now she must make her next move quickly. She left the house and sought out Sean.

311

'I want you to do another job for Tees Shipping,' she said with an engaging smile.

'Very well,' he replied. 'I'm only too willing if it will raise the dividend on my shares.'

'Oh, it will that, if you are successful. I want you to go to London and contact an agent who represents the most important wine-producing family in Spain. I know that their usual shipper can no longer oblige and want you to get that trade for Tees Shipping.'

'But I know nothing about wine,' Sean pointed out.

'You don't need to. All I want you to do is to make sure we get the contract to ship their wine to England. You negotiated the sale of the shares in the *Ironmaster* successfully. Now I want you to make sure it is our ship which fills the void left by my uncle's switch to the iron trade.'

The statement was out before Lydia could halt it. However, Sean showed no sign of realising what she had said. Did it matter if he had? He knew nothing of her strained relationship with Uncle Nathan.

But Sean had noticed and noted. Was there a link here with what he had learned in Whitby? How did she know of her uncle's dealings in sufficient detail to be able to step in and take up the trade he was abandoning? David Drayton? Was she using him? Was there some ulterior motive in her actions? And what of the *Ironmaster*? Surely Mr Bolckow wouldn't allow the ship to be diverted to another trade? But did he know? If not, why had Lydia acted on her own?

Questions whirled in Sean's mind but he had no answers. He needed an ally, someone who would listen to the facts and his suppositions and help him draw conclusions.

'All right, I can see that, but if the question of wine comes up, and it's likely to if I'm dealing with an expert, I'd be stumped to sound authoritative. It would be safer if I had someone with me who had some knowledge of wine.'

Lydia looked thoughtful for a moment. 'Maybe you are right. I want no queries. The agent must see that we know how to handle the product and that we have some under-standing of the types of wine. Kevin could help. He displayed some knowledge when we dined at the Langtons'.'

'Very well.' Sean breathed more easily. The suggestion had come from Lydia, but he had his ally.

'See him today. You must leave for London tomorrow. I cannot afford to miss this opportunity.'

That sounded personal, as if this enterprise was for her benefit alone. What had she in mind?

Sean had marshalled his thoughts by the time he and Kevin boarded the train for London. He was going to have ample time to recruit an ally.

As they proceeded south, Kevin listened intently while Sean acquainted him with what he knew of Lydia, and what he had gleaned in Whitby. He voiced his suspicions and theories.

'There it is, Kevin. Throughout all this Lydia seems to be using people for her own ends, though I think that only becomes apparent when you look beneath the surface, and I believe it is not in her true nature. But have we the right to interfere?'

Kevin gave a little shake of his head. 'Tricky. We have all found Lydia to be a genuine person so far, kind, con-siderate, friendly. From what you learned in Whitby, and supposing the account of a row with her uncle after her father's death is true, her actions could be aimed at revenge.'

'Is there anything we can do?'

'If we don't, we'll have to live with the consequences. I know how thin the line can be between survival and utter destruction. My obsession with revenging Seamus's murder nearly led me to commit a heinous crime myself which would have affected many others. Lydia may never resort to what I was planning to do but she will still have to live with her actions for the rest of her life. If she is seeking revenge other people will be hurt, maybe even destroyed by what she does.'

When Jonas Drayton entered his son's office, David knew immediately that his father had something important on his mind and that whatever it was had exciting implications. He did not speak but leaned back in his chair and waited for his father to disclose whatever it was. Jonas sat down opposite his son.

'David, now Nathan Middleton has committed everything he has to the ironstone trade, I think we should seize the opportunity to acquire his Spanish wine trade. I want you to go to London and seal an agreement with the Zabaleta Wine Company's agent to take over Middleton's shipments.'

David already knew that his father had set his mind on this move and there was no question of not agreeing to carry out his request. Besides it would be a great asset to the business to have this trade. 'Very well, Father. I'll go tomorrow.'

'May I ask who has obtained the contract to take over the shipments formerly handled by Mr Nathan Middleton's company?' It was a disappointed David who put the question in the office of the agent for the Zabaleta Wine Company. He had arrived in London full of confidence that he would return to Whitby with a solid addition to the Drayton business. But he'd been too late.

'Certainly, Mr Drayton. The two Irishmen gave no indication that the deal should be kept secret. The contract has gone to Tees Shipping. Their negotiators were pleasant, made us a good offer, and I was convinced our future prospects would be good with them.'

David was hardly hearing the final words. Tees Shipping? Lydia! She had used the knowledge he had disclosed in his letters to snatch this particular trade from under his nose. She knew that his father was interested in

314

taking it, yet she had not done the honourable thing and held back. *Two* Irishmen? One must surely be Sean Casey whom he had met in Whitby. The other? He did not know. If Casey was negotiator for Lydia, how close were they? Close in business? Or was there more to the relationship?

'I'm sorry we have missed having the pleasure of dealing with the Zabaleta Wine Company,' said David regretfully. 'As a matter of interest, can you tell me where the two Irishmen are staying?'

'Yes, but I can assure you they will not think of selling you their rights.'

'I did not have that in mind. I was merely interested in their trading activities and thought it might be advantageous to both our companies to see if there is any area in which we might work for our mutual benefit.'

Though such a thing was farthest from David's mind, his assertion produced a result.

'That is a commendable attitude,' replied the agent, 'particularly as they have just beaten you to the contract. The Irishmen are staying at the Mitre Tavern in Fleet Street.'

David rose from his chair. 'Many thanks.' He extended his hand. 'Maybe we can do business some time in the future.'

The agent shook hands. 'There is always that possibility.'

David had many things to occupy his thoughts as he walked to Fleet Street. There was much he needed to find out.

He had no trouble in locating the two Irishmen, for they were enjoying a celebratory meal in the tavern's dining room.

Sean's cheerful smile, as he exchanged a quip with Kevin, changed to more than a casual surprise when he saw David approaching them.

'Good day, gentlemen,' he said pleasantly when he reached their table.

'Good day to you,' returned Sean. He glanced at Kevin. 'This is Mr David Drayton from Whitby. Mr Drayton – Kevin Harper, a colleague and good friend of mine.'

The two men exchanged pleasantries, Kevin trying to sum up the man who had figured in some of the things Sean had told him about Lydia. His quick assessment was favourable. There was something about David Drayton that spoke of a man of integrity, an impression which was swiftly confirmed.

'You do not seem surprised to see us,' commented Sean, 'which can only mean one thing. That you knew we were here.'

David gave a slight bow in acceptance of Sean's perspicacity. 'That is true.'

'And that means you want to speak with us.'

'Yes, I need some questions answering.'

'Then please join us. As you see, we have only just started our meal.' Sean looked across the room, and saw a waiter watching them in anticipation of being of service now that the two Irishmen, who had tipped him handsomely for one of the better tables, had been joined by a third man. Sean raised his hand. In a flash the waiter was at the table. 'Please set a place for this gentleman and serve him with what he wants.'

'Yes, sir.'

Kevin made room for David beside him. His place was soon set with cutlery and a glass, and he quickly made his choice of food.

'Because you came here to find us you must have got the information from the agent of the Zabaleta Wine Company.'

'Yes, and was surprised to learn that two Irishmen representing Tees Shipping had forestalled me on a deal my father particularly wanted to secure. I assumed one of the Irishmen must be you, Mr Casey, for not long ago you were in Whitby looking for investors in a ship to be owned by that same company. Of the other Irishman I had no knowledge.'

316

'I am sorry you were disappointed, Mr Drayton, and that you have had a wasted journey.'

'It may not be wasted,' replied David, then paused while the waiter poured some wine. 'But that will depend on the answers I get.'

'And whether I can give them.'

'That is right. But I have a feeling you can.' He cast a glance at Kevin which Sean interpreted as a question.

'You can talk freely in front of Kevin. He knows as much as I do. He has a share in the new ship and so Tees Shipping is of interest to him as well, though he knows no more than I have told him.'

'I suppose Miss Lydia Middleton is the reason you are here?' queried David. He noted a surprised reaction in Sean's eyes which was disguised almost as soon as it appeared. He gave a wry smile and went on, 'Oh, I know that she is behind Tees Shipping. She told me herself when she was in Whitby recently, at the same time as you, Mr Casey.'

'Were we?' Sean was cautious.

'I saw you together on the west pier.'

'Oh.'

'I thought then that you and Lydia were more than friends, but I saw her later and she convinced me otherwise.'

'Let me assure you that is the truth. I am a great admirer of hers, and at one time that admiration might have gone further, but I realised my heart was with an Irish girl and still is.'

'And that girl is now in Middlesbrough,' put in Kevin.

David nodded, pleased to have this news and to know that there had been no serious relationship between the Irishman and Lydia. He realised that if he was to have answers to queries about Lydia's behaviour he would have to reveal more of his own.

'I don't know whether Lydia ever told you about me,' he said, 'but we go back to childhood.' He went on to tell

317

them about his father's opposition to his marriage to Lydia and the reasons for the course of action he had taken. 'Now Lydia tells me that she took the opportunity to form Tees Shipping in order to break down my father's opposition, but there is something about it all which troubles me. This venture into the wine trade seems a deliberate move to take over her uncle's contacts. Why? And how is she going to do that? She has only one ship and that is committed to the iron trade.'

'The answer to the second question is, we don't know,' said Kevin. 'She has disclosed nothing to us but was adamant that we get this trade.'

'As to why, all we can assume is that she wants to make things difficult for her uncle if his switch to the iron trade goes wrong,' suggested Sean.

'That would put her in a position to inflict further harm,' added Kevin.

'Why would she want to do that?' asked David cautiously.

Kevin gave a wry smile. 'You tell us, Mr Drayton. From what Sean learned in Whitby, there were some doubts about why, or even how, Miss Lydia's father died, and apparently there were family rows and threats resulting from that. You were in Whitby at the time, you must have heard talk.'

David nodded, and went on to confirm what Sean was told by Potter. 'And I do know how she hated her uncle after her father's death. It changed her in some ways, changes which I hope the passage of time will eliminate because the dear, sweet girl that I love is still there.'

'Exactly,' agreed Sean.

'We all like Lydia,' confirmed Kevin. 'Sarah won't hear a word against her.'

'And my Eileen, since she arrived from Dublin, has taken to her too.'

'This is all very well, but admiration gets us nowhere. We need to know what she is up to. And if she is bent on avenging her father, how she hopes to achieve it.' There was distress in David's voice.

'I begin to see that she has used, and will go on using, people for her own ends,' pointed out Kevin.

'Then she needs to be stopped one way or another,' cried David.

'And we can't do that unless we know what she is doing and planning.'

Chapter Seventeen

Anxious to receive Sean's and Kevin's reports, Lydia hurried to the station. Coming on to the platform, she saw a handful of people awaiting the train's arrival. They stood or strolled, trying to hide their impatience, they read notices for the fourth time and glanced in the direction from which the train would come.

Was that a low rumble? She looked along the track. It must have been. Others were looking that way too. It grew louder and louder. The engine came in sight. Nearer and nearer. Excitement heightened amongst those on the platform. They watched with something akin to awe the iron monster breathing smoke as it hauled its carriages with ease into the station. The shattering noise was flung back by the walls. The engine's speed decreased. There was a hiss of steam. The clash of metal on metal rang out the full length of the train as the links between the carriages clattered against each other. Carriage doors swung open. Passengers stepped on to the platform. Mothers tried to calm exuberant children, and men struggled with luggage. Lydia ran her gaze over them, trying to identify her men among the throng of people.

Sean! Kevin! They were there. She raised her hand and waved. Her excited anticipation of good news was suddenly changed to surprise. David! What on earth was he doing here with Sean and Kevin? She stood still and waited.

Passengers stepped around her, but three men, smiling broadly, stopped in front of her.

'Ah, sure now, I wonder why the little lady is looking so surprised?' said Sean, putting on a serious expression which could not disguise the twinkle of mischief in his eyes. He glanced at David. 'Would you be knowing now, Davey?'

Lydia cocked an eyebrow at Sean. 'As if you didn't know.' She turned to David. 'This is pleasant but most unexpected.'

'For me too,' he replied, allowing his eyes to speak of his continued admiration for her. He kissed her on the cheek. 'I met these two gentlemen in London and decided I may as well accompany them to Middlesbrough and see you before returning to Whitby.'

The answer sounded a little too glib to her. She felt there was more to this than there appeared.

'It's nice to see you, David, but Sean and Kevin have important news for me. Can I see you later?'

He ignored her question. 'Indeed they have, and it does, or rather did, concern me.'

Lydia glanced queryingly at Sean and Kevin. What had gone on in London?

'If there is no one in the waiting room,' Sean indicated a door close to the station exit, 'shall we talk in there?'

'Very well,' Lydia agreed and led the way.

The room was empty. It was austere but boasted a large table in the centre and several chairs. The walls were painted a light brown and hung with prints of Middlesbrough Farm, the villages of Linthorpe and Marton and, appropriately, a drawing of the railway suspension bridge across the Tees. Kevin quickly arranged four chairs for them.

But Lydia had little time to note her surroundings. 'Well?' she said as she sat down. She looked directly at Sean for an explanation.

'Kevin and I completed your mission successfully,' he started.

321

'This is excellent news.' She smiled her thanks to them with a feeling of relief that David's presence did not spell doom to that prospect.

'Kevin and I were having a meal at the tavern where we were staying when David came in.'

'Not by chance, I may add,' he said. 'I was in London to secure the Zabaleta contract but was told that Tees Shipping, represented by two Irishmen, had beaten me to it. Knowing that you, Lydia, were running Tees Shipping and were hoping you would eventually impress my father with what you had achieved, I was curious. I obtained the address where these gentlemen were staying and sought them out.'

'And was your curiosity satisfied?' she asked.

'Yes and no. I accept that you beat me to your uncle's trade with Zabaleta and that I was defeated fairly. But I was curious as to how you were going to deal with it when you had only one ship, and that committed to the iron trade out of Whitby to Middlesbrough. These two gentlemen could not supply me with an answer. I believed they were not holding anything back from me but were genuinely not privy to your plans. So curiosity got the better of me and here I am.'

Lydia gave a little laugh. 'My plans? Well, they are mine and no one else's.'

'Lydia, we have completed a deal to ship Zabaleta's wine,' said Sean. 'We have to fulfil that agreement. Before Kevin and I left for London you said it was imperative that we secured the contract, and you assured us you had everything in hand. But, as David says, how are you going to do it with our only ship committed to moving ironstone?'

'Try to switch it and Mr Bolckow and Mr Vaughan will block the move,' Kevin pointed out. 'Together they hold more shares than you, and with ironstone shipments booming the other shareholders will rally to their side.'

'What you say is perfectly true,' she agreed calmly, 'but

you will see, they will agree to my plan to put the *Ironmaster* to the Spanish wine trade.'

The three men were astonished by her air of certainty. They glanced at each other as if hoping that one of them could supply an answer.

Lydia gave a little chuckle. 'If you can hold your curiosity in check until tomorrow evening, I will hopefully enlighten you then.' Taking further control she went on, 'What I suggest is that you get David a room at the Middlesbrough Hotel. While you are there book us a private room for a meeting at seven o'clock tomorrow evening. We will all be there plus Luke. I hope then that I shall be able to answer your questions.' She eyed them all in turn but no one said any more. She rose from her chair. 'Very well, gentlemen, there is no more to be said now.' She started for the door.

'Lydia.' David's voice pulled her up short. She turned slowly to face him. 'Will you dine with me this evening?'

She gave the sort of pause which made him wonder if he should have made the invitation, then smiled at his uneasiness. 'Certainly, David. I would love to.' The relief on his face amused her all the more. 'But don't think that wining and dining me will persuade me to tell you any more. That is for tomorrow evening.' She walked out of the room.

Lydia's steps were brisk. She was elated. Thank goodness David had not contacted Zabaleta's agent first. If he had, all her plans would have gone awry for she dare not hold back the secret she and Luke shared any longer.

Her mind was so set on the future that she was oblivious to the hustle and bustle along the streets leading to the Bolckow and Vaughan rolling mill. But as she neared it she became aware of the thunderous noise coming from the mill, of the tall chimneys belching smoke into the air, of the smell and the grime which filled the air. She thought of Whitby and longed for the tang of the sea air, the breeze fresh from the ocean filling her lungs, and the cry of the seagulls lazy in their flight. 'Soon, soon,' she whispered, filling herself with an urgent longing which would not be denied.

Reaching the jetty used by the ore ships, she saw Luke and waved. He immediately left Bob Chase, to whom he was talking, and came to her.

Before he reached her he could tell from her obvious excitement that she had good news.

'They've done it!' she cried.

Without breaking his step, he swept his arms round her waist and whirled her round.

'Then we are safe when we break the news to Mr Vaughan,' he cried, his faced wreathed in smiles. He too longed to be back in Whitby. This would give them the chance, for the *Ironmaster* could switch her port to Whitby and trade from there.

'And Uncle will face ruin!'

The triumphant note in his sister's voice alarmed him. His face became serious. 'Lydia, things are going well for us. We can use Tees Shipping to expand, free from the shackles of the iron trade. Don't let a vendetta ruin everything.'

'It won't,' she replied forcefully. 'When Uncle Nathan comes crashing down everything will be so much better.'

He knew it was no good arguing with her when she was in this sort of mood, besides he wanted his uncle to know that they held his future in the balance, but such drastic measures as his sister envisaged . . . He was not sure.

'Luke,' she went on, 'go now and arrange a meeting for us two with Mr Vaughan tomorrow morning. Don't give any hint as to what it is about but say it is important.'

He nodded. 'Very well. Where's Sean? I thought he might have been with you.'

'He and Kevin are taking David to the Middlesbrough Hotel.'

'You mean David Drayton? What's he doing here? And why with them?'

Lydia explained quickly. When she told him about the meeting tomorrow evening, she added, 'That makes it all the more essential that we see Mr Vaughan in the morning.'

'Lydia, come home to Whitby. I'm sure Tees Shipping will be proof enough for Father.' David put his plea as he strolled arm in arm with her towards the green fields of Linthorpe.

The evening was warm. Though the light was beginning to fade, the sun still held sway in the west.

'I can't, not yet. There are things I have to do first.'

'Do them from Whitby if you need to. Surely you want to get away from all this?' He glanced over his shoulder and with a nod of his head indicated the ugly consequences of industrialisation beside the river.

'Yes, I do, and I will as soon as I can.'

'That can't be soon enough for me.' He stopped and turned to her. His arms slid around her waist and he pulled her gently to him, all the while his eyes expressing a feeling she could not mistake. 'I love you, Lydia. I want to make you a home in Whitby.'

'You shall, my love, but not just yet.'

'What is holding you back? We can overcome Father's objections with what you have achieved.'

'There is more,' she said, 'as you will see tomorrow evening.'

'What more have you to offer?'

She laughed. 'I told you earlier today you would learn no more this evening. And you won't.' She pushed herself on to her toes and kissed him. 'Be patient, my love.'

She would have slipped from his arms but he held her. His lips met hers passionately. 'I love you, Lydia.'

She returned his kiss with equal fervour. 'That's a promise for the future,' she whispered.

'And the future can't come quickly enough for me. I hope this meeting will speed that up.'

'It probably will. But it depends on what happens to-morrow morning.'

'Tomorrow morning?'

'I thought that would arouse your curiosity.' She laughed. 'And don't look so expectant. I'm telling you no more, so don't raise the question when we dine this evening.'

Excitement gripped both Lydia and Luke the next day as at nine o'clock they approached the home of Mr John Vaughan.

'Mr Luke Middleton and his sister,' said Luke when the door was opened by a maid.

'You are expected, sir, miss. Please come in.'

They stepped inside and she closed the door.

'May I take your coats? Come this way, please.' She led the way to the large drawing room. 'I will tell Mr Vaughan that you have arrived. He will be with you in a minute.'

'Thank you,' said Luke.

'Should I take your bag, sir?'

'No, thank you. I will need it.'

The maid retreated and a few moments later the door opened and Mr Vaughan came in.

'Good day to you both.' He greeted them with a smile. 'Your request yesterday intrigued me, Luke, and I have been puzzling over it ever since, especially as you said it was so important. And it intrigued me all the more, Miss Lydia, when your brother said you would be here too. So let us sit down and you can tell me what this is all about.'

Lydia sat down but Luke remained standing for a moment.

'May I, sir?' He indicated that he would like to place the bag on the table.

'Certainly.'

Luke opened the bag. He took out a cloth and laid it on the table to protect the surface. Then one by one he took

326

out four pieces of stone and placed them carefully on the cloth.

As he was doing so, Lydia kept her eyes on Mr Vaughan. She saw him lean forward and peer curiously at the stones. He reached out, picked one up and turned it over in his hand, examining it with care. When he looked up, she saw in his eyes the light of recognition mingled with excitement.

'You know what this is?' Before Luke could answer he replied to his own question. 'Of course you do. You've been handling it ever since you came to Middlesbrough and no doubt before that in Whitby. Where did you get it? You wouldn't be bringing it to me if it was from one of your shipments.'

'In the Eston Hills.'

'What?' Mr Vaughan raised his eyebrows in surprise.

'Lydia and I went for a picnic there. We were walking the hillside when she tripped over a heap of stones hidden by the grass. Some were scattered. When I went to help her to her feet I noticed these. We looked further and found evidence of more. We came across a small quarry. It looked as though stone had once been taken from it for making roads. There was ironstone there.'

'This could be a find of great importance.' Mr Vaughan's voice was charged with emotion. 'If there is more, if it has indeed come from a big seam, then it could alter our whole operation along the Tees. Its close proximity to the works could save us a lot of money. I'll get a map, you must show me where you found it.'

He hurried from the room and when he returned a few minutes later was accompanied by Mr Bolckow.

'I'm sorry to disturb you, Henry, but this is a matter of supreme importance,' he was saying as the two men came into the room.

Mr Bolckow exchanged greetings with Luke and Lydia. As he did so he saw the stones on the table. For a moment he stared at them then said, 'Ironstone.'

'Yes,' said Mr Vaughan. 'Miss Lydia and Luke found it in the Eston Hills. They are about to show me where.'

Luke removed his bag and, as Mr Vaughan unrolled his map and spread it on the table, Lydia placed a stone on each corner of the paper to hold it flat.

'Show us,' directed Mr Vaughan.

They examined the map.

'This is approximately where we had our picnic.' Luke indicated an area and Lydia agreed.

'We walked this way.' She traced a route with her fore-finger.

'We hadn't gone too far before you fell.'

'Maybe about here.'

'And then a little further on and a little higher up the slope we found the quarry,' Luke glanced at the two men who had been following their story with intense interest. 'I don't think we can be more precise than that.'

'Never mind,' said Mr Vaughan. 'What you have shown us is very interesting.'

'It could be of enormous significance,' said Mr Bolckow as he and his partner sat down. 'Is it anywhere near where you have been looking, John?'

'Not too far away. That is one reason why, though I am excited by this news, I am also a little cautious. It doesn't do to get carried away and then be disappointed.' He turned to Luke and Lydia to offer an explanation. 'Before you arrived in Middlesbrough I had investigated the possible existence of ironstone inland from the Skinningrove mines, which had come into our hands, and from other workings along the coast, but without success. It has been a case of trial and error, a little knowledge and a certain amount of luck, but all three never led to anything worthwhile. This may be just another of those times but let us hope it isn't.'

'You'll investigate right away?' queried Mr Bolckow.

'Immediately, Henry, if these two young people will accompany me to the Eston Hills.'

'We are at your service, sir,' said Luke.

'Good.'

'Will you take Mr Marley?' asked Mr Bolckow.

'Yes. It will save time if he is with us.' Mr Vaughan rose from his chair and went to the bell-pull beside the fireplace. 'Mr Marley is a mining engineer,' he explained to Luke and Lydia as he returned to his seat. 'He has been involved with my earlier investigations. We were due to make some more, but your find will direct us to a place where we know there is definite evidence of ironstone.'

The door opened and a maid came in. 'You rang, sir?'

'Yes. Tell James to bring round the carriage. We will fetch a gentleman from the town and then take a trip into the Eston Hills.'

Once in the hills, Lydia and Luke soon found the spot where they had had their picnic. From there the direction of their walk was easily traced.

Mr Vaughan and Mr Marley paused every now and again to pick up and examine stones. Lydia could sense their mounting excitement.

'You say there was a quarry, Mr Middleton,' called Mr Marley. 'Let's go to it now.'

Luke led the way and in a few minutes they were looking into the depression. Mr Marley paused, surveyed the scene for a moment and then hurried to one of the areas where stone had been exposed. He examined it, and removed more soil. After a few anxious minutes, he called to Mr Vaughan, 'This is better than we have found elsewhere. I think we ought to move westward.'

The eagerness in his voice caused the others to follow him and within a few minutes they were staring in wide-eyed amazement at a huge piece of solid rock lying bare before them.

'Unbelievable,' gasped Mr Vaughan.

'If this outcrop continues we have made a discovery of enormous impact,' cried Mr Marley. 'This way.'

329

Their explorations over the next hour gave them all the proof they needed, and it came without their having to do any boring for the ground was pitted by numerous rabbit and fox holes which made it easy for them to follow the line of the ironstone.

At the final moment, when any doubt about the extent of the stone was gone, Mr Vaughan's exuberance was allowed to boil over. 'Ironstone! Here! So close to our works!' His eyes were bright with a vision of the future. 'It will transform Middlesbrough and the river. And it's all because of you two.' He grasped Luke's hand and shook it vigorously. Turning to Lydia, he embraced her and kissed her on the cheek. His laughter was infectious as he shook Mr Marley's hand, and congratulations rang across the hills from a small group of excited people who barely recognised the truth behind John Vaughan's next words.

'The eighth of June 1850 will be a day etched on our minds forever!'

They all cheered.

'What happens now?' asked Lydia as some sort of calm settled on them.

'I have to obtain leases on the land. I will do that this afternoon, after we have returned to Middlesbrough and I have informed Mr Bolckow. I ask you all to keep this quiet until I have done so. I will not try to deceive the owners, but, with the quantity of ironstone still undetermined, I will secure advantageous terms. Then we start quarrying. So much appears to lie near the surface. We'll soon have a tramway laid down to take the stone by trucks to the railway where it will be transported to our furnaces at Witton Park.'

'So this find means that shipments of ironstone from Whitby will cease?' queried Luke.

Mr Vaughan tightened his lips. 'If the ironstone here is in the quantities we need, then I am afraid it will.' He shook his head sadly. 'It will cost you your job, Luke.' He added as a further thought struck him, 'And it will mean the end of Tees Shipping.'

'It won't do that, Mr Vaughan,' replied Lydia quickly with a note of determination in her voice. 'I have made provisions should this ever happen. The *Ironmaster* can be switched to other trading as soon as she is no longer wanted for the ironstone. But that will depend on none of our investors wishing to withdraw.'

Mr Vaughan recognised his obligation and her determination to succeed. 'I am sure that no one will want to withdraw. Certainly I will continue with my investment, and I am sure Mr Bolckow will also. After all, we owe you a huge debt for what you have found. And, I might add, I am sure he will agree that you deserve a royalty on the ironstone we extract. Say a penny a ton?'

'Sir, you are more than generous,' replied Luke.

'What sort of timetable do you envisage?' asked Lydia.

'Ah, a young woman with an eye to the future,' said Mr Vaughan with a smile. He rubbed his chin thoughtfully. 'Let me see. If there is no trouble over the leases, and I expect none, then I can start making arrangements to open a new quarry. Mr Marley will have to do some more investigating as to best place to start, there'll be men to engage for the work, the rails and trucks to be made for the tramway ... If everything goes smoothly, the end of August or beginning of September should see the first ore being moved.'

'Will we know before then if the shipping of ore from Whitby is likely to cease?'

'We should know that once we have seen what the first quarrying yields. Middle of August, would you say, Mr Marley?'

'Yes, sir. I suspect the young lady is anxious to know so that she can make provision for the future of the ship she mentioned.' He glanced at Lydia and saw her nod of assent. 'I should be able to give you some idea in, say, a month or six weeks' time.'

'I would appreciate that, Mr Marley. Can we definitely say a month?'

He looked thoughtful for a moment. 'Very well,' he agreed.

When Lydia and Luke entered the room at the Middlesbrough Hotel which Sean had booked for her proposed meeting, she could sense an atmosphere of expectancy. She smiled to herself. She knew how she had built up their curiosity with her mysterious hinting. Now she was going to burst it like a bubble.

She didn't even sit down at the chair they had arranged for her but drew herself up straight and announced, 'I am sorry, everyone, but I have nothing to tell you.'

There was an immediate outcry. 'What do you mean?' called Sean.

'What are we doing here?'

'You promised a disclosure.'

'Did you know this, Luke?'

'Only this morning,' he replied.

'What's going on, Lydia?' asked David.

'It's simple, I have nothing to tell you.'

'What about the agreement with Zabaleta?'

'We'll fulfil it.'

'I thought you were going to tell us how?'

'I will tell you in a month's time.'

'A month!'

'There will still be plenty of time to make the shipment after that. We won't lose anything, and nor will Zabaleta.'

'What will be different then?' asked Sean. He was beginning to suspect further intrigue to add to the suspicions which had been aroused in Whitby.

'Probably nothing,' replied Lydia. To stop any more questioning she added quickly, 'Sean, book this room for a month's time. All of you, be here then. I'd like you to be here too, David, even though it means coming from Whitby.'

332

She turned quickly and hurried from the room. Luke followed, not wanting to come under questioning from the others.

Chapter Eighteen

My Dear Lydia,

The pleasure of seeing you in Middlesbrough was only marred by the fact that you did not see fit to confide in me who one day hopes be your husband. I console myself with the belief that it concerns your need to ensure Tees Shipping is a success in order to impress my father.

I am worried that, having obtained the agreement with the Zabaleta Wine Company, you will not be able to meet that agreement.

I hope you know what you are doing!

Since I got back to Whitby I have learned from Isobel that your uncle is so enthusiastic about the iron trade he has secured a loan on his house in order to invest in another ship. It seems that he is throwing everything into this enterprise. In fact, he has tried to persuade Father to do so as well but he is resisting all your uncle's blandishments.

Father was disappointed that I was beaten to the Zabaleta trade and wonders who is behind Tees Shipping. He is going to get a shock when he finds out, but surely he can have nothing but admiration for what you have done. Don't ruin it all by over-reaching yourself. Be careful.

I will continue to write until I see you again in a little under a month.

Love,

David

Lydia was elated when she finished reading the letter. Uncle Nathan was getting himself into a financial position of which she might be able to take advantage. She re-read a paragraph. The words hit her forcibly. The house! If her uncle had used it to secure a loan then the bank would hold the deeds. If they foreclosed when her uncle was in financial trouble the house could be sold on. She hoped against hope that the discovery of ore in the Eston Hills was not discovered until she was ready to make the disclosure.

The prime movers were reliable. She knew that Mr Vaughan and Mr Bolckow would say nothing until the moment suited them. Mr Marley, employed in a responsible position, would say nothing until his employers wanted him to. The people she feared might disclose their true activities were the quarry workers but, with their bosses placing no particular emphasis on what they were doing, and the fact that they had already been involved in unsuccessful trials, she calculated they would not realise the true significance of their work. She also reckoned that the same attitude would prevail among those who commented on the activity in the hills. Nothing had come of previous attempts to find ironstone closer to the Bolckow and Vaughan works.

Nevertheless, she spent an uneasy month. She distracted herself with visits to Sarah and Eileen, found relaxation in their chatter, and delighted in playing the piano, especially accompanying Eileen whom they discovered had a good singing voice. These visits were an oasis among the worry and anxiety.

The friends assembled at the Middlesbrough Hotel at the appointed time, hoping that on this occasion there would be no further anticlimax.

'I have important news for you,' Lydia informed them. 'It will soon be public knowledge but until it is I would ask you to keep it to yourselves.'

The air became charged with a tension as she allowed her words to hang in the air.

335

'The day this knowledge is revealed to the world the *Ironmaster* will be on her way to Spain to take on board our first shipment of Zabaleta wine.'

'She can't be!' Kevin protested, though he could tell by her attitude and the firmness of her voice that Lydia meant every word she said. He exchanged a look of surprise with Sean. 'She's tied into iron trade.'

That brought a murmur of agreement from Sean who then added, 'What will Mr Bolckow and Mr Vaughan say about that?'

'They already know,' replied Lydia calmly.

'And they agreed?' Sean and Kevin exclaimed together.

'Yes.' She smiled at their surprise.

'But I thought the *Ironmaster* was busy supplying them with ironstone?' David was curious, as he had been since he missed the Zabaleta trade.

'That will soon be taken care of. In fact, it has been ever since the day Luke and I went on a picnic in the Eston Hills. Remember, Sean, you wouldn't come?'

'What has that day to do with the *Ironmaster* switching to the wine trade?' asked David.

'Because on that day we discovered ironstone in the Eston Hills.'

'What?' Gasps of amazement came from the three men.

'Is this true, Luke?' asked Sean.

'Yes.'

'But you never said anything about it when you got back. Surely you were excited?'

'Of course we were,' put in Lydia quickly, not wanting her brother to say too much. 'But we couldn't say anything until we had seen Mr Vaughan and he had investigated the extent of our find.'

Sean's thoughts had been tumbling, trying to grasp at something that had been said. It was true that Lydia and Luke had invited him and Eileen to accompany them to the Eston Hills but they'd had other plans. So that date was fixed firmly in his mind – two months ago. But large-scale

336

activity in the hills had only begun a month ago. What had happened in the intervening time? He felt sure that Mr Vaughan would have investigated the find as soon as he was notified because a supply of ironstone on their doorstep would be an immense asset to the Bolckow and Vaughan enterprise. But it appeared that Lydia and Luke had delayed telling him of it. Why?

'This news is going to be a blow to those shipping iron out of Whitby,' commented David.

'They'll find other trade no doubt,' said Lydia dismissively.

'It is to be hoped so,' said David. 'If they've invested heavily they could be ruined.'

'Well, we needn't worry, we have the Zabaleta trade and it will give us a base to expand from. It may be more advantageous for Tees Shipping to trade out of Whitby and London, but that will need our shareholders' approval. If I have your agreement on that, I will return to Whitby tomorrow, Tuesday, with David in the *Ironmaster* and visit the other investors.' Lydia glanced round everyone and was pleased to receive their consent.

'Good. Then I can tell you that the announcement about the ironstone find in the Eston Hills will be made on Friday and quarrying will begin soon.'

'This is going to put me out of a job,' said Sean. 'After all, Luke employed me on Mr Martin's behalf and he'll no longer want men on the Tees.'

'I'll be in the same boat,' said Luke. 'But I think, with her ambitions to extend the operations of Tees Shipping, my sister will need my help.'

'Well said, brother,' replied Lydia. She turned her eyes to Sean. 'Of course there'll be work for you, Sean, operating out of Whitby. You showed your ability selling shares in the *Ironmaster* and capturing the wine trade. I'll be in need of a skilled negotiator with a smooth Irish tongue. What about you, Kevin? Will you come to Whitby?'

'I think not, Lydia, but thanks for the offer. I'm satisfied

337

with my position with Mr Langton.'

'And no doubt influenced by the presence of Sarah?'

'Of course.' He bowed at the inference.

'Very well, everything is settled.' She rose from her chair, bringing an end to the meeting.

Sean and Kevin left with Luke.

David came over to Lydia. 'Why did you ask me to come from Whitby for this meeting? Nothing about it concerns me.'

She met his gaze and replied, 'But it does. You came from London with Sean and Kevin because your curiosity was aroused. I was not able to answer you then so, as I knew I would be giving an explanation now, I thought you ought to be here. And, more importantly, I wanted you to have further evidence of what I was doing and how others are reacting to it. What you have heard and seen should help to break down your father's opposition to our marriage, especially when he sees the *Ironmaster* sail into Whitby with that first consignment of wine.'

Luke parted from Sean and Kevin outside the Middlesbrough Hotel and made his way to the jetty which had become so much a part of his life and where he had proved to himself that he could stand alone. He thought of Lydia's manoeuvring to place herself in a position from which she could threaten their uncle. Would nothing satisfy her but to see Nathan beg for mercy? This could jeopardise her other desire, to build a firm that would fulfil their father's ambitions. Was she prepared to sacrifice that for the sake of revenge? He felt sure their father would not have wanted that. He had been too good a man. But how to save her from the path she seemed determined to tread?

'You're thoughtful, Sean,' observed Kevin as they walked towards the Market Place.

'There's something I don't like about all this,' he returned.

'If it's going to ease your mind then talk to me. You know I'm a good listener.'

Sean relayed how his suspicions about Lydia had grown since he and Kevin went to London.

His friend listened carefully and then said, 'You think that all her moves had but one thing behind them – to bring about revenge on her uncle because she thinks he caused her father's death?'

'Yes. But somehow that doesn't fit with the girl we know.'

'True,' agreed Kevin. 'But, you know, we can be affected by death in strange ways, especially if we have been close to a person. Sometimes we see events quite differently from other people and it's difficult to persuade us otherwise.'

'Then it's the impressions clouding Lydia's mind that we have to obliterate?'

'If we can, but we will have to be careful. We cannot interfere in what are really private matters,' Kevin cautioned.

'But we could make observations, suggestions?'

'Yes. It's just a matter of how we go about it.'

'Do you think we could approach Luke?'

'That might be a good idea,' Kevin agreed. 'If your ideas have any foundation he should know. He and Lydia are close. But we might meet a barrier there. He could be in agreement with what she is doing.'

'Well, let's go and see him.'

'I think it might be best to wait until Lydia has left for Whitby. She said she was going tomorrow with David.'

'But if she seeks her revenge when she is in Whitby, we'll be too late.'

'I don't think she will go that far yet. She said she wanted to get the shareholders' approval to switch to the wine trade and work out of Whitby and London. I believe she will wait to tackle her uncle until Friday when the announcement about the ironstone finds in the Eston Hills is made. Then she will disclose she is behind Tees Shipping, the firm that took his wine trade, leaving him nothing to fall back on.'

Lydia enjoyed the voyage to Whitby. It was as if she was no longer on a working vessel, plying its way to the old Yorkshire port for another cargo of ironstone. This vessel was taking her on the final step to achieving her heartfelt ambition. The thought of that elated her and she was in high spirits.

David was pleased with her mood, though he did not know the real reason for it. He found her tender, loving, excited, constantly talking of the future of Tees Shipping and what she was going to achieve.

On reaching Whitby he escorted her to the Angel Inn where she took a room for the night.

'Where from here?' he asked.

'I am going to go to see the people who hold shares in the *Ironmaster*.' She pre-empted his offer to escort her by adding firmly, 'There's no need for you to come. I want to do this alone.'

'Very well. Dinner this evening?'

'That would please me,' she replied.

'I'll be here at seven.'

'I look forward to that.' She kissed him on the cheek, sealing her statement.

After settling in her room and refreshing herself, Lydia strolled from the inn. She made her way to the bridge where, with the tide in, she took in the activity on the river. She breathed deep of the salt air, so different from the grimy atmosphere by the works beside the Tees. She listened to the mingled noises, the creak of ropes, the swish of water, the buzz of conversation, the shouts of sailors, and over it all the cry of the seagulls as they glided smoothly on the currents of sea air. This was her home and soon she would be here permanently, her uncle ruined, her father avenged.

She made her round of the shareholders who all expressed surprise when she revealed that she was behind the founding and running of Tees Shipping. She assured them that its future was safe, in spite of the fact that ironstone had been found local to the Bolckow and Vaughan works and that shipments of ore from Whitby to the Tees would gradually come to an end. She told them it was vital that none of this information was made public until after Friday.

Delighted that they were all satisfied, she made her way to Chapman's Bank.

She had a feeling of satisfaction and achievement as she walked inside, anticipating the outcome of her interview with its owner, Mr George Chapman.

After making her request to see him, she was ushered into his office by one of his clerks. Mr Chapman was a small man whose rotund shape betrayed his liking for good food and wine. His round face bore a jovial expression as he rose from his desk to greet Lydia.

'Good day, my dear. I'm pleased to see you again. Are you back in Whitby permanently?'

'Not yet, Mr Chapman,' she replied. 'But I hope to be soon.'

'I was deeply sorry that I could not help at the time of your father's death.'

'Mr Chapman, think nothing of it. Luke and I understood your position perfectly.'

'And I must say, I admired the way in which you strove to clear your father's debts.'

'Thank you.' She withdrew her hand from his. 'You may be able to help me now.'

'If I can, I will. Please, do sit down.' He held a chair for her and, when she was seated, moved behind his desk. He leaned back in his chair and rested his hands on its arms. 'Now, what might I be able to do for you?'

'I believe you have the deeds to my uncle's house, took them when he wanted to raise money to invest in the iron trade.'

Surprised, Mr Chapman raised an eyebrow. 'You seem pretty certain of your facts, young lady.'

'Oh, I am, Mr Chapman. I was only uncertain as to which bank my uncle was dealing with, but I knew that in my father's day he used your bank so thought it most likely the deal had been done with you. I see by your reaction that I was right.'

'In that case it will be no use denying it,' he replied. 'And I don't suppose it's any good asking where you got your information?'

Lydia gave a wry smile. 'No, it isn't, but let me hasten to assure you that it did not come from anyone within your bank. I don't want your suspicions to rest on anyone you employ, for that would be wrong.'

Mr Chapman pursed his lips and nodded. 'Well, I'm thankful for that, and also that you're being so forthright. Please go on. What interest is it of yours?'

'I would like to buy that house from you.'

'But first your uncle would have to default on his loan and I'm sure . . .'

'I am afraid, Mr Chapman, that it is entirely likely that will happen.'

'You amaze me, Miss Middleton. But tell me, in that unlikely event, how do you propose to fund your purchase?'

'Luke and I have shares in a ship. I will trade those for my uncle's house.'

Their eyes never left each other's face. They were both trying to read what lay behind those carefully blank expressions.

'A ship, Miss Middleton?' Mr Chapman spread his hands in a gesture that was dismissive, yet there was curiosity in his eyes. Lydia recognised that spark.

'Mr Chapman, please let me give you more details of this vessel and how I come to have shares in her.'

The banker could not refuse her request, nor did he want to. He was intrigued.

Lydia quickly informed him of the essential facts of her

involvement with the *Ironmaster*, Mr Chapman listening carefully.

'Well, Miss Middleton, I must say your father would have been proud of the way you and your brother have picked yourselves up since you left Whitby.'

'Thank you, Mr Chapman. It is gratifying to hear you say so.'

'The vessel you talk of is in the iron trade?'

'Yes.'

'From what I hear that trade is bringing in a steady income.' He paused thoughtfully for a moment. 'This could be a good proposition for the bank.'

'And if for the bank, then for you. You *are* the bank are you not, Mr Chapman?'

He smiled. 'You are a shrewd young woman. Yes, I am interested.'

'If that is so, then I must be honest with you. I would not want you to think ill of me if your expectations of making steady money from the iron trade were dashed later this week.'

Mr Chapman was surprised. What was this young woman up to, telling him that the ship would bring him a good return and then, almost in the same breath, saying the income from it could disappear? 'I'm listening,' he said brusquely.

'I will be taking the *Ironmaster* out of the ironstone trade.'

'But . . .' He was bewildered.

'Ironstone has been discovered in the Eston Hills.' Lydia made her announcement sharply, cutting off his protests.

'What?' he gasped in surprise. 'If that is so then no more shipments will be needed from Whitby.'

'Correct,' she replied. 'I give you this information so that you will see my offer is a genuine one. I would not want to close a deal with you without your knowing this. You would have found out, and when you did would think I had purposely withheld information from you.'

343

'So you are offering me a ship without the steady income from the iron trade?' He started to shake his head.

'That is right,' she agreed, 'but I have in place another one which in the long run could prove more lucrative, for there will always be a demand for wine.'

'Wine?'

'Yes. I have made a deal with a Spanish wine company to be the sole shipper of their products for many years to come.'

'I repeat, you are a very shrewd young woman. You obviously had prior knowledge of the discovery of iron-stone and acted upon it.'

Lydia smiled and offered quietly, 'Luke and I discovered it.'

'You did what?'

'It's true, Mr Chapman. Of course it needed expert verification though Luke, who of course had been dealing with ironstone shipped out of Whitby, was pretty certain we had come across a big find. The official announcement will be made on Friday so I would ask you to say nothing about this until then. No use alarming the other shipowners making the voyage between here and Middlesbrough with ore. Besides, the trade won't cease just like that, its decline will be gradual.'

'I won't say a word.' He narrowed his eyes and cocked his head. 'But tell me, Miss Middleton, if this ship can bring in a good return, why do you want to exchange your shares in it for a house? Surely that does not make financial sense?'

'Well, Mr Chapman, from what I hear my uncle, being so heavily committed to the iron trade, could be in difficulties once news of the discovery of ironstone is made public.'

'He could.' Mr Chapman nodded his agreement. 'And it's more than likely he'll be unable to redeem the deeds.'

'My grandfather had that house built. It was my father's home, and mine and Luke's. If my uncle is not able to recover the deeds from you, the house could pass out of the

344

Middleton family. I would not like that to happen. That is why I came to you with this offer.'

'It is noble to want to keep the house in the family and, though I say it again, your father would be proud of you.' He gave a little nod, accepting the unspoken thanks which showed on her face. 'But tell me one more thing. It appears that you have been running Tees Shipping, and that is unusual in itself.'

Lydia broke in with a merry laugh, 'Because I am a woman?'

'Well, you must admit it is, though I must also say you have been running it successfully from what you have told me. But who will do that now?'

'Oh, I shall, with Luke. We will be moving back into Whitby and the ship will work from here and London. The other shareholders in Middlesbrough want us to run the company, and I have persuaded the Whitby shareholders to give their approval too. I must add that when we get a second ship Luke and I will have shares in it. In the meantime we will be paid a wage, to be approved by everyone.'

Mr Chapman's head nodded at each piece of information she delivered. 'Good, good. Then there is no more to be said. I will have the necessary documents drawn up for both parties. Shares for deeds.'

'May I collect them later today? I return to Middlesbrough tomorrow.'

'Certainly, I'll have them drawn up immediately.' He stood up and offered his hand.

Sean wore an anxious frown when he spoke to Kevin. 'Eileen saw that I was troubled by something and she was concerned it might be about our future. She pressed me to tell her what it was.'

'And you did?'

'Yes.'

'If you're worried because you told her, don't be. I was in the same boat, Sarah sensed something was wrong.'

345

'You told her?'

'Yes.'

There was a sense of relief in Sean as he asked, 'What now?'

'I suggest the four of us try to decide what to do next.'

Their meeting later that day only served to heighten their concern for Lydia, but they did decide to put their doubts to Luke before his sister returned from Whitby.

Expecting a pleasant social evening at the Langtons', Luke walked into the drawing room in a bouyant mood but his lively greetings faded when he saw his friends' serious expressions.

'Why so glum? What's the matter?' His gaze swept across them, seeking an answer.

Kevin, who had been elected spokesman, saw no reason not to come straight to the point. 'Luke, we are worried about Lydia.'

He put on a mystified expression. 'Why? There's nothing wrong, she's perfectly healthy.'

'It's not her health we are worried about.'

'Then what?' he queried, glancing swiftly round the solemn faces.

'We feel that behind all that is happening there is an ulterior motive.' Kevin went on to explain what they suspected and why.

Luke's mind was thrown into turmoil. He wanted to be loyal to his sister, but if other people had noticed that her actions could have a hidden motive ... But even as these thoughts were churning in his mind he found himself defending her. 'But from what you say you have no evidence that she is intending anything but what is honourable. All you are doing is making suppositions and drawing the wrong conclusions.'

'We hope that is true,' said Sarah. 'But the things we have observed do cause us to wonder.'

'No need,' he replied sharply, hoping he sounded convincing.

'Luke, I have not known Lydia as long as the others,' put in Eileen, 'but I have come to like her a lot. I see her as a sweet considerate person as well as one with a good head for business. I would hate to see such a person pursue a course which could spoil her.'

'Not merely spoil, destroy,' Sean said to add weight to the argument.

'This is all ridiculous,' snapped Luke, 'and I would ask you all to wipe such ideas from your minds.'

'Can you deny that your sister would like to avenge your father's death? And what about you? Haven't you had such thoughts?' Kevin put the question so strongly that it forced Luke into an admission.

'Of course we have. It was only natural after what happened.'

'And we think that desire still burns in Lydia, maybe even in you both,' said Sean.

Luke saw concern in the Irishman who had befriended them when they first came to Middlesbrough.

'I think I can read in your expression that it does,' said Kevin.

Sarah saw protests rising to Luke's lips and pre-empted them. 'Revenge can be a very dangerous thing. If revenge is in Lydia's mind then we must stop her. Please listen to Kevin's story of how, in the same situation, he nearly embarked on a course which would have shattered the lives of many people, including me. He would also have destroyed himself.' She glanced across at Kevin.

He took up the story and related how his desire to avenge Seamus's murder had nearly led to his committing the same crime, and how he had been prevented from doing so. 'I had no proof, I was prepared to act on mere supposition. Then I realised the potentially devastating consequences of my actions.' As he spoke he saw that his words were having an effect on Luke, sensed that he had never been as strongly in favour of revenge as his sister. 'Think carefully about it, Luke. Only you among us know if we are

347

anywhere near the truth. Only you can say whether we should take this matter further.'

The room fell silent as they awaited his response.

Luke avoided the eyes which were on him. He looked down at his hands resting on his knees. Ran his tongue over his lips.

'I know that you mean well and I thank you for your concern. I'll not deny that Father's death and our subsequent visit to my uncle left us with a desire for revenge. The loss of our home, turned out by our uncle because he felt it was rightly his, only heightened our feelings. More so Lydia's than mine perhaps. She was very close to Father so I admit the desire for revenge.'

'And Lydia's subsequent actions?' prompted Sean.

'I must agree with you. I have tried to reason with her but she would not listen. I believe her desire for revenge is overwhelming.'

'And she has come to use people for that end?' asked Sarah.

'I believe so.'

'But this isn't the real Lydia, not the friend I like and respect,' she added.

'I know,' said Luke with unmistakable sadness in his voice.

'Then we must do something to preserve that person. Make the real triumph over the false, for the path she is following can only lead to self-destruction.'

Chapter Nineteen

Lydia came down the gangway from the *Ironmaster* with a radiance which matched the bright sunshine and clear sky. It was in marked contrast to the drabness of the industrial landscape around her. Wasteland stretched downriver, dark smoke straggled into the air where it hung, hardly moving, in the absence of a breeze. Raucous shouts from the shore workers, waiting to unload the ironstone from Whitby, greeted the newly arrived sailors. Noise pounded out across the open ground from the rolling mills then reverberated from the warehouses, sheds, and buildings strung along the river. The clatter of metal on metal when buffer struck buffer, as trucks were positioned to be filled with ironstone, added to the unholy din.

Luke saw that his sister was oblivious to it all. There was triumph in her attitude, delight at something well done, and he knew that she had had a successful visit to Whitby.

'Luke! Thank you for being here.' She gave him a special hug which confirmed that she was well satisfied with what she had accomplished.

'It is good to have you back.' He stepped away but still held her at arm's length so that he could look into her face when he said, 'No doubt you persuaded our shareholders that going into the wine trade is an auspicious move?'

'Indeed I did,' she returned. Her smile broadened even more as she added tantalisingly, 'But there's more.' She twisted out of his hold and linked arms with him. 'Come, walk me to West Street and I'll tell you.'

'I should be here.'

'Bob's capable.'

Luke knew this was true. He glanced towards the group of men near the stern of the ship, saw Bob and indicated to him to take charge. Bob acknowledged the signal.

'Right,' said Luke. 'Now what have you to tell me apart from the fact that all our shareholders are happy?'

Brother and sister started away from the jetty.

'I paid Mr Chapman's bank a visit and saw Mr Chapman himself.'

'What on earth for?' asked Luke mystified.

'I got him to take our shares in the *Ironmaster*.'

Luke stopped, his face clouded with disbelief. The laughter in Lydia's eyes did nothing to alleviate his bewilderment. 'You what?'

'I got him to take our shares in the *Ironmaster*.' She repeated the words a little more slowly and with emphasis.

'What do you mean? That we no longer have an interest in the ship?'

'Oh, we're still interested in her but we have no shares in her.'

'I don't understand.'

'Then take a look at this.' Lydia opened her handbag, drew out an envelope and handed it to her brother.

He took it carefully as if it contained something unsavoury.

Lydia laughed. 'Go on, open it.'

Luke turned back the unsealed flap and extracted some sheets of paper. He unfolded them and, as he read the first few lines, his eyes widened in astonishment. He looked up at Lydia with disbelief. 'These are the deeds to the house we used to live in.'

'Yes. And now they are ours!' The note of triumph in her voice was unmistakable.

'Mr Chapman exchanged these for shares in the

Ironmaster? I don't believe it.'

'It's true. I persuaded him that Uncle Nathan was unlikely to redeem them. I hope you approve of what I have done?'

Luke was still bewildered but he managed to give his consent and add, 'No doubt you did this by telling him of our discovery in the Eston Hills, so he would know Uncle Nathan faced a disastrous future and therefore he was better off taking our shares in the ship?'

'Exactly. And I told him, as I told all our shareholders, that our discovery should not be talked of until the news was officially released.'

'So does Uncle Nathan know that the house belongs to us?'

'Oh, no, not yet. That blow will fall when he learns that his investment in the iron trade is doomed.' Her voice was filled with elation as she savoured the anticipated confrontation and victory.

But Luke saw the coldness that had come into her eyes with that vision of her uncle subdued and beaten by her own burning desire for revenge. He recalled the warnings of his friends.

He did not speak.

Lydia frowned. 'Luke, you are pleased to have the house?'

'Of course.'

'Then what's the matter?'

Luke hesitated. He was about to voice his true thoughts, but at this moment considered it better not to. He passed off his lack of excitement by saying, 'If we have no shares in the *Ironmaster* we will have nothing on which to build the company you've always desired, and where are we going to obtain an income?'

'We will have something for discovering the ironstone, remember?' He nodded. 'As for the company – well, I was running it, as you well know. I have told Mr Chapman and the Whitby shareholders that you and I will

351

continue to run it for a wage to be agreed.'

'What?' Luke was astonished by her audacity.

She smiled. 'I think I can persuade Mr Bolckow. He's a shrewd investor. He was satisfied with the job I was doing and I believe he'll want it left that way. Then, as we progress, we'll get another ship in which I'll make certain you and I have shares, and so it will go on from there.'

Luke saw the light of ambition in her eyes and with it a ruthless streak he had never noticed before. His sister was changing before his eyes but he knew it was no good pointing this out for she would only deny it. In her present frame of mind she would not be diverted from the course she had set. He could do nothing but fall back on the proposal made at the Langtons'.

'Sarah has invited us to visit this evening,' he informed her.

'Good. You and I can regard it as a celebration.'

The others were already there when she and Luke arrived. Lydia detected a slight uneasiness in the air but dismissed it as a false impression. However she found it confirmed when, after a query about her visit to Whitby, Luke deliberately brought the matter of their shares into the open.

'I think you should tell them that you and I no longer have shares in the *Ironmaster*.'

While Lydia shot him a withering look she noticed that the four friends exchanged glances of astonishment. 'It's only temporary.' She spoke quickly, trying to dismiss the information as of no concern.

'I think we should know more,' said Kevin.

There was no escape when the others backed him.

'It's a private matter. Chapman's Bank in Whitby will hold the shares.'

'That is not much of an explanation,' said Sean. 'Are you holding out on us? Keeping back something you know, like you did with the discovery you made in the Eston Hills?'

Lydia stiffened. 'What are you accusing me of?'

352

'Deliberately withholding vital information so you could turn it to your own advantage.'

She jumped to her feet. The words hammered in her mind. What did her friends know? And how? Had Luke ...? He couldn't have. She glared at Sean. 'After what Luke and I have done for you, I thought you'd be a loyal friend. How can you suggest such things? Come, Luke, I have no need to sit here and listen to this rubbish.'

He did not move from his chair. 'I think you had better sit down and listen to what has to be said.'

She stood defiantly.

'Please, Lydia. It is for your own good.' Sarah's tone was soft but persuasive.

Lydia sat down slowly, still hostile. 'You have no proof of what you say,' she said, eyes fixed intently on Sean.

'I know the date you went for your picnic. You said that was the day you discovered the ironstone.' He presented his facts slowly and with deliberation so that she could not mistake what he was saying. 'If you had revealed your find to Mr Vaughan then he would have investigated immediately because your news would have been of vital concern to him and Mr Bolckow. But he did not start his investigation until some time afterwards. There was quite a gap between discovery and investigation. The only conclusion we can draw is that you and Luke deliberately held back the information for your own purposes.'

He paused. When she did not react to his words, he continued. 'Within that time word spread about the need for more iron ore. More shipowners turned to the trade, among them your uncle who went into it heavily. I learned when I was in Whitby that you had had a serious falling out with him and were overheard threatening revenge. Therefore I could only conclude you had deliberately withheld the information about the ironstone to lure him into the trade. And I also noted that within that period you sent myself and Kevin to London to capture what had been your uncle's wine trade.'

Lydia drew herself up, eyes narrowed with anger. 'You are very clever with your theorising. I could deny it all but what would be the point? I can see by your faces that you believe this to be the truth. And I see that you have cornered Luke. So I'll ease your minds – you are right. And I'd do it all again to avenge my father's death!'

'I don't think you have any proof that your uncle caused that,' Kevin reminded her gently.

'One way or another he was to blame and deserves punishment. And now I'll tell you something else. You may as well know everything. I exchanged my shares and Luke's for the deeds to the house Uncle Nathan lives in. It was our home until he turned us out. Now I'll turn *him* out.'

'Please, Lydia, don't pursue revenge. Bitterness is eating into you and changing you,' cried Sarah. 'Stop before it's too late. I don't want to lose the good friend I know is still there inside you.'

'Heed her,' pressed Eileen. 'Kevin was burnt up by the desire for revenge when Seamus was murdered. Listen to him.'

Lydia started to rise from her chair. She had had enough. But when she met Kevin's gaze she knew she must listen.

He told her his story and concluded with a plea, 'I realised what my desire would lead to. Kill Gilmore and it would leave his wife and children in worse poverty than they already lived in. It would also destroy any chance of the life I wanted, even had I escaped the gallows. Would Sarah ever have recovered from the shock? Knowing her as I have come to do, I don't think so. And that would have devastated her father. The ripples would have gone on and on. Sean, Luke, you ... all would have been affected in some way, and that is not to mention my own family who would have borne the stigma of a murderer for a son. Please, Lydia, call a halt to your desire for revenge, now.'

For a moment no one spoke. They all thought that Kevin had made her see sense.

She rose slowly to her feet, looked at each one in turn, a touch of disdain in her eyes. So penetrating was her gaze, condemning them for interfering in what she saw as a personal matter, only Kevin could meet her eyes.

'There is a difference,' she said in a quiet but powerful voice, 'I won't be committing murder.'

'As good as,' he replied. 'You'll be destroying not only your uncle but his family as well. On top of that you'll take something from us, your friends. But more than anything else you'll be destroying yourself.'

She shook her head. 'I'll be doing that if I don't punish my uncle because then I will not have avenged Father's death and he will not rest easy in his grave.' She turned to her brother who had sat silently throughout the whole exchange. Close as she was to him, she sensed his changed attitude. 'You no longer support me.' Her mouth curled in disdain. 'Well, go your own way, but don't think you'll be welcome in what will be my house before long.'

There was sadness in his eyes as he looked at her. 'I am convinced by Kevin's argument. Don't do it, Lydia. Can't you see that even now it is beginning to take its toll? It has driven a wedge between you and me. You can abandon this scheme and bring us close again. But even if you don't, you will always have a brother's love.'

His words struck at her heart. She turned and walked from the room before they could overwhelm her.

As the door closed, Luke glanced helplessly round his friends. 'What more can we do?'

There was a moment's silence in which everyone tried desperately to find an answer.

'I don't want to lose the sister I love. She is still there, I know. We must save her.' The plea was a cry for help.

'I think that now there is only one person who can do that.' The words came slowly from Sarah. Everyone looked at her, hoping that what she had in mind would solve their problem. 'David.'

'He will have to know Lydia's intentions and that might

destroy their relationship completely,' warned Kevin.

'I have only met David on the two occasions he has been to Middlesbrough,' put in Eileen, 'but I would say that his love for her runs deep enough for him to want to save her from herself.' She looked to Luke for confirmation.

He nodded. 'I'm sure you are right.'

'Who's to tell him?' asked Sarah. 'You, Luke?'

He shook his head. 'I think Sean has the most persuasive tongue, but I'll be there to verify what he says.'

They all turned to Sean.

He did not hesitate. 'Sure now, I'll only be too glad to try. It could be advantageous to have Eileen with me. If David takes action he might find female company of help.'

'We must act immediately. Lydia will want to be in Whitby to confront her uncle when the announcement about the find in the Eston Hills is made tomorrow.'

'So she'll leave today?' queried Sarah.

'Sure to,' returned Kevin.

'I believe she'll use the *Ironmaster*,' said Luke.

'So how do we get there first?' asked Eileen.

'There's another vessel, the *Waverley*, unloading now. She'll sail on the same tide,' said Sean.

Luke snapped his fingers. 'Good, with all this worry I'd forgotten the *Waverley*. I know the captain well. He'll oblige me and cram on sail to beat the *Ironmaster*. Everyone in agreement?'

Everyone approved and Sarah reminded them, 'You must get on board without Lydia seeing you.'

'There's no time to lose then,' replied Sean.

Once the *Waverley* had cleared the mouth of the Tees, her master, Captain Merryweather, called for more sail to take advantage of the freshening wind. The canvas was run out, billowing with a sharp crack as the northeaster caught it. Ropes tightened, timbers creaked, and the sea, driven into curling foam by the cleaving bow, swished along the side to be left churning in a white wake.

On deck, the three friends, while anxious about the outcome of their mission, enjoyed the exhilarating sea air.

Eileen realised her former narrow views about remaining in Ireland were banished forever. She would go wherever Sean wanted. She hoped that would be to work in Whitby for Tees Shipping, but it would depend on today's outcome.

Sean saw the light of enjoyment in her face and slipped his arm round her waist to draw her to him. She snuggled close, content to be with the man she loved.

Luke glanced back towards the river and saw the *Ironmaster* meeting the sea. Thankfully they would beat her to Whitby. As he leaned on the rail and fixed his eyes on the coast, his mind was full of concern for his sister. They had shared many voyages along this seaway in their father's ship. Happy, pleasant days when they were so close they were almost able to read each other's thoughts. They had helped each other through trying times and had emerged with laughter on their lips and the promise of a bright future.

The future? Luke shuddered. Lydia seemed bent on destroying it now, oblivious to what she was doing, cocooned in the thought that once she had found revenge all would be well and life would revert to the way she had known it. She did not seem to realise that the past and present shaped the future and there was no going back. Nothing could ever be the same, but there was no need to mar the future by heaping more tragedies on those of the past.

As soon as the *Waverley* was at the dockside and the gangway was run out, the three friends were striding along the quay, leaving a trail of urchins lamenting that the new arrivals had no bags to carry.

They lost no time in reaching the Draytons' offices. They were putting their request to see David to the clerk when a door along the corridor opened. Jonas Drayton, dressed in outdoor coat and hat and carrying a walking cane, came towards them. He stopped.

357

'You!' His eyes fixed on Sean. 'I told you never to come here again. I thought you had heeded me but it seems you haven't.' His eyes swung to Luke. 'I'm surprised to find you with him, though why I should be I don't know. After all you're a nobody just like him.'

Luke drew himself up. His eyes narrowed and his voice was hard. 'You wouldn't have said that once, Mr Drayton, when you thought my sister worthy of your son. Well, I'll tell you this, you're an arrogant old fool who isn't worth talking to. Now, out of our way. We are here to see David, not you!'

'You have no business with my son,' snapped Jonas. 'Get out of here.' His voice rose harshly.

'We will not be moving until we have seen David. You should let him listen, for it concerns his future.'

'Future be damned! You have nothing to say about that.'

'We have a lot to say about it, and we are going to say it, and you are not going to stop us.'

Jonas's lips tightened. How dare these whippersnappers defy him? His body tensed so much that he started to shake. 'Out! Out!' he yelled. 'My son won't listen to you. I'll forbid him! He'll do as he's told.'

'I won't, Father.' The voice was quiet but the words were so full of defiance that they struck like an arrow from a bow. David had come quietly into the corridor to see what all the commotion was about. 'Now let them pass, Father. I will hear what they have to say.' He knew that their presence spoke of something important and that it must involve Lydia or why come to him? He put a restraining arm across his Father's chest and pushed him gently to one side. 'My office,' he said to Luke.

Eileen and Sean slid past Jonas and followed Luke. As they entered David's office they heard him say, 'No, Father, they have come to see me, not you, so you go about the business you were embarking on.'

A moment or two later he came into the office. 'I'm sorry about that,' he said as he closed the door. 'Please find

358

yourselves seats.' He paused a moment as the three friends settled themselves, then went to his own chair behind the desk. 'A contingent from Middlesbrough. This must be important, especially as you all have such grave expressions.'

'I am afraid that we do not come on a very pleasant matter,' replied Luke.

'Lydia?' Unease clouded David's face and voice. 'Something's happened to her?' His eyes flashed across all three, trying to glean something quickly.

'No. Lydia is well and at this moment on board the *Ironmaster* heading for Whitby. In fact, she should be docking before long. When she arrives we have reason to believe she will immediately embark on a disastrous course. We need your help to stop her.' Luke looked to Sean to take over the explanation.

He did so in as few words as possible. He held David's full attention with what he disclosed. When Sean had finished David leaned back in his chair, staring at his friends in disbelief. 'This can't be true.' He shook his head. 'It's just not in her.'

'I agree,' put in Eileen, 'but I believe the shock of her father's death could have displaced some of her tender nature and turned it to hatred. It is now an obsession which must be exorcised by the only way she knows – revenge.'

'Don't forget, on top of Father's death, Uncle Nathan turned us out of the house in which we had been brought up, a home which was very dear to Lydia,' said Luke.

'But it didn't affect you like that.'

'I must confess it did at first, but I managed to curb it. I had my work, that occupied my mind. Lydia had too much time to think.'

David did not reply. Eileen saw that he was tussling with his thoughts, trying to make sense of all that he had heard, attempting to reach a conclusion. She signalled with a slight shake of her head and movement of her fingers to Sean and Luke that they should say nothing.

359

David straightened. 'I love your sister, Luke. Where will she be?'

Tension drained from the room, leaving only the need for instant action.

'I believe she'll go straight to Uncle's office. There's nothing else for her to do.'

'Then we should be there.' David rose quickly from his chair. Ignoring his father, who was still standing in the corridor, he strode into the street followed by his three friends.

Lydia felt the pull of Whitby as the *Ironmaster* sailed between the piers and met the river's flow. This was home. This was where she belonged. This was where her future lay. This was where she would build a trading venture to match or even surpass that dreamed of by her father. This was where she would live, in the house she regarded as rightly hers. She was coming home.

She thanked the captain for a pleasant voyage and smiled at the disappointment on the faces of the urchins who thronged the quay near the foot of the gangway. Though she did not know it this was the second time this afternoon they had been cheated of the chance of luggage.

She strode with a determined step, trying to conquer the flutter of unease she felt inside at the thought of confronting her uncle. She stilled it by looking forward to seeing him squirm, broken and begging, before her.

'I'm here to see my uncle,' she informed Nathan's clerk who recognised her immediately she walked in. He started to rise from his chair. 'There is no need to announce me, I know which room he uses.' With that Lydia was along the corridor. She did not hesitate but flung open the door and strode straight in, swinging it to with a determined push of her hand so that it shut with a bang.

Her uncle, startled and annoyed by this sudden intrusion, looked up sharply. His eyes widened in astonishment to see his niece, well-dressed and facing him with an air of confident authority. 'You! What do you want?'

'All in good time, Uncle. There is much to tell you and much I want you to know. May I sit down?'

He was still annoyed enough to dismiss her out of hand but, because of her attitude, curious to hear more.

'Well, get on with it, I can't give you much time,' he snapped.

'You'll give me all your time until I'm finished,' she said coolly, eyes fixing his, daring him to deny her.

'Now, see here, young lady . . .'

'No. You listen to me.' She was sitting ramrod straight on her chair, her body tense with defiance. He knew she would stand against any efforts to dismiss her lightly. He had to listen. As she was speaking she had opened her reticule without allowing her gaze to waver. She drew out an envelope and handed it to him.

'What's this?' he snapped.

'Open it, it's not sealed, and you'll see.'

He hesitated only a moment, took the envelope and withdrew some papers.

He looked down at the deeds and blanched 'How did *you* get these?' The words were hissed in dismay.

'They are mine, Uncle.' She delivered the information with an air of triumph, spiced with contempt.

'They can't be. They are lodged with the bank.'

She shook her head. 'No, I bought the property from Mr Chapman. The deeds belong to me now.'

'What?' Anger brought colour rising to Nathan's face as he jumped to his feet. 'We'll see about that!' He started to come out from behind his desk.

'Rushing off to the bank will do you no good,' Lydia returned calmly. Nathan stopped in mid-stride and glared down at her. 'Do sit down, Uncle, you'll give yourself apoplexy, huffing and puffing like that. Maybe that's what you gave Father when you wouldn't help him.' She waved her hand towards his chair. 'Do sit down. I have more to tell you.'

361

Reluctantly he returned to his seat. With those deeds she could regain the house, but what else was to come?

There was no time to talk, no time to make a plan of action, all knew they must reach the offices of Nathan Middleton as soon as possible. Breathing hard from their forced pace they entered the building.

'Is Miss Middleton here?' panted Sean.

'Aye.'

The four friends were relieved, but were they too late?

'She's with Mr Middleton, but I won't interrupt them. There've been raised voices already and I don't want the master's wrath coming down on me.'

'We'll see ourselves in,' replied Luke in a tone which would brook no objection. He started down the corridor but before he reached the door to Nathan's office Eileen, who was immediately behind him, grabbed his arm.

'Wait! Listen.'

Luke glanced questioningly at her.

She nodded meaningfully towards the door. 'Let Lydia derive some satisfaction from all she's done.'

David grasped her meaning and approved. 'We'll step in at the right moment.'

Not another word passed between them.

'Damn you, woman. What do you mean, the ironstone trade to Middlesbrough is doomed?' Nathan's voice rose with his demand.

'Exactly what I say.'

'How can it be? The blast furnaces and rolling mills aren't going to close down just like that.'

'They certainly aren't,' Lydia agreed comfortably.

'Well then, what nonsense are you talking? Is this an attempt to scare me?'

'It will when I tell you that ironstone has been found in the Eston Hills close to Middlesbrough. There'll be no need to ship ore from here.'

'I've heard nothing of this,' he said disdainfully.

'No, but you will. It is being announced today.'

'How do you know?' Nathan still sounded unconvinced.

'Because Luke and I found it.'

'You did what?'

'Luke recognised it. Investigations have been carried out and mining will soon begin on a large scale.' Lydia smiled with satisfaction. She could see her uncle was troubled by this news. Now was the moment to shatter him. 'When we made this discovery you were only thinking about joining the iron trade.' She paused, letting her words sink in.

'If I had known about the discovery I would never have committed myself so heavily to the trade.' The true meaning behind her statement made itself felt then. He stared at her in astonishment. 'You purposely withheld the information until I was engaged in the trade?'

She nodded. 'You surmise correctly, Uncle.'

'And I suppose you thought that would ruin me? Well, let me tell you, you have not calculated carefully enough. You see, I can switch back to a lucrative contract with a Spanish wine firm.' His triumph at having balked her scheme was evident.

She threw back her head and laughed.

'I'm afraid you can't,' she said, the note of triumph intensifying. 'You see, I now have the Zabaleta contract.'

'What did you say?' Though he put the question, it was only an automatic reaction to her statement. He knew it was true. Lydia wasn't going to make such an announcement unless there was substance behind it.

'I knew that contract was coming up for renewal. I made sure of it before revealing that there was iron ore in the Eston Hills.'

'So I didn't have the Zabaleta trade to fall back on?' he gasped.

'Exactly. You see, I am Tees Shipping!'

He stared at her incredulously.

'There's no need to go into detail about how that came

about. Suffice it to say that as we talk my ship, the *Ironmaster*, which has just brought me to Whitby, is now on her way to pick up the first consignment of Zabaleta wine.

'You are in a precarious position, Uncle. Your commitment to the iron trade has left you in debt and I can outsmart you on any other contract you try to make.' She revelled in seeing him slump in his chair, his face ashen. 'Now you know how Father felt. Now you have to face the truth about what happened to him. Would you like to walk the same way to the end of the pier? It would be easy . . .'

Her words were cut short as the door burst open. Startled, she swung round. Her eyes widened in disbelief on seeing her friends.

'Get out of here!' she hissed.

'More of you come to gloat?' This from Nathan in a tone of despair.

'No, Uncle, we haven't,' called Luke.

'Damn you, Luke! Don't you want him punished for what he did to Father?'

'You've no proof he did anything.' David's words came accusingly.

'Damn you too, David. You've no right to be here.'

'I have every right as the man who loves you and does not want to see you destroy yourself. As you will be doing if you pursue this vendetta any further. The consequences will spread far. Your aunt and cousins who think so much of you, and never agreed with their father turning you out of the house, will all suffer. And Luke will be devastated at losing his sister for whom he has a high regard as well as a brotherly love.'

'If he had he'd be standing beside me now,' screamed Lydia, trying to stem his words which were disturbing her.

But David did not let up. 'And there are all your friends – Sean and Eileen here, Sarah and Kevin in Middlesbrough, Mr Langton, Mr Bolckow and Mr Vaughan who admire your business acumen and proved it by asking you to continue with Tees Shipping. Do you want to destroy their trust in you? If that goes will they continue to have faith in your enterprises? Won't you feel your life is destroyed? And all because of your need for a revenge which isn't even worth bothering about.'

'How do you know it isn't? Do you know how I felt in here,' she pressed her heart, 'when I lost Father?'

'No, I don't. But I do know how I'll feel if I lose the girl I love.'

'You'll still have me and I'll be coming with a firm which your father will be proud of. There'll be no obstacle to our marriage.'

'You're right, there won't be if it is brought by the girl you were and still are. But if the girl I see before me now comes to me, having thrown away so much and destroyed other people's happiness, there won't be any marriage. I will not ask this girl to marry me as I asked the other.'

Lydia stared at him incredulously. She felt numb. Surely David couldn't mean it? Was this just a ruse to fool her into stopping her pursuit of revenge? He'd see things differently when she had taken possession of the house and witnessed the downfall of her uncle.

The house! Her house! To be living there again would mean so much. She and Luke. He would approve of her actions once he was there. He wouldn't be able to resist the memories of happy family times.

Family. The word spun in her mind. If she went through with this, what would her aunt and cousins think of her? The pleasant relations she had had with them would be tainted, maybe destroyed, forever.

She looked at her brother. She saw love in his eyes but sadness too. There was a distance growing between them lately and she realised that had hurt Luke. She glanced at Sean. There was pleading in his eyes for the return of the girl he had first met in Middlesbrough, two strangers in a strange town, drawn together but knowing there were others who would be hurt if they pursued a relationship. Was revenge the only relationship she was pursuing now?

She looked at Eileen and saw a girl whose love for Sean had never been in doubt. If Lydia had pursued him what consequences would it have had for Eileen? Might she even have destroyed herself? Then wouldn't Lydia have been as guilty as the uncle she condemned?

Her whole world pressed in on her. Words thundered in her mind. Revenge! Father! Love! David!

'Lydia, please think ...' Luke was speaking, the brother whom she'd thought would be standing by her at this moment, revelling in seeing their uncle brought down. Instead he had deserted her. '... the consequences could be catastrophic.'

The room was closing in. She must escape.

She turned sharply for the door. Eileen was in the way. She pushed the girl roughly aside and, flinging open the door, fled down the corridor.

David was the first to react. He ran after her. 'Lydia! Wait!'

But she did not hear. Her feet rapped sharply on the wooden floor. She reached the door, but before she could flee into the street a hand grabbed her arm. She twisted, trying to shake off the tightening grip. A hand closed round her other arm and brought her round to face her assailant. Her eyes were wild, furious at being stopped. Protests sprang to her lips.

'David! Let go!'

He held her tighter. She struggled fiercely.

'Revenge isn't the answer!' he cried.

'It is.' Anger replaced her fury. 'You won't stop me.'

'I must. For your sake. For ours. I love you.'

The others had come into the corridor but they saw it was best not to interfere.

She hesitated. 'If you do love me, you'll let me go.' Her voice softened. He saw she was taking control of herself. 'Please, David, let me go. Let me decide what to do next.'

Still he held her. Should he heed what she said? He stared at her, trying to discover what really lay behind her plea.

Was she fit to be alone? If he let her go, would he lose her? But maybe he would if he forced her to stay. He concentrated his gaze on her, then, overwhelmed by his desire to save her, pulled her to him and kissed her. His undisguised passion cried out for her to realise that she would lose his unbounded love if she chose the wrong path now.

'Please, David.'

His grasp slackened. He let his arms fall by his side.

She looked at him gratefully. 'I must do what I think best.'

Her statement gave no indication of what she meant but he deemed it wisest to ask for no explanation. Instead he said, 'I love you. I want the girl I know to marry me.'

She said nothing but turned away and walked into the street.

David, still hoping she would make the right decision, watched from the doorway until she disappeared among the crowd.

He turned to find anxious faces studying him. He shrugged his shoulders. 'Lydia has to decide for herself to give this up. I can't force her.'

'But we don't know how she might react.' Luke, alarmed, started down the corridor, but David restrained him. 'Let her be. She won't do what you fear. The only way is to let her decide a course of action for herself.'

'And what do we do?' cried Luke, still anxious for his sister.

'Wait.' David turned him back to the office.

The brief interlude with David had been sufficient to stop the pounding in her head and clear her mind so that as she walked down the street, Lydia began to think more calmly. When she reached the bridge she stopped and looked down at the water flowing towards the sea. She watched it swirl and eddy and go on towards its destiny in the ocean's vastness. Where was her destiny? Would it be lost like the waters of the river if she took revenge?

Life went on around her, its daily routine unaffected by the drama in which she had been involved. One she had seen instigated by the loss of a ship far off in the English Channel. It was a drama that was still not concluded, and its conclusion lay in her hands.

Her eyes skirted the buildings to both sides of the river. Her gaze slid across the red roofs rising on the East Cliff. Beyond them, on the cliff top, lay her father. Could her answer lie with him? But all she heard was, 'Your future is in your hands.' Did that future lie here in Whitby, the place she loved? Would this port, pulsating with the commercial life on which it depended, be tarnished by the action she took? Would it ever mean the same to her again?

There was a future for her here. Tees Shipping could operate out of Whitby. Its ship – ships? – sailing the river, tying up at quays teeming with dockers unloading and loading cargoes, bringing wealth to her, to the shareholders, to Whitby. But would it mean the same if it was not shared with David and Luke, with Sean and Eileen?

She could savour her revenge and stand alone. She was strong enough. She needed no one. She wanted to drive her uncle to his final humiliation and watch him evicted from Saint Hilda's Terrace. But would she regret that when she subsequently faced life without the man she loved?

She glanced down at the waters again. She could end it all. Mesmerised, her hands tightened on the rail. She paused. A long pause. Her grip relaxed and she turned away to walk slowly from the bridge.

Her mind was still unfocused. It turned this way and that, so that she did not know the direction she was taking. But someone had been leading her by the hand for when she stopped she was before a row of houses. St Hilda's Terrace. She could see number twenty-one from where she stood.

Memories came flooding back with such poignancy they brought tears to her eyes. Why should Uncle Nathan have it? Why shouldn't she step across the threshold once more, knowing that those memories could be translated into happy times again?

The house was hers. She had the deeds to prove it. All that was needed was to evict her uncle. She started to turn away, ready to retrace her steps to the office in Church Street and exact the final penalty.

Just at that moment she heard laughter and voices. She stopped and looked back. Isobel, Christopher and her aunt had just come out of the house. Their laughter rang with happiness and it seemed to her that the house approved. They would know nothing of the recent dramas that threatened their lives. If she took her revenge their future could be marred forever or even destroyed. And would the house know happiness then?

Before her aunt and cousins could reach the gate and turn in her direction, she hurried away.

David was anxious. The minutes had ticked away. The atmosphere in Nathan's office was taut. Maybe they were wrong in thinking that Lydia would return. But the drama could not be concluded anywhere else. Whatever she decided, she would have to face her uncle again. Unless . . . David had dismissed that thought once but now it had returned. He shouldn't have let her go.

As they waited, conversation was uneasy. Luke and Nathan were hostile to one another but held back from open confrontation.

David felt he should do something, but what? Where was Lydia? Finally he could bear the suspense no longer. He left without a word and paused outside. What good could he do? If he went in search of her he might be looking in the wrong place, and then if she returned he would not be there.

He paced up and down, ignoring the people who passed, searching for a sight of Lydia. A long fifteen minutes later his terrible musing on what might have happened was banished forever in a surge of relief.

'Lydia!' He was beside her instantly, taking her hands in his. 'Are you all right?' The words were inadequate, his eyes searching for a deeper answer.

She nodded in reply to the surface query, but he had seen in her eyes the answer he had longed for.

He grasped her shoulders and looked at her with all the love in his heart. 'I love you,' he whispered. 'Marry me?'

Unable to speak, she nodded again and there was joy behind her tears.

He kissed her and held her close, ignoring the glances of passers-by, some curious, some shocked and disapproving, others pleased at seeing romance.

'I must see my uncle,' she said.

He did not comment or enquire but kissed her again and led her by the hand to her uncle's office.

She looked around everyone and saw relief on their faces.

'I'm sorry. Can we take up as if this never happened?'

Luke gave his sister a hug. Sean's and Eileen's kisses told her that they too had already forgotten the Lydia they had not liked.

She dabbed tears from her eyes. 'Please, will you all leave me with my uncle?' They looked doubtful, fearing what she might do. 'Please,' she begged. 'Everything will be all right.'

When the door closed, leaving niece and uncle facing each other, there was a tense silence. Then they both spoke together. They stopped and Nathan gave a little bow.

'Uncle Nathan, I have carried hatred in my heart for you since Father died and you turned us out of the house. That made me seek revenge. I should never have allowed that to dominate my life, I see now I was wrong, though it will take some time still for me to forget the part I believe you played in his death. But I hope you can forgive any hurt I have caused you in return?'

He held up his hand, a signal to let him speak but also a gesture of forgiveness. 'You have done me less harm than I did you. I will regret to my dying day that I did not help Tristram when he came to me, but believe me, I had no idea what the outcome would be. If I was the cause of his heart attack then I am genuinely sorry. If you and Luke can find it in your hearts to forgive me, I ask no more.'

'That may take time.'

'I'll wait. When do you want to move into the house?'

'If I am to marry David, I shall not need it.'

'What about Luke? He'll want it.'

'I am sure he will agree with the decision I have made, and I have no doubt he will be able to look after himself.' She held up the deeds and dropped them on the desk. 'These are for my aunt and cousins. I have no doubt they were ignorant of your part in my father's death.'

'But I can't repay you.'

'They are yours. Just see that the house remains in the Middleton family.'

'Have no fear, it will.'

'That is some comfort.'

She started for the door but Nathan's words stopped her. 'Your father and grandfather would have been proud of you. You might like to know that I bought the family heirloom.'

'My piano!' Anger that he should possess it began to seethe inside her, despite her resolution to put this all behind her.

It faded when he added, 'You shall have it as my gift to you when you marry David.'

Dangerous Shores

Chapter One

'We have a problem.'

Eliza looked up from the smiling eyes of two-year-old Abigail, wriggling pleasurably in her cradle, to see her husband John come striding into the drawing room. His voice was serious but, she thought, not too serious. Whatever the problem was, it could be dealt with satisfactorily, though it obviously needed thought and attention.

Eliza was always flattered when he chose to consult her, as he did on most matters. Many men she knew made such judgements without even mentioning them to their wives. She appreciated that John looked beyond the convention of 1782 and considered her an equal partner in his life. His love for her was deep and sincere, and she returned that love in full measure. She showed an interest in all he did, especially the running of the small estate he'd inherited from his father, on the Yorkshire coast, four miles south of the thriving port of Whitby. It was there that his father had made his money as a ship's chandler, and where John continued to run the business that enabled him and Eliza to enjoy the peace and tranquillity of Bloomfield Manor, a medium-sized Georgian house with views of the sea.

'What's the problem, love?' Eliza asked when John reached the window. 'I suppose it has to do with the papers in your hand?' she added as she rose from her chair and came to join him.

'It's a wonderful view, isn't it?' was all he said in answer to her questions.

'Wonderful,' she replied, and waited patiently for him to explain what troubled him.

How often they had stood here, gazing across the terrace and over the lawn to the cliff edge beyond overhanging a tiny bay where at this moment the sea lapped lazily. No matter what the season, no matter what the weather or the tumult of the sea, this view always entranced them and inevitably their fingers entwined as they enjoyed it together.

'Well, what is it?' she prompted quietly. 'What has that piece of paper to do with the view?'

John turned to her. As ever she saw love and adoration on his handsome face, but she also saw from the shadows in his deep blue eyes that he was troubled.

'Maybe we'll leave it,' he said quietly, letting go of her hand and running his hand through his thick dark hair; a worried gesture.

'What?' His statement evoked disbelief in her. She stared at him, her eyes wide with shock and curiosity. 'Leave Bloomfield Manor. Why?'

He hesitated as if searching for the right words. 'This,' he said, holding up the papers.

Eliza took them. The top one was a letter written in immaculate copperplate handwriting; obviously executed by someone used to producing clearly legible documents. Her eyes skipped over the words quickly. The shock she received caused her to sink on to the window seat to read the letter more carefully, making sure she had truly understood the contents at first glance. When she knew that she had she looked up slowly to meet John's anxious gaze.

'Well?' she said.

He tightened his lips and shrugged his shoulders. She noticed his quick glance out of the window but could not interpret whether he was deliberately redirecting her attention to the view they both loved and silently saying: 'This is what I want.' She stood up and placed a comforting hand on his arm. Her blue eyes met his, asking him to say something, for whatever he wanted she would agree to.

'I wish Uncle Gerard hadn't done this, then we wouldn't have been faced with a decision that could affect our lives and even Abigail's.'

'Well, he has. We cannot get away from that. I don't think we can walk away from his immense generosity either without considering it carefully.'

'I suppose not. But I hardly remember him. He left Whitby when I was a child. Under a bit of a cloud, I believe. He was twelve years older than my father. Never set foot here again. Sailed the seven seas and, it was rumoured, made a fortune. He finally settled in Cornwall.'

'And now he's died,' added Eliza when her husband hesitated, 'and left everything to, as it says here, "John Mitchell, my nephew and only male relation". According to these figures it's a considerable fortune in money and land.'

'Yes, but note the proviso. I will have to take up residence in his property, and he stipulates that I must reside there for twelve years otherwise everything I inherit will be forfeit. If I were to leave within that time then I would have to make good the estate's worth to its present value.'

'Or you could refuse the bequest,' Eliza pointed out.

'Are you saying that's what I should do?'

'No. I am just pointing out that there is an alternative.'

'And if I do, the whole of my uncle's estate will pass to the government.'

'Do I detect from your tone of voice that you would not like that to happen?'

'It would seem as if we were throwing his kindness back in Uncle Gerard's face. After all, though I have barely met him since childhood, it seems he did not forget me.'

'True. It looks as though he forgot Martha, though, which is strange considering your sister is four years older than you.'

'What would he know of her, not having been in touch with the family? He probably assumed she'd be married with a husband to provide for her by now.'

'He could have bothered to find out. If he had, he'd have known she lost the love of her life when he was drowned on a whaling voyage in the Arctic,' Eliza pointed out.

'Maybe he was planning to. That letter says my uncle died suddenly.'

'It also states he had drawn up his will two years ago; if he had planned to consider Martha, he would have had time.'

'Well, we will never know his reasons for leaving everything to me, but we have a decision to make.'

'I think before we do so you had better go to Cornwall and view the situation and prospects there. After all, it may *sound* very enticing but we don't want to give up everything here and find later we have made a bad move with poor future prospects.'

'You are always the one with the common sense.' John gave a little smile and tenderly reached out to stroke her dark hair and let it run through his fingers, allowing the copper tint to catch the light.

'Will you tell Martha?' she asked.

'Of course, when she gets back from Scarborough in two days' time. I'll have to or she will wonder why I am going to Cornwall. After all, she is living with us and will be affected by our decision.'

'I wonder if she will take kindly to a move, if that is what we decide?' mused Eliza.

'Should that colour our decision?'

'Not really, but she is close to us both and she adores Abigail, so if she feels her roots are here and does not want to move with us, it could be traumatic for her to see us go.'

This worried them both and a thoughtful silence fell until Eliza wisely said, 'This has come as a shock to us and there are a lot of things to consider. Too many for us to reach a quick decision. We really should wait until you have been to Cornwall before we discuss it further.'

'True,' he agreed. 'I know it will be on our minds but let's not worry about it now. There are a couple of maps with that letter, let's have a look at those instead.'

They went to a table and spread them out.

'That must be the house.' John pointed to a couple of rectangles occupying a position close to the coastline.

'It could have as good a view as this one,' remarked Eliza, running her finger along the boundary line to the south of the house.

'Could it ever match it?' commented John wistfully.

'You'll be the judge of that. I suggest you arrange to leave the day after Martha's return. It's no good hanging about in these matters. A decision will have to be made sooner or later. I know your uncle has stipulated that it has to be done within three months – I think, the sooner the better. It would be unfair to keep Martha on tenterhooks.'

The following morning Eliza was already sitting in the dining room over breakfast when John came in.

'I hope our dilemma did not keep you awake?' he said as he sat down at the table after helping himself to a bowl of porridge from the tureen on the oak sideboard.

'I pushed it from my mind,' replied Eliza. 'I saw no point in worrying about it at this stage. What about you?'

'When I woke this morning I had a solution to part of our problem.'

'What was that?' Eliza raised an eyebrow.

'Well, we have a fine house here. The estate, though not big, is well run, and the chandler's business in Whitby comfortably profitable.'

'Which sounds as though you will regret getting rid of it?'

'Yes, I would, in a way. But that would only happen if we *all* moved to Cornwall. If Martha does not wish to leave it throws another light on our situation.'

Eliza looked a little puzzled. 'What are you getting at?'

'If it is to our advantage to move and Martha does not wish to, I will sign over this property and the business in Whitby to her, with the proviso that if at any time in the future any of us wishes to return, we can do so. I think Martha would agree to that.'

Eliza's eyes brightened. Her sister-in-law's position in all this had troubled her, especially if she did not want to leave Whitby. 'And Martha's capable of managing both?'

'She certainly is,' agreed John. 'She has always taken an interest in both aspects of the business, particularly after Jos was killed. I was pleased she did at the time; it gave her something to think about. Now it might pay off.'

'When will you put this to her?'

'Not until after we have told her about the move. I would not want it to influence her decision.'

When the carriage that Martha had hired in Scarborough turned into the drive of Bloomfield Manor, she breathed a sigh of contentment. It was good to be home.

She was thankful that she and her brother John, four years younger than she, were close. They had had their childhood arguments and differences but if anything this had strengthened their loyalty to each other. They'd been thankful for that when their parents died in an epidemic, and Martha was deeply grateful for her brother's support when her sweetheart Jos, whom she was to marry on his return from a whaling voyage, was reported lost with five others in a whale boat while chasing their quarry. John and Eliza had insisted that she come to live with them at Bloomfield Manor and after that the relationship between them inevitably strengthened. Forward-looking like her brother, Martha was not one to sit back and waste her life. Once her period of mourning was over she took a keen interest in the estate and business, something that John was now pleased he had encouraged.

Hearing the crunch of the wheels on the gravelled drive, John and Eliza were at the door by the time the coachman helped Martha from the carriage. Greetings were exchanged with unfeigned pleasure and then Eliza linked arms with her sister-in-law and they walked into the house together while John took charge of two valises.

'You had a good journey?' queried Eliza.

'I did indeed. A most helpful and attentive coachman.'

Who could resist Martha's charm? thought Eliza. Her deportment, elegant without being showy, naturally caught the attention. Coupled with her warm ready smile, it hooked and held the onlooker's deference and brought her many friends. Her deep brown eyes sparkled with the joy of being home again; the touch of her long thin fingers, resting on Eliza's arm, spoke of her love for her sister-in-law.

'Good. And your friend in Scarborough, was she well?'

'Yes, in very good health.' Martha called over her shoulder as John caught them up, 'I got us some business through her husband. He happened to remark he was not satisfied with a quotation for fifty barrels for the ship he was fitting out. Without knowing what the quotation was, I gave him a price. He was astonished we could supply him from Whitby and still undercut a rival.'

'So it's settled?'

'Signed and sealed. The documents are in my bag.'

John chuckled. 'You certainly aren't one to miss an opportunity.'

'The business is important to me.'

They had reached the front door and as Martha went in she did not see the meaningful glances that passed between husband and wife, nor could she realise how significant her last remark was to them.

'I'll take these to your room,' said John, heading for the stairs.

'You refresh yourself and I'll order tea,' said Eliza. 'Evening meal at our usual time.'

Martha hugged her sister-in-law. 'Thank you, Eliza. It's so good to be back. I shan't be long. I expect Abigail is having her afternoon nap. May I look in on her?'

'Of course.'

'I won't wake her,' Martha promised as she hurried after her brother who was halfway up the stairs by now.

When John came down a few moments later he hurried straight to the drawing room to find Eliza.

'What do you think?' he asked.

'It's going to be difficult. You saw how pleased she was to be back and how enthusiastic about the business.'

John nodded. 'I know, but it's better to tackle the problem now rather than wait.'

'You'll have to if you are to go to Cornwall tomorrow.'

Two maids arrived with the tea then and just as they were leaving Martha entered the room. 'Oh, this is nice,' she said, eyeing the tray of scones, but continued over to the window. She stood for a moment, looking out, before she said,

'There's no view like this.' She turned away slowly, as if reluctant to leave the vista, put a scone on a plate and sat down beside a small table on which John had placed a cup of tea poured by Eliza. 'Abigail looks well,' she commented. 'How have you both been while I've been away?'

'Very well,' replied Eliza, and shot a glance at her husband.

'We have something to tell you,' he said.

Martha gave a small frown as she looked at her brother. 'It sounds serious.'

'It is. We have a decision to make which will affect us all.'

'What? We three, you mean?'

'Plus Abigail and all the staff.'

'What has happened?' asked Martha, concern in her voice as she glanced from brother to sister-in-law.

'I have received a letter from a solicitor in Cornwall to say that Uncle Gerard has left me his entire estate. It comes to a considerable sum. In fact, a small fortune.'

For a moment Martha was struck silent by the shock of the news. 'What? Father's black sheep brother? But you hardly knew him. I certainly have only the faintest recollection of him, and you are younger than I.'

'I know. I can hardly picture him either, but there it is. He has remembered me, though why I don't know.'

'Does the solicitor say anything about him?'

'Only that he sailed the seven seas, made money, chose to settle in Cornwall where he speculated in tin, made more money and bought an estate, Penorna, which along with his ready money and his interests in a copper mine he has left to me.'

Martha raised her eyebrows expressively. 'Lucky for you. I'm delighted. You'll never have financial worries now, and nor will Abigail.' She saw that her brother's expression was still serious and filled with doubt, as if there was something he wasn't telling her. 'I can see it doesn't please you entirely. Come on, tell me why?'

'There are certain stipulations to my inheritance.'

'Oh?' Martha looked askance at Eliza. 'And you don't like them?'

'Well, they are not insurmountable but . . .'

'All right, John, what are they?'

'I have to take up residence in his Cornish property and live there for at least twelve years. If I don't agree I get nothing, and if I leave within that time I have to make good the value of the estate.'

'Oh, I see,' said Martha quietly, pausing for a moment after that. 'Have you reached a decision?' she asked finally.

'Not yet.'

'We wanted to wait until we heard what you thought,' said Eliza.

'But it has nothing to do with me.'

'You are very much a part of the family.'

'You are very kind to me, always have been, I couldn't have wished for a better sister-in-law. But this decision is for you and John to take.' Martha added in a cautionary tone, 'How much do you know of this place?'

'The house and land holdings are substantial. The solicitor sent us this map.' John rose as he was speaking. 'Come and see.' He went to the table and rolled it out. Martha and Eliza joined him. He pointed out the boundaries to his sister.

She studied the map and then commented, 'It certainly is substantial, and it looks as if the estate has a wonderful coastline with cliffs and small bays.'

'This is the house.' John tapped the map.

'I thought it must be. It looks as if it will enjoy a wonderful view. What about these?' She pointed to some markings grouped closely together near the western boundary.

'I can only conclude they are the village of Penorna from which the estate takes its name.'

'You must be tempted?' said his sister.

'Yes, but I have suggested that John goes to Cornwall and looks the place and its prospects over first. It is no good deciding now and then finding it's not what we expect,' Eliza put in.

'That sounds a sensible idea,' agreed Martha. 'How soon must you decide?'

'We have three months, but would like to proceed as soon as possible. I have arranged to leave for Cornwall tomorrow,' her brother told her.

'So soon?'

'It's best to get on with things.'

'Of course.'

'I shall take a coach to Scarborough and another to York. I will stay there the night and arrange my onward journey there.'

'How long do you expect to be away?'

'It may take eight to ten days each way.'

'And there is the time John will be in Cornwall,' added Eliza.

'How long that will take God only knows, but I must be certain about everything.'

That night, lying in her husband's arms, Eliza said, 'John, if there is a decision to be made while you are in Cornwall, make it. I will agree with whatever you want to do.'

'Thank you my love. That eases my mind.'

'Hurry back. I'll miss you.'

'I'll miss you too, dearest.' He kissed her neck.

She shuddered. 'Love me again,' she requested with quiet temptation.

Ten weeks later John arrived home to a rapturous welcome. Eliza had heard the carriage wheels and gave a whoop of delight when she saw her husband descend from the vehicle. She flew from the room, flung open the front door and was down the terrace steps and into his arms almost before he had thanked the coachman. They hugged each other amidst much joyous laughter and then lost themselves in a welcome home kiss. Finally, with arms wrapped round each other, they started for the house. As they stepped on to the terrace, Martha came out.

In her room on the first floor she had heard Eliza's shout and judged that John must be home. As keen as she was to welcome her brother back she delayed a few moments in order to let him and Eliza enjoy their own private greeting.

384

Now she held out her arms to him and brother and sister exchanged hugs of greeting.

'You've been away longer than I expected,' commented Eliza. 'I hope it was all worthwhile?'

'Tell you when I've got the grime of travel off me,' he teased.

'We want to know now, don't we, Martha?'

'We do,' she agreed.

He tried to slip away but they grabbed his arms.

'Now!' said Eliza determinedly.

He laughed. 'All right. You'll have to wait for the fine details but it's all arranged. We go as soon as I can settle things here.'

Silence fell briefly on them. Eliza was filled with astonishment, charged with excitement at the prospect of this new venture alongside her husband. Martha's heart sank with disappointment. She did not want to leave Whitby. She loved it here; had thought she was settled for life, and now that old certainty was being thrown into upheaval. But she could not detract from the joy that was emanating from John and Eliza and tried to show some excitement, for their sake.

'Oh, John!' cried Eliza. 'I'll order some tea. You go and freshen up; and then come and tell us all about it.'

When they entered the house he went straight upstairs. Eliza started for the kitchen but was detained by Martha. 'I'll order the tea, you go to John.'

'Thank you.' She gave her sister-in-law a hug.

A quarter of an hour later, as soon as John and Eliza walked into the drawing room, Martha poured the tea. John got comfortable in a chair facing the two young women who were both anxious to hear his account.

'Well?' promoted Eliza, eager for him to start.

'It is a wonderful place. The scenery is magnificent along the coast . . .'

'Better than ours?' queried Martha tartly.

'Well . . .' John drew the word out in an expression of doubt.

'There, I knew it!' Martha seized on her chance, but before she had time to express any more favourable opinions on the Yorkshire coast, Eliza intervened.

'Go on, John. Where did you stay?'

'A local inn in Sandannack. It was somewhat primitive but comfortable enough with good basic food. The locals were a bit suspicious of me, especially when it became known that I was the new owner of Penorna. Seems my uncle was well liked, so of course they wondered if the new owner would be up to his standards. They feared change; just wanted to go on in the way they always had, with no outside interference. It was almost like being in a foreign country. I soon settled their doubts, especially after I had seen the solicitor and he had briefed me on all aspects of the estate.'

'And what is that like?' asked Eliza.

'Wonderful,' replied John with enthusiasm. 'Uncle Gerard turned some rough meadows into good farmland. He allowed the villagers . . .'

'Then the village is ours too?' Eliza broke in. 'Is that Sandannack?'

'Yes. Twenty families live there. They were afraid I might rescind the rights my uncle had given them, such as access across his land to the sea so that they could pursue their fishing. That is only a part-time occupation for most of them as the majority, along with others from neighbouring villages, work in the copper mine.'

'Ours too?'

'Yes. And we also own several houses in Penzance.'

Martha, who had listened in silence, said, 'From the sound of it you could do no other than accept such an inheritance. The only thing that could have kept you here is your love of Yorkshire.'

John looked grave. 'I must admit it still exerts a strong pull, and finding myself so far from home I nearly refused to have anything to do with Penorna, but then I thought it would be wrong not to keep and expand upon what my uncle worked so hard to achieve. And these people had looked up to him as a just and kindly landlord. What might happen to them if I refused to take on the responsibility?'

'Quite right,' approved Martha. 'Uncle Gerard would have been proud of you. Besides, you are making a more secure future for Abigail.' Her voice caught in her throat. 'I will miss her, I will miss you all.' Her eyes dampened, but, being one who had learned to control her feelings in public since losing Jos, she held back the tears. They could flow later in the privacy of her room.

'But you'll come with us?' gasped Eliza.

'You must,' said John.

Martha shook her head slowly. 'No. It's a new life you are making for yourselves. I could not share it fully while my heart is set on the Yorkshire coast, and more specifically Whitby.' She raised her hands to stem the protest and persuasion she saw coming. 'No, don't. You'll never talk me into it. I thought about it a lot while you were away, John, realising that you might take up your inheritance, while there was no way that I could be persuaded to uproot myself from Yorkshire. Here in Whitby I still feel close to Jos. Don't say any more about it. I will move out of the house as soon as I can find somewhere else to live.'

John glanced at his wife and he saw her almost imperceptible nod of agreement and approval.

'Well, Martha, I'm sorry you won't come with us. We will miss you. But there is no need for you to look for anywhere else to live. You must stay here.'

Martha's eyes widened as she tried to grasp what her brother was doing. 'You mean, here in Bloomfield Manor?'

'With what my uncle has left me, I have no need to sell this house or my business. I will assign them both to you. You shall not want, and I will be happy in that knowledge. You are capable of running the estate yourself but get a manager in if it helps, or promote the foreman, Giles Smithers. We've got a loyal staff in the chandlery business and you have a great aptitude for that. Mind you, you might meet opposition from some of the other businessmen in Whitby, but I think you are strong enough to outface them.'

Martha smiled through the tears in her eyes. 'I look forward to the challenge. John, Eliza, thank you, I don't deserve such consideration.'

'You can come and visit us whenever you like, and we can come north to see you,' said Eliza.

Martha gave a wan smile. 'It's a long way.'

Chapter Two

'Have you got the roof sorted for Ben Fowley?' Eliza asked, as she and John rose from the breakfast table.

'The repairs should have been finished yesterday. I'm going to the village this morning to check.'

Eliza glanced at the window. 'You've nice weather for the walk.'

'Wouldn't have gone if it had been any other,' he replied with a grin.

'Come and say goodbye to Abigail before you go.'

'Wouldn't miss that either.' He took Eliza's hand and they went to the nursery together.

When they entered the room, Abigail sprang from her chair and with a five-year-old's shouts of glee rushed to them: 'Mama! Papa! She flung herself at her mother who swept her into her arms and lifted her high, then hugged her tight as they laughed together. From her mother's arms she turned a bright loving smile on her father. John tweaked her cheeks and she giggled. 'How's my favourite girl?'

'Had all my breakfast,' Abigail responded.

Eliza glanced across at the eighteen-year-old governess, Dorinda Jenkins, who gave a nod confirming the child's statement.

'Good girl. Coming to see Papa off?'

'Yes! Yes!'

Eliza allowed her to slide from her arms to the floor, whereupon she took hold of her father's hand.

John selected a Malacca cane from the stand beside the front door, struck a little pose with it and raised a questioning eyebrow at his wife.

'You look very elegant.' Eliza smiled. 'You always do,' she added, admiring his long tailcoat with its high velvet collar. A full-length waistcoat opened at the neck to reveal a white embroidered cravat tied neatly at his throat. Corn-coloured breeches, buttoned below the knee, came to the top of his brown leather boots.

Abigail ran to a chest, opened it and took out a hat. 'Hat, Papa, hat!' she called, running to him.

'Thank you. Be a good girl while I'm away.' John turned to Eliza and kissed her. 'I hope there are no other problems in the village to hold me up. I want to see how the new tenants are settling in at Croft Farm.'

Eliza and Abigail followed him on to the terrace and watched until he reached a bend in the drive where he stopped and waved to them.

Eliza felt a surge of pride. Though, three years ago, she had harboured some doubts about coming to Cornwall, she had kept them to herself when John had returned from his first visit full of enthusiasm. She had known they would be embarking upon a different life from that they knew in Yorkshire, but seeing John's tact in engaging the confidence of his tenants, especially the miners who worked his mine, she soon realised that her worries had been unfounded. It was the same story with the landed gentry of the county, and though she knew that John did not always agree with them over land policies and their treatment of tenants, he was subtle enough not to attract outright enmity. She knew she had played her part in this, too, and in their acceptance into local society. Eliza was quick to observe and note the local etiquette and soon entertained on an equal scale. They were settled in Cornwall now and had a good life here.

She was the one who wrote to Martha, knowing that John, no matter how close he had been to his sister, would not willingly take up a pen. Or had she spoiled him by taking up this correspondence when they first arrived in Cornwall? Gradually the frequency of the letters had dwindled and there had been no exchange at all during the last year. It seemed that lives in both Cornwall and Yorkshire had become too full.

Reaching the end of the drive, John paused. He had two choices: a walk across country or the longer coastal route. He decided on the latter. The day was one of glorious sunshine, with a slight nip in the air that brought sharp clarity to every view. The scenery along the coast, the soaring cliffs, land sweeping down to the sea, bays and coves, had woven its magic spell on him and today he could not resist such a call.

The path took him close to the cliff edge and he could not help but stop frequently to admire the view. Outcrops of rock with the sea foaming round them stood sentinel in some of the bays; in others virgin sand was touched by the lazy waves that scarcely bothered to break. Gulls squawked overhead and plunged like stones to find precarious footholds on the jagged cliffs. Cormorants lurked there, eyes fixed on some prey, before plunging at speed into the sea to emerge triumphant. Two fishing boats dragged their nets while in the distance a three-master beat its way along the Channel. In the three years he had been here John had never tired of the scenery along this coast.

The path swung away from the cliff edge but he knew that after about a hundred yards it would return above a small cove of untouched sand sheltered by towering cliffs on three sides. Here he was brought to a sudden stop. Today footprints marked the sand below. He could not believe it. Whose were they? How had they got there? Then he saw her emerge from the shadow of the cliff to his right: a thin waif of a girl who strolled casually along the water's edge, allowing the waves to lap over her bare feet. She held her dress so that it would not get wet around the hem, then seemingly irritated by having to do so let it go, flinging her arms high in a gesture of freedom and joy. She did a little jig and skipped a few steps before pirouetting on and on along the sward of sand and in and out of the water, ignoring the splashes that wet the thin cotton, causing the dress to cling to her, emphasising the curves of her lithe body.

John's whole attention was drawn to her. He was filled with curiosity and a desire to know more about her. He had to find out. All thoughts of his mission were driven from his mind.

He looked for some way down but could not find one. Then he turned his attention back to the cove. She had disappeared. His eyes swept the bay. She was nowhere to be seen; only the footprints in the sand remained as evidence that she had ever walked and danced there. If she had clambered round the headland on the rocks, had he missed her in its shadow? It was the only conclusion he could come to. Annoyed, his lips tightened with frustration, he resumed his journey.

Throughout the rest of his visits his attention kept drifting back to memories of the girl on the sand. He wondered who she was and if he would ever see her again. But as he turned for home in the afternoon he tried to thrust all such thoughts away. What had commanded his interest anyway? The fact that she was on a beach that he'd thought completely isolated? Was it purely the magic of seeing someone give way to such carefree abandon? Irritated with himself, he spoke out loud, 'Fool! You'll probably never see her again.'

Nevertheless, during the next fortnight, he walked that way every day but saw no one. He began to think she had been a figment of his imagination.

'John, are you ready? Benson is bringing the carriage to the door.' Eliza turned from their bedroom window.

'Coming, love.' He appeared from his dressing room, stopped and stared in loving admiration at his wife. 'You look wonderful.'

'Like it?' she asked, doing a turn so that he could appreciate her full simple dress of white satin with a low round neck and elbow-length sleeves embellished with tiny ruffles. The new fashion of wearing a slightly higher waist than had been usual allowed the dress to fall more naturally in sweeping folds while maintaining the slimmer effect. Her only ornament was a pink belt at the waist and a soft fichu of the same colour around her neck.

'I'm pleased you kept it as a surprise,' John said appreciatively. 'Such elegance suits you.'

Eliza came to him and kissed him on the cheek. 'Thank you for treating me to a new gown. And might I say that you too look very elegant?' She stood back, admiring his dark blue tailcoat cut high at the waist and matching well-fitting trousers.

'I like this new fashion of trousers, especially for evening wear,' she commented.

'So do I,' he agreed, 'though breeches can be more practical throughout the day. What about the rest of me?'

He wore a white waistcoat with six pearl buttons, and a slightly starched linen cravat tied neatly at his neck and held with a pearl pin. His black shoes shone like mirrors.

'Impeccable, as always.'

He smiled his appreciation. 'I'll wear my beaver hat,' he said. 'You?'

'I'm just going to have my kerchief, the one with three pheasant's feathers.'

'Good, then let's go, we don't want to be late.' He opened the door for her.

She glided past him and down the stairs to the hall where she picked up a shawl as a protection for her shoulders against the sharp evening air.

When they emerged on to the terrace Benson jumped down from his seat on the box and opened the coach's door for them. Once they were settled, the coachman took his place again, gathered the reins and sent the horse on its way to Trethtowan Manor, a matter of five miles further along the coast to the west, where their neighbours Selwyn and Harriet Westbury had lived for ten years since their marriage after his father had bought them the run-down estate. Now, through Selwyn's diligence and hard work, the estate and one copper mine provided them with a high standard of living. Harriet had worked hard too, overseeing the renovation of the old house until it was acknowledged as one of the most attractive along the south Cornish coast. Her gift as a hostess made the lavish parties at Trethtowan Manor the talk of Cornwall and gentry would vie for an invitation. This was not such an event; just a friendly evening with neighbours to whom the Westburys had taken immediately. They were eight years older than John and Eliza with two children, James aged nine and Juliana eight. The family had known John's uncle and were delighted that his nephew had decided to come south and run the estate. John and Eliza had found their advice valuable and it had made their transition to their new life much easier. Now they looked forward to a pleasant evening in good company, with good food and easy conversation.

Benson turned the coach expertly through the stone pillars where the ornamental iron gates had already been opened by the gate-keeper who had been warned of the time of the Mitchells' arrival. Benson liked these visits. He knew the servants at Trethtowan Manor well and expected his own entertainment in a warm kitchen where he would enjoy Cook's hearty fare for the servants, washed down by some of the best ale in the county. He drew the horse to a halt in front of the imposing façade and was quickly to the ground to open the door for Mrs Mitchell.

As they climbed the four steps to the covered stone veranda that stretched the full length of the façade, the large front door swung open and a liveried servant stood beside it to greet them with an inclination of his head and a quiet, 'Good evening, ma'am. Good evening, sir.'

John and Eliza accepted the greeting and moved into a spacious, marble-floored hall where two maidservants were standing by to take their outdoor clothes.

'Eliza! John!' Selwyn held out his hands to them as he came from the drawing room. His broad welcoming smile almost hid the scar that marked his left cheek, supposedly the result of a chance encounter with a would-be thief on the lonely moor as he returned home late. Privately he still suspected there might have been more to it than that. Though he could not prove it, he believed it was the result of the disagreement that festered between himself and Jeremy Gaisford of neighbouring Senewey Estate. Tonight, however, Selwyn's eyes sparkled with delight as he kissed Eliza on the cheek and shook John's hand.

Petite Harriet, who seemed to glide across the marble floor, expressed her own pleasure at seeing them and as she escorted Eliza to the drawing room admired her guest's dress, an observation that was heartily reciprocated. On reaching the room, Eliza stepped away from her hostess to admire Harriet's simple white muslin gown that fell in neat folds to her dainty feet. She had dispensed with the usual ruffles on the sleeves, preferring them plain and ending tightly at the wrists.

After seeing his guests comfortably seated, Selwyn went to the decanter and glasses on the sideboard and was pouring Madeira for them all when the door opened slowly and a young lady stepped tentatively into the room.

'Ah, Lydia, my dear,' cried Harriet, rising quickly. 'Come and meet our guests.' She hurried to the newcomer's side and took her arm.

John had already jumped to his feet. He fought to control the gasp of surprise on his lips. The young woman from the beach! It must be. He surely wasn't mistaken even though he had only seen her from a distance. His heart and mind raced. That lithe body he had seen splashing joyfully through the water could not be disguised by a plain pink dress simply cut with a square neckline. The silk shawl that covered her shoulders complemented the beauty of her ivory-skinned oval face. Pale blue eyes sparkled from it in a lively fashion.

'Eliza, I would like you to meet Miss Lydia Booth. Lydia, this is Mrs Mitchell of whom I have spoken.'

The young woman took the hand Eliza extended. 'I am pleased to meet you, Mrs Mitchell. Mrs Westbury spoke of you in enthusiastic terms.'

'I am delighted to meet you too, Miss Booth. You have the advantage of me. My friend has not mentioned you to me.'

'After a brief visit two weeks ago, I only arrived here yesterday.'

As Harriet turned Lydia towards John he realised why he had not seen her since that day on the beach. 'Lydia, this is Mr Mitchell. John . . . Miss Lydia Booth.'

He took the hand she offered and raised it to his lips as he made a slight bow, never taking his eyes off hers. 'It is a pleasure to meet you, Miss Booth. I look forward to hearing more about you.'

Lydia gave a small smile. 'There is little to tell, Mr Mitchell.'

He was unable to make any further comment as Selwyn brought over a tray with five glasses on it. With the wine taken and everyone seated, Harriet offered an explanation.

'Lydia's family were very close friends of mine when we lived in Oxford. Her mother died a year ago and her grieving father just three months ago.' The murmurs of sympathy from Eliza and John were accepted by Lydia with a slight inclination of her head. 'Lydia has a brother, Samuel, whom I'm sorry to say refused to take responsibility for her, leaving her with no home. Selwyn and I talked it over and decided to offer Lydia the position of governess here to our children. She will live as part of our family.'

'It was a most kind and generous offer,' put in Lydia when Harriet paused, 'and I will be ever grateful to Mr and Mrs Westbury.' Her eyes dampened and her voice caught in her throat as she glanced at them.

'Lydia paid us a brief visit a fortnight ago before returning to Oxford to clear out what had been the family home. Her brother now lives in Wales. She only arrived back here yesterday.'

'I am sure you will be very happy with Mr and Mrs Westbury,' said Eliza with a pleasant smile. 'And James and Juliana are delightful children.'

'From the little I have seen of them, I agree with you,' returned Lydia. 'I am looking forward to teaching them.'

'You have done this sort of work before?' asked John.

'No, Mr Mitchell, I have not, but I have had a good education myself including painting and the pianoforte,' she replied, a little coolly, as if detecting an implied doubt of her ability.

If anyone else noticed they made no comment, but John was aware of the reproof in her eyes as she met his gaze in a manner that forced him to look away.

'Have you any children, Mrs Mitchell?' Lydia asked, turning her attention to Eliza.

'One. A little girl of five named Abigail.'

'A nice-sounding name.'

'You must come and meet her and her governess. The children often meet and play together.'

'That is kind of you, Mrs Mitchell. I look forward to it.'

'I don't like leaving things in the air, so should we say next Wednesday at three o'clock?'

Lydia glanced questioningly at Harriet as she replied, 'If Mrs Westbury is in agreement?'

'Of course, Lydia. I'm sure James and Juliana will enjoy the outing.'

Ten minutes later a manservant appeared to announce that dinner was served. Selwyn offered his arm to Eliza and started for the door. John turned to Harriet. As she placed her hand on his arm, he glanced at Lydia who had hung back, prepared to bring up the rear on her own. He offered his other arm to her, which she took with a smile of gratitude.

His gesture made her feel accepted on an equal footing by the Mitchells. Maybe her first opinion of him had been wrong, though nothing in the subsequent conversation had softened her judgment, but now . . .

John was seated opposite her at the table. Throughout the meal, as conversation flowed, Lydia was aware that his eyes frequently strayed to her and felt that she was being assessed and judged.

'Your artistic talent, Miss Booth, was that inherited? Were your mother and father that way inclined?' His questions startled her. She had barely followed the direction of the general chatter, lost in memories of the beautiful beach she had visited on her last trip to the Manor.

Embarrassed by her own distracted manner, she dabbed her lips with her napkin. As she replaced it on her lap she said, 'My mother was an excellent embroideress and made her own designs.'

'Then it must have come from her.'

'My painting could not compare with her talent,' Lydia demurred.

'Did you keep some of your mother's work?' asked Eliza.

'Indeed I did, ma'am.'

'I should like to see it. Embroidery is an interest of mine. Would you care to show it to us?'

'I would be proud to, Mrs Mitchell.'

Eliza glanced at her hostess. 'After dinner, Harriet?'

'Of course, my dear, while the gentlemen have their port and cigars.'

'Oh, but we must see Miss Booth's painting alongside her mother's embroidery, to make a comparison and assess the source of Miss Booth's talent,' said John. He glanced at Lydia. 'I presume you have a painting you can show us, and are willing to do so?'

She felt her cheeks redden for she sensed there was something of a challenge about this request. 'I have, Mr Mitchell. You shall see both, if you wish.'

John inclined his head. 'Thank you, Miss Booth, we will look forward to it.'

As the meal continued Lydia wondered if Mr Mitchell had a genuine interest in art and if so how good a judge he would be of workmanship and talent? She began to feel twinges of apprehension.

When the men rejoined the ladies in the drawing room, Harriet suggested that Lydia bring the embroidery and painting right away. She took the opportunity to compose herself in the quiet of her room, straightened her dress and patted her hair into place. Satisfied with her reflection in the mirror, she selected a tablecloth and a runner for a sideboard that she judged to be among her mother's best work. She had rescued them before her brother got his hands on them, for she knew he would only sell them to get what he could to appease his drinking habit. She turned her attention to the four paintings she had also brought with her. She pondered and then, a decision made, picked up a watercolour of the Isis with the spires of Oxford in the distance. Taking a deep breath, she left her room.

Selwyn had poured some wine and had placed a glass for Lydia on a side table. She thanked him and sat down, being careful to keep her painting from view. Settling herself, she caught a glint of amusement in John's eyes as he asked, 'Are you keeping that a secret, Miss Booth?'

Lydia's lips tightened but quickly relaxed; she must show no hostility to a guest. 'Not at all, Mr Mitchell. I thought you should see the best work first. I did not want my poor contribution to be in your mind when you saw my mother's.' She started to unwrap the tablecloth.

Harriet got to her feet. 'I think I'd better take one end and then we can hold it up before laying it on the floor as we haven't a table big enough in here.'

'Thank you, Mrs Westbury.'

As they unfolded the cloth Eliza gave little gasps of delight. Finally, when the full extent of the design was exposed, Eliza cried out, 'That is exquisite. Simply wonderful! I have never seen embroidery so beautiful. It must have taken your mother hours and hours of painstaking work.' She was on her feet examining the cloth more closely, murmuring her admiration all the time.

Pride surged in Lydia. How she wished her mother could have heard such praise. 'Thank you, Mrs Mitchell, you are most kind.'

'Not at all, my dear, I mean everything I say.' She glanced at Harriet. 'Don't you think it's just beautiful? You'll have seen it before?'

'Only when Lydia's mother was working on it, never in its entirety. Hold this end, Eliza, so I can see the whole cloth.'

'Of course.' She took over from Harriet.

Their hostess stood silently, concentrating on the exquisite depiction of intertwined flowers, mostly roses, that bordered the cloth. The centrepiece was a mass of foliage, a blending of many shades of green that in parts was extended as if to embrace the roses. 'It is a truly imaginative work, beautifully executed. Selwyn, John, come and have a closer look.'

The two men rose to their feet and joined Harriet. Lydia watched them closely, trying to interpret their reactions, but found herself wondering more about Mr Mitchell's than Mr Westbury's.

After a few moments Selwyn spoke. 'It is truly magnificent.'

'There can't be a stitch out of place,' commented John as he bent closer to the cloth.

'There will be one,' said Lydia. 'Mother always made one slip, and beside it would turn a stitch in the pattern into her initial, W, just to show that it truly was the work of one person.'

'How forward-looking. That would make the cloth all the more valuable should it ever come up for sale.'

'I could never sell it, Mr Mitchell.'

'No, I don't suppose you could. From all I have seen and heard tonight, I can tell how much you loved your mother. You must have been very close.'

'Indeed we were, Mr Mitchell. I wish you and Mrs Mitchell could have met her.'

'I wish we could too, Miss Booth,' he returned quietly. Seeing the dampness in her eyes he said more brightly, 'now we must see your painting.'

Thankful for the change of subject, she gave a small smile and reached for her painting. She stood so all could see it when she turned it round. Silence filled the room as the four friends studied a delicate watercolour of a river with the spires of Oxford hazy in the distance. The whole scene was brought alive by her use of the late light, and the flowing water seemed to invite the viewer to follow it towards those distant spires and uncover the mysteries that lay concealed along its banks.

'A truly accomplished work, Miss Booth! You see colours where other people would not.'

Lydia inclined her head in acknowledgement of his praise. 'Thank you, Mr Mitchell. The greens of the leaves and the grass contain many other colours within them.'

'And you have a subtle way of catching them, Miss Booth,' commented Eliza.

'Thank you, Mrs Mitchell. You and your husband seem to have some knowledge of painting. Are you painters yourselves?'

'Not really, but we were both interested in the work of local artists and bought some after we first married.'

'We were fortunate in that there was a small school of painters in Whitby where we then lived. We were able to study their techniques at first hand.'

'You were fortunate indeed.'

'We like to think it developed our appreciation of art.' John turned to his host. 'What about you, Selwyn? And Harriet? I know from our previous conversations that neither of you are artists, but with such a talent as Miss Booth's under the same roof you must develop your interest.'

'Lydia is certainly very gifted, we can see that. But we'd never pretend to be experts in the matter.'

'What really counts, Mr Westbury, is that a painting pleases you,' said Lydia, 'and that you can live with it, day after day.'

'Well, I could certainly live with yours. Couldn't you, Harriet?' He turned to his wife, whose eyes had never left the painting during these exchanges.

'Though I can't pretend to understand all the finer points, I would receive pleasure from that work every time I walked into the room where it hung,' she replied in a voice that reflected how much it had moved her.

'Then, Mrs Westbury, you shall have it,' offered Lydia.

'But I couldn't!'

'You can. Please, in grateful thanks for all you have done for me.'

Harriet spread her hands. 'What have I done? Given you a position as governess.'

'You have given me a home and welcomed me to it when my future looked extremely bleak. It is yours, Mrs Westbury.'

'Well . . . Thank you, my dear. I will always treasure it.'

'Where will you hang it?' asked Selwyn.

'There is just the place in the hall. I will see it every morning when I come downstairs, and during the day when I pass that way. Visitors will see it, too. Who knows, Lydia? It may result in further commissions for you.'

'And Eliza and I will be the first to place one,' put in John.

'I had no intention of taking up painting on that basis.' Lydia gasped at this turn in her fortune. 'I don't really think I'm good enough, but I'll certainly paint one for you.'

'You shouldn't hide or belittle the talent I can see in that picture,' Eliza told her. 'And you must put a fair price on any painting you do for us.'

'But Mrs Mitchell, I couldn't . . .'

'You must. I insist.'

'Then I must paint the subject you request.'

John looked thoughtful for a moment. 'What about a section of the coast nearby? Is that a good idea, Eliza?'

'Delightful,' she agreed.

'That would be pleasant to undertake and would allow for various interpretations,' Lydia agreed.

'I have a place in mind. It is a little bay that has always attracted us.'

'Where would that be?'

'Difficult to explain to you as you are new to the area, it would be better if I could show you. We will arrange it some time.'

Lydia took that last statement as a dismissal of the subject and wondered why a time could not be arranged now, until she realised that in her eagerness she had overlooked etiquette. Arranging a meeting between a man and a woman, strangers until this evening, would be frowned upon unless they were chaperoned.

The thought came back into her mind as she lay in bed that night. She began to wonder if Mr Mitchell had deliberately avoided a firm arrangement. Maybe he did not want to be encumbered with a chaperone? She chided herself for having such a thought, for with it had come the realisation she would like to see him alone on such an occasion. It would be easier to discuss what he wanted with no one else there – but was that her real reason? Good heavens, what was she thinking? Still, there had been something attractive about him. His deep blue eyes, so alert to everything. His full mouth with laughter lines about it. There were many things about him she'd become aware of as the evening wore on, not least his astute mind and gift for intelligent and penetrating conversation that nevertheless could turn to lighter matters and be amusing. There was something decidedly attractive about him, Lydia decided. Stop it, girl, he's a happily married man who wouldn't give you a second look she told herself. But hadn't he cast glances in her direction very often when his attention might have been directed elsewhere? Just imagination, she decided. Best dismiss all such fanciful thoughts and get to sleep.

Chapter Three

'I am so pleased that they have taken to each other,' observed
Eliza as she and Harriet, sitting at the drawing-room window,
watched the two governesses playing with the children on the
lawn at Penorna. 'From what we saw of Miss Booth the other
night, I am sure you have found a gem. Such talent ... I do
hope she will be able to pass it on to your children. She's
charming too, and today has confirmed her ease of manner.'

'Yes, I am highly delighted,' agreed Harriet. 'And so
pleased we could help her. But you are fortunate, with Miss
Jenkins.'

'Indeed. Abigail took to her immediately.' Eliza gave a little laugh. 'I must say I felt a pang of jealousy, but I soon
realised that Dorinda was careful to prevent Abigail from
switching her affection away from me entirely. She knew just
where and when to draw the line.'

'Good. Where affection is concerned, there is always a danger that the governess will get most of it. I have seen it happen before, and even destroy a marriage in one case where the
father received all the parental love and the governess what
should rightly have been the mother's.'

'But surely the parents could have intervened?'

'They should have done. It is not easy, however, when the
governess becomes possessive but is skilful at disguising it
while appearing the model employee.' Harriet looked in the
direction of the children busy chasing after a ball as the two
governesses encouraged them while keeping the play within
bounds. 'I don't think we have any such worries.'

Eliza laughed as she saw Abigail fall, roll over and spring
quickly to her feet again with a merry laugh. 'I don't think we

404

have. They are a happy group.' She turned away to accompany Harriet to the sofa. 'Are you thinking of giving Miss Booth any free time?'

'Selwyn and I were discussing it only last night,' replied Harriet. 'We agreed it was the correct thing to do. After all, she shouldn't be tied to the children all the time.'

'That was the attitude we took ourselves when we engaged Dorinda, and it works well,' explained Eliza. 'She appreciates having complete freedom for one day a week, and Abigail enjoys a full day spent with me. I was going to suggest, having seen today how well Dorinda and Lydia have taken to each other, that if you had the same idea we should agree to give them the same day off and then the two of them could meet if they wished.'

'That's a splendid suggestion. I'm sure Lydia would welcome it, particularly as Dorinda is a Cornish girl who knows these parts and people in Cribyan and Sandannack. If I remember correctly she always has Thursday off?'

'Yes, and we allow her some time on a Sunday afternoon to visit her family in Penzance. Her father is a shopkeeper there and had the foresight to give his daughter as good an education as possible. We were indeed fortunate to find her.'

'Then I shall allow Lydia the same free time. She knows no one in this area so a friendly relationship with Dorinda might help her to settle, though she has an independent streak.'

'I'm sure Dorinda will welcome her companionship.'

The two girls were delighted when, over tea with the children, Eliza and Harriet explained the arrangements. As they were leaving, Dorinda told Lydia that if she walked to Penorna Manor on the Thursday of the following week, she would take her into the village of Cribyan.

As she lay down that night Lydia blessed her own good fortune. She felt sure that she had found a good friend in Dorinda and that she would be happy in Cornwall, though her new life here was in marked contrast to that she had led in Oxford.

The day she was to meet Dorinda dawned bright. By the time she was ready to leave clouds were gathering, though they did not seem threatening. Nevertheless Lydia put her cloak round her shoulders; during the past week she had experienced the way a Cornish wind could bring a chill, even on a warm day, to the exposed cliff-walk. She kept to a brisk pace, enjoying the views of the sea crashing onto the rugged coast and beating on the rocks far below.

She had walked about a mile when her steps faltered and she finally stopped to gaze down on a small bay. Joy at the sight surged within her for it recalled the day during her first short visit when she had discovered this very place and had skipped across its sand and splashed in the sea as it ran around her bare feet, in the sheer ecstasy of having been given a new chance in life. She had thought of it then as *her* bay, and still thought of it as that now. It was special to her and always would be; marking a turning point in her life. She smiled and felt the bay embrace her. Her footsteps were light as she went on her way.

As she approached Penorna she saw Dorinda sitting on a garden seat under the front portico with Abigail beside her.

Seeing the new arrival the five year old jumped from her seat and, face wreathed in smiles, ran to meet her. 'Miss Booth! Miss Booth!' she shouted. 'Have you come to play with us again? Where are Juliana and James?'

Laughing at such enthusiasm, and pleased that she had been accepted, Lydia took Abigail's hand. 'No, I'm sorry, I'm not here to play today. Miss Jenkins and I have a free day and she is going to take me to Cribyan. I've never been before.'

'Can I come?'

This last remark had been overheard by her mother who had come from the house on realising that Lydia had arrived.

'No, you can't,' said Eliza gently. 'This will be a special day like every Thursday. It's the day on which Miss Booth and Miss Jenkins can do as they please.'

'Whatever they want?' Abigail's eyes widened in disbelief.

'Yes,' smiled Eliza.

'I wish *I* could.'

'You will one day, love.' Eliza placed a reassuring hand on her daughter's shoulder. 'Now, let them get on their way.'

Dorinda smiled at her mistress. 'Thank you, Mrs Mitchell, we'll be back by six.'

Eliza nodded and stood with Abigail, watching the two governesses walk down the drive. They fell into step, relishing their freedom and the chance to talk freely. By the time they had walked the four miles to Cribyan they knew a great deal about each other.

Lydia told her new friend how she had lost her parents and of the way her brother had failed her. She had felt herself fortunate when the Westburys, family friends from Oxford, had offered her the position of governess.

'Are you settling in?' asked Dorinda.

'Yes. The Westburys are very kind and treat me well, but I know when they want to be on their own or to be alone with special guests.'

'I am not in quite the same position as you, not having known Mr and Mrs Mitchell before I was employed by them.'

'How did you get the position?'

'The previous governess was from Bristol. Though she was with the family two years she never really settled and eventually decided it was best to leave. I heard of it and applied for the position, as it would bring me nearer home. The Mitchells saw the sense in that too and gave me a chance.'

'How long have you been at Penorna Manor?'

'Eighteen months.'

'And it's worked out well for you?'

'Oh, yes.'

'What will you do when Abigail no longer needs a governess?'

'I'll cross that bridge when I come to it. A lot can happen between now and then.'

'Best way of looking at it,' approved Lydia. 'Mr and Mrs Mitchell aren't from these parts, are they?'

Dorinda smiled. 'No. It's pretty obvious from their accent. They came from Whitby in Yorkshire.'

'Good heavens, so far?'

'Mr Mitchell was left the Penorna Estate by his uncle.'

'Lucky him! What's he like?'

Dorinda eyed her friend with a little smile twitching at her lips. 'Handsome, isn't he?' Her smile broadened when she saw Lydia blush. 'Ah, you've noticed.'

'No one could miss that,' replied Lydia, trying to put on a disinterested attitude.

'Those deep blue eyes sometimes give him a brooding aura but he's a kindly man, considerate, good with children and adores his wife. He would do anything for her.'

'And her?'

'Well, you've seen her – beautiful, wouldn't you agree?'

'I suppose she is.'

'Suppose?' Dorinda looked horrified. 'You know she is! That perfectly shaped face with its high cheekbones. Eyes like cornflowers, and the copper tint in her dark hair makes it so striking.'

'But what is she like as a person?'

'Good to work for. She is always willing to exchange ideas about Abigail's upbringing and education, and expects me to do the same. She is gentle and kind, casts an aura when she comes into a room. Didn't you feel that when they dined with you?'

'Well, I was aware of her but not in the way you are implying.'

'I suppose you were thinking more of him,' commented Dorinda, still with a teasing twinkle in her eyes.

'Not at all,' replied Lydia indignantly. She stopped talking then, thankful that she could change the course of the conversation without seeming to do so deliberately. 'Is that where we are going?'

They had come to the top of a rise. The land ahead twisted down a hillside to a wide shallow valley in which stood a group of about forty houses, mostly of golden flint and thatch. They straddled a stream and extended along its banks. The lazy curling smoke from several chimneys gave the scene an atmosphere of tranquillity.

'How beautiful,' commented Lydia.

'It is, but don't be disappointed when you see that several of the cottages are falling into disrepair. We're now on the

408

Senewey Estate, owned by the Gaisford family, who are not too particular about living conditions for their tenants. They keep repairs and improvements to a minimum but still extract high rents.'

'So why don't the tenants leave?'

'And go where? They are farm workers or miners. A few might find work elsewhere but there isn't sufficient for them all. And they might even find worse conditions under harsher landlords. Better the devil you know than him you don't.'

'I've only been here a short while but I can't imagine Mr Westbury or Mr Mitchell being like that.'

'They aren't, and thankfully there are others like them nowadays. But come on, let's away down.'

Dorinda started down the slope. Lydia paused a moment, lost in her thoughts, then caught up with her friend and fell into step with her.

'Hello, Dorinda!' a voice boomed across a field to the left.

Dorinda waved to a man carrying a scythe over his right shoulder. 'Mr Telfrey,' she explained. 'Paid a pittance as odd job man to the Gaisfords. Five children under the age of twelve, but he and his wife are always cheerful.'

They'd reached the first cottage by now. As they proceeded along the street, Lydia saw that some of the houses showed signs of needing attention: thatch was thinning, or hanging loose in some places; stones in the walls slipping. 'I see what you mean about repairs,' she commented.

'I thought you would,' Dorinda responded. 'In most cases where a property is in good shape, the repairs will have been done by the tenants themselves. Those who can take the attitude that as they are living here, they may as well keep their home as comfortable and as weather-proof as possible.'

'What about the materials?'

'They'll scrat around to find what they want. Sometimes, out of the goodness of his heart, old man Gaisford will graciously provide them – that way he gets his property repaired for nothing.'

'Exploitation,' hissed Lydia, disgusted by what she was hearing. 'Who are these Gaisfords?'

'The largest landholders in the county. They also own several mines to the north. Present head of the family is Mr Miles Gaisford. He has three sons, Mr Jeremy, Mr Charles and Mr Logan. They're all married. Mr Charles and Mr Logan spend a lot of time in London. Don't know what they do there but I'll tell you this – when they come home all hell is let loose. Parties here, there and everywhere as others in the county catch on to their coat-tails as you might say. Mr Jeremy is as wild as they are, if not worse, and encourages them. He'll inherit one day and I dread to think what the estate will be like then. Or how his brat Luke will turn out in the future.'

'They sound a charming family.'

'Steer clear of them is what I say. Ah, here we are.' Dorinda opened the door to a cottage. When Lydia had followed her in she found herself in a shop. The room was not big but it was full of all manner of things: ironmongery, crockery, cloth, clogs, shoes, and food, with open sacks of potatoes, sugar and flour standing against one of the walls. Lydia gazed in amazement at the variety of goods in such a small space. There was not room for a counter for the shopkeeper to stand behind; instead he stood beside a barrel on which he had balanced some scales.

'Good day, Miss Dorinda,' he said with a cheerful tone and a broad smile.

'Good day, Mr Hollis. This is my new friend, Miss Lydia Booth. She's governess with the Westbury family at Trethtowan.'

'Pleased to meet you, miss.' He touched his forehead with a finger.

'And I you, Mr Hollis.'

'Job not arrived yet?' Dorinda asked.

'I'm expecting him any time. It's a wonder you didn't see him on the way in.'

'I'm afraid we didn't. Something will have delayed him – trouble with the cart or maybe his horse; shoe off or something.' She turned to Lydia to explain. 'Mr Hollis gets his supplies from my father in Penzance. They are due in today. I

410

send a letter to my parents via Job.' She pulled an envelope from the pocket in her cape. 'I have it here, Mr Hollis.'

He took the letter. 'I'll see he gets it. Now, are you going through to have a bite to eat with us? Mrs Hollis will be disappointed if you don't. She'll want to catch up on all the gossip and to meet your new friend.'

'Thank you, Mr Hollis. We can't disappoint Mrs Hollis, can we?' Dorinda gave Lydia a wink and made for the inside door.

A rosy-cheeked buxom lady welcomed them as if they were prodigal daughters returned home. When Dorinda had received her welcoming hug she introduced Lydia who received the same greeting. Mrs Hollis fussed around them, making sure they were comfortably seated, then bustled off 'to get that bite to eat'.

Lydia looked around and saw a room that was obviously under the care of a house-proud lady. The furniture was highly polished, the cushions on the hide sofa and chairs fluffed up and placed just right. Brass candlesticks on the mantelpiece shone; the mirror over the fireplace dare not have a speck of dust on it.

Dorinda noted Lydia's wandering gaze and whispered, 'Not all the cottages are like those dilapidated ones we saw. Many others are cared for like this even though it is a struggle sometimes on the wages most of these people earn. That does not stop them from taking a pride in their homes and making them as comfortable and presentable as they possibly can. Mr and Mrs Hollis have the advantage of having their own business, though I suspect the Gaisfords exact a higher rent because of that.'

Mrs Hollis reappeared carrying knives and forks and started to lay the table. She stopped, looked at Dorinda and said, 'You'll be wondering about Colin.'

'I am. Is he not around today?'

'Sorry, my dear, he's not. He's away to the fishing, trying to supplement his pittance from the fields.'

'I'll not see him, then?'

'No, lass, you won't. Maybe next week.'

411

Disappointment clouded Dorinda's face as Mrs Hollis left the room.

'Is Colin your sweetheart?' asked Lydia.

Dorinda nodded. 'He's generally around when I come on a Thursday, but he's been saying for a while he might go to the fishing.'

Lydia sympathised with her friend, but no more was said then as Mrs Hollis reappeared with some plates. She stayed for a while chatting and then disappeared back to the kitchen. This was repeated many times over the next hour during which time she brought them glasses of home-made elderflower wine. Finally she stood surveying the laid table, giving a little nod of satisfaction as if to say, I've thought of everything. She heard a bolt being shot in the shop door and knew that as usual she had timed the meal to perfection. Mr Hollis appeared and his wife greeted him as if he had been away to work.

'I'll just wash my hands,' he said.

Lydia recognised that this whole scenario was one the couple played out every day. She smiled to herself at such eccentricity but then thought, What does it matter? If that routine makes them happy and appreciate each other there's nothing wrong in it.

When Mr Hollis came back, he was rubbing his hands in eager anticipation of the food that was coming. 'Please be seated, young ladies.' He indicated the places at the table where he wanted them to sit.

After the meal, which passed off with pleasant chatter, the two girls insisted on helping with the washing up while Mr Hollis went to reopen the shop. With the clean pots stacked, Dorinda indicated that they should be going.

'I want to show Lydia the rest of the village and then take her back a different way,' she explained. 'We have enjoyed your cooking. Mrs Hollis, thank you for the meal.'

'You are indeed a good cook, thank you for having me,' added Lydia.

'Any friend of Dorinda is a friend of ours. You will be welcome here any time.'

412

As they left the shop, Dorinda collided with a man who was hurrying past, deep in thought. She was sent spinning backwards and bumped into Lydia who would have fallen but for the wall.

In a split second the man had stopped in his tracks and was staring at them. Anger flared in his eyes briefly. It was gone just as quickly when he saw the two young women. 'My apologies.' His hand went to his hat. 'I'm so sorry, I . . .' The words died away to be replaced by an expression of surprise. 'Why, Miss Booth! Dorinda! Are you both all right?'

The two girls had got their breath back. 'Yes thank you, Mr Mitchell,' spluttered Dorinda. She glanced at Lydia who was aware that Mr Mitchell's enquiring gaze had settled on her.

'Oh, yes, I'm unharmed, thank you.'

'I'm so sorry. I was lost in thought, not looking where I was walking. Are you sure you are not harmed?'

'Certain, sir,' replied Dorinda.

'Your cape, Miss Booth, the wall has marked it.'

'It will brush off, Mr Mitchell. Think nothing of it,' Lydia replied.

'I apologise again.' He doffed his hat. 'I hope the rest of your day is pleasant.' He started to turn away, then stopped and turned back to Lydia. 'I have thought of the place I would like you to paint. I will have to show it to you. That is, if you still want to do it?'

'I would love to. It will spur me on to resume painting.'

'Very well then! I will arrange to show you the view I would like.' With that, he turned sharply and hurried away.

The girls stood in silence watching him, then Dorinda placed a hand on Lydia's arm and turned her round. 'Your back's a bit of a mess from the wall,' she said. 'I'll see if Mrs Hollis has a clothes brush.'

While Dorinda re-entered the shop on her quest, Lydia stared after Mr Mitchell. Her thoughts were in a whirl. Had she really read interest in his eyes or was it a figment of her own imagination? She reined in her thoughts. She should not be giving way to such fancies. Mr Mitchell could have no interest in her – he was a happily married man. She certainly should not be entertaining such ideas which could only lead to ignominy and disaster.

They were driven from her mind when Dorinda emerged from the shop triumphantly brandishing a clothes brush. With a few deft sweeps across Lydia's back the dust and grime were banished.

'There!' she said. 'As good as new.' She was in and out of the shop in a flash, grabbed Lydia's arm and started along the street. 'What was all that about?' she asked eagerly, sensing a story.

'What?' returned Lydia in feigned innocence.

'You know very well what I mean. The painting Mr Mitchell referred to.'

'Oh, that,' said Lydia, as if it was of no consequence.

'Yes, that,' insisted Dorinda.

'Mr Mitchell wants me to do a painting for him.'

'I didn't know you painted?'

Lydia knew that Dorinda would persist in her curiosity so told her how she had taken up painting, and what had happened when Mr and Mrs Mitchell had visited the Westburys.

Dorinda listened intently with only a few 'Ohs' and 'Ahs', but when Lydia had finished she added, 'So what are you to paint for him?'

'I don't know. You heard him, he's going to show me.'

'Ah!' This time her words were laden with innuendo and accompanied by a teasing twinkle in her eyes which changed to doubt as she warned, 'Be careful. Don't get involved in anything you might regret – he's a handsome man.'

'Don't worry, Dorinda, I won't. I'm only going to paint a picture. For all I know he might forget about it.' But Lydia hoped he wouldn't.

'Oh, I wonder what's going on there,' said her friend as she and Lydia turned through the church gate. She indicated what appeared to be a serious conversation between two men standing at a cottage door further along the street.

'It's Mr Mitchell again,' said Lydia.

'I know, and I'm wondering what he's doing at Ben Lowther's cottage.'

'Shouldn't he be?'

'It's a free world, or so we like to think,' replied Dorinda with a shrug of her shoulders. 'But Ben Lowther recently got the sack from the Gaisford mine for laziness and belligerence.'

'Bad character then?'

'Not really. He's decent enough at heart. Rumour has it that Jeremy Gaisford was pestering Ben's wife, an attractive lass. Ben got wind of it and tackled him, giving him a bloody nose.'

'And you don't hit the boss's son and get away with it.'

'Right. I wonder what Mr Mitchell is doing there?'

Lydia started along the path to the church.

'Wait a moment.' Dorinda drew her back. 'There's something going on.'

They saw Mr Mitchell and Ben Lowther shake hands, then before Mr Mitchell could turn away, Mrs Lowther appeared.

'She's crying,' commented Lydia.

'Aye, but through a smile. And look how she's grasping Mr Mitchell's hands. If that isn't gratitude, I don't know what is. I wonder what's been going on?' Dorinda paused and then added with determination, 'I'll find out before we leave the village.'

They spent a little while in the church. When they reached the gate to leave Dorinda said, 'We're in luck. That's Ben's brother just come out of the cottage.' She turned in that direction. 'Hello, Jules,' she called pleasantly as they neared the young man who was walking towards them with a jaunty step. 'You look pleased with yourself?'

His smile broadened as he stopped. 'Hello, Dorinda.'

'Lydia Booth,' she said by way of quick introduction.

Jules only nodded his greeting because Dorinda was already asking, 'Well, what's pleased you? You look like the cat who's got the cream.'

'Aye, I do. Ben's been offered a job and a cottage, and I can go too.'

'What? Leave Cribyan?'

'Aye. And glad we'll be to get off Gaisford land and away from that bloody family!' He glanced sheepishly at Lydia. 'Pardon me, miss, but if you knew them you'd agree with me.'

'Where are you going?' Dorinda asked eagerly.

'Sandannack.'

'Village on the Penorna Estate,' Dorinda explained.

'Mr Mitchell's just seen Ben. He'd heard of the trouble and Ben's sacking. He's looking for a few new workers and has four vacant cottages. Ben jumped at the chance to get Jessie away from the pawing hands of Mr Jeremy. My brother asked if there was a chance for me too and when Mr Mitchell said there was, Ben sent young Alec to find me. The deed is done – we're moving out tomorrow. Sal will be glad too. Well, must be off. Maybe we'll meet again, Miss Booth.' He touched his forehead to her and was gone.

'There you are, Lydia, told you I'd find it all out,' said Dorinda with a triumphant grin. 'Seems our Mr Mitchell is a knight in shining armour. And maybe he'll need that armour. The Gaisfords don't like interference and will regard this as just that.'

'But surely Ben is free to choose where he goes and who he works for, and Mr Mitchell who he employs?'

'Oh, yes, but the Gaisfords still won't like it. And accidents can happen . . .'

'You mean, they could make trouble for him?'

'Aye. As I say, they don't like what they regard as interference and will stop at nothing to teach an opponent a lesson. You've seen the scar on Mr Westbury's cheek?'

'You mean, they were responsible?' Lydia looked shocked.

'Rumour has it.'

'And you believe them?'

'Rumour never lies.'

Chapter Four

Three weeks later Thursday dawned bright with the promise of a settled day. Lydia stood at her window, trying to decide what to do. Dorinda had sent her a note yesterday saying that, unlike the previous Thursdays, she would be unable to meet her as she had been called to Penzance where her father was unwell. Lydia hoped that it was nothing serious and at this moment said a prayer for her friend's father's speedy recovery.

With the weather so tempting she decided that she would get Cook to make her a small picnic, take her pencil and sketch-pad, and walk along the coastal path until a suitable scene took her fancy. Half an hour later she left the house and paused for a moment on the veranda, drawing in a deep breath of the breeze that rolled in from the west, bringing with it the salt tang of the wide Atlantic. She stepped down from the terrace and headed for the garden gate where she took the path leading to the cliff edge.

Her mind drifted over the events of recent weeks and she thanked her own good fortune at the way life had turned out for her. She was now truly settled at Trethtowan Manor where the Westburys regarded her as part of the family and were delighted that James and Juliana had taken so readily to their new governess. Yes, she thought, life is good and I am so lucky.

Her spirits were high when she reached the cliff edge and stopped to gaze across the vastness of the calm sea that for once was not in vicious contest with the rocks and cliff face far below. Her mind wandered as she mused on what lay far beyond the horizon and allowed herself to conjure up magical places. She smiled at her own flight of fancy but, coupled with her skill with pencil and brushes, it at least meant her life need never be dull.

How long she stood day dreaming she never knew but suddenly she started out of her reverie. Her fingers itched to put the pencil to work. But where? She glanced around. Maybe a little further along the coast. She had only moved a few steps when the enchantment of the tiny bay she had visited on that first visit to Trethtowan came back to her mind.

She walked for half a mile keeping close to the cliff edge, marvelling at the panoramas continually unfolding beneath her; jutting rock had been eroded to leave arches through which she caught glimpses of the sea; cliff faces were sheered away, leaving precipitous drops softened by sea pinks and stone crop. She loved this coast and saw much that she could paint here but did not cease her stroll until she was looking down into the tiny bay where she had celebrated her change in fortune. Even now she could feel the same exhilaration and joy at the sight. She was lost in her thoughts, oblivious to anything but what she had come to regard as her place.

'Good day, Miss Booth.'

A voice close behind her made her jump. She swung round, a startled expression on her face. 'Oh, my goodness!' she gasped. Then, seeing Mr Mitchell, she quickly gathered her thoughts.

'I'm sorry if I startled you,' he apologised.

Lydia felt her face glow. She felt a strange pleasure in the closeness of his dark blue gaze that seemed to draw her into closer contact. What was in his thoughts as he looked at her? She felt a stirring in her breast. What did she want him to be thinking? Did his thoughts match her own . . .?

'Oh, no, it's perfectly all right,' she spluttered.

He came nearer. 'I think I did, and I apologise. I would not wish to cause you any distress.' His voice was soft and caressing.

Her thoughts swam. How she envied Mrs Mitchell, listening to this man every day. She stiffened herself. She should not be thinking like this. It was with mixed emotions that she heard Mr Mitchell continue speaking, thankfully breaking her own chain of thought.

'You seemed to be lost in contemplation of the bay?' It came as more of a question than a statement. 'It is beautiful, isn't it?'

'It is. This coastline has cast its spell on me.'

'And on me, but I think this place especially.'

'It is charming,' she conceded without revealing her true feelings.

'Strange that we should meet here,' he went on. 'You remember I asked for a painting to hang in Penorna Manor?' She nodded. 'And said I would arrange to show you the view I wanted?' Again she nodded. 'Well, there it is, this bay.'

'Oh.' Her bay! The unexpectedness of it made her start.

'Is that not possible? Too difficult?'

'Oh, no,' Lydia was quick to reply. She did not want any doubt casting on her ability. 'From here?'

'No. There are different aspects all along this cliff path as you will no doubt have seen. All of them are attractive but there is one place that Mrs Mitchell and I especially like. I'll show you. It's a few yards further on.'

Silently she fell into step beside him. John did not hurry, carefully assessing the exact position. Finally he stopped. 'There, looking towards the swing of the cliff that protects that end of the bay. The various rock strata are particularly picturesque and mark this bay out as something special. The cliffs give way to a fine strand of unmarked sand that is especially beautiful just after it has been washed by the sea. And of course there is the water itself which according to its mood can alter the atmosphere of the bay too.'

'And which mood would you want me to paint it in, Mr Mitchell?'

He looked thoughtful as if weighing up exactly what he wanted. 'Well, I think a tranquil mood. That would emphasise the exhilaration exuded by the figure I think should be placed splashing ankle-deep in the sea, arms stretched above her, clearly expressing the pleasure she is feeling.'

Lydia was stunned, unable to speak. Conscious of his eyes fixed upon her, she reddened. Embarrassed that the feelings she had experienced on that particular day were no longer her own, she could only whisper, 'You saw me?'

He nodded and said quietly, 'I did, from this very spot.'

'I did not see you.'

'You were lost in your own world of happiness. I wondered then, and did until we came to dine at Trethtowan Manor, who you were and why you felt such joy.'

'Do you really want me to put a figure in that scene?'

He laughed. 'Not really. In fact, I think any painting of the bay would be more effective executed from the beach itself,' she heard him saying, 'but alas I know of no way down. You must, though?'

'I do.' In her confusion the admission was out before Lydia realised it.

'Well?' he prompted.

'Seeing this view seemed to symbolise my luck that day. I felt I just had to find a way down. I explored and found one. I can understand why you have never found it, though. It is rather obscure and almost hidden by the fact that you have to climb so far down an awkward fissure in the rock face. But I was determined that day.' Lydia made no move towards it, though.

'Well, Miss Booth, aren't you going to show me?'

She hesitated. 'I don't know if I should . . .' She felt bolder now that she was in possession of knowledge he was not. 'Maybe I like having a secret.' The twinkle in her eyes teased him.

'Miss Booth, if you are to paint in the bay itself on my behalf, I must know if it is possible for you to get down there encumbered with equipment without endangering yourself.'

'Though ideally I would like to paint the scene out of doors it is, as you rightly presume, a hazard to take equipment down there. But all I would need is a pad and pencil to draw the scene and make notes. The painting itself could be done in my room.'

'If it is in any way dangerous, I could not countenance your risking your person on my account. Show me, Miss Booth, and let me judge for myself.'

She hesitated a moment and then said, 'Very well, follow me.'

Lydia retraced their steps for about twenty yards and turned into some undergrowth that ran to the very edge of the cliff. She started into it.

'Miss Booth!' called John with alarm in his voice.

She stopped and smiled over her shoulder. 'It's all right, Mr Mitchell. Now you know why you never found the way down.' She went two more yards and then, stooping, pushed aside the undergrowth. 'There you are, Mr Mitchell.'

He came to stand beside her and found himself looking down into a fissure in the cliff that extended downwards for about six feet before it appeared to stop at a solid rock face.

'Follow me,' she said brightly. 'There are good footholds to either side of this shaft, but pick them out carefully and don't slip.' With that she lowered herself down and he followed.

At the bottom of the shaft he was surprised to find there was a ledge wide enough for them to stand on side by side. Though it was gloomy he realised that light was coming not only from above but also from the right. The ledge ran on in that direction and then widened. Lydia started along it and from there the descent became easier with a lessening of the gradient until, with a final turn, it gave on to the beach.

John stopped in wonder. The beauty of the bay, attractive from above, was almost overpowering from here and embraced him with the feeling of entering another world. Towering cliffs swung in both directions in a protective curve, as if saying, This belongs to you two alone. Though he knew Lydia's feet had once marked that stretch of virgin sand, the sea had washed all evidence away and returned its purity. She started forward now. He stopped her. 'Don't spoil it, paint it from here.'

She turned to question his decision but, seeing in his eyes a powerful love for the scene, did not speak. She could tell that this place moved him on many different levels and felt it

421

...ld be wrong of her to query this. Whatever was going through his mind was his to know, and his alone, unless he chose to share his thoughts. She did not move until he broke the spell.

'Getting down was not as bad as I feared. I can see why the path is difficult to find and I don't suppose anyone else ever will unless they have your determination. I am glad you showed it to me, though, and think it wise I should know. At least I will know where to look if ever you go missing.'

Lydia smiled. 'I suppose that is a comforting thought for me too. I won't end up a skeleton in an unvisited bay. You're sure this viewpoint will do?'

'Yes, it is very similar to the one I described but I would like to be reminded of the first time I saw it from here. Now, I think we'd better go.' He would have liked to linger; to share more time with this young woman whom he was finding more and more fascinating, but common sense dictated he shouldn't. When his wife came to mind he realised his love for her had no bounds; she was the mother of his child, the pivot of his life. She'd supported him in everything he had ever done. He could not repay her by giving way to the first attraction he'd felt towards another woman.

John started for the cleft in the rock. Lydia watched him go, struggling with her emotions. Why did she feel a stirring that she had never felt before? A yearning? A need? Had the change in her situation enabled her to look for things out of life she had never hoped for before? He was a handsome man and those magnetic blue eyes drew her to him as they seemed to penetrate to her very soul, but today she had seen a gentler side to his nature and the mixture only added to his fascination for her. He was leaving; she must go too. She followed and insisted on leading the way so she could point out the best footholds, especially in the final six foot of rock.

Once at the top John thanked her for showing him the way. 'What do you intend to do now?' he asked with casual interest.

'I have brought a picnic.' She tapped the bag she had over her shoulder. 'I'll probably do some sketching.'

'You are going down again?' She thought she detected a hint of concern in his voice.

'No. I'll do drawings of my bay from up here. They will help when I start the real canvas.'

'*My* bay, you said.' He fixed his eyes on hers, daring her to look away. 'Shouldn't that be *our* bay?' There was only a slight pause before he added, 'Good day, Miss Booth.' He raised his hat and strode away.

She watched him go, his words ringing in her mind 'Our bay.' Did she mind the intrusion? No, rather she was pleased. She shared something with him. Before her thoughts could drift further along the wrong path she reminded herself that she could hardly mind. After all, the bay was along the stretch of coastline he owned. She was really the intruder.

She saw Mr Mitchell stop and turn. He took a few steps back towards her and then paused. 'Miss Booth, when you have something ready, you must bring it to show my wife and seek her approval.'

'I will, Mr Mitchell.'

He nodded and resumed his walk.

Had that last instruction been a reminder to her that he was married? Had she unknowingly given a hint of her interest in him, causing him to issue a veiled warning?

John's mind was still on Lydia as he turned away from the cliffs and headed towards Sandannack. He had intended to be there already to see if the Lowther families had settled but was not annoyed at the delay. He had been in the presence of a charming person, one with whom he felt comfortable and moreover one who had shown him a means of reaching the bay that had attracted him and Eliza since the first day they had walked this coast together. He must tell his wife of this discovery but doubted he would ever persuade her to take that first precarious climb down. She had no head for such things. Miss Booth had not flinched, nor appeared to see any danger. He admired that side of her personality.

Maybe her exuberance when he had first seen her had resulted from having found a way down that was known to

423

alone. But now she had shared it. Deliberately? Or had the invitation slipped out accidentally? Had he really detected a personal interest in him? He chided himself for vanity, and for besmirching an attractive young woman's mind. But try as he would to thrust such thoughts away, he could not deny that he had felt a spark of attraction towards her. His musings only stopped when he heard the sound of a galloping horse. He looked round to see the hard-ridden animal turn in his direction.

John stopped walking and his nerves stiffened when he recognised Jeremy Gaisford. He saw that the animal was heaving and sweating, but that was typical of the way Gaisford treated his horses. He himself was dust-covered; his jacket unbuttoned to reveal a grubby white shirt worn open at the neck where the cravat hung loose. He was bareheaded and his red hair had been blown into disarray. He pulled the animal to a lurching halt, yelling at it to obey and settle down, sending dust swirling over John.

Gaisford pointed his riding crop at him. 'Lure any more of our tenants away with false promises and you're in trouble,' he yelled, grey eyes fixed angrily on John.

'Those weren't false promises,' he replied, quietly but with undeniable force as he met Gaisford's gaze without flinching. 'There'd be no need for me to offer a man a job if you treated him right.'

'The way I handle my tenants is my business, not yours! Tread warily, John Mitchell! You're still an outsider here, don't start crossing swords with me now.' The menace in Jeremy Gaisford's tone was not lost on John.

There had been an undercurrent of animosity between them ever since the Mitchells had arrived in Cornwall and John had openly criticised the Gaisford's land policy and treatment of some of their tenants. Now it seemed his latest move had angered Jeremy Gaisford to the point of open threats.

'Heed what I say!' Gaisford deliberately wheeled his horse around so that it struck John and sent him sprawling heavily to the ground, driving the breath from his body. For a moment

he struggled to get up, but realising that Gaisford was already
galloping away he lay still until he'd recovered.

'You look a bit out of sorts, John,' observed Eliza as she
crossed the hall to meet him. 'Was everything all right at the
Lowthers'?'

'Oh, yes, they're getting settled. He'd already been to the
mine with my message. He and Jules are starting tomorrow.'

'Good. They'll be glad. So what's wrong?'

John scowled. 'I had a run in with Jeremy Gaisford. He
threatened me and ran me down with his horse.'

'What?' Eliza showed concern. 'Are you all right?'.

'Just a few cuts and bruises. I need a wash and a brush
down.' He started towards the stairs.

'What was it all about?' she asked, accompanying him up
the stairs.

As he washed, she laid out fresh clothes for him and he told
her what had happened.

'This is the first trouble we have had from the Gaisfords
since we arrived,' she commented, 'though I must say they
have never gone out of their way to be friendly and the
Westburys did warn us what they could be like.'

'Selwyn was always suspicious about that attack that left
him scarred. He thought then, and still does, it was retaliation
for the time he stopped Jeremy from beating a young boy who
had accidentally scared his horse.'

'Be careful, John. It's better to keep clear of them. Don't
forget they have quite a following.'

'Young moneyed brats who think if they emulate the
Gaisfords they can ride roughshod over everybody else.
They're the curse of the county.'

She saw he was getting worked up and taking it out on the
cravat he was having trouble tying.

'Here, let me do that.' She came to him with a smile and
gave him a peck on the cheek as she took hold of the cravat.
'Calm down. Forget Jeremy Gaisford.'

He gave a little grunt and raised his chin so that she could
see what she was doing.

said Eliza with satisfaction as she stepped back to
handiwork.

you, my dear.' He picked up his jacket and as he
shrugged himself into it, said, 'By the way, something more
pleasant occurred before Gaisford appeared. I came across
Miss Booth along the coast path. She had her sketch-book and
pencils and was thinking about the picture we mentioned
when we dined with the Westburys.'

'Oh. She was on her own?'

'Yes.'

'Of course, Dorinda's in Penzance.' Eliza's thoughtful
expression vanished as she remembered. 'Had she decided
what she would paint?'

'That pretty little bay we liked so much the first time we
saw it.'

'She'll have to paint it from the cliff top then. There's no
way down.'

'I think that is what she intends to do.'

'I'm sure she'll do a good job but I don't know when she will
get time to do it. James and Juliana will keep her occupied.'

'Busy people always make time.'

'There's truth in that,' his wife agreed.

It was only later, when Eliza was seeing Abigail to bed and
he was alone, that John wondered why he had not told his
wife that Miss Booth had shown him how to reach the bay and
together they had enjoyed its beauty and solitude. It was as if
he wanted to share it with no one but pretty Miss Booth.

The knock on the drawing-room door at mid-morning the following day drew Eliza's attention. She'd been watching seagulls using eddies of warm air rising from the face of the cliffs
to glide upon with barely a sweep of their wings. These birds
were much the same as those she had watched on the cliffs
near Whitby except that Whitby birds had a more distinctive
screech, which she still missed. Hearing gulls always raised a
touch of homesickness in her and a desire to visit Whitby
again, both of which she kept hidden from John. He had
settled here quickly, had thrown himself unsparingly into

426

running the estate and soon shown his tenants that he was a tolerant and helpful landlord. He had made friends quickly among the local gentry and been accepted by most. Eliza had never worried that the Gaisfords had not extended the hand of friendship, that was their affair, and she knew their relationship with some of the other local landowners was no better. It seemed they kept to their own cronies, as she would call them, and if that was how they wanted it then so be it. But now, after John's run-in with Jeremy, she was worried. She knew of the young man's reputation and his hot-headedness. Her husband's compassion for the plight of others had led him to help the Lowther brothers which had stirred Jeremy Gaisford's hostility. Cross one Gaisford and you crossed them all.

It therefore came as a surprise when a maid appeared carrying a small silver salver on which there was a letter.

'This has just been delivered, ma'am,' the maid said as she crossed the room.

'Thank you, Jane.'

As she took the letter, Eliza glanced at the writing. She did not recognise the scrawl etched across the paper but could make out her own name. She would have said it was the writing of an older person. Her attention was drawn back to Jane.

'Ma'am, Miss Jenkins has just returned. She said to tell you she'd be with you in a few minutes.'

Eliza gave a little nod. 'Thank you, Jane. Will you pass me the letter opener from the desk, please?'

'Certainly, ma'am.'

Eager to assuage her curiosity Eliza had the letter opener in her hand before Jane had left the room. She unfolded the sheet of paper and read:

The Gaisford family
Request the pleasure of your company
At their Annual Ball
on 8th August
at Senewey Manor
Carriages 1a.m.
R.S.V.P.

427

Eliza stared disbelievingly at the invitation and re-read it to make sure.

There was no mistaking it, this really was an invitation to the Gaisford Ball. She had heard of it as being *the* event of the county; it outshone every other which would inevitably be compared unfavourably with the Gaisford Ball. She also knew that those attending this particular event always showed off their new dresses and brought out all their most valuable jewellery, vying to be seen as the most opulently dressed and dazzling person there. A sense of achievement seemed to wash over her then – though they had made many friends in Cornwall, it now seemed they had been fully accepted in the county at last. Maybe she and John had read more into his clash with Jeremy Gaisford yesterday than there in fact was. With Jeremy in mind, she recalled that she had heard how before the ball was over, he, his brothers and their friends always ran riot, passing off whatever devilment they got up to as just good fun. Be that as it may, she felt a surge of pride: she and John had been invited. She was eager to tell him, but that meant being patient until he returned from visiting two of the farms. Her thoughts were interrupted by a knock on the door and the appearance of Dorinda.

'Come in, my dear,' Eliza said brightly. 'I did not expect you back today. I told you to make sure everything was all right with your father.'

'I have, ma'am,' she replied, and went to the chair indicated by Eliza.

'How is he?'

'He had slipped and fallen in the shop, scraping his leg rather badly. The doctor was called and has attended to him. Father is to rest it for a few days and when he does get up must only stay on his feet for a few hours at a time.'

'What about help?'

'He has good neighbours who have kept an eye on him since Mother died. They had called the doctor and seen to him but then thought I had better know. They said there was no need for me to stay longer.'

'You are happy with all the arrangements.'

'Yes, ma'am.'

'If you are called back at any time, you must go.'

'Thank you, ma'am. I'll go on my day off next week, and probably also on Sunday, if that is all right, ma'am?'

'Of course it is. Families are important, especially parents.'

'Thank you, ma'am. I'll go to Abigail now. I looked in on her before I came down. She seemed happy with what she was doing and I told her I wouldn't be long.'

Unable to settle to anything, Eliza waited for an hour impatiently before she heard the front door open. She was out of her chair in a flash and across the room. She flung the door open. 'John, come here!' she called excitedly, holding out her hand as she went to him.

Startled by the crash of the door, he looked at her askance, surprised by such exuberance in his wife. 'What is it?'

'Come!' She had him by the hand and was hurrying him towards the drawing room. With the door closed she turned to him and held out the invitation. 'This arrived just over an hour ago.'

He took the letter from her and silently read it then looked up. 'I don't believe this. This is the first time since we came to Cornwall, and I certainly wouldn't have expected it after what happened yesterday.'

'Well, there it is,' said Eliza, excitement dancing in her eyes.

'But this must be from his father, not Jeremy.'

'Yes. Jeremy may be hot-headed but from what I hear he has to toe the line at home.'

John gave a little grunt. 'His father can't be at his side all the time. And he'll support a son against any outsider. Don't you think it strange this should come just after I cross swords with Jeremy?'

'That did strike me, but I thought it might be a peace offering from the family.

'You could be right,' agreed John, but his voice held a note of doubt.

'There's only one way to find out.'

429

'Accept the invitation?'

'Of course. I never entertained the thought of not doing so, and hope you agree with me?'

'Though I have my doubts about the motive behind it, I do agree. We must go, to heal any rifts that have occurred.'

Chapter Five

Jeremy Gaisford tapped his left palm with his riding crop as he strode down the long stone corridor to the great hall of Senewey Manor. Though he lived here with his wife Hester and his five-year-old son Luke, it was still his father's home and he ruled it. Jeremy envied the freedom experienced by his brothers who each had their own smaller estate in another part of Cornwall. He as the eldest would inherit Senewey but meanwhile was tied to it by his father's inflexible command. The fortune that would one day be his outweighed the lack of freedom, for Jeremy liked money and the power and influence it gave him. He especially liked to exert his superiority over the young bucks of the county, who were only too eager to exploit his generosity.

Today his lips were tight with the annoyance that his morning ride would be delayed. On his way to the stables he had been stopped by one of the servants who had run from the house to tell him his father wanted to see him in the study immediately. Summoned that way, Jeremy knew it meant *now* unless he wanted to upset his father and he did not want that.

'Father! Father!'

The child's shout did not halt him. He saw his own son Luke slip his hand from his governess's grasp at the top of the stairs. The eight year old soon reached the hall, ran to his father and grabbed at his breeches.

'Where are you going?' demanded Luke.

'To see Grandfather.'

'Can I come?'

'No! And leave go!' Jeremy snapped, giving his son a little tap with his riding crop.

431

'Why can't I come?'

'Because I say so!'

'But . . .'

Jeremy glared at the governess who had now reached the bottom of the stairs. 'Can't you keep him under control?'

'Sorry, sir! Luke, come here.'

'No!' he screamed at her.

'Come here.' she said more firmly.

Luke's grip on his father's leg tightened. Jeremy's face darkened, his square jaw setting. 'Let go!' he snarled, and with a rough push sent the boy tumbling to the floor. Luke instantly started to cry. 'Stop your snivelling! Be a man!' The governess was crouching beside the boy, trying to comfort him and help him to his feet. She felt like pouring out a tirade at Jeremy but dare not. She knew it would be difficult to find another position in the county if she openly criticised him. With ailing parents to support she dare not lose this position. As Jeremy strode away he called over his shoulder, 'Toughen him up!'

She made no reply. Her glare after his retreating figure gave her some satisfaction. Couldn't he see that his son already was tough; that his crying now was not because he had been pushed to the floor but because his father had not given him even one second of his time? Had he done so the boy would have been overwhelmed with happiness. She knew Luke was sturdy with a hardy streak. Tears very seldom came to his eyes even at the roughest of falls, and there were many of those in the way he played, given his love for adventure and daring. 'Come, Luke, your father's busy, we'll go out and see what we can find to do.'

With that he was on his feet, tears dry and a new light in his eyes. He loved it when they went outside. There were trees to climb, animals to stalk, streams to splash in, and a hundred other things to do.

Jeremy tapped on the thick oak door of his father's study and walked in. Even now there was something awe-inspiring about this large room with its dark oak panelling. Here he had received the first vicious scolding and heavy punishment meted out by his father when he was seven. It had had no physical effect on him; in fact he'd gloried in the fact that he felt little pain, but whenever he entered this room now he recalled his own determination one day to sit in his father's chair where he'd watch the heavy old panelling around him torn out, piece by piece, and with it every memory of Miles Gaisford.

Now Miles sat behind his large mahogany desk facing the door. Though he was of medium build he possessed a force of personality that was felt wherever he was. Jeremy, though used to it, always experienced it, just as he did now walking towards the desk. The thick carpet muffled his steps. He would have preferred to hear them; the sound would have given him some confidence, whereas the silence seemed to be imposed by his father and implied that only he could break it. Miles knew how to dominate men who were much stronger than him physically. Every time he looked at his brutish son he revelled in that thought.

'Sit down,' he ordered curtly.

Jeremy knew he was in for a tongue lashing, but for what reason he did not know.

Miles watched his son closely with eyes that were sunken in a sharp, pointed face. Those eyes missed nothing, quick to sum up a situation or a person, particularly one he was meeting for the first time. More often than not his instant judgement was right.

Born the second son in a middle-class family of minor merchants in the north of the county, Miles had shrewdly courted Rowena, the only child of the owner of the Senewey Estate, knowing it would pass to her on her father's death. He set himself out to show his father-in-law that he would be capable of running such a possession. Delighted by his son-in-law's nimble brain, quick learning and aptitude, Rowena's father gave him more and more responsibility and Miles turned that to greater and greater account as he expanded the assets of the estate. The marriage was no love match but it was convenient for both him and her. Rowena wanted for nothing and knew before her father died that he was satisfied that it was so. She produced three healthy sons and knew that pleased her husband. He ignored the shortcomings in her looks and was not averse to finding satisfaction elsewhere to which Rowena, not wishing to upset the situation, closed her eyes.

As he stared at his bull-like son Miles admired him but would not let him know it. He knew Jeremy was tough, a hard man, quite capable of looking after himself with pistol, sword or fists. A skilful horseman, he rode hard, a trait that his father, a lover of fine horses, frequently criticised. Miles wished he could instil some judgement in his son so he might consider situations carefully before taking action, whether they concerned the running of the estate, their other enterprises, or his personal dealings. He also wished that Jeremy could control the hot temper that went with his red hair.

'What was the meaning of the fracas you had with John Mitchell?' Miles's voice was low but incisive.

Jeremy was surprised. He had never mentioned it. How did his father know? He moistened his lips nervously. 'Mitchell stole two of our employees.'

'Stole?'

'He took the Lowther brothers to work for him.'

'Were they employed by us?'

'Yes.'

Miles's eyes narrowed. 'You sure about that?'

'Yes.'

'Hadn't you sacked them?'

'Er . . .'

'You were conveniently trying to forget that, I see.'

Jeremy said nothing.

'So if they weren't employed by us, there was nothing to stop Mitchell hiring them?'

Jeremy looked uncomfortable. 'I suppose not,' he muttered.

'Yet you threatened him. Oh, yes, I know about that, don't ask me how. And don't think it was Mitchell who told me because it wasn't. Why don't you think before you act?' His father's eyes blazed. 'It's better to have friends among the other estate owners rather than enemies. You'd better mend some fences. You can start by being polite to Mitchell and his wife at the Ball.'

'You've invited them?'

'Yes. They've been here since '85, three years, it's time we were on better terms with them and inviting them to the Ball is a first step.'

'Anyone else coming I should know about?'

Miles gave a small smile. 'Yes, the Westburys have been invited also.'

Jeremy raised his eyebrows. 'I thought after three refusals you crossed people off the list?'

'I know, I know, I've gone against pattern there. The Westburys used to come and, as you point out, would automatically have been left off the list this year, but it has come to my notice that they are very friendly with the Mitchells, so as it is their first time I thought it would be more comfortable for them if their friends came too.'

'Are you up to something?' Jeremy dared to ask, knowing his father could be a devious man and did little unless it was to his own advantage.

'It pays to be on good terms with all the gentry of this county, so see you are polite to the Mitchells and never cross swords with them again. Or, before you do, make sure you are in the right. Don't blunder in as you did on this occasion when you were clearly in the wrong. They have a sizeable estate, a profitable mine, close to the Westbury mine, and own a stretch of coastline. They'd be better friends than enemies. Off with you now and have your ride.' Jeremy took the dismissal obediently and started for the door. 'And treat your horse kindly,' his father called after him.

Two days after they had received their invitation Eliza and John rode over to the Westburys and were delighted to learn that Harriet and Selwyn had also received one.

'We were surprised,' added Harriet.

'Why?' queried Eliza.

'We haven't been for three years,' she said, and went on to explain about the Gaisford rule. 'So this gave us a shock.'

'Tell us more about it?' Eliza urged. Though she was easier in her mind now she knew their friends were going, she realised she would be more so if she had some prior knowledge of what was expected.

The days leading up to the Senewey Ball became more and more hectic but Rowena was in her element. She loved it all and frequently recalled the days when as a little girl she used to peep down from the landing to watch the elegant guests arrive. Then came her own first Ball, and memories of that were always recalled as the day of the latest one drew near. As Mistress of Senewey Manor the burden of organising it fell upon her. She recalled all that her mother had taught her and what she had observed for herself throughout the years. She was thankful that Miles was generous with the amount he set aside for provisions. Like her, he always wanted the celebration to be better than last years.

More servants were brought in. Rowena divided them into groups and placed one of her regular servants in charge of each one to which she assigned a special role for the evening. She paid particular attention to the floral decorations and personally supervised the laying of the tables in the dining room so that the buffet meal could be served to best advantage and guests not be kept waiting. She made sure that every servant knew the part they were playing and made it sound as if the success of the whole rested on that particular task. That way she engaged everyone's interest and made them keen to see that nothing went wrong. Miles oversaw the wines and put two male servants in charge of the cellars. He gave one last look to the estate workers who were to see to the parking of the carriages and that the grooms and their horses were looked after.

As the minutes ticked away towards the arrival of their guests Rowena grew more and more anxious about the weather. When he saw her go out on to the stone veranda for the umpteenth time in the last fifteen minutes, Miles followed her outside.

'Will you stop worrying, Rowena? It's a perfect autumn evening,' he said in a comforting tone.

'Yes, but you know how easily the weather can change and if it rains there could be chaos.'

'It won't rain, the weather is settled, there's barely a hint of wind. It's ideal and will put all our guests in a good mood. Everything is ready.' He took her hand. 'As usual you have done a splendid job, I just know this is going to be better than ever.' He smiled and her mind flew back to the first time he had smiled at her all those years ago – it seemed more than a lifetime. She could still remember it and in that moment had thought, This is love. Of course, in a matter of days she knew it wasn't, and never would be, and that their relationship would instead develop into a mutual respect and understanding that was all they expected and wanted. She had derived a certain type of happiness from it over all these years, and suspected Miles had too.

'Come inside, sit down. your dress is beautiful and suits you as you suit it. Relax with a glass of wine,' he told her. 'Jeremy and Hester will be down in a few minutes. Charles and Emma, and Logan and Fanny, won't be long. They always arrive early for the Ball to have a few words with us before the guests arrive.'

'You're right,' she conceded. 'I can't do any more and I've no control over the weather. I just want everything to be right for you. I know you set great store by our Ball, helping to create and maintain good relationships throughout the county.'

'And tonight we have the Mitchells from Penorna for the first time. I know you'll see they are made most welcome.'

'Why have you never invited them before?'

'I wanted to see how they fitted in first. Mr Mitchell's uncle did so very well but that wasn't to say his nephew would. And they were coming from Yorkshire. Cornwall's a world away – so different. They may not have settled and we Cornish folk may not have taken to them. But they do seem to have integrated well, from what I hear.' They reached a small room off the main hall and took a window seat from where they could see the first arrivals.

Ten minutes later Jeremy and Hester came into the room. Miles frowned upon seeing his son already with a tankard of ale in his hand and wondered how much he had drunk already, but not wanting to start the evening badly for the sake of the ladies, he held back from open criticism. He would have a sharp word before long, though. Leaving the ladies admiring each other's dresses, he poured them a glass of Madeira each. As he was doing so he heard the scrunch of hooves and wheels on the drive. Glancing out of the window, he saw the light from lanterns strategically placed near the entrance to the house reveal two coaches he recognised. 'Charles and Logan are here,' he called over his shoulder.

Jeremy put his tankard down and hurried from the room, ever ready to exchange back-slapping greetings with his brothers and joke with his pretty sisters-in-law whom he knew were not averse to responding flirtatiously.

Family greetings were exchanged heartily, dresses admired, children's welfare queried, wine distributed, the thirty minutes together setting the tone for the start of the evening.

'You look very becoming, my dear.' John, who had had some misgivings about this evening after his altercation with Jeremy, was assiduous with his compliments nevertheless and his eyes reflected his approval of Eliza's dress for he knew she put great importance on her attire and sensed she needed reassurance tonight.

This evening she had discarded her old stiff silks and had had a dress made in the newer cotton that was pouring out of the Lancashire cotton mills. Lighter and less ostentatious, it incorporated discreet padding to give the slimmer female figure a gentle bustle. The dress, of a pale yellow fabric with a small light blue flower motif, fell with only a slight flare from a high waist. Eliza preferred the sleeves long and tight to the wrist, and around her bare shoulders had set a silk shawl, with the simplest of silver necklaces sparkling against her skin. She had been pleased with her own appearance and her husband's praise, returning it when she saw he had replaced his fussy embroidered waistcoat with a severely elegant one of light brown silk. He wore a long jacket, left open at the front, with a high collar and a stock of muslin wound several times round the neck. His matching pale grey trousers came tight to his calves, below which he wore white stockings that were reflected in his highly polished evening shoes adorned with small silver buckles.

Even Benson was bold enough to offer his congratulations on their appearance when he saw them into the coach before leaving Penorna Manor. They drove to the Westburys' as pre-arranged for they preferred to travel on together. Greetings and compliments were made when they arrived and news exchanged over a glass of wine.

As Harriet and Eliza came from the drawing room into the hall with laughter on their lips, Lydia was coming down the stairs.

'Are the children settled?' Harriet asked her.

'They are, Mrs Westbury. Good evening, Mrs Mitchell. I hope you have a pleasant time,' Lydia said, pausing two steps from the bottom.

The two men came into the hall then and she had to stifle her reaction on seeing John.

'Good evening, Miss Booth,' he said pleasantly.

'Good evening, Mr Mitchell,' she replied. Her heart lurched when his eyes met hers. She thought she had detected a hidden interest as he passed her by. She stood still, her mind pounding. He looked so handsome. Then he was gone. She gazed at the closed door, wondering what it would be like to dance with John Mitchell. She was sure he would be an elegant and accomplished dancer. She pictured herself in the most wonderful gown, matching his steps with hers, feeling his hand on hers, his touch on her waist as he whirled her round: the most elegant couple on the floor.

With the sound of the first carriage arriving Miles and Rowena took up position to greet their guests. Servants were on hand to take cloaks, coats and hats while others hovered with trays of welcoming punch. Their three sons and their wives welcomed the guests after their parents and saw that they mingled to create the convivial atmosphere expected at the Gaisford Ball.

'Oh, good, there are a number of people here already.' Eliza expressed her delight as they came in sight of Senewey Manor. She had not wanted to be the first to arrive at this, their first Gaisford Ball.

The coach was directed to its position and the new arrivals escorted to the house where they found people already milling about in the hall and the babble of conversation coming from rooms beyond.

They were greeted by a liveried footman who politely enquired their names, announced them in a loud voice, and directed them to Mr Miles Gaisford and his wife who were amiably receiving their guests.

'Ah, Mr and Mrs Mitchell, how delighted we are to see you. Welcome to your first Gaisford Ball.' Miles took Eliza's hand and raised it to his lips as he made her a small bow. Then he took John's hand in a firm grip.

'It is a pleasure to be here, Mr Gaisford,' replied John.

Miles raised his hands in protest. 'Miles, please. We are near neighbours.'

John signalled his acknowledgement with an exchange of his own Christian name. Eliza thanked Miles for his invitation and when he had said, 'Enjoy yourselves,' she passed on to Rowena's friendly and warm greeting.

As they moved away they were offered glasses of punch. They lingered a while in the hall, wondering which direction they should take, while looking for any familiar faces and awaiting the Westburys who were now being welcomed by Miles and Rowena.

Raucous laughter from a group of men across the hall attracted their attention and at that moment John caught a look from Jeremy Gaisford that he could not read. He saw him speak quickly to the others around him and leave them to come over.

'John!' He extended his hands in greeting and smiled with unexpected warmth. 'It *is* good to see you, and I must apologise for that unfortunate incident a few days ago. I was in the wrong, accusing you of stealing the Lowthers from us. They were perfectly free to move.' As he had been speaking he had shaken hands in what could only be described as an obsequious manner.

Taken aback by what seemed to be genuine contrition, John could do nothing but respond in like manner, particularly as he was a guest. 'Think nothing of it.'

'Good man.' Jeremy slapped him on the shoulder and turned to Eliza. 'Mrs Mitchell, welcome to our home and to your first Ball. May it be one of many for it will be our delight to have your charms continue to adorn it.' He bowed, took her hand and raised it to his lips, all the while concentrating his gaze on her.

She smiled in return and thanked him for his welcome. 'It is a pleasure to be here.'

'Please enjoy yourself, and such an exquisitely dressed lady must reserve a dance for me – that is,' he cast a glance at John, 'if you will allow me the pleasure?'

He inclined his head in agreement.

'Then let me book the second one. The first must be your husband's. Now you must come and meet my brothers.' He led them to the group he had left and made the introductions quickly but without undue haste. They were made to feel at ease, and as the group around them gradually split up with the arrival of more guests found themselves being shown round the house by Charles and Emma.

A large room to the right with chairs set against three walls was to be used for dancing. As the evening was warm the doors had been opened to allow guests on to the veranda that ran along three sides of the house. In a similar room to the left of the hall, again with access to the veranda, tables had been laid with the most tempting array of food. Smaller salons with access from both these main rooms were open for use, and in one of these Emma suggested they sit down while Charles went in search of replenishments for their glasses.

'It is a sizeable house,' commented Eliza.

'Indeed it is,' replied Emma. 'It has been in the family for many years but it was Charles's grandfather who expanded the building, partly with the idea of being able to establish these Balls as a means of cementing relationships within the county.'

Charles caught that last remark as he returned with a maid carrying a tray of wine glasses.

'It worked,' he added, 'and I hope in the present case it is successful. This is your first time, I believe?'

'And enjoying it,' replied Eliza.

'I'm so pleased,' said Emma. 'I hope you continue to do so. The night is still young, there are many hours of enjoyment left.'

As the two ladies fell into conversation, Charles turned to John. 'I'm sorry about that run in you had with Jeremy. He can be impetuous at times.'

'You heard about it?'

'Naturally. I don't condone everything he does but at heart he's a good brother.'

'He's made his apologies and the incident is now forgotten as far as I'm concerned.' Even as he spoke John was wondering if there was an ulterior motive behind these niceties. Apologies seemed so out of keeping with what he had heard of Jeremy and yet the Gaisfords were acting in a friendly manner that could not be faulted.

All thoughts and conversations were interrupted when they heard the musicians strike the first notes to inform everyone that dancing would take place in a few minutes. As the gentle strains continued, the buzz of chatter raised its pitch in anticipation of the pleasure to come.

'We had better take the first dance with our wives,' said Charles with a wry smile, 'but, Mrs Mitchell, may I claim one later?'

'Shall we say the fifth, Mr Gaisford?'

'My pleasure,' he replied.

'Then I shall be bold enough to ask you for that dance too, Mr Mitchell,' put in Emma quickly, a twinkle in her eyes, daring him to refuse. 'I would guess that you are an excellent dancer,' she added, allowing her gaze to run over his figure.

He responded with a little inclination of his head and said, 'I look forward to it.'

442

As they walked to the room set aside for the dancing, Eliza whispered, 'Brazen flirt! Watch your step, John Mitchell.'

'I'll certainly be careful not to step on her toes,' he replied, amused by her unintended pun. 'What do you think of the Gaisfords efforts to be charming?'

'Perhaps they are; perhaps we don't know them well enough.'

'Their reputations say otherwise.'

'Reputations are often exaggerated.'

'Well, we shall see.'

People were milling after them and quickly taking their places for the dance. An atmosphere of enjoyment charged the room from the first note and the guests swung into their first steps. The swirl of dresses sent cascades of colour around the room; every eye observed the better dancers, attractive ladies or handsome men, even as they wove their way in line across the polished floor.

Halfway through the first dance, as they passed each other, Eliza whispered, 'You are being watched.'

'I know,' John replied with a small smile that showed he was enjoying the flattery.

Their positions changed and he found himself opposite Emma.

Her eyes rested invitingly on his. 'You dance well,' she said quietly. 'We must try the waltz,' she added, knowing that during that dance they would stand close together. 'You are familiar with it?'

'Yes, I have danced it, though it is not generally performed in this country.'

'But it is so daring and exciting!' Her eyes twinkled mischievously.

She had been bold enough to make the suggestion and had cornered him so neatly he could hardly refuse. 'It will be my pleasure,' he replied as they moved apart.

'Has that minx got her claws into you?' Eliza quipped as they came together again.

'If dancing the waltz is any indication, yes,' he replied.

Eliza raised her eyebrows. 'The waltz! She must have planned that. You be careful, John Mitchell. I notice you have also been the object of other scrutiny.'

'You shouldn't have married such a handsome man,' he teased.

The dance finished but almost before the floor had cleared the musicians started the second. Jeremy was beside Eliza.

'May I claim my dance, Mrs Mitchell?'

'Indeed you may, Mr Gaisford.'

He led her on to the floor and she was surprised to find that, for a big solid man, Jeremy was light on his feet and an impeccable dancer. They floated around the floor and Eliza felt lost in another world where every other dancer was clumsy.

'You dance divinely, Mrs Mitchell,' he said.

'I could say the same for you, Mr Gaisford.'

'I enjoy it, as I'm sure you do?'

'Yes, I do, and regret that the opportunities rather fell away after we moved from Whitby.'

'That has been our loss, but I'm sure that after tonight opportunities will become more numerous. Other people who give Balls will have noticed you and your husband and the charm you are lending to this occasion.'

'You flatter us, Mr Gaisford.'

'I do not. And I regret that my father did not invite you before. I also regret I caused trouble with your husband, for it must have distressed you?'

'It did, but we have put that behind us.'

'I am pleased to hear it.'

When the dance finished he escorted her back to her husband, who had been dancing with Harriet.

'Thank you,' Jeremy said quietly to her, and then looking at the others as Selwyn joined them, 'I hope you are enjoying yourselves and will continue to do so.' He moved away to speak to some other guests.

John raised a querying eyebrow at Selwyn.

'He's being exceptionally pleasant.'

'Beware of the fox in disguise.'

444

'Oh, come on, you two,' put in Eliza. 'I think you read more into things because of his reputation for hard riding and hard living. Mr Gaisford was politeness itself, considerate, and a divine dancer.'

'Put on for this evening,' replied Selwyn. He allowed his voice to trail away as he saw Miles and Rowena approaching them.

'And how are our new guests enjoying themselves?'

'Very much,' replied John. 'Indeed, it is a splendid occasion.'

'I like to set the standard for the whole county. I hope it makes for good relationships and helps in many other ventures.'

'I'm sure it does, Mr Gaisford,' put in Selwyn.

'You have been here longer than Mr Mitchell and had time to observe us. I believe you should think again about some of the propositions I have put to you in the past which you chose not to take up. Consider how you could have benefited from them. Tell Mr Mitchell about them.'

'Miles! We said no business this evening. Well, certainly not in front of the ladies,' Rowena admonished.

'I am sorry, my dear, and I apologise to you too, ladies.' Miles's eyes swept over Harriet and Eliza. 'And may I add how delightful your dresses are? You both sparkle among so many beautiful gowns.'

'You are a flatterer, Mr Gaisford,' said Eliza. 'I can see from whom your eldest son inherits his charm.'

Miles smiled. 'I saw you dancing with Jeremy. I hope his steps were to your liking?'

'Indeed they were.'

'Then please go on enjoying yourselves.'

The Mitchells and the Westburys made sure that they did. They danced, mingled, and dined from tables laden with every kind of savoury and sweetmeat. The Mitchells were pleased to be introduced by their neighbours to other county gentry, but in the course of conversation through odd words and expressions John was constantly reminded of just how much influence the Gaisfords wielded in the county. It made

445

him wonder why Miles Gaisford had never approached him before this evening, until he realised from other snippets he heard that he had been giving John time to settle and see if he was going to stay permanently in Cornwall. Had he finally reached a conclusion about that? It seemed so, from what he had said to Selwyn earlier. John wondered what propositions he had been referring to and why exactly Selwyn had turned them down? He meant to find out but tonight was not the time.

Chapter Six

'I am going to ride over to see Selwyn,' he announced at breakfast the next morning.

'Curious about those propositions Mr Gaisford mentioned?' queried Eliza, looking up from her scrambled egg.

'Better to be forearmed. After what I heard last night, I reckon the Gaisfords wield more power in this county than we ever imagined.'

'Maybe. You would hear more than I – male talk – but I found them all charming. Did you not, or was your attention focused more on Charles's wife?'

'She certainly went out of her way to flirt.'

'And you enjoyed it.'

'And you'd think there was something wrong with me if I didn't,' he teased. 'Well, I must be off.' He rose from his chair, came round the table to kiss her and headed for the door.

The groom soon had his favourite horse saddled and John put it to a steady pace along the cliff top. The sharp air helped to clear his head of a slight hangover. He was in no hurry. He would enjoy the ride. The sun shone but he eyed the clouds to the west with suspicion; they could spell rain later in the day. He admired the coastal scenery that kept unfolding but nothing charged him with real emotion except the little bay that brought memories flooding back as he automatically halted his horse to take in its beauty. After a few moments he slid from the saddle, tethered his mount, and moved closer to the cliff edge. He stood easily, legs astride and hands clasped behind his back. Relaxed, he felt the bay call to him, offering itself, seeming to say there was more than peace and tranquillity to be had on its shore. He stepped towards the hidden path but stopped. This was foolish. He was letting emotion run away with reason. What more could the bay offer him? He started to turn back to his horse but was halted by a movement far below.

She stepped out of the shadow of the cliffs and waved to him.

He stood transfixed by the unexpected sight. Then he found himself hurrying to find the way down. He moved cautiously, at first, finding foothold after foothold. Eventually emerging on to the strand he found she had moved to a position from which she couldn't be seen from the cliff top.

He walked towards her, his mind in a whirl. What was he doing here? Hesitancy overcame his steps. He felt her eyes on him. Did he read a challenge there or was he giving way to an over-active imagination? A shaft of sunlight moved over her. She stood perfectly still; a thing of beauty.

'Miss Booth.' His mouth was parched, his throat dry. 'I did not expect to see you here.'

'Nor I you, Mr Mitchell.'

'I was on my way to Trethtowan to see Mr Westbury.'

'He was at home when I left. It's my day off, you know, and you require a painting,' she offered by way of explanation.

'Ah, yes, of course,' he stammered.

'Mr and Mrs Westbury told me it was a splendid Ball.' She seemed to be trying to find something to say rather than let a charged silence stretch between them. It was as if she dared not trust herself if that happened.

'Yes, it was.'

'I am pleased.'

'Thank you.'

'I . . . er . . . if I may say so . . .' She hesitated.

'Yes, Miss Booth?'

'Er . . , when you called at Trethtowan on your way to the Ball, I thought you most elegant.' The words escaped despite her better judgement.

'Thank you.' So she *had* noticed. He was surprised by the wave of pleasure that sent through him.

'And Mrs Mitchell, of course.'

The mention of his wife's name shattered John's complacency. What was he doing talking to this young attractive woman in the privacy of a place he had dubbed 'their own'?

'I had better be going.' He turned abruptly and hurried away.

Lydia watched him go, her heart thumping, cursing herself for having reminded him that he was married. She wanted to reach out and stop him. Instead a tear ran down her cheek. He disappeared from her sight. Her mind raced. Oh, why had she fallen in love with this man, a love she must keep secret even from him?

She bit her lip to drive back the tears of regret and picked up her pencil and pad. The resulting painting would be a labour of love.

Reaching the top of the cliff, John paused to get his breath and look back, but Lydia was not to be seen. Regretfully, he swung himself into the saddle and rode slowly to Trethtowan Manor, his thoughts full of the girl on the beach. Certain emotions threatened to overwhelm him and jeopardise the life he loved with Eliza and Abigail.

When he swung from the saddle in the Trethtowan stable yard and handed his horse over to one of the stable lads, he pushed the haunting thoughts from him and hurried to the house where Selwyn greeted him warmly. Once they were ensconced comfortably in his study and had exchanged brief comments about the Ball, John came straight to the reason for his visit.

'Nothing could have served better to cement local relationships than last night's Ball but I still have a nagging suspicion of Gaisford's intentions. We have been here three years and this is the first friendly approach from any of the family. He referred to propositions that you'd turned down and hinted you had been unwise. You never mentioned them to me.'

'Before your time here, John, so there was no point in telling you. I thought Gaisford had given up on me, but from what he said last night, I see he has ideas again.'

John looked puzzled. 'What exactly are you saying, Selwyn?'

'Look, you must have realised that the Gaisfords are powerful in Cornwall. They're the most prestigious family in the
county and have accumulated land and wealth over genera-
tions though Miles's origins were not exalted. Nevertheless
many of the gentry run with him rather than oppose him. If
they do oppose the Gaisfords, they don't do it openly, careful
not to cross swords with them.'

'Not like I did with Jeremy.'

Selwyn gave a little smile. 'Exactly. That run in could have
cost you.' To emphasise his meaning he ran his finger along
the scar on his cheek.

'You mean, the Gaisfords were behind that?'

'Happened before your time, as I said. I could never prove
anything. The attack appeared to have been by footpads, but
it came soon after I had finally refused one of Miles
Gaisford's propositions.'

'What was that?'

'He was keen to buy a large parcel of land including my
mine from me, and when I refused suggested we go into partnership together to raise more sheep. I knew he really had an
idea that there were good copper deposits beneath that land
and the terms he was suggesting for the partnership contained
a clause about other possibilities for development that was
very much in his favour. It was complicated so he thought I
would not notice how it was angled.'

'And were there copper deposits?'

'Oh, yes, good ones. I knew that though but he didn't know
I knew it.'

'But why not exploit them, if it would have made you
money?'

'Money isn't everything, John. I had plenty and still do. We
live comfortably already and a large section of our land would
have been spoilt by further mining. I didn't want that, but
Gaisford did not like my refusal.'

'And you think he tried to persuade you?' John indicated
the scar.

'Yes.'

'Did he try again?'

450

'Oh, yes. I had a horse killed from under me, though it was made to look like an accident. And Harriet was molested by a couple of thugs in Penzance.'

'What?' John expressed his shock.

'Snatched her bag, knocking her down in the process. She ended up with two black eyes and cuts to her forehead and knees, plus of course the shock. She gave as good a description as she could of her attackers but they were never caught.'

'And you think Gaisford was behind that as well? Surely he wouldn't sink so low as having a woman attacked?'

Selwyn shrugged his shoulders. 'Well, it's only my suspicion but all the events occurred when I was not going along with Miles's propositions.'

'There were others?'

'He wanted to buy some facilities I have in Falmouth but I refused, knowing he would try to force me out. I also have two fishing vessels I refused to sell him.'

'So what made him give up?'

'My stubbornness, but really he never gives up because he refuses to be beaten. After what he said last night, I think he has something else in mind, either for you or me or both of us.'

'What can I possibly have that would interest him?'

'Who knows? Look to your assets. I know he was at your uncle several times but Gerard was a wily old bird, if you don't mind my saying so. He outfoxed Gaisford on several occasions and he didn't like it. Your uncle was a very popular man, though, and could have raised a great deal of support, you might almost say an army, if Gaisford had moved against him. Could be that you might become a fitting target to satisfy his need for revenge.'

John grimaced. 'Thanks for the warning but I don't . . .'

'Don't underestimate the Gaisfords. They'll band together if it suits them, and the younger wives are not averse to helping either. Be very wary of their wiles.'

Selwyn's words occupied John's mind for a few days but, as the weeks progressed in the peacefulness of everyday life, they gradually faded from his memory until they were brought sharply back to mind one day in the spring of the following year.

He had set off walking on his weekly visit to the mine. He was halfway there when a rider broke the horizon and came towards him. It was not long before he recognised Jeremy Gaisford who for once was moving at a slow, considered pace. He halted his mount a few yards in front of John.

'Good morning to you, Mr Mitchell,' he called, steadying his horse with a firm hand.

'And to you, Mr Gaisford,' replied John.

'I was just coming to see you.'

John's expression betrayed surprise. He had seen none of the Gaisfords since the Ball. Why should Jeremy be on his way to see him?

'Father would like you to call on him.' The tone Jeremy used was more like a summons than a request. John bristled.

'What's he want?'

'It's his business to tell you. He would have come to see you himself but he's not well.'

'I'm sorry to hear that.' John calmed his tone. 'Maybe it would be better if I waited until he was recovered?'

Jeremy grimaced as he shook his head. 'If Father says now, he means now.'

'You mean, today?'

'Yes.'

'But I have other things to see to, I cannot . . .'

Jeremy did not allow him to finish. 'Look, Mr Mitchell, I wouldn't normally plead with you, but as I said, Father is not well and there is something he would like to get settled with you. So not only he but I would be obliged if you could pay him a visit before the day is out.'

This was a new side to Jeremy Gaisford, one he had never heard of. His father must be far from well for Jeremy to put the request in this way. John looked thoughtful for a moment then he nodded and uttered a brusque, 'All right. I'll be at Senewey within the next two hours.'

'I'm obliged, Mr Mitchell,' replied Jeremy, and without another word turned his horse and put it into a gallop the way he had come.

John watched him for a few moments with a puzzled frown. What could this be all about? What was so important that it couldn't wait until Miles Gaisford had recovered? He turned on his heel and walked back home where he instructed his groom to have a horse saddled. All was quiet as he entered the house by a side door but on reaching the hall he heard voices coming from the drawing room. Entering the room, he pulled up short.

'Mrs Gaisford.' He bowed politely to Emma who acknowledged his greeting with a radiant smile.

'Mr Mitchell. It adds pleasure to my visit to see you,' she replied.

John turned to his wife. 'I did not know you were expecting a visitor.'

'Naughty of me, Mr Mitchell,' Emma put in quickly. 'It was my spur of the moment whim to come visiting. I had seen nothing of you or your wife since the Ball and thought it ought to be rectified. I am going to hold a small dinner party and hope you will be able to accept an invitation when I make the arrangements?'

'That is very kind of you, Mrs Gaisford. I will leave the decision to my wife. You must excuse me, I have an appointment.'

'I thought you were on your way to the mine?' said Eliza, curiosity in the glance she exchanged with her husband.

'I was but had to change my plans.' His expression told her to ask no more.

'Will you be back about the same time?'

'I should be no later.' He turned to Emma. 'Forgive me.'

'There is nothing to forgive, Mr Mitchell. Appointments must be kept.'

As John went for his horse he wondered how much she knew of her father-in-law's summons and whether that forthcoming dinner party was all part of another Gaisford scheme. But to what end?

When he reached Senewey Manor a groom appeared to take care of his horse. Inside the house he was taken quickly to Mr Miles Gaisford's study.

He received a shock. Miles was propped up by pillows and cushions in a large armchair positioned so that he could receive all the warmth from the fire. He was dressed but had a rug around his knees. His skin had a yellowish pallor and his eyes seemed even deeper set in his gaunt face. He was far from the hale and hearty man who had graced the Senewey Ball.

'Mr Gaisford, I received a message from your son.' John glanced in the direction of Jeremy who was standing beside the large mahogany desk. 'And may I say how sorry I am to see you are not well?'

Miles gave a little dismissive wave of his hand. 'Something I picked up when I was in the Indies. It recurs once a year and is not pleasant when it does. There are times when I fear . . .' He gave an even firmer wave of his hand. 'But let's not talk of that. However, I decided I must put a proposition to you before it is too late. Jeremy could see to it but this is something dear to my heart and just in case this illness moves for the worst, I thought it best to deal with the matter now. I thank you for coming so quickly.'

John noted his words carefully. Was Miles trying to play on his sympathy?' 'I cannot envisage that anything concerning me would interest you, Mr Gaisford.'

'Ah, now that is where you are wrong, Mr Mitchell.'

'Well, I can make no comment until I hear of your interest and proposition.'

'Quite right.' He looked in the direction of his son. 'Where are those drinks?' he snapped. 'Don't keep our guest waiting.' Miles lowered his tone as he asked John, 'You will take a glass of Madeira with us?'

'Thank you.'

'Do sit down.' Miles indicated one of the two chairs that had been placed to face his.

John sat down, judging that the other was for Jeremy, who arrived with a tray on which there were three glasses of wine.

454

John took one, making his thanks as he did so. Jeremy turned to his father. 'Do you think you ought to, Father?'

The older man bristled. 'Don't mollycoddle me. When did a glass of good wine harm me? Give it here. And that decanter's nearly empty. Get some more.'

Driven by his father's sharp tongue, Jeremy started for the door.

Miles savoured his drink and then said, 'You have some land that I would like to buy.'

John's instinctive reaction was to say no and point out firmly that he was not in the market to sell anything, but he suspected Miles had more in mind than just buying a piece of land. He wanted to know more about this interest.

'Which piece of land would that be?'

'Map.' Miles waved a hand irritably at his son.

Jeremy turned back from the door, pushed a small table towards his father, plucked a map from the desk and left the room.

'Come nearer,' Miles said.

John shuffled his chair so that he could see the complete map and immediately noted that it covered the section occupied by the Senewey, Trethtowan and Penorna Estates.

'That is the parcel I would like to buy from you.' Miles pointed to a tract someone had marked on the north side of the Penorna Estate.

John made a thoughtful sound. 'Why that particular section, Mr Gaisford, it doesn't border yours?'

'I've bought land north of it and would like to enlarge it so I can run a larger flock of sheep.'

John felt sure there was more to it than that. He had noticed that the western edge of this section bordered the land Gaisford had previously tried to buy from Selwyn, and that was connected with the supposed existence of a rich vein of copper. He wondered if Gaisford was speculating that it ran through to Penorna land as well?

'I'll give you a good price for it. Three hundred.'

John looked thoughtful. His mind was racing. That certainly was a good price. It confirmed that what he suspected

455

was true. There was more to this than acquiring more grazing. 'I don't know, Mr Gaisford,' he replied. 'I'm not sure that I really want to sell any land. You see, my uncle left the estate to me and I'm sure he would want me to keep it intact. Did you, by any chance, offer to buy that land from him?'

'No, I did not. I did not have the land to the north in Gerard's day. It has been a recent acquisition.'

'I am flattered by your offer but I don't really think so.'

Miles's lips tightened in a sharp line. He did not like to be beaten. 'Three hundred and fifty.'

'No, Mr Gaisford, and please don't offer more, it will be a waste of time. I am adamant – I won't sell.'

'A great pity. What about a partnership then?'

'Partnership? Just to run more sheep? Come, Mr Gaisford, that seems an unlikely idea.'

'All right, Mr Mitchell, I'll be honest with you but you can't blame me for trying. I illegally had a survey done. It shows signs of a rich vein of copper running from my land, through Mr Westbury's and into yours. The three of us could form a partnership to exploit our joint assets. Developing together could substantially reduce our costs.'

John's lips tightened. 'May I remind you that by carrying out any survey on my land you were breaking the law. I could take you to court over this.'

'But you won't. It would be no advantage to you to do so, and would only bring down antagonism towards you from many of the local gentry if you sullied the Gaisford name. So you have a chance of making a fortune.'

'Have you approached Mr Westbury?' he asked tersely.

'Some time ago. He wasn't interested but now you are involved he might change his mind. We will . . .'

'Don't presume,' John cut in roughly. He stood up and fixed his gaze on Miles. 'I have no intention of selling land to you, nor will I ever go into partnership with you. I don't think that would be as straightforward as you try to make out. You endeavoured to get me to sell on the pretext of running sheep, hoping I'd fall for it and you would get a much better deal

456

than you were prepared to pay for. Any dealings I have, I like
to be honest and above board.'

Miles's lips tightened. His face began to colour from the
neck up. 'You damned whippersnapper! How dare you speak
to me like that?'

'I speak to people how I find them.'

'Why, you . . .' Miles's face was a mask of fury.

'Good day to you,' John cut in and strode towards the door.

'Jeremy! Jeremy! Get yourself in here!' Miles's shouts
reverberated round the room. 'Jeremy!'

The door was flung open just as John reached it. He did not
stop but strode past an amazed Jeremy.

'Throw him out! Throw him out! Get rid of that insulting
cur!'

Unsure what to do, Jeremy's step faltered. Should he do as
he was bidden or go to his father and try to calm him? Alarm
gripped him. He was shocked to see his father's face turning
purple with rage. 'He's going, Father. Calm yourself.'

'He wants horse whipping!'

Jeremy heard the front door crash shut behind John.

'He's gone. He's out of the house. Just calm down. It's not
good for you to get so worked up.'

'Worked up! Worked up! You weren't here. You didn't hear
what he said. As good as called me a cheat. Me! Miles
Gaisford! How dare he insult me? And I offered him a fortune, too. Ungrateful runt turned me down and insulted me
while he did it.'

'You want me to act on that?'

'Act on it? Do you have to ask? Gather your wits about
you. That man insulted a Gaisford. Insult one and you insult
us all. You hear that?' Miles's voice had risen with fury. His
hands and arms were shaking. 'If I'd been younger I'd have
thrashed him within an inch of his life.' The words started to
come spasmodically. 'I . . . would . . . have taught . . . him . . .
a . . . le . . .sson.'

Alarm struck Jeremy with the stark realisation that something was dreadfully wrong.

'I . . . I . . . w . . . would . . . I . . .'

457

'I know, Father.' He was on his knees, trying to pacify him.

His father stared at him as if he didn't know him. Then he clutched at his chest and fell forward and would have fallen out of the chair if Jeremy hadn't been there.

'Help! Help!' Jeremy's shout echoed beyond the door.

Two manservants burst into the room. They sized up the situation in a moment and were quickly helping Jeremy.

'Better get him upstairs.'

The commotion brought others hurrying to the scene. Rowena, after the initial shock of seeing her husband hardly able to hold his head up, took charge.

'Jeremy, send a rider for the doctor and you'd better send news to Charles and Logan also.'

He ran from the room.

'Hester,' Rowena went on to her daughter-in-law, 'see that the house servants go on with their duties, reassure them that nothing else can be done until the doctor arrives. Inform the governess and see that Luke's all right. No need to tell him what has happened.'

She supervised the servants carrying Miles to his bedroom. As they laid him gently on the bed he groaned and opened his eyes.

'What? What?' the words spluttered their way out. His eyes moved as if he was trying to recognise his surroundings.

'Lie quiet,' Rowena soothed. Satisfied that they could do no more, she signalled the servants to leave the room. She turned back to her husband, who had closed his eyes again, and ran her fingertips gently across his forehead. She felt a little relief when she saw Miles respond with the faintest of smiles for a brief moment. She pulled a chair close to him and sat watching him closely. His breathing was shallow but had settled into a regular rhythm for which she was thankful.

A few minutes later an anxious-looking Jeremy hurried into the room. His mother signalled him to be quiet. He came to stand beside her and placed one hand on her shoulder.

'How is he?'

'Quiet and stable,' she whispered. 'We'll let him be still until the doctor comes.'

It was an hour before he arrived, having been out on another call that had taken him to a remote part of the county. In that hour Miles had remained peaceful, though not responding to any questions from his family. Hester had assured Rowena that the household was operating as near normally as was possible, though a tense atmosphere and concern permeated it. Charles and Logan, accompanied by their wives, had arrived by now to see their father and were perturbed by his inability to show any sign of knowing they were by his bedside.

Still anxious to know the full story of what had happened, Rowena noticed her eldest son signal to his brothers and saw them follow him from the room. She left her daughters-in-law with her husband and hurried after her sons.

Coming on to the landing, she saw them striding purposefully towards the staircase. There was something about their attitude she did not like.

'Wait!' The command came from her like a whiplash.

All three stopped as one and swung round to face their stern-faced mother.

'Drawing room,' she ordered, and swept past them on to the staircase.

They eyed each other but each knew they dared not defy a direct order.

Rowena stood imperiously in the centre of the room, facing the door. 'You seemed to be busy about something,' she said coldly as the door closed.

'Jeremy wanted to tell us some news,' replied Charles lamely.

'I suspect it was to do with what happened to your father and I think he had already dropped a hint to you as soon as you arrived.' She eyed her eldest son. 'Jeremy, you were there. I too want to know what happened.'

'It was that bastard John Mitchell!' he replied with all the venom he could master.

Rowena, knowing his short temper, stared coldly at him. 'That tells me nothing.' Her icy words forced him to get the better of his rage.

'There was a dispute.'

'Explain,' she snapped, irritated by his fencing. 'And don't try to fob me off. I'll know if you are.'

He knew only too well that she would. None of them had ever been able to deceive their mother. He went on to tell them all exactly what had happened when Mitchell visited Senewey at Miles's request.

'So you see, Mitchell is to blame. If he had agreed to a proposition which was highly beneficial to him this would never have happened. He deserves to be taught a lesson.'

Charles and Logan muttered their approval.

Rowena, who had shown no reaction throughout this story, embraced her three sons with a gaze that was cold and penetrating. 'You will do nothing!' The words came with a deliberate emphasis that also indicated there would be dire consequences if they were disobeyed.

Though he had registered that, Jeremy had to voice a protest. 'Mother, our father is lying up there and we don't as yet know whether he will live or die or remain helpless. We *have* to do something about it.'

'Yes, you have, and that is support him, help in his recovery, and don't upset him by any stupid actions you will term revenge.'

'But Father raged against Mitchell!'

'Maybe, but I know your father. It would be a spur-of-the-moment temper. Miles is no hot head. How do you think he gets his way in the county? No, you *don't* use physical means and you *don't* do anything that will jeopardise your father's recovery. That is of paramount importance to us all. Don't any of you forget it!'

Chapter Seven

John was discussing the proposed changes to the garden at the front of the house with his head gardener when their attention was drawn by the sound of an approaching horse. A few moments later the rider appeared and John immediately recognised Selwyn.

'We'll continue this discussion later,' he said.

'Certainly, sir,' the gardener replied and headed for his greenhouse.

John waited for his friend. 'Good morning, Selwyn,' he greeted him brightly as the horse was brought to a standstill.

'Morning, John,' returned Selwyn, swinging out of the saddle. 'Have you heard about Miles Gaisford?' he added as he secured his horse to a rail set to one side for this purpose.

'Heard what?'

'He collapsed yesterday. From what I've heard it sounds serious.'

'What? But I was with him only then.'

'How did you find him?'

'He wasn't well, propped up in an armchair, looking pale, but he had all his wits about him. Dismissed his illness as nothing.' John had noted a questioning look come over his friend's face and knew he was expecting an explanation as to why he'd been at Senewey. 'Miles had summoned me.'

'Summoned you?' Selwyn's curiosity was heightened even more by this revelation.

'Yes. He sent Jeremy on purpose to ask me. I was on my way to my mine at the time but Jeremy was adamant I should go to see his father immediately. Seemed important so I went.'

'And was it?' prompted Selwyn.

'Well, depends how you look at it. Miles wanted to buy some land from me. I was thankful you had forewarned me about the propositions he made to you. After an illegal survey he believes the land contains a rich vein of copper. He got rather het up when I refused to sell and riled at me. You could even say I was verbally thrown out of the house with threats being hurled after me.'

Selwyn pulled a face. 'Miles has a temper but he's good at keeping it under control, though there's no mistaking his displeasure when he has not got his way. But he'll do things subtly to try to get what he wants. Now Jeremy, he'll charge in without thinking . . . but his father and mother generally keep him on a tight rein. If they've made an order he'll very rarely defy them unless he thinks they won't get to know.'

John frowned in concern. 'I hope his altercation with me did not bring a worsening of his condition. I think I'd better go and see how he is. Will you come with me?'

'Of course! He is my neighbour and it is only proper to show concern.'

Recognising the two men as near neighbours of the Gaisfords, the footman who had answered the door met their request to see Mrs Gaisford by showing them into the small reception room close to the front door.

'I will let the mistress know you are here,' he said politely.

A few minutes later, when they heard the door open, both men turned from the paintings they were examining.

'Gentlemen,' Rowena greeted them as she came into the room, allowing the door to swing shut behind her. She held herself erect, perfectly in control of herself and the situation.

'Mrs Gaisford.' They both spoke together. Selwyn glanced at John, acknowledging him as their spokesman.

'We are terribly sorry to hear of your husband's illness. We hope it is nothing serious.'

'His collapse caused us all alarm and anxiety but I am pleased to say that the doctor has diagnosed nothing serious. However, he will require a lot of rest and in future will have to curtail some of his activities. He must not become as angry

462

as he did yesterday. You may remember him becoming so, Mr Mitchell?' She turned cold, questioning eyes on John.

'I do, Mrs Gaisford, and am sorry if our conversation was to blame for what happened.'

She gave a little shrug of her shoulders. 'Who can tell?'

'Indeed,' he agreed, though he knew Jeremy would fully have reported his meeting with her husband and no doubt embellished certain aspects of it. 'Business propositions are not worth getting worked up about.'

'I agree. Mr Gaisford generally does not do so. I can only assume that being indisposed as he was at the time did not help.' As if that was the end of the matter she added, 'I will give him your commiserations.'

John bowed his acknowledgement as Selwyn said, 'And our good wishes for his speedy recovery.'

'Thank you, gentlemen.' She went to the door.

The two men followed and in a matter of moments were riding away from Senewey.

'Did you see Jeremy watching us from the window?' asked Selwyn as they put their horses to a trot.

'I did. I could feel the ice in his stare from that distance.'

'Then beware. He'll blame you for what happened to Miles, particularly if he doesn't make a full recovery. Their father and mother may dominate the Gaisford sons but they can't always be in control of them. The three of them, especially Jeremy, are not averse to using underhand methods that can't be traced back. Watch yourself, John. This dispute has become more than just a suggested land purchase.'

John heeded his friend's words but when nothing untoward happened over the next three weeks he began to lower his guard, especially when word got round that Miles Gaisford was up and about again. Though he would never be the same man, his wiry stamina and natural determination had stood him in good stead. His mind and speech were not impaired and he was, therefore, still able to rule his family with the same authority he had always done. So it was that he curbed Jeremy when his son came to him with the

opinion that John Mitchell should be taught a lesson for
what he had done.

'Raise one finger against him and you'll have me to answer
to! There are other ways of going about this that will not
antagonise members of our community.'

Fuming at this rebuff, the second he had received from his
father where John Mitchell was concerned, Jeremy nursed his
grudge in private. Things would certainly be different when
he took over the Senewey Estate, something he had seen coming sooner than expected until his father made an unwelcome
recovery.

A month had gone by when, one evening, Jeremy swung
out of the saddle at the Waning Moon, a wayside inn used
by travellers on the northern edge of the Senewey Estate.
Two other horses were tethered to the rail. He eyed them
but did not recognise them. Jeremy pushed open the heavy
oak door, lowered his head under the lintel, and stepped
inside. The flagged floor was uneven and strewn here and
there with grasses culled from the edge of the neighbouring
moor. A rough wooden counter stretched the full length of
one wall. Eight rickety oak tables of varying sizes occupied
most of the floor space without crowding it. Sitting at two
of them were eight unsavoury-looking characters who
glanced in Jeremy's direction when he came in but then
returned their attention to their tankards. His gaze swept
over them as he went to the bar. He was satisfied with what
he saw. The landlord, of ample girth and florid features,
acknowledged him without mentioning his name, something
Jeremy had banned him from doing, especially if there were
strangers in the inn.

'Ale,' he said, fishing a coin from his pocket. He glanced at
the two men leaning on the counter nursing their tankards. He
did not know them. No doubt they were the owners of the
horses he had noted outside.

One of them straightened, glanced at him, nodded and
made a gruff, 'Good evening.'

Jeremy acknowledged it. He did not want to get involved in
a conversation but to ignore them completely would only

draw attention to himself. 'Strangers in these parts?' he added, making his statement a question.

'Indeed we are and glad to find this inn. We did not want to attempt the moor at night. Landlord has obligingly agreed to give us a room for the night. We'll continue our journey to St Just in the morning.'

'A wise move,' agreed Jeremy. 'There are treacherous places on the moor and if you don't know them you could be in trouble.' Though he made his tone amiable he was cursing to himself. He had banked on there being no strangers at the Waning Moon tonight. However, that was not an insurmountable problem so long as he was not seen to be associated with any of the other occupants of the room. A little more care must be taken and he knew that the plans he had instigated for any such situation would be observed.

Ten minutes later, after a desultory conversation that carried no significant information, one of the strangers stretched and said, 'We'll stable our horses, landlord, and then away to bed. We've had a tiring day.'

'No need to bother with your horses, Toby will see to them.' Without giving the strangers time to countermand this idea the landlord opened a door behind the counter and shouted, 'Toby!'

A few moments later a lad of about fifteen bustled into the room. 'Yes, Pa?'

'Stable these gentlemen's horses.'

'Yes, Pa.'

'Mind you give 'em a good rub down and feed 'em.'

The lad was gone at that. The landlord eyed the two men. 'I'll take you up now, if you wish.'

One of them yawned. 'Seems I'm ready.'

The landlord picked up an oil lamp and lit it from one of the candles that were burning on the counter. 'Follow me.'

The two men made their goodnights to all in the room and received a few nods in return while Jeremy put his into words.

As the door closed behind the strangers the men sitting at the tables turned their attention to Jeremy. They knew if Mr Jeremy Gaisford was here something was afoot – he wanted

465

some of them for a job. One of them started to say something but he raised a hand, warning them to say nothing until he did. He listened intently to the footsteps on the stairs and crossing the floor overhead. He followed their progress, and was satisfied that the landlord was taking the men to rooms as far from the bar as possible. He grunted with satisfaction to himself. No one spoke until the landlord reappeared.

Jeremy eyed him. 'Settled?'

'Aye, they soon will be. I took 'em a glass of whisky each as a nightcap. Drop of something in it that'll make 'em sleep like babes 'til morning.'

'Good. Then fill up the tankards all round,' said Jeremy.

That brought good-humoured murmurs from all the men. He dragged over a chair to join them.

'I'll only need Davey and Con for this one,' he said, 'so the rest of you drink up and get off home.'

The other six knew better than to show their discontent for they had all been in the same position as Davey and Con at some time or other and knew their turn would come. They also knew that Jeremy preferred only the persons involved in a plan and the landlord to know what was going on; the landlord because he was the lynchpin, the Waning Moon being the place where messages could be left and sent.

Once the room was clear except for the landlord, Davey, Con and himself, Jeremy came straight to the point. 'I want John Mitchell roughing up.'

Davey and Con grinned at each other. This was just up their street and they would be well paid.

'Don't overdo it. I just want him taught a lesson that'll make him reflect. Make it look like robbery.'

'When?' asked Con.

'Any time, but you may want to study his movements before you proceed.'

Both men nodded. 'Leave it to us.'

Mitchell must be taught a lesson for what had happened to his father. Obtaining the land that could yield a good vein of copper could come later. For the present, revenge was all that mattered to Jeremy.

For three weeks Davey and Con kept John Mitchell's movements under scrutiny until it emerged that he visited his mine every Tuesday, his tenants in Sandannack on Wednesday, and those in outlying cottages and farmsteads on Thursday. He always walked to the first two, but because of the greater distance involved he rode to the others.

'It's misty,' commented Eliza, looking out of their bedroom window before going down to breakfast one Wednesday in early September. 'Will you still go to Sandannack?'

John, pulling on his jacket, came to stand beside her. He observed the weather before he replied. 'It looks thin; the sun will soon burn it up. It could turn out to be a pleasant walk.'

They went down to breakfast together, calling to see if Dorinda had Abigail ready to accompany them.

Unknown to them two men, pulling their jackets tighter against the rolling, chilling mist, were moving close to the house.

Con shivered and fished a bottle from his pocket, taking a swig. He smacked his lips as the whisky burned its way down. 'That's better,' he said and thrust the bottle at Davey who was munching a sandwich. He swallowed and then put the bottle to his own lips.

'Think he'll go today?' asked Con.

'Sure. This fog may delay him but it ain't going to last.'

'Then let's get it over with.'

Davey nodded as he took another bite at his bread. 'Aye, and then we can have more comfortable breakfasts.'

An hour later, with the sun winning its contest with the mist, Con gave the dozing Davey a sharp dig in the ribs. He was immediately awake, stifling a protesting grunt when he saw John Mitchell emerge from the house, pause on the veranda to observe the sky, kiss his wife and walk down the steps and along the drive.

The two men waited until Mrs Mitchell returned inside which she did when her husband was lost to sight round a curve in the drive. From previous weeks they knew which direction their quarry would take when he reached the end and so set off through the tree-covered ground to their right to be in position to pick John up on his walk to Sandannack.

'When are we going to take him?' asked Con.

'In the hollow, we decided, but on his way back.'

'Why not as he's going?'

'He'll be missed sooner if he doesn't arrive in Sandannack.'

'Think anyone there will bother?'

'They might. I hear he's liked in the village. Someone might be curious.'

Con grunted and nodded. He always let Davey take the lead.

Reaching the first house, they saw John start his rounds. When they were satisfied that he was following the usual pattern they headed for the inn, a small establishment on which, with John's financial support, repairs were being carried out. They called for some ale and took a corner seat where they spent time over their drink. Towards noon, after a second tankard of ale, they left the inn and strolled a mile out of the village to a small hillock that would keep them from view of anyone on the road they knew that Mitchell would take to return home. The day had turned out warm so, with a pie and some apples which they had brought with them, they lay down and satisfied their hunger.

Only three people drew their attention until, shortly before three o'clock, footsteps were heard crunching on the stony track. Their intended victim. They exchanged glances and nods, indicating that each knew what their next move should be. They waited until John had passed from sight and then rose to their feet. They cut away from the track into a little gully that they knew would obscure their presence. Moving swiftly to out-run John, they circled back towards the track. Two miles from the village it dipped into a hollow, each side of which was strewn with large boulders that had fallen from an outcrop of rock. Neither man spoke but Davey indicated that they should take up the positions he had indicated when planning their strategy. He would be on John's right when he entered the hollow and Con on his left; boulders would hide both men.

The air was mild and still and John's footsteps were unmistakable as he approached the hollow. His spirits were high. It had been a good day for him and it had been made special when several of his tenants expressed their gratitude for the repairs he was having done to their houses before winter. Satisfied tenants made good workers and he knew he would see their appreciation reflected in their work. His mind was far away when suddenly a broad-shouldered man confronted him. He had a neckerchief tied tightly around the lower half of his face and was brandishing a cudgel. The abrupt appearance of the man from behind a boulder startled John. His arms automatically came up to defend his face but it was the blow from behind that pitched him to the ground.

'Perfect,' muttered Con who had delivered the blow.

'Aye, now let's give him something to remember,' snarled Davey. He felt pleasure as he drove his foot hard into John's midriff.

'Hold it,' said Davey sharply, stopping Con who was stamping on John's thighs. 'Let's see if he has any money. It has to look like robbery.'

'Aye.' Con grinned at the thought of lining his pockets. He dropped to his knees and started rifling through John's pockets. He found some loose change and then, with a cry of triumph, held up a small leather pouch drawn tight by a leather throng. He pulled it open and spilled ten sovereigns into his palm. 'Look at these!' he yelled, springing to his feet.

Davey's eyes brightened when he saw them. 'Five for you and five for me,' he whooped and grabbed his share. Then he froze. 'Listen!' His fierce intonation and changed expression froze Con.

'What?' he whispered, seeing alarm come to Davey's eyes.

'A horse!' he said and then, realising the hoof beats were coming from the direction of the village, added, 'A rider! Let's get out of here!' He started running for the slope. Breathing heavily, the two men reached the top, flung themselves over the ridge, lay flat and twisted round so that they could look down into the hollow.

The hoof beats grew louder. When the track dipped into the hollow the rider came into view.

'A girl,' hissed Con, seeing a young lady riding side-saddle at a steady trot. 'Let's take her!'

Davey gripped his arm firmly. 'No! Do that and we'll be finished! Jeremy Gaisford will find out and then we'll be done for. No more jobs and no more money.' He knew that thought would hold Con in check. 'Lie still and watch.'

Alarm and apprehension shot through Lydia when she saw a huddled figure on the ground as she dipped into the hollow. Automatically she pulled her horse to a halt and looked anxiously around. This was a perfect place to be waylaid and footpads had been known to set one of their number lying prone as a decoy. She saw no sign of anyone else but there were plenty of hiding places behind the boulders. She sat still for a few moments, casting cautious glances around her and letting her eyes stray back to the figure lying face down on the ground. She could detect no movement. Maybe whoever it was was dead. Alarm and horror gripped her.

Then she chided herself for the way in which she was behaving. If this person was hurt he needed attention. She inched her horse forward, her eyes on the figure but alert for any movement to left or right. She drew her mount to a halt and looked down at the man, his face hidden. This was no decoy; there was an ugly gash in the back of his head and blood had made a stain in the dust and soil. She slid quickly to the ground and dropped to her knees. She gripped his shoulders and turned the man over. There were bruises on both cheeks, one eye was puffing and there was a deep cut on his forehead. But she recognised him at once.

'Mr Mitchell!' Alarm filled her when she saw who it was. What could she do? What should she do? Get help, but where? Ride back to the village? But that would mean leaving him here; she could not do that. Ride to Trethtowan Manor? That would take longer but ... her flying thoughts were interrupted by a groan from John. She felt relief at hearing it. He was alive! 'Mr Mitchell! Mr Mitchell! Can you hear me?' His eyes flickered. 'Oh, thank goodness!' She watched him, willing his eyes to open properly.

His eyelids fluttered and after a few moments settled and remained open. He stared towards the sky, seeming to be

470

having difficulty in focusing his eyes, then he turned his head, winced at the pain, and looked at her. For one moment he seemed puzzled but he said, 'Miss Booth?' in a way that seemed to ask, 'What are you doing here?'

'Yes, it's me,' she replied gently. 'You are hurt. We must get you home.'

That idea pleased John but when he moved he winced and let out a cry as pain seared his side. He lay still and looked at her with querying eyes. 'What happened?' he mumbled.

'I don't know. I came across you as I was going back to Trethtowan. I would say you were attacked.'

That observation struck a chord with him. 'I was. A man confronted me but I was struck from behind, so there must have been two of them.'

'And it looks as though they did more damage than that blow on the back of the head.'

'It feels like it.'

'Maybe they would have done even more if I hadn't come along.'

'Thank goodness you did. Did you see them?'

'No. What about you?'

'Well, I saw the one who confronted me but he had a neckerchief over his face.'

Lydia was pleased that throughout these exchanges John seemed to be gaining strength. Now she ventured to make a suggestion. 'We have two options. Either I leave you here and ride for help, or we see if with my help you can get on my horse and I will take you home.'

'That's what I'll try. If you leave me here they may return and finish me off. 'Feel in my right-hand pocket, Miss Booth.'

She did as she was told. 'Nothing, Mr Mitchell.'

'Nothing? There should have been a leather pouch with ten sovereigns in it.'

'So it was robbery?'

'It looks like it.' Though John had agreed with her assessment of the motive for the attack, he privately wondered if there was a deeper reason for it, one that stemmed from Jeremy Gaisford. 'Now let's see what I can do.'

471

It was a struggle and very painful but with her help and his determination John got to his feet. She held him up while he steadied himself for a moment. His legs felt weak where they had been stamped on and his right side felt as if it was one massive bruise.

'I might have a problem getting on to your horse,' he said, gritting his teeth against the pain.

Lydia looked around. 'Do you think we could get you on to that slab of rock? Height might be an advantage if I bring the horse alongside you.'

'A good idea! Let's try.'

She assisted him to the rock and helped him on to it. A few minutes later, in spite of the pain and discomfort, John was successfully seated on the horse. Walking beside him, in case he needed her shoulder to steady himself, Lydia took the reins and encouraged the horse into a walking pace.

Once he had assumed as comfortable a position as possible he put the question, 'How did you come to be on this track and on your own today? It's not Thursday.'

'Mr and Mrs Westbury were taking the children to see their grandmama in Penzance and that left me free. A friend of mine has just come to Mousehole for a month, I haven't seen her for five years. She had asked me to visit. As I was free today, Mr and Mrs Westbury suggested I ride over. I was on my way back.'

'Lucky for me! I might have laid there for a long time, or else the robbers might have completed their job.'

Lydia shuddered at the thought.

'I think they probably heard your horse and left before you appeared,' said John, 'but let's talk of more pleasant things. I need my mind taking off these cuts and bruises. How is the painting coming along?'

'I am highly satisfied so far. I was going to contact you. I would like you to view what I have done so far, but I wanted to do that in the bay itself.' Lydia pulled herself up. Had that sounded too bold? 'But it will have to be put off until you recover. You cannot possibly scramble down until you are completely well again.'

'You are right, but the thought of what is to come will aid my recovery.'

Lydia's heart skipped a beat. Was there something behind that statement or was she letting her imagination run away with her?

John wondered if anything lay behind the fact that she was suggesting they should meet in the bay, albeit to view her painting.

Lost in their own thoughts, they both lapsed into a charged silence.

The clatter of the hooves on the cobbles as Lydia led her horse into the stable yard at Penorna brought a groom hurrying to see who was arriving. Startled by the sight of Mr Mitchell led on a horse, he reacted quickly when Lydia said, 'Get Mrs Mitchell, there's been an accident.'

The brief message brought Eliza in a high state of concern hurrying from the house. By the time she'd reached the stable yard Lydia and another groom had helped John to the ground and were supporting him to the back door.

'John!' Eliza's voice was filled with shock at seeing the cuts and bruises on her husband's face, and the state of his clothes. 'What happened?' Her eyes flashed from him to Lydia, wondering how she came to be with her husband. She was by his side at once, taking over from the groom whom she told to fetch a doctor quickly.

'I was attacked,' John replied, wincing as a sharp pain stabbed through his side.

'About two miles from Sandannack,' said Lydia. 'I came across him on my way back from Mousehole,' she added by way of an explanation for her presence.

John stopped in his tracks and grasped at his ribs.

Alarm coursed through Eliza. 'We'd better get you to bed.'

Each step up the broad staircase sent a pain through his ribs even though he had support on both sides. They reached the door of the bedroom.

'Thank you, Miss Booth, I'll manage from here.'

Lydia detected a touch of coldness in Eliza's voice and wondered what the other woman was thinking. She nodded and went to the stairs. She hesitated at the top and looked back down the corridor. Eliza was manoeuvring her husband through the doorway but managed to glance in Lydia's direction. Their eyes met for one brief moment but neither could identify the expression in the other's.

By the time she reached the bottom of the stairs, Lydia had come to a decision. She would wait to hear the doctor's report. If she didn't she would have an uneasy time until she learned of the extent of John's injuries. But what would Mrs Mitchell think if she did wait? But why shouldn't she? Surely it was only courteous and neighbourly? Lydia sank down on to a chair opposite the stairs.

She had been sitting there nearly ten minutes when a maid come into the hall and showed surprise on seeing her.

'Oh, Miss Booth,' she gasped, recognising her from her visits to see Dorinda.

'Sorry if I startled you.'

'That's all right, miss, but come and sit in the drawing room.'

'No, I'm all right here.'

'Would you like a cup of tea, miss? You look pale. From what I hear it must have been a terrible shock for you to find Mr Mitchell.'

'It was. I would love a cup of tea, if that would be all right?'

'I'm sure Mrs Mitchell would approve.'

The girl hurried away, leaving Lydia marvelling at how quickly gossip circulated among servants. The girl could only have known about Lydia's finding John from the remark she'd made in the presence of the groom as they were helping him into the house.

Twenty minutes later she was still sitting there but had finished two cups of tea from the teapot when she heard a door open and close upstairs and footsteps approach the top of the stairs. She saw Mrs Mitchell appear. Her step faltered for a moment when she glanced down and saw Lydia.

474

Eliza glided swiftly down the staircase, noting the tray set on a small table beside her. Reaching the hall she said, 'Miss Booth, I am so sorry. Forgive my bad manners. I should have ordered tea myself and told you to go to the drawing room, but I hope you will understand the distress I felt on seeing my husband in that state.'

Though there was every indication of friendliness, Lydia felt the explanation was not as warm as it should have been. 'There is nothing to reproach yourself for, Mrs Mitchell. I hope you don't mind my waiting? I was anxious to hear about Mr Mitchell's condition.'

'He has some terrible bruising on his body and legs, but how serious it is we won't know until the doctor has been. Do you want to wait until then?'

'If that is all right with you?'

'Of course.' Eliza felt she could do nothing but agree. 'It might be a good idea. You will be able to carry a full account to Mr and Mrs Westbury.' Besides, she thought, it will give me a chance to learn how exactly you came to find him. 'Do let us go to the drawing room. Mr Mitchell has settled and had drifted into sleep when I left him. We can only await the doctor.' She led the way into the room and when they were seated comfortably began: 'From the few words my husband spoke it seems it was lucky that you came along or his beating might have been worse, even fatal. He thinks you disturbed the robbers.'

'I am not sure about that, Mrs Mitchell. There was no one to be seen when I arrived and saw him lying on the track. I did not even know who it was until I turned him over. He was lying face down. It may well be true that my horse alerted them to my approach and they made off, otherwise I suppose they would have hidden your husband behind some boulders.'

'It sounds as though they had chosen their place well. Thank goodness you did disturb them! My husband may not have been found for days if they had concealed their handiwork. How fortuitous that you came along. You were alone?'

Realising that Mrs Mitchell thought it strange that she should be riding alone Lydia quickly offered her explanation.

She had just finished that when there was a knock on the door and a maid entered the rom.

'The doctor is here, ma'am.'

Eliza was on her feet immediately. Seeing Lydia began to rise also, she said as she headed for the door, 'Wait here, Miss Booth. I'll let you know the result of the examination as soon as the doctor has made it.' Then she was gone. Lydia sank back on her chair, reproved. Was Mrs Mitchell harbouring suspicions? Did she really believe that Lydia had been visiting a friend in Mousehole, or did she think that she was on her way to an assignation with John? Lydia pulled herself up sharply. This was purely the work of her own vivid imagining, surely?

How long she battled with these thoughts and others like them she did not know but they were banished quickly when the door opened and Mrs Mitchell walked back in. Lydia immediately jumped to her feet.

'It is not as bad as we feared, Miss Booth. There is a lot of bruising, especially around the ribs, but none are broken. It is the same with his legs. He'll have some pain for a little while but should be up in two days. He'll have to take things steadily for a while until the bruising and aches disappear. Though it is a bad gash on the head, the doctor thinks there is no concussion. The black eye and facial cuts will leave no scars.'

With every word Lydia felt more relief. She tried to control the tremor in her voice as she said, 'I'm so relieved. I will inform Mr and Mrs Westbury.'

'Thank you, Miss Booth.'

Eliza escorted Lydia to her horse and as she rode away stood watching her thoughtfully.

Was that young lady's story about being on her way back from Mousehole true? She could have chosen another route to Trethtowan Manor. She was attractive, too, something John had surely noticed. He had been very keen on her doing a painting . . .

Eliza, deep in thought, walked slowly back into the house.

476

Chapter Eight

'It's a pleasant morning,' said John, eyeing the sky as he and Eliza strolled on to the terrace after breakfast. 'I'll take a turn in the garden.'

'Are you sure?' she asked with concern, though she was pleased he wanted to make the effort. 'It's only ten days, John.'

'I feel a lot better.' He had become impatient with his slow recovery and this morning the aches and pains were so much less. 'I must try sometime. Walk with me?'

'Of course! We'll get our coats.' She turned to the door and he followed her. His request struck a chord with her. *He wants me with him. I should never have harboured suspicions. It was only natural he should mention how Miss Booth helped him, and there has been nothing else to deepen my unfounded doubts.*

'Had enough, John?' she asked after half an hour, detecting that even at this leisurely pace her husband's steps had slowed.

'I think so, but it's been very pleasant. I'll try to venture a little further every day.'

A week later he announced, 'I'll walk over to Trethtowan and have a chat with Selwyn today.'

'You do that. It will be a change for you.'

Though Selwyn and Harriet had visited John, the two men had never had the opportunity to talk privately about the attack and John was eager to compare notes with his friend.

'Ah, my dear John, it is good to see you've managed to walk this far,' Selwyn greeted him with great delight. 'How are you feeling?'

'Well,' replied John.

477

'Come inside, sit down,' Selwyn urged, considerate for his welfare.

'May we sit outside? It's such a pleasant September day.'

'Of course.' He started towards the seat on the canopied terrace that stretched the full width of the house. 'Drink?'

'Chocolate would be fortifying.'

'Certainly. I'll be back in a moment.' Selwyn hurried inside and returned in a few minutes accompanied by his wife.

'How good to see you here,' greeted Harriet with a broad welcoming smile. 'Don't get up. I hope you haven't tired yourself, walking this far?'

'No. I've been gradually working up to it. Today when I woke up I felt so much better, and here I am.'

The three friends relaxed in each other's company and chatted amiably over their chocolate.

When she had finished hers, Harriet rose from the seat. 'I'm sure you men would like to talk on your own. If you'll excuse me, I have some letters I must write to be ready for collection tomorrow.'

The two men got to their feet.

'Will you dine with us before you set off home, John?' Harriet asked. 'We have some fine cold beef.'

'That is kind of you and I appreciate being asked but I told Eliza I would not stay.'

'Very well. Why don't both of you come the day after tomorrow, about this time?'

'I'm sure Eliza would like that.'

'We'll see you then.'

When she had gone the two men settled back on their seats.

'Selwyn, I have never heard any details of the attack on you, but in the light of what happened to me recently, do you mind talking about it?'

'Of course not! I thought it was in the past and since there has not been a recurrence I was inclined to forget it. Now, after your experience, we should probably exchange notes.'

'You said you suspected the Gaisfords might be behind it, especially as it followed an offer they had made to buy some land from you that you turned down?'

'Yes, but I had no direct evidence to connect them with the attack.'

'But doesn't it seem strange the attack on me should follow a similar pattern? I had just turned down Miles Gaisford's offer to buy my land.'

Selwyn frowned. 'I did not realise it was such a close similarity. I thought the Gaisfords were blaming you for Miles's seizure because there'd been an exchange of words that grew heated. I'd no idea what the subject was.'

'My refusal to sell may well have sparked Miles's upset,' John commented.

'It's possible,' Selwyn agreed gravely.

'Tell me, did you see your assailants?' John asked.

'I saw one but could not recognise him again, his face was covered. While he confronted me I was struck from behind so there must have been two of them.'

'Exactly what happened to me,' John confirmed, a touch of excitement in his voice.

'So you are thinking they must have been the same two men?'

'It seems more than likely.'

'But you can't link them with the Gaisfords?'

'No. And even if I were able to confront them, they would deny it.'

'Most certainly, and the Gaisfords would then see to it that your name was blackened in the county. Accusing someone without proof does not go down well hereabouts.'

John's lips tightened in exasperation.

Selwyn saw it and said, 'Don't do anything rash, it's not worth it. They are a powerful family. But if you quietly take notice of what happened to you, though I know you won't like doing that, relations with the Gaisfords may move into calmer waters, like they did with me. Oh, they continued to make offers to buy the land but they eventually saw I was determined not to sell. I have no doubt they will approach you again, more than once. If you weaken, they will eventually put more pressure on me to sell. They want to link our land with theirs.'

479

'Selwyn, you have my firm assurance that I will not sell.' His friend's firm delivery left Selwyn in no doubt that he meant what he said. 'Now, I think I had better be going.' John rose to his feet. 'Thank you for your hospitality.'

'You are welcome any time. I'll see you the day after tomorrow.'

Before John had time to move James and Juliana raced round the corner in a game of chase. They were followed by Lydia, who was laughing joyously at something that had gone on before. She pulled up when she saw the two gentlemen and her merriment died away. The children ran to their father.

John and Selwyn laughed with them as they circled about shouting, 'Hello, Mr Mitchell! Hello, Mr Mitchell!'

'Oh, I'm sorry,' Lydia gasped. 'Children, calm down, calm down!'

'It's all right, Miss Booth,' said Selwyn. 'It's good to see them happy and enjoying themselves.'

'Good day, Miss Booth.' John's eyes met hers.

'Good day, Mr Mitchell,' she replied, embarrassed that she should have been caught with such a dishevelled appearance after her run with the children. 'How are you? I hope fully recovered from your ordeal?'

'I am, Miss Booth, and it is very remiss of me not to have thanked you myself before now for all that you did for me that day.'

'It was only what anybody would have done, Mr Mitchell.'

'Perhaps, but you did it with such care.'

Lydia blushed and could make no answer. Instead she turned her attention to the children. 'James, Juliana, come on, you've some art work to do.'

While James pulled a face and Juliana shouted, 'Oh good, good!' Lydia ushered them into the house, pausing at the door only long enough to look back at John and say, 'I trust Mrs Mitchell is in good health?'

'She is, thank you, Miss Booth.'

With that she was gone, but the look she had given him lingered in his mind as he walked home.

Two mornings later when John and Eliza were about to leave for Trethtowan, a letter was delivered to them.

'It's from Martha,' said John, recognising the writing. He broke the wax seal that held the paper and unfolded it. He smiled as he said, 'She's got her money's worth.' He held up the paper for Eliza to see the sheet cross-covered with close writing which carried the narrative back between the original lines.

'Read it to me,' said Eliza, who was choosing which bonnet she should wear for the walk to the Westburys, for they had decided that on such a pleasant day the exercise would do them both good.

Martha, in the first part of the letter, merely gave them news of herself and happenings in Whitby. Then their attention was caught and held as John read: '"And now I come to more serious things. Some problems have arisen within the business and I would value John's opinion on them. I do not want to set them down on paper and so would be grateful if he could visit me here. I do not wish to cause alarm, nor for him to set out immediately. The problem can wait certainly a week or two, but it could be advantageous for it to be solved within four weeks."'

John stopped reading and then added, 'That seems to be it. Then she send her felicitations to you and Abigail and trusts that we are all in good health.'

'You must go,' said Eliza without hesitation. 'It must be something important if Martha requires your assistance. When will you go?'

'Let's talk about that on the way to Trethtowan.'

Although Eliza would have preferred him to go by coach because of the time of year he decided to travel north on horseback to make use of the freedom. As there were some matters that needed his attention at the mine and in Sandannack, which could not be left until his return from Whitby, he would leave in four days' time.

When the Westburys were informed of his intended visit to Yorkshire they reassured John that they would make sure all was well with Eliza in his absence, even going so far as offer-

481

ing her a place with them until his return. This she declined, thinking the upheaval too much apart from which, with Abigail, Dorinda, and all the servants, she certainly would not be alone.

'You will look after Mama for me, won't you?' asked John, squatting on his haunches as he took hold of his daughter's hands.

'Of course I will, Papa.' Abigail looked serious as she made her vow. 'How long will you be away?'

'I don't know. It depends on what your Aunt Martha wants, but I'll be back as soon as possible. Give me a hug to remember you by.'

Abigail flung her arms round her father's neck and hugged him tight. He kissed her on the cheek and, as she released her hold, straightened up and looked with loving eyes at his wife. 'You are sure you'll be all right?'

'Of course,' Eliza replied firmly. 'Don't worry about us. You concentrate on your mission. I hope the problem is easily solved. Give Martha our love, and hurry back.'

'I will.' He kissed her and would have lingered but she was more practical.

'Off with you or you won't reach your planned first stop before night fall.'

He swung into the saddle; Eliza and Abigail accompanied him out of the stable yard then went on to the terrace from where they watched until they returned his wave before he rode out of sight.

'Jeremy, a word after breakfast.'

He knew that was a summons and immediately feared a reprimand. But since Miles's recovery some of the snap had gone out of his criticism even though his mind and speech were still as alert as ever.

When Jeremy entered the study his father indicated a chair to him. Miles's gaze was cold and penetrating as ever.

'I may be less active than I was but I still have it all up here,' he tapped his head, 'and I have my sources of informa-

482

tion. It came to my notice two days ago that Mr Mitchell had been robbed by two thugs a few weeks back. Had you anything to do with that?'

'No.'

Miles's eyes narrowed. He slapped the top of the desk with the palm of his hand, sending the noise ricocheting from the panelled walls. 'Don't lie to me! I can read you like a book.' Jeremy flinched under the whiplash of his father's tongue.

'Mitchell had to be taught a lesson for what happened to you!'

'He had not! I take some of the blame for your over-reaction on myself. I ranted and raved that day ... I shouldn't have done, but I was ill and hadn't all my wits about me at the time. I've told you before, there are ways and means other than violence to attain our objectives.' He paused to let the significance of his words sink in. Jeremy nodded, looking contrite. 'Now, it has also come to my notice that Mr Mitchell has gone to Whitby.'

'For good?' Jeremy was always surprised by his father's omniscience and wondered how he got to know such things.

'No, a visit to his sister.' Miles gave a little smile at the fact that he knew something that had escaped his son. 'You wonder how I know? When will you learn to quiz servants in a subtle way? They love to tittle-tattle about their employers and are only too ready to air their knowledge to their peers from other estates. You learn a lot that way. Not all of it's useful but sometimes one little fact can be.'

'And what do you make of the fact that Mitchell has gone north?' queried Jeremy.

'We made him a tempting offer for that section of land; let us make an even more tempting one to his wife in his absence.'

'You think she might sell without her husband's knowledge?' Jeremy showed his surprise.

'Few women will turn away from the prospect of money and jewellery.'

'What exactly have you in mind?'

483

'I'll get your mother to set up a little supper party for three with Mrs Mitchell as our honoured guest, a kindly gesture because her husband is away.'

Jeremy smiled. He remembered how his father had concluded the purchase of some land along the coast that included a useful haven for small vessels in a similar manner. 'You are a wily old bird.'

'I've told you before, there are more ways than one.'

'But what if she doesn't bite?'

'Then I will put another plan into action. In case that has to be implemented I want you now subtly to find out the situation at Mitchell's copper mine. Are they likely to employ more men? How is production? Any chance of opening up new workings? Whatever you can find that might be useful. I must have such facts as soon as possible so that if Mrs Mitchell refuses to act without her husband, my second plan will be in place when I judge the time to be right.'

'Ma'am, a rider from Senewey has just brought this.' The maid held out a silver salver on which there was a sealed sheet of paper.

Eliza took the paper as she asked, 'Is the man awaiting an answer?'

'No, ma'am.'

'Thank you.'

When the maid had left the room Eliza broke the seal and unfolded the letter to read: 'Mr and Mrs Miles Gaisford request the pleasure of your company at supper on Wednesday 3rd April at 5p.m.'

She turned the sheet over so that she could check how it was addressed. She saw it bore only her name. So the Gaisfords must know that John is away, she thought. Was this purely a gesture of good will? Near neighbours being solicitous for a woman alone? She let her reasoning run. Would John approve of her accepting? Was there any good reason why she should not go ... and would she be slighting the Gaisfords if she did not?

484

A week later Benson drove his mistress to Senewey. Eliza was welcomed there most effusively by Rowena and Miles and quickly realised she was the only guest.

Over a glass of Madeira the Gaisfords learned that John had gone to Whitby at the request of his sister who had some queries about her business there for which she required her brother's advice. The conversation continued to flow pleasantly across many topics throughout the lavish meal taken at this time of day, as was the custom for families of such standing. Eliza was impressed and remarked upon the succulent pigeon pie and the tempting orange cheesecakes. The meal was leisurely and lasted two hours. Finally, feeling well satisfied, she accompanied her host and hostess into their elegant drawing room where the curtains had been drawn, lamps lit, and the fire raised to a warming blaze. Once they were comfortably seated and the servants had withdrawn, Miles judged it a good time to put his proposition to Eliza.

'Mrs Mitchell, you may know that some time ago I offered to buy some land from your husband?'

'Yes, I do. He would not sell.'

'That is true. I am particularly anxious to purchase that land in order to extend my northern holding.'

'But our land does not adjoin yours, Mr Gaisford, so any extension would be limited by the fact that Mr Westbury's land lies between,' Eliza pointed out.

Miles knew now that he was dealing with an astute woman. Very few wives, his own Rowena excluded, would have been as interested in their husband's land management, or indeed in any other of his economic affairs. Such things would have been left entirely to the men. But it was now obvious to him that the Mitchells had a shared interest in business. That suited him for he could now discuss the matter further; an uninterested wife would have meant any pursuit of the matter would have been useless.

'Correct, Mrs Mitchell, but if I am able to purchase your land I believe it would give Mr Westbury more incentive to sell his to me. Being able to link both pieces of land to mine would enhance my property without in any way detracting from yours. Mr Mitchell and Mr Westbury are not using that land for any specific purpose.'

'At the moment,' put in Eliza.

'Do you think Mr Mitchell has plans for it?'

'Not that I am aware of.'

'Then let me make you an offer?'

'I think that had better wait until my husband returns.'

'Do you know how long he will be away?'

'No. That depends on the nature of the help his sister requires.'

'He could be away for a considerable time?'

'It is possible.'

'If that is so it may be too late to complete the sale of the land. You see, Mrs Mitchell, I must not and cannot leave the money I am prepared to use for this purchase idle. That is not profitable. If your husband were to be absent for long I could not wait. It is a case of acting on the offer I make you now.'

'That puts me in an awkward position. There are many matters on which my husband seeks my advice and I know would allow me to act upon.' She left a thoughtful pause but it was sufficient for Rowena to interject.

'Then you and I are fortunate in our choice of husbands, Mrs Mitchell, for Mr Gaisford involves me in his affairs even more than he does our eldest son who will eventually inherit. Mr Gaisford has talked to me about his proposal, and I can tell you it is a very generous and a lucrative one for you.'

'Let me put this to you, Mrs Mitchell, and then I will say no more. I will not press you now for a decision because you will want time to consider it, but I would like an answer within the week so I can make a good start to 1786,' Miles told her.

Eliza listened very carefully to his proposition. Though he made no comment, Miles was delighted by her attentive expression. When he had finished he sat back in his chair. 'There it is for your consideration, Mrs Mitchell. We will say no more about it now. After all, this was really a social occasion. I apologise for turning to other matters.'

'That is perfectly all right, Mr Gaisford. I will think about your offer and if I consider that I should act upon it, I will do so as there will be no time to contact Mr Mitchell by letter and receive a reply in the next week.'

'I leave matters in your hands, Mrs Mitchell.'

Rowena turned the conversation to the embroidery she was doing and had purposefully left in sight so that it could become a talking point if necessary. The evening continued pleasantly and Eliza found herself seeing the Gaisfords in a more favourable light.

When she took her leave and was being helped into her out-door clothes, Miles excused himself for a moment and hurried into his study. He returned a few moments later with a small red leather box. He held it out to Eliza. 'A little memento to express our thanks for sharing a most pleasant evening with us.'

She hesitated. 'I couldn't, Mr Gaisford. It is I who should be thanking you.'

'And we accept your thanks,' put in Rowena. 'But we would like *you* to have a tangible reminder of this evening.'

'The evening itself is sufficient.'

'Please?' From Miles's expression Eliza knew he would be offended if she did not accept. She took the box and opened the hinged lid to discover a string of pearls resting on a bed of red velvet.

She gasped then looked at Miles and Rowena in amaze-ment. 'Mr and Mrs Gaisford, this is more than kind. I really don't know what to say.' Her words trailed away as she looked down at the shining pearls again.

'Then say nothing,' said Miles quietly.

'Enjoy wearing them,' said Rowena, and patted Eliza's arm.

She sat back in the carriage as it headed for the ornate gates at the end of the long drive. 'A bribe, more like,' she muttered to herself. Then her thoughts turned to the more than gener-ous offer which was almost double that which had been made to John.

It was uppermost in her mind the next morning when she woke and continued to occupy her while she dressed. By the time she was ready to go downstairs she had resolved to consult Selwyn. After all, the Westburys had told John they were there to help her if need be while he was away, and she could forewarn Selwyn he too was likely to be approached again by Miles.

She called for Abigail and waited while Dorinda tied a ribbon in her hair, then mother and daughter went down to breakfast.

'I'm going to see Mr and Mrs Westbury this morning, do you want to come and see Juliana?'

'Oh, yes, please.' Abigail's eyes lit up. She had got on well with Juliana ever since their arrival in Cornwall and they had become firm friends. James being older had always adopted a superior attitude but Juliana had told Abigail to take no notice; that was just boys.

'You go into breakfast. I'll be there in a moment.' Eliza rang the bell that stood on a table at the bottom of the stairs. A few moments later a maid appeared and was sent to inform Benson to have the carriage ready to drive to Trethtowan Manor, after which she was to tell Dorinda that they would leave in half an hour.

Whenever these outings occurred the governess looked forward to them for it meant an exchange of gossip with her friend Lydia.

The drive was pleasant and once they were at the Trethtowan Estate the two governesses, at the instigation of Juliana and Abigail, took the girls for a walk in nearby woods.

'I hope I am not interrupting anything,' Eliza apologised when her friends had welcomed her.

'Not at all,' replied Harriet. 'We are always pleased to see you.'

'Well,' said Eliza as they walked into the house, 'I have something to tell you and I want your advice.'

'Only too pleased if we can give it,' replied Selwyn as Eliza slipped off her coat and handed it, together with her bonnet, to the maid.

'That's a beautiful string of pearls,' commented Harriet. 'I have not seen them before.'

Eliza gave a little smile. 'They are part of my story.'

'Oh?' Harriet was puzzled and eager to know more. What did they signify, and how did they figure in this advice Eliza had mentioned?

Harriet and Selwyn looked at her enquiringly once they were seated in the drawing room. They listened to her story with obvious amazement as it unfolded.

'That is an extraordinary offer,' commented Selwyn when she had finished.

'And no doubt, from what Mr Gaisford said, you'll be getting one too.'

'It will be very tempting if I do . . .'

'Don't be hasty,' his wife warned.

'A pity John isn't here,' Selwyn muttered.

'It is,' agreed Eliza, 'but we can't wait until he gets back. I say *we*,' she added quickly, 'because I think we should act together on this.'

'Quite right,' confirmed Selwyn. 'We know it's all about the possibility of finding copper on our land. And on top of his offer, I reckon those pearls are something of a bribe.'

'Exactly what I thought,' said Eliza.

'Such a price for the land is very tempting, however,' commented Selwyn.

'John was adamant about not selling before,' said Eliza in a tone that conveyed he might still have the same attitude.

'Then don't sell,' said Harriet, picking up on her feeling.

'But what if he returns and wishes I hadn't missed such a good offer?'

'There is another way of looking at it,' pointed out Selwyn. 'If it is that valuable to Gaisford then it is just as valuable to us. If our land has good copper deposits we can exploit them together without the Gaisfords. But I was not in favour of despoiling the landscape and nor was John, so in spite of this very tempting offer why don't we stick by our principles?'

There was only a momentary hesitation before Eliza spoke again and when she did her tone was full of resolve. 'Then don't sell! Miles Gaisford won't like it but he'll have to live with it. I'll write to him when I get back home. And I'll return these pearls.'

'Don't do that,' warned Harriet. 'He'll take it as an insult, for he will know that you have seen it as a bribe, whereas to all intents and purposes it was merely a gift to commemorate a pleasant evening.'

Eliza nodded. 'I suppose you are right.'

With goodbyes said and Abigail and Juliana acknowledging that they had had a good time, Lydia stood with her hand on Juliana's shoulder watching the carriage drive away. But her thoughts were all on the news just imparted by Dorinda. Mr Mitchell had gone to Whitby and it was not known when he would be back. She felt that something had been snatched away from her for she had expected to arrange, somehow or other, to meet him in their bay to get his approval of the painting.

Rowena watched her husband with keen eyes as he broke the seal on the letter that had just been delivered from Penorna Manor. It could only be one thing – an answer from Mrs Mitchell. She saw Miles's scowl and the way it darkened. His lips set in a tight line as he flung the paper on to the table. It slid across the polished surface to Rowena. She picked it up and read the polite refusal of her husband's offer.

'Damn the woman!' he hissed. 'Why wouldn't she sell?'

'Because she doesn't want to,' replied Rowena calmly.

'We could have made a fortune out of the copper deposits on which the Mitchells and Westburys are sitting!'

'I know it's a setback to your ambitions but we are well off as it is. Don't go getting yourself worked up about it. You know what happened last time.'

'I won't.' She saw a glint in his eye. 'I have an alternative plan in readiness.'

'And what is that?'

'Better you don't know.'

Rowena gave a little inclination of her head. She knew that the Gaisfords had employed underhand methods in the past and, as her husband rightly said, it was better she did not know of them now.

'Where have you been?' Miles asked as Jeremy strode on to the terrace after handing his horse over to one of the grooms.

'Getting the information you wanted,' he replied, a touch of satisfaction in his voice.

'Well, what is it?'

'Tell you in a minute.' Before his father could say anything Jeremy was away into the house. He returned after a few minutes with a glass of whisky in his hand.

'You drink too much,' his father criticised. 'It'll be your downfall.'

'Something to celebrate.' Jeremy grinned and raised his glass.

Miles was irritated by this carefree attitude when important things were at hand. 'Well?' he snapped.

'Mitchell's mine is below production. They are looking to recruit miners but it seems there are few unemployed hereabouts. Fishermen and farmers won't go underground even though there may be more money at it.'

'Are they looking to expand?'

'Not at present. There has been talk of it in the past but since Mitchell came that seems to have been dropped. He doesn't seem interested in expansion but does like to keep present production to capacity.'

'So if that capacity dropped he may be forced to open up another seam. That could be made costly for him and . . .'

'. . . it might be better for him to sell that copper-laden land you want.' Jeremy finished for him.

'Exactly.'

'So what is the next move?'

'We wait until Mitchell returns.'

'Why until then?'

'Because he's likely to act on what I plan. After the way he proceeded when he learned about the Lowthers, I'm almost certain he'll do the same again.'

'You are going to plant someone on his workforce?'

'You are getting the idea. Details can be finalised later. What you have to do is to recruit one of our workers on whom you can rely.'

'Leave it to me.' Jeremy grinned.

'See that whoever you get is absolutely trustworthy and will never talk.'

'I shall.'

Miles eyed his son. 'Where did you get your information?'

Jeremy smiled with the pleasure of knowing he could out-fox his father on this one. 'That is for me to know and only me, but I'll tell you this: my sources are very reliable.' He raised his glass in mock salute then drained it, stood up and walked briskly into the house.

His father watched him, tight-lipped, and wondered what the future held for his eldest boy who would so often act without thinking. He almost wished Logan had been the eldest.

Chapter Nine

Nostalgia swelled in John and tightened his throat at first sight of Whitby. The feeling that he was home heightened as he neared the town and saw the red-roofed houses climbing the cliffside towards the old church and ruined abbey. He took the track that led to the East Side. He was thrilled to see the bustling activity on the quays below where ships were loaded and unloaded. As he was swept up into Whitby's life, once so familiar to him, he felt a little twinge of regret that he had ever left his birthplace for the other end of the country. But then he tightened his lips and stiffened his determination not to let such sentimentality get out of hand.

He rode along Church Street and turned into the yard of the White Swan. The clatter of hooves brought a stableman and boy hurrying from the inn's stable.

The man pulled up short on seeing John. 'Mr Mitchell!' he gasped in surprise.

'Aye, it's me, Bob,' replied John with a broad grin. 'You haven't seen a ghost.' He swung out of the saddle.

The boy had taken the reins and Bob took John's proffered hand. 'It's good to see you, sir,' he said, and glancing at the boy ordered, 'Charlie, take good care of that horse. Rub it down and feed it.'

'Aye, aye, sir.' Charlie waited until John had taken his saddlebags and rolled cape then led the horse away.

'Here for long, sir?'

'Not sure yet. I'll let you know when I want my horse again.'

Bob nodded. 'How are Mrs Mitchell and that nice little girl of yours?'

'Very well,' replied John, sensing a tug at his heart at the mention of them. 'Jake Thorburn still landlord here?'

'Aye, sir, he's just inside.'

'I'll have a word.'

'Do you want a fresh horse to go to Bloomfield Manor?'

'Please.'

'It'll be ready in a few minutes.'

John headed for the inn while Bob went to the stable to see that Charlie was giving due attention to the horse belonging to someone who had once been a good customer.

A short while later John swung from the saddle in front of the house that had long been his home. He had lived his boyhood there and later brought his bride to this place. Abigail had been born here, and they had all welcomed his sister here in her days of sorrow. It held so many memories, happy days, only a few tinged with sadness and anxiety. As he started up the four front steps the door opened.

'John!'

His face was instantly wreathed in smiles. 'Martha!'

Then they were in each other's arms. The intensity of their hug betrayed the extent to which they had missed each other.

'I saw you from the window.' Martha's eyes were damp as she stepped back to look at him. 'You look well,' she said. 'A little tired maybe, but that is only to be expected after your long journey. Whitby air will soon put you right.'

'It obviously keeps you young,' he said as they went into the hall pushing the door closed behind them.

'You see what you wish to see,' she laughed.

'Truly, you haven't changed,' he insisted while admiring her aura of serenity. Her taste in dress was simple but fashionable and she always wore the colour that suited her best – light blue emphasised by the darker hue of the thin shawl draped neatly round her shoulders. He was pleased to see she wasn't wearing her business troubles, whatever they were, on her sleeve.

He had dropped his saddlebags and cape on the floor of the hall and tossed his hat on to a chair. As he shrugged himself out of his woollen jacket Martha rang a bell twice and after a very brief pause rang it again three times in quick succession. The signals had the desired results. A footman and maid duly appeared.

'This is Mr Mitchell, my brother,' she said. 'Robert and June,' she added, turning to John who acknowledged the new servants as they paid him a respectful welcome. 'Robert, take Mr Mitchell to the room we have ready for him. June, tea in the drawing room in ten minutes.'

When John came down to the drawing room after he had restored himself he found it empty. His immediate action was to walk to the window. How many times had he stood there and looked out just like this? He felt his heart beat a little faster – the view still moved him.

'It is still a glorious sight,' said Martha quietly as she came to stand beside him.

He started. 'Oh, I didn't hear you come in.'

'You were far away. Is it the view?'

John gave a little smile. 'It's still wonderful.'

'Nothing to match it in Cornwall?' She turned her eyes to him as he continued to look out of the window.

There was a moment's hesitation before he replied, 'There's a tiny bay . . .' He sounded wistful.

She noted the tone of his voice and the dreamy look that had come to his eyes but made no comment. A little flutter of anxiety touched her, though. Was there more behind his expression than he was telling her? Could she still read her brother like a book? Her thoughts were interrupted when a knock on the door was followed by the arrival of tea.

Brother and sister sat opposite each other with a low round table between them. She poured the tea and he had already taken a scone, looking at it with relish. 'You still have Mrs Binns cooking for you, I see. How I used to enjoy her scones.'

'Well, now you can enjoy them again.'

He spread some butter and then raspberry jam on the scone. Before he took a bite he said, 'What's the trouble in the business?'

Martha gave a slight, dismissive wave of her hand. 'That can wait until tomorrow. It will be better explained at the

495

office where there are all the necessary documents. What I want now is to hear all about Cornwall.'

The rest of the afternoon and evening were spent in John's detailed description of his new life in the far-off county.

When she undressed for bed Martha thought about the many things he had told her and linked some of them to that wistful look she had noted shortly after his arrival. She would not question him about it but she locked the facts away in her mind.

'Right, Martha, tell me something about what is troubling you here,' prompted John over breakfast the next morning. 'I know the relevant documents will be at the office, but let me hear what you believe is wrong now.'

Martha hesitated, which struck him as being slightly strange, because his sister had always been one to come straight to the point. Something truly must be wrong if she had to consider how best to tell him. He knew that her sipping at her coffee was only a delay while she mustered her words. She glanced down at her empty bowl and then met his enquiring gaze. 'I have stepped into something we had never before contemplated and it has brought me only trouble,' she told him. 'I wish now I had never done it.' In the touch of guilt that had come to her voice there was also a cry for help.

'All right. Whatever you've done can be undone, or least a solution found,' he said reassuringly. 'Just begin at the beginning.'

'Business was going well. Oh, there were those who resented a woman moving into a man's world, but no one really acted against me in any tangible way. People undercut my prices, but that's to be expected in trade. I made sure our service was better than most. I also saw a way in which I thought we could give better service and maybe even expand our field. I decided to build a ship.'

John raised his eyebrows. This was a surprise but, not wanting to interrupt his sister's flow nor give her any inkling of what he was thinking, he made no comment.

'We pay for our goods to be transported and I thought if we could do that ourselves we would be more profitable. I thought if we built a vessel of the right size we could get into smaller harbours and expand our trade to places that at the moment are only supplied overland.'

John nodded. He could understand her reasoning.

Martha gave a small wistful smile. 'I also dreamed of sailing on her to Penzance and giving you a surprise.'

'You certainly would have done that! So what has gone wrong?'

'I went carefully into the costing and got Mr Smithers to check the figures.'

'So you still have Stewart. I'm pleased to hear it.'

'The ever-faithful manager! The business would not be the same without him.'

'So, you did the costing, Stewart checked the figures, and you were happy enough to go ahead?'

'Yes.'

'What is the size of the vessel?'

'A one hundred-tonne sloop.'

John nodded and pursed his lips thoughtfully. 'Big enough to sail the coast yet small enough to get into creeks and small waterways.'

'Yes.'

'How far has the building gone?'

'About halfway. That's the trouble . . . she should have been finished by now. She's six months behind schedule.'

'What?' John's expression of shock could not be hidden. 'And I suppose that is costing you money?'

'Exactly. At this rate the venture will never be profitable.'

'Who's building her?'

'Carson and Son.'

'Who are they?' John frowned.

'A new firm, set up eighteen months ago.'

'Why did you choose them?'

'I thought newcomers would be keen for business and want to show what they could do. Besides, they were recommended to me by Mr Wesley Horton.'

497

'Ah!'

'You sound as if you don't like him?'

'Never did.'

'But why?'

John shrugged his shoulders. 'Never could quite put my finger on it, it was just one of those feelings. He was always friendly enough on the surface but I believed he could be a bit underhand, though I had no real proof. Was it general knowledge that you were to have a ship built?'

Martha gave a little nod. 'I never kept it a secret. Our staff would hear of it. Friends knew of it, and you know how it is, things have a habit of becoming general knowledge in Whitby.'

'What has been Horton's attitude to you running a business? After all, he's in the same trade.'

'Yes. I can't say he has been helpful other than by recommending Carson.'

'And after a while things started to go wrong there?'

'Yes. You don't think Mr Horton could be behind the delay?'

'It's a possibility. He could be stealing your idea and having a ship built himself to go after the same trade.'

Martha's lips tightened at the thought that she might have been duped. 'What can we do?'

'First of all, don't become distressed about it. I'll look into the reason for the delay and tell Carsons to get on with the job.'

'I'm sorry about this, and for dragging you all the way from Cornwall, leaving Eliza and Abigail.'

'Think nothing of it. It is better this way than letting the situation here go too far. I would like to see all the documents relating to the building of the ship before I visit Carson's.'

'Very well! We'll go to the office whenever you are ready.'

Half an hour later John was exchanging greetings with Stewart Smithers. A few minutes later he welcomed the moment when his sister announced she had some paperwork to do and would be occupied for an hour. It enabled him to have a chat with her manager about the business and about the situation arising out of the slow delivery of the sloop. He saw

498

nothing untoward in what Smithers had to tell him except that the manager did not trust the excuses made by Carson's, and the fact that they were ever-ready to demand more money to finance the work.

Studying the contracts and payments, John saw that the situation was at a point where it would soon be over-budget.

'You look very concerned, John?' commented Martha on her return.

'The situation is decidedly tricky but I'll say no more now. We'll go and take a light luncheon at the Angel.'

They left the office situated on the east side of the river and threaded their way through the hustle and bustle of the thriving port. John realised how much he had missed it. They crossed the bridge and were soon at the Angel.

'Where's Carson's yard?' asked John later as they left the inn.

'Farthest one, upstream on this side of the river.'

'There certainly seems to be plenty of shipbuilding going on,' he commented as the sound of hammers and saws heralded much activity. All the yards were extremely busy constructing every manner of vessel, in keeping with Whitby's high reputation in this trade. He stopped at Carson's yard. Three ships were under construction there. Workmen were laying the keel on one. A second had reached the stage of having its deck beams and carlings fitted, but there was no work being done on the third which had reached the stage ready for hold shelf-pieces to be fitted.

'Which is yours?' John asked.

'The one on which they aren't working.'

'And whose is the one of similar design but at a more advanced stage?'

'I don't know, but I do know it was started after mine.'

'If yours was first, it should be the more advanced.'

'I pressed Mr Carson on that and he told me that when the timber arrived for the next stage of construction it was not suitable. Said he would have to wait for a new consignment.'

'That seems to me a lame excuse and points to bad management. He should have had sufficient timber to swap between the ships under construction so there was no delay on either of them. Certainly yours should now be further ahead than it is.' John paused a moment in thought then added, 'Why don't you go back to the office and leave this to me? I'll see you there shortly.'

Martha, knowing her brother, did not press him for further explanations but agreed.

When she had gone John strolled further into the yard and passed himself off as a possible customer. He was examining Martha's ship when a voice made him turn to see a thin man of average height studying him with eyes John would have described as shifty, though he wondered if his assessment was being coloured by the fact that his sister's ship had not been completed on time.

'Can I help you, sir?'

At least the man was polite though his voice held a note of suspicion.

'Mr Carson?'

'Yes, that's me. You looking to have a ship built?'

'I might be in the market in a month's time so I'm looking around. I heard tell you are new in Whitby?'

'Yes. These are our first three vessels. Are you from these parts?'

'No.' John decided not to reveal any more just yet.

Mr Carson looked surprised. 'But yet you come to Whitby for a ship?'

'I'm exploring all possibilities, but knowing Whitby's reputation for building good stout vessels, I would not be averse to having one built here.'

'Was my yard recommended?'

John had been trying to lead him to put that question. Now he had. 'Yes, by Mr Wesley Horton.'

'You know him?' Mr Carson's voice levelled into a more amenable tone. 'That's his . . .' He stopped as if he should not divulge any more but John had noted the inclination of Carson's head in the direction of the vessel that had progressed quicker than Martha's.

'You don't seem to have the space to take on another commission.'

500

'You said you would possibly be interested in a month's time?'

'Yes.'

'Well, I can speed work up on that one and have it cleared to suit your timescale.' So Horton's ship was priority, John noted.

John nodded. 'And that one?' He indicated Martha's vessel. 'Is that an order or one you are building to sell?'

Carson pulled a face. 'It's an order but I can delay it.'

'I wouldn't want to step on anybody's toes . . .'

'I can fix it, sir. The order has been placed by a lady! Now I ask you, sir, what is trade coming to when a woman moves into a man's world? We don't want them so what's it matter if I do a little delaying? And with you knowing Mr Horton, I don't mind giving you priority. It's easy to make excuses for the delay on that ship, especially as the person in question falls for everything I say.'

'Really?'

'Oh, yes.' He gave a laugh that showed he thought he was conducting a clever campaign.

'Well, Mr Carson, I have a vested interest in that ship you are delaying.' John's sudden rapier-like tone startled Carson. 'I want her finished in a month and no longer else I can legitimately deduct sufficient from the payments due to you to recompense Miss Mitchell for the trade she has lost. I have no doubt you will report my visit to Mr Horton with whom you are obviously in cahoots.' John saw denial rising to Carson's lips and quickly put in, 'Don't refute it, Mr Carson, I'm sure I'm right and you may as well know now that I am Miss Mitchell's brother. Not only that, I myself have powerful trading connections. No doubt Mr Horton will assure you that's untrue but he does not know the extent of my new connections since leaving Whitby. So, Carson, you could face ruin. Finish our ship or else . . .' He let the threat hang in mid-air. 'I'll be back.' John did not wait for him to speak but turned and strode purposefully away.

Carson stood watching him in confusion. He knew determination when he saw it and that Mr Mitchell was the type of man who would carry out his threat if the work was not completed in the time specified. He could well face ruin. But what about Mr Horton? Dare he upset him? He swung round and hurried to the Horton vessel. In a few moments the men working on it were relocating themselves on the Mitchell sloop.

Once out of sight of the shipyard John slowed his step. He smiled to himself when he heard the sounds of work behind him cease. He stopped, listening intently. When he heard the first hammer blow taken up by others he turned and moved quickly back to the yard. He stepped quietly up to Carson who was so intent on shouting new instructions to his workforce that he did not realise John was there until he said, 'That was very wise of you, Mr Carson.'

He started but John was already striding away, leaving the shipbuilder to ponder his words.

Martha looked askance at her brother when he walked back into the office.

'I don't think you'll have any more bother with Mr Carson,' he commented with a knowing smile. 'And I don't think Mr Horton will try to outsmart you again. By Mr Carson's actions Horton will know we have seen through his ploy.' He went on to tell her what had transpired at the yard.

'But won't Mr Carson just employ more men?'

'I doubt he'll be able to. You've seen that all the shipyards are working to full capacity. Carson won't find another skilled man in Whitby.'

'But what will happen when you leave?'

'I'll stay to see your ship launched. Let Carson see me around the town.'

Martha's eyes brightened. 'You will?' she asked in a voice filled with excitement.

'I'll write to Eliza tomorrow, tell her I'm delayed but will be home for Christmas.'

Pleasure surged through Eliza when a maid brought her a sealed sheet of paper and she recognised the writing as John's. She broke the seal with eager fingers and unfolded the letter. Her heart sank when she read that her husband would not be home for at least a month, and probably a week longer taking into account his travelling time. Though disappointed, she understood his reasons and only hoped that nothing else would happen to delay his return. This had been their first spell apart since marrying and she had not realised how much she would miss him. The days to his return seemed to stretch endlessly ahead.

Chapter Ten

Three days later Miles Gaisford was sitting on the terrace enjoying the sunshine as he gazed across the undulating fields that sloped to the distant edge of the cliffs. He felt deep satisfaction that he had turned his inheritance by marriage into one of the largest estates in Cornwall, and if he counted in the two estates assigned to his younger sons, though bought and financed through the wealth he had generated, the Gaisfords truly had become powerful and rich landowners. If only he could buy the land he so coveted from Westbury and Mitchell! He had seen his opportunity when Mitchell had gone to Whitby but had not reckoned on the inflexibility of Mrs Mitchell. Who would have thought a woman would resist so much money *and* a pearl necklace? Well, his second plan must be used and now, seeing Jeremy returning from his morning ride, was the time to implement it.

He pushed himself slowly from his chair, stepping over to the balustrade. With one hand on the stonework, he signalled to his son. Jeremy slowed his horse to a walk and turned it towards the terrace. Miles gave a little nod of satisfaction and returned to his seat.

'Morning, Father,' Jeremy called as he pulled his mount to a halt and swung from the saddle. 'How are you this fine morning?' he asked, striding on to the terrace.

'Been better, been worse,' returned his father gruffly, but Jeremy was pleased to detect an undercurrent of satisfaction, as if something had initiated a decision.

'What is it?' he asked, slapping his riding crop into the palm of his left hand as he flung himself down into a chair beside his father.

'Mr Mitchell is away for at least another month.'

Jeremy eyed him with curiosity. 'How do you know that?'

Miles's lips twitched with satisfaction. 'I've told you before, use your ears and cultivate gossip.'

Jeremy nodded, knowing it was useless to press for more information; he would not get his father to divulge his sources. 'So does this mean that we are going to . . .'

'Yes, it does,' Miles interrupted, knowing what his son was going to say. 'Now it's up to you to see that everything is in place by the time Mitchell returns.'

'The bait will be ready. Mr Mitchell will bite and be hooked,' said Jeremy with a smile of satisfaction.

'Good. See that nothing goes wrong.'

Undeterred by the threat of rain, Jeremy rode across the wild expanse of moor to the village of Cribyan. Most of its men were working in the Gaisford mine three miles from the village but some had been delegated three days ago by Jeremy to repair two cottages in the village. One of them was Jim Lund. As he rode past Jeremy raised his finger in a signal and knew from the nod he received in return that Lund had got the message. Jeremy rode on through the village and was on the moor again when the rain struck. He cursed the weather, booted his horse into a quicker pace and hunched his shoulders against the rain.

Twenty minutes later he dropped from the saddle in front of the wind-lashed Waning Moon. He hurried inside, sending the door crashing behind him. Water dripped from his clothes on to the stone floor as he threw his cape from his shoulders and sent spray across the floor when he shook his hat. At the same time his glance surveyed the room. The landlord stood behind the bar chatting with the only other occupant of the inn.

'G'day, Mr Gaisford,' greeted the landlord. 'Not so hot out there?'

'Far from it, Tom,' replied Jeremy. He turned his gaze to the other man. 'How are things at Creaking Gate Farm, Jos?'

'Exactly that, Mr Gaisford, creaking, and if I doesn't get myself back they'll be creaking all the more.' With that he drained his tankard and hurried out into the pouring rain.

505

Ten minutes later Jeremy was starting his third whisky when the door burst open, letting in a blast of rain-driven air that propelled a cursing Jim Lund into the room. He shook himself like a dog and spray flew everywhere.

'Cut it out, Jim,' snapped Jeremy, glaring at the new arrival.

Jim made no reply but threw off his rain-sodden jacket and slumped against the bar. Tom was already pouring him some ale.

'Give him a warmer,' called Jeremy.

''Preciate it,' called Jim. As soon as the whisky was in front of him he drained the glass and felt warmth drive down his throat and through his body. 'That's better,' he said, smacking his lips. He picked up his tankard, crossed the stone floor and sat down opposite Jeremy.

He had closely watched this strong, broad-shouldered young man every moment since his tempestuous arrival. Strong-framed and muscular, these attributes had been further honed by a rough, tough life and were evident in Jim's height. Though this was not a man he would care to tangle with physically, Jeremy knew Jim could take orders and carry them out to the letter. And his other great asset was that he would keep his mouth shut. He realised he was on to a good thing, doing unsavoury jobs for Jeremy Gaisford.

Jim met his searching gaze. 'The job you mentioned has come up?' he asked.

'Yes. Still want it?'

'I don't yet know what it is,' replied Jim cautiously.

'I'll tell you about it only if you decide to do it.'

Jim grunted. He generally knew what a job entailed before accepting it but when Jeremy had first mentioned the possibility of something big he had not divulged its exact nature.

'Well?' prompted Jeremy. 'It will pay well. More than the last one . . . considerably more because it will have to be done over a greater length of time.'

For a moment Jim looked thoughtful, then deeming it wisest to keep on the right side of Jeremy Gaisford, he agreed.

Jeremy gave a nod of approval. During the next two hours, over four tankards of ale and two whiskys each, the plan was laid and finalised, but only after Jeremy had agreed to Jim's recruiting two other men whom he vowed would follow him to hell if necessary and were as tight-lipped as he was.

Hearing the rattle of a horse's hooves on the drive, Eliza looked up from her embroidery to see a horseman appear from behind the avenue of trees that lined the early part of the drive.

'John!' she gasped, dropping her needlework on the seat and springing to her feet. Joy surged in her heart and she rushed to the steps of the terrace, calling to Abigail who was playing ball on the lawn with Dorinda. 'Abigail, Abigail! It's Papa!'

Startled, the child froze with the ball in her hand. She looked bewildered and then the significance of what her mother had said struck home. 'Miss Jenkins! Miss Jenkins! It's Papa!' She was already racing to her mother who had come down the steps on to the lawn. They held hands and hurried towards the rider. Smiles wreathed their faces as John pulled to a halt, jumped from the saddle and held out his arms to them both.

'John!' Eliza felt such strength and comfort in his embrace and experienced a welcome sense of being protected again.

'It's good to be home,' he replied huskily, then dropped down to hug Abigail. 'How's my girl? Been good? Looked after Mama?'

Abigail laughed with joy. 'Yes! Yes!'

John straightened up, kissed his wife again, picked up the reins and led his horse as they all walked towards the stables, happy to be together again.

From a distance Dorinda had watched the reunion. She wondered how Lydia would view Mr Mitchell's return, for she had wondered if there was more behind her friend's casual enquiries about him than merely wanting a decision on her painting.

Later, when John had refreshed himself and taken a meal, he answered all Eliza's questions about Martha's welfare and the

507

trouble in Whitby. At the end of his story he eyed her questioningly. 'Something's troubling you. Has anything gone wrong while I have been away?'

Eliza bit her lip.

'Begin at the beginning,' he prompted.

First she told him about the invitation to dine with Miles and Rowena.

He frowned when she mentioned the gift of pearls. 'You refused them, of course?'

'No. When I went to warn Selwyn that Mr Gaisford might approach him with another offer to buy his land, I told him about the gift and he and Harriet advised me to accept them as it would be a slight on the Gaisfords' hospitality and generosity if I were to return them, even though we both suspected the gesture was a bribe. As tempting as the offer to buy the land was, though, I refused.'

'Good. If he sees that land as valuable to him, then it is just as valuable to us. Do you think Selwyn will sell on the back of the increased offer?'

'No,' she replied firmly, to leave no doubt in his mind. 'We agreed to stand together against Miles's proposal.'

'Good. Have the Gaisfords made any other move?'

'No. Miles seems to have accepted my refusal with equanimity.' Eliza added slowly, 'But there is something else I have to tell you.'

'Trouble?'

'Well, not really, not so far as we are concerned. The mine is working well but not to full capacity. We needed more men.' She paused a moment, gathering her thoughts. 'You remember the Lowthers and the action you took there?' He nodded. 'Well, a similar situation arose. It came to my notice that a man called Jim Lund and two other Gaisford workers had been unfairly dismissed and evicted from their cottages. I got our mine manager to get them to meet me at the mine, interviewed them and took them on. They were amiable, strong, willing and grateful, and I have not had a bad report of them since.'

'Good.' He gave a little smile. 'We are doing well out of the Gaisfords.'

508

'I hope it continues that way.'

'You have nothing to worry about now I'm back.'

The following day, on rising, John looked out of the bedroom window. Judging the weather to be settled fair, he said. 'I'll visit the mine today and probably call in on Selwyn on the way.'

'So soon?' asked Eliza from the bed. She stretched seductively. 'You've been away so long, must you go now?'

'I'm not tied to any time,' he said quietly as he moved towards her, his eyes devouring her as she slipped the bed clothes aside.

An hour later he whispered in her ear, 'I think I must go this time,' then added. 'There's always tonight.'

She twisted in his arms and kissed him passionately. 'A reminder until then.'

Those words rang in his mind as he rode away from Penorna yet he turned his horse along the cliff track that would take him past the bay. He was still waiting for Lydia's painting of it. Did he hope that she was there now? He stopped, swung himself from his horse and ventured close to the edge so he could see the bay better. Its beauty seemed to strike him anew. The golden sand was unmarked, the azure sea lazily lapping; he knew he would always find peace and tranquillity here and it would always have a special place in his mind and heart. He swung himself back into the saddle and put his horse to a gallop, venting his unacknowledged annoyance that Lydia was not there. 'Ridiculous,' he muttered. 'There was no reason for her to be.'

He slowed his horse eventually and was deep in thought as he approached Trethtowan, a thought that still occupied his mind as he arrived at the house. The door opened as he finished tethering his horse at the top of the drive, knowing a groom would come to collect it.

'Miss Booth!' he said, a touch of surprise in his voice to see the object of his thoughts standing before him.

'Mr Mitchell!' Her voice shook; she blushed.

He noted it and liked it. He took in her high-waisted pink gown with the narrowest of brown braid trim running down the bodice in two rows from a high neck around which was set a circle of white frills. The natural wave of her short brown hair was unencumbered by a bonnet and bounced freely as she came to the top of the steps before the front door.

'Miss Booth, it is good to see you looking so well.'

'I am, Mr Mitchell, thank you. I understand you have been in Whitby. I hope your visit was pleasant.'

'Indeed it was, Miss Booth. And how is my painting coming along?'

'Very well, or at least I think so, but I would like your opinion, preferably on site so that you can compare what I am trying to achieve with the real scene.'

'Very well, Miss Booth. Which day is suitable for you?'

'The day after tomorrow is my free day.'

'Then we shall meet there at eleven o'clock.'

Lydia inclined her head in gracious acceptance but her eyes were locked on his. It was John who broke the contact and in a faltering voice which he instantly attempted to firm, asked, 'Are Mr and Mrs Westbury at home?'

'They are in the drawing room. If you'll follow me?' Lydia turned quickly back to the house and in a few moments was announcing Mr Mitchell's arrival to her employers.

'You're back!' cried Selwyn, dropping the book he was reading to the table beside his chair and jumping to his feet to greet his friend warmly.

Harriet welcomed John with a beaming smile as he took her hand and raised it to his lips. 'It's good to see you home and looking so well.' She rose from her chair. 'Let me ring for some chocolate.'

'That would be pleasant,' he replied, 'and will fortify me for my ride to the mine.'

With the chocolate at hand John asked Selwyn if he knew any more about Jim Lund's dismissal than he had already learned from Eliza.

'It seems he refused to do a dangerous job underground. The mine manager's instant dismissal of him was backed by

Jeremy Gaisford, and the same applied to two other men who sided with Lund.'

'Know anything about them?' John asked.

'When Eliza was thinking of employing them I did some enquiring. Seems they are all good workers. I never heard that there had been any complaint against them before. I gave these facts to Eliza and she acted accordingly. I could see no reason to deter her.'

'Thanks, Selwyn. I appreciate that.'

When Lydia returned outside after seeing John to the drawing room she stood on the terrace, leaning on the balustrade and gazing across the countryside while seeing nothing. Her mind was on the boldness she had displayed by suggesting that Mr Mitchell meet her in their bay in two days' time. She was hoping the weather would be as fine as it was today and that led to her picturing the meeting in her mind ... She had to pull her thoughts together sharply. What was she expecting to happen? Had she really seen in John's eyes a personal interest in her or was that just wishful thinking on her part? Was she letting herself slip beyond the boundaries of decorum even by thinking this way? She straightened, chided herself, slapped her hands hard on the stonework in self-reproof and walked, tight-lipped, into the house.

Although when he left Trethtowan John's mind was on what Selwyn had told him, it soon became occupied with pleasanter thoughts of the charming young lady who had appeared before him a short while ago. He felt sure he had read interest in her eyes and it flattered him. But was he right or was it purely his imagination wishing to pique the interest of a younger woman? No, it was not that; he tried to convince himself Lydia really had shown interest. Then his mind began to spin in confusion as he remembered what had happened in his own bedroom but a short while ago. Eliza! If she could have read the thoughts he had recently had about Miss Booth, she would have been devastated. He should never have commissioned that painting but such things just happened and, unprompted, one thing naturally led to another. Now he was to meet Miss Booth in the special place that had woven its magic around them both. He should call the meeting off, he knew. He wrestled with that thought, but by the time he'd reached the mine he knew he wouldn't.

John discussed the mine's production and men with his manager, Bert Wallace, who told him he was pleased Mrs Mitchell had approved the employing of three workers dismissed by the Gaisfords.

'They are good men, Mr Mitchell,' he said, 'and Lund is skilled with dynamite. We have had to use a small stick once since his arrival and he handled it perfectly.'

'Why Lund?'

'Our usual handler, Pat Welburn, had suffered a badly cut hand the previous day and we thought it might be an impediment if he was handling dynamite. Lund came forward and said he could do it. I hadn't any alternative so told him to get on with it. I tell you, he was most competent. No flurry. He exuded confidence, and the other men could feel that so it settled their minds. As you know, explosions underground can be tricky; nobody likes them really. I'll be using him again later this week. The section his explosion opened up looks promising but another blast will tell us if it is worthwhile pursuing further. So our expansion will not be held up by waiting for Welburn's recovery.'

Good. Then Gaisford's loss was our gain,' commented John with satisfaction. 'Will you continue to use Lund after Welburn's hand is better?'

'Yes. it's good to have two men competent with dynamite.'

'How did Welburn damage his hand?'

'He and Lund were working on a section in which some timbers needed replacing. Lund stumbled and the end he was carrying slipped; Welburn took the full weight but the trouble was his hand was trapped. Nasty, but fortunately nothing broken.'

John nodded. 'See that he loses no pay because of it.'

'He will appreciate that, sir. Thanks.'

512

As John rode back to Penorna he was thankful that nothing worse than a damaged hand had occurred during his absence ... and then his mind drifted to that meeting in two days' time.

Early-morning mist lay like a ghostly hand across Penorna but it was a phenomenon that John had witnessed on a number of occasions and he knew it would soon clear. Saying that he was going to visit two of his tenant farmers, he left the house immediately after breakfast.

As he'd thought the mist gradually dispersed during his walk and by the time he reached the bay had completely cleared. The wintery sun shone down from a clear sky. He stood above the bay, drinking in the colourful beauty below that was matched by the azure of a tranquil sea.

He'd started for the path down when a prick of conscience stopped him. A tight feeling in his stomach troubled him and his mind had misgivings about what he was doing here. Thoughts battled within him: to approve a painting; to meet a beautiful young woman; in friendship, nothing more; as patron of a work of art; to test himself; to purge himself of the desire he knew he had been growing; to put an end to a relationship that could only spell disaster for both of them ... But there was no relationship, not really, and did he not wish there was? He could turn back from it now, but then this place that held so much enchantment for him would be marred for him, never to be magical again, never to be filled with the joy it had filled him with from the first day he had seen it. Seen her.

He slid carefully down the slope hidden by bushes and undergrowth, negotiated the outcrops of rock successfully and dropped the last few feet on to the sand. He recovered his breath as he stood gazing across the strand to the cliffs that enclosed the bay, bringing peace and seclusion.

After a few minutes he walked slowly across the sand to a group of boulders that at some time in the past had tumbled from the cliff to lie in confusion at its foot. Reaching them, he chose a position from which he couldn't be seen but from which he could see Lydia start the first part of the descent. Only his footprints marked his passage.

Lydia felt a surge of excitement as she gathered up her artist's materials and unfinished painting. The day had developed as she had hoped, sunny but fresh with clear skies. A day to feel joy and gladness in the heart – and she was going to meet a man with whom she had fallen in love. He did not know it; she could never tell him, he was married. And yet as she reminded herself of these things another part of her did not care. She could love John from afar, but would that be enough? She told herself that it would have to be and was determined to draw joy from it.

She left the house with a brisk light step which slowed as she neared the bay. Her heart was racing. Would she be first or would John be there already? Maybe he wouldn't come? Maybe he had forgotten? There could be a thousand and one reasons for him not to appear.

There were footprints in the sand! Her thoughts went topsy-turvy and her heart raced. New sensations surged through her. She wanted to be with him, be there in front of him with his eyes fixed only on her. Without hesitation she scrambled down to join him.

He saw her! Emotions were heightened, leaving him confused. He felt as though he should hide or walk away from this situation but he knew he did not want to. Besides, his footprints betrayed his presence. He rose to his feet and automatically went to meet Lydia. At first his steps were slow and then his eagerness to see her overcame his good sense and he hurried to join her. All he could think of was seeing her again. He reached the far side of the bay before she was at the bottom of the cliff. Knowing exactly where she would emerge, he waited. The moments ticked by. It seemed an eternity. Then she was there, negotiating the last few feet and an awkward drop.

'Mr Mitchell,' she called. In that moment, with her mind diverted from her descent, Lydia stumbled. Her materials flew from her hands as she tried to steady herself and stop the painting from falling too. She managed that but did not save herself from toppling backwards and sliding the few yards to the final drop. She cried out as she plunged down. Everything seemed to whirl around her and she tensed herself against the impact. Instead she felt strong arms envelop her and a firm body take her weight. The painting slipped from her grasp and dropped to the sand.

'Miss Booth! Are you all right?' John's voice was full of concern.

She gasped for breath and struggled to hide her embarrassment. 'Oh yes. I ... er ... I ...'

'Just sit quietly for a moment. You've had a shock.'

She became aware that he still held her. How comforted and protected she felt. She looked up at him. 'Oh, Mr Mitchell, I'm sorry.'

He gave a little reassuring smile that turned her heart over as he said quietly. 'You have nothing to be sorry for, you did not fall on purpose. Thank goodness you weren't hurt.' He thought he should release his hold on her but having her in his arms sent a feeling through him he did not want to lose, and she did not seem to want to move away. His eyes met hers and unspoken words flowed between them, charged with meaning that neither of them could deny. Slowly their lips came together in a passionate kiss.

When they parted, John's voice was full of embarrassment and apology. 'Miss Booth, I'm sorry.'

She put a finger to his lips. 'Don't be. I'm not. Say no more about it.'

'But ...'

'You were going to say that it shouldn't have happened because you are a happily married man. I know that, Mr Mitchell. What has already happened, and anything that might, will always be a secret locked away in my heart.'

'I should have stopped ...'

'No, you shouldn't,' she interrupted. 'I will be so bold as to say I've dreamed of that happening ever since the first time I met you. It is I who should have resisted such thoughts.'

'Miss Booth, there can be no future between us.'

'I know that, and would not want to break up a happy marriage.'

He looked askance at her. 'You mean, you want a relationship between us to develop nevertheless?'

'If that is what you would like and it can remain a secret, known to no one.'

'Miss Booth, you know what you are saying?'

'Yes. I cannot deny I fell in love that moment I saw you. I cannot explain why. It was as if an arrow had pierced my heart, releasing every emotion of love that was there. Don't deny me my feelings, I would be devastated if you did and I could no longer experience my love for you. I think you are gentlemanly enough not to do that.'

John hesitated, torn between what he knew he really should do and what he wanted – to love this attractive young woman who made his heart sing every time he thought about her. 'Miss Booth,' he said gently, 'I cannot deny that I was attracted to you from the first moment I saw you, but being a married man I was afraid to let such an emotion have an outlet. Yet I think you and I both sensed the attraction between us.'

She nodded but did not speak. She knew he was wrestling with his conscience. She waited, tense in the knowledge that his decision could tear her heart out.

'Miss Booth.' John's voice was quiet but she sensed the emotion in it. 'I can offer you no more than a secret love. I love my wife. I would not want to hurt her.'

'And I do not wish to usurp her place,' Lydia said quickly but with firm assurance.

'In company there must be no sign of our feelings for each other. Outside of that, perhaps from time to time we can meet here or in an old empty cottage in the little valley that lies close to the boundary between Penorna and Trethtowan Estates.'

'I know it.'

John gave her a questioning look and she nodded. There was no need for further words to seal what passed between them; the touch of their lips did that.

516

Chapter Eleven

The early January snow of 1786 had disappeared except for a few pockets. 'I'm going to the mine this morning,' John announced at breakfast. 'They may be going to blast, see if the seam that is being worked runs further west. If it does there's a possibility it goes even further. Another piece of dynamiting will show us everything. If it is positive it will take us into land that Gaisford wants to buy.'

Eliza came to the stable yard to see her husband leave. He was ready to mount his horse when she stopped him, kissing him on the cheek and saying, 'If you go down that mine, be careful.'

'I will,' he reassured her.

'Good morning, Wallace,' called John as he halted his horse and the mine manager came out of his hut to meet him.

'Morning, sir.' He eyed his employer with a sense of satisfaction that the good will and investment in the mine Mr Mitchell's uncle had established had been continued by his nephew. In the years since John Mitchell's arrival a good rapport had built up between himself and the miners.

'All set to blast today?'

'Aye, sir. Welburn was keen to do it, but on examining his hand I decided to leave it to Lund. The cut hasn't healed properly.'

'Was Welburn satisfied with your decision? I don't want to lose him.'

'Yes. He saw sense when I explained why I thought he should not handle explosives for at least another two weeks.'

'Good.' They started to walk towards the mine-shaft. 'Pumps working?'

'Aye, sir! That new one you had installed six months ago is a great improvement. it's pushing out about five hundred gallons a minute and enabling us to go where we would never have been able to before. Like the seam where we'll be blasting today.'

'And if we find new ones, as we hope, that will mean greater production and more profit. I'll see to it that it puts more money in the men's pockets.'

'That's generous of you, sir.'

'Not at all, they are responsible for it.'

'But it's your investment.'

'We are all in this together, Wallace.'

'It's a pity all mine owners don't share your attitude, sir. Cornwall would be a better place if they did. Exploitation of miners is rife in the county as owners line their own pockets.'

'Greed, I'm sorry to say, Wallace.'

'Aye. And it'll get worse at the Gaisford mines when Mr Jeremy takes over. I hear tell his father isn't too well again.' Wallace pulled himself up sharp then, thinking he had said too much. 'Sorry, sir, I shouldn't be criticising my betters.'

'Don't apologise, Wallace. I sympathise with your opinion.' John left a little pause and then added, 'I didn't know Mr Miles wasn't well again.'

'A recurrence of the trouble he had a while back, shortly before you went north, sir.'

John nodded and their conversation halted as they had reached the shaft head. Several miners in flannel trousers, shirts and heavy boots were already queuing to descend. Light-hearted banter passed between them to take their minds off the grim conditions in which they would work. There'd be no light except from the candles secured by lumps of clay to the convex crowns of their resin-impregnated felt hats. They would descend on wooden ladders to the first workings, about three hundred feet below, and then walk along a tunnel that gradually decreased in height and width until for the final yards they'd have to crawl. The air would progressively turn fouler and the temperature soar until it became unbearable to wear their shirts, and once work started the dust would make it hard to breathe at times. Yet there was a camaraderie second to none among these men, and also among their families for many wives would be working as bal maidens at the pit head, some in the dangerous occupation of crushing the copper ore with large hammers on iron anvils, their heads protected from flying chips by large hats covering their faces.

John Mitchell's workers knew they were luckier than most, for he did his best under the circumstances to provide them with some safety measures underground, and on the surface had erected open-sided sheds to afford workers some shelter from the weather. He also gave the children easier tasks whereas many other employers gave age or sex little consideration when allotting work on the surface, and expected young boys to work hard alongside the men below the surface.

The Penorna miners valued the fact that their employer sometimes joined them below ground even though he left the active work to them. They appreciated his understanding that they were the experts in this arduous task and he was not.

The straight descent was precarious, the ladder narrow though firmly secured to the rock and every man under instruction to report immediately any loose hold he might note.

Reaching the line they would be working on today, John asked to be shown exactly what was to happen. Bert Wallace led the way along the tunnel past a line of men. They eyed John, nodded, or touched their felt hats in respect. He nodded back or gave a word of encouragement. When the tunnel narrowed he and the manager were alone until, after crawling the last few yards, they emerged into a small area that had been widened enough to hold five men and made high enough for them to kneel upright.

Jim Lund and his two assistants were already there. Bert Wallace made hasty introductions, momentarily stopping the two men who were striking the bit to make a hole for the explosive. As Art Preston and Wes Maidstone resumed their task, Lund explained what he wanted to achieve.

'I'm placing a medium-sized charge there to open suffi-cient rock face to let us see what lies beyond and what it is likely to lead to. If it is satisfactory then I'll open up a large area in which the men can work.'

John nodded his understanding. He watched, feeling all the while the choking dust rise from the continual battering the rock face was undergoing, but he was determined not to retreat until it was necessary.

After a while, covered in dust, Art raised a hand and a sweat-covered Wes stopped hammering at the bit and drew a deep breath of relief in spite of the dust-laden air. Art glanced at Jim who shuffled to the hole that had been beaten in the rock. He examined it carefully and raised his thumb. With a glance at John and Bert he said, 'I'll get it ready now.'

The other four knew this was a signal for them to retreat. This they did without any haste as that could lead to a fatal loss of concentration in manoeuvring through the narrow tun-nel back to the main hall where the miners were waiting to move in after the rock had been blasted open. The manager made sure that they were all out of danger and then waited patiently for Jim to appear after he had completed packing the explosive to his liking.

It seemed like an eternity to the waiting miners who gave a little cheer when he eventually appeared, not by way of greet-ing but as a release of pent-up tension.

Jim cast a quick glance along the tunnel and, satisfied that no one should be in danger, crawled a few feet back the way he had just come. Then he scrambled back quickly and every-one knew that the trail of gunpowder that would reach the fuse and dynamite had been lit. Men clamped their hands over their ears, some remaining upright, pressing back against the rock face, while others preferred to crouch as if to protect themselves against a foe. An uncanny silence descended on the tunnel; even the movement of dust in the air seemed to be stilled. Tension heightened. Minds queried, shouldn't it have gone off before now? Something must have gone wrong. Is Lund going to have to go back? Then all thoughts were shat-tered by an explosion that sent air-waves sweeping back through the tunnel, buffeting the men that stood there. Dust swirled and thickened until each man could hardly see his neighbour. The crash of falling rock reverberated back through the tunnel. Slowly the noise died away; dust began to settle; men looked eagerly at each other from grimy faces.

John stepped back towards the narrow tunnel that would lead them to whatever the explosion had uncovered.

Bert Wallace touched his arm. 'Not yet, sir! Lund goes first – a tradition of his that he has never broken. If things haven't gone as planned he wants to know first.'

John nodded and wiped dust from his lips.

Lund was already crawling through the tunnel. Everyone waited anxiously until his head reappeared and they saw his face wreathed in a broad smile. He scrambled to his feet and held up both thumbs which raised a relieved cheer that rippled along the tunnel. There would be hard work ahead but it meant that there would be more ore to mine and continued employment.

The manager got into urgent conversation with Lund then turned to the rest of the men. He called two of them forward and put them in charge of two gangs. The first would go into action widening the narrow part of the tunnel and then the second gang would move in as soon as was practical to clear the chamber opened up by the charge. But first he wanted to see for himself the result of the blast. He glanced at John. 'You coming through, sir?'

'Try keeping me back,' he replied with a grin. He followed his manager through the narrow tunnel to find the rock face of the chamber torn apart, but Lund's skill in placing the dynamite had made sure it had not undermined the stability of the chamber roof. Men could safely work to clear it and get to the ore that had been exposed.

'It looks to be a rich vein, sir,' called Bert with delight.

'It does,' agreed John, pleased with the way he had adapted to this life which was so different from the one he had led in Whitby.

He summed up their position underground in relation to the surface and judged in which direction Selwyn's land lay. If the ore they had uncovered now spread in that direction then Gaisford's assessment had been correct. It would also mean that if Selwyn was in agreement, he and John could join the two mines and work the new veins underground, using the present outlets, without marring the surface as Gasiford would have done.

John drew the manager and Lund to one side. 'This is a good sign. I think there might be more ore to the left of this chamber and the tunnel we will be driving now to get this ore out.'

'It is possible, sir,' agreed Wallace. 'In fact, I would say more than likely, but if we go too far that way we will be getting into Mr Westbury's land.'

'Yes, I know. There might be an advantage in joining up with him, if he is agreeable, but leave all that to me. We won't tackle the next blast until I have discussed it with him. if he doesn't like the idea we can try another direction.'

'Very good, sir.'

Already they could hear the men making a start on widening the narrow part of the tunnel.

When John and the manager finally climbed out of the shaft on to the surface they breathed heavily on the pure clean air.

John's lips tightened. 'I wish I could do more to eliminate the dust from down there but until someone invents a more powerful air pump I can't. And I don't like to see young lads of seven or eight working the pump. Get some older ones on.'

'But the families of those lads depend on their contribution to the household.'

'Give them some other work on the surface then.'

'But, sir, we are working to capacity up here.'

John cast his eyes over the constant activity: boys and girls trundling ore from the pit head to the bal maidens who wielded hammers to break it up; boys bent double jiggling large sieves, and women dressing the ore. He gave a little shake of his head. This was far from satisfactory; employment should be less exacting than this. He knew his uncle must have been a man who looked ahead. Maybe he could be the same. But he could never do what he really desired for his workers, that would cost far too much money. Still, he would do what he could. He had already seen that their cottages were better maintained and the wages he paid, while far from what he would have liked, were better than most other employers provided. It was conditions at the mine that troubled him most but there was little he could do about underground working. Maybe there was more he could do on the surface.

John screwed up his face in thought then said, 'Wallace, those boys at present employed on the air pump, set them on with some carpenters to make those open-sided sheds more weather-proof for the bal maidens. They're still exposed to driving rain and wind at the moment. And let's try and give them something more solid to stand on. It can't be good for them to be working on wet ground.'

'Yes, sir!' Bert's reply was brisk, indicating approval of what would be seen as revolutionary by some mine owners.

'I've heard that two of the big mines have built what they are calling drys – rooms where the miners can have a wash down and change into clean clothes before leaving for home.'

'I've heard tell of them too, sir.'

'Look into it, Wallace, and I'll do the same. We'll compare notes then and see if we can do anything similar here. I've been here long enough now to be able to make changes and hopefully improve conditions.'

'Yes sir! This is very thoughtful of you. Everyone will appreciate any changes for the better.'

'Don't say anything about this last idea until we have looked into it because it will have to be financed from the profits I can see being made if Mr Westbury and I join up below ground. But we want to move fairly quickly so that once the carpenters have finished work on those sheds we can turn them on to constructing the drys.'

'Very good, sir.'

'I look forward to hearing your calculations of the yield that was revealed today.

'I should have a good idea in a couple of days, sir.'

'Good.' John walked to his horse, satisfied with the way things had gone below ground and with the development of his ideas for improvements on the surface. He had a strange feeling that his uncle's influence was still being exerted around here and that he was only doing what Gerard would have done himself had he lived.

Bert Wallace watched him go, thankful that Mr Mitchell was walking in his uncle's philanthropic footsteps.

Eliza was pleased to see her husband riding towards the house and acknowledged his wave as he turned his horse towards the stable yard. Nevertheless a flutter of anxiety swept through her on seeing his dust-covered appearance. She knew he had been below ground and realised the danger he would have been in. She had heard people talk about conditions in the mines and was always anxious when John left to visit his even though she knew he did not always go below ground. She wondered why he had been there today.

She allowed him time to wash and change before she went into the house. He was coming down the stairs as she stepped into the hall. She sensed excitement in him as he took her hand and they went to the drawing room together.

'We discovered another good vein today,' he said, and went on to explain how this had come about. 'It seems likely it will join with Selwyn's. I'm going to have a word with him about it.'

'So Mr Gaisford was right!' commented Eliza.

'Yes.'

'I'm going to propose to Selwyn we break through. If the result is what I think it will be, we'll form a partnership in one big mine.'

'Won't new diggings mar the countryside which is the one thing you both swore to avoid?'

'I believe that if we share each other's shafts we will have enough access without making more, which is what Mr Gaisford would have done had we sold to him. I'll go to see Selwyn in the morning.'

The fine weather tempted John to walk to Trethtowan; he felt closer to the countryside and its beauty on foot than he did when he rode. It also gave him time to think. Today two things occupied his mind: the news and proposals he was bringing Selwyn, and his own relationship with Lydia Booth.

From a distance he saw Lydia leave the house with her artist's materials and canvas and judged that she would be going to their bay. Keeping to their agreement, neither acknowledged the other openly. To wave from such a distance would have indicated to others that there was a close friendship between them, and neither wanted public speculation about that.

He saw Selwyn busily poring over some papers on the terrace but when his friend looked up and saw him, he gathered the papers together and came to meet him.

'Good day, John,' he called. 'What brings you here this fine day?'

'I have news, Selwyn. Can we walk in the garden?'

'Of course,' he agreed, wondering what the news was that had brought such excitement to John's voice.

They fell into step, strolling in the rose garden down lavender-lined paths and on into the herbaceous area beyond. As they circled the lily pond John unfolded his story. When he had finished relating the facts about yesterday's blast he posed the question: 'Are you agreeable to my blasting through to your land?'

'Yes, why not?' Selwyn had become more intrigued as John's story had unfolded and he saw the possibilities of their working a large mine together. 'I suggest we first attempt a tunnel wide enough for a man to crawl down and make an examination. Then, if that proves successful, we'll move into a large-scale operation.'

'That is what I was going to propose. Do you want me to drive the tunnel from my side?'

'That would seem to be the sensible thing to do as you have been blasting there and, from what you have said, already have a good idea of the direction to take.'

'Very good. I'll discuss this with my manager and dynamite-handler tomorrow.'

'Then let me know when you propose to blast and I'll see my men are well clear.'

John felt that ease of mind that only comes when events fall into place. Advances at the mine heralded the possibility of greater profits. Besides that his visit to Whitby had been successful, and though it had had its nostalgic moments he had looked forward to returning to Cornwall, to Eliza and Abigail and now a third woman in his life. All was good with John's world and he strode out with a light step.

Reaching the bay, he did not hesitate but descended the steep path quickly. At the bottom he stopped and looked around him, mystified. There was no sign of Miss Booth nor any footprints in the sand. He had seen her with her art materials and had felt sure she would be here. Perplexed, his heart sinking, he turned his head this way and that, searching from where he stood. No one, no sign of movement. His lips set in a line of disappointment. He shrugged his shoulders resignedly and had started to turn back to the path up the cliffside when teasing laughter rippled from behind him. He spun round and saw a vision of beauty emerge from a narrow cleft in the rock face.

'From the look on your face I know you care.' Her soft tone caressed him, like gentle music on his ears.

His eyes devoured her. He did not speak but held out his arms.

She came to him and let him enfold her.

There were three customers in the Waning Moon when Jeremy Gaisford, paying his weekly visit, shut the door quickly behind him to keep out the rising wind blowing in from the west. Though it howled around the eaves and corners it carried no threat of rain, but Jeremy had been glad he had chosen his long coat with its large collar which he had turned up as he crossed the high moor. Now he turned it down and shrugged himself out of the coat. He gave a brief curt nod to the three men inside, two of whom were strangers, and showed no sign of recognising Jim Lund. He was pleased to see him there, of course, for it meant that the man must have some information.

'Evening, landlord,' said Jeremy, as he came to the counter. 'A tankard, if you please.'

'Aye, sir.' He drew the ale. 'Wind rising this evening, wouldn't like to be at sea.'

'Nor I, landlord.' He took his ale and went to sit at a corner table that gave him a view of the room. He eyed the strangers and concluded they were travellers, pausing on their journey to slake their thirst. He judged they would want to be at their destination before nightfall and so would not be long in leaving. Ten minutes later he was proved right for the men put on their coats and hats, bade the landlord good night and left.

Jim Lund picked up his tankard and crossed the room to sit opposite his employer.

'Another drink each, Tom,' called Jeremy.

The landlord nodded, drew the ale and brought it to them. Jeremy handed him a coin and told him to have one himself. Tom, not invited to join them, knew something very private was about to be discussed.

'Well?' prompted Jeremy.

Jim leaned forward. 'Today we blasted in the chamber I told you about before.'

'And?'

'We uncovered a vein that looks very promising. When that has been properly opened up, Mr Mitchell is talking about blasting on its west side.'

'And if he does, that could join him up with Westbury,' Jeremy said thoughtfully.

'Aye, and if they decide to open up their mines into one and work together they can use the shafts each already has to ship the copper out. That will save expense.'

'They'll work together for certain. It will be no good Father trying to buy that land from them now they know what lies beneath the surface.' Jeremy paused, set his lips tight in thought, then slapped the table hard. 'All right, put the next part of the plan into operation as soon as you think it wise. You know what I want.'

Two days later John visited his mine again and discussed the plan to blast a small exploratory tunnel in the direction of the Trethtowan workings.

'If that is successful in telling us what we want to know, then carry on,' he instructed Wallace and Lund. 'I'll warn Mr Westbury to keep his workers clear of that particular area from tomorrow until he hears from me again.'

After he had left, the two men went below ground and planned how they would go about making the necessary blast to open up a small tunnel. Wallace left much of the actual final arrangements and placement of the dynamite to the expert – Lund.

The following day Wallace saw that the necessary area underground was clear of miners and then joined Lund and his two assistants. Preston and Maidstone were already at work making the hole Lund required for his dynamite. Wallace had little to say but observed the meticulous care Lund took. He was not surprised when later that day, after the explosion had been made, there was a reasonable hole through which he could crawl to make his examination. He re-emerged with a broad smile on his dusty face.

'It's good. Looks like a rich vein links the Penorna and Trethtowan mines.'

'Do you want us to carry on then?' asked Jim.

'Aye. Plan to make the next blast tomorrow.'

After he had gone Jim examined the chamber they were in and the tunnel he had just created. By the time he left the mine he knew exactly what he was going to do and as he walked home he smiled at the thought of the Gaisford money that would soon be jangling in his pocket.

John was on the terrace the following morning when his attention was caught by the sound of a galloping horse. When the rider came in sight he immediately sensed trouble. His fears were heightened when he recognised his mine manager's horse and saw that the rider was a grime-covered youngster.

'Mr Mitchell! Mr Mitchell!' he yelled, hauling on the reins. 'Trouble at the mine!' The horse struggled against the tight reins and the boy fought for control. 'Bad rockfall. Mr Wallace said to come at once.' The horse was still champing at the bit, seeking to free itself.

John leaped down the steps and raced for the stables, shouting over his shoulder, 'Wait for me.'

When he emerged from the stable yard a few minutes later the boy immediately turned his horse alongside John's and matched his gallop stride for stride.

'What's happened?' yelled John.

'Not sure, sir! Something to do with Jim Lund's blasting.'

'How bad? Anyone hurt?'

'Don't think so. Mr Wallace had the tunnels cleared but I think it's a bad fall.'

John realised the boy knew no more and, with the horses at full tilt, concentrated on reaching the mine as soon as possible.

Men from below ground were gathered at the pit head in groups. Surface workers stood idly by their work spots. Overall there was a buzz of speculation. John spotted Wallace and Lund, who seemed to be arguing, close to the shaft head. With concern in his eyes he rode straight over to them and dropped from the saddle.

'What happened?' he demanded.

'Explosion went wrong, sir,' replied his manager.

'How wrong? Anyone hurt?'

'No one, sir. All the tunnels were cleared beforehand.'

'Good,' John said with obvious relief. Injuries and loss of life were the last things he wanted. 'So what's the damage?'

'Bad, sir.' He hesitated a moment as if reluctant to disclose the facts, then realised he had no choice. 'Yesterday Lund opened up a small tunnel as agreed. It turned out to be as we'd hoped, indicating that there is a rich vein joining the Penorna and Trethtowan workings. We decided to open it further today.'

'So what went wrong?' John shot his question at Lund.

'After examining what we had achieved yesterday, sir, I decided that it was possible not only to open that small tunnel further but also to enlarge it into a workable chamber from which it would be easier to access the Trethtowan mine. I hoped I could at the same time enlarge the way to what was our working chamber . . .'

'But that would mean using dynamite dangerously in excess of what we have been using,' rapped John angrily. 'And what exactly do you mean by what *was* our working chamber?

Lund's lips tightened. 'It's completely blocked now, sir. The roof caved in.'

'What?' John's face showed his shock. He glanced at the manager for explanation. 'Didn't you supervise this?'

'Yes, sir! We had agreed on what should be done, and that did not include opening up the way to our chamber at this stage – that could have come later.'

John turned on Lund. 'So you went against . . .'

'Sir,' he broke in. 'I thought it safe to do so, and that it would save time.'

'You should have stuck by our original arrangements,' snapped Wallace. 'You knew that you were going to have to use more dynamite in a very restricted area.'

'All right,' broke in John. 'What's done is done. We cannot put it back to what it was. Just tell me how this is going to affect production?'

'We will have to turn men to clearing a tremendous fall if you still want to join the two mines, but that is going to take time.'

'So that will affect our output?'

'Yes. Unless you take on more men especially to do the clearing, but that would prove costly.'

John nodded thoughtfully. 'Let's just get people back to work and I'll give some thought as to what should best be done.'

'Very good, sir.' The manager hurried away and soon had the Penorna employees back at their respective jobs.

'Not you, Lund,' John said as the dynamite-handler started to walk away. 'I want you to tell me exactly what you did and what happened.'

He listened carefully to what Lund had to say and when he had dismissed him called over Preston and Maidstone. He questioned them and found their version of events corroborated Lund's.

John had much to think about as he rode slowly home.

Eliza heard him come in and left her parlour to rush down the stairs to greet him. 'What happened, John?' Seeing his distress, she led him to the drawing room where she poured him a glass of whisky. He accepted gratefully, sat down and told her what had happened.

'Let us be thankful that no one was hurt,' she comforted him.

He nodded. 'That's the positive way to look at it.'

'It's the only way. When you've made a proper assessment you'll have to decide if it is worthwhile clearing this rock fall.'

'It puzzles me why it happened at all. Lund seemed so competent. When you hired him, did you have any recommendations?'

'Mr Wallace and Mr Welburn had heard that the Gaisfords thought highly of him.'

'Then why sack him?'

'Belligerent to Mr Jeremy, it was said.'

'And the other two?

'Supported Lund.'

John played with his glass thoughtfully.

Eliza eyed him. 'You have something on your mind, what is it?'

'The circumstances of his dismissal and engagement were very similar to the Lowthers'.'

'But the Lowthers are good workers, aren't they?'

'Yes, I have no complaints against them. I was merely drawing the comparison with the way Lund came to us.'

Eliza looked puzzled.

531

'Supposing the Gaisfords set up the dismissal of Lund and his friends, knowing we were likely to engage them. After all, we had done the same when the Lowthers were sacked.'

'You mean, they were planting them on us for a purpose, to cause trouble because you would not sell the land?'

'Yes.'

'But the Gaisfords would know you already had a competent dynamite-handler in Mr Welburn. You weren't likely to hand that job over to Lund.'

'Right, but Welburn was injured and *that* happened while he was helping Lund.'

'You think Lund arranged that injury?'

'He could have.'

'So that he was in a position to cause this rock fall?'

'Exactly.'

'But you've no proof.'

'And never will have. They're too smart for that.'

'What are you going to do about Lund and the other two?'

'Keep them on, but keep an eye on them too. I had better appraise Selwyn of the situation. I'd rather do it before he hears about it from anyone else.'

When John had acquainted his friend with what had happened and went on to theorise about Lund's part in it, Selwyn was inclined to agree and also approved of his decision not to sack the three men.

'We'll have to assess what can be done. If we think it's still financially viable to clear the fall in order to make one big mine, we shall share the expense of the clearance even though the fall is on your side,' said his friend.

'That is generous of you. I'll arrange a meeting with you at the mine.'

Jeremy Gaisford received Jim Lund's report at the Waning Moon with delight and paid him generously. He was amazed that Mitchell had not sacked Lund, however.

'Be careful how you behave. One false step now could

arouse Mitchell's suspicions. See that Maidstone and Preston understand that. You might still prove useful to me.'

Jeremy rode home in good spirits but they vanished when he recounted in detail what Lund had accomplished and saw his father's face darken with anger.

'Fool! Did you countenance causing such damage?'

'I left that to Lund.'

'Did you not instruct him in what I wanted doing?'

'Yes.'

'*Exactly* what I wanted?'

'I told him to cause a rock fall that would disrupt the mine.'

'Is that all?'

'Yes. What else did you want?'

Miles scowled. His lips tightened with irritation.

'When will you learn to follow my instructions to the letter? Why don't you pay attention to detail? Why don't you listen? Are you incapable?' With each question he thumped the arm of his chair. 'I distinctly told you that any disruption was to make Mitchell think it would be better to sell to us, not to wreak such havoc that it would make him suspicious we still wanted to buy. Who would buy from him now when to put such havoc right would cost a fortune?'

Jeremy felt his pulses racing. 'Why blame me?' he snapped. 'I didn't lay the dynamite.'

'No, but it was your responsibility to see that Lund understood exactly what was expected of him. You're an incompetent fool! I wish Logan were the eldest. God knows what will happen to this estate when *you* get your hands on it. More's the pity my hands are tied by a trust that states the eldest son must always inherit Senewey. Damn whoever laid that down!' Miles was shaking as he spat the words out. He glared at his son. 'Get out! Get out now!'

Angry words sprang to Jeremy's lips but he thought better than to voice them and started for the door. 'And you're a coward! Daren't stand up to your own father, frightened to say what you think.' Stung by his words, Jeremy swung round. His face was a mask of hatred. He saw Miles's hands pushing against the arms of his chair. He was half out of his seat. Their eyes met, Jeremy's filled with enmity, his father's with disgust. 'Get out! Get . . .'

The words choked in Miles's throat and were replaced by a gurgling sound. He clutched at his chest and slumped back in his chair. His eyes widened. Jeremy felt their gaze penetrating his very soul. He stepped towards his father, then he stopped. A small smile of contempt mingled with satisfaction as he ignored Miles's attempt to reach out to him.

'My help? You want my help now?' he mocked. 'You've just been telling me how useless I am. Well, I'm not going to risk that happening again.'

He smiled as he watched his father die.

Chapter Twelve

Landowners from all over the county came to pay their last respects to Miles Gaisford. They filled the small church and filed out to join Senewey Estate workers and miners who had had to wait outside in the bleak damp March wind that blew in from the Atlantic. Not many truly mourned this man's passing but they were all there out of respect for Cornwall's foremost family and for Rowena who they noted was escorted by Logan – had Jeremy taken over Senewey completely? They knew Miles had kept a tight rein on certain aspects of his sons' lives, especially the running of the estate. Now, many of them wondered what the future held for Senewey with Jeremy at the helm. Not least among them John Mitchell.

He had paid his own respects and was turning away when Jeremy's cold voice stopped him.

'Mitchell, what a pity you didn't sell that land to my father. now you are faced with an expensive disaster. Not only that, he would still be alive today if you had obliged him.' He charged the last sentence with accusation.

It sent a chill through John. 'What do you mean by that?'

'Your refusal brought on the attack from which he never fully recovered and that finally brought about his death. You are to blame, Mitchell, and I'll not forget it.' Jeremy gave John a dismissive look and turned away to accept condolences from a sympathiser, easier in his mind now that he had put the blame on someone else.

John was tempted to accuse him of instigating the recent disaster at the mine but without proof it was too dangerous. As he left Senewey, John wondered what the future might bring. His thoughts were centred on the troubled relationship with Jeremy Gaisford, but it was another relationship that was to turn his world upside down, 10 April 1786 would always live in his memory.

Mr Mitchell, I have something to tell you but first I want you to see the finished painting.'

'Finished? I was not expecting it so soon.'

'There was a reason why I pressed on with it, Mr Mitchell.'

'Mr Mitchell?'

'A wise precaution. If we used Christian names in private then their use might become too familiar to us and we might slip up in company.'

He nodded his understanding and agreed that they should continue in the same way. He did not like the formality but saw the wisdom of Lydia's reasoning, and he wanted nothing to mar the joy of their weekly meeting in private.

'So, let me see the painting.'

With its back to him she unwrapped the canvas carefully. She was watching his face carefully when she finally turned it round and saw John's expression change to one of wonder and joy.

He stared at the painting for what seemed an age, then looked up slowly and locked eyes with her. 'That is wonderful. You have captured the very essence of our bay. It will always bring you close to me whenever I look at it.' As he was speaking he came to her. She knew exactly what was going to happen then so turned the painting to one side and allowed it to fall gently back on to the sand. He kissed her passionately as his arms enfolded her. Lydia accepted his kiss, feeling safe in the comfort of his love. When their lips parted she laid her head against his chest and shivered while his fingers gently stroked her neck. 'John, I said I had something to tell you.' She paused, half expecting him to prompt her, but lost in the joy of holding her he did not. She went on without any preamble, 'I am going to have a baby.'

For a moment his world stood still, blocking out her words, but in that moment the enormity of what had happened bit deep. He had betrayed Eliza, dear precious Eliza around whom his life had hitherto revolved. The woman who had supported him in everything he did, had borne his beautiful daughter, shared so much with him and with whom he wanted to go on sharing life. Why on earth had he allowed his interest in Lydia Booth to develop this far?

She read something in his expression that she'd hoped she would not see. 'You are angry . . . you don't want this child?' She looked up at him with accusing eyes.

He pushed her away but only far enough for him to hold her by the arms and look into her eyes. 'I'm not angry, but are you sure? I thought we . . .'

She did not let him finish. 'So did I, but it has happened.'

John shrugged his shoulders in acceptance. 'Are you happy about it?'

She nodded. 'Yes. I will always have something of you now.'

The sincerity of her reply smote his heart. 'I love you, Lydia Booth,' he whispered, drawing her close. He kissed her again, but when their lips parted practicalities were foremost in his mind. 'I must think what to do for the best. I want no scandal to fall on you.'

'It won't, and no stain will touch you if you agree to what I propose.'

'You've thought it out?'

'Yes. I love you too much to come whining to you, expecting you to solve my dilemma.'

'Our dilemma! We have caused this, we will see it through together.'

'I will leave Cornwall . . .'

'You can't!' he protested. 'I could not bear never seeing you again.'

'Nor I never seeing you! Hear me out. I will put it about that I am needed by my brother whose wife is having a baby and is extremely ill. I'll say he now lives in the North of England in a small village nobody's ever heard of, close to the Scottish Borders. No one will check that. I won't really go there; he wanted nothing to do with me when our parents died

537

so he'll show no concern for me now. I'll find somewhere else to go to have the baby. When I return I will say that the baby is my brother's but as his wife has died and he won't take any responsibility for it, I have agreed to bring it up.'

'I don't think anyone will question that, but we do have to find you somewhere to live. I have property in Penzance but if you move into one of those houses it could look a little suspicious. You know how people speculate.'

'Then I will have to find somewhere else.'

'You will need money to buy a house. I will provide that, and make you a regular allowance.'

'That is as I expected, but there is a condition to my return that you won't like. You'd better hear it now before making any more promises.' Her eyes were fixed intently on him so that she would not miss one moment of his reaction to what she was about to say. Wary of her words, he gave a questioning frown. 'You will have no personal contact with the child!'

A chill struck at his heart. 'What?'

'You will have no personal contact with the child!' she repeated in a voice so full of determination that it shocked him.

John spun away from her in disgust. 'Impossible!'

'I insist on it or I do not come back.'

'You can't mean it?' he cried, his face darkening.

'I do. it's the only sensible thing to do.'

'It's not!' His voice was sharp, matched by an expression clouded with anger. 'I will not be denied the right of seeing my own child grow up.'

'I'm not denying you that but there will be no personal contact.'

'I won't agree,' he stated resolutely.

'If you don't you'll wreck your marriage, wound Eliza and Abigail, and destroy our love for each other.' Lydia's voice broke with anguish. 'Be sensible. If you have a personal relationship with this child, it is more than likely your wife will get to know.'

'How, if we keep it secret?'

'*We* may be able to do that, but we can't expect the child to do so. It would see you, know you, and something would slip out in all innocence.' He looked doubtful. 'How would you explain your visits to a child who would want to know who you were? And that's another thing . . . you will not be able to visit me either.'

'What?' Astonished disbelief swam in John's eyes. 'So you are putting an end to our relationship, destroying our love?'

'No, I'm not!' she cried with an urgency that pleaded with him to understand. 'You love your wife and daughter. You don't want to hurt them. In my love for you, nor do I. If our child saw you in their company and inadvertently let slip that it knew you, don't you think they would begin to wonder why?' Her reasoning held him silent. 'You can see I'm right,' Lydia went on. 'Having no personal contact would ensure that did not happen. You can see him or her only from a distance. Passing in the street, there must be no acknowledgement. it is the only way. I insist on it, for the sake of our child I will not have hurt. It is for the good of us all.'

As she was speaking, the implications behind her reasoning began to make sense. Not only did John see that but, in her frankness and concern for all, he sensed a new bond of trust would be forged between them if he accepted.

'Maybe you are right.' Though there was a touch of doubt in his voice it had all but vanished from his mind and was completely obliterated when she spoke again.

'I *am* right, John. It's the only way if we are to remain near each other.'

He gave a small nod of acceptance, drew her close and kissed her.

Lydia felt relief to her very soul.

He looked thoughtful. 'Have you thought about where you will go to have the baby?'

'No. I haven't had much time to get used to the idea myself.'

'I think I have a solution, a place I know will be reliable and not a word will ever be breathed about. The secret will be safe forever.'

She looked at him with eager expectancy. This was the one aspect of her pregnancy that had troubled her, but one that she had been determined to solve to their advantage. Now a solution might be within her grasp.

'You will go to my sister in Whitby. It is far enough away from here for no one to know. Martha and I are very close. She will help, and say nothing about you and the baby. She knows how to keep a secret even from my wife with whom she gets on well. She will know reliable people who will help with the birth and say nothing afterwards. How does that sound to you?'

'It's a gift from heaven.' Lydia's eyes shone brightly.

'Very well. I will accompany you to introduce you to my sister and offer her an explanation. You'll find her a very understanding person. I know she will not apportion blame.'

'But how will you explain your need to go to Whitby again?'

'There was some trouble in the business so I can quite openly pay her a visit again. After all, even though I draw nothing from the business, I still have an interest in it. While I am in Whitby I will set up an account into which I will put money so you can purchase a house on your return to Cornwall. It will also serve as a place to deposit your regular allowance.'

'That's wonderful.'

'But there is still the problem of where you can stay between your return to Cornwall and the purchase and setting up of your new household.'

'I think I can solve that. As you know, my family were friendly with the Westburys in Oxford. It was through that friendship that I was given the job of governess when times were hard for me. I am sure they will let me come back to them for a short while.'

'That certainly would be a solution,' he agreed.

'I can only ask. But that still does not give us a place to meet without the child knowing?'

'Hopefully one of my properties will become vacant and if it does we could have that as our meeting place. Now, the

540

sooner we go to Whitby the better, so no one here gets any inkling of your condition.'

'We cannot be seen leaving together.'

'I know, so here's what I propose. I will go by coach from Penzance, leaving next Thursday morning. I'll go only as far as Truro where I will stay at the Lion until your coach arrives two days later. I will join you there for our onward journey to Whitby together. I'm sure Mr and Mrs Westbury will take you to Penzance.'

'I will tell them the day after tomorrow that I have heard from my brother and wish to leave their employment.'

'That sounds satisfactory, but why not tomorrow?'

'Because I am delivering the painting to you then and have no doubt that they will want to accompany me to see your reaction. We don't want to risk their mentioning my leaving then.'

'Wise,' he agreed. 'So, after your visit, the next time I see you will be a week on Thursday in Truro.'

Lydia picked up the painting. 'I think we had better go. I'll bring this to your home tomorrow to present it to you and your wife. And, remember, act as if you have never seen it before.'

'Trust me. And, Lydia, it will mean so much more to me now.'

They parted with a kiss of promise and love.

'Ma'am, Mr John is here.'

The shock of this announcement brought Martha quickly to her feet. Dropping the book she had been reading, she was halfway across the drawing room when her brother walked in.

'John! How delightful!' She embraced him affectionately. As she kissed him on the cheek her attention was drawn to a well-dressed young lady standing in the doorway beyond.

John felt Martha's surprise. He stepped over to the new-comer and said, 'Martha, I want you to meet Miss Booth.'

Lydia, who had been apprehensive about this meeting, in spite of John's continual assurances during their journey together from Truro, took a tentative step into the room.

541

Martha moved to greet her with one hand held out. 'Miss Booth.' Her soft voice with its gentle accent helped to ease Lydia's concern but she saw curiosity in that gaze nevertheless.

'I am pleased to meet you, Miss Mitchell.'

Martha detected nervousness marring that pleasant voice. Questions were pouring into her mind but she could not ask them now. She shot a quick glance at her brother and saw something in his eyes as he looked at Miss Booth that set alarm coursing through her. She held it in check as she said, 'And I you, Miss Booth, welcome to my home. Won't you sit down?'

'Thank you.'

Martha indicated a chair and sat down herself when Lydia was seated. 'What brings you on this unexpected visit?' she asked, turning her eyes on her brother who had remained standing.

John had rehearsed this moment many times since he had made the decision to seek his sister's help.

'I would like you to accommodate Miss Booth for a little while.' The words came out not at all as he had planned for they had a nervous timbre to them that he knew would arouse his perceptive sister's curiosity. He went on quickly before Martha could say anything. 'Miss Booth is a dear friend who needs help. I would be grateful if you could do this for her.'

Tension had seeped into the room, in spite of John's efforts to keep it at bay. Martha, sensing that her brother did not want to offer a full explanation in front of the young lady, knew there was only one way to bring him relief and took it.

'Then I had better show her to the guest room and inform the staff that we will have visitors for a few days.' She stood up. 'Miss Booth.'

Recognising this as an invitation to follow, Lydia got to her feet. As she started after Martha she cast John an embarrassed plea to make sure everything would be accepted by his sister.

Martha paused in the hall to ring a hand bell that stood on a small oak table at the bottom of a staircase whose ramped banister of fine oak resting on handsome matching balusters gave a sense of permanence and security. That feeling persisted when a maid appeared, neat in her black dress and white apron, and Martha said, 'June, this is Miss Booth who will be staying with us. She is to have the first guest bedroom and you are to give her your special attention. I will acquaint Mrs Barton.'

'Yes, ma'am,' replied June. 'I'll take that, miss,' she added when she saw Lydia go to a valise.

'Thank you,' she replied quietly.

'Mrs Barton is my housekeeper. I will introduce you later,' explained Martha.

Lydia followed her up the stairs and was glad that there were no further questions as Martha kept the conversation going about the ease of their journey from Cornwall.

'I hope you will be comfortable here,' she said as she turned the knob on a heavy oak door that opened easily.

Lydia stifled a gasp when she found herself inside a large corner room with windows that gave a view of two different aspects of the garden and landscape beyond. The room was decorated in yellow giving it a bright sunny atmosphere that was reflected in the pristine white bedclothes. A dressing table was set neatly with all the necessary accoutrements and a large wardrobe was ready to store any clothes. Martha opened a door in one wall and Lydia saw it was a toilette area.

Jane, catching Martha's small wave of dismissal, had already left the room when Lydia said, 'Miss Mitchell, thank you for your kindness.'

When she replied, 'I love my brother very much,' it carried a wealth of meaning and Lydia knew that if she hurt John she would create an enemy for life in this woman. 'Freshen up, make yourself comfortable and come and join us in the drawing room in, say, twenty minutes. I'll order some tea for then.'

Lydia gave a small nod. She offered no further explanation of why she was here; John would do that. Martha sought none for she too knew that it had to come from her brother.

She hurried down the stairs, made a quick visit to the kitchen and then returned to the drawing room. The door had hardly clicked shut behind her when she said in a demanding tone that had some anger in it, 'An explanation, John, please.'

He hesitated. This was a confrontation he had already gone over and over in his mind but now, facing his sister, he was embarrassed and all the words had fled from his mind.

'The beginning is a good place to start,' snapped Martha. The touch of irritation in her voice was accompanied by the reproach in her eyes and he knew she had already surmised some of the truth.

'I fell in love,' he said lamely.

'You what?' Her voice rose. 'I thought you loved Eliza?'

'I do.'

'So what is going to happen? Has this woman turned your head? She's a pretty little thing, I'll grant you that, but . . .'

'She's more,' he cut in.

'How can you say you love Eliza and still fall for this woman?' his sister demanded in disgust.

'I assure you it's possible,' he replied tersely but with marked conviction. He ignored his sister's protest and added, 'I'm staying with Eliza and she will never know of my relationship with Miss Booth.'

'And I suppose you are going to say she'll never know about the baby?' Martha gave a derisory shake of her head. 'Don't look surprised. These things happen, and why else would you bring her here but to avoid a scandal in Cornwall? What explanation did you give Eliza for your own visit?'

'A follow up on my last.'

'Very convenient for you,' returned Martha sarcastically. Then, regretting her tone, softened her voice as she asked, 'What do you want me to do?' She glanced at her fob-watch. 'Miss Booth will be joining us for tea in fifteen minutes.'

'I'd like you to look after her until after the baby is born.'

'You think that by your coming here, no word will ever get back to Cornwall?'

'How could it? Your servants need never know that Miss Booth's child is mine. I have merely brought the daughter of a friend here for your help, as far as they are concerned. You can even use the story we are using when Lydia returns to Cornwall.' He explained that.

'We'll see, but they can be adept at putting two and two together.'

'I know that a timely word from you will suffice to stem any gossip. They are loyal to you because you treat them well and would not want to lose their employment with you or have you spread word that would preclude them from obtaining other work in this district.'

'You are very perceptive.'

'Then you'll help?'

'Who am I to refuse my brother? And of course I owe you something in return for you saving me from Mr Horton's machinations.'

'That never entered my head.' John exchanged a small knowing smile with her.

A knock on the door heralded June and another maid with the tea. As they were leaving Martha said, 'June, will you tell Miss Booth tea is served?' A few moments later Lydia tentatively entered the room.

'Come in,' said Martha in a tone that still held some hostility. 'Sit down there,' she added, indicating a chair. She saw Lydia glance anxiously at John. 'My brother has told me everything,' she said tersely. 'You are welcome to stay here, and rest assured you will be well looked after with no scandal. I have friends who will attend the baby's birth, and all my staff know how to be discreet. I will think up a story to tell them, maybe even say your brother would not take you in after an indiscretion.'

The draining of tension from Lydia was visible. 'Miss Mitchell, how can I ever thank you – except to assure you that no harm will come to your brother's marriage. I love him too much to let that happen.'

'See that it doesn't, Miss Booth. Though I don't condone what has happened, I will have to come to terms with it and you and I will have to get to know each other better.' Martha started to pour the tea and John handed it to Lydia along with a scone and some jam. In a more relaxed atmosphere, in the

545

company of John and his sister, Lydia felt the last of the tension draining away, even though she knew she would have to work to win this woman's full confidence.

Later, after Lydia had retired, John explained about setting up an account for her, and though she knew that her brother would be cautious about how he acted, Martha issued another warning that nothing he did should jeopardise what Eliza and Abigail should have by right.

Two days later, deeming it wise to make this a short visit, John left for Cornwall.

Eight months later a baby girl was born in Whitby and Lydia christened her Tess. With her returning strength, she broached the subject of returning to Cornwall.

'You'll spend Christmas here and not return south until 1787 brings better weather for travelling. As much as John might want to see you and his daughter, he would not want you to place yourselves at risk.'

Martha and Lydia had become close by now and Martha was delighted that they would share Tess's first Christmas together. Though she wanted to see John and show him their daughter, Lydia knew the wisdom of her words and delighted in the fact that she was giving her friend so much pleasure by staying over Christmas.

Knowing nothing of what was happening in Whitby, John spent some anxious days, especially when he knew the birth would be imminent, but he submerged those anxieties in a display of love for his wife. When the time had passed and Lydia did not return he tried to convince himself that it was because of the inclement conditions and longed for the finer days and warmer weather.

He hid any anxiety and enjoyed a family Christmas with Eliza and Abigail who, now at six, was beginning to approach the festivities with an adult outlook. She eagerly helped her mother and father with the seasonal food distribution they made to their employees. It was a gay time at Penorna Manor where John and Eliza maintained the tradition set up by his uncle of a special feast for the household on Boxing Day.

Abigail willingly served the staff who had grown to admire and love this girl who showed signs of turning into a beautiful young lady, with the same complexion as her mother, deep blue eyes and copper-tinted hair, and her father's amiable disposition.

It was not until late March that Selwyn and Harriet, on a visit to Penorna Manor, unwittingly gave John the news he wanted to hear.

'You remember Miss Booth who resigned her position as governess to go to look after her sister-in-law?' said Harriet.

'Of course they do,' chided her husband. 'They have her painting hanging in the hall.'

Harriet dismissed his observation with a wave of her hand. 'We recently agreed to her coming back to us while she found somewhere local to live. Well, she arrived yesterday with a child.'

'What?' Eliza asked with surprise.

Reading the implication she supposed was there, Harriet gave a small laugh, 'Oh, not hers, Eliza. Her sister-in-law died in childbirth and apparently Miss Booth's brother wanted nothing to do with the baby, a little girl. Miss Booth agreed to take her and her brother has financed the purchase of a house and will make her a monthly allowance.'

'That's very noble of Miss Booth,' commented Eliza. 'How long will she be with you?'

'She intends to buy a house in Penzance as soon as possible.'

John's heart had been racing. Lydia and his child were close! He had to curb his own desire to ask questions.

'Has she named the child?' asked Eliza.

'She's called Tess.'

John savoured the name. He liked it. Then his mind was brought sharply back to the conversation for Harriet was continuing to speak.

'She's a beautiful baby and Miss Booth says she is so pleasant and happy.'

'I'm surprised she came back to Cornwall,' commented Eliza.

'When she left us she said she might as she had been happy here. Her brother's attitude to his daughter was such that Miss Booth thought she should move far enough away for him to have no influence over the child.'

It was a fortnight before John received further news of Lydia and Tess. It came innocently, one day after he had returned from the mine, when Eliza informed him that she had had a visit from Harriet and among the news she'd brought was the fact that Miss Booth had now left Trethtowan and was residing in a house in Market-jew Street in Penzance. To avoid any hint of suspicion, John curbed his impatience for another eight days before he went into town, ostensibly to examine his properties there. It did not take him long by casual indirect enquiries to learn where the newcomer to Market-jew Street was living.

Lydia had been adamant about him having no contact with the child but surely seeing his daughter while she was so young would not affect any future situation.

He rapped hard on the brass knocker and a few moments later the door was opened by Lydia. Her expression contained surprise, pleasure, wariness and a hint of annoyance. 'Mr Mitchell!'

'Lydia, I just had to come.'

Anxious that she should not be seen, she said, 'You'd better come in.' She moved to one side and quickly closed the door once he had stepped inside. 'What are you doing here?' she demanded. 'I told you, no contact with our child.'

'Tess,' he corrected. 'I heard about your arrival at Trethtowan and the move to Penzance. I curbed my impatience to see you and Tess then but I could wait no longer.' He reached out and spanned her waist with his hands. Lydia's annoyance because he had broken her condition melted. She relaxed in his arms and met his lips with equal desire.

When the kiss ended he said, 'Where's Tess?'

She took his hand and led him to the stairs. A few moments later he was standing beside a cot gazing at his peacefully sleeping daughter, her head on a pristine white pillow.

'She has your eyes, your hair and your nose.'

Lydia chuckled. 'You see what you want to see.'

'No. She's beautiful, just like you.'

Hearing voices, Tess twisted her head and gave them a wonderful smile. Moved by it, John reached down and touched her hand with his forefinger. Her tiny fingers came tightly round his and she gurgled at him.

'She likes you already,' whispered Lydia, pleased by her daughter's reaction. A few minutes later, when she saw Tess's eyes begin to close, she said, 'I think she's ready to sleep.'

When they went downstairs Lydia took John into the drawing room where a fire burned brightly. 'Thank you for making this possible,' she said.

'It is the least I could do,' he replied sincerely. 'Are you managing?'

'I want a maid and a cook.'

'You will engage them?'

'I have already done so. They were recommended by Dorinda whom I contacted after I moved here. They start tomorrow so it is as well you called today or I would have turned you away at the door.'

'You wouldn't!'

'Oh, yes, I would. You know the conditions I made and nothing must change them. You must never visit here again. Mrs Foxwell, the cook, and Mary Cunnack, the maid, are respectable women and have accepted my explanation that I have had to take my brother's child because he is incapable of doing so after the death of his wife in childbirth. But I would not want to try to explain your presence here.'

'Then I will have to arrange for one of my houses to become available for us.' He drew her to him and looked deep into her eyes. 'I cannot bear to be away from you too long.'

'I feel the same, John.' She hugged him. 'Oh, it is so good to see you and have your arms round me again. But we must be careful. We must avoid raising any suspicion.'

'We will, my love.' He kissed her tenderly. 'How much does Dorinda know?' he asked as they drew apart. 'You were very friendly.'

'We still are. But she knows no more than anyone else.'

'Good, keep it that way.'

'Now,' she said, 'I have a letter for you from your sister. I'm sorry I have not been able to get it to you before now, but Martha said it did not matter when I gave it to you.' She rose from her seat to get her reticule from the table.

'How is she?'

'Very well! You have a remarkable sister. I don't think she wanted us to leave. Tess became a favourite with her.'

'I know she will miss you both.'

She handed him the letter. He broke the seal and unfolded the sheet of paper.

'I'll get some tea while you read that,' Lydia offered.

24th February 1787

My Dear John,

These past months have been a delightful time for me. Lydia is a charming person and we got on extremely well after a few awkward days. I realise how much she loves you, and that in that love for you there is no rancour or jealousy towards Eliza. I believe she will do everything in her power to see that your wife never learns of this relationship. See that you keep it that way otherwise so many lives will be ruined and many people will be terribly hurt, not least the innocent Tess. What can I say but that she has been a great joy to me? I was sorry to see both of them go. Although I offered her and her mother a home here, I fully understood that Lydia wants to be near you. Even though I understand there is to be no personal contact, which I think wise under the circumstances, you can take part vicariously in your daughter's upbringing and from a distance watch her grow into the charming young woman I know she will become.

I suggest, dear brother, that you destroy this letter. If it fell into the wrong hands it could have far-reaching results. Though you may think it is in a safe place, you never know. Besides, there is no reason to keep it! Fire it.

My thoughts will often be with you and that dear little girl.

Your loving sister,
Martha

He read it again and was tearing it up and dropping it into the flames when Lydia returned.

'Oh, you're burning it,' she commented as she crossed the room to place the tea tray on a low table in front of a settee.

'It was better destroyed,' he replied, straightening and turning to join her on the settee. 'It contained nothing untoward but our relationship could have been surmised by anyone seeking to make trouble.'

She nodded and started pouring the tea.

'Martha wrote highly of you.'

'It was she who was wonderful.'

'She wanted you to stay. Would you have liked that?'

'I wanted to be near you, and I wanted you to have Tess close even though I still expect you to adhere to my conditions.' She saw his eyes cloud with disappointment. 'It's for the best, John, it really is. But if you'd rather, I will go back. Martha said I could if ever the need arose.'

'Don't think about it. We will be careful. I don't want your life destroyed. It will be better for us once one of my houses becomes vacant.'

'The sooner the better.'

As he walked away from the house John's mind was full of regret that there could be no personal contact for him with Tess, but that was dismissed in the hope that from afar he could watch her grow up and bloom as beautifully as Abigail.

Chapter Thirteen

'Race you!' Abigail shouted as she set her horse to a gallop. Her laughter swept back to her mother and father.

'No!' shouted Eliza, but the alarm in her voice was lost on the wind.

'Let her go,' laughed John, pleased at the exuberance he saw in his daughter. 'Seventeen tomorrow, she's bound to be full of life. She'll be all right, she's a good rider.'

'I suppose so.' Eliza sighed. 'She's always been older than her years.'

'And prettier by the day,' said John. 'Some day soon a young man's going to come along and sweep her off her feet.'

'Perhaps we should be doing more to encourage someone who would be suitable,' answered Eliza wistfully, reminded of her own youth and feeling sorry that she would, in the not too distant future, see Abigail leave home.

The years had been good to them. They had had the pleasure of seeing their daughter grow up, influencing her development and view of the world. They knew they owed a great deal to Dorinda Jenkins, too, and although they anticipated the day when Abigail would no longer need a governess, did not look forward to telling her so. That task was taken from them when Abigail was fifteen and Dorinda reluctantly had to give in her notice and move to Penzance as her father was ill and needed full-time attendance.

The estate prospered and the Mitchells were liked by their tenants. When the rock fall was cleared after two years and the Penorna and Trethtowan mines joined, the yield was even better than expected and the joint business cemented the friendship between the two families.

Their prosperity was eyed jealously by Jeremy Gaisford who was thwarted at every turn when he secretly tried to cause disruption and havoc for them, even endeavouring to drive a wedge between the two families, but John and Selwyn were wise to what he was attempting. On the occasions when John was roused to anger and confronted Jeremy face-to-face, Gaisford vehemently denied that he was involved and renewed his own accusation that John was responsible for his father's death.

Because he was a Gaisford and Miles Gaisford's lasting influence was still felt by many, Jeremy relished the power he wielded in his father's stead. He regarded any challenge to it as a personal affront. Whenever their paths crossed, whether in company or not, he went out of his way to bait and insult John. By ignoring this, he only angered Jeremy all the more.

Their feud was now widely known throughout the county. Though many realised the blame lay at Jeremy's door, they dare not voice their opinion aloud for without his father's stern hand to guide him, Jeremy now ran wild. His brothers, while loyal to the family name, did not condone his unruly ways and now saw that his running of the estate would lead to ruin for he had none of his father's acumen and foresight. Though they protested at some of his decisions and offered their advice freely, they always received the same answer: 'I'm running things now, not you, and don't forget you only have your own estates under sufferance. They are part of Seneway, I can take them back any time.'

Thoughts of Jeremy were far from John's mind today as he rode along the cliff top beside his wife. Nor did his mind drift to Lydia Booth. She had made sure that her personality and charm won her many new friends in Penzance who, like her staunch ally Dorinda, never doubted that she had relieved her brother of a child he was unable to raise.

Discretion had always been foremost in their minds and in that atmosphere their love for each other had never waned. Lydia was content, in her love for him, to have it that way. She wanted nothing more than to love him and to raise their child, knowing that their friendship did not intrude on his happiness with his wife.

Today, on the eve of Abigail's seventeenth birthday, all seemed well in John Mitchell's world.

Abigail urged her horse faster, enjoying the sensation of speed as she always did. In the company of her parents she kept the urge restrained but on her own the full gallop was what she liked best. Today was an exception for she was filled with excitement about tomorrow when her seventeenth birthday would be celebrated with a party at Penorna. She felt the urge to throw off the shackles of restraint and revel in her own youth and daring. Hoofs tore at the turf as her favourite horse sensed her desire. Her smile broadened and laughter rang from her lips.

She glanced back as the path twisted and saw that her parents were out of sight. She laughed louder in the joy of pounding hoofs. Ahead the track dipped into a hollow where she knew it veered close to the cliff edge, but she gave that no thought. She had ridden this way many times and had never considered the danger. The path rose slightly before it dropped into the hollow. She topped the rise and her eyes widened with horror, driving out the laughter, at the sight of a rider coming with equal speed towards her. She hauled hard on the reins, attempting to take her animal out of the rider's path and away from the cliff edge. Everything moved into a whirling kaleidoscope of horseflesh crashing against horseflesh, but her skill had avoided what would have been a devastating head-on collision. She kept control as her horse swerved away, and brought the animal round aware of the second horse crashing to the ground, its rider thrown to the earth with a momentum that took him over the cliff edge. His scream of horror split the air. Horrified and shaken, she hauled her mount to a halt and was off the saddle almost before it had stopped. She was at the cliff edge, peering down, scared that she would see a broken body on the rocks far below. The sharp realisation that that was not the case was reinforced when she saw a figure clinging to a narrow stone ledge, his legs dangling over a sheer drop. Terror-filled eyes stared up at her from a face drained of colour. Abigail dropped to the ground and flattened herself.

'Hold on!' she shouted, and inched forward until she could reach down. She strained her arm, forced her fingers as far as she could, but it was no use; the space was too much, she could not possibly reach him from here. She viewed the rock face between them. A yard down, a horizontal ledge of rock to her left offered a chance if she could lower herself down to it, but there was no way of knowing how secure it was. Any instability could send her hurtling to oblivion. But that thought was banished from her mind when she saw his fingers slip slightly, sending clods of earth tumbling past his head. 'Hold on,' she encouraged. 'I'm going to try to reach that ledge.' She saw that he knew what she intended to do.

Dismissing the terror she was experiencing, Abigail slid slowly over the edge of the cliff, sending earth spinning away. She paused, tested, and then inched down with care until she felt solid rock beneath her feet. The ledge. But would it hold? Would it take her weight and that of them both if she managed to get a hold on the man?

Abigail dampened her lips in an attempt to pluck up the courage to make her next move. She met the man's pleading gaze that was full of hope. With that strong in her mind, she gave him an encouraging smile. She focused her mind on her next move and pressed against the rock with her feet. Although bits of earth were scuffed away, she was encouraged by a feeling of solidity. Turning and lowering herself the last few feet with extreme care she lay flat on the ledge, resisting the temptation to look further than the young man who barely clung to life. She shuffled herself forward and reached towards him. Her fingers closed round the left sleeve of his jacket and even through the cloth she could sense the hope rise in him.

'I'll hold on while you reach for that rock just above you to the right,' she said. 'Test it.' His eyes flicked to the rock. She tightened her grip on his sleeve. 'Now!' she called sharply. He grabbed, she felt the extra weight shoot up her arm, then it

555

was eased. Her eyes were intent on the rock. It held. 'Good,' she called with relief. After a moment's pause she added, 'Can you ease yourself up a little?' He swallowed hard and then, still staring anxiously at the rock, did so. It held. 'Hold tight while I get a grip on your arm instead of your sleeve.' Concern had welled up inside Abigail, for she had seen the cloth beginning to tear under his weight. 'Now!' she changed her grip and sensed some easing of the strain. 'Good,' she said encouragingly. 'Pull on the rock when I pull on your arm, and try to get your knee up on this ledge.' Realising what she was trying to do, he nodded. 'Now!'

The combined leverage drew him slowly up. Stones and earth were falling away but the rock and the ledge held firm. He drew his right knee up, felt for the ledge, then as he pressed down hard Abigail pulled on his arm. He attained the ledge and after a moment of anxiety about his solidity they both sighed with relief.

Abigail glanced at the top of the cliff. It was in reach if they could kneel. She pointed this out to the man and he nodded. 'You first,' she said with an authority that wouldn't brook opposition. He got to his knees, reached out and pulled himself up. In a few moments she was lying beside him at the top of the cliff, breathing deeply after the exertion but mostly from a sense of huge relief.

The sound of galloping horses drew them back to reality. She sat up and saw her mother and father, faces lined with worry, arriving with a riderless horse between them. They were out of their saddles and crouching beside her in a moment. 'What happened?' Are you all right?' The urgent plea for information was directed at Abigail but their eyes took in the young man who was struggling to his feet. Who was this?

Eliza frowned at her own thoughts. Luke Gaisford? What had he done to her daughter?

John was troubled too, his thoughts ran wild. He had not seen Luke for nearly ten years, not since his father had sent him away to school, but the Gaisford features were unmistakable. Why had he attacked Abigail? It was all right Jeremy directing his hatred at John, but to fill his son's mind with antagonism against all Mitchells was going too far. Such thoughts flashed through his mind in the few seconds it took to help Abigail to her feet.

'Sir, ma'am.' The young man was speaking. They both looked askance at him for his gentle voice was filled with the patent desire to reassure them. 'This young lady has just saved my life.'

They stared at him in amazement. 'What?' said John.

'If this is your daughter, as I suppose it is, she risked her life to save mine.'

John and Eliza turned their attention on Abigail to seek an explanation. She straightened up from brushing down her soiled clothes with her hands and merely shrugged her shoulders.

'What happened?' queried Eliza, her heart all of a flutter at what lay behind the young man's words.

'Let me explain, ma'am,' he said. He went on to relate what had happened and emphasised Abigail's bravery.

As Luke was speaking she had been studying him. She thought him to be about her own age. He was handsome with a strong jaw, a straight nose, eyes that held a green tinge but were sharp and bright and glistening with a love of life and adventure. She noticed his long fingers as he unconsciously adjusted his cravat while he was speaking, all nervousness thrust aside now and replaced by a confidence that was razor-sharp. At the same time his posture settled into its customary self-assurance. Abigail, still wondering who he was, nevertheless found herself attracted to him – a feeling she had never experienced before.

'Sir, ma'am, you have a brave daughter. And thank you both for returning my favourite horse.' He turned to Abigail. 'What you did showed complete disregard for your own safety. I will be ever in your debt as I do not know how I could repay you.'

'Don't try then, but come to my birthday party at Penorna tomorrow at four,' replied Abigail, hardly realising she had made the invitation.

Eliza was about to intervene when she caught her husband's slight shake of the head and said nothing. John had seen a light in his daughter's eyes that he had never seen there before and knew this was no time to intervene.

Luke picked up the reins, patted his horse with comforting hands and swung himself into the saddle. He turned his mount, checked it and said, 'Sir, ma'am.' His eyes turned back to Abigail. 'Until tomorrow then.' She smiled up at him.

They watched him ride away, upright, in command, comfortable in the saddle.

'That was a brave thing you did,' commented her father.

'You might have been killed,' said Eliza in a tone that held a touch of admonishment.

'Well, I wasn't, Mama,' replied Abigail sharply. 'I couldn't see him fall to his death. He was lucky to get the hold he did but could have slipped at any moment; there was no time to wait for help.'

'You know who he is?' asked John.

She shook her head. 'No. I wondered if you did?'

'Luke Gaisford.'

'What? Mr Jeremy's son?'

'Yes.'

'He's a lot handsomer than his father . . . must get his looks from his mother.'

'That may be,' chided her mother, 'but he's still a Gaisford, and you've asked him to your party!'

Penorna was in a festive mood. Abigail at seventeen was a beautiful and popular young lady. Many guests from all over the county remarked upon it on their arrival in the main hall where they were welcomed by the Mitchells with a glass of warming punch. Passing on, they drifted into two rooms set aside for their comfort or chose smaller ones for more intimate conversations or to renew old acquaintance. The dining room had been laid out with mouth-watering dishes of every kind to form an ongoing buffet throughout the evening. The warm balmy air had enabled the glass doors leading onto the terrace from various rooms to be opened wide, enabling the guests to mix more freely. All of them looked forward to a pleasant evening, especially when the dancing started in the large main salon that had been cleared for the purpose, leaving a few chairs round its perimeter for those who wanted only to watch and comment on who was with whom, and speculate on concealed relationships.

'I think we have met all the guests,' commented John. 'We may as well join them. Enjoy the party, you two.' He smiled at his wife and daughter. 'I'll just have a word with Albert.' He crossed the hall to the door where their head butler was standing. 'I think all the guests have arrived but if I have overlooked someone and there are late arrivals, you know what to do.'

'Yes, sir! How long, sir?'

'An hour.'

'Very good, sir!'

Abigail, disappointed that Luke had not come, wandered off and was soon surrounded by friends and well-wishers. Throughout the night and earlier today visions of him kept haunting her mind. In her thoughts she had pictured herself dancing with him, but that was not to be; he appeared to have taken no notice of her invitation.

After three-quarters of an hour the dancing started. The second dance, a quadrille, was under way when the front door was flung wide with a crash and Jeremy Gaisford strode in, brushing Albert aside without ceremony. Luke, close behind, cast the butler a look of apology and rolled his eyes skywards in a gesture of contempt for his father's rudeness. Hearing the music, Jeremy made straight for the open doors to the main room. He stood in the doorway, feet astride, arms held loosely by his sides, as he surveyed it. He then clasped his hands behind his back and rocked on his feet; a commanding presence who had already captured the attention of several people near the door. Knowing that there was no love lost between the Gaisfords and the Mitchells they were all wondering why Jeremy and his son had gate-crashed the party, for they were certain they were not there by invitation.

'Mr John Mitchell!' Jeremy's voice boomed across the room, reverberating off the panelled walls.

In confusion at this unexpected intrusion the musicians gradually stopped playing and the dancers, uncertain what was happening, missed their step, bumped into each other, several only saved from falling by their partner. Chaos broke out around the room followed by a tense silence.

'Mr John Mitchell!' Jeremy roared again.

Abigail saw Luke standing behind and to one side of his father. Her heart missed a beat. He had come! He hadn't ignored her! But why was his father here making such a scene?

'Here, Mr Gaisford,' John shouted from the side as he started to make his way to the centre of the floor while dancers cleared a path for him. He walked towards Jeremy with deliberate steps. 'What do you want here?' And so that everyone knew he added, 'An uninvited guest.'

Jeremy, eyes fixed firmly on John, waited until he was close, then asked in a less belligerent tone but loud enough so that everyone could hear, 'Where is your daughter?'

'That is no ...' Before John could finish the sentence he was interrupted.

'I am here, Mr Gaisford.' Abigail pushed her way through a group of people and walked towards him. She felt his eyes fixed upon her as if he was trying to probe her very soul but did not shy away. Her footsteps did not falter. Reaching her father's side, holding herself erect and with her eyes fixed firmly on Jeremy, she said, 'What is it you want, Mr Gaisford? You were not invited, I believe.'

'Invited or not, I had to come,' he said quietly. He looked at John and was about to speak to him, when he decided otherwise. Instead he raised his voice so that everyone in the room could hear. 'Ladies and gentlemen, I want you all to know that you are celebrating the birthday of a very brave girl who yesterday saved my son Luke from certain death!'

For a moment there was a stunned silence, then a buzz of exchanges and questions rippled round the room. 'What is

560

this?' 'What does Gaisford mean?' 'What happened?' 'Death?' What's he talking about?'

'Ladies! Gentlemen! Please, I have more to say!' Jeremy's voice brought silence to the room again. 'My son was thrown from his horse and went over the cliff side. He got a hold but could not pull himself back. He hung above a sheer drop, which would have meant certain death but for Miss Mitchell's actions. Without thought for her own safety, she went over the cliff and succeeded in getting him back.' He turned to Abigail. 'Miss Mitchell, my family will be forever grateful for what you did yesterday. If ever you need help, do not be afraid to ask us for it.' He faced John. 'Mr Mitchell, you have a brave daughter, and beautiful too. You are a lucky man. You too are lucky, Mrs Mitchell,' he added, glancing at Eliza who had come quietly to stand beside her husband and daughter. 'Mr Mitchell, we have had our differences in the past. Can we bury them now?' Jeremy held out his hand.

Detecting a sincere desire in the gesture, John took his hand in a firm grip. 'They are condemned to the grave,' he responded.

Clapping in approval of the end of this known feud broke out in the room, gathering in volume.

'Mr Mitchell,' said Jeremy quietly, still shaking hands, 'my wife is outside in the carriage. May I bring her in to make her own thanks to your daughter?'

'Of course,' replied John. 'Goodness me, you shouldn't have left her waiting outside.'

Jeremy gave a wry smile. 'We weren't invited,' he said in a jocular tone.

'Well, you are both invited now.' The two men hurried into the hall, strode outside and in a few moments were escorting Hester Gaisford into the house. She was presented to Abigail who was already talking to Luke. Eliza had called to the musicians to resume and the quadrille set people dancing again. She then took charge of Mrs Gaisford and left the men to cement the new relationship between the two families.

After the last guest had gone in the early hours of the morning, John, Eliza and Abigail flopped down at the dining-room table and ate a late supper, which, because of the attention they'd paid their guests, they had been unable to do earlier.

John gave a little laugh. 'Strange,' he said, 'how an accident can end such bitterness between two families.'

'And Abigail's bravery,' put in Eliza.

'Oh, yes, but that wouldn't have been manifest if it hadn't been for the accident.'

'And I might never have met Luke,' put in Abigail dreamily. 'He's asked me to go riding with him the day after tomorrow. I've said yes. I hope that is all right?'

Eliza and John exchanged glances and John knew that she was leaving the decision to him.

'Of course.' He'd realised from the moment they had all watched Luke ride away after Abigail's rescue of him that his daughter had grown up; she was a woman and prepared to face all the challenges that could bring, including affairs of the heart. He realised, and he knew Eliza would too when they spoke of it in the privacy of their room, that a time would come when they would have to let her go. To do so lovingly would always bring her home. In the meantime they could only warn her, advise when asked, and give her their unstinting understanding and love.

'Of course,' he repeated, and then added, 'but don't forget he's a Gaisford. That family have always had a wild streak, and none more so than his father. Beware of that in Luke. It may appear it isn't there now but these family traits can lie dormant for years before they suddenly erupt. Just beware, Abigail.'

'Does Miss Booth still visit you?' Eliza put the question when she and John were spending an evening with Selwyn and Harriet.

'Oh, yes,' replied Harriet. 'She comes once a month. As you know, I encouraged her to do so soon after she returned to Cornwall . . . when was it? Ten years ago.' She gave a shake of the head. 'How time passes! It seems but yesterday. She likes to come and hear news of James and Juliana. She was here last week.'

'She is well?'

'Yes.'

John's nerves had tightened at the mention of Lydia. He concentrated on his food and avoided been drawn into the conversation lest he make some slip. It had been the same throughout the last ten years whenever Lydia's name was mentioned. They had been years of careful planning, meetings that would not attract attention, excuses made for being away from Penorna, so that two people, deeply in love, could express that love for each other. And yet throughout all that time John had found his love for Eliza had never weakened. It was a mystery to him that he could love two women with such intensity at the same time; yet he found he could and blessed his ability to do so, for it brought a richness to his life in spite of the intrigue. He drew strength from the fact that Lydia always assured him she was happy and wanted life no other way. Showing interest in Eliza and Abigail, she salved the guilt she and John shared towards them. They found reassurance together in watching their daughter grow, though he regretted having no closer contact with her. She came sharply to mind now when Eliza asked, 'How is the child?'

'Tess is a fine girl. She'll be eleven in December. Miss Booth is doing a wonderful job with her. Her brother owes her a great deal.'

John felt a flush of pride and had a sudden strong desire to admit to being her father but sensibly kept quiet; too many lives would be shattered if ever the truth came out. He changed the course of the conversation. 'Is it true that Jeremy Gaisford is not well?'

'So I've heard,' replied Selwyn. 'But what do you expect, the way he drinks?'

'I hope that is a trait he hasn't passed on to Luke,' said John with some concern.

'You are thinking of Abigail?' put in Harriet.

Eliza grimaced. 'Yes. She's seen a lot of Luke this last nine months, ever since she saved his life.'

563

'I suppose it was a natural coming together after that, and he is a handsome young man.'

'Indeed,' agreed Eliza. 'And always charming whenever we have met him.' She glanced at John.

'I agree. But a Gaisford is a Gaisford. What runs in that family's blood?'

'There are always good apples as well as bad ones,' said Selwyn in an attempt to reassure his friend.

'I don't think you need worry about Abigail,' put in Harriet. 'She's a sensible, self-assured young woman who I'm certain can take care of herself.'

'I hope you are right,' mused Eliza.

'Have no doubt about it,' Selwyn added his conviction. 'And if ever it came to a love match, with both of them being only children the result could be the most powerful land-owning family in Cornwall.'

These were words John was to recall in the spring of 1798 when he paid his last respects to Jeremy Gaisford. At the graveside of the man who had been his enemy first and latterly his friend, he wondered what the future held in store for eighteen-year-old Luke.

Luke watched the coffin lowered into the cold Cornish earth with mixed feelings. His father had been a hard-driving task-master but there was something about him that Luke was drawn to; that he admired and tried in some ways to emulate. As he'd moved into his teenage years, he'd found it easier to do. It stemmed from the time when his father started to treat him more as a man than a boy and shared many a fast ride with him, leading him to down a tankard of ale and swallow a dram of whisky after it. Jeremy knew if his son was like his father, other natural instincts were there too and would never be denied when they surfaced. So he was more than pleased when Abigail Mitchell entered Luke's life. He fostered the relationship through which he could see a legitimate means of achieving his own father's thwarted ambition to acquire the Penorna Estate. Luke accepted his father's ultimate aim but for himself it was only a secondary interest; he was more interested in the girl.

He glanced across the grave and his eyes rested on Abigail. The sombre black she wore did nothing to detract from the beauty of this young woman he had sworn to have. There were others among the great crowd gathered here to pay their last muted respects who Luke knew would come eagerly to his bed, some with an eye to becoming Mistress of Senewey, others simply for the fun of it. He wished Abigail Mitchell was at his side now, but that would have to wait while mourning was observed, and even then he could not be sure she would walk up the aisle with him. They had become close since she had saved his life, but she had never allowed their friendship to move beyond that.

Abigail sensed someone looking at her and, glancing in the direction of the chief mourners, saw Luke's gaze fixed on her. Their eyes met briefly and he quickly looked away but in that moment she read desire. She shuddered. It felt different from other times she'd observed that look. This time she sensed it was cold and calculating, and behind it lay the intention that one day he would break down the barrier she had hitherto held between them. That barrier had been erected on her father's warning, and though she had a great admiration for Luke, who in her presence had shown her every respect, Abigail was wary of him for at times she sensed something disturbing beneath his outwardly pleasant demeanour.

The day after the funeral Luke strode into the dining room for breakfast. He was surprised to find his mother there already, seated at the table enjoying some porridge.

'Good morning, Luke,' Hester said brightly.

'Good morning, Mother,' he replied tersely as he went to the sideboard to help himself to a glass of milk. He had no need to order porridge from the attending maid for he knew that once he appeared she would scuttle away to the kitchen to return in a few minutes to serve it piping hot. 'Too ill to attend the funeral but here you are as large as life.' His voice dripped with sarcasm.

'I had no respects to pay to your father because of the way he treated me after your grandfather's death. Until then I had accorded him the dignity that went with the position of husband, but after Miles's death his behaviour ran wild. He wanted me for only one thing, and supply it I had to even if he had been with his other women.' Hester gave a grunt of contempt. 'For God's sake, Luke, don't look at me like that. It was bend to his will or be thrown out. Jeremy would have ignored the scandal, but think of the stories that would have been spread about *me*. I had to stay and give him outward respectability even though people knew how rotten to the core he was.' She looked hard at her son. 'I only hope and pray you do not turn out like him, Luke.'

He made no comment but said, 'Mr Archbold the solicitor will be here at eleven. Please be in the drawing room for the reading of the will and to hear what I have to say afterwards. Uncle Charles, Uncle Logan, Aunt Emma and Aunt Fanny have been invited to be there too.'

Hester eyed him with suspicion but said nothing. She would know at eleven what the future held for her. No doubt she would be well provided for by her husband for the help she had given him.

Uncles and aunts arrived within a few minutes of each other, were shown to the drawing room and announced by the maid delegated for the duty. Luke and his mother made their greetings amiable, and their relations showered Hester liberally with commiserations and concern.

Luke played the perfect host with a charm that did not deceive either of his aunts. Neither of them had fallen under his spell as many women of their age had done, and they had privately voiced their opinion to each other that there was more behind this gathering than the mere reading of Jeremy's will. Luke was older than his eighteen years. So far he had hidden in his father's shadow but now, as the hereditary owner of Senewey, he had real power that they judged he would be tempted to use.

They made no comment on it but shrank from the formality of the setting. Luke had supervised the seating; six straight-backed chairs faced a small table behind which stood a similar chair. There had been no attempt to make this an informal

566

occasion. The only concession to that was when he personally showed them to the chairs in which they should sit and served them each a glass of Madeira. He also placed one on the table. It was at almost that precise moment the maid opened the door and announced, 'Mr Archbold, sir.'

A man bustled nervously in. His slight stoop, brought on by advancing years, made him seem smaller than he was. Sharp eyes darted about from one to the other as if summing them all up as he came towards Luke. The young man greeted him with outstretched hand. Mr Archbold took it and winced at his strong grip.

'Mr Gaisford.'

'Mr Archbold. You are indeed a good time-keeper.' Luke glanced at the clock on the mantel-piece.

'Eleven is eleven, sir.'

'Precisely. Let me take your coat and hat.'

The solicitor removed them and passed them to the maid who had waited to receive them. With a brief, 'Thank you, sir,' he took his document case from Luke who had held it for him meanwhile.

'You know my mother?'

'Indeed, indeed.' Mr Archbold quickly went to Hester and shook her proffered hand while nervously offering his commiserations on her loss.

'And my uncles and aunts?' Luke introduced them in turn and the solicitor renewed his acquaintances quickly.

'Your seat, Mr Archbold,' said Luke, showing him to the chair behind the table. 'And a glass of wine.'

'Most kind, sir, most kind.' He shuffled behind the table, took a sip of his wine and opened his document case. He withdrew a sheaf of papers that caused Logan and Charles to grimace in surprise at each other. It looked as if they were in for a long reading.

But their expectation was short-lived. Mr Archbold took another drink of his wine, cleared his throat and said, 'Ladies and gentlemen, this won't take long.' He picked up a sheet of paper, glanced at them all as if checking that he had their full attention, and then read: '"This is the last will and testament

567

of Jeremy Gaisford. Being in sound mind, I leave everything I own to my son, Luke. Signed in the presence of Mark Crossley and John Golding, householders in Penzance. Dated 5th May 1797."'

The silence that filled the room was palpable. It spoke volumes. No mention of anyone but Luke. They were all in his power. How would he wield it? Their lives were almost literally in his hands. Though they were outwardly calm, Logan and Charles were quaking. They did not own their own estates; they worked them for their own livelihood and gain but the land was part of the Senewey Estate and could be taken back at any time. Father and brother had never exercised that right. What about nephew?

Emma and Fanny looked shocked and indignant. Not to be mentioned in the will they took as a slight, but worse than that they knew their destiny was now in the hands of an eighteen year old they didn't much like and definitely did not trust.

Hester sat as if frozen. No provision for her. The husband to whom she had become a plaything, suffering abuse of every kind whenever the drink took hold, had not provided one penny for her future security. Her fate now depended on a son of whom she had become wary.

'Thank you, Mr Archbold! If I show you to the dining room you will find some refreshments there. When I am ready you and I will continue with our business.'

Luke rose from his chair. The solicitor followed suit and trailed after him. Luke returned a few minutes later to be met by a buzz of indignant observations. He ignored these. He went to the chair behind the table recently vacated by Mr Archbold and held up his hands for silence. Then he sat down and looked round all the faces staring expectantly at him. He gave a little smile, enjoying the power he wielded over his relations.

'Well, there it is, I own everything,' he said smugly.

'No doubt you already knew the contents of the will and wanted to savour your triumph in front of us,' said Logan, his voice sharp with disgust.

'I did know of it, Uncle Logan, the day after Father died.'

'Eager to grab it all.' Logan did not hide his own contempt.

'Careful, Uncle.' There was a chill in Luke's words. His aunt's gesture of warning in placing her hand on her husband's arm was not lost on him. 'It seems my aunt has more sense than to rile me.' He glanced at his other uncle. 'What about you, Uncle Charles?' His uncle gave a resigned shrug of his shoulders. 'Nothing to say?' mocked Luke. 'And you, Aunt Emma?'

'What will be will be,' she replied sharply. 'What about your mother? Your father should have made provision for her after all she did for him.' She glanced at her sister-in-law who gave her a weak smile of thanks while mouthing the word silently.

'Your concern touches me. No doubt you all want to know what I am going to do about my mother.' He turned his gaze on Hester. She saw no affection there, only a cold contempt. 'I can never forgive you for not preventing Father from beating and abusing me. You will live in the West Wing on a small allowance I shall make you and will never again venture into the rest of the house. That is for my sole use.'

Words of reproach sprang to her lips but she remained silent, lanced by his hostile eyes. Besides, she knew any protests would be useless.

He turned to the others. 'Now what am I to do about you four?' He paused thoughtfully, knowing they were quaking with anxiety inside. 'As you will have gathered, I am seeing Mr Archbold again shortly. I will instruct him to assign the estates you now occupy permanently to you.' He saw relief sweep through his uncles and aunts. 'Possession of them by the Senewey Estate is hereby revoked. They will be yours to run as you please, but in future there will be no financial support from Senewey or from me.'

'But being able to fall back on support from Senewey is essential,' protested Logan.

'Now it stops. You will have to manage without that cushion.' Luke's voice was so firm, his expression so adamant, that Logan knew it was no use even trying to negotiate.

Silence fell on the room. Luke glanced at each of them in turn and then said, 'That is all. Mr Archbold will draw up the necessary documents and let you have them for signature as soon as possible.' He rose from his chair, a gesture of dismissal. 'If you wish for them there are refreshments in the dining room. Mr Archbold will have finished his. I will be busy with him for quite a while so I'll say goodbye now.'

Chapter Fourteen

Seated in the drawing room, Mr Archbold shuffled his sheaf of papers nervously. Annoyance clouded Luke's eyes.

'Get on with it, man,' he snapped irritably.

'Er . . . yes, yes.' He picked up a sheet of paper, glanced at it, and as if annoyed with himself pushed it to one side and chose another. An expression of relief came to his face. 'First of all we have the papers dealing with the farm holdings . . .'

'Mr Archbold, do we have to detail everything?'

'Well, sir, it is the only way you will know exactly what you are worth.'

'Summarise it, Mr Archbold, summarise it!' Each word became stronger as if Luke felt it necessary to hammer it into the solicitor's mind.

'You really should have all the details, Mr Gaisford.'

'Spare me those, Mr Archbold. Just tell me what I am worth and what ready money is available.'

'I am afraid there is very little of the latter. Almost next to nothing in fact.'

'What?' Luke's face darkened in angry surprise.

'Your father was a heavy spender. He got through a lot of money and in actual coinage left you little.'

'Then I will have to put that right by selling some land.'

'I am afraid you can't do that, sir.'

'Why not, it's mine?'

'True, sir, but you are prevented from selling land by an entail in your great grandfather's will.'

'What? That old bastard's tied me down?'

'If you put it that way, sir, yes.'

Luke's lips tightened.

'If you are thinking of increasing your flocks of sheep, I must tell you that when I was working out your assets and sought expert advice on the farming side of the estate, I was told that the grazing land could not sustain any more and that the flocks you have now are not in good shape.'

'Why not?'

Mr Archbold gave a gesture of helplessness with his hands. 'I am no agricultural expert, Mr Gaisford.'

The irritable shake of Luke's head dismissed that angle.

'We'll have to increase the output from the mine then.'

Mr Archbold grimaced. 'I'm afraid not, sir. Your father did that and now the copper is running out.'

'But he had another harbour built!'

'True, and that helped with his initial raised output, but he had not taken into account that the supply of copper was finite. The harbour he already had could have dealt with the copper over a longer period but he wanted to exploit it faster and thought the answer was another harbour. That harbour is about to become redundant.'

Now Luke knew why his grandfather and father had been keen to buy Penorna and Trethtowan land: copper. Their own mines were almost worked to extinction.

'I can raise rents, or are you going to tell me that can't be done either?'

'It can be done, sir, but I am afraid if you do so you will have trouble on your hands. You see, your father received a petition from his tenants concerning the state of their dwellings – they had seen what Mr Mitchell and Mr Westbury were doing for their tenants. In order to placate his own Mr Jeremy signed an agreement that rents should not go up until after repairs had been undertaken on their dwellings, and that these repairs would be completed by the end of next year.'

'My father seems to have made a fine mess of things,' said Luke with contempt. 'Any more bad news?'

'That just about sums it up.'

'He's left me in a bad way then?'

'Well, sir, the straight answer is yes, but you still have some income from the farms and rents, and a little from the mine.'

Luke looked hard at Mr Archbold. 'No word of my precarious position must get out. The Gaisfords have been an important family in Cornwall for many years; it must remain so. I will see to it that our fortunes are revived. In the meantime I must keep my word to my mother and my uncles.' He went on to instruct the solicitor what he wanted him to do.

'I am sure under the circumstances allocating their two estates to your uncles is a wise move as they will no longer be able to call on Senewey for financial help.'

'See that the necessary documents are drawn up and signed as soon as possible.'

'That will be done within the next two days, sir.'

'Good. I think you had better leave me all those other documents to peruse in my own time, see if they can help me find a solution to my precarious financial position.'

'Very good, sir! May I just remind you that much of your income should be set aside to meet the cost of renovations agreed to by your father, for replenishing stock on the farms, and to tide you over once the copper has run out.'

Luke nodded. 'Or I find a new source of income.' He smiled to himself. He had two possibilities already in mind. Maybe he would need only one of them or he might exploit them both, just for the hell of it.

Both might take a little while to accomplish but he would be patient and in the meantime exist on the income he could achieve on his current assets. Nevertheless the next day, with the weather set fair, he took a ride along the coast to the small harbour his father had constructed.

He slipped from the saddle on the cliff top, tethered his horse and walked to a point from which he could survey the harbour and its location within a sheltered cove.

The cliff dropped away sharply before him and swung round on either side into headlands that towered over the cove. His father had made use of that when he had positioned the stone harbour below with its two piers curving towards each other, offering protection from the stormy seas that could pound this jagged coast. The harbour satisfied him, but he was concerned about access to it. He strolled along the cliff edge, studying the possibilities, until he reached a position, which gave him his answer. He stopped when he realised that from here he could see winding paths climbing to the cliff top at both ends of the cove. Because of the contours they had not been noticeable from any other point but this. He felt elated. It could not have been better! He must examine the place more closely. He hurried along the cliff top to his right and was even more satisfied when the nature of the terrain hid the path from his view. He almost missed the point where it came out on top of the cliff, and this pleased him all the more.

He wound his way down to the cove and when he reached the bottom felt almost overpowered by the towering cliffs above him. He hurried on to the harbour wall that had been built into the cliff and saw that it ran in both directions to meet the paths from the cliff top so that there was one continuous route in a loop from top to ship or vice versa. He nodded with satisfaction. He made his way along the right-hand pier and on reaching the end saw what wonderful protection the two piers gave to the harbour. A vessel would be safe here from even the most monstrous waves running into the coast. But he was more interested in the shoals of rock that jutted out into the sea from the foot of the cliffs to right and left, and in the access from them to the harbour wall that ran along the bottom of the cliff. Again he nodded with satisfaction. This could be the answer to his financial dilemma and, coupled with his other idea, could make him a rich man. Visualising his future, Luke studied the scene again. Those shoals, so close to the harbour, were dangerous. He climbed thoughtfully to the cliff top and rode away.

He had ridden a mile when he checked his horse and sat deep in thought for a moment. A decision reached, he turned his mount and with a whoop put it to a gallop that he did not stop until they reached the Waning Moon. Luke swung from the saddle and strode inside. He took in the scene as he walked to the bar. Two men sat at a table in one corner of the room, deep in conversation. He did not know them but they were well dressed and he judged some trade was being discussed or a plot being hatched to outwit a neighbour. The man he took to be the landlord was rearranging some tankards behind the bar.

'Good day, landlord,' he said, his eyes summing up the man.

'Good day, Mr Gaisford.'

'You know who I am?' said Luke, a little surprised that the landlord of a lonely inn should know him.

'Tell a Gaisford anywhere. In your case I see something of your father in you so you must be Mr Luke.'

'Shrewd man. But I really shouldn't be surprised, knowing my father frequented this establishment.'

'He did that, sir, and we did business together, so if you need anything at all, you let Tom Mather know. Now, sir, welcome to the Waning Moon. Your first drink is on the house.'

'That's very civil of you, Tom. A tankard of your best, if you please.' He glanced at the two men in the corner.

As Tom placed the full tankard on the counter, he lowered his voice and said, 'They're from over St Ives way, on their way back from St Just.'

'Make it your business to know all your customers?'

'Aye, sir, I do. It pays to know who I'm dealing with.'

'Wise! Now, this business you conducted with my father, what was it?'

'A bit of all sorts, but chiefly I put men his way he could use for various enterprises. The Waning Moon was their regular meeting place.'

'So you could do the same for me, if and when the time comes?'

'Aye, I could sir. Have you something in mind? Taking up where your father left off?'

Luke shook his head. 'This has nothing to do with what my father did and it may be a little while before I can implement

575

my plans, but when I do I will need men who can be trusted and who will keep their mouths shut.'

'You will be able to rely on the men Tom Mather gets.'

'Good. No doubt we will do business then.'

Luke was highly satisfied with his day as he turned it over in his mind on his way home. The foundations were laid for one plan, now he must implement the other.

'Another invitation?' Eliza put the question to Abigail who had just unsealed the sheet of paper one of the maids had brought to the dinner table.

She glanced quickly at the neat writing so elegantly laid out. 'From Martin Granton, a ball at Granton Manor in three weeks' time,' she replied, excitement dancing in her eyes for this meant dancing and she loved that.

'This is the fourth ball in the last six months,' observed her father. 'Sydney Leigh, George Morland, David Gillow ... you are a popular young lady.'

'Would you want me to be anything else, Papa?' said Abigail with a coy smile.

'No, but they are all cronies of Luke Gaisfords and I hear tales about their wild ways.'

'Rumours are always exaggerated. I find them most polite, especially Martin. Besides, Luke has not associated with them since his father died, and you've seen how thoughtful he is when he has taken me out riding.'

'I will grant you that, but I still think still waters run deep. And he is a Gaisford.' Seeing that his wife and daughter had finished their meal, John laid down his napkin and stood up.

He escorted them to the drawing room where they had just sat down when they heard the maid cross the hall to answer the front door. She appeared a moment later to announce that Mr Luke Gaisford was here to see them. John and Eliza exchanged a quick glance and each wondered what merited this unexpected visit. Abigail sensed her heart race a little at the mention of Luke's name and she too wondered what had prompted his arrival.

'Show him in,' John instructed.

Luke strode in, confident and in charge of the situation. There was a smile on his face yet apology in his eyes that underlay his words. 'Ma'am, Sir, Abigail.' He looked at each in turn and then included them all when he said, 'My apologies for intruding at this time of day but I thought I should waste no time. As I have now thrown off my mourning, I am calling to ask if you, sir, will give me permission to seek the privilege of escorting Miss Abigail to the ball at Granton Manor?

'You knew she would be invited?' asked John cautiously, surprised that Luke should call so soon after the invitation had been received.

He gave a little smile. 'Sir, I have been unable to attend any of the balls over the last nine months period of mourning but I hear about them all and the talk is always of how popular Miss Abigail is so I concluded that she was sure to be invited to this one. I received my own invitation this afternoon. As I wanted to be sure that no one pre-empted me, I rode over here at the first opportunity.'

'You are an enterprising young man,' commented John. 'My daughter has just now received her invitation to attend the ball, while we were dining.'

'Then indeed I am fortunate in my timing, sir. Of course, my fate hangs not only on your permission but also on Miss Abigail's acceptance.' He cast a glance at her.

She felt a thrill run through her when she read challenge in his eyes.

'I will be delighted to accept, with my father's permission.' She turned her gaze from Luke to her father who saw in it an appeal that he couldn't refuse. His daughter had always been able to twist him round her little finger, even in his sternest moments.

'Very well.'

'Thank you, sir, and you, ma'am.' Luke turned his smile on Eliza whom he knew had been studying him carefully. If there was any uneasiness in her mind he wanted to alleviate it. 'I will call for Miss Abigail and have her home at a reasonable hour. I promise she will have a splendid time.'

577

'I'm sure she will, Mr Gaisford. Though you have previously accompanied my daughter when she is out riding, a great deal will rest on your conduct at this ball for I am sure there will be others in the future.'

'Indeed, Mrs Mitchell! I understand your point. Have no fear, Miss Abigail will be well looked after. Now, I have intruded on you for too long, I will take my leave.'

'Stay, take a glass of Madeira with us before you leave,' John offered.

'That is kind, sir.'

'Sit down.' John indicated a chair as he rose from his to go to the decanter and wine glasses standing on the oak sideboard.

Luke sat down, placing his hat and riding crop on the table beside his chair.

'How is your mother, Mr Gaisford?'

'Not too well, ma'am. She has never really got over my father's death. She is turning into a recluse, confining herself to one wing of the house, not even wanting to mingle with me or any friends who call.'

'I'm sorry to hear that. Death affects people in different ways. I hope she can soon shake off her despondency and resume as near normal a life as possible.'

'Thank you, ma'am. I will convey your wishes to her.' Luke looked up and took the glass of Madeira from John who had served his wife and daughter first. 'Thank you, sir.'

John got his own glass and sat down. 'How are you settling down to running the estate? A heavy responsibility for one so young.'

'Very well, thank you, sir. When I returned home after my schooling I learned a lot from my father.'

'I heard tell that prospects were not too good at Senewey mine?'

'Rumours, sir, rumours, no doubt brought about by the fact I cut back on the workforce. My father had over-employed.' Luke hoped his excuse sounded feasible even though it was only partially true and he was in fact keeping more men on than he should to disguise the fact that the copper seams were running out. 'You seem to be running a very efficient estate, sir.'

'My uncle had left a property that was already running efficiently. I thought if I kept my tenants and workers happy they would continue to see that it did so. Which is exactly what they did.'

'You were lucky indeed to have such loyal employees.'

The conversation drifted across various topics for another ten minutes before Luke politely announced he must leave and intrude on them no longer.

As he rode away he was happy with his visit – Abigail had been invited to the ball and he had learnt much about Penorna Estate and had been able to draw some detailed conclusions about the wealth that she would inherit.

The door of the Waning Moon crashed open propelled by Martin Granton who took one step into the room and stopped. A quick glance told him what he wanted to know and he called over his shoulder, 'He's here!'

'Has he got them lined up?' Sydney Leigh almost sent Martin staggering as he pushed past him.

George Morland and David Gillow, arms round each other's shoulders, ran in and headed straight for the bar, shouting, 'Luke!' They untangled their arms and took up position on each side of Gaisford, clapping him on the back. 'Good to see you! Where have you been?'

Sydney, who had drained a tankard in one gulp, wiped his hand across his mouth and said, 'I know. That beautiful filly's got him bewitched.'

'Bewitched and bewildered,' slurred David, reaching for a tankard before Sydney could grab it.

'Keep filling them, landlord.' Sydney eyed Tom who had been forewarned by Luke about his four friends. 'They'll drink a lot, they'll get a little merry and be a bit boisterous, but they can hold their liquor. Pranksters but not troublemakers.'

'What do you want us here for?' asked Martin, eyeing Luke.

579

'Get your tankards and come over here.' He started for a table in one corner of the room.

The others followed but Sydney stopped and looked back. 'Remember what I said, landlord?'

'Aye, sir, no dry tankards.'

'Correct.' He turned and almost tripped but managed to keep his tankard level and not spill a drop. He staggered to the table and dropped into the only vacant chair. 'Well?' he said, shaking his head woozily as he stared at Luke.

'Sober up,' said Luke, and raised an eyebrow towards Martin who he regarded as his closest friend and who never took as much drink as the others.

Sydney sat up straight, saluted and said, 'Yes, sir.' The serious expression he had adopted vanished in a snigger which quickly turned to outright laughter. 'Thought I was drunk, Luke? You've never seen me drunk.' He looked round his companions. 'Has any of you seen me drunk?'

'No,' they all agreed in one voice.

'Good, that's settled! Now, Luke, what is this all about? Why meet on this Godforsaken moor? Never been here before.' Again he looked round. 'Anyone else been here before?'

'I have,' said Luke.

'You don't count 'cos you must have been. Must have known the landlord kept good ale. It is good ale, isn't it?' He looked around for general agreement and then eyed Luke again. 'Well, what are we here for?'

'I want you to know this place because if you are drinking with me this is where it will be done for the foreseeable future.'

'Hey, we ride the county, remember,' protested George.

'I don't until . . . well, I don't know.'

'Oh, I see, the filly's got him roped.' He gave a little grin.

The others stared at Luke, wanting confirmation or denial.

'So what if she has? There are big stakes to play for and I'm prepared to do my drinking here so Abigail doesn't hear about it. Play along with me and you won't regret it. I'm not going to be hogtied all my life. You can drink wherever you like but with me it's here. And one other thing: you keep this to yourselves. To all intents and purposes I am not riding with you anymore.'

'Ah, putting on a good show for Mama and Papa with the Penorna Estate as the prize,' said David, tapping his nose knowingly.

'Keep your suppositions to yourself, and the rest of you don't speculate with anyone. You will all benefit in the long run, I don't forget my friends.'

Martin made no comment. A vision of Abigail ran through his mind while his heart sank. To pursue her now would be to incur the wrath of his old friend, and that could be disastrous. Luke Gaisford, who always had to have his own way, would not rest until he had sated his desire for revenge on all those involved and that would include Abigail herself. Martin could never let that happen.

John let himself into the house in New Street that he and Lydia had used as their meeting place. Throughout December and January the weather had prevented him from taking Christmas gifts to her and Tess. Now, with a snap of warmer weather in the February of a new century making the ride to Penzance possible, he was taking the opportunity to do so.

He had been in the house no longer than ten minutes when he heard a sharp and persistent hammering on the front door that carried the sound of urgency. He hurried along the hall and, on opening the door, was shocked to see a distraught Dorinda standing on the step. His mind raced to consider the possible reasons she might be here. She was Lydia's friend and could only be here in connection with that. But how had Dorinda known about this house which he and Lydia had kept such a secret?

The alarm in her eyes eased a little when she saw him. 'Mr Mitchell, thank goodness you are here,' she cried with relief. 'We hoped the change in the weather would bring you to Penzance. I'm afraid I have some bad news.'

'Come in, come in,' he urged, and led the way to the drawing room. 'What is it?' he called over his shoulder as he closed the door.

'Lydia, sir. She is very ill.'

'What?' Alarm surged through him. 'I must go to her!' He started for the door but stopped and swung round to face Dorinda. 'You know about us and this house?'

'Just a few minutes ago I learned of it and Lydia swore me to secrecy. It's safe with me, sir. A promise to a dying person must never be broken.'

'Dying? Oh, my God! Quick, tell me?'

'Lydia caught a chill. It turned for the worst. She's been in bed for ten days, growing weaker and weaker.'

'Didn't she get the doctor?'

'Yes. He's called several times. He last visited about half an hour ago but gave no hope for her recovery.'

'There must be!' cried John, his face taut with anguish. 'Take me to her!'

'That's why I'm here. Lydia wants to see you.'

'Where's Tess?'

'Lydia asked Mrs Foxwell to take her out of the way, and the maid has been sent home. Lydia wanted the way clear for your visit so no one but me would know of it.'

'Come on. Let us hurry.'

Reaching the house in Market-jew Street, Dorinda led the way upstairs. At the bedroom door she whispered, 'I'll see if everything is all right, sir.'

He nodded and she slipped into the room. A few moments later she reappeared.

'You can come in, sir.'

When John stepped into the room he received a shock. Lydia lay against the pillow, her face pale and gaunt. The bloom he remembered on her face and had always carried in his mental picture of her had gone. Though she tried to muster a smile, her expression remained wan and lifeless.

He heard the door close and was immediately on his knees at the bedside. Taking her hand in his, shocked to find how thin it was as if the flesh had wasted away, he gazed into her eyes, searching for something that would tell him what he feared was wrong. 'Lydia, what has happened to you?' His voice was ragged with distress. 'Why didn't you send for me?'

'I couldn't John, that would have betrayed our secret.' Her words came scarcely above a whisper.

'I could have done something,' he protested.

'You couldn't.' The finality of her statement alarmed him and wrung his heart.

'I must!' Tears welled in his eyes.

'No, John, you can't. Mrs Foxwell has looked after me. She couldn't have been kinder.' The words croaked in Lydia's throat. He felt her grip on his hand tighten. 'I hoped and prayed that the weather would relent and I would see you one more time. God has been good and granted me that wish.' As she said those words she seemed to find a little strength. 'Kiss me, John, and then go.'

'I cannot leave you like this,' he cried, his heart rent by pain.

'You must. There is nothing you can do except what I ask.' The pleading in her eyes could not be denied.

'Anything, my love.'

'I am happy that I have seen you again and felt your lips on mine. I know that you love me.'

He was about to speak when she stopped him. 'You must keep up the pretence. Your wife must never know about us, but promise me you will see that Tess is cared for?'

'That is a promise I will never break.'

'Kiss me again and go.'

'But . . .'

'That is what I want you to do. I don't want you to see me die. I want you to remember me as I was when we shared so much joy. Don't forget me.'

'I won't ever do that, and Tess will be there to remind me.'

Her smile then was as radiant as he had ever known it. He realised she knew the end was near. She reached up and stroked his cheek, finding consolation in the contact. He leaned over and kissed her, allowing the touch to linger until she whispered. 'Go.'

He hesitated but her wisdom prevailed. Two hearts met for the last time as he glanced back and received her smile, encouraging him to face the future in the way she wanted him to.

He found Dorinda waiting for him at the bottom of the stairs and steeled himself for what he knew was to come. There were tears in her eyes as she said, 'She's not long for this world, sir.'

'I'm afraid she is not.'

'She has been happy here, sir. And I have lost a dear friend.'

'Will you take care of the arrangements when the time comes?

'Certainly, sir.'

'You know with whom she was friendly in Penzance. Please inform them. Will you also inform Mr and Mrs Westbury and let them know the date of the funeral?'

'Certainly, sir. What about her brother?'

'I will see that he is informed.'

'Very good, sir. What about Tess? I can take her until you decide what to do.'

'That is very kind of you. It would solve the immediate problem.'

'It is the least I can do. Lydia was a very good friend to me and gave me great support when my father died. I know you will want what is best for Tess but if it becomes necessary, I can take care of her.'

'That is very good of you.'

'I could not see that darling child abandoned.'

'That will never happen, Dorinda.' As he was speaking John had been fishing in his pocket. He withdrew a wad of money that had been intended for Lydia. 'This will meet any expenses. I will call after the funeral to settle anything outstanding.'

'Yes, sir.'

As he rode home John felt as if part of life had been torn from him. 1800 would be the darkest year of his life. He wept openly but by the time he reached the Manor had control of his feelings once again.

Two days later Selwyn and Harriet Westbury rode up to Penorna where they were welcomed warmly by Eliza and John.

'We come with sad news,' announced Harriet as they entered the drawing room. 'We have received word that Miss Booth, whose painting hangs in your hall, died two days ago.'

'No!' Eliza frowned. 'She wouldn't be very old?'

'No, she wasn't,' replied Harriet. 'And the child she was caring for, little Tess, is still very young.'

The words were like arrows to John's heart and it took all his strength of will to prevent a breakdown but he managed to ask, 'How did you hear about it?'

'You remember she was very friendly with your governess, Miss Jenkins? Well, they renewed that friendship when Miss Booth came to live in Penzance. It was Miss Jenkins who informed us.'

'What will happen to the child?' asked Eliza.

'The obvious thing would be for her to go to her father, but if he didn't want her when she was born, he's not likely to want her now. So it looks as if the poor little girl will end up in a home.'

The picture that conjured up in John's mind almost made him scream but he restrained himself by remembering his promise to Lydia.

'When is the funeral?' asked Eliza.

'The day after tomorrow at St Mary's in Penzance, eleven o'clock,' replied Selwyn.

'We ought to go, John. She will be part of this house as long as her painting hangs here,' suggested Eliza.

'Would you like us to bring the carriage and then we could go together?' Harriet offered.

'That would be kind,' Eliza accepted.

Two days later a sombre service was conducted by the solemn-faced rector who praised Lydia for her goodness in taking responsibility for the baby her brother had abandoned at birth, and for the excellent job she had since done in raising Tess. He pointed out her involvement with church affairs and how she had enriched people's lives with her personality and their homes with her paintings.

John listened to it all with a lump growing in his throat. He stood beside Eliza and Abigail, with a heavy heart, and watched the coffin lowered into the ground. Across the grave he saw Dorinda holding the hand of his daughter, Tess. He felt certain he could see tears in the child's eyes and ached to give her comfort and tell her who he was, that he would always look after her. But he almost heard a warning word from beyond the grave: You will only confuse and hurt our daughter and shatter other lives. It will hurt me too. If you love me, don't do it.

I won't, my love, he whispered silently for answer and his grip tightened on Eliza's hand.

As people moved away, Dorinda brought Tess close to the graveside and, bending down, said something to her.

'Tess, you know Mr and Mrs Westbury but you don't know Mr and Mrs Mitchell and their daughter Abigail who live at Penorna Manor.'

'Mama used to point it out to me when we passed by on our way to see Mr and Mrs Westbury.'

For a moment Dorinda was alarmed by her use of the word 'Mama', but realised that other people would think Tess's usage the natural thing to do, the child having known no other mother.

Tess looked seriously at them. 'Mama told me not to cry because she was going somewhere where she will be happy.'

'That's right, Tess, she will be,' said John, crouching down and taking hold of her hand. Thrilled at the contact, the first he had had with his daughter since that baby grip on his finger, he looked into her eyes, so like her mother's, and a lump came to his throat. 'You are a brave girl and must go on being so. Your mother would want you to.'

She smiled at him. 'I will be, Mr Mitchell.'

'I remember you as a baby,' said Eliza.

'Do you, Mrs Mitchell?'

'Yes, I do, and you have grown into a charming girl.'

When the carriage reached Penorna, Selwyn and Harriet refused the Mitchells' proferred hospitality. John led his womenfolk into the house.

'Come down and we'll have a glass of Madeira,' he said. Five minutes later, alone in the drawing room, he was thoughtfully pouring three glasses of wine while grappling with the problem of what to do about Tess. It was something that would have to be resolved quickly. He could not rest on the good graces of Mrs Foxwell for long. The door opened and Eliza and Abigail came in. They accepted the glasses of wine and sat down.

'You know, I can't get the thought of that child out of my mind,' said Eliza. 'What is to become of her?'

'It's a problem,' said John.

'How old is she?' asked Eliza.

He looked thoughtful, as if trying to work it out. 'Let me see, I would think she'll be thirteen, maybe fourteen.'

'Fourteen,' mused Eliza, giving a little nod of her head. 'Not too young, I suppose. In some ways it could be an advantage . . .'

'What are you getting at?' asked John.

Eliza did not answer his question but put one to her daughter. 'What do you think, Abigail, would you like a personal maid of your own, a waiting maid?' The unexpectedness of the query brought a moment of charged silence then Abigail broke it with an excited cry.

'Oh, yes!' Then it dawned on her what lay behind her mother's query. 'You mean, Tess?'

'Why not?'

'Isn't she too young?'

'I don't think so. She struck me in the short time we saw her as being older than her years. My maid Sally can help to train her in the basic tasks, and any refinements you can school her in yourself.'

'Oh, yes, please.' Abigail was even more delighted now that the advantages had been pointed out to her.

'What do you think, John?' Eliza asked.

His mind had been racing. Had the answer to his dilemma unwittingly been given by his wife? Tess and he would be here under the same roof and, though he would have to be extremely careful about their relationship, he would at least be able to keep an eye on her and see that she was well cared for.

'That's sounds a feasible idea. If it is what you both want, I will arrange it with Dorinda.'

Chapter Fifteen

When John walked into the dining room the following morning Eliza and Abigail were already there.

'Are you both still in favour of the girl coming here?' he asked as he went to the oak sideboard to help himself from a silver tureen.

'Yes,' they both agreed.

'No doubts during the night?'

'No,' replied Abigail quickly.

'None,' said Eliza.

'We don't want to get her here and then either of you have regrets,' warned John as he sat down with his plate of porridge.

'What's this all about?' queried Eliza. 'Are you having doubts?'

'No,' he replied sharply. 'I just wanted to be certain you were both still in favour of having her. I shall send word to Dorinda this morning, telling her that we would like to discuss Tess's future and will send a carriage for them the day after tomorrow.'

Later that day Dorinda was surprised when a footman appeared in the shop and handed over a note from Penorna Manor. She asked him to wait and took the paper into the house before breaking the seal.

Dear Miss Jenkins,
In the matter of Tess's future, Mrs Mitchell and I believe it might be beneficial for her to come to Penorna as personal maid to Miss Abigail. Please give this some thought. I am sure you will view this suggestion with Tess's interests at heart.

If you are agreeable I will send a carriage for you the day after tomorrow at ten in the morning so that we can discuss the matter further.

John Mitchell

Reading the note again steadied her thoughts. Tess to leave her! Dorinda had grown attached to the girl during her frequent visits to Lydia and had watched with interest as she grew into an attractive, pleasing child. There would be a gap in her own life if Tess left Penzance. Dorinda brought her tumbling thoughts under control and chided herself for being selfish. She should be thinking of what was best for Tess. She knew only too well, from her own experience, that the child would be going to a well-run house and home. She would have more space there than she would have in the little house behind the shop in Penzance. Personal maid to Miss Abigail Mitchell would be a reasonably good position to have, and, though she would not know it, Tess would also be under the watchful eye of her father.

With her decision made, Dorinda folded the note, put it in the pocket of her dress, and returned to the shop.

'Please tell Mr Mitchell I will be ready at ten o'clock the day after tomorrow.'

Tess's bright smile when she came into the shop after visiting a friend touched Dorinda's heart and drove the thought of losing her to the forefront of her mind again. Could she bear to let her go? She had no need to tell Tess about Mr Mitchell's proposal, after all. She could send the carriage away without Tess even knowing, but would that be fair? Could she live with her own deceit?

'You look as if you've had an enjoyable time?' said Dorinda to postpone making a decision.

'I did, thank you. Gertrude is such fun.' Tess smiled, recollecting her friend, and then adopted a serious expression as she added, 'I think she was trying harder because she didn't want me to be sad about Mama.'

'She's a good friend,' Dorinda agreed. 'Go through and take your coat off. I'll be with you in a minute. I want to talk to you about something.'

'That sounds serious?' said Tess with a grimace.

'It is and it isn't.' Tess recognised Dorinda's reply as being one of her favourites when answering a question.

As Tess entered the house Dorinda spoke to her shop assistants, thankful that she had two such loyal workers. They had been invaluable when she had taken over Jenkins's Emporium on her father's death and set about restoring its fortunes, with considerable success.

Tess had dumped her coat in the small room between the shop and the house and was waiting in the drawing room.

'Tell,' said Dorinda, taking the girl's hand as she sat down beside her on the sofa. She knew it was no good skirting the issue so came straight to the point. 'I have had a note from Mr Mitchell who asks if you would like to be personal maid to Miss Abigail Mitchell?'

Tess stared at Dorinda in stunned silence.

'Leave you?' She frowned and her eyes pleaded for explanation.

'Well, yes. You would have to live at Penorna Manor. Miss Abigail would like you to be her own maid, but only if you would like to go.'

Tess was confused. She liked Dorinda, whom she had known for most of her life. In the days since Lydia had been ill she had found comfort and deep friendship here, a friendship that held an undercurrent of love. Now it was being suggested she should leave.

Troubled, she asked Dorinda, 'Does this mean I won't see you again?' There was a catch in her voice.

Dorinda smiled. 'No, love, of course not! You can come and visit me whenever it is possible.'

'But when would that be?'

'No doubt you will get some free time, but that can all be arranged with Mr and Mrs Mitchell.'

'But I wouldn't know what to do,' protested Tess in some distress.

'You're a bright girl, you'll soon learn.'

Tess looked at her again. 'What would you do?'

'I am not being offered the position,' Dorinda replied gently. 'You will have to decide. All I will say is that you would be going to a beautiful home with plenty of space, something I don't have in a house behind a shop. And I am sure you could be happy there. I was when I was governess to Miss Abigail. I suggest we go to see Mr and Mrs Mitchell. Mr Mitchell said in his letter that he would send a carriage for us the day after tomorrow. I agreed to go because I thought you should learn more about the position and see Penorna for yourself before you decide.'

Tess nodded. 'Very well,' she replied.

Dorinda recognised the doubt in Tess's voice, but she also knew that if she tried to persuade her, the attempt could do more harm than good. Tess was strong and sensible enough to make up her own mind.

Dorinda was thankful when she looked out of her bedroom window and saw that the morning scheduled for their visit to Penorna was bright and holding every promise of staying that way. The countryside and the house would look inviting rather than show the dour complexion they adopted when Atlantic gales drove rain and mist over them. She badly wanted Tess to gain a good impression of the place for she knew from her own experience that Penorna had much to offer. What a person took from it depended very much on them but, knowing Tess, she believed the girl could derive much from a stay at the Manor.

She was pleased when she went downstairs to find that Tess was already there and dressed carefully to present herself smartly to Mr and Mrs Mitchell.

'You've beaten me,' Dorinda said brightly. 'All ready to go.'

'I thought I may as well get ready when I got up,' replied Tess.

'Quite right! I'm pleased you chose that dress. It's as pretty as you,' commented Dorinda, admiring the pale blue, high-waisted dress that hung almost straight to the tops of Tess's black shoes. The neck-line was high and the slightly puffed shoulders lengthened into sleeves that ended tight at the wrists.

Tess looked troubled. 'You don't think Mama would mind?'

'You looking pretty?'

'Well, it's not long since . . .' Her voice faltered.

'Of course she wouldn't,' Dorinda was quick to reassure her. 'She would want you to look your prettiest.'

'And Mr and Mrs Mitchell won't think it wrong of me?'

'No, I'm sure they won't.'

The carriage arrived on the appointed minute and the coachman could not have been more polite and considerate as he saw Dorinda and Tess comfortably seated. He gave Tess a sly wink and responded with a broad smile when he saw his gesture had replaced her worried expression with laughter.

Dorinda took the child's hand in hers, thinking to reassure her but also drawing comfort herself.

'I've never been in such a carriage before,' Tess whispered, excitement in her voice. She looked around her, admiring the polished wood, the clean iron and shining leather. The sway of the carriage, the clop of the horse's hooves and swish of its tail, caught her attention. When she saw people stare at the passing vehicle with curiosity and envy, she felt like a real lady.

The route to Penorna took them at times close to the edge of the cliffs. The sea below shone blue and green, tipped with dashes of white; the horizon was far away and the sky big and blue. Tess felt almost overpowered by such space and freedom after the confines of Penzance which she had escaped only occasionally.

The coachman manoeuvred the horse and carriage skilfully through the open iron gates that admitted them to a driveway leading through a wood. The track burst out of the trees eventually into a wide-open space of manicured lawns that led gently towards a house that made Tess catch her breath.

It's size did not overwhelm, but it was large enough to impart an air of spaciousness and calm. Tess stared wide-eyed at it until her thoughts of what might lie ahead were interrupted by Dorinda.

'It's lovely inside.'

Tess merely nodded and the carriage drew up in front of four steps leading on to a stone veranda that stretched along the front of the house. The coachman was quickly to the ground, and on helping them out informed Dorinda that the carriage would be here, waiting when they were to return to Penzance. At that moment the front door opened and a maid only a little older than Tess appeared. Dorinda, knowing Mr Mitchell's meticulous timing in such matters, was not surprised.

'Follow me, please,' said the maid pleasantly while eyeing Tess with some curiosity.

She led the way along a corridor and up four steps into the large entrance hall where Tess noticed the two large doors, the upper half of which were glass, that gave out on to the veranda. She was disappointed they had been made to use the servants' entrance but then stifled the feeling; after all, Dorinda showed no signs of caring.

The maid knocked on a door, hesitated, then opened it. 'Miss Jenkins and Miss Booth, sir.' Tess now felt a flush of pride at being given her title for it made her feel like an adult. The maid stood to one side beside the door and indicated to them to enter.

Dorinda ushered Tess into a room that almost overwhelmed her with its size. Did people really need so much space to live in? The thought was forgotten almost as soon as it had come when her attention was drawn to Mr Mitchell who had risen from his chair to greet them with a warm smile. Mrs Mitchell occupied a chair next to that vacated by her husband, and Miss Mitchell was sitting in a window seat.

'Miss Jenkins, Tess, do sit down.' John indicated the sofa.

'It will have been a pleasant ride this morning,' commented Eliza amiably.

'It was, ma'am,' replied Dorinda.

'Did you enjoy it, Tess?' asked Eliza as she weighed up this girl who looked so smart in her pretty blue dress. How tragic that she should lose the person she regarded as her mother and with no loving father to turn to either.

'Oh, I did, ma'am,' replied Tess brightly.

'Good.' John had taken his seat again and Abigail had drawn up a chair beside her mother. 'Do you know why you are here, Tess?' He was finding it hard not to take this charming child into his arms and reveal the truth to her, but Lydia's words came strongly to mind.

'Yes, Mr Mitchell,' replied Tess who had seated herself prim and properly with her hands resting in her lap, just as she knew Dorinda would want her to. 'Dorinda told me.'

'What do you think to the idea? Would you like to come here and be Miss Abigail's personal maid?' asked Eliza.

John was on tenterhooks. What if Tess did not like the suggestion? She might leave and then maybe he would never see her again.

'Yes, ma'am, but I don't know what I would have to do.'

'I have given her some idea, ma'am,' put in Dorinda, 'but of course I do not know what you expect of her.'

'I am sure you will soon learn, Tess,' Eliza reassured her. 'My personal maid Sally will teach you, and my daughter will tell you what she wants.'

'It won't be hard,' put in Abigail, 'and you will have a room to yourself on the floor above mine.'

A touch of doubt floated into Tess's eyes. 'Will I still be able to see Dorinda?'

'Of course you will,' added John quickly. He sensed Tess was on the point of accepting and did not want anything to overturn her decision. He looked at Eliza. 'That will be possible, won't it?'

'Of course it will. You will have one day a week free after you have done your early-morning chores, and Sunday after morning service will also be free time for you.'

'And if ever you accompany me to Penzance there may be the opportunity for you to call on Miss Jenkins then,' Abigail pointed out.

Tess turned to Dorinda. 'What would you do?' she asked.

'I am not being offered the position,' she replied gently. 'You will have to decide. All I will say is, you would be coming to a beautiful home and I am sure you would be happy here. I was when I was governess to Miss Abigail.'

Tess nodded. 'As long as I can still see you.'

'Of course you can,' reiterated John.

She looked directly at him and from her eyes he read, Don't break your promise, but he already knew he never would. If only he could tell her the truth, he knew she would love and trust him. Tess turned to Dorinda again. 'All right, if you think that is best for me, and it is what Mama would have wanted me to do?'

'I'm sure it is,' Dorinda said. Her eyes met John's for one fleeting moment then and both knew that from afar Lydia had guided Tess to the right decision.

The carefully chosen staff at Penorna Manor welcomed Tess with open minds and helped her to settle in quickly. They liked her unassuming personality and willingness to help any of them if the necessity arose, though they were aware that, like themselves, she would eventually be guarded about her position in the hierarchy of the servants' hall. Sally, who was twenty-two and had been in service since she was twelve, coming to be Mrs Mitchell's lady maid when she was seventeen, took Tess's training seriously but imbued it with so much fun that Tess settled to it quickly. She was a fast learner and asked plenty of questions so that she was soon taking on responsibilities many of her age would have balked at.

Abigail was delighted with the way Tess kept her room spotless, cleaning the carpet with the use of damp tea-leaves and a brush, polishing the furniture and carefully dusting the ornaments. She was amused by the way Tess quickly assumed an air of authority by getting one of the housemaids to assist her in making the bed just the way that Abigail liked it. She thought her father and mother had found a gem when Tess had put away her dresses in a more orderly manner than the housemaid had previously done.

John too was delighted with the way Tess settled in, but dare not be over-enthusiastic or show her any special consideration, nevertheless, he experienced joy that his two daughters should be living under the same roof and that they got on so well, albeit as servant and mistress. As time passed he sensed a deep affection for Abigail growing in Tess, and that Abigail appreciated Tess's thoroughness and thoughtfulness.

Although initially apprehensive about moving to Penorna to work for strangers and wondering if she would really have free time to visit Dorinda, Tess soon lost her doubts. Mr and Mrs Mitchell, knowing it would enable her to settle in quickly, made sure that visits to Dorinda were encouraged, and whenever time allowed Abigail took Tess with her while visiting Penzance. Though both were unaware of it for some time, these expeditions further strengthened the bond between mistress and maid. Tess had a pleasant if small room handily above Abigail's. She was pleased that it was at the front of the house with a view across beautifully kept lawns to the small wood through which the main drive ran. The ornamental gates to the road were just visible beyond the trees. In the snatches of time she took for herself she loved to look out of this window, especially at any new arrivals at Penorna and in particular when she was able to see guests in their finest clothes, though none came close to her beloved Abigail.

But one person visited frequently and Tess took an instinctive dislike to him. After eighteen months she was clear in her own mind: she did not like Luke Gaisford. If she had been asked why she could have given no good reason, it was just a feeling. There was something about him that did not quite ring true. Could she fault his treatment of and attention to Abigail? Not really, but in her own heart she thought he was too effusive, too glib, and she did not like the way she had seen him look at Abigail. His visits to take her riding or walking became more and more frequent, and if ever there was a party anywhere in the county Luke Gaisford was always the first to ask Abigail to be his partner.

Three days before Abigail's twenty-second birthday, she and Luke rode out from Penorna Manor.

'That's a fine animal,' she commented. 'When did you get it?'

'Three days ago, from a dealer in Bosovern. Had my eye on it quite a while.'

She eyed it up and down then said with a challenging smile, 'Still not good enough to beat mine.'

He chuckled. 'We'll see,' was all he said, but his eyes told her he would rise to the challenge.

She knew she would have to be alert for the moment he threw down the gauntlet, but for the time being she would enjoy the more sedate ride. Abigail shuddered with pleasure at the feel of the gentle breeze caressing her cheeks. She loved this sort of day; small pure white clouds drifted lazily across the bright blue sky, never interfering with the sun. The gentle ride brought a feeling of contentment and she knew that an exhilarating gallop later would bring with it a sense of adventure, but no matter which she was glad she was sharing them with Luke Gaisford.

They kept to the cliff path that afforded them views across a calm sea that challenged the colour of the sky. They skirted the Trethtowan Estate and on reaching Senewey land increased their pace to a trot.

A few minutes later Abigail was jerked out of her reverie when Luke shouted without warning, 'Race you!' and put his mount into a pounding gallop.

Though caught unawares, Abigail rose to the challenge and put her own horse in pursuit. She was sure to catch him, she always did. But today she soon realised that Luke was on a very different horse from usual. She saw immense power in the animal ahead of her though she was not going to admit defeat yet. Flying hooves cut the earth and Abigail revelled in the turn of speed and the brute strength beneath her. But no matter how she exhorted her mount to greater efforts, she realised she would not catch Luke.

The track dipped into a hollow. He pulled his mount to a halt there and even before it had stopped moving he was out of the saddle and striding towards Abigail, letting his mocking laughter fill the air. Goaded by it, and filled with the exhilaration of her own swift ride, she fought her horse that wanted still to run. As she brought it under control Luke grabbed the bridle and steadied the animal.

He came to her side, laughter in his eyes. 'Beat you!' he announced triumphantly. He reached up and with his strong hands clasped firmly round her waist helped her to the ground. He did not let her go then but looked down into her flushed face. Their eyes met and held. Not a word was spoken as their lips came together sweetly and naturally. Abigail's arms slid round his neck as she returned his kiss.

'Payment to the winner,' she said softly as their mouths parted.

'I want more than that,' he whispered. 'Marry me, my love?'

She met the intensity in his eyes. A charge ran between them for an instant and then in a moment of overwhelming joy Abigail said, 'Yes, I will.'

He hugged her close; his lips found hers again and passion flared between them.

When they moved apart they automatically held hands and strolled through the hollow.

'You have made me very happy, Abigail.'

'No more than you have made me.'

'May I have your permission to ask your father for your hand when we return to Penorna?' he asked quietly.

'Of course,' she replied with an excited tremor in her voice. 'Why wait?'

Tess was at her window when the two riders burst from the wood at a gallop. Instead of riding towards the stables at the back of the house, they came straight for the front. There was joy on their faces and laughter in their eyes as they pulled their horses to a dust-stirring halt. Luke jumped from his saddle and was instantly beside Abigail, reaching up to help her to the ground. His hands closed round her waist and he continued to hold her, even when her feet were on the ground. He

599

looked down at her and she met his gaze lovingly. His lips met hers and Tess saw her accept his kiss with equal fervour. She shuddered. Something had happened today. There was a wild joy in the couple as they climbed the steps to the front door, side by side.

'Let me see if Father is in his study,' suggested Abigail when they entered the house. Luke followed her across the hall. She knocked on the door and opened it far enough to look round it. John was at his desk. He looked up and said, 'Come in,' at the same time giving a little indication with his hand, but she ignored both gestures and instead turned back into the hall. 'He's in,' she whispered, then stepped aside to allow Luke to enter the room. She closed the door behind him.

'Good day, sir. I am sorry to interrupt but may I have a word?' he began tentatively. As they had ridden back to Penorna he had wondered what would be the best way to approach Mr Mitchell. By the time they had reached the house he had nothing firm in mind and now found matters had taken their own course.

With this query John's full attention became riveted on the young man. He sensed what must be coming, or why hadn't Abigail accompanied him? 'Do sit down, Luke.' He indicated a chair on the opposite side of his desk.

Luke tried to relax as he sat down. He fell quiet and then realised that Mr Mitchell was waiting for him to speak. 'Sir, I . . . er . . . I would like to ask you for your daughter's hand in marriage.' The words were out before he realised it.

John held a moment's silence. 'You have asked Abigail?' he said finally.

'Yes, sir.'

'And she accepted?'

'Yes, sir.'

John looked thoughtful for a moment. 'There is no need to ask you about your prospects and whether you will be able to provide for my daughter in the way to which she is accustomed. I know Senewey, and have heard about the way you have pulled it round since your father's death.' Luke breathed a sigh of relief to himself. His efforts to hide the true state of Senewey's finances had paid off. 'There is something I must do before I give you my answer, however, and that is to have a word with Mrs Mitchell. That may as well be done now, so if you will wait here I will go to her.'

'Yes, sir.'

As John rose from his chair Luke, out of respect, did likewise. John left the room. Finding the hall empty he guessed Abigail must have joined her mother in the drawing room. He found that he was right.

'Papa?' There was a look of eager expectancy in her eyes as Abigail jumped up from her chair.

John raised one hand to calm her. He looked at his wife. 'Abigail has no doubt told you that Luke Gaisford is with me, and why?'

'Yes,' replied Eliza, her eyes fixed firmly on her husband, trying to read his decision from his expression. 'And?' she prompted.

'I haven't given him an answer yet.'

'Oh, Papa!' chided an anxious Abigail.

'I wanted a word with both of you first,' he went on, ignoring his daughter's reproof. 'Do you really know him, Abigail?'

'I do, or I would not have given him permission to ask you.'

'He's a Gaisford, remember . . .'

Abigail looked exasperated. 'You're always harking back to old times. Luke's different. You cannot judge the son by the father.'

'But blood does run deep, and who knows what hidden Gaisford traits still lie undiscovered in him.'

'Couldn't there be good traits too?' demanded Abigail.

Eliza saw that this situation could grow heated, which might turn family relationships sour. She did not want that so intervened with a question of her own. 'Do you love him, Abigail?'

'Oh, yes, Mama, of course I do.' She put such intense feeling into her reply there was no misunderstanding it.

Eliza looked at John with an expression that said, That is all that matters.

601

'Your mother seems convinced. I believe there are other matters to take into consideration, but if you feel so strongly about Luke then I will have to give my approval.'

'Papa!' She flew into his arms and hugged him tight. 'Thank you, thank you!'

'But you must promise us that if any doubts arise, you will tell us?'

'None will, Papa.'

He patted her on the shoulder. Abigail turned to her mother who had risen from her chair to hug her. 'Thank you, Mama.'

'Be happy,' Eliza told her.

'I will.'

'And remember your father's warning: a Gaisford is always a Gaisford.' Eliza gave a little pause, then added. 'But I pray Luke may be the exception.'

John was already at the door. Abigail wanted to rush after him but her mother laid a calming hand on her arm. A few moments later John and Luke reappeared and from Luke's nervous expression Abigail knew he still had not been told the decision.

'Good day, Mrs Mitchell,' he said politely, a gesture that Eliza acknowledged with an inclination of her head.

'Well, Luke,' said John, 'it seems you have my permission to marry my daughter.'

For one brief moment the words did not sink in then the ecstatic smile on Abigail's face confirmed what he had just heard. Luke's face lit up with a broad smile.

'Thank you, sir, thank you!' He rushed to take John's outstretched hand and then Eliza's. 'Thank you too,' he said, and she accepted a kiss on the cheek. As he turned from her mother Abigail came into his arms and they exchanged a triumphant kiss.

'I think this calls for champagne,' said John, going to the bell pull.

A few minutes later a toast was drunk to the young couple's future happiness.

Tess heard voices and went to the window of her room. She saw Luke mount his horse and say something to someone just out of sight. She guessed it was Abigail when she saw him blow a kiss. He turned his horse and in a matter of moments had put the animal into a gallop. Just before she lost sight of him in the wood she saw him sweep his hat off and wave it above his head in a way that had all the signs of someone who had just achieved something he dearly wanted.

Tess learned what that was fifteen minutes later when, having heard Abigail come upstairs, she went to help her mistress out of her riding clothes.

Hearing the door open, Abigail swung round. Her face was wreathed in a broad smile; there was joyous excitement in her eyes. She grabbed Tess and whirled her round and round. 'Oh, Tess, I'm so happy. I'm going to be married!'

She felt a nervous wrench in her stomach at the news. Abigail had her attention fixed on someone Tess did not like. Luke Gaisford! His name plunged like a spear through her mind. She wanted to cry out, No! He's not good enough for you! Miss Abigail, don't marry him! But she dare not. It was not her place to pass an opinion; it would mean nothing if she did. How could she mar the joy that enveloped Abigail? Besides, she did not want to lose Abigail's friendship and put their growing relationship on a mere mistress-and-maid level. It would sadden Tess and hurt her deeply if that happened. She quickly gathered her wits and, with fingers crossed behind her back, said, 'I'm so pleased for you, miss, and I hope you will be very happy together.'

In another part of the house two people were expressing their own doubts.

'I detect you aren't happy with this engagement, John?' Eliza put the question as he closed the door to their bedroom.

'Luke's a Gaisford, Eliza, and bad blood can run deep.'

'I know, but so far he has shown no signs of being like his father. He has always been very polite whenever he has been here, and he has always been most attentive to Abigail.'

'I agree. I cannot fault his behaviour or his attitude. He is properly considerate of our views and restrictions,' said John, but with a touch of reluctance that he had to agree there.

'And Abigail has assured me that Luke has given up drinking and no longer runs with the wild crowd he used to, although they remain friends,' went on Eliza. 'I have discreetly checked up on this when I have taken tea around the county and it seems that Luke avoids all the places he used to frequent. People say he seems to have turned over a new leaf since his father died, and is only interested in the running of the estate nowadays.'

'But he's still a Gaisford.' John's lips tightened. 'Old habits can be resurrected. I wish Abigail could see it.'

'We've pointed it out to her ever since she started seeing more of Luke.'

'I know, and short of putting an outright ban on her associating with him, we thought she would see the type he really was. Instead she seems to have reformed him.'

'We could have refused her permission to marry.'

'I don't think that would have done any good.' John gave a reluctant smile. 'You know as well as I that Abigail can be headstrong and stubborn if she wants to. She would probably have cocked a snook at convention, walked out and gone to him. Then we would have lost her for good, and we would not want that. All we can do is give her our blessing and offer her our continued love and support.'

Two days later, having helped Abigail to dress for her party, Tess remarked as she stepped back to view her mistress, 'That was a good choice of dress, miss. It suits you. You look so beautiful. Everyone will envy Mr Gaisford.'

'Thank you, Tess, and thank you for having this dress so beautifully ironed.'

Tess could not deny the happiness her mistress was feeling. She watched discreetly from a corner of the passage that led into the main hall at the moment the engagement was announced to the crowded room. It sent new joy through the guests who poured congratulations onto the happy couple.

From her position Tess caught the question that was put several times: when will the wedding take place?

As she wandered back to her room it rang in her mind and brought another to the fore. What will happen to me? Her answer was to recall that Dorinda had told her she could always go to her. Yes, that would be her best solution.

But she received a different answer the following afternoon. Abigail had slept late, and after a light luncheon with her father and mother, had gone riding on her own. Tess had taken the opportunity to straighten her mistress's room. Noticing the water jug had been chipped, she obtained a replacement from the kitchen and was returning along the landing when she heard voices she recognised as Mr and Mrs Mitchell's coming from the bedroom where the door was slightly ajar. She heard her name and halted her step.

'Tess? Well, I suppose Abigail will want to take her with her after she and Luke are married. After all, it's better to have a lady's maid she knows,' said Eliza.

Softly spoken though they were, the words thundered in Tess's mind. Go to Senewey Manor! Oh, no! As happy as she was with Abigail, she did not like the prospect of living at Senewey, nor being under the authority of Luke Gaisford about whom she was still uneasy.

'We must draw comfort from the fact that Tess will be with her. When the time comes, I'll have a word with her and ask her to report anything disturbing directly to us.'

Tess's heart was racing. It was obvious Mr and Mrs Mitchell had doubts of their own about this marriage. Why hadn't they refused permission for it? It was apparent they hadn't and that they were relying on her to stay near Abigail in case of any trouble. From loyalty to Abigail and her parents she could not refuse to go to Senewey.

Chapter Sixteen

At Luke's urging a date was soon fixed, but he had to agree
with Abigail's wishes, instigated by her father and mother,
that the wedding day be in six months' time. Abigail was
happy enough with that because it gave her time to enjoy and
savour all the parties during their engagement period and
revel in the preparations for an August wedding.

Luke resigned himself to wait, soothed by the thought of
the dowry which would relieve his ever-worsening financial
position. But before the happy day he knew he would have to
further some other schemes he had in mind.

He met his four friends regularly at the Waning Moon,
sometimes more than once a week. It became 'their' place, a
travellers' inn where they could have a private room for an
evening's drinking, stay the night and face the world in peni-
tent sobriety the next day.

Although Tess still harboured doubts about Luke as a suitable
husband for Abigail, whom she had come to love and admire
all the more, she kept them to herself. But after what she had
overheard, she resolved to sharpen her vigilance when she
removed to Senewey.

Unaware of Tess's misgivings, Abigail was pleased that the
girl appeared to be swept up in her own joyous mood for she
felt a strange affinity to her maid.

Although Eliza and John would have preferred a quiet wedding they knew it could not be so. Since coming to Cornwall
their stature had grown and, though their acceptance into

Cornish society had been slow, it was founded on admiration and trust, especially after the reconciliation with Jeremy Gaisford on Abigail's seventeenth birthday. The gentry would expect a big wedding, especially as the bridegroom was from the oldest family in Cornwall on his mother's side. So the preparations were thorough. Eliza determined that everything should be stylish and correct.

The week before the wedding was one of glowering skies and rain swept in by a south-westerly wind that in the dark hours seemed to be howling a warning. At least Tess, lying awake in the darkness, took it that way. It accentuated her own troubled state. She saw nothing but disaster ahead in this marriage and feared what might happen if Abigail's deep love for Luke was betrayed, but there was nothing she could do about it.

She slipped out of bed early on the day of the wedding; there was much to get through before the ceremony at noon but the first thing she did was to go to the window. When she drew back the curtains she saw a bright morning with no evidence of the inclement weather of the past week. Was this an omen? Did the heavens shine on the wedding after all? Had her own suspicions been unfounded? She did not know the answers and there was no time to worry now with so much to be achieved before the ceremony.

Tess had done most of the packing for Abigail's immediate requirements for the two weeks she and Luke would spend at Senewey Manor before, taking advantage of the fragile peace with Napoleon, they left for a wedding trip to France. She would complete that immediately and see that all her own things too were ready to move to Senewey Manor. She had been apprehensive when Abigail had told her that Luke had agreed to her still being employed as her maid after the wedding but hid that feeling, knowing she wanted to remain close to her mistress.

When she went to Abigail's room she found her already up and arrayed in her undergarments over which she had slipped a lace robe.

'Good morning, miss,' Tess greeted her.

'With an exciting day ahead, I woke early, Tess, so left my bed. A day dress for breakfast, please.'

Tess quickly chose one and in a matter of minutes Abigail was on her way downstairs. Tess glanced round the room and decided to get her own breakfast before tidying up.

She was not long away and had resisted the kitchen staff's desire to know what Abigail's wedding dress was like, telling them she did not want to spoil the surprise and they must all wait and see.

By the time Abigail returned Tess had brought some order to the room and immediately turned her attention to the preparations for the wedding. Time would fly and there was the carriage ride to Penzance to consider.

When the moment came, Tess knelt on the floor and helped Abigail into a pair of pale blue shoes. She then carefully took the wedding dress from its hanger, handling the garment as if it was the most precious piece of delicate glass. They were both awe-struck by its beauty and not a word passed between them as Tess helped Abigail into the deep rose brocade silk dress. Its patterned bodice came tight to the waist and fell in smooth lines to the floor. The round neckline finished at discreetly puffed shoulders, and the sleeves came tight to the wrist. Abigail gave herself a little shake that sent the dress shimmering.

Tess stood back and looked at her with open admiration. 'Oh, you do look beautiful, miss.'

'The head-dress, Tess,' said Abigail, her voice quivering with excitement.

Tess eased the garment from its box and placed it carefully on her mistress's head. The white bonnet had a low crown, a brim decorated with intertwining green leaves and yellow rosebuds, and had a delicate white waist-length veil neatly fastened to it. It still allowed Abigail's coiffure to show, the hair swept back on either side of a middle parting.

'Just right,' said Abigail, gleefully appraising herself in a full-length mirror. 'Thank you, Tess. And thank you for all you have done to make this occasion happy for me. I hope you too will be happy at Senewey.'

'Thank you, miss,' Tess replied, though she still had misgivings about that.

'As I have already told you, a special carriage is arranged to take you there later in the day. When you arrive you will report to the housekeeper, Mrs Horsefield.'

Any further conversation was halted by a knock on the door. Tess went to it quickly and on opening it saw Mr and Mrs Mitchell.

'May we come in?' Eliza asked.

Tess glanced back at Abigail whom she knew must have heard the request. She nodded and Tess stood aside, holding the door ajar. Eliza and John stepped into the room and came to a halt. They stared in wonder and admiration at their daughter.

'Beautiful!' The word was drawn out as John stared at her in amazement.

'You look wonderful,' said Eliza, her own face wreathed in admiration.

John found himself wondering would he ever see his other daughter looking so beautiful in her wedding dress?

John was filled with pride as he walked down the aisle of St Mary's Church, Penzance, with his beautiful daughter attracting everyone's eyes. Seeing Luke's expression of adoration as he turned to greet her, he wondered if he had judged this young man too harshly and offered a silent prayer that Luke's attitude would never change. His daughter's happiness was paramount to John and he only wished he could openly express the same for Tess.

No one could fault the parson's handling of the service, and the homily he directed at the bride and groom not only expressed his hopes for their future happiness but also dwelt for a few moments on the duties of man and wife towards each other.

The church was full, with places at the back especially reserved for the staffs of Penorna and Senewey so that they could make a quick exit once the actual ceremony was over. Tess managed to gain one from which she had a good view of the ceremony which she watched with mixed feelings. She wanted to be happy for Abigail but her misgivings about Luke Gaisford had worsened the nearer the wedding day drew. She could not deny, however, that the couple looked radiantly happy and that Luke could not have been more attentive to his bride.

It was also a happy laughing pair who emerged from the church to be greeted by many casual sightseers and were soon joined by the congregation flowing out of the church to shower congratulations on them.

The carriages taking the staff back to their respective manors were already leaving, those to Penorna to be ready to serve the wedding guests on their arrival; those to Senewey to await the arrival of bride and groom later in the day.

As he came out of the church John caught a glimpse of Tess in one of the last Penorna carriages. He felt a sharp tug at his heart and a sense of his own injustice filled him. Tess should be beside him now, occupying her rightful place among the guests as Abigail's sister. The thought was driven from his mind, though, as Eliza slipped her arm under his and said, 'A lovely occasion. A pity Luke's mother was not well enough to attend.'

'Yes,' he agreed. 'Here's their carriage arriving.'

The crowd milled even closer around bride and groom. Congratulations, well wishes, advice both serious and humorous, filled the air but all were lost on the couple who had eyes only for each other. It took them ten minutes to reach the carriage after its arrival. Once it was away the other vehicles that had been lining up moved forward; the first for the bridesmaids and Martin, the best man. This was followed by one for John and Eliza, and then for the other guests.

The joyful mood continued at Penorna where no expense had been spared to make everyone feel this was a special day, one to be remembered. Wine flowed freely, there was food aplenty, and no one lacked for conversation. Inevitably bride and groom were separated as demands on their attention grew. Luke found himself confronted by Martin, Sydney,

610

George and David. Each in turn shook his hand, offered their congratulations and wished him well for the future.

'Will that include a resumption of our meetings at the Waning Moon?' Martin asked.

'Of course,' replied Luke emphatically. 'You'll see me turning up at the inn soon after my return from France.'

It was late afternoon when John managed to extricate himself from a conversation with two landowners from the north of the county and went in search of Eliza.

He interrupted her chat with two friends from St Ives and drew her to one side. 'It will soon be time for Tess to leave for Senewey. Should I have a word with her about Abigail?'

'If you think it wise,' she replied, but a slight nod signified her approval. 'Don't put too much responsibility on the girl. We don't want to give her the impression she will be spying for us.'

'I'll be careful.'

He found Tess in Abigail's room. She was surprised when John walked in and looked sheepish, as if she had been caught somewhere she shouldn't have been.

'I was just making a last check on some of Miss Abigail's things, sir.' Tess blushed as she added quickly, 'Er . . . I mean, Mrs Gaisford's things.'

John smiled at her embarrassment. 'That was very thoughtful of you, Tess. I'm sure everything will be in order. You learned quickly and you have always been very efficient and I am pleased with the way you have both got on so well.'

'Sir, Miss Abigail has been very easy to deal with.'

'I'm glad. Now it will soon be time for you to be going to Senewey. Robert will have a carriage ready for you in ten minutes. Before you go, I want to give you one last instruction. If ever you are worried about my daughter, in any way, come and tell me. No one else – only me, or Mrs Mitchell if I am not here. I don't want you to feel you'll be spying on her or Mr Gaisford but if you are at all uneasy . . .'

He left the sentence unfinished but from her expression knew that she had read his meaning.

'I will, sir.'

'Thank you, Tess.'

As he left the room John so wished he could turn back and tell her the truth about herself, how much he had loved her mother and now loved her.

Tess went to her room. She looked round her, sad to be leaving. She had been happy here. The Mitchells' kindness, especially that shown her by Mr Mitchell, had helped to ease the loss of her dear mama, as Tess had always called her aunt.

She picked up the valise which Dorinda had given her when she left Penzance, and went to the door. She paused, looked behind her for the last time and then left her sanctuary, determined to cope with the new life that faced her and to keep a watchful eye on Miss Abigail's welfare. She gave a little nod – yes, to Tess she would always be Miss Abigail, no matter that now she was legally Mrs Luke Gaisford.

Robert was kindness itself when he drove Tess to Senewey Manor. He kept up a light stream of chatter to try to brighten her move. He did not envy her residing in the Gaisford residence even though she was going to continue as the bride's lady's maid. He did not like the house himself but made no comment about that even though he sensed Tess shudder when it came in sight.

Her spirits plummeted but in a few moments she'd pulled herself together, determined not to let a mere house get her down, even though after Penorna this one seemed dour and dreary. It appeared to have no feeling of life about it and Tess wondered how much of that was due to the people who had lived there in the past and those who lived there now.

Robert drove into a courtyard at the rear of the house and pulled the horse to a halt at a small door. He helped Tess down to the ground and carried her bag inside.

'I've been here before. I'll show you where to go,' he whispered.

Tess thought their footsteps striking the stone floor sounded like harbingers of doom. They came to another door which he opened and Tess followed him into a small lobby which she noticed thankfully was carpeted. She didn't like the echo-ing sound here. Robert knocked at a door to the left and opened it on a command to come in.

'Good day, ma'am,' he said politely, 'I've brought Tess Booth, Mrs Gaisford's, that is the *new* Mrs Gaisford's person-al maid as arranged.'

'And good day to you, Robert,' she said, rising from an armchair near the window that looked out on to a small walled garden. 'Ah, so this is Tess about whom Mrs Gaisford talked so highly.'

'It is,' replied Robert. He turned to Tess. 'This is Mrs Horsefield, the housekeeper.'

Tess felt uncomfortable in front of this woman who pre-sented a formidable figure as she eyed her up and down, but ventured to say, 'I was told to report to you, ma'am.'

'You're younger than I expected,' said the housekeeper.

'I'll be sixteen in December and I'm a good worker, ma'am.'

'So I've been told. See that you remain so.'

'I will, ma'am.'

'Mrs Gaisford has told me that she wants you to devote your entire time to being her personal maid so she must think highly of you. See that you don't let her trust in you down.'

'I won't, ma'am.'

'Because Mrs Gaisford wants it that way, the only other person you will report to will be me.'

'Yes, ma'am.'

During this exchange Mrs Horsefield had gradually appeared less formidable; her features had lost their first severity and assumed a more kindly expression.

'I'll show you to your room and explain some things to you on the way.' She turned to Robert. 'You'll take a tot before you leave?'

'That is very kind of you, Mrs Horsefield. It will certainly help me on my way.'

'Very good! I'll deal with Tess and soon be back.'

As she said goodbye to Robert, Tess wondered how many tots he had previously taken with Mrs Horsefield, but what did it matter? It was none of her business and it did make the housekeeper seem more human and not the harridan that Tess had feared. Maybe it wouldn't be so bad at Senewey after all.

She followed Mrs Horsefield from the room and fell into step beside her in the corridor.

'This is the staircase you will generally use unless it is absolutely essential for you to use the main one,' the housekeeper said as they climbed to the first small landing. Here she opened a door that led on to a wide corridor, luxuriously carpeted. She crossed this and took Tess into a small vestibule that led into a big room furnished with a large sofa and four armchairs that Tess felt she would be lost in. The walls were papered with a small floral pattern against a yellow background and on each wall there was a gold-framed seascape. 'This is Mrs Gaisford's sitting room,' explained Mrs Horsefield, and then opened a door on the right. 'This is her bedroom. You will be responsible for these two rooms.' The bedroom was as large as the sitting room. Apart from the huge bed there was a wardrobe, chest of drawers, dressing table, oval card table and four chairs, two easy chairs, and small table to each side of the bed. The two large windows looked out onto lawns and flower gardens beyond which lay wild moorland.

When they returned to the sitting room Mrs Horsefield hesitated. 'That door leads into Mr Gaisford's sitting room and beyond it is his bedroom. You will never venture through that door. Tully, Mr Gaisford's manservant, looks after those two rooms. You'll meet him later, as you will all the staff. I'll take you to your own room now.'

They returned to the stairs. As the mistress's maid Tess merited a small bare room which held a single bed, small table, chest of drawers, chair and wash stand. It was lit by a sash window that looked down over the courtyard.

'Everything has been prepared for you here, Tess. Now, I will return downstairs and send Alice to show you the rest of the house. She'll be with you in fifteen minutes.'

'Yes, Mrs Horsefield. I'll be waiting.'

The housekeeper nodded. 'I hope you will be happy with us at Senewey Manor.'

Tess put her few belongings away and had just finished making the bed to her liking when there was a knock on the door.

She looked up expectantly when it opened but the person who entered was not at all as expected. In her mind she'd pictured a middle-aged woman who had worked for years as a general maid for the Gaisford family. Instead she saw a thin waif of a girl of about her own age tentatively edging into the room, as if afraid of what might confront her.

'Tess Booth?' she asked in a voice that was scarcely above a whisper.

'Yes, that's me,' said Tess brightly to reassure the girl that she was not an ogre. 'You must be Alice.'

'Yes, miss.'

Tess grinned. 'No need to call me miss, I'm only a maid like you.' She stepped past the girl to close the door.

'But you're a personal maid,' said Alice with some awe.

'I am, to the new Mrs Gaisford, but I'm still a maid like you and don't you forget it if we are to be friends.'

Alice's smile wiped the solemnity from her face. 'You want to be friends with me?' she asked eagerly.

'If you want to be friends with me?'

'Oh, I do. There's no one here of my age and it gets lonely at times.'

'Then you and I will be friends,' replied Tess, equally grateful, realising that there might be a time when she really needed a friend at Senewey. 'Mrs Horsefield said you are to show me round the house.'

'Yes, but first I have to give you these.' She thrust the things she had been holding towards Tess.

'What are these?'

'Dresses like mine,' replied Alice. 'We all have to wear the same here.'

'Oh, I didn't know that.'

'You have to try them on, and if they don't fit I have to pin them and take them to the sewing room.'

Tess shrugged her shoulders. 'In that case, I may as well try them on now and if they need altering we can take them there when you show me round.'

Tess slipped off her own frock and shrugged herself into the first of the three dresses that Alice had brought. Alice tried to hide her embarrassment at Tess's openness by saying, 'I wish I was like you.'

'What do you mean?' asked Tess.

'You aren't skinny like me.'

'Maybe you are better in other ways.'

'I doubt that. I'll never be a personal maid.'

'I knew nothing about it until I was engaged to be Mrs Gaisford's personal maid before she was married. She insisted I come here with her.'

'You were lucky.'

'I learned quickly.' Tess looked down at Alice who was deftly pinning the bottom of the dress. 'I couldn't do what you are doing so skilfully.'

'I'm sure you could.'

'No, I've never done anything like that.'

'My mother taught me. I helped her. She did some dressmaking in St Just.'

They quickly adjusted the three dresses and Alice agreed that the several aprons were suitable.

'Come on, I'll show you the house, now?

They delivered the dresses to the sewing room first. The three sewing maids were friendly and Tess was told the alterations would be completed by noon the next day. The housemaids eyed her suspiciously but without any rancour; the kitchen staff were more friendly, though with all the preparations for the following day's party going on they had little time to give her. The head cook, who Tess realised ruled this domain, told her she would only be allowed in the kitchen when she was answering a request from Mrs Gaisford. She also informed Tess that staff mealtimes were to be strictly adhered to. When they left the kitchen, Alice showed her the staff dining room.

She then conducted Tess through the rest of the house, telling her where she was allowed to go and which areas were out of bounds. In the hall, which was oak-panelled and from which a wide staircase lined by an elaborately carved banister led to the upper floors, Alice indicated a long corridor leading to the right.

'Off there is the West Wing. You have no need to go there. It is where Mrs Gaisford, Mr Luke's mother, lives. You may catch a glimpse of her occasionally but she lives very much on her own and has her own maids.'

Tess looked around and then Alice lowered her voice. 'They say that when Mr Gaisford inherited, he insisted his mother should live in that wing and keep to herself.'

'Is there something the matter with her?' asked Tess.

'Not that I know of! I did meet her in one of the corridors once by accident and she asked me who I was. She seemed kind enough, but I know no more. My advice to you is, don't ask questions. Keep strictly to your work for the new Mrs Gaisford and all will be well. My only other piece of advice is, don't cross Mr Gaisford, he has a quick temper.'

'I wouldn't have thought that from what I have seen,' said Tess, hoping this would prompt Alice into saying more. But all she added was, 'You haven't worked for him and you haven't seen him at home. They tell me there's something of his father in him.'

Tess said nothing further but locked the information away in her mind.

'It's time we were leaving, love,' whispered Luke in Abigail's ear in an attempt to draw her away from conversation with Martin.

She gave a small nod as she said, 'That's a pity. I was just revelling in Martin's compliments. You must visit us soon after we get back.'

'Senewey used to be a second home to me whenever I was home from school,' replied Martin.

'You were at Rugby with Luke?'

'Yes, and Sydney and David and George. We all went there together and gained a reputation for being the Cornish Five.'

'A reputation that stuck for a while after your return,' commented Abigail with a knowing smile.

Martin threw up his arms in denial as he said, 'We reformed.'

'Reputations stick,' she teased. 'Who knows what you get up to now?'

'We really must go,' put in Luke.

Abigail took his arm, flashing Martin a dazzling smile that set his heart racing. When it became known that the bride and groom were about to leave for Senewey the guests made their way outside to give them a send off. Laughter and shouts of congratulation rang through the air as the carriage started to move. Abigail threw her bouquet in the air and a great cheer rang out when it was caught by George's sister.

The newly weds sank back on the seat with contented sighs.

'All so wonderful,' said Abigail, taking Luke's hand in hers. 'Your mother and father did us proud.'

'Thank you. I'm sorry your mother was not able to be there. I must see her before I change out of my wedding gown.'

Luke hesitated only a moment before he realised he could do nothing but comply. Besides, it would be for the best. His mother may keep very much to the West Wing nowadays but there was always the possibility that Abigail would come across her by chance, careful as she was to avoid her own son.

When word ran through the house that the carriage was approaching the staff quickly gathered in the entrance hall where they were marshalled by Mrs Horsefield to form a welcoming party.

The housekeeper greeted the happy couple and then introduced each member of the staff to Abigail. When they had dispersed she turned to Luke and said, 'Your mother?'

He nodded and led her to the door giving access to the West Wing. Here he took her through a sitting room into a medium-sized hall from which a staircase rose.

As soon as he looked inside he said, 'Mother, I've brought Abigail to see you.' He stepped to one side to allow his bride

618

to enter. She detected delight in Mrs Gaisford's voice when she greeted her and there was no disguising the brightness that came to the older woman's eyes.

'Mrs Gaisford,' said Abigail as she crossed the room to embrace Luke's mother and greet her with a kiss.

Hester reached out for Abigail's hands and held them affectionately as she said, 'How beautiful you look, my dear.' The light in her eyes left Abigail in no doubt that the compliment was given genuinely.

'I'm sorry you were not able to be at the wedding.'

'So was I, but my health is not good and if I had had trouble during the service it would have upset everybody. I was better here, thinking of you and my son and hoping you will be good for Luke. He has a tradition to live up to, and that on top of running an estate is not easy.'

'Now, Mother, no preaching,' cut in Luke.

Abigail saw a flash of resentment cross her mother-in-law's face but as befitted a woman of breeding she brought her reaction so quickly under control that it was hardly noticeable.

But it made Abigail wonder if all was not as it should be between this proud, frail woman and her son.

Chapter Seventeen

Although she did not like Senewey Manor as much as the house at Penorna, Tess was determined to settle quickly and thankful she had already made a friend in Alice. The arrival of the bride and groom after the reception at Penorna set Senewey into a whirl of excitement that continued throughout the following day with a party that went on into the next morning. Tess was pleased to see Abigail so radiantly happy and hoped it continued for a long time.

Even though she was swept up in her love for Luke, Abigail was pleased to have Tess's familiar presence close by to negate the unfamiliar surroundings. She was also pleased and excited to tell her, 'You are coming to France with us.'

Tess stared at her with disbelief, 'Me? Going to France?'

Abigail laughed. 'Yes. Mr Gaisford is allowing me to take you as my personal maid rather than relying on hired servants there.'

'Oh, miss, that's wonderful! I never dreamed . . .' Tess's words faded away. Then, with the idea sinking in, she said, 'I've never left England before.'

'Nor have I, Tess. But Mr Gaisford has been to France so he will see that we are all right.'

'I hope so, miss. I'm not sure about foreigners, but this is exciting.' Her eyes were bright at the prospect of a new experience.

When Tess broke the news to Alice, her new friend was not envious but said she would want to know all about it when Tess got back.

In the ensuing days Tess was careful to see to Abigail's every need and be meticulous about packing for the wedding trip. Throughout this time she saw little of Luke until the day they left for France when he came to see that the trunks and valises were securely packed on the coach in which Tess would travel alone during the week-long journey from Penzance to Dover.

He acknowledged her and asked, 'Have you been on the sea before?'

'No, sir.'

He grimaced. 'Well, if you are going to be sick, keep right away from me.'

'Yes, sir.'

'And make sure this luggage arrives safely.'

'Yes, sir.'

The responsibility he had thrust upon her made Tess nervous but by the time the two carriages had reached the port she had determined not to let it worry her and to enjoy her first trip abroad, though how much freedom she would have there she did not know.

The hustle and bustle at Dover took her mind off the pending crossing to France and it was only brought sharply back to mind when the ship left the harbour. Tess was thankful that the sea was smooth for the first time she left English shores and in fact found pleasure in the ship's motion.

At Calais Luke organised two coaches to take them to Paris, Tess travelling, as she had done in England, in the coach that carried their luggage. It was a lonely journey for her but she made the most of it by taking an interest in all she could see from the windows. An overnight stay in Abbeville was a welcome break, and though she became the object of curiosity when she went to dine with the servants at the establishment chosen by Mr Gaisford, she coped well in spite of the language difficulty.

It was different in Paris where they had rooms in one of the best hotels in the city for here Tess came across people with whom she could communicate more easily, though their smattering of English left much to be desired. She was pleased that she could now attend more readily to Abigail's needs for she did not like to be idle. Nevertheless her time was divided between bouts of strenuous activity and what might have been periods of sheer boredom had she let them become so. Whenever an opportunity arose during daylight she ventured out to see the city, being careful to keep to places frequented by crowds of people. She spent a considerable time in the magnificent Gothic cathedral of Notre Dame, overawed by the soaring architecture but saddened by the ravages of the recent Revolution on this holy building. She had thought that the church in Penzance was wonderful but it could not compete with this. The majestic façade of Les Invalides held her attention for many minutes, and the lively river traffic as she walked by the Seine made her think for a moment of the port where she'd grown up. Signs of the huge upheaval of the Revolution were still everywhere to be seen but she was fascinated by the work that was going on under the Napoleonic revival.

The evenings were long for her. After she had seen to Abigail's needs, before she and Mr Gaisford visited Luke's friends in the city or spent time at a theatre or restaurant, Tess's time was free. In anticipation of this Abigail had provided her with several books. She had started Anna Maria Porter's *Octavia* on the way here, and still had *The Gipsy Countess* by Elizabeth Gunning, *Tales of the Cottage* by Mary Pilkington, and *Angelina* by Mary Robinson, to start.

After Paris they moved on to Chartres where after Abigail and Luke had visited the cathedral on their first day, Abigail told Tess that she must find the opportunity to see it too. Two days later when Luke took Abigail by carriage into the neighbouring countryside, Tess quickly cleared away her mistress's clothes and tidied the room before leaving for the cathedral.

She had caught a glimpse of it as they arrived in the town but, after Notre Dame in Paris, had not expected to see another such sight. She stood for a long time taking in the carvings above the west doors above which rose three magnificent stained glass windows that were outdone only by the breathtaking rose window above them. The glory of those windows became evident when she went inside and saw the light come streaming through them. Awe-struck she just stood and stared, trying to decide whether she preferred this to the beautiful rose window in Notre Dame.

How would she ever be able to convey all this beauty and magnificence to Alice when she got home?

Tess found there was more to come when they went to Rouen where she walked in Joan of Arc's footsteps leading to the stake. Then it was on to Amiens for a few days before going on to Dieppe.

They arrived in the early afternoon and Luke excused himself to Abigail, saying that he had some business with a man who had been recommended as being able to put some business his way. Abigail decided to take the opportunity to have a rest after the bustle of the days they had spent. Seeing her mistress was comfortable, Tess retired to her room to remain on hand when needed.

'It looks as though you haven't been successful,' commented Abigail when Luke returned, wearing a puzzled frown.

'I wasn't,' he said irritably. 'I was told in England that this man would be in Dieppe, now I'm told he's in Calais.' He looked thoughtful for a moment. 'I'll have to reassess the situation when we get there.'

As Tess's coach trundled the last few miles into Calais she reflected on the master's attitude to Abigail throughout their sojourn in France. She could not fault his attention to his wife whenever she had been able to observe it. Everywhere they had been, he had commandeered the best accommodation and seen to her every comfort. He paid little attention to Tess but she knew he had observed her contributions to his wife's well-being, and, remembering Alice's warning, had given him no cause for complaint.

Riding in the leading coach, Luke took Abigail's hand in his. 'I hope you have enjoyed the last eight weeks?'

'Immensely,' she replied with a smile. 'Your arrangements have been marvellous and I have enjoyed every minute of our trip. I only wish it could go on.'

'Alas, my love, tomorrow we have to re-enter the real world.'

'Ah, well, we have wonderful memories.' She leaned towards him and kissed him. 'Thank you.'

'Abigail.' She straightened at the sound of a serious note in his voice and was disturbed to see a severe expression on his face. 'I didn't tell you this because I didn't want to spoil the little time we had left, but from what I was told in Dieppe I may have to be in Calais for a few days.'

'Why?'

'The man I had to see, Monsieur Defarge, had told a subordinate to deal with me. When I explained my business proposition he did not hold out much hope, but I insisted I should see Mr Defarge himself. I was not going to be pushed aside by a subordinate! If Defarge does not want to do business then I will have to stay in Calais a little longer and find someone who does.'

'Then I'll wait with you.'

'No! It would be far better if you went ahead. Godric will have brought the coach from Senewey to Dover and everything is arranged for our journey back. As I will not be with you, your lady's maid can ride with you.'

'But I don't like you deserting me like this.' There was a steely note to her voice and criticism in her eyes.

Luke bristled with annoyance. 'You are going to have to get used to it,' he retaliated. 'We are back to serious concerns which may take me away from you quite often.'

Abigail did not reply but turned to gaze out of the window. Their first harsh words had marred the end of what she had viewed as the perfect start to her marriage. Was reality dealing its first blow? Was a Gaisford trait revealing itself? Her father's warnings came to mind. But she knew from the harsh determination in Luke's voice that there was nothing she could do about his decision to leave her now, and it was extremely unlikely that she would be able to do anything about it in the future.

It was late afternoon when they arrived at their accommodation. Tess followed them inside and immediately sensed the tension between them. She wondered what had happened during the coach journey. Luke ordered a meal to be brought to them and, apart from arranging a room for Tess, left her to fend for herself.

'You still sulking about tomorrow?' he demanded towards the end of the meal during which Abigail had shown no inclination to talk.

'Not sulking. Hurt that you are deserting me and leaving me to find my own way home.' She cast him a withering look that condemned his ungentlemanly behaviour.

'You'll have Tess, and Godric will be at Dover. It's not as if you are going to be on your own.'

'You are my husband and you should be seeing me home.'

'Yes, I'm your husband, and the sooner you realise that I'm under no obligation to you, the better it will be. I've told you, I'm likely to be away quite a lot so you'd better get used to it. I have business to attend to.' The anger in his eyes shocked her. This was not the man who had courted her.

'What's got into you, Luke? I've never seen you like this.'

His eyes narrowed. 'You never question what I do, when I do it or what my motives are. Remember that and life at Senewey will be good.' He pushed himself to his feet and looked down at her with hard eyes. 'For now, remember we are going to be apart for a while after tonight. I'll be back!'

He swung past her and was out of the door before she could say anything, but the welcome he expected when he returned was clear to her.

Abigail sat staring at the table. What had gone wrong? What had she done? Nothing wrong as far as she knew. Since the wedding everything had seemed like paradise, but now ... Was it the thought of their mundane life back in Cornwall that had annoyed Luke? But surely that was of his own making. Life needn't be that way after all. Had the fact that he had been unable to see Monsieur Defarge in Dieppe altered his mood? What business matter could cause such a drastic change in him?

A knock on the door interrupted her thoughts. In answer to her response Tess opened the door tentatively.

625

'Do you require me, miss?' she asked, seeing Abigail on her own.

'Come in, Tess,' replied Abigail.

Tess sensed the unhappiness in the room and connected it with the absent Mr Gaisford.

'I won't want you any more tonight and will manage for myself in the morning. You have been told what time to be ready to leave for the ship?'

'Yes, miss.'

Abigail did not bother to correct her. She knew that Tess still regarded her as her Miss Abigail though was always careful in front of Luke to address her as Mrs Gaisford.

'Ten o'clock,' Tess added.

'Mr Gaisford will not be accompanying,' said Abigail. Tess was aware of the catch in her mistress's voice though Abigail quickly disguised it. 'He is detained in Calais on business. Therefore you and I will travel together when we reach England.'

Though this was a plausible explanation Tess was not convinced, but it was not her place to comment.

'Very well, miss.' She started for the door.

'Thank you for all you have done for me on this visit to France. I hope you have enjoyed seeing another country.'

'I have. It has been wonderful, but I will be glad to be back in England.'

Abigail gave a little nod. 'I think I will be too.' She gave a wan smile that dismissed any excitement she might have felt about her return to Senewey.

It disturbed Tess and as she returned to her room she wondered what had happened between Abigail and Luke.

Following the instructions he had received in Dieppe and confirmation of how to find Rue de St Quentin from the concierge, Luke hurried to his destination. He found number four to be an unpretentious house that showed no evidence it harboured the headquarters of an illicit trading gang. If the luxurious trappings inside were anything to go by, though, hopefully he was going to reap the same rewards from a venture that was new to him. The servant who had admitted Luke asked him to wait in the hall and then went up a wide staircase. A few moments later he appeared on the landing and called in a thick accent, 'Will you come this way, sir?'

Luke hurried up the stairs and followed the man along the landing where he knocked on a door, hesitated a moment and then opened it. 'Monsieur Gaisford,' he announced and stood to one side to allow Luke to enter.

A small man rose from an easy chair situated to one side of a richly ornamented fireplace. Surprised that this man was not as tall as he had imagined, Luke felt he would easily be in command of their discussion, but that feeling was immediately forgotten when he absorbed the air of authority that emanated from this man. His steel blue eyes held hypnotic power as they searched Luke's face and assessed him mercilessly. This was not at all the sort of man Luke would have associated with a notorious band of smugglers operating along the Normandy coast.

'Monsieur Gaisford.' The man held out his hand and started to speak in French. He stopped and then said, 'Ah, I see from your eyes that you do not understand. I will start again and we shall conduct our business in English. I believe you were looking for me in Dieppe. Louis Defarge.'

Luke was astonished by the steely grip such a small hand possessed. 'Monsieur Defarge! You received word from Dieppe very quickly.'

The man smiled. 'No sense in setting up methods of communication if they are not efficient. The message I received was that you wanted to see me on the recommendation of a mutual friend, Joseph Boilly. Let me offer you a glass of wine.' He poured it while he listened to Luke's explanation.

'He was a friend of my late grandfather . . . much younger, of course, more my father's age . . . but I recalled his visits to the family home in Cornwall. I remembered hearing talk of certain activities along the Normandy coast. I also recalled the name of a Frenchman, a name that seemed unusual to a Cornish youngster. It stuck in my mind. Recent enquiries on my part have linked you with those activities.'

'Ah, monsieur, you have linked memory with diligent search. But let us not be evasive. When you speak of activities, you mean smuggling.' He left a small pause that allowed Luke to nod his agreement. 'And what is your interest?'

'I want to get involved.'

'Why?' The question was blunt.

It made Luke realise he was dealing with a man who would readily detect any lie. 'I need to increase my income.'

'You are looking at a risky trade to do that.'

'You seem to have done well out of it,' commented Luke, letting his eyes wander across the room's rich furnishings with an unmistakable implication. Immediately he realised he had made a mistake.

'You should not assume that any appearance of wealth is all derived from illegal trading,' replied Monsieur Defarge coldly. 'If you think you are going to make a lot of money by smuggling, you are mistaken. You should forget it and think again.'

'But . . .'

Monsieur Defarge held up one hand to stop him. 'I know there are already smuggling gangs in Cornwall – no, I have had no dealings with them – and you would find it very precarious setting up against them.'

'I could do it.'

'I admire your confidence if not your judgement.' Defarge rose to refill their glasses.

'I have a small harbour which would be ideal for running contraband.' Luke went on quickly to describe it and Monsieur Defarge let him.

'It is obvious you have had no previous experience of smuggling, nor have you any idea of the best situations for it. Your harbour may seem ideal to you but have you ever thought how easily it could be blocked by preventive cutters? And with preventive men in position on the cliffs, you'd have no escape but be caught red-handed. Any captives would be likely to squirm out of the noose by talking, and that would do me no good. I'm sorry, Mr Gaisford, I can't do business with you. Besides, my dealings are along the Essex and Yorkshire coasts. I don't wish to expand my English trade.'

'I can . . .'

Again Monsieur Defarge interrupted. 'No, Monsieur Gaisford, no attempt on your part will make me change my mind.' As he had made his own position clear he had seen Luke's face darkening and realised that not far below the surface of this Englishman was a seething anger that could explode. He was about to offer Luke another glass of wine but thought it wiser not to. 'But let us part in friendship.' He stood up in a gesture of dismissal.

Luke, tight-lipped and furious at being rebuffed, rose. He ignored Monsieur Defarge's proferred hand and stormed from the room.

The Frenchman watched him go and shook his head sadly. That young man's lack of self-control could be his downfall – and a threat to his associate.

Abigail spent an anxious time waiting for her husband to return. She had loved every minute spent with him until this evening and the disturbing character trait that had manifested itself. Had she caused it to emerge? But she could think of no reason to lay the blame on herself. Was it something that had happened in Dieppe? Why hadn't Luke revealed to her that their visit to France would entail business as well? Why the secret? The more she tried to unravel what had happened, the more agitated she became. She started pacing the room, twisting a handkerchief between her fingers.

The sound of heavy footsteps in the corridor froze her to the spot. Though she expected it she still jumped as the door crashed open and Luke strode in, slamming the door behind him. He was breathing heavily and she shrank from the wild angry look in his eyes. His lips were set in a hard determined line. He flung his cape to one side and grabbed her by the shoulders. She could smell drink on his breath as he bent to kiss her and turned her head away.

'Not in drink,' she retaliated, fearful and repelled to see him in this state.

He grasped her chin so that she could not escape and pulled her head round to face him. 'Any way and any time I want.'

Lips that were hard and fierce met hers. Gone were the tenderness and gentleness that she had known from him. Now they expressed only one thing. He pushed her viciously away so that she fell upon the bed. He stood over her, eyes filled with pleasure in what he would take.

'No!' she started to shout, but her cry was stifled by the blow that brought blood to her bottom lip.

'Quiet,' he hissed. 'I'll have what I want, and don't you ever refuse me.' His hands closed round her and nothing she could do stopped him from tearing her clothes from her.

The following morning Tess had seen the luggage was put on the carriage that would take them to the quay and was waiting outside when Abigail and Luke came out of the hotel. She hid her reaction when she noticed the mark on Abigail's lip and the attempt her mistress had made to hide it with an extra dusting of powder. She was also aware of a tension between husband and wife in spite of Abigail's attempt to smile as if nothing had happened. In marked contrast, Luke's attitude was one of smug satisfaction.

Their conversation on the way to the quay was stilted and Tess knew that she had only been allowed to ride with them because it was a short journey. She was glad when they reached the ship and she could escape from the tense atmosphere. She felt relief that it was an English ship and the banter between the sailors was understandable. She was able to exchange some words with them. They were helpful with the luggage and warned her that the crossing might be a little rough. She was concerned when she saw that the parting between Abigail and Luke was not as she would have expected. She felt sure that there was some resistance in Abigail's attitude to her husband's goodbye kiss. But she wondered if her imagination had been playing tricks on her when the mistress stood by the rail, waving to Luke on the quay.

Though they each kept their own counsel both women would have agreed that the arrangements for their journey to Cornwall were impeccable. That part of their return went smoothly, and they only suffered from two days of inclement weather.

Even the dour walls of Senewey seemed to offer a welcome on their return. Abigail hoped this was true and that the unpleasantness in Calais was an isolated instance due to drink. She only hoped Luke was not reverting to the reputation that had surrounded him before they met.

Chapter Eighteen

The news that the Senewey carriage was coming up the drive ran through the house like a fire-storm. Mrs Horsefield, knowing the day when Godric had expected to return, had briefed the staff to assemble in the hall immediately the carriage was sighted.

As the coach pulled up two footmen came down the steps and were on hand to assist Abigail from it. Though taken aback, they controlled their surprise to see Tess in the master's place in the coach.

Catching the merest flicker in their eyes, Abigail readily offered an explanation. 'Mr Gaisford has been delayed in Calais on business; he will be back in a few days.'

'Yes, ma'am,' they replied in unison.

While she went into the house through the main door, Tess hurried to the servants' entrance. She would be ready and waiting in Abigail's room by the time her mistress arrived.

'Ah, that is that,' she said when she did so. 'The staff all seem to be in good heart and nothing untoward has happened while we have been away.'

'That is good, miss.'

'Help me out of my outdoor clothes and find me a comfortable day dress. Then off you go and settle in. You can see to my unpacking tomorrow. I want to have a wash and a rest after those last tedious miles.'

Tess found a suitable dress, left it hanging outside the wardrobe and went to her own room, thankful that she too could now take a rest before getting back into the routine at Senewey.

Abigail stretched herself out on the bed and let the tension of the journey drain out of her, but it was not long before her thoughts were turning to the honeymoon and how the joy of it had been marred by Luke's actions in Calais. He had apologised with heartfelt repentance the next morning but that had not and could not wipe out the memory. She felt defiled and knew that regaining her trust in him would take some time, if it ever happened at all. A great deal would depend on Luke. She realised being rebuffed in business had led him to drink and that had taken effect in the worst possible way as far as she was concerned. Her mind became troubled. Could it happen again? Had his taste for drink, which he appeared to have controlled before the wedding, returned? And if it had, could the consequences be the same on other occasions? It was a thought that constantly troubled her as she awaited her husband's return.

Tess had been in her room an hour when there was a light knock at the door. She opened it to see Alice.

'Come in.' Tess greeted her with a smile that told her friend she was pleased to see her, as did her embrace when the door had closed.

'It's good to see you again, Tess,' said Alice. 'Did you have a good time, apart from work?'

'Oh, I did. We saw so many wonderful things.'

'I must hear all about them. I haven't time now, but I just had to come and say welcome back.' Alice hesitated a brief moment and her eyes brightened with excitement. 'And to tell you I have a sweetheart.'

'What?' The surprise on Tess's face was quickly suffused with pleasure as she asked, 'Tell me, quick, before you go.'

'Met him at a fair in Sennan. Leo Gurney. Three years older than me. Father's a fisherman. Leo helps him. Tell you more later! I must hurry.'

Tess hugged her. 'I'm happy for you.'

As the door closed on Alice, Tess wondered if she herself would ever feel the joy that her friend was so obviously experiencing.

Two weeks later Abigail was sitting on the terrace before the house when she heard the pounding of hooves. Looking up from her embroidery, she saw a familiar figure urging his horse on now that the house had come into view. Excited by the sight of his lithe powerful figure and thrilled by his easy control of the horse, the love for him she had felt before their wedding was revived.

Luke's eyes were bright with pleasure, laughter on his lips, as he swung himself eagerly from the saddle and swept her up in his arms. His mouth met hers in firm but gentle passion that was more like the Luke she knew and loved. She must hide any uneasy feelings from him or her marriage could be wrecked.

'It's good to be home and have you in my arms again,' he said, holding her so that he could look into her eyes.

Searching for any evidence of recrimination for what had happened in Calais, he saw none. She must have forgiven him. He was filled with joy and relief. He did not want to lose Abigail; there was too much at stake. Nevertheless he felt he had to make amends by apologising. 'I'm sorry for what happened in Calais, my love. It was the drink.'

She put a finger on his lips. 'I know.'

A groom came round the corner to take his horse. Abigail took Luke's arm and led him into the house. He was home.

While he washed and changed, he answered her question: 'Were you successful in France in whatever it was you had to do?'

'No, is the blunt reply. You may as well know, I was trying to conclude some business deals I believed necessary to keep us on a sound financial footing.'

'So does it mean we are in bad straits?' she asked with concern.

He laughed. 'It's not yet come to that, but we would have been a lot better off if I'd succeeded. Maybe we'll have to be a little bit careful until I can look into other possible enterprises here. My father spent heavily and did not leave me in such a good financial position, as people think. Don't look so worried, love.' He came to her, took her hands and pulled her from the chair. 'I will take care of things.' He kissed her reassuringly then took her hand and said, 'Let's go down.'

When they entered the drawing room he let go of her hand and went to the decanters on the sideboard, selected the one containing whisky and poured himself a good measure.

Abigail tensed. Was the old habit back? 'Don't start drinking again,' she said. The words were out almost before she realised it. She bit her lip, regretting what she had said; wishing she could snatch the words back; recalling his warning to her not to tell him what he should or should not do. She saw anger flare in his eyes but he replaced it with a mocking smile as he raised the glass in her direction. He knew she had got the message.

That evening passed pleasantly and when they went upstairs he surprised her with the present of an exquisite pearl necklace. Though it was on her lips to question the wisdom of such expenditure, Abigail knew it was wisest not to. To ask his true financial position would not be correct, it was the man's prerogative to look after that side of their lives. That night their love-making was gentle and tender.

Two days later Luke strode into the Waning Moon.

'Good day, Tom.'

'And to you, Mr Gaisford! It's good to have you back. The usual, sir?'

'Aye, Tom! A tankard of good ale, none of that French muck.'

The landlord chuckled. 'That didn't go down well then?'

'It didn't. Have my friends been coming in?'

'Aye, they have. Every Thursday without fail. Other times as well, though not always together on those occasions, but certainly they all came every Thursday, because you said you would be here the first one after your return.'

'So they'll be in tomorrow?'

'Aye. I'll be surprised if they aren't. Generally about three o'clock.'

Luke took a good draught of his ale, put his tankard down and wiped the back of his hand across his lips. 'That was good. You can be filling another, and get one for yourself.'

The following afternoon Luke delayed his arrival at the Waning Moon until four o'clock. The corner table around which his friends were grouped was already littered with empty tankards. When he swept through the door they all burst into roars of welcome which soon became ribald suggestions about the recent groom's activities.

Luke grinned but did not rise to their insinuations. He greeted each man in turn with his own barbed comments. Martin called for ale for his friend only to see that Tom had already anticipated the order and was on his way with a foaming tankard. After he had placed it on the table he cleared the empty ones away.

Luke settled himself to try to answer all the questions that were flung at him, and he in turned quizzed them all for news of events in the county.

'I heard your lady was back in residence at Senewey over a week ago, but when you didn't show up here and this lot had not heard anything I thought it must be a rumour,' said George.

'What you heard was correct,' replied Luke.

'Then what the devil kept you from the Waning Moon?'

'I was in France.'

For a brief moment silence fell as if they were trying to comprehend what he'd said.

'You were still in France and Abigail was here?' quizzed Sydney.

'I had business in France but she came back as scheduled.'

'I hope the business made the separation worthwhile,' quipped David.

Luke frowned. 'It didn't,' he snapped, irritated to be reminded of his own failure. His lips tightened. 'It was only a minor setback.'

'What were you trying to arrange?' asked Martin seriously.

'Nothing of great importance. As you all know, the mine is not as profitable as it was and I was trying to set up something else in its place.'

'Tell us,' Martin urged.

Luke gave a little shake of his head. 'No. It's over and done with.'

'All right,' said George, accepting the refusal for them all. 'Well, tell us, are you going to frequent the Waning Moon every Thursday or has the little lady tightened the knot?'

Luke threw back his head with raucous laughter. 'There's no lady that can tie Luke Gaisford down.'

'So your abstinence before the wedding was a blind?' said George.

'What do you think? A wife's property becomes her husband's. Penorna is my prize as well as the lovely Abigail!'

'You wily bastard,' rapped David. 'You loved where money is.'

'Naturally.'

'Why didn't I think of that?'

'Because you aren't sharp enough,' countered Luke, 'and you aren't as handsome.'

'You might have to wait a long while before Abigail gets Penorna,' warned Martin, upset to hear Luke's motive for marrying her.

Luke did not respond but called for more ale and then suggested that in future it would be more convenient for them to meet on a different night each week.

They did not query his reasons.

Life at Senewey settled down. Though Abigail largely left Mrs Horsefield to continue running the house as she had always done, she made some changes in its routine by subtle suggestions to the housekeeper that allowed things to alter smoothly, with the stamp of authority now belonging to the mistress of the house.

Because Luke had warned her that there were times when he might have to be absent, attending to the management of the estate and its assets, Abigail made no verbal objection when he was away from home. Besides, wasn't sharing a bed more passionate after an absence? There were times when she felt sure that drink had passed his lips but she never questioned it, for it never again reached the stage where it took him over.

Three months after their return from France, Luke made a suggestion during their evening meal. 'I think we should give a ball here at Senewey.'

Abigail looked up from her plate and saw he was watching her with interest. Her eyes widened with delight. 'Can we?' she cried with enthusiasm.

'Why not? Besides, the county will expect it. They'll have been waiting on tenterhooks to see how the new mistress of Senewey will cope with such an event.'

'Now you are making me nervous. All eyes will be on me!'

Luke smiled. 'You'll cope, my love, unless I'm very much mistaken.'

'Thank you for your faith in me! I'll not let you down. When will it be?'

He looked thoughtful for a moment. 'Though I didn't take a lot of notice at the time, I think Mother used to start about three months beforehand – there's a lot to do. Finish the meal and then we'll go to my study and fix a date.'

Twenty minutes later they were poring over his notebook that he had marked into days. As Luke flicked over the pages she noticed that there were many more of what she took to be appointments and notes than she expected to see, but she felt it was wisest not to comment. It was not her place to pry but to trust her husband to be working for their good. Luke stopped turning the pages. 'Here we are.' He stabbed a page with his finger. 'How about Friday the twelfth of March? We can dance into the next morning without intruding into the Sabbath.'

'Yes,' she agreed.

He picked up a pencil and made an entry then withdrew a sheet of paper from a drawer. 'There's no time like the present. Let me write down what is to be done. First, the musicians!'

'The same group as we had for the wedding?'

'Yes, but that was only small section of them. This will be a much bigger event. I'll send my man into Penzance tomorrow to engage them. If they can come on that date we'll go

638

ahead with everything else. Consult with Mrs Horsefield, she's done it all before. There will be the food, the allocation of the rooms, the lay out, and the decorations to obtain. You'll probably need extra staff.' He pencilled some notes.

'But what about the expense?' Abigail asked tentatively, knowing she could be risking an outburst or at least a rebuke.

'Don't worry about that,' he replied considerately. 'Certain aspects of the estate are not contributing what they should but I have other things in mind. You are not to concern yourself. Now we must consider a guest list.' He started to write and the list grew longer and longer.

'So many?' she queried doubtfully.

'It will be expected from the foremost family in the county. We must be careful not to insult anyone by leaving them out.'

Nothing more was said until the next day when Luke announced that the musicians had been hired and Abigail could go ahead with the other arrangements. As it was late she waited until the following morning to tell Mrs Horsefield. Deeming it correct to inform the housekeeper first, she kept the information from Tess but told her to tell Mrs Horsefield she wanted to see her. 'I'll be in the drawing room.'

When the housekeeper arrived she said, 'You wanted to see me, ma'am?'

'Yes. Mrs Horsefield, we are to have another ball here at Senewey.'

Mrs Horsefield's eyes lit up. 'Oh, ma'am, it will be like old times. The house will be alive again with so many people. This is exciting.'

'I have some ideas, but I will need your help.'

'Yes, ma'am.'

'We may as well start discussing things now.'

The housekeeper drew on her past experience and also absorbed some of the suggestions that Abigail made so that by the end of the session they had a broad outline of what the arrangements would be. Abigail took Mrs Horsefield's advice on the extra staff that would be needed and left her to engage them.

Satisfied with this preliminary session, she went to her room where she found Tess putting away some clothes that had been brought by the laundry maids.

'We are going to have a ball here,' Abigail announced. 'And Mr Gaisford has said I have to have a special gown made.'

Tess caught the enthusiasm in her mistress's voice and responded with equal fervour, especially when Abigail told her, 'During the next few days I want you to help me get the invitations ready.'

Chapter Nineteen

Over the ensuing weeks excitement mounted at Senewey Manor; it meant more work for everybody. The staff enjoyed doing something different, though for the efficient running of the Manor routine had to form the basis of their lives. Abigail's enthusiasm seemed to galvanise them into wanting to make this, her first ball as Mistress of Senewey, a success. Mrs Horsefield's organising skills, as befitted a first-rate housekeeper, were even more in evidence but she was careful not to assume the authority that was rightfully Abigail's. So they worked well together.

The main worry for Abigail was not whether it would be a success but why Luke was showing so little interest. She knew he was occupied with the running of the estate and that he had some financial problems but when she broached the subject he dismissed her worries. Though she was not sure she was getting the truth she dare not pursue the subject for she had seen a spark of hostility in him that alarmed her.

As Abigail's confidante Tess became involved in much of the preparations particularly as a quick and able message-carrier for her mistress.

'Tess, the invitations all went out and we have been receiving replies, but I found this one addressed to Mrs Gaisford. It must have been mislaid in the sorting. Run with it to the West Wing now.'

Tess took the sealed sheet of paper and hurried from the room. She went via the servants' staircase to the main hall and was halfway down the corridor to the closed doors to the West

Wing when a voice she instantly recognised as Mr Gaisford's barked at her from the main hall and froze her in her tracks.

'You! Where are you going?'

She turned nervously to see Luke, dressed in his riding clothes, glaring at her.

'Well?' he demanded again. 'Tongue tied?' He stepped towards her.

'I . . . er . . . I . . .'

'I can't stand here all morning. You know you shouldn't be down here.' His eyebrows knitted together in an expression that was meant to put fear into Tess. 'Now off with you! If I catch you in this part of the house again it will be the worse for you.'

Tess bit her lip, trying to hold back the tears that threatened to flow. She seemed riveted to the spot yet knew she must go. He appeared to be barring the way though there was plenty of room for her to pass. With an effort she forced herself on. As she slid past him Luke gave her a switch with his riding crop across her back that made her flinch and released her tears.

'Remember what I said,' he rasped as she scuttled away, thankful that she had put the invitation into the pocket of her apron.

Unthinkingly, she burst into Abigail's room. It seemed the natural thing to do. Abigail swung round from the window and immediately her look of surprise became one of concern when she saw the tears of pain and terror flowing down Tess' cheeks.

'What's happened?' she cried as she rushed to the girl.

'Oh, miss, Mr Gaisford . . .' she faltered.

'Calm down, Tess,' said Abigail gently as she put her arm round her maid's shaking shoulders and led her to the sofa. 'Sit down and tell me what has happened.' She took a handkerchief from her pocket and handed it to Tess.

She sniffed, dabbed her eyes, gave a last sob and looked mournfully at Abigail. 'Oh, miss . . .' Her words choked her.

'Take your time, Tess.' Abigail rose from the sofa and went to a carafe, poured a glass of water and handed it to the girl before sitting down again.

'Thank you, miss.' Tess took a sip of the water. She swallowed hard and stiffened her back. 'I'm sorry.'

'Now tell me, quietly and calmly, what happened?'

Tess drew a deep breath and related the incident in the corridor leading to the West Wing.

'My husband struck you?'

'Across my back, miss, with his riding crop.'

'What?' Astonished disbelief showed on Abigail's face. 'You are sure? You haven't dreamt this?'

'No, miss,' replied Tess indignantly. 'Why should I make it up?'

Abigail did not reply. She knew her maid too well to doubt her. She wished she could retract the question. 'You say he told you you shouldn't be in that part of the house?'

'Yes, miss.'

'Didn't you tell him I had sent you with a message for Mrs Gaisford?'

'I didn't get a chance, miss. I had the note in my pocket . . . here it is.' She handed it to Abigail.

'All right, Tess. Say nothing of this to anyone.'

She nodded. 'I won't, miss, of course I won't.'

'I'll go and see Mr Gaisford immediately.'

'I think he'll have gone riding, miss.'

'Very well, I'll see him later. You stay here until you feel better. I'll take this invitation to my mother-in-law myself.'

Abigail was fuming at Luke's treatment of Tess as she hurried along the landing, down the stairs and across the hall. She slowed her footsteps along the corridor to the West Wing and tightened her grip on herself. She could not allow Hester to see her in this condition. What had happened had nothing to do with her. She was not responsible for her son's actions. Abigail paused at the connecting door, straightened her dress and took a deep breath. By the time she walked into Mrs Gaisford's drawing room she was in control of herself.

'Ah, my dear, how nice to see you.' Hester's smile was warm and welcoming and held genuine pleasure. It immediately made Abigail wonder if Luke's stated reasons for his

643

mother keeping to herself was the full truth. Hester, though frail, certainly did not look ill and the greeting she gave Abigail did not speak of any desire to be left on her own. 'Do sit down. I hope this is a social visit?'

'I've brought this, Mrs Gaisford.' Abigail held out the invitation which Hester took with curiosity.

Abigail sat down opposite her mother-in-law and watched her as she opened the paper.

Hester read the words. Sat for a moment staring at them, read them again then looked up slowly. Abigail saw tears in her eyes.

'Thank you, my dear.' The catch that came into her voice after that brief moment of pleasurable excitement was not lost on Abigail. Why such sadness? she wondered. Had it brought back memories of her younger days when she herself would organise such events and be the belle of the ball? Abigail could picture this woman, whose lined face would once have been as smooth as silk, as a lively attractive person full of self-assurance. Was she sad at the thought of what had been or was there something deeper behind this?

'Had you heard about the ball?' asked Abigail tentatively.

The older woman nodded. 'The girls who look after me told me the house was buzzing with excitement that the Senewey Ball was going to be revived. They were the foremost balls in the county for many, many years. I can remember the first one I came to as a young girl of fifteen ... Oh, it was such an exciting time for someone as young as I.'

'Didn't Luke come and tell you himself?'

'Not him!' snapped Hester.

The touch of contempt in her voice startled Abigail. 'Maybe he was relying on me to do so, possibly by this invitation. I'm sorry it got mislaid,' she apologised. 'But you have it now. You'll come?'

Hester hesitated then gave a sad little shake of her head. 'I'm not well enough, my dear.'

'But you could sit down and meet people. I'm sure you would like to meet old acquaintances?' protested Abigail, feeling that Hester had made an excuse that would not stand up to scrutiny.

She gave a wan smile. 'Maybe, but I don't think so.'

'We'll see again nearer the day,' Abigail suggested, believing this was probably not the time to press the matter further.

Hester gave a small nod and changed the subject. 'Are the preparations going well?'

'Yes. Mrs Horsefield is a great help in guiding me in what should be done.'

'She always was a stalwart. She loved such occasions and knew the Gaisfords wanted to outshine everyone else. You won't be getting much help from Luke?'

Once again Abigail detected that sour note towards her son. 'He has the estate to run.' She hoped that excuse would satisfy her mother-in-law, but before she received a response they both were startled as the drawing-room door crashed open and Luke stormed in, his face a mask of fury.

'What are you doing here?' he shouted, glaring at Abigail.

Puzzled by his animosity she said, 'I came to visit your mother and invite her to the ball.'

'Did I not make it plain that she was to be left on her own?' he demanded.

'Surely you did not mean that literally?' countered Abigail.

'I did,' snapped Luke. 'In future, see that you adhere to my wishes.'

'But I see no reason . . .'

'Out!' he broke in, pointing at the door with his riding crop.

Abigail shot a glance at Hester and saw such a troubled expression in her eyes that she immediately rose from her chair and headed for the door after casting her a glance of sympathy. She heard Luke's footsteps behind her and fury at the treatment she had received boiled over when she heard the door slam behind them. She swung round to face him, anger in her eyes. 'Don't you dare treat me that way again!'

'I'll treat you how I like and don't you forget it!'

Abigail was shocked by the viciousness of his reply. It conjured up memories of Calais all over again, and that frightened her. She could feel her heart thumping, but something was telling her not to seem afraid but to keep calm. She could not do that in the face of his hostility and commanding posture, however. 'Don't you threaten me, and don't ever use your crop on Tess again.'

Luke's eyes flared into red fury. He grabbed Abigail's neck and pushed her hard against the wall. His face came close to hers as she struggled for breath. 'I've told you before, don't tell me what I can and cannot do. But I'll tell you one thing more – *keep away from my mother*. I make her an allowance and allow her to have the West Wing but she has no right to enter the main house. I have had no love for her since she refused to raise a hand in my defence. My father loved to lash out at me. Keep away from her.' He relaxed his grip on her throat and stepped back.

Abigail doubled up, gasping for breath, her hands at her throat where he had held it in a strong-fingered grip. She raised her head slowly, eyes filled with horror. 'A son in his father's image, I see. Thank goodness we have no children, nor ever will have.'

Luke smirked. He raised his crop under her chin and pushed her head back into a position from which she had no escape but was forced to look into his eyes. 'Oh, yes, my love, we will,' he hissed to burn his expectation into her mind. 'And don't you forget it!' His eyes narrowed. 'And we'll act as if none of this ever happened. We will be the perfect couple, the Gaisfords of Senewey. And Senewey will have a son and heir. In case you are inclined to forget, here is a little reminder.' He stepped back and struck her shoulder hard with his crop.

Abigail stifled the cry that sprang to her lips but could not disguise the pain on her face.

'You will act like a dutiful and loving wife to Luke Gaisford or there'll be worse to follow.' He laughed in her face, wheeled away and strode off down the corridor.

She slumped against the wall, grasped her shoulder and bit her lip, trying to stem the pain. Her eyes, fixed on Luke's retreating back, burned with hatred but she recalled the smell of drink on his breath. Had that caused his cruelty to her or was it because she had visited his mother? Or maybe something else entirely had caused his anger?

She pushed herself from the wall, tenderly touched her neck, straightened her collar and adjusted her dress. With a heavy sigh she walked slowly along the corridor to the adjoining hall. Thankful that it was deserted, she climbed the stairs with slow weak steps, her mind still trying to fathom exactly what had gone wrong within their marriage. Thankful that Tess was no longer in her room, she sank into a big armchair close to the window.

Linking what had just happened with the event in Calais, she realised that drink had been involved in both cases. That could be the immediate cause but it may not be the root of the matter. She thought back to Calais. There an anticipated business deal had not taken place and she had sensed Luke's expectations had been high. That could have led him to try to drink his disappointment away. Had some recent business arrangement here upset him or was he merely angry that he had found her with his despised mother?

Even as so many thoughts tumbled in her mind, she could not deny that her love for her husband still ran deep. She drew hope from that and believed his love for her would overcome the dangers of drink that brought out a cruel, sadistic side to his nature. She convinced herself she could fight such a foe but realised she would have to nurture their relationship subtly.

When Tess came to help her dress for the evening nothing was said about the earlier incident. Abigail tried to keep the mark on her shoulder covered but was not wholly successful. Tess's gasp made her realise that she had seen it.

'Miss, what happened?' Tess asked in horror.

'Nothing,' replied Abigail dismissively.

'But . . .'

'I tripped and fell against the wall,' she said in a tone that stated that was the end of the matter.

Tess dare not pursue it though she knew the mark on her mistress resembled that on her own back. It had been made by a riding crop.

When Tess was putting her clothes away, after Abigail had left for her evening meal, she wondered if this was something she should report to Mr Mitchell but concluded that it could only bring more trouble down on Abigail at the hands of Mr Gaisford.

The earlier confrontation in the corridor leading to the West Wing was never mentioned during their meal together. Luke could not have been more considerate and attentive to his wife. Was he feeling remorse? Was this was a way of saying sorry? But if that were the case Abigail thought he would have been more effusive, whereas tonight he was once again the Luke she had come to love and still did. She noted that there was no smell of drink on his breath and that he did not take any wine with his meal and avoided it again when they went to the drawing room.

He showed more interest in the forthcoming ball tonight. Abigail was pleased, and while they were on the subject plucked up the courage to mention the question of his mother's invitation, but not so as to confront him directly. 'I'm sorry if I misunderstood about inviting your mother.' She felt sure he would hear the thumping of her own heart.

'It's not that I object to her receiving an invitation but she really isn't well enough to attend. If she did she might be an embarrassment to herself and that would be unpleasant for everyone,' he replied quietly.

Abigail had no answer to that and was forced to let the matter drop. Luke's words had come quietly and reasonably, he seemed very much under control, so she concluded that drink had been the cause of the outburst in the West Wing. And tonight he had taken none.

Their love-making that night was prolonged and full of tenderness and Abigail knew he hoped the result would be a son and heir.

As the day of the ball drew nearer and nearer an air of expectancy seemed to settle over the house. Excitement gripped the staff; they went about their daily tasks with a new vigour so that they could get back to the preparations for the ball. Together Abigail and her housekeeper planned where to put the tables in the dining room so that the food would be easily available to everyone; which chairs should be put around the edges of the main chamber to be used for dancing; which rooms would be available for relaxation and gossip; and so many other things that would help to make this ball the talk of Cornwall.

'Another fitting day, Tess,' Abigail reminded her. 'So make preparations to go to Penzance.'

'Yes, miss. I've had it in mind. I'm looking forward to seeing how your dress looks now.'

'So am I.'

'Will I be able to see Dorinda, miss?'

'I don't see why not. We'll make it our business to see her and we'll call at Penorna on the way back. I haven't seen mother and father for a long while.'

'I think you will look lovely in that dress,' remarked Tess as their coach drew away from Penzance.

'Thank you,' replied Abigail. 'Not a word to anyone about it. It has to be a complete surprise.'

'I won't say a word, miss. Oh, I have enjoyed my day.'

'I'm pleased you have. We'll do it again next week. But we haven't finished today yet. We have time to call in at Penorna.'

Memories of her happy childhood and the joy of moving into the adult world filled Abigail's mind when the house came into view. Though she had been born in Whitby and knew her father's sister still lived there, she could remember little of it. Penorna was her real home.

She was out of the coach as soon as its wheels stopped, leaving Tess to renew acquaintance in the servants' quarters. Abigail sped across the hall to the drawing room, threw open the door and so startled her mother that she pricked her finger with the needle as she made the next stitch in the tablecloth she was embroidering.

'Abigail!' Eliza dropped her work on to the table beside her and was on her feet to exchange a loving hug with her daughter. 'This is a pleasant surprise. I'm so glad to see you. You don't visit often enough.'

'Life is so busy, Mama.'

'I know, love. It's just me wanting to see more of you. How are you? You are looking well.'

'I feel well.'

'And Luke?'

'Busy on the estate and trying to solve some problems.'

'Problems?' asked Eliza as she went to the bell pull.

'Oh, I don't know what they are,' replied Abigail, not wanting to disclose that they concerned his finances for she knew little more than that and Luke had assured her that they were not serious. 'He says there is no need to worry.'

There was a knock on the door and a maid entered. 'You rang, ma'am?'

'Chocolate for us both, please. Preparations for the ball will be keeping you busy?' Eliza said to her daughter.

'Oh, yes! It is all so exciting. I'm on my way back from Penzance where I've been for a fitting – my ball gown.'

'Oh, tell me,' pressed Eliza. 'What's it like.'

'No, Mama,' laughed Abigail. 'It is to be a surprise. Only Tess and I will have seen it before the ball.' She changed the subject. 'Where's Papa?'

'He's gone to the mine. I didn't want him to go.' A serious expression replaced Eliza's excitement at seeing her daughter. 'He hasn't been too well this past week. Off colour generally but he said he felt a little better this morning. He felt well enough to go to the mine on a routine visit. He thought getting out would do him good.'

'I hope it does,' said Abigail with concern. 'Has he had similar symptoms before?'

'Not that he has said, but you know your father – he's not one to complain about his health. Now tell me more about your life at Senewey?'

Mother and daughter spent a pleasant hour before Abigail thought it was time to be leaving. Word was sent to Tess and she was at the coach when Eliza and Abigail came on to the terrace.

'You and Papa will be coming to the ball?'

'Wouldn't miss it for the world,' replied Eliza. 'Hopefully your papa will feel more like himself by then.'

Eliza came to the coach, had a brief word with Tess, and stood watching their departure until they were lost to sight beyond the small copse.

Chapter Twenty

'Quick, Tess, quick! I can hear coaches coming,' called Abigail as Tess started fastening the buttons at the back of her gown.

Her nimble fingers sped through the remaining buttons. 'There, miss,' she said as she moved round to face Abigail with a critical eye on the dress.

'See who's arriving,' said her mistress, making swift gestures with her hands towards the windows.

Tess was there in a flash, focusing on the first of two coaches that were pulling up at the front of the house. She watched the occupants alight. 'One of Mr Gaisford's uncles in the first coach.' There was a pause as she waited for the passengers to alight from the next. 'And the other uncle in the second coach. Both accompanied by their wives.'

'I'd better hurry,' cried Abigail, finishing smoothing her dress. 'Am I all right, Tess?' she asked, patting her hair.

'You look beautiful, miss, and that dress is going to make everyone stare.'

Abigail shot to the door. She gave a brief pause and said, 'Thanks for all your help, Tess.' Then she was gone.

The maid smiled at the closed door. Her mistress was so excited, but who wouldn't be on such an occasion? Would Tess herself ever be as excited over something? How she wished she could share things with her mother, but stoically she fought that feeling as she recalled how fortunate she was to have Abigail as her mistress and to be treated by her more as a sister than anything else. She looked round the room which was scattered with clothes. She would tidy up later. Now, from a secluded corner of the landing, she watch the guests being received by the master and mistress. She hurried from the room and was in her place in time to see Abigail starting down the stairs.

She had come quietly to the top of the flight and paused there to survey the scene below. Two footmen stood beside the door and four maids hovered nearby, ready to attend to the guests' outdoor clothes or serve any other needs. Luke was greeting his Uncle Charles and Aunt Emma while Uncle Logan and Aunt Fanny waited to offer their felicitations. Luke had told her of his cold relations with his father's brothers and she had witnessed only a slight thaw at their wedding. She wondered just what the atmosphere was like in the hall at this moment. There was only one way to find out but she was not going to miss the chance to make an impressive entrance. Abigail took each step slowly. The movement caught the attention of those below. They all looked up and the conversation stopped; their attention was riveted on her. She knew immediately she had caused a sensation. Her eyes flicked over the group but settled on Luke. It was his approval she wanted. She saw it in his eyes. They not only endorsed her choice of dress, it was as if he was seeing her for the very first time. He not only approved of her whole appearance, it was as if he wished to devour her. It sent her heart racing and her mind reeling. She held their attention until she reached the bottom of the stairs and crossed over to them with a warm smile and friendly greeting. Their comments were more than approving.

Emma and Fanny were most taken by Abigail's Empire-line sheath gown. The high waist came to just under the line of her breasts and was banded with a ribbon of deep blue in contrast to the pale shade of the dress. A woven braid in a Greek key pattern bordered the hem of the gown and the small train. Tiny puff-shouldered sleeves sprang from a low, wide neckline. A single row of pearls hung from her neck to a pendant at her cleavage. Abigail carried a cashmere shawl casually draped over one arm and held an embroidered reticule in her left hand. She had taken particular care with her hair, its Grecian style, in keeping with the design of the dress, enhanced the features of her face perfectly.

Abigail could see approval in the aunts' eyes, and maybe just a little jealousy. Was it because she had outshone them or because she was mistress of Senewey? Maybe it was just because she was younger.

As more guests were beginning to arrive the Gaisfords moved off, leaving Luke and Abigail to greet the newcomers. But before that he managed to get in a quick word. 'You look lovely. What a magnificent dress!'

'Thanks to your generosity,' she said, with an inclination of her head to express her thanks.

'And what an entrance,' he chuckled. 'You stunned them. I approved of that.'

She felt his hand squeeze hers and was pleased.

'You don't look so bad yourself. I prefer the fashion for trousers though I see that not everyone has switched from breeches,' she said, noting that two of the arrivals were so attired.

There was a wide variety of fashions on display but everyone had taken care with their appearance, wanting to present themselves as well as they could. But no one received more compliments than Abigail.

As the new arrivals dwindled to a trickle she began to grow worried and Luke sensed it.

'Something wrong?' he asked.

'Mother and Father haven't arrived yet. I told you Father hadn't been well. I hope he hasn't suffered a set back.'

'There's still plenty of time,' Luke reassured her.

Five minutes later he drew her attention to the door. 'Here's your mother with the Westburys.'

The relief that swept over her was replaced by concern when she saw Eliza was on her own. 'Where's Papa?' she asked after greeting their neighbours.

'He was sick this afternoon and did not feel up to all this evening's excitement.'

'Is he all right?'

'Yes. I was going to stay but he insisted I should come. He told me to tell you that it's only a mild attack and he sends his best wishes to you both for a memorable evening.'

'Thank you, Mrs Mitchell,' said Luke. 'I hope Mr Mitchell is well again in the morning, but if there is anything we can do, please don't hesitate to ask.'

'That is kind, Luke. I'm sure he will feel better in the morning. Now, don't let this for one moment upset or spoil this evening. Your father wouldn't want that, Abigail. And let me admire your dress!'

She could do nothing but take her mother's word that there was no need to worry. She could not go among her guests with a troubled expression and was soon swept back into the gaiety of the evening. She moved comfortably among the guests who were all too ready to compare this ball with such events in the past. Opinion was generally favourable. The evening was a success.

The ball proceeded smoothly. Ladies exchanged news and gossip, men opinions on the state of the nation, the county and the ambitions of Napoleon.

At one point, with the hour heading towards midnight and Abigail dancing with Martin, Luke took the opportunity to draw his two uncles into a private room.

Not knowing the reason, Logan remarked, 'You certainly are keeping up the Senewey traditions of throwing the best ball in the county.'

'That was the idea, but it may become increasingly difficult to keep the Gaisford name to the forefront in other spheres.'

'What do you mean?' asked Charles.

'Sit down, let me charge your glasses.' As Luke went to a table on which there stood a decanter and several glasses, Charles and Logan exchanged glances in which curiosity was mingled with wariness. They thanked him when he brought them wine and responded when he raised his glass and said, 'The Gaisfords.'

Charles pursed his lips and without taking his eyes off Luke, said, 'You haven't brought us in here just to toast the family name. And I smell trouble in your previous statement.'

655

'The Senewey Estate is in a precarious financial position . . .' started Luke, only to be interrupted by Logan.

'Oh, come on, nephew, you don't expect us to believe that?' He gave a grunt of derision.

'It's true.'

Charles guffawed. 'With all the assets you have?'

'Look around you,' suggested Logan with a smirk. 'This ball will have cost you! Then there's your wife's dress and those pearls round her neck, your honeymoon in France . . . oh, *you* aren't short of a penny!'

'Father left little money,' snapped Luke, irritated by his uncles' attitude. 'He'd run the mine almost out; the land won't sustain more sheep; he had neglected most of his property so I'd have trouble if I raised rents. My income only just keeps us solvent but that picture will soon change for the worse.'

'So why all this show of opulence?' demanded Charles.

'To keep up the Gaisford reputation and our standing in the county.'

'So what has this to do with us?' asked Logan.

'I hear that since I gave you your estates, you've turned them round and . . .'

Charles gave a loud contemptuous snort. 'So you want us to help you out?'

'You *are* Gaisfords.'

'You didn't take that into account when you severed us from the estate,' put in Logan. His eyes narrowed. 'You'll get no help from me.'

'Nor from me,' added Charles quickly. 'What you did to us turned out to be a blessing. We both realised we had been too ready to fall back on Senewey. Cutting us off as you did made us look seriously at our situation and to make the most of our assets, some of which we had neglected to develop. Well, things turned out well, and though there is much more still to do we are at least solvent and heading for some nice profits. Thanks to you and your hasty judgement we are doing nicely and the future looks bright.' He started to rise to his feet as if that was the end of the matter. Logan followed suit.

'Wait!' cried Luke. 'You're Gaisfords. Doesn't that mean anything to you?'

'Yes, it does, but in our own way and on our own terms.' Charles's voice was cold. 'Father never really saw eye to eye with us. Jeremy was always the favourite because he was the one who would inherit. We didn't matter. He made no provision for us in his will. Oh, yes, he allowed us our small estates, but made sure that they were dependent on Senewey. You broke that yoke and,' he added sarcastically, 'we both thank you for it. But don't expect us to help *you* out.' He spun round and headed for the door, followed closely by his brother.

'You're Gaisfords!' yelled Luke, his eyes burning with anger. 'Gaisfords!'

The door slammed behind them and he was left staring at it.

'You bastards,' he hissed, anger turning to hatred. 'I'll show you. I don't need you! Senewey will survive and you'll regret it!' He started for the door, stopped, swung round and went to pour himself a full glass of wine. He drained it and poured another. His hands were shaking; wine slopped over the rim. He cursed. Fury burned deep within him. He sensed the onset of one of the terrible moods he had witnessed in his own father. Luke's mind fought against the recurring visions he suffered of those times that Jeremy, suffering some setback, had taken it out on him, a child or youngster unable to defend himself. He drained his glass and placed his hands firmly on the sideboard, needing the sensation to strengthen his will against the red mist that threatened to spin him into the same hellish regions that had consumed his father.

Abigail, in light-hearted conversation with some guests but alert to what was going on around her, had noticed Luke draw his uncles aside. The move puzzled her for she knew that her husband was not on the most friendly of terms with them. She had heard that his father's death had brought about a rift within the Gaisford family and that there was little communication nowadays between uncles and nephew. In fact, it had only been at her insistence that they had been invited to the Gaisford Ball. So now, as the door closed on them, she wondered what was afoot; what could have drawn them together? A reconciliation? She kept her attention on the door as she moved among the guests.

It opened. Abigail, in conversation with George Morland, tried to read something into the fact that Luke had not come out with his uncles and that they both emerged talking earnestly. There was about them an air of smugness that spoke of victory. She excused herself from George and started over to the side room. Why was Luke still in there? She was halfway to it when the door opened. She stopped, eyes fixed firmly on her husband. Alarm coursed through her for she was sure that he was struggling against anger. As he stood and surveyed the room and put his hand on the door jamb as if to steady himself, she sensed drink was behind the movement and there was still a long night ahead of them. She saw him set off in her direction and his step was steady, but was he keeping himself in check?

The fury that had contorted his expression when she first saw him had been almost disguised by the time he reached her, but what lay beneath? And, smelling drink on his breath, she inwardly shuddered.

'Shall we dance, my love?' he asked.

She took his arm, a signal of assent. As they walked to the main hall they nodded or passed a few words with their guests without stopping. She could tell Luke did not wish to be drawn into talk at this moment. Throughout the cotillion she realised he was using this interlude to calm his reaction to whatever had happened with his uncles behind the closed door. When the dance finished he escorted her over to her mother who was talking to the Westburys, and then excused himself. She saw him beckon to one of the manservants and take a glass from the proffered tray before going in search of George Morland.

Though she danced with other guests, exchanged gossip, enjoyed the refreshments, accepted compliments about the success of the ball, Abigail's eyes kept drifting to her husband. Misgivings began to grow in her at the amount of drink he was consuming. That it showed no sign of taking effect made her even more uneasy for beneath his seemingly ice-cold attitude seethed a volcanic temper. What might lie in store if someone, even she herself, upset Luke tonight? She tried to keep her mind off the possible consequences but they still haunted her when, after the departure of the final guest, with the cold streaks of dawn heralding another day, she made her way to her room.

During the last twenty minutes she had not seen Luke at all and was ill at ease when, on passing his door she heard angry mutterings and curses within. She did not pause to try to make sense of the words but moved quickly and silently to her own room. After locking the door she leaned back against it with a sigh.

Gathering herself together, she walked across the room. She felt a strong desire for Tess's companionship and wished she hadn't told her maid that she would not be wanted until later in the morning. As she started to undress, her mind turned to her father. She hoped he would soon recover from his indisposition. She recalled her mother's reassurances but still wondered about the extent of her father's illness and hoped that nothing was being kept from her. She would go to Penorna later in the day.

Abigail started, the run of her thoughts interrupted by a faint sound from the door. She swung round and stared at the moving handle. Her heart started to thump. The door resisted the attempt to open it. Though she knew she had locked it there remained the fear that it would open. There was a harder tug at the door followed by a low curse.

'Abigail, open this door!' Luke's voice was low but commanding.

'No,' she returned, her voice trembling.

'Open it!'

'No. Not now, Luke.'

'Open it!' The command was followed by a thump on the door.

She did not answer.

'Do it or it will mean deep trouble for you.' This threat held a note of menace that she feared would mean worse for her than she'd suffered in Calais.

'No.' She tried to sound confident. 'You've had too much to drink.'

Luke fumed. His hammering on the door made her recoil. 'Don't criticise me! Open this door! Immediately!'

'No!'

The silence was intimidating, a portent of what tomorrow might hold.

'Bitch! You'll pay for this!' His fist drove at the door one more time then she heard his footsteps move away, the curses he rained down on her fading into the distance.

As she turned towards the bed she found herself trembling, whether with rage, fear or both she did not know. A lovely day, concluding with a splendid ball for which she had been showered with compliments, had been ruined. She flung herself on the bed and sobbed herself to sleep.

She woke five hours later and immediately recalled how that locked door had saved her from a catastrophic encounter with Luke. She shuddered. Yet still beneath her feeling of loathing lay love for her husband. How could such extremes exist side by side? Drink, she supposed. But she knew the habit, which he had allowed to slip back into his life, did not always precede violent conduct towards her. There had been times when his loving had been tender and considerate despite his drinking, and at those times hers in return satisfied them both. So why had that violent outburst threatened her a few hours ago, and previously in France?

She suddenly realised she must look a sight. Tess must not see any evidence of her tears. She sprang from the bed and, knowing that Luke would not dare to cause a scene now, unlocked the door and started her toilette.

A familiar knock sounded on the door.

'I hope you slept well, miss?' said Tess brightly, entering the room.

'I did, thank you.'

'It was a splendid ball,' her maid commented. 'And you looked so beautiful, no one could match you.'

Abigail laughed softly at the adoration in her voice. 'I don't know about that, everyone had made a special effort to look their best.'

'I was sorry that Mr Mitchell wasn't there.'

'He was not well. I must go to see how he is after I have had something to eat. When we have finished here, will you inform them in the kitchen that I will be down in a few moments and also tell Godwin to have a carriage ready to take me to Penorna?'

'Yes, miss. I hope you find Mr Mitchell recovered.'

'I hope so too.'

Tess glanced around the room to make sure her mistress had what she wanted. She would come back to straighten everything later. She started for the door.

'Tess, do you know if Mr Gaisford is up yet?'

'I saw him riding away about half an hour ago.'

Abigail felt some relief at this for it meant there would be a short interlude before she came face to face with him.

As soon as he left the stable yard Luke stabbed his horse into a gallop. He had been curt with the maids when he'd snatched a quick breakfast and the grooms were not sorry to see him ride away. Something had upset their master and they preferred him out of the way at such times.

A problem he'd thought would be solved last night was still with him. He cursed his uncles. Had they no care for the Gaisford name, which would be stained if his financial position were not regularised? Precarious as it already was, it would be worse when the debts incurred by that lavish ball were added to it. The weather matched his mood. Glowering clouds were swept eastwards by a strong wind that buffeted the rider and rippled the pools of rain left in the rutted track. He took a narrow bridle path that led to the cliff-top a mile away. High above a sea churned into whitecaps by the wind he gentled his horse to a walking pace and rode on until the harbour built by his father came in sight. Luke stopped his horse and controlled its restlessness in the pummelling wind. He sat in the saddle for a few minutes, contemplating the scene, before his attention was held by the fast-running sea, pounding the cliffs and sending spray high in the air. Its vicious unrelenting power seemed to surge through him, filling him with a sense of excitement and mastery of his own destiny. Harness such power and he could solve his petty problems. His eyes narrowed in resolve; a faint smile lifted the corners of his lips. He slipped from the saddle, tethered his horse and walked along the cliff edge. He turned off the track along the headland that sheltered the harbour from the brute force of the sea. Reaching the end, he stopped to survey the scene. The headland dropped away before him. To his left the sea swirled into the harbour; to his right the cliffs swung down but a hundred yards into their descent to the sea were broken into a series of huge step-like sections that finally gave on to a strand of sand stretching another hundred yards or so before it ran into a barrier of soaring cliff. He studied this area carefully for some time before he was satisfied that it would be possible to negotiate a way from the sea to the top of the cliffs via the step formation. The thoughtful mood held him until he reached his horse again and swung himself into the saddle.

Exhilarated by the plans that had formed in his mind, he spurred his horse on urging it to go faster and faster, enjoying the pounding of its hooves and the sweep of the wind through his hair. Luke let out a whoop filled with excitement even though he knew that what he had in mind still needed much careful planning. He would take the first tentative steps when he reached the Waning Moon.

Chapter Twenty-One

Though there had been a touch of anxiety in her mind as the carriage left Senewey, memories of a happy childhood and growing up in the beautiful setting of Penorna Manor flooded back to Abigail when Godric guided the horse up the long drive. The house seemed to send out a welcome stability in contrast to the uneasiness Abigail was beginning to feel at Senewey. But now there was her concern for her father, to shadow this homecoming.

She entered the house unannounced and went straight to the drawing room. Finding it empty, she climbed the stairs quickly and hurried to her father's room. She gave a light knock on the door and tentatively began to push it open as she called out, 'May I come in?'

'Of course,' came the reply.

She recognised her mother's voice and detected a note of relief mingled with joy.

'Oh, we are so pleased to see you,' said Eliza, hurrying to hug her. She kept hold of her daughter's hand as she turned back to the bed.

Alarm surged through Abigail when she saw her father's pale, drawn face. 'Hello, Papa.' She took his hand and leaned forward to kiss him on the cheek.

'Hello, love.' John mustered a smile and his eyes brightened a little but his voice lacked its usual strength.

Abigail glanced at her mother. 'How long has he been like this?'

'Nearly three weeks.'

'What?' Anxiety bit deep. 'Why didn't you let me know?'

'Your father forbade me. He knew you were embroiled in all the preparations for your first ball at Senewey and did not want to distract you,' Eliza explained.

'That was naughty of you, Papa,' Abigail rebuked him mildly. 'You'll have had the doctor?' she asked her mother.

'Oh, yes, he's puzzled by your father's illness, though, particularly as it is persisting and does not seem to be responding to the medicines prescribed. So all we can do is to keep him warm in bed and give him plenty to drink.'

Abigail saw that her father was making an effort to keep his eyes open. When, a few moments later, she saw them shut, she took her mother's hint that they should leave him.

On the way to the drawing room Eliza ordered chocolate to be brought in a few minutes. As they settled Abigail realised that, until now, she had not noticed the worried lines on her mother's face; last night she had disguised them with powder and paint. Now in the harsh daylight they were newly noticeable.

'Mama, you are worried. Is there something you are not telling me?'

'Not really. It's just that this illness is dragging on and your father seems to make no progress. He's failing daily. I'm hoping now he's seen you he will improve. When you walked in I thought he might be revived, but you saw he was soon drifting into sleep.'

Abigail saw her mother was fighting back tears. 'Mama,' she said firmly, 'when I've had my chocolate I'll go back to Senewey, collect a few things and return to stay with you.'

'But you can't leave Luke.'

'I can and I will. This is an emergency. If it helps Papa to get better then it will be worth it. Besides you need my help.' As she added, 'Luke will understand,' she wondered if he really would after what had happened last night.

'Well, it would be a great comfort to me, if you are sure?' replied her mother gratefully.

'I am,' said Abigail forcefully. She gave a little pause then added, 'Luke was out when I left but as soon as he returns I'll come back here. Will it be all right to bring Tess in case I have to stay awhile?'

'Of course! You must have your maid with you. She can have her old room; it's not in use. I'll have it made ready.'

'Thanks, Mama.'

'No, it is I who should thank you. I'm sure it will do your father the world of good to have you here.'

As soon as she had had her chocolate Abigail left for Senewey. She instructed Godric to keep the carriage in readiness to take her back to Penorna, and summoned Tess.

'Make ready to go with me,' she instructed. 'My father is not well and I must be at Penorna. You are to come too. You'll have your old room.'

'Yes, miss.' Tess felt a surge of excitement at the prospect of returning to the house she had come to love, but it was tempered by the bad news of her old master's illness. 'I hope Mr Mitchell will soon recover. I'm sure it will do him good to see you.' She went about her task of packing quickly and efficiently, consulting her mistress about what she would like to take. With that seen to Tess hurried to her own room to gather her clothes then went in search of Alice.

'I'm going to Penorna,' she informed her.

Alice looked glum. 'How long for?'

'I don't know, it will depend on how long Mr Mitchell is ill.'

'I'll miss you, Tess.'

'And I'll miss you, but you'll have Leo Gurney.'

'Aye, when I can manage some time off and that isn't often. I'm frightened he'll find someone else.'

'I'm sure he won't.'

'I hope you are right. And I hope Mr Mitchell recovers so that you will soon be back here.'

They hugged and then Alice went off to resume her tasks. Tess, after reporting to Mrs Horsefield, went to busy herself in Abigail's room while awaiting their carriage trip to Penorna.

Abigail hoped that they could leave soon but knew she should wait until Luke returned. She was thankful when she heard him enter his room in the mid-afternoon, and hastened to knock on his door.

When he opened it he showed surprise. 'Abigail! Come in, come in.'

Relief swept over her. His expression was amiable and his tone lacking in animosity.

He closed the door behind her and before she could speak, said, 'I must congratulate you, my dear, on the splendid way you organised the ball.'

'I had Mrs Horsefield's experience and advice to guide me.'

'Nevertheless you had the final word and I know there were certain things you instigated. Everyone was talking about it. Thank you for keeping up – no, improving on – the Gaisford tradition. I am grateful to you.'

Abigail was astonished, though she kept that hidden. This was not the Luke she had expected after she had refused him last night. She could smell drink on his breath still but his demeanour was pleasant and the light in his eyes held no animosity. Something must have pleased him this morning.

'Thank you, Luke, I am happy it was a success.'

'Indeed it was. Some guests were expressing the hope we could hold another one before the end of the year.'

She gave a little smile. 'That's a good recommendation, if they want more.'

He laughed. 'Aye, but they don't think of the expense. We'll see.'

'Luke, there's something I need to ask you.'

'Oh? That's a serious expression,' he broke in lightly.

'I'm afraid it's a serious matter. You were aware that my father was not well enough to attend the ball?' He nodded. 'I have been to Penorna this afternoon. He's not at all well. I know Mama is terribly worried though she won't admit it. I said I would go over to be with her until Father is on the mend.'

'Of course you must go.'

Abigail was so taken aback by the quickness of his assent that she had to stifle a gasp. 'Oh, Luke, you don't mind?'

'No. You must be there.'

'What about you?'

'I'll be all right. I hope it won't be for long and that your father is soon well again.' He came to her and took her in his arms. 'Don't worry about me. Just get your papa well. Until then I'll miss you.' He kissed her gently on the lips.

She looked up at him. 'Thank you,' she said quietly. Her eyes became coy. 'I think you had better have something better than that to remember me by.' Her lips met his with a passion that promised much on her return.

He came to see her leave, sending his good wishes for a speedy recovery to her father. As the carriage drove away she looked back and saw him still standing watching it. She waved and he raised his hand. Abigail settled back on the seat wondering at Luke's enigmatic personality. He had not mentioned last night; it was as if it had never happened. The person who had hammered at her door and shouted curses was no longer evident. In his place was the kind and considerate Luke she had known before their wedding. His violent mood swings seemed to be linked to drink, but also to unexpected bad news. As much as she loved her husband she dreaded his reaction to the next problem he encountered.

After the carriage had disappeared Luke, lost in thought, strolled slowly into the house. He really did not like Abigail leaving Senewey for an unknown length of time but at present, after his walk on the cliffs and visit to the Waning Moon, it would at least give him time to himself to lay plans for what he had in mind.

The coastal location he had examined would suit him ideally for it presented the situation he wanted and was handy for Senewey, which would be central to his scheme. His visit to the Waning Moon had proved satisfactory for, without Luke's revealing anything of what he had in mind, Tom had assured him that he could recruit five trustworthy men who for a price would do any job asked of them and keep their mouths shut. Luke would meet them tomorrow afternoon at three o'clock on the cliffs above the harbour.

On an afternoon when a strong wind had abated to a pleasant breeze and the sun shone from a sky strewn with puffy white clouds that obeyed the whims of the breeze, Luke arrived on the cliffs an hour before the meeting. He tethered his horse and spent the time surveying the area again, analysing its potential and weighing advantages against disadvantages so that by the time the five men arrived he had made his decision.

They came on foot, a rough-looking crew with only one small man among them. Luke judged him to stand at five foot six whereas the rest were no less than six foot and burly with it, not that the small man lacked strength; he looked as powerful as his companions.

When they came to a stop in front of him one man stepped forward.

'Mr Gaisford?' he asked, his tone suspicious.

'Yes,' replied Luke, eyes boring into the man, exerting his authority, letting him and his companions know who was in command here and would be ruthless with them if his instructions were not carried out to the letter. 'You the leader?'

'Aye, sir, Josh Ebbs.' He touched his forehead with the broad forefinger of his right hand. He held himself erect, with a wild defiant air that Luke reckoned had led him into many a scrape, evident from the scar down his left cheek and a nose that had been clumsily set after a fight.

'Right, Josh, name the others.'

'Harry Leland.'

Luke was pleased at the way this man met his scrutiny without dropping his own eyes, a strength of character that Luke hoped would be matched by his loyalty. He stood as tall as Josh and emanated the same strength but there the comparison ended; Harry's face was unmarked except for the lines beginning to age him.

'Wes Outhwaite.'

Luke nodded at a man who was only slightly smaller than the first two. His face was leathery and deeply tanned, marks of toil in the open, farmwork or fishing, it didn't matter to Luke. What did was the pose the man adopted which was that of a man alert and ready to give a good account of himself if the necessity arose.

'Pete Masters.'

Luke was looking at the youngest of the group. He reckoned him to be in his twenties but he had an air of strength and willingness to use it on command, whatever that entailed. His eyes were sharp and his ready smile made Luke wonder if he could ever be fired to anger.

'Titch Vasey.'

The small man who stood in front of the others grinned, touched one finger to his forehead and did a little jig by way of introduction. 'Ready, Mr Gaisford, sir! I can be in and out where these monsters can't get, and as quick as a flash of lightning.' He puffed out his chest, proud of what he could offer. Luke knew he would be the joker of the party and that if caught in any misdemeanour would turn his round face into a picture of cherubic innocence.

'That's us, Mr Gaisford,' Josh concluded the introduction.

Luke eyed them all for a moment, taking in their thick jerseys, woollen trousers tucked into heavy boots, and woollen caps clamped to their heads. 'You look as though you will be capable of the job I have in mind. Tom will have told you that I require the utmost loyalty and tongues that don't wag. If they do you'll feel the long hand of punishment, but holding them still and doing a good job will render you well paid. Don't doubt me on this. I never go back on my word.'

'We understand, Mr Gaisford.' Josh spoke for them all. 'You can depend on us. What is it you want us to do?'

'That will come later. For the moment, come with me and I'll tell you what I want you to do during the next two weeks.' As they walked along the cliff above the harbour Luke told them something about it. Then he led them towards the headland where he stopped.

'There is a shelf of rock running a short distance out to sea and back towards the harbour. That makes gaining access a little tricky but a good boatman will soon master what is required without mishap.' He turned along the coast and pointed out the run of rocky terraces that descended to the strand of sand. 'What I want you to do during the next two weeks is to explore them and find two ways that can be used to reach the top of the cliffs from that stretch of sand. Then I want you to do the same from the harbour.'

They all would have liked to know what lay behind this command but knew they should follow Josh's example and ask no questions.

'There is one other thing. You have seen that entering that harbour from the sea will require skill. Do you know of two men who could handle that?'

Josh did not hesitate. 'Wes has two brothers, both fishermen, skilled with boats. They'll go anywhere.'

Luke nodded and looked at Wes. 'That right?'

'Aye, Mr Gaisford.'

'Can they keep their mouths shut?'

'They can be dumb like me.'

'A boat?'

'Two if required, sir. They'd rather use their own; they fit them like a pair of gloves.'

'Excellent. Names?'

'Andy and Morgan.'

'Recruit them.'

'Yes, sir.'

'Good. I'll meet you here in two weeks. Same time.' He strode away, and as he passed each man touched his forehead. Luke liked to exert his authority on his subordinates.

Tess felt a sense of coming home when the carriage drew up at Penorna. When she'd left Penzance for the first time she was very apprehensive but he had settled here quickly thanks to the kindness and thoughtfulness of the Mitchell family and their staff. Now she looked forward to meeting Mr and Mrs Mitchell again and to being in her old room. She hesitated when she got out of the carriage and watched Abigail hurry up the steps.

Her mistress stopped and turned to her. 'Come along, Tess.'

'But, miss . . .' It was obvious that Tess was thinking she shouldn't be using the main entrance even though she was with her mistress.

'Come along, you aren't at Senewey now.' Abigail's smile of encouragement held a touch of amusement when she saw Tess's doubt turn to pleasure.

'Yes, miss.' She hurried after Abigail with a light tread.

Eliza, who had heard the approaching carriage, was hurrying down the stairs when Abigail and Tess entered the house.

'Wonderful to have you,' she said, grateful to have someone else to share the responsibility of nursing a sick man. She hugged her daughter and then turned to Tess who had stood back modestly. 'Welcome back, Tess.'

'Thank you, ma'am. I was sorry to hear about Mr Mitchell.'

Eliza smiled an acknowledgement and said, 'You are in your old room.' She linked arms with her daughter and set off up the stairs.

'Yes, ma'am,' returned Tess, and turned her attention to the luggage that was being brought in from the carriage.

Finding her father asleep, Abigail stayed a few moments watching him and then went to her own room where Tess was already unpacking. An hour later her mother appeared to tell her that John was awake.

'Hello, Papa,' said Abigail as she entered his room.

'Abigail, it is good to have you here. Your mother tells me you are staying awhile?'

She was shocked at the effort it took him to say these few words, but pleased that his eyes were brighter and he'd mustered a smile, faint though it was.

'I'm here to help out and give Mama some rest. And to get you better.'

He reached out and took her hand but there was no strength in his grip. 'Have you brought Tess?'

'Yes,' replied Abigail.

'Good. She shouldn't be left alone at Senewey and you need her here.'

'It's all taken care of,' said Eliza reassuringly.

John gave a little nod of satisfaction. 'Bring her to see me sometime, she was part of this household.'

'All right, Papa.' Abigail could see that the effort her father had had to expend had drained him. 'Rest awhile. I'll sit with you.'

He nodded, gave a wan smile and adjusted his head more comfortably on his pillow. As his eyes flickered shut Abigail glanced at her mother and mouthed quietly, 'Go and have a rest.'

Eliza slipped from the room.

John remained stable for three days. Fully conscious, he could speak to them but it was an effort and each conversation was short-lived. On the fourth day, when Abigail was sitting with him, he became restless and tossed his head on his pillow, grimacing and muttering as if he was searching for something.

Abigail went closer. 'Papa, Papa,' she said quietly with a touch of alarm and urgency in her voice. 'What is it?' His words in reply were indistinct. She leaned closer, looking into his eyes. They were wide open but he did not seem to see her. Instead he appeared to be looking beyond her as if seeing something she could not. His lips moved. 'What do you want, Papa?' Muttered words came fast. Abigail frowned as she strained to catch their sense. What was that? Tess? Was that what he had said? It couldn't be. Was that the same word? Tess. But why should he mention her? She could think of no reason. John's mutterings faded away to nothing and he lay at peace.

A short while later Eliza came into the room and saw her husband peacefully asleep. 'Has he been all right?' she asked quietly when she joined her daughter, sitting in the window catching the sunlight of a bright day while she read *The Farmer's Boy* by Robert Bloomfield

'He's been tossing and turning a bit. Not for long, but he was muttering which he has never done before.'

'What was he saying?'

'It was difficult to make out but I think I caught the name Tess.'

'Tess?'

'Yes, but I couldn't be certain and I can see no reason why Father should mention her name.'

Eliza looked thoughtful. 'Remember when you arrived he asked if Tess was with you, and seemed relieved that she would not be alone at Senewey?'

'So he did. I wonder why he was concerned?'

Eliza gave a little shake of her head. 'I don't know, unless it was that he thought it would be better for you to have her here.'

'Maybe in his delirium that thought had come back to him and he was wondering again if Tess was here?' Abigail suggested.

'We'll say nothing about what has just happened but I'll make an excuse to bring her in to see him.'

'She asks after him each day so you could use that as your excuse.'

The following day Abigail was once again sitting with her father when her mother came into the room.

'How are you feeling, John?' she asked as she came to the bed.

'A little better, thank you, now that I have my two lovely ladies with me.'

Eliza sat down on the opposite side of the bed to Abigail and took his hand. 'Flatterer,' she said, pleased that he was interested enough to make such a comment.

After a few minutes she let go of his hand and said, 'I'm going to leave you, John, I'll be back in a few minutes.'

He nodded and she left. When she returned she ushered Tess into the room. With one hand on the girl's shoulder she led her to the bed.

Tess was shy about seeing Mr Mitchell in bed and showed her unease.

'Mr Mitchell,' said Eliza, using the formal code of address in front of a servant, 'I have brought Tess to see you. She is always asking after you.'

'Ah, Tess, how nice to see you.' John's eyes brightened as they rested on her. He reached out to her.

Tess, wondering if she should take his hand, looked up at Mrs Mitchell with query in her eyes. Eliza read her dilemma, smiled at her and nodded. Tess took his hand and had the strangest sensation that he was comforting her rather than she consoling him.

'Is it pleasant to be back at Penorna, Tess?' he asked.

She nodded. 'Yes, sir.'

'Good, good.' He managed a smile but his mind suddenly cried out for her to say 'Father' instead of 'sir'. His lips trembled, about to say the word, but he forced it away; there were two other people here who should never know. 'I am pleased you have come to see me.'

'Thank you, sir.'

He looked hard at her. 'When you go back to Senewey, continue to look after Abi . . . Mrs Gaisford.'

'I will, sir.'

'Good. That pleases me.'

Tess, not knowing how to reply, merely nodded.

He let his hand slide from hers. Eliza smiled at her. 'Off you go, Tess. You have done well.'

'Yes, ma'am.' Tess looked back at the slight figure in the bed. 'Goodbye, sir.'

'Goodbye, Tess.'

Abigail's eyes were on her father. She saw him watch Tess every step of the way across the room until the door closed behind her. Did she see a flicker of interest in him? Of pride or admiration? It must have been her imagination; there was no need for him to feel anything for Tess. But hadn't there been times when she herself had felt closer to this girl than the mistress–servant relationship warranted? She dismissed such fanciful wanderings when her mother spoke. 'Abigail, I'll sit here awhile if you would like a walk in the garden. The fresh air will do you good.'

'Thank you, Mama, it will.'

She left the room after giving her father a kiss on the forehead and telling him she would not be long. Collecting a light cloak, she strolled on the terrace where she paused to breathe deeply of the crisp air and admire the well-kept gardens that had always captured her attention. She left the terrace and crossed the lawn towards what was known as 'the hidden garden', an expanse of grass paths and small individual garden 'rooms' with seats surrounded by tall yew hedges, making the whole area one of seclusion and peace. She had almost reached its entrance on the north side when she heard the sound of a horse's hooves. She stopped and looked towards the drive, awaiting the appearance of the rider who would come into sight once he had ridden out of the wood.

He came riding at a trot. Her heart skipped a beat. Luke! He had been once before and promised to come again soon, but as whole days passed her disappointment had grown. Now it was banished. There was joy in her heart as she hurried in his direction. He saw her and waved, slowing his pace until they met on the drive. He was out of the saddle and sweeping her into his arms almost before she realised it.

'It's so good to see you, Abigail,' he whispered close to her ear as he hugged her. Before she could answer their lips met and passion, heightened by absence, soared between them.

'I've missed you, Luke,' she whispered when their lips parted.

'How's your father?' he asked, leaving the next obvious question unspoken but knowing she knew that he was really asking, When are you coming back to Senewey?

'He's not really any better. He has his good days but mostly they are bad.'

Luke looked glum but said, 'You must stay if you think it helps.'

'I'm sure my being here gives him heart, and I know Mama is grateful for my presence.'

'If that is the case then you certainly must not think of coming home yet.'

Abigail, a little surprised by his easy compliance, said, 'You are so understanding. Thank you. I will make it up to you as soon as I return.'

He smiled, a twinkle in his eyes as he said, 'I'll see you do. Were you going for a walk?'

'Just in the hidden garden.'

'May I accompany you?' he queried light-heartedly.

'I'll think about it,' she replied coyly.

'Don't think about it too long,' he teased, taking her arm. 'Tell me what you have been doing.'

675

'My visits haven't been as frequent as I wished but I have been working on something I think will solve most of Senewey's problems.'

Her eyes brightened with excitement. 'Tell me.'

He shook his head. 'No, not until I think it's the right time.'

'Luke!'

He shook his head. 'No, and none of your charming wiles will make me talk.'

Try as she might, she was no wiser when he'd left Penorna than when he'd arrived but she was pleased to see Luke in such a good mood and hoped that whatever his scheme was, it would bear fruit to keep him that way.

Chapter Twenty-Two

As he rode home Luke was not sorry that Abigail would be absent from Senewey for a while longer. It would give him continued freedom to concentrate on his plans.

At his second meeting with Josh Ebbs and his gang he had met Wes Outhwaite's brothers Andy and Morgan. He was impressed by them, for they had chosen to arrive by boat to demonstrate their skills in the fast-running sea that made entry to the harbour tricky. They made it look easy but he knew it was not.

They left their boat in the harbour and climbed the cliff to join the others. Wes introduced them.

'Andy.'

The fisherman touched his forehead and stuck out his hand. There was only a moment of reluctance on Luke's part before he shook it, feeling a strong grip, fingers callused from working oars and lines. He saw a face weathered by wind and sea, and strength in the thick neck set on broad shoulders.

'Morgan, youngest of the family,' said Wes when he saw doubt in Luke's eyes. 'He may be only seventeen but he'll do a man's job and more if required.'

'Aye, I will that, sir,' said the youngster eagerly.

Luke saw the enthusiasm of a boy desiring to enter and be part of a man's world.

'See that you do,' he said, 'and even if your brother has already told you I'll repeat it: not one word of what we do and what you see must pass your lips.'

'They are sealed, sir,' replied Morgan emphatically.

The men then reassured him that they had planned routes from the strand and harbour to the cliff top, and on examining them Luke was pleased with what they had done. Both ways were usable but would not be obvious to anyone on the cliff top. As curious as the gang was to know what Mr Gaisford was planning, he would not reveal anything to them then. 'You will know more when you meet me at the Waning Moon four nights from now,' he had told them.

He had one more essential part of his plan to fit into place and as he rode home from Penorna he hoped that would be settled tomorrow.

Luke turned the collar of his coat up against a wind driving threatening clouds that as yet had not decided whether to douse the warm earth. He eased himself in the saddle and turned over in his mind what he had chosen to say to his friend. Martin Granton lived at Granton Manor, a small Elizabethan house that had come into the family in the early-seventeenth century. It had suffered mismanagement later in the century, from which it had never truly recovered. When Martin was left as sole heir on the death of his parents he had struggled to maintain it, but pulling the estate round was a hard task when financial resources were limited. It was this latter fact that Luke hoped to turn to his own advantage.

He eyed a building that was showing marked signs of needing repair. He felt sorry for his friend and hoped he could stem his own slide towards a similar penury. He halted his horse at the side of the house and tethered it to a wooden railing placed there for this purpose. At one time a groom would have hurried out to see to it. Luke patted the animal as he walked past and up the stone steps to the terrace. The balustrade was badly weathered and in some places the stonework showed signs of imminent collapse unless something was done soon to save it. Reaching the front door, he pulled hard on the metal bell-pull. A few moments later the door was opened by a manservant. At least Martin was managing to keep up some appearances.

'Good day, Mr Gaisford,' the man greeted brightly.

'And to you, Roger! Is Mr Granton at home?'

'He is, sir,' replied Roger and stood back to allow Luke to enter. 'He's in his study, sir.' He started across the hall from which all the furniture but two chairs had been sold to raise money.

Luke halted him with, 'It's all right, Roger, I'll announce myself.'

'Very good, sir.' He turned in the direction of the servants' quarters at the back of the house.

Luke tapped on the door and hearing the call of 'Come in', entered the room.

Martin, who was sitting behind a large oak desk, jumped to his feet when he saw his friend. 'Good to see you, Luke,' he said with a smile as he came over to shake hands. 'Glass of Madeira?' he asked, starting towards a sideboard standing near a large window that looked out on to the garden in which one man was battling to curtail the prolific growth.

'Not for me, thanks.'

Martin stopped in his tracks and swung round, surprise on his face. 'What, Luke Gaisford refusing a drink?'

'Just this morning.' Luke smiled, sitting down in one of the two armchairs drawn up opposite each other in front of an ornate fireplace.

'This must be a serious occasion?' said Martin, taking the other chair.

'It is,' replied Luke. 'Are you still in need of financial help?'

Martin gave a grimace. 'You know I won't accept charity.'

'I'm not offering it,' replied Luke. 'What I am about to tell you is strictly between us. We have been good friends all our lives. I'm closer to you than to the others. You I trust implicitly.'

'You are right there, but what's this about? You know whatever you tell me will go no further.'

'I am not as well off as I appear.'

'What?' A puzzled frown betrayed Martin's disbelief.

'It's true,' said Luke.

'But the expense of the ball?'

'Oh, yes, that's cost me dear, but the county expects it of the Gaisfords.'

'But . . . your other assets?'

'Very precarious.' Luke went on to elaborate.

'If things don't turn for the better you are soon going to be in the same position as I am,' returned Martin.

'Yes, but I am going to do something about it. In fact, I have laid plans already.'

'Why are you telling me all this?' asked his friend with marked curiosity.

'Because you could benefit too from what I have in mind.'

'Me?'

'Yes. But once again I want you to swear that you will not tell anyone, even if you turn my proposition down.'

'I'm not likely to if it is going to make me some money. You can trust me to keep my lips sealed. But why are you offering whatever it is to me?'

'You need money. You and I have shared a few adventures together, ridden hard, drunk hard. You have never been afraid of a fight or of danger.'

Martin gave a laugh as memories came to mind. 'That's true. So what have you planned?'

Twenty minutes later a tense silence had come over the room. Martin stared at his friend. His mind was in turmoil as he grappled with Luke's proposition. Something warned him not to become involved, but the enticement of easy money was strong and Luke's scheme piqued his taste for adventure, especially when he would be involved in it with his friend. If this worked out he could be looking at a much brighter future for Granton Manor.

'Wait a minute, Luke.' He held up his hands to stop Luke saying anything more. 'I hate to bring this up but I think it is better to do so now rather than later. I hear Mr Mitchell is not well. Suppose he dies. Aren't you likely to come into a size-able fortune then through Abigail?'

Luke gave a wry smile. 'I must admit the thought has crossed my mind, but I have already gone a way down the road I have described and been bitten by the adventure of it.'

'So what is the next move?'

'Are you in?'

Martin nodded. 'Yes.'

'Good.'

When Luke stood up, Martin did likewise. They clasped hands, sealing their pact.

'We meet on the cliffs above the old harbour four nights from now, seven o'clock,' Luke declared. 'Come by way of Senewey. We'd better go together the first time you meet the men I've recruited.'

'Are they trustworthy?' asked Martin cautiously.

'They know what will happen to them if they aren't,' replied Luke, his voice cold and menacing.

A shiver ran down Martin's spine as he realised this was also a warning to him.

The men were already on the cliffs when Luke and Martin arrived. They stared in silence as the two riders slid from their mounts.

'You all doubtless know Mr Granton by sight but he won't know you.' Luke went on to introduce each man in turn. 'Mr Granton will be working with us and providing some of his buildings for storage. We also have mine on Senewey and some at the Waning Moon, as well as the caves accessible from the harbour.'

'This sounds like a smuggling job?' said Josh, making his comment a query.

'No, it's not. That would have required a much bigger and more detailed organisation, involving more people and increasing the possibility of betrayal. What I am about to reveal to you involves only us and you all know what will happen if you break your word to me to keep silent. What I have in mind will leave no trace apart from a few broken timbers.'

'Wreckers!' More than one man gasped at the idea.

Luke nodded. 'Aye, it's been done before, so tradition tells us. I'm reviving the practice for our benefit. We'll all make money from it.'

'You'll want no survivors?' queried Joss, having heard tales of the brutality of previous wreckers.

'That's right,' replied Luke, committing these men to something they had not thought about when they assembled on the cliff a short while ago. 'Is anyone against that? If so, let him go now! But woe betide him if he betrays us later.'

The men looked uneasy, whether at the thought of leaving no survivors or the threat to themselves neither Luke nor Martin could be sure, but no one walked away.

'Good,' said Luke. 'We will place lights on the main headland and a minor one high above the far side of the harbour. Ships thinking there is a safe passage between them are likely to sail closer to the brighter light and that will put them in danger from the shelf of rock that runs out from the foot of the cliffs. The Outhwaite brothers will be stationed in the harbour ready to row out to the wreck, take on board what they can and ferry it back to the harbour. The rest of us will be at the foot of the cliff ready to exploit the strand and the ways you have explored of climbing the terraces.'

'How are we to know what cargo a ship will be carrying?' asked Titch.

'Doesn't matter! Ships heading for the south coast and the Thames always carry valuable cargoes. After each wreck we'll store the goods and wait awhile before gradually disposing of them. I will make out that I've set up a trading company, but that part of the operation needn't concern you, except for transporting the goods to their destination when I have concluded a transaction with an interested party.'

'How do we know what you receive in payment?' queried Andy, a touch of suspicion in his voice.

'You'll have to trust me, just as I have to trust you not to talk. Any more questions?'

'Are we to be here every night?' asked Pete Masters.

'No. Once we have taken a ship we will lie low until I deem it safe to operate again. You'll get a message via Tom at the Waning Moon. We can't guarantee when a ship will be lured by the lights, it will depend what is happening on board and on the gullibility of the captain. I believe we are more likely to be successful in foggy or stormy weather. Any of you expert weather readers?'

'Aye,' said Wes Outhwaite, 'brother Andy's an expert. Needs to be as a fisherman.'

'Right, Andy, you read it for us.'

'I'll do my best, Mr Gaisford. How should I let you know?'

'Granton Manor will be nearer you. Let Mr Granton know and he'll inform me. You can tell the rest of the men, and that night we'll meet on the cliffs here at dusk.'

'Right, Mr Gaisford!' He glanced skywards. 'Now we are all here, I suggest we meet in two days' time.'

Martin raised an eyebrow in surprise. 'You think the weather will be to our advantage then? It looks so settled.'

'Trust me, Mr Granton.' Andy gave a little smile.

'It will be interesting to see if you are right,' countered Martin amicably.

Two days later in mid-afternoon the sun was still shining when Martin arrived at Senewey Manor.

'Looks as though Andy will be proved wrong,' he said with a grimace as he joined Luke on the terrace.

They settled down with their whiskies and an hour later went inside for a meal. They were halfway through it when they both paused while cutting at a slice of beef. They exchanged glances, querying what they had heard.

'Is that the wind?' said Martin tentatively.

The windows rattled for answer.

'That was sudden,' said Luke. 'It was so calm when we came in and there was no sign of a change.' He got to his feet and went to the window.

Martin had to allay his curiosity and left the table to join him. They did not speak as they stared unbelievingly at the dark clouds rolling towards them across a sky that but a short time ago had been clear. As if to prove this was reality a streak of lightning seared the horizon and thunder rumbled threateningly. The wind would not be left out and shrieked at the house, trying to batter a way in.

'Extraordinary,' muttered Martin. 'There was no sign of this when we came in.'

'Has Andy got a sixth sense?'

'Else he's a magician.'

'It's uncanny but it's exactly what we want. That wind will be turning the sea into a maelstrom. Come on, let's finish our meal. We'll need to eat our fill for what this night holds ahead.'

With black turbulent clouds filling the sky, darkness came earlier than expected. Luke and Martin wrapped themselves up to contest the wind and rain that had started to lash land and sea. The wind seemed to be angry at their intrusion when they stepped outside and went for their horses. Hunched in the saddles against the bruising weather they kept their animals to a walking pace, only breaking into a trot when Luke, who was leading the way, felt it was safe to do so.

There was no sign of anyone when they reached the cliff above the harbour and tethered their horses in the shelter of a huge boulder. Leaning into the wind, they hurried towards the headland. They had almost reached it when a figure stepped into their path.

'Here, sirs.' Josh's words were torn away by the wind. As he turned from them, Luke and Martin knew the others must be seeking shelter in a hollow to their right. So it proved but any protection from the elements was minimal.

'We've a good night for it, sir,' said Josh as they joined the others. 'The sea's running high. Any vessel driven on to that shelf won't last long in this.'

Luke nodded, sending water streaming from the hat crammed tight down on his head. 'Andy, are you a wizard or something? A short time ago there was no sign of this weather.'

'I feel it in my bones.' Andy grinned, pleased that he had been proved right, though he'd never doubted he would be.

'Let's get organised,' said Luke, stamping his authority on the situation. 'Morgan, you get off to the cliffs at the far side of the harbour, light the lamp and then join your brother at the boat in the harbour. You both know what to do from then on.

The light on this headland will be lit when we see Morgan's light, then take up your positions as planned. From then on you'll have to use your own initiative but you know where to conceal any goods. Don't forget, don't take everything – leave something as evidence that the rest could have been swept out to sea. And remember, no survivors live to tell the tale. The whole crew could easily have been lost in the wreck and drowned.' He emphasised the last word to remind them of what should be done.

Morgan hurried away around the cliff top. His brother Andy accompanied him until he took the path to the harbour and the boat. Everyone else waited until they saw Morgan's light appear then occupied themselves as pre-arranged. Josh lit the light on the headland then joined the others who were making their way to the strand to take up position close to the foot of the headland. Luke and Martin remained on the cliff top so that they could oversee operations even though the driving rain made visibility poor. But watch they must, for theirs was a vital role. The minutes ticked by and ran into half an hour and still they waited, buffeted by the wind and slashed by the rain. Only the thought of the rich pickings to come kept Martin from walking away as his conscience pricked him with the thought of no survivors . . .

'There!' Luke's cry startled him.

Martin's eyes strained to penetrate the blackness that had intensified with the merging of sea and sky, with only the sound of the sea pounding at the rocks and swishing up the sand to indicate that they were not one.

'Where?'

'There!'

He followed Luke's raised arm and pointing finger. A light! Then it was gone. He held his breath. Visible again, he realised it was swaying, dipping and rising. A light on a mast-head? In that direction it was all it could be. 'A ship!'

Luke was already bending to the lantern. Sheltering as best he could, he managed to light it at the third attempt. The note of triumph in his voice was unmistakable. He picked up the lantern and held it high, a signal to the Outhwaite brothers in their boat in the harbour and to the man whom they knew Josh would have set as a lookout. From their high vantage point they could now signal the ship's progress to the waiting men until it came into sight.

Time seemed to drag and the light at sea did not seem to move any nearer. It would disappear and then reappear in the same place as the powerful waves dictated its progress.

'It's closer!' cried Martin.

Luke trusted his judgement and swung the lantern twice. They could still not be certain that it was heading for the coast to seek shelter from the driving sea and the striving wind.

The minutes passed. 'It's running in!' shouted Martin.

Luke swung the lantern three times, paused, and seeing the light seeming suddenly to sweep nearer, raised his lantern and swung it quickly three more times. He put the lamp down. Now it was up to his men to pick up the ship which he was certain was running for the safety the two lights on the cliff falsely offered.

The ship's hull took on a solid shape surmounted by masts and rigging that pierced the dark sky. A sail hung torn and bedraggled, evidence that the crew had not been able to deal with it before the storm struck. Lifted by an enormous wave, the ship seemed to be thrown into a deep trough, but by skilful seamanship or a miracle it survived only to be pounded anew by the sea, angry that it had not gained a victory, and the wind screeching at its escape. Their anger turned to triumph when the ship lurched as if struck by a huge hand. There was the tearing sound of timber as the hull hit the underwater rock. The vessel attempted to go on only to drive the wound deeper, allowing water to pour in. The ship reeled and tilted. A sharp cracking sound penetrated the maelstrom of noise and a mast broke, toppled, and dragged the tattered sail with it. It fell with a crash into the sea, dragging the ship further over and more quickly to its doom. Cries of horror and pleas for help were torn away by the howling wind as the merciless wreckers moved in to take their booty.

The ship broke in two. Half of the main mast was swept out to sea then beaten back by the current towards the strand. The rest was breaking up on the rocks. The Outhwaite brothers dealt with that section, loading their fishing boat with cargoes as quickly as they could in the circumstances, but their sailing skills enabled them to make three runs before the break up of the ship made any more impossible.

From the sand Josh directed the operation of getting as much booty as they could on shore before the stern broke up completely and was swept away to deeper waters. Before the goods were taken up the cliff, he ordered his crew to make sure no one had survived the doomed ship, just as the Outhwaite brothers were doing on the other side of the headland.

Martin had been mesmerised by the spectacle of the ship's death throes. He felt chilled by it but also triumphant for they had accomplished what they had set out to do. Now all that remained was to see what goods it had been carrying and to hide the cargo as quickly as possible.

Master of the whole operation, Luke had not only felt excitement but been gripped by the immense power that was his. He could send ships to their doom and men to their deaths. In his frenzy of excitement, he had an ungovernable urge to act as executioner himself. Standing high on the cliff, unsubdued by the howling wind, unbowed by the lashing rain, he felt like a god.

'Come on.' Martin broke the spell but it had left a deep impression on Luke.

They hurried along the cliff top and awaited the arrival of the first man from the beach. Harry Leland appeared, carrying a wooden case on his shoulder. He dropped it to the earth with relief and drew air deep into his lungs. Martin was quickly on his knees, prising the lid open.

'Brandy!' he called triumphantly.

'There's a few more cases like that,' cried Harry. His exhaustion forgotten, he hurried to return to the sand.

Before dawn the storm had blown itself out; all the cases and boxes had been hidden in prearranged places to be removed at a time and date when Luke gave the order. Little evidence that a ship had foundered was left. Whether it was found sooner or later it would only be regarded as a ship lost with all hands in foul weather. The storm would have been reported and the ship's owner would presume it was to blame.

Luke told the men to meet him at the Waning Moon the following night, an order Martin had to turn down due to a prior commitment.

The following evening Luke made sure he was first at the inn and occupying the back room, telling Tom to direct the others there and to keep the ale flowing. Discussion of their first venture as wreckers was filled with triumph, hilarity, analysis, and suggestions for improvements, though all realised that much depended on how events turned out on the night. All the men were relieved that all hands had been lost when the ship broke up and no one had had to commit the ultimate act, but Luke warned them that in future they must not turn away from it. If they did it could scupper the chance of any future operations and endanger their own lives. The sombre mood that his warning brought was dismissed in a moment when he announced that they would move the goods in two days' time to destinations from which he could set about arranging their sale and disposal. After which their pockets would jingle.

They were all in a more than amiable mood when they left the Waning Moon, and took no notice of the other people in the bar. Two sat deep in conversation at one of the tables, talking no notice of them, and two at the bar appeared to take only a mild interest in the men loudly enjoying themselves in the back room.

Chapter Twenty-Three

During the next three weeks Luke visited Abigail three times. On each occasion, fearing his arrival would signify an insistence it was time for her to return to Senewey, she was pleasantly surprised to find that he was in an amiable, in fact buoyant, mood. Curious, she probed him about this when they were alone but he refused to be drawn, merely saying, 'All is well, you have nothing to worry about. My financial problems are taking a turn for the better.'

His euphoria was the result of being able to dispose of the looted cargo under the guise of a trading company he said he had founded, explained away to people in the county by the fiction that he was diversifying and expanding his assets. He was generous in his payments to Martin and his 'employees', knowing that this was the best way to keep their tongues silent.

As he rode home after a fourth visit, Luke's thoughts drifted back to the night of the wrecking and he felt an urge to feel that fierce excitement again. Knowing from which cove the Outhwaite brothers operated their fishing enterprise, he rode there on the off chance that he would find them. He was rewarded by seeing them checking their lines.

After greetings had been exchanged, Luke put the important question to Andy. 'Can you predict the weather pattern for the next few days?'

Andy looked thoughtful as he glanced at the sky, studied the clouds and wind direction. He scratched his head. 'Signs are a bit confusing, as they have been over this whole week. I've seen them like this before then give way to fog.'

'So you are saying that we could expect fog in the next few days?' asked Luke eagerly.

'Aye, could be.'

'Then I think it's time to light the lamps again. Will you spread the word to meet at the Waning Moon tomorrow night?'

Andy glanced at his brother. 'Morgan, you can do that.'

'Aye, I'll away.' The youngster was off, driven by the excitement of what he viewed as a new adventure.

The following night plans were made, though they all agreed there was little new to do to improve the operation. Much depended on how the next ship reacted when it struck the rocks. Following Andy's new prediction that fog would roll in over a calm sea, they met on the cliffs two nights later.

Because of the fog Luke employed two lights close together, hoping they would entice a captain looking for a safe passage closer to the coast. It was shortly after midnight that his judgement paid off. One moment they were staring into a clammy blanket of fog; the next a dark mass visible through the night sent their pulses racing: a ship was heading to its doom.

Timbers ripped apart; masts shattered, broke and crashed to the tilting deck. Cries of horror and shouts for help were muffled by the fog as confusion reigned on board. Sailors who had not been killed by the initial breaking up were thankful for the calm sea. If they could escape the jagged rocks there was still hope for them. But that hope was short-lived. Powerful grips held their heads below water until they were pushed away to their end in a watery grave.

Luke, Martin and their gang worked hard to hide the cargo. Finally they left for their respective dwellings with instructions to meet at the Waning Moon two nights later. Everyone was highly satisfied with their night's work.

When he parted from Martin and rode to Senewey, Luke experienced once again that euphoria that had gripped him on the cliffs as he'd watched a ship come to an inglorious end at his command. Once again he had wielded the power of an executioner.

690

The meeting at the Waning Moon, where they used the back room as usual, was one of jubilation. They had high expectations of the cargo's value, enhanced by much hard drinking and hilarity.

As they left together, Luke made an observation. 'You were a bit subdued tonight, Martin. Something troubling you?'

He was silent for a few moments then let his doubts be heard. 'Is it really necessary to get rid of the survivors?'

'What else are we to do?'

'I don't like this killing.'

'Getting cold feet? Think of the money that will save Granton Manor.'

'Is it worth it? And I shudder at the way the others joke about holding a man under water.'

'You aren't actually doing it so shut it out of your mind. Besides, you are in too deep now to get out.'

Martin shrugged his shoulders. 'I suppose so.'

Luke did not like the tone of regret in his voice. 'And don't think of going to the authorities.' He made sure his words carried a chill warning.

The next day Luke was still in a euphoric mood when a hard-ridden horse disturbed the silence around Senewey. Luke, who was on the terrace blindly staring across his land while reliving the sight of the ship breaking up, recognised one of the grooms from Penorna.

The rider spotted him and turned his horse to bring it to a halt at the foot of the steps. Breathing heavily after his fast ride, he swung from the saddle and thrust a letter at Luke, 'From Mrs Gaisford, sir,' he said as he removed his hat.

Luke said nothing but broke the seal and read the few words quickly. 'Tell Mrs Gaisford I'm on my way.'

'Yes, sir.' The man turned back to his horse and galloped away as Luke hurried to the stables before briefly returning to his room in the house. A few minutes later he was back at the stable and mounting the horse that stood ready for him. Without a word, he left Senewey at a gallop. Abigail's brief message, 'Father died last night' was imprinted on his mind.

How much had Mitchell been worth, and how much would Abigail inherit? Maybe there had been no need for him to become the leader of a gang of wreckers after all.

The sound of the galloping horse brought a groom hurrying out to take charge of his horse. Luke ran into the house. 'Where's Mrs Gaisford?' he called to a maid who was crossing the hall towards the kitchens.

'Upstairs in Mrs Mitchell's room, sir.'

Luke raced up the stairs and knocked on the third door along the landing. It was opened by a red-eyed Abigail, her face drawn and pale with the expression of someone overwhelmed by circumstances.

'Oh, Luke!' Her wail sounded like a deep cry for help as she flung herself into his arms.

He held her tight. 'I'm here, love, I'm here.' He saw beyond her. In the room a man was standing by the bed.

'Your mother?' he queried.

'She's so ill,' Abigail whispered as she took his hand and led him into the room.

The man at the bed turned to them.

'Doctor Fenchurch,' Luke acknowledged in a low voice.

'Mr Gaisford,' returned the doctor. 'I'm so glad you are here, for your wife's sake.' His sombre expression struck Luke then.

'Mrs Mitchell?' he queried anxiously, glancing towards the bed. He saw a woman aged before her time, a face so pale that alarm coursed through him. Eliza's eyes were closed, her breathing shallow. He felt Abigail's grip tighten on his hand.

The doctor nodded. 'On one of my early visits to Mr Mitchell, Mrs Mitchell told me she too was experiencing some pain. I examined her and the diagnosis was not good, but she made me promise to tell no one while her husband was ill.' He glanced at Abigail. 'She did not want to add to your worries.'

'Why not?' cried Abigail. 'I could have helped.'

'I pointed that out,' the doctor went on, 'but she insisted and I had to respect my patient's wishes. The strain of the succeeding weeks took its toll in spite of your insistence, Mrs Gaisford, that she took more rest.'

'I thought her deterioration was caused by worry over Father's illness and that she would recover in time,' sobbed Abigail.

The doctor grimaced. 'I'm afraid not, Mrs Gaisford. On top of her illness, the shock of losing her husband has been too great even though she'd begun to expect it. We cannot tell how much her mental attitude has contributed to what we see now. Thankfully she is unconscious and will have no pain that I can tell. I'm afraid there is nothing more we can do.'

'Oh, no!' Abigail wailed and sank against Luke's side. His arm came round her to offer support as the tears flowed and sobs racked her body.

'Nothing?' he queried.

The doctor shook his head. 'Sadly we do not yet know enough about our mental composition and how to treat its reaction to severe trials. The desire and will to live depends largely on the individual. I'm afraid with the death of her husband, Mrs Mitchell appears to have given up.'

'Mama!' Abigail slipped from Luke's arms and went to her mother. She took Eliza's hand. It was so cold. She was aware that her mother did not even know she was there. The hand went limp; Eliza's breathing became shallower and then stopped completely. The doctor stepped to the bed and felt Mrs Mitchell's pulse, then laid her hand gently back on the bedclothes. 'She's gone,' he said quietly.

'Oh, no!' Abigail collapsed sobbing on the bed, her arms reaching out to her mother as if she would prevent her journey in death.

Luke started to go to her but Doctor Fenchurch raised a hand to stop him and mouthed silently, 'A moment or two.' Luke waited until the doctor nodded and then went to his wife. He put his hands on her arms and gently prised Abigail from the bed and on to her feet. 'Come, love,' he said gently, and led her, weeping, from the room. They waited on the landing for the doctor.

He came out a few moments later and, glancing down into the hall, was thankful that Mrs Downing, the housekeeper, was there awaiting news. They went down and when he had

693

informed her of what had happened and she had passed her commiserations to Abigail, assuring her that she was willing to do all she could, the doctor said, 'Will you look after Mrs Gaisford while I have a word with Mr Gaisford?'

'Certainly,' she replied, and accompanied Abigail to the drawing room.

The doctor and Luke went into the study. 'Two deaths on the same day is bad enough, but when it is your father and mother it could be devastating. Mrs Gaisford will require every care and attention, especially from you, the only relative she has left. She should not have the worry of the funeral arrangements which I suggest are made as quickly as possible. If it will help, I will set them in motion today. It is a matter of where you would like the burial to take place? I would suggest the little church at Sandannack. It is the estate village and I'm sure Mr and Mrs Mitchell would like to be buried there, but of course that decision rests with your wife.'

'I will have a word with her and let you know later today.'

'Do that and I will put things in motion.'

Luke saw the doctor out and went to the drawing room. 'Give me ten minutes, Mrs Downing, and then come back.'

'Very good, sir.' She left the room.

He sat down beside Abigail whose distress showed in a face drained of all colour, the pallor of exhaustion evident in her eyes. He took her hands in his. 'What can I say, love, what can I do?'

She looked pleadingly at him and whispered hoarsely, 'Comfort me.' She fell into his arms, sobbing. He held her until the tears eased, then gently pushed her away so he could look into her eyes. 'I will have to leave you for a short while.'

Before he could say any more, she grabbed his arm and cried out, 'No, Luke, no!'

'There are things I must see to,' he explained. 'Mrs Downing will be here. I won't be long.'

She bit back the tears, and when Mrs Downing appeared Luke left immediately.

He rode swiftly to Granton Manor where he was immediately admitted to Martin's study. After acquainting him of the situation at Penorna and receiving his friend's commiserations, Luke asked him to take charge of the storage and disposal of the cargo from the wrecked ship. He rode back to Penorna where he found Abigail composed if subdued.

Finding that she had drawn on her inner strength and seemed determined to cope, he put forward the doctor's suggestion and received her agreement that the funeral should be at Sandannack. Luke left to see the doctor, calling on the way to arrange a date with the parson. The doctor had already informed the undertaker who was always engaged for the Gaisford funerals.

Though the following week was a trial for Abigail she came through it remarkably well, and believed she had done so because of the support she had received from Luke. They rode back to Senewey together. Luke had arranged for her father's will to be read there once the last of the sympathisers had paid their respects. With that completed they led the solicitor, Mr Wagstaff, into Luke's study. He poured each of them a fortifying glass of Madeira.

The solicitor cleared his throat, glanced at the papers in front of him and said, 'Because Mrs Mitchell died as well there are certain bequests made to her in Mr Mitchell's will that are no longer applicable. She was not entitled to make a will unless her husband approved, a right which was not pursued, so everything will be regarded as being disposed of by Mr Mitchell's. Which means, everything will go to you Mrs Gaisford.'

At this announcement Luke's pulse raced. His financial problems were solved at a stroke for what a wife held was by rights her husband's and could be disposed of or used as he wished. He heard the solicitor speaking again.

'But it is not as straightforward as that. Mr Mitchell made everything over to his wife, with the proviso that she could not dispose of any of the assets but only enjoy the interest on them for life. It would have made her a good living, I must say. That condition would have continued to operate until her death. Once that occurred all assets were to go into a trust for his daughter.'

These words numbed Luke. He was well and truly tied. He could not now lay a finger on any of the Mitchell assets, which he would have diverted to uphold the Senewey Estate.

'Under the terms of this will,' the solicitor went on, 'Mrs Gaisford has the use of the income from the Penorna Estate, but only in set yearly amounts. It will provide Mrs Gaisford with a good living similar to that her mother would have enjoyed. I think your father saw it as a nice addition to anything Mr Gaisford allows you, ma'am.' He cleared his throat. 'Before I conclude, I must add that Mr Mitchell made some bequests from the ready money available which he saw was sufficient to cover them. These bequests are in varying amounts to members of the Penorna staff. There is only one person who isn't, though she was at one time and continues to be Mrs Gaisford's maid. To Tess Booth Mr Mitchell left the sum of five hundred pounds.' He looked down at a document and quoted, '"in recognition of her faithful duty to my daughter"'. He paused and then glanced at them. Letting his eyes rest on Abigail, he said, 'Will you inform her, ma'am? And I think you had better advise her what to do with the money. It is a considerable sum for such a person.'

'I will, Mr Wagstaff.'

Luke said nothing. His silence concealed an intense fury. His dreams lay shattered. He said very little as he saw the solicitor from the house then stormed into the drawing room, slamming the door viciously behind him. Abigail flinched then swung round from the window where she had gone to stand when the solicitor left. The crash eliminated all thoughts of why her father had left so much money to Tess. She saw Luke's face darken with anger.

'That damned father of yours!'

'Don't you talk of him like that,' snapped Abigail, drawing herself up boldly. She guessed what Luke was hinting at and had it confirmed when he hissed, 'Tied everything up so I couldn't get my hands on it!' There was hatred in his tone.

Now she saw a Luke she did not recognise. Gone was any consideration for her in her bereavement. In these circumstances she had to stand up to him. She was alone now. There was no one else to help her and she had experienced his dark side in the past. Now he was heading for the decanters on the sidcboard.

'And would you have taken it?' she demanded. His answer would show where Luke's real loyalties lay.

'Damn right I would. Senewey is what matters!'

'I thought you told me things were turning out better for you?'

'Penorna would have made sure of that.'

'Then I'm glad my father protected it. Penorna means so much to me.'

He drained his glass and poured another.

'Luke, don't!'

He glared at her in fury. 'I've told you before, don't tell me what to do!' He drained his glass at a gulp and in defiance of her wishes filled it again.

Abigail knew where this could lead and was pleased when he announced he was going out. She was even more relieved when, from the window, she saw him ride furiously from the stable yard. She felt sorry for the animal for in his rage Luke would ride it hard. She hoped that by the time he returned he would have ridden the anger out of himself. But in case he hadn't, tonight she would lock her doors as a precaution. Abigail rang for a maid and asked her to find Tess and tell her to come to the drawing room.

She was sitting on the sofa when Tess arrived. Her mistress asked her to sit on the chair opposite hers, saying, 'I have something to tell you.'

Tess sat down, placing hcr hands primly in her lap. Wondering what this was about, she looked straight at Abigail.

'As you probably know, Tess, the solicitor has been here to read my father's will.'

'Yes, miss.'

'Well, in it my father left you five hundred pounds.'

This was almost beyond Tess's comprehension. She just stared at Abigail,

'Do you understand what I have said?'

'Er . . . yes, miss.'

'Well?'

'So much money!' gasped Tess.

'It is indeed.' Then Abigail had to put the question that had been puzzling her. 'Do you know why he should do this for you?'

Tess shook her head, 'No, miss. The master was kind when I first came to Penorna, but so was Mrs Mitchell.'

Abigail said no more about it but in her mind linked this with the name her father had muttered when he was ill. The association puzzled her.

'What do you want to do with the money?' She asked.

'I don't know, miss. What can I do?'

'Would you like me to see to it for you?'

'Oh, please, miss.'

'I'll ensure that Mr Wagstaff puts it into a reputable bank.'

'Thank you, miss. Oh, could I give a hundred pounds to Dorinda? She was always kind to me, especially when poor Mama died.'

'That is a kind thought, Tess. I'll arrange it and then you and I will go together to tell her. And, Tess, it might be as well to keep word of your good fortune to yourself. Some unscrupulous people might try to play on your good nature.'

'I will, miss.'

Tess lay on her bed, snatching some time to herself before she prepared Abigail for bed. She was bewildered by her good fortune and found it hard to believe that she now possessed so much money. One question haunted her: why had Mr Mitchell done this? She could find no answer.

A knock on the door interrupted her thoughts. She swung off the bed, straightened her clothes with a swift brush of her hand and opened the door.

'Alice! Come in.' She closed the door behind her friend. 'Come to tell me what you've been doing on your free day?'

They sat down side by side on the edge of her bed.

'I met Leo.' Alice's eyes brightened at the memory. 'We walked on the cliffs and down to the beach where his father keeps his boat. The fishing has been good lately and they have been asked to supply fish to the Waning Moon, an inn on the moors used chiefly by travellers though some of its former reputation still clings to it.'

'What was that?' asked Tess.

'I can only tell you what Leo told me. It seems it was a rough place frequented by a gang of smugglers. It has brushed off that image lately but Leo wonders if it has quite disappeared.'

'What do you mean?' queried Tess, who loved listening to Alice's tales.

'Well, Leo told me that on one occasion, when he and his father had delivered fish and had stayed for a tankard before setting off home, a gang of men in very high spirits came from a back room. They had to pass through the bar to get out. A rough-looking crew, said Leo, all except one. He was much smarter than the others and that is why he caught Leo's attention, though it was only for a moment as he led the others out.' Alice paused.

Tess could tell that she was dying to tell her something so prompted, 'Well, go on?'

'Leo said it was Mr Gaisford.'

'What?' Tess frowned. 'It couldn't be.'

'Leo said he would swear on the Bible.'

'But Mr Gaisford wouldn't associate with such men.'

'That's what I said, but Leo would have it that the man he saw was Mr Gaisford.'

'Did he know any of the others?'

'A man called Josh Ebbs and two fishermen. Not personally, but he recognised Ebbs as a man he saw get into a fight in St Ives. Apparently he has an unsavoury reputation. Leo said that if the others were running with him they would be up to no good.'

'So why was Mr Gaisford with them?'

Alice shrugged her shoulders. 'Who knows?'

'If you hear any more, you will tell me?' pressed Tess.

'Of course! You are my friend.'

This conversation drove all thoughts of her own good fortune from her mind and, in her concern for Abigail, remained to haunt Tess.

As he rode hard for the Waning Moon, Luke sent curses ringing to the heavens that would have doomed John Mitchell to hell had Luke the power. A fortune snatched from his hands by his cunning father-in-law! He would now have to endure the sight of Penorna prospering under the efficient manager John had left in place. The only way Luke was ever likely to get his hands on it was through a son. Abigail was sure to make her child her heir, and with her out of the way the child would be under Luke's influence. But he needed money now and wanted something else to take his mind off the blow he had been dealt by a measly-mouthed lawyer.

He burst into the Waning Moon, startling Tom who was behind the bar drawing two tankards of ale.

'A tankard and a bottle,' Luke shouted as he blundered to a corner table. Chairs clattered as he flung himself down on the corner settle.

Leo Gurney glanced at his father who raised an eyebrow in contempt for Mr Gaisford's boorish behaviour. Leo locked this away in his mind. Here was something to tell Alice, and he noted more when the innkeeper took the tankard, a bottle and a glass to Luke.

'Pass the word for a meeting. Tomorrow night, Tom.'

The landlord was surprised that this order was so openly given, though it would mean nothing to the other occupants of the bar.

It might mean nothing but it had raised Leo's curiosity, especially as he assumed that the meeting would be with Josh Ebbs and the others he had seen in their company. He could have a fine tale now with which to impress Alice!

The following afternoon Leo told his parents he was away to Sennen and might be late back. Instead he arrived at the Waning Moon shortly before dusk, ordered a tankard of ale and took it to a corner table from which he could observe the door without being too conspicuous. Two other men came in and settled themselves at a table. Ten minutes later a man came in, took a tankard from the landlord, and made his way to the back room. Leo was alert; he couldn't be sure if this man was among those he had seen before but things were definitely beginning to happen. Three men came in together then, two of them the fishermen he knew by sight. He recognised the next man to arrive – Josh Ebbs. Now he was certain something was afoot, especially when Ebbs too disappeared through the same door. Two more men arrived, one much smaller than the others. He did a little jig at the bar while he called for two ales and enquired if they were the last to arrive.

'Two more,' Leo heard the landlord reply, and guessed one of them would be Mr Gaisford.

He was proved to be right a few minutes later when Luke Gaisford arrived and went straight towards the door to the back room. Tom immediately placed a bottle and two small glasses on a tray and filled two tankards. Leo guessed this was their routine. He saw Mr Gaisford open the door, momentarily halt his step and say, 'Open a window and get this damned fug out of here!' He heard a chair scrape as the door closed behind Mr Gaisford. The landlord put the two foaming tankards on the tray and went to the back room. When he returned Leo noticed he carried one glass and a full tankard. Leo took it that the second man must not be coming. He finished his own drink, bade the landlord goodnight and left the inn.

Once outside he allowed his eyes to adjust to the darkness and then made his way quietly round the building. As he had hoped and expected, the sash window of the back room had been raised. He crept quietly to it but was disappointed that a curtain had been drawn across, however that mattered little; what he wanted now was to hear what was said.

Ten minutes later he had heard enough to shock and leave him bewildered as to what he should do next.

If he told his mother and father it would brand him as a liar, for he had not been to Sennan and they would never trust him again. If he went to the authorities, would they even believe him? If they investigated further, Mr Gaisford would be in serious trouble and that could lead to ruination for Leo's own family, such was the power of the local landowner. He had told Alice about his first sighting of Mr Gaisford at the Waning Moon, maybe he should confide in her?

He was no nearer a decision by the time he reached home but after a restless night decided that, because he was meeting Alice the next day, the last option was the one he would implement.

Chapter Twenty-Four

Tess, her arms full of clean clothes from the laundry, staggered when Alice raced round the corner of the corridor leading from the domestic wing and bumped into her.

'Alice!' she gasped irritably, just saving the clothes from falling.

'Oh, sorry, Tess. I was miles away, wondering how I was going to tell you . . .'

'Tell me what?'

Alice glanced up and down the corridor. 'Not here, Tess.'

'Why?'

'Leo and I have a problem.'

Tess stared at her. 'You're not . . .' She let her words trail away but the inference was not lost on Alice.

'Of course not,' she snapped. 'I'll come and see you this evening when I finish,' she said, and hurried away leaving Tess staring after her wondering what that was all about.

She found out later when Alice recounted what Leo had told her when they'd met the previous evening.

Tess was flabbergasted by the story. 'This can't be true,' she said doubtfully while at the same time finding no reason for Leo to make up such a tale.

'That was what I thought but he swears it is. He doesn't know what to do about it.'

Tess looked thoughtful. She had never really conquered her dislike of Mr Gaisford and still wished Abigail had never married him, but she had and if Tess went to her with this story, what sort of reception would she receive? A wife would not tolerate such accusations against her husband, not without proof. But how to get it? And did Tess really want to act? Wouldn't her mistress's life be shattered if Tess were able to prove that her husband was the leader of a gang of wreckers? Maybe it would be better if she left well alone.

She pondered a few moments longer while Alice watched her anxiously. Then, a decision made, Tess said, 'Let's not do anything at the moment. Give me a little more time to decide what is best. Tell Leo to keep what he heard a secret, and if he finds out any more to let you know. We need proof. I think if the three of us witness a wrecking we stand a good chance of convincing Mrs Gaisford. Ask Leo if he can find out when there is likely to be another attempt, and warn him again not to say anything about this to anyone.'

When Alice saw Leo and told him what was wanted he wondered how he could find out when the gang would be active again. Then he remembered something he had overheard but had regarded as insignificant at the time. He had heard Andy Outhwaite being congratulated on his weather predictions.

The next morning Leo walked in the direction of the beach on which he knew the Outhwaite brothers kept their boat. Seeing them working on the timbers, he wandered over and after exchanging greetings, said, 'Repairs? Did you run into trouble?'

'Caught a rock,' said Andy. 'That young brother of mine wants to learn to avoid them,' he added with a touch of light-hearted contempt.

'He shouldn't have told me to go in closer,' Morgan retaliated.

'Will you have it ready to sail later this week?'

'Must fish tomorrow. We'll not get out for two days after that. Fog will be rolling in.'

How innocently information can be given away. Leo, who guessed that fog could provide good conditions for the wreckers, had got what he wanted but stayed chatting for another ten minutes.

After he had sauntered out of sight he quickened his pace and headed for Senewey Manor. He knew he could be rebuffed when he made a request at the servants' door to see Alice, but he had to take a chance.

His enquiry was passed to Mrs Horsefield who, when he reassured her it was a matter of urgency and that he would not make a habit of calling at the house, sent for Alice and allowed them five minutes. It was all he needed.

Alice was surprised to see him but his news that a suspected wrecking might take place the day after tomorrow alarmed her.

When Alice passed on this message, Tess battled with a dilemma. She knew the authorities should be informed of any law-breaking, but would they believe the word of a working girl against that of a landowner, a member of Cornwall's respected family? If they did, disgrace would come upon the Gaisford family and that would include Abigail too. Could she do this to the young woman who had befriended her?

Early that evening she was going to the mistress's room to turn down the bedclothes for the night when raised voices beyond the door brought her to a halt.

'You'll do as I say!'

'Not when you're saturated in drink!'

'Whenever I want!'

'Why are you drinking more these days?' There was open criticism in Abigail's tone.

'I'll drink if I want to.'

'What's made you do it this time?'

'What do you mean, this time?'

'It always seems to be when something has upset you . . .'

'And hasn't your damned father upset me? Not even a mention in his will.'

'So that's it? Money. You thought Penorna would rescue Senewey.'

'Why else did you think I married you?'

'Luke!' There was horror in her voice. 'You don't mean it! You can't?'

'I do!'

'It's the drink talking . . .'

'It's me. There's only one thing I want from you now – a son.'

'No, Luke!'

The sound of a vicious slap followed by a hard blow resounded through the door. Tess stiffened. Her hand flew to the door-knob but never reached it. If she opened that door the consequences could be far worse. Mr Gaisford would know what she had heard and could easily blacken her character so no one would believe anything she said. She closed her ears to the cries and protestations of her mistress and walked away, but her resolve to find proof of what Leo had heard hardened.

She spent a miserable hour before she returned to tap lightly on the door and await permission to enter.

'May I turn down the bed, miss?' Tess asked as she walked in, noticing the bed clothes in a dishevelled state.

'Yes,' called Abigail who was sitting in front of her dressing table, wiping her face and peering in the mirror. Though there was an attempt to give the usual bright reply, Tess noted the catch in Abigail's voice. That, together with the evidence she saw through the mirror, alarmed her. Abigail was trying to disguise some marks on her face with powder but she could not obliterate the cut on her forehead.

'Miss, are you all right?' cried Tess. 'You're cut. What happened?'

'It's nothing, Tess. I fell and knocked myself on the bed,' replied Abigail, trying to dismiss her concern. 'I grabbed the bed clothes to save myself, but didn't.'

Tess did not accept what she saw as a poor excuse for the state of the bed but it was not her place to comment. 'Miss, those bruises are . . .'

'Forget them,' snapped Abigail.

'I can't. I was in the corridor and heard . . . oh, if only your father was still alive!' cried Tess, the words blurted out before she could control them.

Abigail swung round on her stool. 'What do you mean?' she demanded.

706

For a moment Tess looked embarrassed then she knew there could be no holding back; it would be better if the truth came out. 'When we left Penorna after your wedding, your father asked me to report to him anything untoward that happened at Senewey.'

'He did what?' Shock ran through Abigail.

'He wanted me to look out for your welfare.'

'How could he do such a thing?'

'He was only thinking of you, miss. I don't think he was too keen on Mr Gaisford, and nor am I.'

'What tales have you carried to him?' cried Abigail in disgust.

'None, miss,' Tess protested quickly. 'I thought if I did it might make things worse for you with Mr Gaisford.'

'That was thoughtful of you,' replied Abigail sarcastically.

'But now, miss, after what I heard tonight, and judging by your face, I wish your father was still here.'

Abigail looked sharply at Tess and hardened her stare. 'You must tell no one, understand? No one!'

She shrugged her shoulders, a gesture of hopelessness. 'Who is there I can tell?'

'So that solves your problem.'

'Not entirely, miss.'

'What do you mean?' asked Abigail suspiciously.

Tess hesitated nervously.

'Out with it,' demanded Abigail, irritated by this.

Tess went on to relate her suspicions about Mr Gaisford's activities. As her story unfolded doubt filled Abigail's expression.

'Rubbish, Tess,' she finally exclaimed. 'These are just fanciful ideas that a young man has dreamed up for some reason of his own. Mr Gaisford wouldn't even go to a place like the Waning Moon.'

'But Leo swears he did overhear these things. He is sure the wreckers will be on the cliffs above the Gaisford harbour that has never been used, the first night there's fog.'

'Tess! That's enough! I don't know why you have got caught up in these foolish accusations. Now, let me hear no more of this nonsense.' Abigail turned back to face the mirror.

'Yes, miss.' The mistress was subdued and did not speak again as Tess went about her tasks. She left the room without a word.

Abigail sighed as the door closed. She stared at herself in the mirror but her mind turned elsewhere as thoughts came crowding in. Could there be some truth behind it? What had Tess to gain? In fact, how could Alice and Leo profit? They would only bring down Luke's wrath upon them, and she well knew that it could be of a terrible nature. If they were planning to attempt blackmail they would never have drawn Tess into it; involving a third party would have been too risky. She wondered what they would do now that she had told Tess to forget everything? Was Luke really capable of the desperate action Tess had mentioned? Abigail was sure he had financial troubles but would he resort to wrecking to solve them? She fingered her bruises and shuddered at the thought that he could be capable of anything. She spent an uneasy night as she battled with thoughts of what she should do next. By daylight she had decided that her only possible course was to seek help from Martin Granton. Close as he was to Luke, she did not believe that he would be involved in such a scheme and she knew he could be relied upon to give her sound advice.

When she'd left Abigail Tess sought out Alice. 'I've told Mrs Gaisford,' she said, but nothing about what she had overheard from the corridor or about Abigail's facial injuries.

'Oh, Tess, what will she do?'

'She doesn't believe me, said it was nonsense and I should forget it.'

'But Leo wouldn't lie to me,' Alice protested.

'I know he wouldn't,' soothed Tess.

'What can we do? Should we forget it? I don't know whether Leo will. He may go to the authorities.'

'He can't!' Tess was alarmed by this possibility. 'Tell him not to. Well, not yet. We need proof. We'll have to witness a wrecking ourselves.'

708

'What?' Alice was alarmed by the prospect.

'It's the only way,' Tess insisted. 'What did Leo say? Clear day tomorrow then fog the next two days?'

Alice nodded.

'You see him tomorrow and arrange that if it is foggy the following night, we'll meet him. Get him to arrange the place.'

Abigail avoided Luke at breakfast, and when she heard him go out, ordered the groom to get a horse ready for her. In doing so she remarked on the absence of Mr Gaisford's horse.

'He left for Penzance, ma'am,' came the information.

Abigail was pleased for it meant that the way would be clear for her to visit Martin.

She rode quickly to Granton Manor and was relieved to find him at home.

'This is a pleasure,' he remarked with a warm welcoming smile when she was shown into his study. He came from behind his desk, took her hand and raised it to his lips. 'You are looking particularly charming this morning.'

'I don't feel it,' she returned, and the worried expression that crossed her face then troubled Martin.

'Something on your mind?' he asked with concern as he indicated a chair.

Abigail bit her lip. 'It concerns Luke.'

'Luke?'

'Yes. I don't know whether to believe what I have heard or not. You are his best friend and a dear one to me. I could think of no one else to turn to, as you will soon realise ...' She paused as if gathering her thoughts.

'Begin at the beginning,' he prompted gently.

'Tess, my personal maid, is friendly with Alice, one of our house maids. Alice is courting Leo Gurney.'

'I know the Gurneys – fishermen, I believe.'

'That's right. Well, Leo told Alice that he had seen Luke at the Waning Moon with a gang of undesirable men he later learned were wreckers.'

'What?' Martin showed outward disbelief while his mind was racing with the possible consequences of this. He had never expected that a casual sighting could be their undoing.

'That's exactly how I reacted. But I cannot see what Leo has to gain by spreading false information. No one would take his word against Luke's.'

'So you think there could be some truth in it?' Martin still seemed surprised.

'Well, it seems Leo delved some more and swears that he overheard them plotting to cause another shipwreck. What am I to do, Martin?'

It was a plea for help he could not sidestep. Could he use it to try to turn his friend away from this nefarious trade that could only lead to doom for them all?

Martin gave a little shake of his head. 'Why would he get involved in something like this?'

'I know he's had some financial worries. Maybe he saw this as a way of solving them.'

'Surely not. He would know it was a dangerous game?'

Abigail gave a grimace. 'He's not been himself lately. Gets very irritable easily, as if he has a mountain of worries. Do you know anything?'

Martin shook his head. 'Luke always was a volatile person. He would take risks at school, and that was what endeared him to us, but they were calculated risks. He always liked activity and excitement. Whenever a new escapade came to mind he was charged with an energy that was almost over-whelming. We all saw that you had a calming effect on him and hoped with that and maturity he would settle down. Now it seems that for some reason he hasn't.'

'Can we save him from himself?' Abigail queried uneasily.

Martin hesitated. 'That could be difficult. If he is the leader of a wrecker gang he has stepped beyond the law, and with a number of men involved it will be difficult to do what you ask.'

'We must try,' she cried.

'I think for the time being you mustn't approach him or tell anyone else. Instruct the others who know to say nothing at this stage. I will see if I can find out anything more.'

She nodded. 'If you think that is the wisest thing. You are a good friend, Martin.'

'Go home and try to lead as normal a life as possible. Don't let Luke suspect that you know anything about his activities. Such knowledge could spell danger for you if it is true.'

He led her outside. When they reached her horse Abigail turned to him with tears in her eyes. 'Thank goodness you are here, Martin.'

He smiled, overwhelmed with guilt at the trust he saw in her eyes.

Wondering what she would think if she knew how he too had been sucked into Luke's scheme, he watched as she rode away.

Afterwards he walked slowly back into the house, knowing that he was faced with momentous decisions that would shape not only his future but that of others. But one thought began to predominate: Abigail must come out of this unharmed.

Two days later Tess spent an uneasy time closely watching the weather. It appeared to be settled as it was a calm sunny day but she felt almost relieved when in the late afternoon wisps of fog started to curl in from the coast. When it started to thicken about five o'clock, she quietly sought out Alice, helping in the kitchen.

'Tonight, ten o'clock,' she said and received a nod in acknowledgement.

As the hour drew near Tess spent an anxious few minutes after preparing Abigail's bed and room for the night, hoping she would not be wanted any more. She was relieved when the mistress dismissed her and she was able to hurry back to her own room. After donning suitable footwear, she fastened her cape around her shoulders. Careful to ensure that there was no one to see her, she hurried down the back staircase and out of the servants' door. She was pleased to see that Alice was already at the corner of the house. There would be no time lost in waiting. The girls fell into step and took the path that led to the coast. The fog was thick but they knew their way and reached the fork in the track, where Leo had said he would meet them, without mishap. They were disappointed to find that he was not there and spent some anxious moments stamping their feet to keep warm in the damp clinging fog.

'Where is he?' muttered Alice between teeth chattering with cold and nervousness.

The fog swirled and broke a little. In those few moments Tess's eyes tried to pierce the gloom but the fog closed in again, seeming denser than ever.

'We'll see nothing in this,' moaned Alice. 'He could walk past us and not see us.'

'I can see you.' A voice, ghostly through the fog, startled them.

They spun round, grasping at each other for reassurance. No one there! They stared into the fog that swirled, anew mocking them.

'Here.' The voice, muffled by the fog, seemed to come from another direction.

They whirled round again. A dark outline began to emerge. They felt relief when it took on human form and with one more step revealed itself to be Leo.

'Where have you been?' snapped Alice, realising that he had come from an unexpected direction.

'Been scouting around for an hour. Thought it best I be knowing something definite before you got here.'

'Have you learned anything?' asked Tess.

'Aye. They've lit lamps on the headland and two others on the cliffs at the opposite side of the harbour. Two men are ready with a boat in the harbour, two are on the headland – Mr Gaisford and one other I couldn't identify. His back was to me. The rest have gone down to the beach to the right of the headland.'

'What do we do now?' asked Alice anxiously.

'I've found a place where we will be sheltered and yet be able to see if a ship is lured in. Come on.' Leo led them along the headland turned on to a rise on their right and then down into a small hollow facing out to sea. 'Settle here,' he advised.

Pulling their capes around them, they sought a comfortable place.

'How long are we likely to be here?' asked Alice, beginning to think this was not a good idea.

'Who knows?' said Tess. 'Be patient.'

Abigail looked out of her bedroom window. Fingers of fog swirled, thinned, and disappeared to leave only ghostly moonlight. Her thoughts turned to what Tess had said. Could she be right? The fog rolled in towards the house, turning the moonlight into an eerie glow and gradually obliterating it; an ideal night for wreckers if the old stories were true. But these days? There was doubt in her mind but still the possibility tormented her. Martin had told her to do nothing, to wait to hear from him. But she hadn't so far and this waiting was too hard. She had to do something. She had to know. If Tess was right, this was likely to be a night for wreckers to go abroad.

There was only one way to find out; only one way to lay that ghost. Abigail stepped quickly to her wardrobe. She grabbed a thick cape which she flung round her shoulders; wound a kerchief round her neck and tucked it inside her cape which she fastened at her throat. Outside the house she recalled that Tess had mentioned the Gaisford harbour that had never been used so hurried in that direction, thankful that the fog had thinned a little by now. She heard the slap of the sea against the cliffs before she could see it and slowed her steps to orientate herself. She felt sure she was not far off where she wanted to be, but what should she do now? Where should she go? She tightened her lips in annoyance. What on earth was she doing out here? Why had she come? She should be fast asleep, safe in bed. She started to turn for home then stopped. A rent in the fog exposed a light further along the cliffs. Beyond that moonlight for a brief moment flirted with the water in the harbour. Was that new light there for some nefarious purpose? Did Tess's story have some foundation? If there were to be a wreck then the wreckers would be looking somewhere near the bottom of those cliffs. Could she find a way down?

She sought about her in desperation and in so doing noticed a second light along what she knew to be a rocky headland.

She recalled seeing a small stretch of sand to the right of it. Could that be where she would find the wreckers? Was that where she would discover the veracity of Tess's story? Abigail started off quickly but soon slowed her steps, reminding herself that she should be careful. There might be men posted on the cliff top. She must not be caught.

Twenty cautious steps later she received such a shock that she would have cried out but for the strong hand that had come from behind to clamp itself on her mouth. The other arm had closed round her waist in a firm hold.

A voice close to her ear said, 'It's all right, Mrs Gaisford, I'm a friend – Leo Gurney. Tess and Alice are with me. Don't make a sound or we'll all be in trouble.'

Abigail relaxed her stiffened body and gave a little nod of understanding.

Leo released his grip and whispered, 'This way, ma'am.'

In a few steps she was beside Tess and Alice.

'Miss!' Tess greeted. 'Thank goodness Alice saw you. If you had gone much further you might have run into Mr Gaisford.'

'What?' Abigail gasped, not wanting to believe this confirmation of what Tess had told her.

'I think he's nearer the end of the headland,' said Leo, 'and there's someone else with him.'

'Who?'

'I don't know. Never saw his face.'

'Then it's true?' said Abigail, sinking into despair. 'I must stop him!'

Leo grabbed her. 'Sorry, Mrs Gaisford,' he apologised. 'I had to stop you for your own sake and for ours. Show yourself even to Mr Gaisford and I reckon you'll not see the light of another day.'

'What?' cried Abigail, indignant at the implication behind his words.

'Mrs Gaisford, your husband may be the gang's leader. If he won't sacrifice you for the safety of all, the rest of the gang will turn on him and then it will be the worse for everyone. These men will be desperate to silence tongues. We've got to let matters take their course for now, and then if we want to go to the authorities we can all bear witness to the truth.'

'But I can't see my husband commit . . .'

'Miss,' broke in Tess, 'let's wait a while. It's the only thing to do.'

'Martin! There!'

He glanced in the direction in which Luke was pointing. He could see nothing but fog. 'You must have damned good eyesight.'

'There!' Excitement raced through Luke. His whole body felt a feverish thrill at the power that swelled in him. He could douse the lights now and the ship might alter course; leave them and it would surely sail to its doom. He had power over life and death, power to which he must keep returning, power which would condem some but which, if wielded wisely, would save others from the gallows. 'There! See it now, Martin?'

'Yes.'

They watched in silence for a few moments.

'She's coming our way!' said Luke, grabbing Martin's arm. 'It's a watery grave for her and her crew. No survivors!'

Martin was shocked by the glee in his friend's voice for it confirmed his inner suspicions: Luke was delighting in the murderous side of their venture as well as its financial rewards. Martin was overwhelmed by a desire to walk away from this whole filthy enterprise but he knew he could not. If he attempted it, it would be he who ended up with his head held under the sea until he drowned.

The ship came on towards them, looming larger and larger.

'She's going to founder nearer the beach!' called Luke. 'Come on, we'll get down there.'

Realising the implication behind his words, Martin was reluctant to follow, but he had to otherwise he would be a marked man. They were soon at the terraced face of the cliff that would give them ready access to the beach and to the men already there, awaiting the vessel fast sailing towards her end.

Not far from Luke and Martin four figures stood as if in a trance. Each one felt the urge to shout out and halt the ship in its tragic course but they were rooted to the spot by the spell of doom. A movement close by startled them and they saw two figures suddenly materialise and climb quickly along the cliff to their right.

'They're going down,' said Leo, knowing the lie of the land from his earlier foray.

'Are we going too?' asked Tess.

'We'll have to if we want full proof of what is happening.'

But no one moved. It seemed as if the three friends had silently relinquished authority to Abigail, and she knew it. She appreciated their concern for her and for what the expected discovery could do to her. She sensed that if she called a halt to this they would respect her decision, leave her to deal with it privately and say not a word. But she could not walk away from what would happen on the beach; she had to know the truth. 'We must go down,' she said.

'Very well, ma'am, follow me,' said Leo. 'Keep close and be careful. The descent can be tricky in parts. Don't make a noise . . . and, whatever you do, don't be seen.'

They slipped away into the fog, their attention divided between finding footholds and observing the ship. It was momentarily cloaked by the mist that soon drifted away, allowing them to see the vessel on course for destruction. It was close to them by the time they'd reached the beach without mishap. Leo ushered them into the shelter of some rocks from which they could see the ship only as a darker mass in the fog that had thickened round it again. They saw figures moving about near the cliff face. The ship was looming over them now and they froze. The next instant the vessel foundered and brought with it the splintering sounds of timber and the crashing of masts as she heeled over. Shouts rent the air. Cries for help dwindled from the helpless vessel as it broke up.

Figures moved from the foot of the cliffs, ran along the beach to the vessel and clambered on board, risking being lost themselves as it made a last attempt to right herself. The fog swirled away from the moon, allowing it to bathe the scene in a white light.

Abigail gasped to see the frenzied activity and had to stifle the cry that sprang to her lips when she saw fighting break out. There was no attempt to rescue the crew. Instead she saw men forcibly dragged into the sea and held under. She wanted to intervene but then was struck dumb in horror as she recognised Luke among the attackers, urging the others on, fending off an assault that resulted in his heaving his attacker overboard and then jumping in after him to make sure he drowned. Shouts of triumph, alarm and terror filled the night air. Not even the rolling fog could muffle them nor hide the horrific sights. Abigail shuddered. She felt Tess slide a hand into hers. Alice trembled in Leo's arms.

'Abigail!' A whisper so close by startled them all.

They swung round in alarm.

'Martin!' Abigail's soft exclamation was filled with horror. 'You and Luke?' They must be together or why was Martin here? When she had spoken to him at Granton Manor he had not revealed that he was a member of Luke's gang, yet here he was at the scene of a wreck. The thought almost overwhelmed her. She had betrayed what she knew and suspected; now no doubt Luke would come to know of it and she feared the consequences. 'Martin! You've betrayed me!'

Shocked by her accusation, he stepped forward and grabbed her by the shoulders. 'I haven't. There's much to say but you are all in too much danger now.'

'It'll be worse when you expose us.'

'Never!' he cried, desperately wanting her to believe him.

'If you aren't in league with Luke, why are you here?'

'It's a long story, but I want no part of what is going on now. The gang will be coming this way to go up the cliffs. I know another path further along the beach which they don't. Trust me! Come on . . .' He took Abigail's arm and hustled her away. The others followed. They kept as near to the rising land as they could, using it as camouflage to lessen discovery, but the wrecker gang was too preoccupied to think that anyone else might be on the beach.

'Why did you . . .'

Martin halted her. 'We'll talk later. Another two hundred yards and we'll be clear of the route they will take to the top.'

When they'd passed that mark he still urged them on. Another two hundred yards and they came to a cleft where the cliffs started rising again at the end of the strand.

'It's a bit of a stiff climb but manageable,' he informed them. 'I'll go first to show you the best way. You, young man, bring up the rear.'

'Yes, sir! Leo, sir.'

'Right, Leo, make sure no one falls.'

'Won't you be missed?' asked Abigail with concern.

'It's easy to go astray in a mêlée. I'll think of some explanation later.'

'What's Luke doing?'

'Talk later,' he said. 'We must get . . .'

'Wait!' Tess urged. 'I heard a cry! Listen.'

Above the surge of the sea on the beach they heard splashing.

'Someone's floundering,' said Leo quietly.

They listened with deep concentration. The splashing sounds continued and then they heard a gasp for breath followed by a scrambling across shingle and the sound of someone falling to the ground, followed by a groan.

'There!' whispered Tess.

They saw a figure struggling to get up.

Martin and Leo rushed forward.

The figure started and dropped to its knees, as if giving up. 'No! No!' He shuddered and threw up one arm to ward off the expected blow.

Martin was kneeling beside him. 'We are friends,' he said vehemently. 'Friends!'

The man stared at him in disbelief.

'Come on.' Martin got one arm under his right shoulder and Leo supported him on the left. They stumbled up the beach to join Abigail, Tess and Alice.

The man started in bewilderment on seeing three females.

'No time for explanations now,' said Martin. 'You are safe. Can you make the top? That's a nasty gash on your forehead, and there's another on your thigh.'

'Not surprising after being held under water and being left for drowned. I fooled them into believing it. But don't worry, I'll get to the top. I'll do anything to escape that murderous crew and see they get what they deserve.'

His remark sent a chill through Abigail. Here she was, helping a witness who could condemn her own husband to the gallows.

Chapter Twenty-Five

The climb was hard but the sailor met the difficulties resolutely, ignoring the reopening of the wound on his thigh. Aided largely by Leo while Martin helped the ladies, he reached the top. They all collapsed on the grass, drawing gulps of air into their heaving lungs. Silently they fought to steady their nerves and forget the horrors they had witnessed.

After a few minutes Martin had scrambled into a sitting position when he heard Abigail say, 'What are we going to do now?' Sensing her helplessness before the dilemma that faced her, he said in a comforting tone, 'We'd better get away from here before we decide.' He got to his feet and helped her from the ground. The others followed suit. He turned to the seaman. 'I'm Martin Granton,' he said, then introduced Abigail who took over to give the names of the others.

'Noel Ford, Captain of the *Lady Jane* – the vessel you saw lured to her doom by that pack of scoundrels!' Anger and bitterness resonated in his voice.

'Captain?' asked Martin.

'Aye. You think I'm too young? Maybe, but I've been at sea since I was ten. I worked hard, determined to become captain before I was twenty-five. I succeeded. At twenty-three this was my first command. Now I'll have to prove I was not to blame for losing my ship. Thank God I have you all as witnesses.'

'We've got to find you a safe hiding place,' put in Martin quickly before anyone could comment on Ford's remark. 'The wreckers will soon be swarming all over this area.'

While Leo took the lead, Abigail dropped back to walk with Martin at the rear. She touched his arm and slowed her pace to open up a gap between them and the others.

'Where are we going to hide him?' she asked anxiously.

'Senewey and Granton are out of the question. Penorna is a possibility but I'd rather the hiding place were more remote. Maybe Leo can help.' He called softly to the fisherman who dropped back. 'Leo, we need to decide where to hide Captain Ford. It will only be a temporary measure. We can't go to Senewey, Granton or Penorna. Have you somewhere where you keep your boat?'

'Aye. We have two boathouses on the beach, little more than shelters for the boat. Nobody else uses them. I'll put it right with Father.'

'Good. It will only be for a short while, to give him a chance to recover and for us to decide what to do because his first reaction will be to go to the authorities. Take him to the beach and wait with him there until I return from escorting the women to Senewey. Don't tell him anything until I get there.' After another half-mile he halted the party at a fork in the track. 'Captain Ford, I want you to go with Leo. He'll shelter you until I get back. I'll explain everything then, but for now I must see the ladies get home safely.'

The seaman nodded. He must bow to Martin's superior knowledge of the district. He did not want to stumble on the wreckers and was besides drained by his terrible experiences. After witnessing his crew being murdered and having been on the verge of death himself, he felt both physical and mental exhaustion.

Martin left Abigail and her maids at the servants' entrance to Senewey, warning them to say nothing to anyone and await word from him.

Reaching the beach used by the Gurneys, Martin saw that the two buildings were in a dilapidated state but would at least provide shelter. Double doors hung limp on their hinges, stonework was crumbling. In a corner of one shed the roof had fallen in. Leo was standing close to one of the doors. When Martin went inside he saw that the young lad had made the seaman as comfortable as possible, propping him against a boat and covering him with a piece of old sail.

Thinking him asleep, Martin asked Leo quietly, 'How is he?'

Captain Ford caught the words and replied, 'Safe, thanks to you.'

'Tess should take the credit,' said Martin as he and Leo came to the sailor. 'She was the one who heard you in the sea. No one else did.'

'Then I am grateful to her. I hope we shall meet again.'

'We must see to your recovery first,' said Martin gently. 'That is a nasty gash on your forehead but at least it has stopped bleeding. How is your leg?'

Noel Ford winced as he sought to ease it. 'Hurts like hell after that climb, but it has stopped bleeding since Leo got me here. I think you'll have to get a doctor, though. The sooner the better. Then I can call those blackguards to justice and prove it was not my own incompetence that caused the wreck. I must clear my name and save my career.'

Martin hesitated then said, 'I have some explaining to do myself. It is important that you listen carefully.'

The serious note in his voice caught Captain Ford's attention.

'We were not on the beach by accident.' Martin's bold statement alarmed him.

'You weren't part of that gang?' he asked, a tremor of fear in his voice.

'Please listen,' Martin requested, and went on to explain why exactly they were at the scene of the wrecking. When he had finished his story, he added, 'So, you see, there is more at stake here than merely bringing these men to justice. For my part I regret ever becoming involved, but rest assured I took no part in what happened tonight after your ship struck. I was sickened by what was going on and sought to leave the whole vile undertaking.'

Captain Ford nodded. 'You are an honourable man, Mr Granton, otherwise you would not have committed yourself to my rescue. With my death there would have been no one to

722

bring an accusation against the wreckers, and you could have resolved your problem with your friend without anyone else knowing. I also see that if I pursue my quest for justice, with support from you and the others, I will be endangering all your lives and Mrs Gaisford's name will be besmirched forever. I need to consider my next move carefully. Why not leave me here and come back in the morning?'

'I'll stay with him, Mr Granton,' offered Leo.

Ford smiled. 'You needn't do that. I couldn't get far in my present state.'

Leo looked askance at Martin, but seeing him nod knew that he too had to trust this man.

When they went outside the fisherman said, 'I'll bring him some breakfast in the morning, sir.'

'Good. What about your parents?'

'I'll fix it with them.'

'Very well. I'll be back in the morning.'

As he made his way to the cliff top where he and Luke had left their horses, Martin was still wary of running into one of the gang.

Luke leaped from rock to rock until he reached a position from which he could survey the beach. The breeze that had made itself felt in the last few minutes was beginning to tear rents in the fog and reveal the whole scene bathed in ghostly moonlight. He stood with feet apart and body braced, revelling in the knowledge that he had been responsible for such destruction and killing. He chuckled deep in his throat then threw back his head and laughed aloud, letting the sound fill him with the sweetness of success.

He watched his men moving the cargo along the beach and up the cliff towards its allotted hiding places. He surveyed the wreck, lazily swaying in the sea, and knew that even if it were seen before the waters claimed it as their own, it would merely be regarded as an unfortunate casualty of the fog. No evidence of deliberate wrecking would remain. Satisfied that all was going to his liking, he wondered where Martin was. No doubt he would be taking care of the salvage.

723

Luke climbed steadily to the cliff top, pausing frequently to look back on the scene with a high degree of satisfaction. Reaching the horses, he hoped nothing had happened to his friend in the general mayhem. He was sure it hadn't; Martin was capable of looking after himself. Well, there was no point in waiting, he would see him tomorrow.

He climbed into the saddle and urged his horse recklessly along the track.

At Senewey he quickly unsaddled the horse himself, as was his practice when he had been out late, threw a blanket over it and went into the house. He hung his redingote and hat in the lobby and went quietly up the stairs. He had taken two steps along the corridor that passed Abigail's room to his own when he stopped. His eye had caught a mark on the carpet. Annoyance tightened his lips. Someone wasn't keeping the place clean. About to move on, he dropped to one knee instead to examine the mark more closely. He reached down and fingered it. Damp! It had been made recently. And something in it felt rough. He brushed his hand firmly across it. Sand! Who had been out tonight? And then he wondered where, and what exactly they might they have seen. He straightened up thoughtfully and went to his room.

Tess sat on her bed, wondering how Abigail was reacting to the knowledge that her husband was the leader of a band of wreckers. She glanced at the coat she had thrown on the bed and thought she had better put it away. As she picked it up she remembered being a little way behind Abigail on their climb up the cliff and seeing a neckerchief lying in front of her. It must have come loose in the effort of the climb and slipped unnoticed from Abigail's neck. She remembered picking it up and stuffing it into her own pocket where it had lain forgotten until now. She must return it at once. Abigail might be wondering what had happened to it and worrying it was lying somewhere, evidence of where she had been.

Tess slipped from her room and hurried quietly through the house. Turning into the corridor that led to Abigail's room, she pulled herself back instinctively. Her heart was thundering. Mr Gaisford was in the corridor! She should get quietly away, she knew, but what was he doing on his knees, examining the floor? Tess peeped round the corner again. He was rubbing his hand on the carpet. He rose slowly, muttering to himself. She wished she could have heard what he was saying. He paused a moment and then continued on his way. When she saw him enter his own room Tess breathed more freely. Though she knew she should return to hers, curiosity got the better of her. When she reckoned Mr Gaisford was settled, she moved silently to the spot he had been rubbing and ran her own hand over the carpet. Sand! It must have come from Abigail's shoes. Could Mr Gaisford be wondering how it came to be there? Could he possibly think his wife had been at the scene of the wreck? Alarm coursed through Tess. Abigail must be warned!

'I must see you, miss,' whispered Tess, tapping at the mistress's door.

The note of alarm and concern in her voice made Abigail unlock the door.

'What is it?' she whispered.

'I brought you this. You dropped it as we were climbing the cliff.' Tess held out the neckerchief which Abigail took.

'Oh, my goodness. A good job you saw it. But by the look on your face there's more to this visit than that?'

'Yes, miss. It's what I've just seen and discovered.' Tess went on to relate her experience of the last few minutes.

'Oh, no!' gasped Abigail when she had finished. 'I never thought of that.'

'Mr Gaisford can't know it's you.'

'But as the mark is in this corridor, he may conclude I left it.'

'Give me the shoes you were wearing. I'll clean any sand off them then there'll be nothing to link you to it. Other people could have used that corridor. Me, for example. We must be careful not to give him any reason to suspect you.'

'I must warn Mr Granton of this latest development and find out what he's doing about that unfortunate Captain Ford.'

'In the morning, miss. You can't do anything now.'

725

When Tess came down the following morning to attend to Abigail she found her, in spite of yesterday's revelations, in control of her self. Nevertheless Tess felt duty bound to warn her, 'Miss, if you are going to see Mr Granton today, be careful, Mr Gaisford may want to see him too.'

'I shall, Tess. Thank you for your concern.'

With those words in mind Abigadil paused at the door to the dining room, wondering if Luke was there. She drew herself up. He had to be faced some time and the outcome of their meeting could have a profound effect on her future. She opened the door and went in.

Luke rose politely from his chair, looking rested and composed. 'Good morning to you, my dear! I trust you had a good night?' He flashed her a dazzling smile.

Abigail almost overreacted. Was this the same man she had seen on the beach? 'I did, thank you. I trust you did too?' She sat down and a maid immediately came forward to pour her coffee as she always did.

'I had a splendid night. Don't think I've ever slept better.'

Abigail glanced at the maid. 'I'll have my usual, please.'

'Yes, ma'am.' The young woman left for the kitchen.

As soon as the door closed, Luke directed his attention to his wife. 'I have a problem for you to solve, my dear.'

Abigail cocked one eyebrow at him as she took her first sip of coffee.

'When I came home last night, I found some sand on the carpet in our corridor. You know I don't like such sloppiness. I want you to find out who made it and why they hadn't cleaned it off immediately.'

'Sand? Well, I'll see it's dealt with but is it worth all the fuss of finding out who left it?'

'I want to know.'

'It may be difficult to discover. Whoever did it may not even know they did so.'

'You investigate and find me the culprit!' His eyes narrowed and she could not evade his scrutiny as he declared. 'I will expect an answer when I get home.'

'Very well.' Abigail nodded. 'Will you be late?' she added casually, hoping he would not sidestep the question.

'I have to see Martin this morning and then I must go to St Just and St Ives on business so may not be back until the day after tomorrow. You'll have plenty of time to solve our little puzzle.' He laid his napkin on the table and stood up just as the maid returned with Abigail's breakfast. 'I must away, my dear.' He came to her and kissed her on the cheek.'

When the door closed she sagged with relief. She knew who had unwittingly made that mark – she had herself. Thank goodness Luke had automatically thought it must have been a servant. She would have to make a pretence of questioning them all but could not throw the blame on anyone. But if she had no evidence to lay against anyone, might Luke suspect her? If so then she was in great danger for he would fear that anyone abroad that night might have witnessed the wreckers at work. She was relieved. She still had some time to play with but could not make her first move until this afternoon. She must give Luke time to be clear of Granton Manor before she sought out Martin.

Martin was heading for the stables when he heard the sound of an approaching horse. He went to the front of the house and saw Luke. His lips tightened. Damn! How long would he stay? Martin needed to see the captain of the *Lady Jane* as soon as possible.

'Morning, Martin,' called Luke as he brought his horse to a halt. 'What happened to you last night? Your mount was still there when I left.'

'Didn't think to wait, did you? Anything could have happened to me in that affray,' he muttered sarcastically.

'I knew you could take care of yourself.'

Martin ignored the remark and said, 'For all you knew a knife might have split me open.'

'Apparently it didn't, so stop being grumpy. It was a good night's work.'

'Was it?'

727

'You should have been there to see the cargo. You'd be dancing a merry jig now if you had. We'll make a lot of money out of this one and that should make you happy.'

Martin's face took on a grim expression. 'I don't like this slaughtering of the innocent.' The words were out before he realised it. He silently cursed himself for being a fool. Luke would not tolerate a weak link.

His friend's eyes narrowed.

Martin had seen this look in them before. He knew he should take it as a warning. A break with Luke now could prove catastrophic. He had to be sure he didn't endanger other people.

'Sick of it?' Luke queried. 'You know why we could leave no survivors.'

Martin held up a hand. 'Yes, I know. But I thought some of the men got too carried away last night.'

Luke laughed out loud. 'Squeamish now, are we? I can't restrain them, Martin, it's part of what makes them such good wreckers. You and I don't have to kill like they do so take no notice of their handiwork. Just think of the money which will save Granton Manor.'

Martin was almost on the point of saying, 'You *did* kill, I saw you. And I've seen the blood lust in your eyes before. I've seen the demons take over.' But he held his tongue. To speak now would to betray everything, and he knew if he did so he would not live long. Instead he asked lamely, 'Why are you here this morning? I thought we were not to meet again for a week?'

'Friendly concern, old boy.' He clapped an arm round Martin's shoulders. 'I wondered what had happened to you.' Luke glanced curiously at his friend. 'What *did* happen?'

'I was in the sea, fighting one of the sailors. We were getting deeper and deeper into the water and he was getting the better of me when a hand grabbed him, pulled him off and pushed him under. The tide swept me away then and I came ashore further down the coast.'

Luke nodded. 'Thank God you made it safely back. I can't afford to lose my old friend. Now that I'm satisfied you are all right, I must be on my way. Off to St Just and St Ives.'

Martin had no need to ask him why. He knew that when they met in a week's time Luke would have buyers lined up for the commodities he would pass off as the fruits of legitimate trading.

As soon as Luke had gone Martin hurried to the stables and in a matter of minutes was riding for the Gurneys' boathouse. He was thankful when he saw Leo talking to his father outside the shelter.

'Good day, Mr Gurney,' he said amiably.

'Good day to you.' He eyed Martin. 'I don't like what my boy has got himself into, sir, I'll tell you straight, and all I can say is, I think you should go to the authorities immediately.'

'If we do that, Mr Gurney, innocent people will be hurt and lives will be shattered. All I want is time to work this out. If I can't, I'll lay everything before the authorities myself. Please, Mr Gurney, bear with me.'

'Pa, please do as Mr Granton asks. Alice is one of the people who would be affected.'

Mr Gurney pondered his son's plea. 'What about him in there?' He indicated the shelter. 'He's calling for justice for his crew.'

'I explained things to him last night when we brought him here.' said Martin 'I'll have another talk with him. How is he?'

'I don't like the look of that leg,' put in Mr Gurney. 'He needs proper care and attention.'

'Right, I'll see to it,' said Martin, not knowing what he would do but realising that he had to put on a show of authority and reassurance. 'Now I'll have a word with him.'

In spite of the captain's pleas for him to go to the authorities, Martin persuaded him to wait a few days. He agreed on condition that if Martin couldn't find a solution by then, he would seek official help.

It was an anxious ride back to Granton Manor but he was still no nearer solving his problem by the time he walked into the house.

He was still battling with it when Abigail arrived.

'Thank goodness you are here,' she said when she was shown to his study and they were alone. 'I have a problem.'

'So have I,' replied Martin.

'Did Luke visit you this morning?'

'Yes.'

'Did he say anything about what he found at Senewey last night?'

'No?' Alarm came into Martin's eyes.

Abigail quickly told him about the mark on the carpet. 'I can't blame any of the staff and that will lead him to one conclusion – it was made by me.'

'We've got to do something to dispel that idea.'

'We have time to think of it. He's likely to be away until the day after tomorrow.'

'Oh, thank goodness.' Martin heaved a great sigh of relief. 'He didn't tell me that. Meanwhile I've got to decide what to do about Captain Ford. He needs medical attention and can't get it where he is. I've got to move him, but where to?'

They turned over some possibilities. It was only when they were trying to keep their spirits up with a cup of tea that Abigail had an idea.

'I know someone in Penzance who might help.'

'Who?' asked Martin.

'You probably don't know her. Dorinda Jenkins was my governess until she went to look after her ailing father, a shopkeeper there. After he died she kept the business on. When she was my governess she became friendly with another one at Trethtowan named Lydia Booth. Miss Booth left her situation there when her sister-in-law was ill in childbirth. Alas, she died. Because her brother would have nothing to do with the child, Lydia brought her back to Cornwall and settled in Penzance. Dorinda and Lydia renewed their friendship then and Dorinda grew fond of the child too. Unfortunately Lydia died and it was thought it might be a good idea for the child, who was nearly ten by then, to go into service. She came to Penorna as my personal maid. You've met her – Tess.'

'The girl who was with you last night?'

730

'Yes. She alerted me to the whole sorry tale when Leo told her friend Alice. Oh, I didn't believe it at first, but there were certain things that made me wonder.'

'So that's how you came to be on the beach?'

'Yes. Now I can see a possible solution to helping the captain. I think Dorinda might do it, especially if we take Tess along to ask.'

Martin got to his feet. 'You and I will ride into Penzance now and see Miss Jenkins.'

'No, Martin, that could be a waste of time. You take a coach and pick up the captain. I'll go to Senewey to prepare Tess. You come via the house and then we'll all go to Penzance together.'

'But what if Miss Jenkins won't agree to help?'

'Then we'll just have to bring him back and think again, but I think she will.'

Within the hour Abigail and Tess were climbing into the coach at Senewey.

The captain remembered them. After they had settled down he addressed Tess directly. 'I believe I have you to thank for my survival.'

'Me?' She looked puzzled.

'Yes. I'm told if it hadn't been for your sharp ears, I might not be here now. No one else heard me in the sea.'

Tess blushed at the warmth of his glance. 'That was nothing.'

'It was a great deal,' he said. 'Thank you.' His thoughts were responding to the attractive girl whom he judged was only a year or so younger than himself.

'You'll not do anything to betray my mistress, will you?' she cried.

'I'll have to explain the loss of my ship and clear my own name of any blame, but for your sake I'll try to avoid any mention of your mistress,' he replied quietly.

The ride to Penzance was not an easy one for the captain; the movement of the carriage jarred his injured leg and sent pain shooting through him. At the particularly rough sections of road it took all his willpower to stop himself from crying out. At one point it was so bad he instinctively grabbed Tess's hand for support. For the briefest of moments she was inclined to pull it away but instinct told her he needed her help. She held his hand tightly, sensing his suffering. Even under these circumstances his touch brought feelings to her she had never experienced before. Though she knew that the sooner they reached Penzance, the better it would be for the sailor, still a part of her was wishing this journey could go on forever.

Although Martin needed to concentrate on handling the horse he managed to carry on a low-voiced conversation with Abigail who was sitting on the box beside him.

'Knowing what you do now, will you return to Senewey?'

'What else can I do? I am Luke's wife. He does not know I witnessed the wrecking and appeared perfectly normal this morning.'

'Be careful, Abigail. You may not have experienced it yet but Luke is highly volatile.' He glanced at her as he spoke and caught a grimace on her face that alarmed him. 'You have already seen his unpleasant side?'

Denials sprang to Abigail's lips but she held them back, realising that Martin had guessed the truth and knowing in her heart of hearts that she badly needed a confidant she could trust. She felt a closeness to this man despite his long association with her husband.

She nodded.

'Has he mistreated you?'

Abigail bit her lip. 'Yes.'

'On more than one occasion?'

She nodded, tears welling in her eyes. She wiped them away. She must not break down now. She glanced through the coachman's window and saw that Tess and the captain were engrossed in conversation inside the cariage.

'Abigail, you can't go back to Senewey.'

'I must. I'm his wife.'

'Then you will be in danger. I've seen blood lust in Luke's eyes recently. It's a heightening of a trait I have seen in him before, even when we were at school. I'm worried for you, Abigail.'

The tremor in his voice reflected the feelings he had kept hidden from her; it made her wonder if deep down there had been reciprocal feelings within herself. She automatically laid her hand on his arm as she said, 'And you will be in danger too. He will learn of your part in saving the captain, I'm afraid.'

'I can take care of myself. It is you I'm worried about.'

They fell into a charged silence.

The coach rumbled into Penzance. Following Abigail's directions, Martin brought the vehicle to a halt outside Miss Jenkins's shop.

'Come on, Tess,' called Abigail as she eased herself down. With a reassuring smile at Captain Ford, Tess slipped out of the coach and followed her into the shop. Within a few moments one of Dorinda's assistants had brought her from the house. She expressed delight at seeing her friends and quickly ushered them into her drawing room. She realised from their serious expressions that something was troubling them.

'Dorinda, we need your help ...' Abigail explained the captain's plight as clearly and concisely as possible. 'He needs to be kept hidden otherwise he could be in great danger. Can you help us?'

Dorinda glanced from one to the other. She could not avoid the pleading expression on Tess's face. 'I'll do what I can. Bring him in.'

Relief swept over them all. Tess hugged Dorinda and said, 'Oh, thank you,' with such heartfelt meaning her old friend wondered what lay behind it.

'Wait a moment!' Dorinda called them to a halt. 'I'll send my assistants to the storeroom then they won't see anything from the shop window. When the way is clear, bring him to the side door.'

They made a show of saying their goodbyes to Dorinda in the shop. Outside they awaited her signal and then quickly took Captain Ford to the side door where Dorinda awaited them. She assessed his condition at a glance and led the way upstairs to one of her spare bedrooms. They left Martin, who had brought clean clothes from Senewey, to attend to the captain and see him comfortably to bed.

Back in the drawing room, Abigail further explained their reasons for bringing the captain to Dorinda and swore her to secrecy.

When Martin came downstairs he announced, 'Captain Ford is going to need a doctor. Do you know of one who can be trusted to keep his presence here a secret?'

'I will attend to that,' said Dorinda confidently. 'I'm friendly with Dr Bushell who was widowed four years ago. I can trust him.'

Tess remembered Dr Bushell and was pleased at the implication she read behind this, but made no comment.

'Good.' Martin addressed Tess. 'Captain Ford was asking to see you before you left.'

Her blushes did not go unnoticed by Dorinda who looked enquiringly at Abigail when the door had closed behind Tess.

'It was Tess who saved him from the sea,' she explained. 'She was the only one who heard him.'

Tess knocked tentatively at the bedroom door and then entered shyly. Captain Ford smiled and held out his hand. 'I want to thank you again for saving my life.'

She took his hand and felt the same sensation as she had experienced in the coach. 'I only said I'd heard something.'

'No one else did,' he pointed out. 'And if you hadn't, I might have perished there. I will always be in debt to you.'

'You can repay me by getting well and not endangering the lives of my mistress and friends.'

'I must clear my own name but I'll do it without implicating them, I promise, though I might need a witness . . .'

'Then use me, not them.'

He looked at her with open admiration. 'You are such a loyal person.'

Her face reddened as she met his gaze. 'I must go.' She let her hand slip from his.

'Please come and visit me again?'

'I will,' she promised with an encouraging smile.

On reaching Senewey Manor Abigail invited Martin to partake of some refreshments and he accepted readily. Tess hurried away to her own room then went to find Alice to reassure her that Captain Ford had been taken care of and she herself had nothing to fear so long as she told no one of what had happened.

As they settled at the dining room table the contrast between this quiet domestic scene and the enormity of the dilemma that faced her was almost too much for Abigail to bear. Her world, the one she had dreamed about when she'd married the handsome heir to Senewey, lay in ruins around her. She felt bereft, with no one to turn to who could truly help her unless it was this man, the one who had saved her last night. But Martin had his own problems to contend with too. Luke would see any help he offered her as a betrayal of him, and Luke's machinations could be deadly.

The question that occupied both their minds was voiced by Abigail. 'What should we do? Face him with the truth or say nothing and hope he never learns of it?'

'I think both of those would be dangerous. You would be on a knife-edge all the time, and I know Luke would be sharp enough to detect it and want to know why. You already know what *that* could mean for you.'

'I'll have to risk it. I can't walk out on my own husband. Think of the scandal.'

'Isn't that better than what you may suffer at his hands?'

Abigail shrugged her shoulders as if resigned to staying and accepting the consequences. 'What about you? You've been part of this horrible affair. Luke is not just going to let you walk away. You would be too much of a threat to him. And I think, in clearing his name, Captain Ford is bound to reveal so much of the truth that the finger will be pointed at Luke. That could implicate you too.'

'I can only think it would be safer for me to leave. Come with me, Abigail, don't try and outface Luke.'

'But he might never know I witnessed what happened. And if I left too, it could look like marital desertion. That you and I were lovers.'

'Oh, that we were!' Martin immediately made a gesture as if to pluck back these words. He knew he should never have uttered them, but they were out and in a way he did not regret it for he saw sympathy in Abigail's eyes and knew that she had guessed something of his feelings before now.

She reached out and took his hand. 'Another place, another time, who knows? But we must play the cards we've been dealt. I cannot run away even under these circumstances.'

'Luke will not be back until the day after tomorrow,' Martin pointed out, then added a final piece of advice. 'In the meantime, think things over very carefully.'

Chapter Twenty-Six

When he had gone Abigail felt very alone. She needed someone to talk to who wasn't directly involved in what had happened. How she wished her parents were still alive! Had her
father seen traits in Luke that she, love-struck, had been blind
to? Had the old rivalries between the families still troubled
him even though there had been that reconciliation on her
birthday? And had this led him to ask Tess to contact him if
she observed anything untoward? Why hadn't she herself
heeded her parents' doubts? Why hadn't she been aware of
Martin's feelings towards her – if only he had pressed his case
then, what might have been ... She realised it would have
made no difference, though. Her love for Luke at that time
had been all consuming. Now she was lost without that
certainty in her life.

By late afternoon she was no nearer solving her problem
but then a name began to impinge on her mind – Mrs
Gaisford. Luke's mother might help her. Abigail knew all
was not well between mother and son, but would Hester talk
against him? She recalled Luke's behaviour when she had
visited his mother. Shuddered at it, in fact. Once again she
wondered what lay behind his isolation of Hester, his reason for forbidding his wife to talk to her. There was only
one way to find out. Abigail made her way to the West
Wing.

'Ah, my dear, I'm so pleased to have your company,' Hester
greeted her warmly.

'And I am pleased to see you, Mrs Gaisford,' replied
Abigail, taking a seat opposite her mother-in-law.

'How have you been?' asked Mrs Gaisford.

'Very well.'

Hester gave a little knowing smile. 'Maybe, but I think something is troubling you.'

'Very shrewd,' said Abigail with a grimace.

'And that look tells me it concerns my son. You can tell me, if you like?'

Abigail did not answer immediately.

'It is best to begin at the beginning. Don't spare my feelings. I know what my son can be like.'

Almost before she knew it, the words were pouring out of Abigail and the sordid story lay before Mrs Gaisford.

Hester shook her head sadly. 'I feared things would go this way. I hoped not. But I have seen much of my husband's character reproduced in Luke, and unfortunately all his worst traits. I suffered greatly at his hands, both physically and mentally. Oh, Jeremy was the catch of the county when I was young – he was a Gaisford, after all. I soon realised he had married me only to outdo his rivals.' Hester gave a wistful smile. 'I used to be the belle of every ball then. You would not think so to look at me now, but young men courted me in droves and Jeremy did not like it so swept me off my feet, and up the aisle. The biggest mistake I ever made! My life became a misery to me. I had to be there whenever he wanted me. I had to do his will. He would mock me and flaunt his liaisons with other women, knowing I dare not do anything about it. I tried once. That's when the beatings started. They were worse when he was in drink, and at those times he was cruel to Luke too.'

She shook her head sadly at the recollection and dropped it in shame as she added, 'And I did nothing about it, frightened to turn Jeremy's wrath even more fiercely against me. I turned Luke away when he sought protection in front of his father and afterwards he did not even seek it in private, thinking I was privy to all that was happening. And that is why I am here now, shut away from everyone except the two servants charged to see my basic needs. Luke is punishing me for not lifting a hand to save him from his father. I could see the ill

738

treatment was having a marked effect on him, but hoped you would have a steadying influence on him and make him into the man I always believed he could be. And now he has revived the notorious trade of wrecking and taken lives to line his own pockets. He has sunk too far. His father was bad but would even he have done this?'

'What should I do, Mrs Gaisford?' Abigail pleaded.

She hesitated only for the briefest of moments. 'Leave! Go, my dear, go!'

'But I'm his wife.'

'Give that no countenance. If you stay, your life will be a misery to you as mine was to me. In fact, I believe in your case it would be worse. My husband never killed, but from what you saw Luke do on the beach there's no telling how far he will go. He could harm you. Leave him to take the consequences once this sea captain sees justice done.' A catch came to her voice as she added, 'I wish I'd had the courage to leave my husband. Don't make the same mistake.'

'Thank you for listening, Mrs Gaisford, and I'm sorry to bring you such news.'

Hester dismissed the apology with a wave of her hand. 'I'm pleased you did. I see my son at his true worth. I long ago stopped trying to make excuses for him.'

'And thank you for your advice.'

'Heed it, my dear. Go and don't look back. Only remember me.'

Abigail hugged and kissed her, and said, 'I will, Mrs Gaisford. Goodbye.'

With a saddened heart, Hester watched her daughter-in-law leave.

Abigail's new determination quickened her step as she returned to her room. Mrs Gaisford had made her see that the only course for her was to leave. She called for Tess and was already changing into her riding habit when the girl appeared.

'Tess, I want to pack our essentials. You and I leave here tomorrow morning.'

739

The order set Tess's mind into a whirl. 'Where are we going, miss?'

'I don't know. I'm on my way to see Mr Granton now to discuss that. Unless this trouble blows over very quickly we won't be coming back here. At least, not for a considerable time.'

Tess sensed urgency in her mistress's words. In a way she was not surprised they were leaving; she knew there would be danger here after what they had witnessed, and was glad that they would not be under Mr Gaisford's continued scrutiny, but her heart was wounded by the thought that she might not see Captain Ford again.

'Tell no one about this, Tess, no one! Just have everything ready.'

During the few minutes Abigail had to wait impatiently while the under-groom prepared a horse for her, she fought to keep her mind focused on the decision she had made. She rode fast to Granton Manor and was quickly shown into the drawing room to await Martin.

He hurried into the room at the servant's summons. 'Abigail, what brings you here so soon?'

'I'm leaving, Martin, early in the morning. I thought you should know.'

'I'm glad. I think it's the best course for you.'

'What about you? I feel I'm deserting you.'

'Don't think that.'

'But it worries me to think about what might happen to you.' She caught his gaze and added impetuously, 'Come with me, out of danger.' He hesitated. 'Why not?' Abigail prompted.

'There is no reason why I shouldn't . . .'

'Then do it. Don't leave yourself at Luke's mercy.'

'Where have you planned to go?'

'I was at a loss at first but on the way here an idea came to me. I have an aunt in Whitby, father's sister Martha, of whom I have only faint memories. Whitby's on the Yorkshire coast, surely far enough away from Luke.'

'But does he know of her?'

'I don't think so. He took little notice of the wedding invitations, only providing a list of the people he wanted inviting. Aunt Martha was ill at the time so could not come. When Father and Mother died I wrote to her at our old home Bloomfield Manor, but of course the letter did not reach her until after the funerals. My aunt replied but as far as I know Luke did not see the letters.'

'Was she never talked about?'

'Luke was never interested in my background. I was only five when we came here and I think he regarded me as virtually Cornish. His only concern was for the Gaisfords.'

'I must admit that, though I knew your mother and father were not from these parts originally, I never knew their origins.'

'Then we shall go to Whitby and seek help from my Aunt Martha.'

'No one must know where we are going. We must make our departure as secret as possible. I'll take my two-horse carriage and drive it myself. We do not want to make your leaving Senewey obvious so I propose I come to the servants' entrance at ten tonight and bring you here so we can set out early in the morning. I have had to deplete my staff and those still in my employ I can trust implicitly.'

'I will have to bring my maid. I cannot possibly leave Tess behind with no protection when Luke realises I have left.'

'His actions would be too terrible to contemplate. You must bring her, of course.'

'What about the captain, the Gurneys and Alice?'

'We are going to have to let matters here take their course. Captain Ford knows the full story. We must trust to his discretion in whatever action he takes. I'm sure the Gurneys will look after Alice.'

She nodded, realising there was nothing more they could do. Now all she wanted was to get as far away from Senewey as possible.

On reaching the Manor, Abigail quickly informed Tess of their plans.

Though she was in full agreement that her mistress should

seek safety from her husband, Tess's heart sank: she would not see Captain Ford before they left. The thought brought such a sense of loss she was bewildered. Such feelings to be caused by a stranger.

'What about the sea captain, Miss? And Dorinda and Alice and Leo?'

'There must be no communication with any of them. We two and Mr Granton are in grave peril from Mr Gaisford. I believe it will be better for the others concerned if we leave here and they do not know where we have gone.'

'But Captain Ford will be in danger!'

'Only if Mr Gaisford discovers him. With us out of the way there's little chance of that.'

Martin was on time and they loaded the carriage quickly with Abigail and Tess's belongings, which they had kept to a minimum. Though they couldn't be absolutely sure, they thought no one had observed them.

When they reached Granton Manor, Martin summoned Mrs Duckworth, his cook housekeeper, and instructed her to see to the immediate needs of Mrs Gaisford and her maid.

'I will see to it, Mr Granton. I'll call Marcia.'

'She's the only maid we have,' he offered by way of explanation to Abigail.

Mrs Duckworth hurried from the room and returned in a few minutes with the maid who knew which rooms were to be given to Mrs Gaisford and her maid.

Mrs Duckworth was following them out when Martin called her back. 'I will be leaving early in the morning with Mrs Gaisford and her maid. I don't know how long I shall stay away but I want you and Marcia to look after the house until I return. I am sure you are wondering what this is all about. You are a trustworthy person, Mrs Duckworth, so I think you deserve an explanation. Because of certain events, which I need not go into, Mrs Gaisford is in great danger so I am taking her where I hope she won't be found. You must tell no one of this, especially Mr Gaisford. If he or anyone else comes looking for me, you do not know who was here or where I have gone.'

'Very good, sir! You can rely on me.'

'Instruct Marcia and I will tell Roger.'

'Will he be staying on as groom while you are away, sir?'

'Yes, the horses will still need attention.'

'Of course.'

Martin hurried to the stables where Roger had taken the carriage. He was already taking the horse from the shafts.

'Roger, I want the two-horse coach ready for seven o'clock in the morning. I will be driving it myself.'

'Yes, sir.' The groom was surprised. It was very rare for Mr Granton to drive the coach, though Roger knew he was capable of doing so. It looked as if this might mean a long absence.

His supposition was confirmed when Martin added, 'See that the valises in the carriage are transferred to the coach and leave space for mine also. And make the inside comfortable for Mrs Gaisford and her maid.'

'Yes, sir! Will you be gone long?'

'I don't know. And listen, Roger – you know nothing if anybody comes questioning you. I've gone away, you know not where, and on no account reveal that Mrs Gaisford and her maid have been here. There is a perfectly good explanation, you will hear it one day when I return.'

'Yes, sir! My lips are sealed.'

'You are a good man, Roger. See to things here while I am away.'

'I will, sir.'

At seven o'clock the next morning, Martin took up the reins. He nodded his thanks to Roger, Mrs Duckworth and Marcia. The four servants were all that remained of a once grand household. They and their master held each other in mutual esteem. It was a sad parting but they trusted him to return one day when it was safe to do so.

Luke rode up the drive to Senewey highly satisfied that he had received orders for most of the goods salvaged from the *Lady Jane*. There were always customers for brandy, wine, lace and tobacco, the goods shipped to Spain and from there to

England. Though there had been rumours of ships wrecked on the coast recently no one treated these as being deliberately caused; the days when ships were lured to their doom were thought to be long since gone. No one questioned the trading venture that Luke had set up, either. His enterprise was proving highly profitable so far. There would be other ships heading up the Channel, other nights spent watching men fighting for their lives while he held their fate in the palm of his hand. Now, home again after two nights away, there was only one thing he was in need of. He went straight to his wife's room. No one there!

His lips tightened. He swung out of the room and down the stairs. The drawing room was similarly empty. His examination of the study, dining room and ground-floor reception rooms proved unfruitful too. Abigail was not on the terrace, so where was she? She should have been here awaiting his return! He stormed through the house to the servants' quarters and Mrs Horsefield's room.

Luke flung the door open, startling the housekeeper who sat at her desk sorting some bills for payment. 'Where's my wife?' he demanded angrily.

Mrs Horsefield rose from her chair. 'Sorry, sir, I did not know you were back.'

'Well, I am,' he snapped. 'Where is she?'

'I thought she had gone to join you, sir.'

'Join me? Well, she didn't. Did she not tell you where she was going?'

'No, sir. I didn't know she intended leaving. It was only after her bed had not been slept in for two nights that I thought she must have gone to join you.'

'Not slept in?' Luke frowned. 'Does that maid of hers know anything?'

'She's not here either, so I conclude she has gone with Mrs Gaisford.'

Luke's face darkened. 'Where the devil are they?'

'Could the mistress have gone to Penorna, sir?'

'She isn't in the habit of doing so.'

'I have known her ride over there on the odd occasion.'

'Have you?' Luke looked thoughtful. 'But never taking her maid?'

'No, sir. Maybe because you were away she thought to stay over.'

Luke nodded. Calmed a little by this possibility he left the room without another word. He hurried to the stables and rode from Senewey as if the hounds of hell pursued him. But the manager and skeleton staff at Penorna knew nothing.

Anger seethed in Luke. Where was she? Why take her maid? That seemed to indicate she intended staying away, unless she had gone to Penzance taking her maid to help with some shopping or whatever. But all the Senewey carriages were at the Manor. He had subconsciously noted that when he went to the stables. She could always have been picked up by one of the Westburys. She had not seen a lot of them since her marriage but occasionally one of them visited, clinging to the friendship of childhood days.

In a state of pent-up anger he rode quickly to Trethtowan Manor, only to be told that none of the family had seen Abigail for two months.

Luke fought to conceal his rage. He turned for home but, when he came to the fork in the track pulled hard on the reins, bringing the animal to an earth-tearing halt. He was not far from Granton Manor; he may as well tell Martin that his share from the last wreck would go a good way to solving his financial problems.

The house looked dejected; it certainly needed restoring. Luke strode through the yard, seeking some sign of life. There was none visible and because of it the house seemed to have a forlorn air. Luke tugged at the metal bell pull. A few moments later a maid timidly opened the door.

'Mr Gaisford to see Mr Granton,' he stated.

'Mr Granton is not at home, sir.'

Luke's lips tightened. 'Where is he then? When will he be back?'

'I don't know, sir.'

'Useless girl,' he snapped. He pushed past her and said, 'Get your housekeeper, she may know.'

Marcia scurried away, glad to leave the matter in Mrs Duckworth's hands.

She appeared in the hall. 'It is as Marcia said, sir,' she got in before Luke could question her. 'Mr Granton went out early. He did not say where nor when he would be back. I'm sorry I can't help you further, sir.'

Luke cursed, ignored her courtesy and stormed out of the house, slamming the door behind him. Fuming, he stopped at the top of the steps, slapping his riding crop against the palm of his hand. Didn't anyone ever tell their servants where they were going?

He strode to his horse, climbed into the saddle and rode to Senewey.

There was still no sign of his wife there, nor was there the following morning. Frustration did not help Luke's temper and his staff suffered the lash of his tongue anew when they could provide no answers. Where was Abigail? How could anyone disappear so completely?

He rode to Granton Manor where once again Marcia told him that Mr Granton was not at home.

'Did he return yesterday?' Luke demanded.

'No, sir,' replied Marcia automatically, then feared she had innocently imparted information she should have kept secret.

Luke paused when she'd shut the door, realising for the first time the fact that his wife and friend had disappeared at the same time. Could there be anything in that? Making sure the groom wasn't around, he went to the carriage house. He knew Martin's carriages. One was not there! Luke frowned. Was that significant? He gave a little shake of his head. A missing carriage did not mean the missing pair were together, yet it was strange that both had left their homes about the same time. He sought out Roger. 'Your master took the coach. Was anyone with him?'

'No, sir.'

'So why did he need it?'

'Don't know, sir. He did not say.'

'Did he tell you where he was going or when he would be back?

'No, sir.'

Luke gave the groom a curt nod and left. If the man knew anything he was not saying. Luke was reluctantly beginning to believe that Abigail and Martin were together.

He must find them, deal with Martin and bring his wife back – no scandal must be allowed to besmirch the Gaisford name.

He searched Abigail's room for something that might direct him to her whereabouts but found nothing. It was an angry and frustrated man who went to bed that night. His sleep was disturbed by haunting dreams. Faces swirled under water, came close to condemn him and floated away; waves broke, their spray merging to form female flesh. She turned her head. Abigail was accusing him! Luke sat up in bed, sweat pouring from him, shouting her name. Moonlight streamed through the window. Wide-eyed, he swept his gaze around the room but he was alone.

Shaking, he slipped from the bed and went to the window. What was the meaning of his dream? He drew the cool night air into his lungs and focused his mind. Men he had killed. Abigail on a beach with accusation in her eyes. Was she haunting his conscience? Or had she been on the beach? That mark in the corridor near her room. Sand . . . was that why she had fled, knowing what would happen if he found out the truth? Had she gone to Martin for help and he, knowing her fate if he confided in Luke, could not bring himself to betray her? To track Martin ought to be the easiest option as they'd been friends for so long but since his parents had died he seemed to have no close relatives in the county and his friends were all Luke's too. He wouldn't approach them. Luke was at his wit's end.

With daylight he was in the saddle and riding to see George Morland but a casual query about Martin's connections drew no response. It was the same with David Gillow and Sydney Leigh. It seemed that Martin's wider connections were a mystery.

Fury stalked Luke for two days; he was making no progress. It seemed Abigail and Martin had disappeared off the face of the earth. Martin knew the truth about those wrecks. Even if he hadn't revealed it to Abigail, Luke sensed that somehow she knew of it too. They were both a danger to him. He must find them.

Dorinda came up to Captain Ford's room with his breakfast tray. She found him out of bed fully dressed.

'Captain Ford, what are you doing?' she cried. 'Get back into bed at once.'

'I'm so much better, Miss Jenkins.' He smiled as he took the tray from her and placed it on the table. 'I'll enjoy that,' he added, eyeing the bacon and egg and wedge of white bread.

'You know what the doctor said, a full week in bed,' she admonished.

'But that was at the start of my illness when he did not know how well I would progress.' Before she had time to protest any further he went on, 'I have to find Tess. She said she would visit me and she hasn't.'

'Maybe she hasn't had the opportunity.'

'Perhaps, but I have a feeling it's more than that. I have to find out. I know from what Mr Granton told me that she works at Senewey Manor for Mrs Gaisford. Tell me how to get there?'

'I will not. I know what you were told. It is too dangerous for you, as you are well aware. I thought you wanted to see justice done?'

'I do, and I will.'

'You won't if you confront Mr Gaisford.'

'But I must see Tess.'

'You can thank her again for saving your life when you have brought those wreckers to justice.'

There was a knock on the house door. 'I'll have to go,' Dorinda said.

She admitted the doctor with the news that Captain Ford was out of bed, fully dressed and wanting to know the way to Senewey Manor.

He hurried up the stairs followed by Dorinda. 'What's this nonsense?' he demanded as he burst into the room.

'Good morning, doctor,' Captain Ford greeted him pleasantly. 'I'm glad you are here. You can confirm that my leg is very much better.' He stood up and started to unbuckle his breeches. Dorinda gasped and fled from the room.

Ten minutes later she came back in answer to the doctor's call.

'Captain Ford is right. His wounds have healed remarkably well. A strong constitution always helps. He can go about his business.' The doctor halted Dorinda who was about to speak. 'I don't want to know what that is. I have kept, and will continue to keep, his presence here a secret since it was you who asked me. I don't need to know anything else.'

Dorinda blushed. 'Thank you.' When the doctor picked up his bag she added, 'I'll see you out.' When they reached the front door she added, 'Come and dine with us this evening.'

'It will be my pleasure. Thank you. You are a remarkable woman, Miss Jenkins. Oh, by the way . . . you were governess to the present Mrs Gaisford, I believe?' Dorinda nodded. 'There's a rumour going round that she and her maid have disappeared and that Mr Gaisford is almost out of his mind with worry looking for them. There's another curious thing. I had reason to see Mr Granton, but when I called at the manor I was told he was away and it was not known where he had gone nor when he would be back. There may of course be no connection between the two events . . .' He gave a little grunt. 'I shouldn't be spreading rumours but I knew you use to work for the Mitchells.'

Panic was rising in Dorinda. Had Luke Gaisford discovered his wife knew the truth and taken steps to silence her and Tess, and maybe Mr Granton as well?

She hurried up the stairs and found Captain Ford in high spirits, consuming his breakfast with enjoyment. 'There, I told you I was better, Miss Jenkins.' His voice trailed away when he saw her concern. 'What's the matter?'

'The doctor has just told me it is rumoured Mrs Gaisford and Tess are missing.'

'What?' Captain Ford was on his feet, food forgotten.

'And when the doctor called on Mr Granton, he was told he was away as well and the housekeeper did not know when he would be returning.'

'You mean, they are together?'

Dorinda shrugged. 'I'm not saying that, but it seems strange that they are all missing at the same time.'

Noel Ford started for the door. 'I must find Tess before she comes to harm.'

'Wait!' Dorinda's sharp tone stopped him. 'Where are you going?'

'To find Mr Gaisford.'

'And what will you gain by that?'

'I'll throttle the truth out of him.'

'And gain nothing. Don't go rushing blindly into this. By confronting Mr Gaisford, you'll be revealing who you are and then he'll make sure you don't live to bring evidence against him.'

The chill that brought over him made the captain realise that Dorinda was right. It would be foolish to dash into this situation without thought.

'You fear for Tess?' she continued.

'Yes. And the others, of course.'

'Then, let's approach this sensibly. If, as it seems, Mr Gaisford is looking for them, then they have as yet come to no harm. They had good reason to flee.'

'But where? They could be anywhere.'

'True, but let's try and reason this out.'

'What do you know of them? If Mrs Gaisford and Tess are with Mr Granton, isn't it likely he would take the lead? Do you know of any connections?'

'Not really.'

Noel threw up his hands and looked heavenwards in despair.

'That may not be a bad thing.'

'But . . .'

'Hear me out,' interrupted Dorinda. 'Being in service as a governess and then running my shop, I hear a lot of chatter.

Few people know anything of Mr Granton. It seems he has no close family left. He came into Granton Manor after his parents died and spends all his time there. He has few friends within the county apart from those of his schooldays. That was all he wished for.'

'I can try them.'

'No! Mr Gaisford was one of that close circle so there would be danger for you in contacting any of the others. Because there seems to be little to lead us further after Mr Granton, we must think about where Mrs Gaisford might take them, to whom she might turn. Besides, that's the line you must follow in case Mr Granton isn't with them.'

'So where?' said Noel, desperation in his voice.

'Mrs Gaisford would want to get as far away as possible.' Dorinda paused thoughtfully. 'I went to be governess to Abigail just after Mr and Mrs Mitchell came to Cornwall. Abigail was five . . .'

'Where did they come from?' asked Noel, grasping at what might be a possible lead.

'Whitby in Yorkshire.'

'Might she have gone to relations there?

'It's possible. She had an aunt there.'

'Is she still alive?'

'I don't know. It's a long time ago.'

'What's her name?'

'I don't know. All I do recall is that she was Mr Mitchell's sister. It's possible she is still in Whitby, if she is alive. But even then, she may have married and have a different name by now. Oh, there are so many imponderables.'

'But if this is my only lead I must pursue it,' replied Captain Ford determinedly.

'How will you travel?'

'I'll go to Falmouth, find a ship and work my passage to London. I'll sail onward from there to Whitby or one of the ports nearby. If there's the opportunity in London I'll give the owner of the *Lady Jane* a shock; no doubt by now she will have been declared lost with all hands.' He looked at Dorinda with admiration in his eyes. 'Thank you for all you have done. I will be ever grateful to you. Wish me luck.'

'I'll do more than that. I'll pray for your success, and that you'll find Tess again.'

'I promise I will, and bring her back to you.'

Chapter Twenty-Seven

Though he did not believe that Martin would betray him, because if he did he would only be implicating himself, Luke still felt uneasy about his friend's absence, especially as the housekeeper at Granton Manor insisted she did not know when her master would be returning. He did not want to link Abigail's disappearance with Martin's but suspicion nagged at Luke and the possibility of Martin and Abigail being together held the prospect of calamity. His need to find them was desperate.

He paid a second visit to the Westburys.

When the door was opened by the maid at Trethtowan Manor, he said, 'Mr Luke Gaisford would like to see Mr and Mrs Westbury.'

'One moment, sir,' she replied. 'Please step inside.' She held the door for him before hurrying to Mr Westbury's study.

A few moments later Selwyn greeted him, privately wondering what brought Luke Gaisford to this house again so soon. After all, it wasn't as if the two families were on the best of terms and the disputes he had had with Luke's father still rankled in his mind.

'Mr Gaisford,' he greeted Luke without noticeable enthusiasm. 'What brings you here so soon?'

'I am pursuing a new line of enquiry about Mrs Gaisford's absence.'

'You've had no news of her?'

'No, and it's most worrying.'

'I'm sure it is. But why come here? We told you only days ago that we knew nothing.' There was a note of irritation in Selwyn's voice now.

'I know, but it might help me if I learned something of her origins.'

'Then you had better come into the drawing room.' Selwyn led the way. 'Harriet, Mr Gaisford is here seeking our help again,' he said as they entered the room.

She looked surprised. 'What more can we possibly tell you than we did on your last visit?' she said coldly. She had never been an admirer of Luke, nor indeed of any of the Gaisfords. She wished John Mitchell had forbidden his daughter's marriage but Abigail had been a head-strong girl and, as her father had said at the time, it was better to keep her love rather than suffer an estrangement.

'Do sit down,' said Selwyn.

As Luke took a chair, he said, 'I know nothing of my wife's origins and if I did it might help me to find her. I was only very young when the Mitchells came to Cornwall so did not take much notice of any talk at the time. Abigail was only two then, I believe, and I suppose could not remember much about life before coming here. I know you were friendly with the Mitchells when they arrived and wondered if you knew where they originated?'

'You think Mrs Gaisford might have returned to her roots?'

'It is a possibility. I've got to search everywhere. I know an aunt was invited to our wedding but was ill and could not come. I know nothing more about her or where she was living at that time.'

Hester eyed her husband. She wondered if they would be doing Abigail a disservice if they divulged the little they knew. But she did not catch his eye and Selwyn was already answering Luke.

'The Mitchells arrived here from Whitby when Mr Mitchell's uncle left him the Penorna Estate. That would have been in 1782.'

Hester kept her annoyance hidden but from the look of satisfaction in Luke's eyes she knew he had grasped the information that had slipped out so easily. Whitby.

Seeking to elicit more, he asked, 'Did this aunt live in the town itself?'

'We don't know,' put in Harriet quickly before her husband could speak. Almost too quickly for Luke's liking.

'Do you know if she was married? It is no good my looking for a Mitchell if she was.'

Once again Harriet quickly answered, 'We don't know.'

'Mrs Westbury,' said Luke smoothly, 'did you ever hear of Mr and Mrs Mitchell being invited to a wedding?'

'No,' she replied haughtily. 'Though for all we know she may have married before they came here. We have told you all we know.'

For a brief moment Luke's lips tightened. He realised he had been politely told to leave. He said in a tone that matched Hester's for coldness, 'Thank you, Mrs Westbury. You have both been most helpful.'

He rode home already planning the details of his journey north tomorrow.

About the time Luke was leaving Senewey, Noel Ford was claiming a berth in the fo'csle of the *Sunbeam*, a brig heading for London. She had put into Falmouth with a sick crewmember and her captain was only too pleased to find a sailor willing to fill his place. Noel kept his true identity a secret, willingly serving as a deckhand to get a passage to London. In favourable weather the brig made good progress up the Channel. He felt exhilarated by the sway of the ship, the wind in his face, the slap of the sails and the creak of the ropes. This was where he belonged, and this was where he would be once again, back in command the next time, his name cleared of the taint of negligence.

The Thames was heaving with shipping. Masts seemed to terrace the sky everywhere he looked. Ships were unloading goods from all over the world, stevedores straining their muscles to stow cargoes in time to catch the tide while lighter boats were ferrying passengers to and fro across the navigable river that made London the commercial capital of the world.

Work finished, paid off, an offer to sign on refused, Noel Ford paused at the top of the gangway. The quay was overflowing with people pursuing their everyday jobs amongst the array of warehouses and jetties. Passengers were hurrying to their ships, pickpockets eyeing up their next victim, girls seeking another customer. The smell of dung from the dray horses was added to the smell that rose from the murky waters of the river, to mingle with the stench from the factories, breweries and tanneries belching smoke to join that of the multitude of domestic chimneys covering the city in a cloying black soot. Noel shuddered; the sooner he was out of this filth and on the open sea the better.

He hurried along the quay, seeking the offices of shipping companies that sailed north from the Thames. His enquiries at the third one proved successful; he could work his passage on a collier due to call in at Whitby on its way to Newcastle for its next load of coal. The ship would sail in three hours and the captain expected him to be there an hour beforehand.

Noel was thankful that he still had time to visit the offices of Harland Shipping. He ignored the two clerks who stared at him open-mouthed when he walked in and went straight to the door of an inner office where he walked in without cere-mony.

The portly, red-faced man seated behind his oak desk looked up, scowling at the intrusion. Words of admonishment died on his lips unspoken. He gaped at Noel in utter disbelief. 'Captain Ford!' The words came in a whisper.

'You are not seeing a ghost, Mr Harland,' Noel announced. 'I'm very much alive.'

Mr Harland swallowed hard. 'What . . .' He choked with emotion, took a deep breath and then the words poured out. 'The *Lady Jane* was reported lost with all hands on the Cornish coast, evidenced by a piece of wood that drifted ashore. What the devil happened? Why were you so near the coast? Incompetence, I assume, Ford. Sheer incompetence on your part!'

'No, sir,' Noel broke in sharply to stop this tirade. 'We were lured on to the coast in fog by wreckers, sir.'

'What? Don't try to cover your own stupidity by telling such tales. Wrecking was suppressed decades ago.'

'It's back, sir. The villains murdered my crew in cold blood. I nearly lost my own life, but managed to fool my would-be killer and was helped to escape. It is a long story, sir, one I cannot disclose in full now. I'm on my way to Whitby where I hope to trace some witnesses to the wrecking and so prove my innocence.'

'Whitby? You talk in riddles. How can Whitby be connected with a wreck in Cornwall?' grunted Mr Harland with disdain.

'I'm not sure it is but I have hopes.'

'A wild goose chase, more like. I should have you arrested for incompetence leading to loss of life . . .'

'Give me a chance to prove my innocence first?'

'What, and let you walk out of here never to return?'

'Sir, I needn't have come here at all but thought you should know the truth before you took further action with your insurers. I want to prove my innocence and to captain a ship for you again.' The light in Noel's eyes spoke of his sincerity.

'And you believe you can find the truth in Whitby?'

'I hope so, sir.'

'It seems a tall order to me.' Mr Harland eyed him for a moment. 'Very well! I'll retain my faith in the man I promoted to captain before his time. See that my faith is not misplaced.'

At about the same time as Captain Ford was sailing down the Thames as a deck-hand on the *Pelican*, Luke Gaisford was riding north and a coach was approaching Whitby.

The journey from Cornwall to Yorkshire had been made with little difficulty, though it had been long and tedious. Martin had handled the horses well and been solicitous for the comfort of both Abigail and Tess at every nightly stopover.

Having shared the horrors on the beach, the tension and uncertainties of the aftermath and their closeness in the coach, Abigail and Tess were by now far closer than they had been previously, more like friends than mistress and servant, though Tess did not presume upon Abigail's kindness.

They had reached York one late afternoon and Martin decided it would be better to stay the night there and face the rest of the journey refreshed. Upon making enquiries he was directed to the tavern in St Helen's Square. Here they found the comfortable accommodation they sought and stabling for the carriage horses. After a hearty breakfast the next day, they set out for Whitby, each entertaining their own hopes and thoughts.

They were thankful that the day, though somewhat cloudy, did not threaten rain, especially when the trackway took them on to the high wild moors. Anticipation mounted as they twisted and turned their way through the valley of the Esk, following the river down to Whitby where it ran between high cliffs into the sea. Red-roofed houses climbed skywards. Ships lay at quays on the east bank; hammers resounded from the shipbuilding yards; the whole town alive with activity as people hurried about their final tasks before heading for home or the many inns.

Martin enquired for the best coaching inn and was met with a choice when the man eyed his coach and informed him, 'White Horse in Church Street for the horses; Angel across the river for the ladies.'

Martin did not hesitate; he negotiated the coach through the crowds flowing across the bridge in both directions. As he turned into the Angel's yard an ostler and his assistant were instantly at the horses' heads, steadying them as Martin brought them to a stop.

'Stabling for the night, sir?' came the enquiry.

'Not sure. It may be longer.'

'Very good, sir! They'll be well looked after.'

Martin turned to the coach but already two liveried boys had hurried from the main door and were assisting Abigail down. One of them escorted her to the inn with Martin accompanying them. The second boy smiled at Tess and took one of the cases with which she was struggling.

Tess felt important when he said, 'Follow me, miss. I'm sure you will be comfortable at the Angel.' As they entered the inn he called to two younger boys, 'Bring the rest of the luggage from the coach.' They scampered off. 'Have to tell them everything,' he whispered confidentially to Tess. He put her case down near a desk at which Martin was speaking to the landlord.

'That will be ideal,' said Martin gratefully. He turned to Abigail. 'I have booked you a room which has an adjoining one suitable for a personal maid. I will be three doors away.'

This was much better than she had expected and Abigail thanked both Martin and the landlord.

'Will you require a meal this evening, sir?'

'Yes,' replied Martin.

'We have a special room for travelling servants so . . .'

'No.' Abigail halted him. 'Tess will dine with us.'

'But, miss, I . . .' Tess started, but was cut short.

'We have shared so much over these last few days, you will not dine alone.'

Tess glanced at Martin who smiled and approved of Abigail's action. 'Of course you must, and whatever happens from now on we will see it through together.' He turned to the landlord. 'You may be able to help by telling us if anyone called Mitchell still lives at Bloomfield Manor?'

The landlord hesitated thoughtfully. This was a strange travelling party. The gentleman had booked in as Mr Granton, he had booked the lady in as Mrs Gaisford, but the younger female who had been given a room for a maid had addressed her mistress as 'miss' and the three of them were going to dine together. They did, however, *look* highly respectable.

'Yes, sir! There is a Miss Mitchell in the town. Bloomfield is a modest estate but she also runs a merchant business in Whitby quite successfully.'

Abigail felt a tremor of excitement run through her. This must be her aunt. Never married and still lived at Bloomfield Manor. Did this signal a change in their fortunes?

'Can you direct us to the Manor?' Martin asked.

'Certainly. You will be going tomorrow, sir?'

'Yes, I suppose so.'

'I think the best thing, if you are agreeable, sir, would be to send this boy to direct you. Billy's father is one of the gardeners there.'

759

The lad grinned, pleased he would be relieved of other duties for a while tomorrow.

'That's very good of you, landlord.' Abigail turned to the boy. 'Very well, Billy, be ready at half-past nine.'

The following morning, with Martin driving the coach and Billy sitting beside him, they travelled south along the coast road from Whitby. After about four miles Billy indicated some ironwork gates ahead. 'Bloomfield Manor, sir. The house lies nearer the coast. Stands on the cliffs with wonderful views out to sea.'

'You seem to know it well?'

'Been up here with my father, sir.'

When the house came in sight they saw that it was of only medium size but had the appearance of being loved and well cared for.

'Look after the coach and horses, Billy,' Martin instructed him as he drew to a halt in front of the main door. Abigail alighted from the coach. As she cast her eyes over the building, she had a strange feeling of coming home. She turned to Tess. 'You are to come in with us.'

Martin tugged at the bell pull.

Each of them wondered what awaited them when that door opened.

At that very moment a ship was beating in towards Whitby. Noel Ford surveyed the old town clinging to the cliffs, its red roofs climbing towards the venerable church and ruined abbey, and wondered if it was here that he would find those who could prove his innocence, and also the girl who had tugged at his heart strings.

A neat little maid looked askance at the three people standing on the steps of Bloomfield Manor attended by a boy she recognised as the son of one of the gardeners.

'We would like to see Miss Mitchell, if she is at home,' said Martin pleasantly.

'Whom shall I say is calling, sir?'

760

'Mrs Gaisford, Mr Granton and Miss Booth,' replied Martin, finding that the easiest way to make it known who they were. To try and explain that Tess was Abigail's personal maid would only complicate the situation and he wanted to keep it simple for Miss Mitchell.

They were soon admitted for she was especially curious about the names Gaisford and Booth.

While she was crossing the hall Abigail's sense of recognising her surroundings became sharper. They walked into a comfortable drawing room and she knew she had been there before.

A well-groomed, immaculately attired elderly lady rose from her armchair. She held herself erect, someone clearly in charge of her every emotion. Her eyes were piercing. She looked the visitors over, quickly summarising them, confident in the knowledge that her first impressions were generally correct. She could not fault what she saw as the gentleman introduced them, but was caught by the expression on Mrs Gaisford's face. It was one of extreme curiosity, as if she was trying to recall the dim and distant past and match it with the present.

'Do sit down.' Martha indicated some chairs. 'You'll take chocolate?'

'Thank you, ma'am,' replied Abigail politely.

Before Martha took her own seat the door opened and the chocolate was ordered. She was aware that Mrs Gaisford had surveyed the room quickly and was now looking at her with even deeper curiosity.

'Miss Mitchell, it would appear even from here that you enjoy a marvellous view from that window. Do you mind if I take a look?'

Though she was struck by the unexpected request and wondered why this question had come before the purpose of their visit was revealed, Martha agreed. Sensing that Mrs Gaisford's companions too were surprised, she watched Abigail go to the window. No one felt inclined to break the atmosphere that descended over the room. Abigail stood perfectly still, gazing out of the window, then slowly turned

761

round. She fixed her eyes intently on Martha. 'I remember looking out of that window. I have lived here,' she said quietly. Her eyes never left the lady before her. 'I believe you are my Aunt Martha.'

Martha frowned for answer then said tentatively, 'Abigail?'

'Yes.'

'But . . . Gaisford?'

'You were invited to my wedding.'

Martha was lost for words. She held out her arms. 'I was ill,' she recalled in a falling voice. 'Then your father and mother . . .' Her eyes filled with tears. 'It was too late to come. You poor child, I should never have left you unvisited.'

She hugged Abigail lovingly. There was a knock on the door. Martha straightened up, drew a deep breath and, taking a handkerchief from her pocket wiped her eyes. Abigail realised she did not want the servants to see her so moved.

'Come in,' she called.

A maid appeared with the chocolate and placed it on a low table in front of Miss Mitchell.

Once the door had closed again, now totally in command of her feelings, Martha asked, 'What brings you to Whitby?' She started to pour the chocolate.

'It is a long story, Aunt, but first I must properly introduce my travelling companions. Mr Martin Granton, my very dear friend, and Miss Tess Booth, my maid.' She notice her aunt start at this. Assuming she was surprised to have a servant sitting with them, Abigail quickly added, 'She is more than that, she is a friend as well.'

Realising how her niece had viewed her response, Martha inclined her head in acceptance of this explanation whereas her real reaction had been one of suppressed shock. Tess Booth! This must be the child who'd been born in this very house, her brother's child! A young woman. She was maid to Abigail, her own sister, yet first she had been introduced as a servant and then as a friend. It hit Martha like a thunderclap then. These two young women did not know they were sisters! Martha stiffened, holding back the revelation that sprang to her lips. Why did they not know? John must have had his reasons for wanting the relationship kept secret. Now she was the only one who possessed that secret. Her mind was spinning when Tess came to her side to help hand out the chocolate and sweetmeats.

Once Martha was settled back in her chair, she said, 'Now, tell me why you are here?'

'We need your help, Aunt,' said Abigail. 'I fell in love with a handsome young man named Luke Gaisford, heir to the biggest estate in Cornwall. Father and Mother had their doubts about him, I believed at the time because of hostility Father had experienced at the hands of Luke's father. There was a reconciliation when I saved Luke's life in a riding accident when we were seventeen. But he always had a wild reputation.' She glanced at Martin, wanting him to endorse that.

'It's true, Miss Mitchell. Five of us went to Rugby from Cornwall. Oh, we certainly acquired a reputation there and Luke was a natural leader. That reputation clung to us all when we left school but it held most tenaciously to Luke, who seemed to want to carry it on. We all thought when he met Abigail she would have a calming effect on him, and she did for a while, but a leopard doesn't change its spots. The unsavoury side of Luke which he inherited from his father soon emerged.' He glanced at Abigail whom he wanted to take up the story, for he did not know how much she wished to reveal to her aunt.

Abigail explained how the relationship had deteriorated, how she came to hear of Luke's activities but would not believe that he was a wrecker until she saw the evidence for herself, what that had led to and how they were now in danger for their lives. 'We hope that Luke will not be able to trace us and that the sea captain Tess saved will bring my husband to justice.'

'You wish that on your own husband?' asked her aunt.

Abigail hesitated, battling with the feelings this question had aroused. 'He should be tried,' she said slowly, 'but I don't wish him to hang.'

'Why didn't you go to the authorities in Cornwall?'

'If I could explain,' put in Martin. 'The Gaisfords are extremely powerful there. Their word is far more likely to be believed than ours. We saw that our lives were threatened and would continue to be until Captain Ford had recovered and laid his allegations. We had no idea when that would be and thought it best to leave Cornwall in the interim.'

'You are far enough away here but determination has a long arm. You must stay at Bloomfield with me out of danger.'

'Oh, Aunt, we are so grateful!' cried Abigail. 'I did not know to whom I could turn, then I thought of you and hoped we might find you still here.'

Martha dismissed that observation with a wave of her hand. 'I'm very glad you did. Now I'll have the opportunity of getting to know my niece. I'll ask my housekeeper to have rooms prepared. Mr Granton, will you and Tess see to the transfer of your belongings from the Angel?'

'Certainly, ma'am! It is most kind of you to offer me accommodation as well but I can easily stay at the inn.'

'No, I won't hear of that. I think it best if all of you remain together.'

When Martin and Tess had left Martha said to Abigail, 'Tell me about Tess. You introduce her as your friend and personal maid. Those terms seem somehow incongruous.'

'When her mother died and her father would have nothing to do with her, Tess was brought to Cornwall by an aunt who was once governess to our neighbours' children. I don't know whether Tess even knows the true story because she always referred to Miss Booth as her mother.'

The truth? Martha thought. How near Tess was to that by calling Miss Booth her mother! And Martha knew how Lydia would have relished being called that. Her respect for her old friend grew now she knew that for John's sake Lydia had kept the truth a secret.

'When Miss Booth died, Father suggested that Tess should come to me as my personal maid,' Abigail explained.

Martha nodded. The reasons behind John's actions were clear to her.

'Tess fitted in very well and we became close. I found she was very easy to confide in. In fact, there were times when we seemed more like sisters.' Martha tensed at that but Abigail did not notice. 'She looks after me wonderfully well and I'm glad she was with me at Senewey.'

'Good, good,' was all the comment Martha offered. She was left wondering what her best course of action might be. To reveal the truth might destroy Abigail's opinion of her father, but didn't Tess have the right to know the truth? Martha would battle with these questions further.

Noel Ford stepped ashore oblivious to all the activity of the busy port. He eyed the people going about their daily lives. At that moment a young man carrying a sheaf of papers was hurrying past him. Noel grabbed his arm, bringing the man to an unexpected halt. His face clouded with annoyance and he was about to confront Noel when the seaman spoke first.

'The best inn in the town?' he asked.

'For what?' demanded the young man.

'Rooms where the best people would stay,' said Noel, having reasoned that if the people he sought had come to Whitby, they would seek the best accommodation.

'The Angel, across the river,' replied the man, anxious to be on his way to deliver the papers for his employer.

'Thanks.' Noel released his arm and the man hurried away to be lost in the crowd.

Noel crossed the bridge and entered the Angel. 'Good day, landlord,' he said heartily to the man behind the counter who was examining the visitors' book.

He looked up enquiringly at the man who confronted him.

'You may be able to help me,' Noel went on. 'I am looking for a gentleman and two young ladies.

The landlord eyed him suspiciously. 'I am not in the habit of imparting names or information about our guests.'

'It is imperative that I trace them,' pressed Noel. 'I can give you their names. Mr Granton, Mrs Gaiford and ...' He stopped. He realised he did not know Tess' surname. 'Oh, I don't know the other surname, I only know her as Tess.'

The landlord looked thoughtful, uncertain about disclosing their whereabouts. The door opened then and he felt a surge of relief when he saw Mr Granton coming in.

'Sir, this man . . .'

His words faded when Martin, looking surprised, greeted Noel. 'Captain Ford, what on earth . . .'

The question was cut short by Noel's exclamation of: 'Tess!'

She stopped in her tracks. A moment's disbelief was dismissed in her cry of, 'Captain Ford. What are you doing here?'

'I need my witnesses so I came to find you.'

'How did you know we were in Whitby?' asked Martin.

'When Mrs Gaisford's family first came to Cornwall, Miss Jenkins was appointed her governess. She remembered that they had come from Whitby where she seemed to think there could be an aunt. It was the only lead I had. I thought I'd try my luck and it has proved to be correct.'

'Then you had better come with us,' said Martin. He told the landlord, 'We are leaving. Make out our bill while we collect our things. I am most obliged for your help and for making us so comfortable.'

'All part of the service, sir. I am sorry you are going, but maybe we will see you again sometime.'

Twenty minutes later he was driving his coach back to Bloomfield Manor.

Inside the coach Tess and Captain Ford sat in a strained silence in which each of them could only guess what the other was feeling in the shadow of the unknown future that hung over them all.

Abigail was more than surprised when Captain Ford walked in. After his introduction to Martha he told his story. When Noel had finished explaining how he had found them, Martin came out with the ominous observation that if Captain Ford had found them so easily, so could Luke.

Chapter Twenty-Eight

In the gathering darkness the rising land beyond Pickering seemed to present a formidable barrier to Luke Gaisford as he approached the market town from York. He knew from previous enquiries that he faced a journey across wild moorland so, as much as he would have liked to press on, deemed it wise to stay in Pickering for the night rather than face unknown hazards in the dark. He was pleased with the good progress he had made and estimated that if his quarry had used Martin's coach their journey would have been much slower than his. He felt sure he must have closed the distance between them considerably.

The next morning, fortified for his ride, he left Pickering in high hopes that his quest would soon be brought to a satisfactory conclusion. Abigail would return with him, a chastened wife subject to his rules and whims, and Martin with his lips sealed by the threat of being named the leader of the wreckers, for who would not believe the word and integrity of Luke Gaisford, head of the foremost family in Cornwall?

Reaching Whitby, he followed his instinct that Martin would choose the best inn to house Abigail. A stable boy raced out of the stables when he heard the clop of horses' hooves in the yard. A few moments later, his horse taken care of, Luke entered the inn, booked himself a room for a stay of unknown length and then made his enquiry.

'I am seeking a gentleman accompanied by a lady and her maid. It is a matter of life and death that I find them as soon as possible. Have they stayed here recently?'

767

As soon as Luke had made his reservation, the sharp-minded landlord had connected his name with that of the lady accompanied by another gentleman. His mind was filling with possibilities, foremost among them was that this man was a husband pursuing an absconding wife and her lover. He might be able to make something out of this. After a few moments of thoughtful consideration, he made the standard reply that he used until he saw how a situation might develop. 'I am not in the habit of revealing what I know about my clients, sir.'

'It sounds to me as if you are confirming these people stayed here.'

'I did not say that, sir.'

Luke gave a little smile. 'I rather think you did. Maybe that will help you to recall?' He pushed his bribe discreetly across the counter.

The landlord quickly slid it out of sight. 'Well, sir, I do remember three people who would fit your description. They stayed here for one night.'

'Recently?'

The landlord pursed his lips. Luke slid another coin to him.

'Two nights ago.'

'Are they here now?'

'No, sir.'

Luke's eagerness was dampened but he put another question. 'Do you know where they went?' He did not wait for further pondering; another coin was proffered.

'Yes, sir, Bloomfield Manor.'

'Bloomfield Manor?' said Luke, looking puzzled.

'Yes, sir! Miss Mitchell's place.'

Luke grasped at this information. Mitchell? Abigail's maiden name! So she must have known about and found a relative. 'Where is this manor?'

'South of Whitby, about four miles.'

'You can direct me to it?'

'Of course, sir.' The landlord's hand covered another coin and he went on to give Luke the directions.

Luke thanked him and said, 'My room, landlord.'

A few moments later, ensconced in his room, he was considering his best course of action.

When Martha sat down to breakfast with Abigail, Martin and Captain Ford, Tess having resumed her position and duties, she asked if they had any plans.

'No,' replied Abigail. 'If Captain Ford's observation of yesterday is correct, maybe we had better move on.'

'That won't solve your problem for good. Your husband may still keep up his pursuit and you would always be looking over your shoulder then,' Martha pointed out.

'I can't keep running,' put in Captain Ford. 'I came to find the witnesses who will prove me innocent of negligence and save my career at sea.'

Abigail looked worried; this could mean facing Luke again with all that entailed. She looked appealingly at Martin.

Seeing she was going to abide by his opinion, he said gently, 'We can't keep on running, Abigail. I think it would be better to face Luke here where we know we have the support of your aunt.'

'You can count on me in anything you decide. I would like you to stay. I think it is the best course for you,' Martha confirmed.

'Don't desert me now,' pleaded Captain Ford.

Abigail, whose first instinct had been to keep as far away as possible from Luke, saw it was not the answer. She nodded. 'But what if he does not come?'

'I daren't consider that,' replied Captain Ford. 'I think he will.'

'So do I,' agreed Martin. 'We are a potential danger to him and always will be while we are alive.'

'You think he will go that far?' asked Abigail in alarm.

'As far as I am concerned, yes,' replied Martin. 'After all, I was part of his gang. In your case, Abigail, he does not know you were a witness to the wrecking, and the same applies to Tess, so he may conclude that we are together as lovers. He does not yet know that the captain of the *Lady Jane* is alive and that could be a great asset to us.'

'So all this puts you in a strong position when he finds you,' said Martha. 'I think you've got to let that happen.'

The morning sunshine was warming the gentle breeze blowing from the sea when Luke rode boldly up the drive to Bloomfield Manor. He viewed the house's exterior derisively, thinking it small compared to Senewey, but it looked well cared for and spoke of money not being a problem. His enquiries had elicited that Miss Mitchell, apart from her servants, lived alone and ran a successful merchant's business in Whitby. An unusual woman then, he realised.

That proved to be true. He recognised from the way she held herself and her delivery when she greeted him that here was a strong personality.

Martha Mitchell was alone when she came into the drawing room where he had been shown by a maid.

'Mr Gaisford,' she greeted Luke as she pushed the door to behind her.

'Miss Mitchell,' he returned, meeting her searching gaze calmly.

'Do sit down, sir, and tell me the purpose behind this visit from a man who is a total stranger to me. And one who, from his accent, is not from these parts?'

'Miss Mitchell, I will not bandy words with you but confront this delicate matter head on.' He saw her give a little nod of approval and recognised that she was a person who liked straight talking, no doubt from her years spent working in what was almost exclusively a man's world. 'I believe you recognise my name and that you have my wife, your niece, staying with you.'

'And I will give you a straight reply, Mr Gaisford. Yes, Abigail is with me.'

'Then I am relieved to have found her and hope I am in time to save her mental condition from worsening. I must take her home immediately to familiar surroundings which will help her to a full recovery.'

'Mental condition, Mr Gaisford? I can see nothing wrong with my niece's state of mind.'

770

'But to leave her own husband without a word! And after the strange way she has been acting lately, that does seem to signify an upset mind. I would be most gratful if I could see her.'

'All in good time, Mr Gaisford. At the moment Abigail is walking on the cliffs with a friend.'

'A friend?' He made his query sound surprised.

'Yes. A Mr Granton.'

'Ah, Martin, my oldest and dearest friend! Now, Miss Mitchell, does that not indicate to you the instability of my wife's mind? Why else would she leave Cornwall accompanied by a man who has been my loyal companion since boyhood?'

'It would indicate to me that she was seeking a trustworthy person's protection.'

'Protection? What tales has she been telling you?'

'Of cruelty. Of beatings.'

'What?' Luke feigned surprise and shock. 'Miss Mitchell, do I look like a man who would risk bringing scandal on the family name?'

'Ah, Mr Gaisford,' said Martha with a glint of triumph in her eyes, 'you are just the sort of man to risk anything – if you think you can get away, with it.

'Miss Mitchell, I resent that implication.' A note of hostility had entered Luke's voice. 'And I demand to see my wife.'

'I have told you, Abigail is not in.'

'Then I shall have to find her.' He was out of his chair and striding towards the drawing room door when it opened.

Martha was also on her feet and seized control of the situation immediately. 'Ah, Captain Ford, meet Mr Gaisford. Mr Gaisford, Captain Ford of the *Lady Jane*.' She saw the Captain stiffen but immediately respond to her frown and slight shake of her head, an indication to him to do nothing. He merely acknowledged Luke's terse greeting as he pushed past, intent on finding Abigail and Martin, and stormed out of the room.

Luke came out of the house and was about to mount his horse when he saw her. Tess. She had emerged from a door at

771

a lower level of the house near the corner and was carrying a basket, its contents covered by a white cloth. A picnic? Was she taking refreshments to Abigail and Martin? If so, then she must be going to a pre-arranged rendezvous. Not realising she was being observed, she headed for a path that disappeared into a wood. Beyond he could hear the distant sound of the sea.

Luke followed and, because the path was quite overgrown, was able to keep a discreet distance away without losing sight of her. He was halfway through the wood when he pulled up and stood stock-still. His mind whirled and then focused on the words that now rang like a death knell in his ears: 'Captain Ford of the *Lady Jane*.' The *Lady Jane*? It couldn't be! Impossible! None of the crew had survived. But now there was doubt in his mind. Martin was here, too, and he was implicated in the wrecking. It could not be coincidence that these two men were together. But how, and why were they here? Did this give him the reason for Martin's departure from Cornwall? Had he now two threats to deal with or were there more? But if the two most closely involved witnesses, Captain Ford and Martin Granton, could not testify, the second-hand nature of the evidence of the others would count for nothing, he reflected. Luke continued along the path. He had lost sight of Tess but it was obvious that she would have gone this way.

'Miss Mitchell, if that was the man behind the loss of my ship, I want my revenge as you well know. Why stop me?' raged Captain Ford, as the door slammed behind Luke.

'Because he would simply have denied every accusation you threw at him. It would have been his word against yours. There could well have been violence done here in this room which would have got you nowhere. Besides, he might well have dealt finally with you and then me there and then, which would have left no one to alert the others. I let slip that my niece and Mr Granton were walking on the cliffs. He showed no sign of connecting you with the ship he wrecked, though I deliberately mentioned her name. Off with you, then, and follow him! I have a hunch that it may work strongly in your favour as he tries to persuade my niece, one way or another, to return with him to Cornwall.'

Noel did not wait another moment and was just in time to see Luke disappearing into the wood.

'Martin, where is this all going to end?' asked a distressed Abigail. 'We are walking these cliffs as if all was well with the world and yet our future is overshadowed by a dark cloud which we can do nothing about.'

'We are waiting for a development that will dispel that cloud forever.' He tried to sound reassuring, to promise her that all would be well, even though he privately harboured doubts about the outcome.

'You really think there will be a reckoning here? That Luke will find us?'

'Yes.'

'Then let it be soon.' Abigail's plea seemed to be thrown to Heaven. Then she added, 'I hope it will not be too dreadful.' Distress and despair at the thought of the outcome turning in favour of her husband made her blanch and shudder.

Martin instantly took her hand, offering comfort. 'I wish I had opposed Luke from the start, pursued you for myself, but I was weak, too ready to bow before his dominant personality, so I stepped aside. I have loved you since first meeting you. That is why I never looked elsewhere.'

She met his admiring gaze frankly and there was a touch of regret in hers as she raised a hand to his cheek. 'You are a dear friend, Martin. Who knows what might have been?'

They heard a rustling sound and turned to see Tess emerging from the wood fifty yards away. Her face broke into a broad smile when she saw them. She thought what a striking couple they made and wished with all her heart that her mistress had chosen this man instead of Mr Gaisford.

'What's this?' asked Martin, noting the basket Tess was carrying.

Abigail smiled. 'I arranged a picnic for us and asked Tess to bring it here about this time. That is why I manoeuvred our walk to end here where the path from Bloomfield meets the one along the cliff edge.'

'Splendid,' said Martin enthusiastically, 'and what a wonderful view. How did you know about it?'

'A childhood memory. When I mentioned it to my aunt she brought me here to show me that memory had served me well.'

'Your picnic, miss,' said Tess.

'Thank you, Tess, I'll take it,' said Martin.

'Everything is in order at the house?' asked Abigail as she turned along the cliff path.

'Yes, miss. Enjoy your picnic.' Tess hurried away.

'Thank you,' Abigail called after her.

Tess raised her hand in acknowledgement without looking back.

'You have a truly devoted servant there,' commented Martin.

'She's more than that,' replied Abigail. 'She is a true friend, though she never oversteps the mark.'

'Where are we going to have this?' he asked.

'There's a hollow a few yards along here.' Abigail started along the cliff path to reach a depression in the ground close to the cliff edge which gave them views of the sea breaking on the rocks far below. Today they swelled gently, washed towards land by an undulating sea that stretched to the horizon in a dazzling expanse of blue.

They settled themselves comfortably with Martin dancing attendance on Abigail, and she wondering how she had ever mistaken Luke's attentions for a proof of love.

Tess made for the house, wishing such trouble did not hang over them. She should not be entertaining dismal thoughts on such a pleasant day. She thought instead of Captain Ford. She sensed that he had some feelings for her, but did they purely stem from the fact that she had saved his life? She found herself hoping not, which made her examine her own feelings. He was a handsome man, engaged in a trade that carried a thrill of adventure which automatically gave him a dashing aura. She smiled to herself; she should not become carried away. Nevertheless she allowed her thoughts to develop. What if their feelings towards each other were to be spoken aloud? What if he proposed? How would she answer? Could she really say she was in love with him? Was she?

Her happy speculation was interrupted by a noise ahead. She stopped. Who could it be? Caution took hold. She stepped away from the path and quickly sought cover in some bushes. A few moments later a figure appeared. Mr Gaisford! He had found them! Panic gripped Tess. How did he come to be on this path, one that would lead him straight to her mistress? What had happened at the Manor? Her every instinct was to warn her mistress but now Mr Gaisford was between them. If she crashed through the undergrowth he would hear her, yet she had to do something. Panic was rising in her when she heard the crack of a twig. Someone else was coming! She crouched lower, then relief surged through her when she saw Captain Ford. She rose from her hiding place and the sight of her stopped him in his tracks. He raised a finger to his lips and then held out his hand in an indication for her to come to him.

Tess stepped lightly on to the path and he came to stand beside her. His hand automatically sought hers to offer reassurance as he asked, 'What are you doing here?'

'I brought a picnic for Mrs Gaisford and Mr Granton.'

'You know where they are?'

She nodded.

'You saw Mr Gaisford?'

'Yes. Are you following him?'

'Explanations later! Come on.' Still holding her hand, he led the way forward.

They reached the junction of the paths and he looked askance at her.

Tess indicated the way she had gone to meet Abigail and Martin. He nodded and gestured again for quiet. They moved on cautiously until they heard raised voices. Another five yards made the voices more distinct and they rounded a bend in the path to see Luke standing on the edge of a hollow overlooking the sea.

'. . . and such a cosy setting,' he said in a mocking tone. His voice turned cold and threatening then. 'Try to steal my wife, would you, Martin?'

'No, I . . .'

'Or were you running away from something else? Well, both issues can be settled as one.' He jumped down into the hollow. Though Martin had half expected this he was surprised by the swiftness with which Luke acted.

Luke's blow took him high on the cheek with such force that it knocked him to the ground. His head stuck a stone and he lay still, close to the edge. Luke, eyes wild with the lust to kill, let out a cry of triumph as he moved towards the inert form of his former friend. His intention was clear and Abigail grasped his coat.

'No!' she screamed.

He glared at her with eyes blinded by blood lust. It was a look she had last seen on that beach in Cornwall. He tried to shake her off but she held on to his arm. 'You are coming home with me to act the dutiful wife, and woe betide you if you don't. He knows too much. He'll never see Cornwall again.' Still held by Abigail, he struggled towards Martin.

'If you kill him, you'll have to kill me too,' she yelled. 'I was on that beach!'

Luke stared at her. Suspicions that he had tried to suppress were now confirmed. 'Then you'll have to die too!' He swung round on her so forcefully that she was forced to drop his arm. She tripped over Martin's outstretched hand and fell. Gloating triumph fired Luke's eyes. All reason was gone.

'And you'll have to kill me too!' a voice boomed behind him.

Luke swung round. 'Ah, the captain who managed to survive. Well, this time you won't,' he yelled with a wild laugh.

Noel jumped at him but Luke stepped aside just as Noel hit the ground. He swung a vicious kick at the captain that brought a gasp of pain from him as it took him in his ribs. He fell back against the side of the hollow. Luke moved in, planning that in a few moments three bodies would lie broken on the rocks far below, waiting for the sea to take them.

Abigail, still dizzy from the vicious blow he had dealt her, was struggling to get to her feet and screaming at him to stop.

He reached out to grasp Noel's shirt.

The rock struck his forehead. Taken completely by surprise Luke staggered backwards under the severity of the blow, lost his balance, and with arms flailing felt the ground crumble away under his feet. With a scream he fell to the fate he had intended for the others.

It was a dishevelled and wounded party that reached Bloomfield Manor, shocking Martha by their appearance. Once she had seen to their needs and they were seated in the drawing room with a reviving drink, she heard all the details of what had happened.

'You were right, Miss Mitchell, to stop me from confronting Mr Gaisford here,' said Captain Ford. 'Although it was a tragic end, I think it was probably the best one. With respect for your loss, Mrs Gaisford.'

'And no doubt best for me too, the way my life would have gone if Luke had survived.' Abigail rose from her chair. 'I must bring Tess in and reassure her that I attribute no blame to her.'

She returned with a tearful Tess, still murmuring apologies.

'Come and sit here with me,' said Martha, who occupied a sofa on her own. She took Tess's hand in hers. 'From what I hear you did a very brave and necessary thing. You should not suffer any regret.' She patted the girl's hand comfortingly and continued to hold it for a minute. Then she fished a handkerchief from the sleeve of her dress and handed it to Tess who wiped her eyes, stopped her tears and smiled wanly.

'Miss Mitchell is right, Tess. If it hadn't been for you I would have lost my life,' said Captain Ford. You saved me, and not for the first time.'

Martha, who had held Tess moments after she was born, felt anew a sense of responsibility for her. Realising the feeling behind Captain Ford's words she asked him, 'What will you do now?'

'If you will all give me written statements, I will go to London and clear my name with my employer. In order to spare Mrs Gaisford, I shall request that none of this is made public and that the owner merely reports that the wreck was caused by inclement weather. I am sure he will agree. I will request another command and ask him to allow it to sail out of Falmouth so that I will be near Tess, who I suppose will be returning to Cornwall with Mrs Gaisford?'

Tess's heart leapt. Captain Ford wanted to be near her! She wanted to be near him too.

'Is that what you will be doing, Abigail?' asked Martha.

'I think so, Aunt.'

'You know, you can stay here with me if you think Cornwall will hold too many bad memories for you.'

'I know, but it holds happy ones too. After all, I have lived in Cornwall for most of my life. I know it's a little soon after what has just happened, but in Cornwall I will be close to the man I should have married in the first place.' Her eyes met Martin's and she saw there the answer she wanted. 'There will be three estates to administer once we are back,' she went on quickly, 'and I must bear the responsibility of breaking the news to Luke's mother.'

'From what you have told me I am sure she will under-stand, though that will not ease the loss of a son for her.' Martha paused a moment then, looking at her niece, said, 'Abigail, come and sit the other side of me.' She did as she was bidden, and when she'd sat down Martha took her hand. 'Before you go back to Cornwall there is something you and Tess must know.'

They all looked at her curiously.

'What I am going to tell you is a secret that I have kept for a long time. Before I tell you, I want you to promise me that you will not think less of a certain person I shall name.'

Abigail said, 'I promise.'

Tess nodded.

'Good. From what I have seen of you both in the short time you have been here, I know you will keep your word.' Martha went on to tell them the whole story of her brother and Lydia Booth. 'He thought no less of your mother, Abigail, and did the right thing by your mother too, Tess, who demanded nothing. From what I saw of Lydia who stayed here with me while she awaited her confinement, she was a kind and loving woman. To save you and your father from public censure, Tess, she pretended she was your aunt. I am pleased to hear you always addressed her as Mama, which indeed she was.'

There was a charged silence as each of them tried to take in this revelation.

Abigail was stunned. Her father had betrayed her mother! How could he have loved someone else? Her mind set against him, but then she remembered he had never altered in his affectionate behaviour towards her, he had always been the kindest, most considerate and loving husband and father. She could not fault him in his paternal duties so she really had no cause to condemn him. How must he have felt, having Tess in his household yet never being able to acknowledge her as his daughter? Now she understood why he had asked to see her when he was dying.

Tess was bewildered. The man who supposedly would have nothing to do with her was not her father after all. The man who was had been kind to her. Now she knew why. How she wished she had just once been able to call him by his proper name, but she understood why it hadn't been possible – too many people would have been hurt, too many lives shattered. Her dear aunt had in reality been her mother, and now Abigail was not just her mistress but also her sister.

When Martha rose from her chair to announce she was going to sit on the terrace for a while before getting ready for the evening meal, Captain Ford and Martin tactfully followed her.

Speechless, the meaning of their aunt's words sinking in, Abigail and Tess stared at each other. Then as one they held out their arms to each other, realising now why they had often felt a special bond between them, one they were both determined to make even closer now, as they knew their father would have wished.